EVELYN WAUGH

CONTENTS

INTRODUCTION

In 1943 the distinguished American critic Edmund Wilson belatedly read *Decline and Fall*. No Anglophile, he had ignored it for fifteen years. Now that he had got round to it he confessed that he was delighted, especially with 'that hair-raising harlequinade in a brazenly bad boys' school' at the beginning of the book. The latter part of the book, he thought, leaned a little too heavily on Voltaire's *Candide*, but his regret at this falling-off did not prevent him from crediting the novel with the virtues of 'spontaneity' and 'audacity'. Not long afterwards *Brideshead Revisited* appeared and Wilson found it a serious disappointment; in his opinion the author had simply lost his way, or perhaps his audacity and spontaneity. There is certainly room for disagreement about the merits of *Brideshead Revisited*, though it should be acknowledged that despite its relative heaviness and a certain sentimentality it is, like all Waugh's books, a novel of undoubted individuality and power. On the other hand most readers would accept without much demur Wilson's judgment of *Decline and Fall* and its pre-war successors, *Vile Bodies*, *Black Mischief*, *A Handful of Dust*, and *Scoop*.

'Spontaneity' and 'audacity', though not inaccurate characterizations, are nevertheless inadequate. One needs at least to add 'hilarity', and even that does not quite cover the case. Waugh himself once made the point that hilarity is by no means necessarily an accompaniment or product of happiness. The audacities of his first novel – written when he was twenty-five – are touched by the first hints of a farcical desperation that will increase with time. His hilarity – or rather, his power to produce hilarity in the reader, for *Decline and Fall* is a book that for over fifty years has retained its ability to make readers writhe with laughter – has a certain dark, even menacing quality. For example, nobody could possibly mistake *Decline and Fall* for one of Wodehouse's deftly, daftly plotted tales. That world of genial innocence, in which crafty servants, descended from ancestors in Roman comedy, do the necessary thinking for their masters and get them out of scrapes caused by their own incapacities, or by the moral demands of ferocious aunts, is not, except in that both deal with the bizarre adventures of upper-class youth, Waugh's world. One cannot imagine Bertie Wooster reduced to prep-school teaching or expect to find in Wodehouse an aristocratic entrepreneur who owns a chain of Latin American brothels; and nobody in Waugh lives in a near-paradise like Blandings. There is no such earthly paradise in Waugh, and anything approaching that dignity is either an illusion or a thing of the past. Any houses that could be thought by their old-fashioned owners to have a claim to that title are pulled down, as Margot Beste-Chetwynde destroys King's Thursday, or as Brenda Last, in *A Handful of Dust*, sets in train the ruin of Hetton. Such acts of vandalism, along with many other dreadful but amusing instances of modern irresponsibility, provide reasons or excuses for the melancholy that gives Waugh's hilarity its peculiar resonance.

Evelyn Waugh later constructed an elaborate myth of lost Catholic aristocracy, founded on the fact, indubitable though of varying significance depending on where, as to religion, you stand, that English patrician families had at some point in the past, and notably under Henry VIII, fallen into apostasy. He himself was born into a secure Protestant middle-class professional family. His father was a respected publisher, his elder brother a successful writer. He suffered the education proper to his class, in preparatory and public schools of impeccable though not magnificent status. He was to remark that such an education at least enabled people to accept prison conditions more cheerfully than the lower classes.

Oxford in the post-war years, the epoch celebrated in the first pages of *Brideshead Revisited*, was for him, as for many, a wonderful relief, and he found there congenially dissipated companions, some of them much richer and grander than he. There were among them those who, tolerating his gloomier eccentricities, remained his friends in later years.

Following an academically inglorious Oxford career he took for a time the course, not unusual for lively but impecunious academic failures, of becoming a preparatory school teacher.

Though it brought him rewards he could not have foreseen at the time, this was hardly the career he would have chosen. He found piecework in London, writing for the journals, working briefly for the paper he later exploited under the name of the *Daily Excess*. Meanwhile he kept up a serious interest in art, being himself a talented draughtsman. He attended an art school, though briefly, and at one time he thought of apprenticing himself to a cabinet maker. Thus did the influence of William Morris survive into the era of Ronald Firbank.

He was attracted by the Pre-Raphaelite Brotherhood, and his first extended piece of writing was an essay on that group, privately printed in 1926. Pursuing that interest, he published in 1928 his first book, a biography of Gabriel Rossetti – a competent work which was received with respect. Its sobriety is in strong contrast to the mood of *Decline and Fall*, which was published later in the same year. Christopher Sykes, in his biography of Waugh, makes the ingenious suggestion that Rossetti and his circle appealed to Waugh not only because he liked their work but because he saw in Rossetti's insomnia and drugtaking an image or prediction of his own fate. At any rate the existence of this sober twin of *Decline and Fall* reminds us that Waugh could be simultaneously serious and hilarious – not that *Rossetti* is at all dull. Waugh was right to note in his diary that it was 'quite amusing in parts'.

Another diary note, dated 3 September 1927, records that he had 'begun on a comic novel'. Despite his apparently rather hectic social life he must have applied to its writing the same speed and efficiency that, as the diaries suggest, he showed when working on *Rossetti*. By the time of his first marriage, in June of the following year, he was reading proof. Early in October 1928 he noted that he had seen *Decline and Fall* on a best-seller list; but although there was a second printing in that month print runs were small, and the sales were in fact rather modest.

*

Decline and Fall fantasticates many personal experiences and has many in-jokes, some of them presumably inaccessible to anybody outside a very small circle of friends. However, they do no harm. Waugh had a mischievous habit of introducing the names of people he had met, and distributing them with apparent irrelevance among his characters. Philbrick, conferred on that fantastically versatile criminal, the butler at Llanaba, was the name of an Oxford undergraduate contemporary with Waugh, who, as it appears, had for some reason given him the nickname of 'Philbrick the Flagellant'; it caught on, and under severe provocation the injured Philbrick revenged himself by assaulting its author. The name Fagan, awarded to the Headmaster of Llanaba, had belonged to a young woman whom Waugh had introduced, disguised as a boy, into a strictly male Oxford party. The burglar Crutwell is named after the Dean of Waugh's college; he disliked Waugh, who detested him in return, and ensured that his name would be attached to some unlikeable character in every novel up to *Scoop*. Crutwell is still remembered, the loathing only slightly mitigated by compassion – he is described as 'a wreck of the war' – in Waugh's autobiography, *A Little Learning*. More obviously, Jack Spire of *The London Hercules* is Sir John Squire of *The London Mercury*, whom Waugh had met.

The first edition of the novel was illustrated by some of Waugh's own drawings, and one of them depicts the brothel quarter of Marseilles, which he had visited with his brother Alec. In this drawing one *louche* establishment bears the sign 'Chez Otoline' – a jest which Lady Ottoline Morrell, a famous literary hostess, either missed or thought fit to ignore. Some names, Miles Malpractice for instance, are substitutes for others which, being too pointed, too identifiable, were changed at the request of the publisher. Other persons, some well known, appear under names which do not resemble their real ones, for example David Lennox, the fashionable photographer, is recognizable as Cecil Beaton. The games with nomenclature, along with the deft verbal caricatures, reflect that passion for teases and practical jokes which also animated and gave the characteristic quality of outrage to Waugh's comic plots.

There are more innocent borrowings. The grammatical definition Paul Pennyfeather finds in the textbook given him to read in prison – 'a syllable is a single sound made by one effort of the voice' – is an example drawn from work Waugh himself set for a class of dull students at Arnold House, the preparatory school in Wales where he taught for two terms in 1925. That dreary experience was, as it turned out, an essential preparation for the writing of *Decline and Fall.* For Arnold House, one need hardly add, is the original of Llanaba Castle.

In his autobiography and in his diaries Waugh has quite a lot to say about his time there, and some of his remarks may surprise readers of *Decline and Fall.* In his pre-fictional accounts of the school he calls it 'depressingly well conducted'. It is true that he failed to win the respect of the headmaster's powerful wife, 'Mrs Vanhomrigh' – pronounced, he explains, 'Vanummery'. In fact her name was Banks; why, in a supposedly factual account, he gave her the unusual name of Swift's friend Hester Vanhomrigh I have not seen explained. There is evidence that Mr Banks was no Fagan but a perfectly sane and respectable schoolmaster, and that Waugh himself, though perhaps not a very effective teacher, was at least popular with the boys. So much can be gathered from the testimony of the writer Derek Verschoyle, who was a pupil at Arnold House when Waugh was there. He provided Christopher Sykes with a rather elegant account of his schooldays, and of his relations with Waugh, whom he found quite amiable, though useless at games. One of the new master's prescribed tasks was to teach Verschoyle to play the organ, an instrument with which Waugh was unfamiliar. Readers of *Decline and Fall* will remember that Paul Pennyfeather is likewise required to teach young Beste-Chetwynde the organ, and that their relationship, though friendly, had grave consequences for Pennyfeather. It led to his involvement with Beste-Chetwynde's mother Margot, later Lady Metroland, who planned but failed to marry him, and instead allowed him to be arrested and imprisoned for offences very much hers and not his. Thus, it seems, did plausible fragments of memory cohere to form fantastic jokes and plots.

Waugh says that when he was starting the novel he reread the diaries he kept as a schoolboy at Lancing, and no doubt they were helpful, but his more recent experiences at Arnold House were clearly more important. He fantasticated them, writing rapidly but with the fastidious care that is characteristic of all his work. It is visible in the plotting, in the dialogue, and in the writing of every sentence. His highest claim, put forward with a kind of proud modesty, was to good craftsmanship; his stated aim in writing novels was to make finely finished objects, like a good cabinet maker. The remarkable quasi-autobiographical passage at the beginning of his novella *The Ordeal of Gilbert Pinfold* (1957) is perfectly just: 'It may happen in the next hundred years that the English novelist of the present day will come to be valued as we now value the artists and craftsmen of the late eighteenth century ... Among these novelists Mr Gilbert Pinfold stood quite high.' Mr Pinfold claims for his books that they are 'well made'. But he admits that craft alone may not be enough, that the novelist needs also a touch of the demonic. Pinfold–Waugh had this gift also. Pinfold in his sickness weaves paranoid fantasies that strike the reader, though not, on the whole, Pinfold, as hilarious. Waugh deployed in fiction all the comical social prejudices, as well as the taste for ruthless teasing and practical joking, with which, in life, he assaulted others as well as himself. But however demonic or fantastic the motive, the product must be well made. One feature of the craftsmanlike, the well-made, is that it is manifestly so, there is no need to boast about it; and, that one still modest passage in *Pinfold* apart, Waugh hardly ever does so. Equally there should be no appearance of labour; yet we know that he did revise and polish, not least when writing *Decline and Fall.*

One instance of such revision is the character of Mr Grimes. Alternately in the soup and landing on his feet, he weaves his way through the book, rather as the absconding bounderish major will do in *Vile Bodies* – sometimes gloomy, always threatened, but in the end a rather heroic survivor. He is the sort perhaps more often met in the interwar years than before or after, hanging on and making a living somehow – marginal, unscrupulous, likeable, almost 'a capital fellow' ('capital fellows *are* bounders' as Waugh, who knew many of them and celebrated some, himself remarked). Grimes is based on a master at Arnold House, whose bounderishness at first amused Waugh, though he soon decided he was boring. The distance between this person and Grimes was indeed considerable; as the story developed the fictional character acquired a glory and a pathos that removed him far from his original. In the earliest version of the novel Grimes, like his model, was candidly a pederast, having a special relationship with young Clutterbuck. Only discreet traces of his pederasty remain in the final version, as when Grimes fixes the heats on the day before the school sports, giving Clutterbuck many victories ('he's a splendid little athlete'). They may be more effective for being unobtrusive, and indeed would hardly, in 1928, have been condoned if they had been otherwise.

Waugh's first idea was to have Grimes flee from the understandably repellent prospect of marriage to Fagan's daughter, only to be decapitated by the Irish Mail as it roared through Llanaba station. But he came to see that what he needed was not a defunct Grimes, who carelessly lost his head just as, earlier, he had lost his leg, but a Grimes who always emerged from the soup and landed on his feet, who had the marvellous durability of the genuine bounder. In his usual ruthless way he transferred the fate of decapitation to silly, unbounderish Prendergast, who became the victim of the foolishly liberal policies, deplored by Pennyfeather and also, we feel, by the author, of a wet prison governor. And so Grimes escapes and inevitably turns up at King's Thursday to join the white slave racket.

Turning up is, of course, a structural device in *Decline and Fall*: Philbrick is everywhere, Fagan turns up as boss of the hospital where Paul has his fake operation. Another whose turnings up are introduced with cruel insouciance, is the young Lord Tangent, grazed by a bullet from the pistol lent by Philbrick to Prendergast for use as a starting pistol at the phoney sports. Later we are casually informed that the foot has swollen up and turned black; then that it has been amputated. Some time after that we learn of the boy's death (which, as it happens, he himself predicted at the outset: 'Am I going to die?') and of the lamentations of his mother, Lady Circumference, described in *Vile Bodies* as 'the organ voice of England, the hunting-cry of the *ancien régime*'. 'It's maddenin' Tangent having died just at this time,' she says, fearing that people may wrongly suppose the death of her son to be the reason for her declining to attend Margot Beste-Chetwynde's second wedding.

So it goes: chance collisons, absurd but sometimes fatal sequences of incident, in a small world where it is useless to seek a rational or just concatenation of events, or an account of human relations dictated by probability or decency. In *Vile Bodies* the cosmopolitan Jesuit Father Rothschild is permitted to observe that the behaviour of modern youth arises from 'a fatal hunger for permanence', a piece of moralizing Waugh seems later to have regretted. Certainly there is nothing of the kind in *Decline and Fall.* There the young vandalize, fornicate, cheat at cards. In a Victorian novel such as Trollope's *The Way We Live Now* we would be invited to experience distaste or horror at such goings-on; fornication is beyond forgiveness, almost beyond mention, and even cheating at cards is treated with unqualified dismay. There is in Trollope's novel a young man, Sir Felix Carbury, member of a very smart, very corrupt set, who by sleeping in after a debauch omits to elope with an heiress. One can just about imagine what Waugh would have made of that situation, and indeed of the young man; in Trollope he is made out to be uniformly detestable, but Waugh, even if his treatment allowed us to think likewise of Sir Felix, would not himself have said so.

It is not only the very young who escape; their elders – white slave traders, vain and useless politicians, adulterers, epicene photographers, inhuman architects – are not censured. Indeed all these people are made more interesting than Paul Pennyfeather. Only the dull are honest, perhaps for want of wit. Paul, though impelled by chance events into association with so fast a set, is not qualified to belong to it, as Peter Pastmaster lets him know at the end. He travels impassively through a world of deception, folly, treachery and fraud, a world in which the rituals of punishment are as meaningless as those of love. If the proper responses to such a world are either despair or hilarity he displays neither. He is simply manipulated by it, and he does not belong. Yet he doesn't belong, either, with Prendergast, who is much more naive and stupid.

Paul's world is, or ought to be, that of his friend Potts, with whom he exchanges serious letters. Yet Potts's association with the boringly worthy League of Nations causes him to betray his friend. There is a sense in which the characters of *Decline and Fall* are divided into those who are strong, careless sinners, those who do not count at all, and those who, like Paul, are neither hot nor cold, who are not strong or assured enough to sin but whose innocence is not of a kind to ensure that they acquire merit.

Paul is certainly a kind of Candide, a victim, unresisting, unvirtuous. He has no Pangloss, no absurd philosopher, to advise him, though he does seem to accept that, such as it is, venal and absurd as it is, the world in which he finds himself is the best of all possible worlds. In the opening scene, the Bollinger gang, not exactly reading men, roar, break windows, smash china, deface a Matisse, destroy a piano, stone a fox to death with champagne bottles, and so on. Yet when they attack Paul it is he, not they, who suffers at the hands of the authorities; their removal of his trousers exposes him to a capital charge of indecency. Sent down by the comically venal dons, he accepts his fate without effective protest – he is even ashamed of himself for saying 'God damn and blast them to hell' as he ignominiously departs – just as he accepts with resignation the disastrous consequences of the glass-breaker Alastair Digby-Vane-Trumpington's later interventions in his life. When Dr Fagan asks him why he left the university so suddenly he accurately, but without using available excuses, admits that he was sent down for indecent behaviour; Fagan finds the confession a reason for reducing Paul's exiguous salary. He replies in exactly the same way when questioned by Prendergast.

In love with Margot, he is ignorant and incurious about her trade, easily becomes a scapegoat, and is condemned as very wicked, a distinction he doesn't deserve. He hardly seems to resent his luck, and enjoys the rigours of prison, especially solitary confinement. When the treacherous Margot finally visited him to explain that their marriage is off, he was 'greatly pained to find how little he was pained' by the news. No doubt there is here some reflection of the feeling, not uncommon at a time when the Great War was a recent memory, that one was simply at the mercy of forces uncontrollable by the individual will; yet to feel that is to be the type of personality known as Laodicean: lukewarm, neither cold nor hot. We are allowed to think Paul's destiny appropriate; reinstated as a humble student of divinity, he enjoys reading about outrageous and fiercely condemned ancient heresies. 'Quite right to suppress them.' Here at last was a world which made some sense without threatening or involving him personally in its wickedness and its retributions.

Such interests are not so remote from Waugh's own as might be thought. Paul, reading about ancient heresies in Scone, is imitating or parodying John Henry Newman, who spent a long vacation in Oxford reading about the Monophysites, and so for the first time came to doubt 'the tenableness of Anglicanism': 'here,' he wrote in *Apologia Pro Vita Sua*, 'in the middle of the fifth century I found, as it seemed to me, Christendom of the sixteenth and nineteenth century, reflected. I saw my face in that mirror and I was a Monophysite.' Heresy and apostasy were prominent among Waugh's later overt preoccupations, though he was never, as Newman may have been for a moment, a Monophysite (believing that Christ had only one nature).

After his conversion to Rome he was able to give expression to his quite orthodox religious preoccupations, for example in *Helena* (1950), a novel about St Helena, daughter of the British King Cole, mother of the first Christian emperor Constantine, and discoverer of the True Cross. The pure factuality of Catholic Christianity, symbolized by the plain unadorned wood of the Cross, was the true reality; anything else masquerading as that was absurd or a fraud. Departures from the Christian facts – by other religions, from the hot-gospelling of *Vile Bodies* and the foot-reading of *A Handful of Dust* to what was called, with much distaste, 'humanism' – were heresies, and those who professed them were apostates; it would be quite right to suppress them if, in this less satisfactory age, that were possible. In later life he came to believe that even the Vatican was betraying the truth; the abandonment of the Latin mass distressed him greatly.

But an enjoyment of human absurdity, including his own, long sustained him. It is brilliantly evident in *Pinfold*. He still loathed apostasy, including its secular variants, and he could hardly approve of the bounders who apostasized from honour in the evacuation of Crete. His war trilogy indeed contains many bounders; few of them are capital fellows but they are still very amusing.

His final diary entries have still a sardonic wit, occasionally associated with a bold declaration of Catholic truth in circumstances where others might not think to find it in evidence. Writing of Timothy Evans, a man of subnormal intelligence executed for a murder he did not commit, he comments that Evans, a lapsed Catholic, had been hell-bent until his conviction, when he returned to the faith and 'died shriven'. Himself bored almost to death, he was still witty: 'All fates are worse than death,' he noted. There is something about such observations, though they doubtless reflect a deeply held conviction, that reminds one of absurd and unfair destinies described in the novels – the fate, for instance, of little Lord Tangent, or of Prudence in *Black Mischief*, who is inadvertently eaten at a cannibal feast by her lover Basil Seal. Presumably she was unshriven at the time.

In Muriel Spark's story 'The Portobello Road' a girl is murdered; and another woman reacts to the news by exclaiming how lucky the victim was to have been to confession the night before. She is said to be 'speaking from that Catholic point of view which takes some getting used to'. This is true enough, and in some ways novels written from that point of view also take some getting used to. Waugh himself would presumably have had no difficulty with the idea that the murdered girl had been lucky, and would also have agreed with Mrs Spark, whom he warmly admired, that there is some active but obscure relation between fictive plots and a divine plot that is absolutely true but which we cannot understand.

Why, it may be asked, does God allow dirty tricks in his scenario for the world, as when Jacob–Israel cheats Esau out of his blessing? Why is Hosea commanded to marry a prostitute? Why does Samson have to marry two unsatisfactory gentiles and have his eyes put out to ensure the defeat of the

Philistines? Why are the four women named in Matthew's genealogy of Jesus all in one way or another apparently unsuitable? And so on. Mrs Spark reflects on such matters when considering the divine purpose of a bitterly divided Jerusalem in *The Mandelbaum Gate.* As to Jacob's treachery, she remarks that 'the mighty blessing, once bestowed, was irrevocable', and that God has no interest in fair play; he wasn't, as she comments, educated at Eton. Another Catholic novelist, Graham Greene, at any rate in some moods, like that prevailing in *The End of the Affair*, also, though more gloomily, contemplates the apparently irrational and sometimes cruel incursions of grace into the lives of sinners, arbitrarily determining their plots and their fates.

Decline and Fall was of course written before Waugh's conversion, but with hindsight we can think of it as Catholic *avant la lettre*; it plays many tricks of the sort Mrs Spark is thinking about. Moments of decision or indecision, of no significance on a human scale of values, turn out to have immense importance. Paul, on his wedding day drinks a toast to Fortune and then stays on, slightly against his better judgment, for another drink with his evil angel Alastair; so he is still there, as he need not have been, when the police arrive to arrest him. Even then he does not understand the extent of the catastrophe this trivial slip entails; it is left to the boy Peter Pastmaster to do that. Or think of Prendergast, victim of the good intentions of the liberalizing prison governor; how appropriate that news of his death should be passed around to the tune of 'O God our help in ages past'.

If you accept that the world is a fallen world, subject to apparently random and wanton intrusions of sense or reality, it becomes easier to accept as hilarious what otherwise seems rather to be a cause for despair. At the time of *Decline and Fall* Waugh would probably not have expressed a view of fiction similar to Muriel Spark's, but it happened that his kind of writing, and the assumptions on which it was based, were consonant with a view of that sort, and the deeper structure of his plots was to become more evident in later work. Thus, as I say by hindsight, we can make this first novel out to be Catholic. Of course he might have explained Esau's disappointment differently, perhaps as what was deserved for being thick, or a bore, like Sir Humphrey Maltravers, or a wimp like Prendergast, or a crook like the bishop, Prendy's patron, who approved of 'modern churchmen who drew their pay without the necessity of commitment to any religious belief'.

Waugh's novel has in common with the relevant chapters of Genesis that, as Grimes remarks when he arrives at King's Thursday to get in on the 'places of entertainment' racket, it is a small world. With the larger world, with society more largely considered – the idea of a larger community, requiring concern for unemployment, homelessness, famine – Waugh had very little to do; like Mrs Thatcher, he hardly believed there was such a thing as society in that sense. So Virginia Woolf's remark that Waugh's early satire showed no interest in social conditions was true enough. It was important to him, however, to have a view of the social order which provided him with social (and no doubt racial) inferiors. The poor he expected, he said, to cheat and lie, though presumably they did so less interestingly than the rich. His plots avoided all considerations of general welfare; they reflected Jacob's inspired fraud, making no provision for the indigence of stupid Esau. You can't help feeling that in *Decline and Fall* the narrator is not on the side of Pennyfeather, nor on that of the greedy dons, nor on that of the forces of law and order.

Conscience of the ordinary kind is represented, in the earlier books, as an unenviable possession of the middle classes. Paul is the sort of person who might occasionally feel a twinge of it. Trumpington had, with aristocratic insouciance, deprived him of his entire income, and, measuring Paul's worth, had offered him compensation of twenty pounds. Thereupon Paul has a crisis in which he undergoes what he supposes to be the struggle of conscience appropriate to his social position. He believes that 'by any ordinary process of thought, the money is justly mine. But ... there is my honour. For generations the British bourgeoisie have spoken of themselves as gentlemen, and by that they have meant, among other things, a self-respecting scorn of irregular perquisites. It is the quality that distinguishes the gentleman from both the artist and the aristocrat. ... Now I am a gentleman. I can't help it: it's born in me. I just can't take the money.' Paul, thus tamely distancing himself from his aristocratic friends (and from the artist who is writing the passage?) is quickly corrected by Grimes, who, despite his dubious origins, has the proper instincts of aristocrat or artist. He has already got the twenty pounds; Paul gets his small blessing whether he wants it or not. Grimes of course is a gentleman too, a public school man, but has learned how to live with it.

I have never been quite happy about his performance – his 'agony' – at the dinner given by Paul in the Hotel Metropole at Cwmprydygg. It is understandable that he should take a poor view of marriage, but this philosophizing sounds out of character: 'There's a home and family waiting for every one of us. We can't escape, try as we may. It's the seed of life we carry about with us like our skeletons, each of us unconsciously pregnant with desirable villa residences . . .' Grimes is surely pregnant rather with 'places of entertainment', and so finds himself more at home in the ambience of the Beste-Chetwyndes than Paul does; and unlike Paul, when he wants out he can always arrange it.

Philbrick is another independent figure, crossing all boundaries: butler, millionaire, intimate of the famous criminal Crutwell; a creature adapted to this world. So is Dr Fagan, professional snob, benign monster of prejudice: 'from the earliest times the Welsh have been looked on as an unclean people. It is thus that they have preserved their racial integrity. Their sons and daughters rarely mate with humankind except their own blood relations.' This is outrageous, but so is the whole book. Like Dr Fagan we 'look forward to each new fiasco with the utmost relish'. In a world providing a preview of chaos theory there are fiascos in plenty, arising, often enough, from apparently trivial causes, and related to one another by a sort of demonic craftsmanship.

Decline and Fall is full of distinctive voices and distinctively absurd ways of behaving, all beautifully interrelated. Hindsight may enable us to find in it the promise of narratives both more hilarious and more solemn to come, but it is itself an original masterpiece. It is clear evidence for the truth of the praise its author awarded himself in the opening pages of

Pinfold: he undoubtedly stood 'quite high' among the most gifted craftsmen of his time.

*

The modest success of *Decline and Fall* was eclipsed by the publication, two years later, of *Vile Bodies* – not, he insisted, a sequel to *Decline and Fall*, despite the reappearance of some characters from the earlier book. He was working on this new novel when his wife suddenly left him for another man. Waugh was deeply shocked. The novel, much affected by his distress, appeared in January 1930, three days before he was granted the decree nisi that ended his marriage. That was not the end of the story, for after his conversion to Catholicism Waugh, desiring to marry again, had to wait for the marriage to be annulled in Rome, which did not happen until 1936.

The writing of *Vile Bodies* in 1929 was much affected by the author's wretchedness and disgust at his wife's desertion. The follies and indulgences of upper-class youth, which made the book what one reviewer called 'a revue between covers', now acquired a darker tone. Father Rothschild's remark about the 'hunger for permanence' that lay behind the socially outrageous conduct of the set in which Adam Fenwick-Symes finds himself is a hint of this darkening.

Though never quite a Bright Young Thing himself, Waugh knew that world and recognized similar tendencies in his own behaviour. 'The test of a young man's worth,' he wrote some years later, 'was the insolence with which he could carry off without mishap. Social outrages were the substance of our anecdotes.' In *Vile Bodies* such outrages were not without consequences. It is a wilder book than *Decline and Fall* – a comic vision of the sort of people who by their mode of life may bring upon themselves enormous calamities. At first they are, to use a favourite expression of their own, merely bogus, their lives amusingly reduced to selfish fantasy. But later misconduct is seen as such, and seen as destructive and, in certain phases, evil.

Their conduct may owe something to the change of spirit brought about in those who were too young to be involved in the recent war; or to the decline of religion and the consequent withdrawal of moral sanctions. The story contains allusions to religious activities that are themselves bogus, or made so in the telling: Mr Melrose Ape's evangelism, the ubiquitous but ineffective Father Rothschild, the ridiculous film about John Wesley. It also suggests that the entire country is in a phase of futility and irresponsibility. Some of the manifestations of this mood Waugh clearly enjoyed, just as he enjoyed such characters as the drunken major, Nina's crazy father and Rosa Lewis, whose hotel was the original of Shepheard's Hotel.

Much in the prevailing spirit of aimless to-ing and fro-ing, Waugh went to Belfast to enjoy a motor race, which he used in his story as a means of destroying the unhappy Miss Runcible. He sent the adulterous Nina and Adam, who pretends to be her husband, to spend a traditional Christmas in Nina's childhood home. And he steered the book to its conclusion, a war that leaves nothing intact, not cities, not money, not men.

So in the end *Vile Bodies* is not merely a Firbankian tale about dissolute youth and outrageous gaiety but also a black morality. Rebecca West classified it under the heading 'the literature of disillusionment', along with *The Waste Land.* It might also be said to be a characteristic work of *l'entre deux guerres*, the first has happened already, the second is prefigured in the desolate scene at the end.

The novels that followed *Vile Bodies* still have amusingly corrupt characters like Basil Seal; *Black Mischief* and *Scoop* are quite as hilarious as their predecessors. Even *A Handful of Dust*, Waugh's sombre masterpiece, is sometimes cruelly funny. *Put Our More Flags* remembers some of the old characters but is animated more by the author's impatient reaction to the slackness and dodging of the period known by most as the Phoney War, and by Waugh as the Bore War – 'that odd, dead period before the Churchillian renaissance' – and his longing for military action. Waugh used his old trick of scoring off friends and enemies by giving their names to undesirable characters in his stories, which is why the terrible evacuated children in this book are named after Cyril Connelly, the bon vivant who edited a journal of whose war policies, or defiant lack of them, Waugh disapproved; but his motive, as so often, was really just mischief. He enjoyed a cautious but not frigid relationship with Connelly, and even contributed to *Horizon* his notable novella *The Loved One.*

It may well be that the most significant character in *Put Out More Flags*, this 'elegant potboiler', as Waugh called it, is not the incorrigible Seal or Alastair Digby-Vane-Trumpington, but Ambrose Silk. Trumpington enlists in the ranks, partly to avoid messing with temporary officers, but mostly from a sense of patriotic duty. Waugh approves of patriotism, and makes the death of the character Cedric Lyne an image of the courage that it makes possible. But his deeper respect is reserved for the epicene Ambrose Silk: 'I alone bear the weight of my singularity,' he says; and this seems to be a kind of motto for the author himself as he moved on inexorably towards his version of the religious life.

Frank Kermode

SIR FRANK KERMODE has been Northcliffe Professor of Modern English Literature at University College, London, King Edward VII Professor of English Literature at Cambridge and Charles Eliot Norton Professor of Poetry at Harvard. His many books include *The Sense of an Ending*, *Romantic Image* and a memoir, *Not Entitled.*

SELECT BIBLIOGRAPHY

THE NOVELS OF EVELYN WAUGH
(all published by Chapman & Hall)
Decline and Fall, 1928.
Vile Bodies, 1930.
Black Mischief, 1932.
A Handful of Dust, 1934.
Scoop, 1938.
Put Out More Flags, 1942.
Brideshead Revisited, 1945.
The Loved One, 1948.
Helena, 1950.
Men at Arms, 1952.
Officers and Gentlemen, 1955.
The Ordeal of Gilbert Pinfold, 1957.
Unconditional Surrender, 1961.
(*Men at Arms*, *Officers and Gentlemen*, and *Unconditional Surrender* form a trilogy later published in a revised version as *Sword of Honour*, 1965.)

STORIES
Mr Loveday's Little Outing and other sad stories, 1936.
Work Suspended and other stories, 1949.
(Both published by Chapman & Hall)

BIOGRAPHY
Rossetti, his Life and Works, Duckworth, 1928.
Edmund Campion: Jesuit and Martyr, Longman, 1935.
The Life of the Right Reverend Ronald Knox, Chapman & Hall, 1959.

TRAVEL
Labels. A Mediterranean Journey, Duckworth, 1930.
Remote People, Duckworth, 1931.
Ninety-two Days, Duckworth, 1934.
Waugh in Abyssinia, Longman, Green & Co., 1936.
Robbery Under Law: The Mexican Object-Lesson, Chapman & Hall, 1939.
When the Going Was Good, Duckworth, 1946.
A Tourist in Africa, Chapman & Hall, 1960.

AUTOBIOGRAPHY

A Little Learning. The First Volume of an Autobiography, Chapman & Hall, 1964.

LETTERS

The Letters of Evelyn Waugh, ed. Mark Amory, Weidenfeld and Nicolson, 1980.

DIARIES

The Diaries of Evelyn Waugh, ed. Michael Davie, Weidenfeld and Nicolson, 1976.

ESSAYS etc.

The Essays, Articles and Reviews of Evelyn Waugh, ed. Donat Gallagher, Methuen, 1983.

BIOGRAPHIES

STANNARD, MARTIN, *Evelyn Waugh. The Early Years, 1903–1939*, Dent, 1986.

—*Evelyn Waugh: No Abiding City, 1939–1966*, Dent, 1992.

SYKES, CHRISTOPHER, *Evelyn Waugh: A Biography*, Collins, 1975.

CRITICISM

STANNARD, MARTIN, *Evelyn Waugh: The Critical Heritage*, Routledge & Kegan Paul, 1984.

CHRONOLOGY

DATE	AUTHOR'S LIFE	LITERARY CONTEXT
1898	Birth of Alec Waugh, Evelyn's brother.	
1903	28 October: birth of Evelyn Waugh to Arthur and Catherine Waugh in Hampstead.	James: *The Ambassadors.* Shaw: *Man and Superman.*
1904		Conrad: *Nostromo.*
1905		James: *The Golden Bowl.* Forster: *Where Angels Fear to Tread.*
1908		Forster: *A Room with a View.* Bennett: *The Old Wives' Tale.* Grahame: *The Wind in the Willows.*
1910	Attends Heath Mount Preparatory School.	Forster: *Howards End.*
1911	Begins keeping a diary.	Lawrence: *The White Peacock.* Beerbohm: *Zuleika Dobson.*
1912		Beerbohm: *A Christmas Garland.* Brooke: *Collected Poems.* Shaw: *Pygmalion.*
1913		Lawrence: *Sons and Lovers.* Proust: *A la Recherche du temps perdu* (to 1927). Conrad: *Chance.*
1914		Joyce: *Dubliners.*
1915		Ford: *The Good Soldier.* Conrad: *Victory.* Buchan: *The Thirty-nine Steps.* Woolf: *The Voyage Out.*
1916		Joyce: *A Portrait of the Artist as a Young Man.*
1917	Alec Waugh's *Loom of Youth* published. Evelyn attends Lancing College, Sussex.	Yeats: *The Wild Swans at Coole.* Eliot: *Prufrock and Other Observations.*
1918		Brooke: *Collected Poems.*
1919		Shaw: *Heartbreak House.* Beerbohm: *Seven Men.* Firbank: *Valmouth.*
1920		Pound: *Hugh Selwyn Mauberley.*

HISTORICAL EVENTS

Emmeline Parkhurst founds the Women's Social and Political Union.

Russo-Japanese war. Franco-British *entente cordiale.*
Liberal government in Britain: Campbell-Bannerman Prime Minister. First Russian revolution.

Asquith becomes Prime Minister.

Death of Edward VII.

Coronation of George V. Agadir crisis. Industrial unrest in Britain.

Outbreak of World War I.
Asquith forms coalition government with Balfour.

Easter Rising in Dublin. Lloyd George becomes Prime Minister.

Bolshevik revolution in Russia. US joins war.

Armistice. Women over 30 gain vote.
Versailles peace conference.

League of Nations formed. Prohibition in the US.

DATE	AUTHOR'S LIFE	LITERARY CONTEXT
1921		Huxley: *Crome Yellow.* Pirandello: *Six Characters in Search of an Author.*
1922	January: attends Hertford College, Oxford, as a Scholar reading History. Begins contributing graphics, and later pieces to undergraduate magazines.	Joyce: *Ulysses.* Eliot: *The Waste Land.* Housman: *Last Poems.* Fitzgerald: *The Beautiful and the Damned.*
1923		Cummings: *The Enormous Room.* Firbank: *The Flower Beneath the Foot.* Huxley: *Antic Hay.*
1924	Leaves Oxford with a third-class degree. Begins novel, *The Temple at Thatch.* Makes film, *The Scarlet Woman.* Attends Heatherley's Art School, London.	Forster: *A Passage to India.* Shaw: *Saint Joan.* Ford: *Parade's End* (to 1928).
1925	Schoolmaster at Arnold House, Llanddulas, Denbighshire (January–July). Destroys *The Temple at Thatch* on Harold Acton's criticism. Attempts suicide. Writes 'The Balance'. Begins as schoolmaster in Aston Clinton, Berkshire (September).	Fitzgerald: *The Great Gatsby.* Kafka: *The Trial.*
1926	*P.R.B.: An Essay on the Pre-Raphaelite Brotherhood 1847–1854* privately printed. 'The Balance' published.	Faulkner: *Soldier's Pay.* Nabokov: *Mary.* Henry Green: *Blindness.* Firbank: *Concerning the Eccentricities of Cardinal Pirelli.*
1927	Sacked from Aston Clinton (February). Story for *The New Decameron* commissioned; writes 'The Tutor's Tale: A House of Gentlefolks'. Temporary schoolmaster in London, also contributing to *The Daily Express.* Meets Evelyn Gardner (April). Writes *Rossetti, His Life and Works.* Takes carpentry lessons. Proposes to Evelyn Gardner (December).	Woolf: *To the Lighthouse.* Hemingway: *Men Without Women.* Dunne: *An Experiment with Time.*
1928	Begins writing *Decline and Fall. Rossetti* published (April). Marries Evelyn Gardner (June). *Decline and Fall* published (September).	Lawrence: *Lady Chatterley's Lover.* Woolf: *Orlando.* Yeats: *The Tower.* Lewis: *The Childermass.* Nabokov: *King, Queen, Knave.*

CHRONOLOGY

HISTORICAL EVENTS

Establishment of USSR. Stalin becomes General Secretary of the Communist party Central Committee. Mussolini marches on Rome. Coalition falls and Bonar Law forms Conservative ministry.

Baldwin becomes Prime Minister. Women gain legal equality in divorce suits. Hitler's coup in Munich fails. German hyper-inflation.

First Labour government formed by Ramsay MacDonald. Hitler in prison. Death of Lenin. Baldwin becomes Prime Minister again after a Conservative election victory.

Locarno conference.

British general strike. First television demonstrated.

Lindbergh makes first solo flight over Atlantic.

Hoover becomes US President. Stalin de facto dictator in USSR: first Five Year Plan. Women's suffrage in Britain reduced from age 30 to age 21.

DATE	AUTHOR'S LIFE	LITERARY CONTEXT
1929	Mediterranean cruise with his wife (February–March). *Vile Bodies* begun. Marriage breaks down (July). Divorce (September).	Faulkner: *The Sound and the Fury*. Cocteau: *Les Enfants terribles*. Hemingway: *A Farewell to Arms*. Henry Green: *Living*. Priestley: *The Good Companions*. Remarque: *All Quiet on the Western Front*.
1930	*Vile Bodies* published (January). Received into the Catholic Church; *Labels, A Mediterranean Journal* published (September). Travels to Abyssinia to report coronation of Haile Selassie for *The Times* (October–November); travels in East and Central Africa.	Eliot: *Ash Wednesday*. Faulkner: *As I Lay Dying*. Nabokov: *The Defence*.
1931	Returns to England (March). *Remote People* completed (August) and published (November). *Black Mischief* begun (September).	Faulkner: *Sanctuary*. Woolf: *The Waves*.
1932	Working on film scenario for Ealing Studios (January–February). Writes 'Excursion in Reality' (March). *Black Mischief* completed (June) and published (October). Sails for British Guiana (December).	Huxley: *Brave New World*. Faulkner: *Light in August*. Betjeman: *Mount Zion*. Nabokov: *Glory*.
1933	Travels in British Guiana and Brazil (January–May). Writes 'The Man Who Liked Dickens' (February). Meets 'white mouse named Laura' Herbert at Herbert family home in Italy (September). 'Out of Depth' and *Ninety-Two Days* written (October–November).	Malraux: *La Condition humaine*. Stein: *The Autobiography of Alice B. Toklas*.
1934	In Fez, Morocco, begins *A Handful of Dust* (January–February). *Ninety-Two Days* published (March) and *A Handful of Dust* completed (April). Expedition to Spitzbergen in the Arctic (July–August). *A Handful of Dust* published (September). Begins *Edmund Campion: Jesuit and Martyr* (September); writes 'Mr Crutwell's Little Outing' and 'On Guard'.	

CHRONOLOGY

HISTORICAL EVENTS

Wall Street crash. First year of the Depression.

Gandhi begins civil disobedience campaign in India. Nazis win seats from the moderates in German election.

Britain abandons Gold Standard.

Unemployment in Britain reaches 2.8 million. F. D. Roosevelt's landslide victory in US presidential election.

Hitler becomes Chancellor of Germany. Roosevelt's 'New Deal' in US.

Riots in Paris; Doumergue forms National Union ministry to avert civil war. Dollfuss murdered in attempted Nazi coup in Austria.

DATE	AUTHOR'S LIFE	LITERARY CONTEXT
1935	Completes *Campion* (May); writes 'Winner Takes All' (July). Travels to Abyssinia to report on imminent Italian invasion for *The Daily Mail* (August–December).	Isherwood: *Mr. Norris Changes Trains.* Eliot: *Murder in the Cathedral.* Odets: *Waiting for Lefty.* Graham Greene: *England Made Me.*
1936	Writes *Waugh in Abyssinia* (April–October). Annulment to first marriage agreed by Rome (July); engagement to Laura Herbert. Returns to Abyssinia to report on Italian occupation (July–September). *Waugh in Abyssinia* published. *Scoop* begun (October).	Faulkner: *Absalom, Absalom!* Nabokov: *Despair.*
1937	Marriage to Laura Herbert (17 April); honeymoon in Italy. Decides to rewrite *Scoop* (July). Moves into Piers Court, Stinchcombe, Gloucestershire (August).	Hemingway: *To Have and Have Not.* Orwell: *The Road to Wigan Pier.* Sartre: *La Nausée.* Betjeman: *Continual Dew.* Steinbeck: *Of Mice and Men.*
1938	Birth of daughter, Teresa Waugh (March). *Scoop* published (May). Two trips, both with Laura: to Hungary (May) and Mexico (August–October). Writes 'An Englishman's Home' and begins *Robbery Under Law: The Mexican Object-Lesson.*	Graham Greene: *Brighton Rock.* Beckett: *Murphy.* Orwell: *Homage to Catalonia.*
1939	Completes *Robbery Under Law*; writes 'The Sympathetic Passenger' (May). Begins *Work Suspended. Robbery Under Law* published (June). Birth of son, Auberon Waugh (November). Joins Royal Marines (December) and abandons *Work Suspended.*	Joyce: *Finnegans Wake.* Eliot: *The Family Reunion.* Steinbeck: *The Grapes of Wrath.* Henry Green: *Party Going.* Auden: *Journey to a War.* Isherwood: *Goodbye to Berlin.*
1940	Expedition to Dakar, West Africa (August–September). Transfers to Commandos in Scotland (November). Birth and death of daughter, Mary Waugh (December).	Hemingway: *For Whom the Bell Tolls.* Graham Greene: *The Power and the Glory.* Dylan Thomas: *Portrait of the Artist as a Young Dog.* Faulkner: *The Hamlet.* Henry Green: *Pack my Bag: A Self-Portrait.* Betjeman: *Old Lights for New Chancels.*

CHRONOLOGY

HISTORICAL EVENTS

Italy invades Abyssinia. Anti-Jewish Nuremberg laws passed in Germany.

Spanish civil war begins. Abdication crisis in Britain. Hitler and Mussolini form Rome–Berlin Axis. Moscow 'Show Trials' begin. Blum forms Popular Front ministry in France.

Japanese invade China. Baldwin retires and Neville Chamberlain becomes Prime Minister.

Germany annexes Austria. Munich crisis.

Nazi-Soviet pact. Germany invades Czechoslovakia and Poland; Britain and France declare war (September 3).

Germany invades Norway and Denmark. Churchill becomes Prime Minister. Dunkirk. Italy declares war on Britain and France. Fall of France. Battle of Britain. The Blitz.

DATE	AUTHOR'S LIFE	LITERARY CONTEXT
1941	Sails for service in Egypt (February); raid on Bardia (April). At Battle of Crete (May). Disillusioned with war. July–August, on circuitous route home, writes *Put Out More Flags*. Rejoins Royal Marines (September).	Acton: *Peonies and Ponies.* Fitzgerald: *The Last Tycoon.*
1942	*Put Out More Flags* published. Transfers to Blues, Special Service Brigade; birth of daughter, Margaret Waugh (June). *Work Suspended* published (December).	Anouilh: *Eurydice.* Sartre: *Les Mouches.* Camus: *L'Etranger, Le Mythe de Sisyphe.*
1943	Transferred to London (March). Father dies (June).	Davies: *Collected Poems.* Henry Green: *Caught.*
1944	Given leave to write (January); begins *Brideshead Revisited* (January–June). Birth of daughter, Harriet Waugh (May). On British Military Mission to the Partisans in Yugoslavia (from July).	Eliot: *Four Quartets.* Anouilh: *Antigone.* Camus: *Caligula.* Sartre: *Huis Clos.*
1945	Returns to London (March). *Brideshead Revisited* published and *Helena* begun (May). Demobbed; returns to Piers Court.	Broch: *The Death of Virgil.* Betjeman: *New Bats in Old Belfries.* Orwell: *Animal Farm.* Henry Green: *Loving.* Mitford: *The Pursuit of Love.*
1946	*When the Going was Good* published (selection from previous travel books). Travels to Nuremberg (March) and Spain (June). Writes 'Scott-King's Modern Europe' and *Wine in Peace and War.*	Rattigan: *The Winslow Boy.* Cocteau: *L'Aigle à deux têtes.* Henry Green: *Back.* Dylan Thomas: *Deaths and Entrances.*
1947	Visits New York and Los Angeles for projected film of *Brideshead Revisited* (January–March). Writes 'Tactical Exercise'. Writes first draft of *The Loved One* (May–July). Birth of son, James Waugh (June). Visits Scandinavia (August–September).	Mann: *Doctor Faustus.* Camus: *La Peste.* Diary of Anne Frank is published. Henry Green: *Concluding.*

CHRONOLOGY

HISTORICAL EVENTS

USSR is invaded. Japanese attack Pearl Harbor. US joins war.

Fall of Singapore. Germans reach Stalingrad. Battle of El Alamein.

Germans retreat in Russia, Africa and Italy.

Allied landings in Normandy. Red Army reaches Belgrade and Budapest. Butler's Education Act.

Hitler commits suicide. Germany surrenders. World War II ends after atom bombs are dropped on Hiroshima and Nagasaki. United Nations founded. Attlee forms Labour government.

Nuremberg trials. 'Iron Curtain' speech by Churchill. Beginning of Cold War.

Independence of India and Pakistan. Warsaw Communist conference.

DATE	AUTHOR'S LIFE	LITERARY CONTEXT
1948	*The Loved One* published (February). Begins lecture tour in USA (October).	Eliot: *Notes Towards the Definition of Culture.* Graham Greene: *The Heart of the Matter.* Faulkner: *Intruder in the Dust.* Henry Green: *Nothing.* Acton: *Memoirs of an Aesthete.*
1949	Returns from America (March). 'Compassion' published.	Orwell: *Nineteen Eighty-Four.* De Beauvoir: *The Second Sex.* Graham Greene: *The Third Man.* Mitford: *Love in a Cold Climate.* Miller: *Death of a Salesman.*
1950	Birth of son, Septimus Waugh (July). *Helena* published. Last visit to America.	Hemingway: *Across the River and into the Trees.* Eliot: *The Cocktail Party.* Henry Green: *Doting.*
1951	Middle East tour for *Life Magazine* (January–March). Writes *Men at Arms* (June–December).	Salinger: *The Catcher in the Rye.* Powell: *A Question of Upbringing* (the first of the 12 novels comprising *A Dance to the Music of Time* (1952–75). Mitford: *The Blessing.*
1952	Writes *The Holy Places* and 'Love Among the Ruins'. *Men at Arms* published (September). Christmas in Goa.	Beckett: *Waiting for Godot.* Miller: *The Crucible.*
1953	Begins *Officers and Gentlemen* (March).	Hartley: *The Go-Between.*
1954	Voyage to Ceylon and mental breakdown (February). Contributes to "U" and "non U" debate. Death of his mother (December).	
1955	*Officers and Gentlemen* published (May). Trip to Jamaica, writing *The Ordeal of Gilbert Pinfold* (from December).	Nabokov: *Lolita.* Miller: *A View from the Bridge.* Graham Greene: *Loser Takes All, The Quiet American.* Murdoch: *Under the Net.*
1956	Moves to Combe Florey, Taunton, Somerset.	Beckett: *Molloy.* Camus: *La Chute.* Faulkner: *Requiem for a Nun.* Mitford, Waugh, Betjeman et al: *Noblesse Oblige.*

CHRONOLOGY

HISTORICAL EVENTS

Marshall Aid: US contributes $5.3 billion for European recovery. Soviet blockade of West Berlin: Allied airlifts begin (to 1949). State of Israel founded. Apartheid introduced in South Africa. Yugoslavia under Tito expelled from Comintern. National Health Service inaugurated in Britain.

Federal and Democratic Republics established in Germany. People's Republic of China proclaimed. Korean war begins (to 1953). NATO founded.

McCarthy witch hunts – persecution of Communists throughout US.

Conservatives return to power in Britain. Burgess and Maclean defect to USSR.

Death of George VI: accession of Elizabeth II.

Stalin dies and is succeeded by Khrushchev.

Vietnam war begins. Nasser gains power in Egypt.

West Germany joins NATO.

Suez crisis. Invasion of Hungary by USSR.

DATE	AUTHOR'S LIFE	LITERARY CONTEXT
1957	*Pinfold* completed (January) and published (July). First plans for *Unconditional Surrender* (July).	Camus: *L'Exil et le Royaume.* Pasternak: *Doctor Zhivago.* Pinter: *The Birthday Party.* Nabokov: *Pnin.* Spark: *The Comforters.*
1958	Travels to Rhodesia (February–March), collecting material for—	Betjeman: *Collected Poems.*
1959	*The Life of the Right Reverend Ronald Knox* published (October).	Spark: *Memento Mori.* Eliot: *The Elder Statesman.* Graham Greene: *The Complaisant Lover.* Beckett: *Endgame.*
1960	*A Tourist in Africa* published.	Spark: *The Ballad of Peckham Rye.* Updike: *Rabbit, Run.* Pinter: *The Caretaker.* Betjeman: *Summoned by Bells.*
1961	*Unconditional Surrender* published (September). Trip to West Indies with his daughter Margaret (November–February).	Graham Greene: *A Burnt-Out Case.* Albee: *The American Dream.* Huxley: *Religion without Revelation.* Mitford: *Don't Tell Alfred.* Spark: *The Prime of Miss Jean Brodie.*
1962	Working on *A Little Learning.* Begins 'Basil Seal Rides Again' (August).	Albee: *Who's Afraid of Virginia Woolf?* Isherwood: *Down There on a Visit.*
1963	Publication of 'Basil Seal Rides Again'.	Stoppard: *A Walk on Water.* Pinter: *The Lover.* Spark: *The Girls of Slender Means.*
1964	Serial publication of *A Little Learning* (June–July).	Sartre: *Les Mots.* Ayme: *The Minotaur.* Isherwood: *A Single Man.*
1965	War trilogy revised and published as *Sword of Honour* (September).	Pinter: *The Homecoming.* Albee: *Tiny Alice.*
1966	Evelyn Waugh dies on Easter Sunday, 10 April, at Combe Florey.	Albee: *A Delicate Balance.*

CHRONOLOGY

HISTORICAL EVENTS

Macmillan becomes Prime Minister. Treaty of Rome: Common Market established.

De Gaulle elected President of the French Republic.

Castro becomes premier of Cuba.

J. F. Kennedy elected US President. Congo crisis. Sharpeville shootings in South Africa.

Berlin wall is constructed.

Cuban missile crisis. Anglo-French agreement on the construction of Concorde.

Assassination of President Kennedy. Profumo affair. Macmillan resigns; Douglas-Home becomes Prime Minister. Britain refused entry to Common Market.

Wilson becomes Prime Minister. Martin Luther King is awarded the Nobel peace prize. Fall of Khrushchev.

DECLINE AND FALL

To
Harold Acton
in Homage
and Affection

CONTENTS

PRELUDE

MR SNIGGS, the Junior Dean, and Mr Postlethwaite, the Domestic Bursar, sat alone in Mr Sniggs' room overlooking the garden quad at Scone College. From the rooms of Sir Alastair Digby-Vane-Trumpington, two staircases away, came a confused roaring and breaking of glass. They alone of the senior members of Scone were at home that evening, for it was the night of the annual dinner of the Bollinger Club. The others were all scattered over Boar's Hill and North Oxford at gay, contentious little parties, or at other senior common-rooms, or at the meetings of learned societies, for the annual Bollinger dinner is a difficult time for those in authority.

It is not accurate to call this an annual event, because quite often the Club is suspended for some years after each meeting. There is tradition behind the Bollinger; it numbers reigning kings among its past members. At the last dinner, three years ago, a fox had been brought in in a cage and stoned to death with champagne bottles. What an evening that had been! This was the first meeting since then, and from all over Europe old members had rallied for the occasion. For two days they had been pouring into Oxford: epileptic royalty from their villas of exile; uncouth peers from crumbling country seats; smooth young men of uncertain tastes from embassies and legations; illiterate lairds from wet granite hovels in the Highlands; ambitious young barristers and Conservative candidates torn from the London season and the indelicate advances of debutantes; all that was most sonorous of name and title was there for the beano.

'The fines!' said Mr Sniggs, gently rubbing his pipe along the side of his nose. 'Oh my! the fines there'll be after this evening!'

There is some highly prized port in the senior common-room cellars that is only brought up when the College fines have reached £50.

'We shall have a week of it at least,' said Mr Postlethwaite, 'a week of Founder's port.'

A shriller note could now be heard rising from Sir Alastair's rooms; any who have heard that sound will shrink at the recollection of it; it is the sound of the English county families baying for broken glass. Soon they would all be tumbling out into the quad, crimson and roaring in their bottle-green evening coats, for the real romp of the evening.

'Don't you think it might be wiser if we turned out the light?' said Mr Sniggs.

In darkness the two dons crept to the window. The quad below was a kaleidoscope of dimly discernible faces.

'There must be fifty of them at least,' said Mr Postlethwaite. 'If only they were all members of the College! Fifty of them at ten pounds each. Oh my!'

'It'll be more if they attack the Chapel,' said Mr Sniggs. 'Oh, please God, make them attack the Chapel.'

'I wonder who the unpopular undergraduates are this term. They always attack their rooms. I hope they have been wise enough to go out for the evening.'

'I think Partridge will be one; he possesses a painting by Matisse or some such name.'

'And I'm told he has black sheets on his bed.'

'And Sanders went to dinner with Ramsay MacDonald once.'

'And Rending can afford to hunt, but collects china instead.'

'And smokes cigars in the garden after breakfast.'

'Austen has a grand piano.'

'They'll enjoy smashing that.'

'There'll be a heavy bill for to-night; just you see! But I confess I should feel easier if the Dean or the Master were in. They can't see us from here, can they?'

It was a lovely evening. They broke up Mr Austen's grand piano, and stamped Lord Rending's cigars into his carpet, and smashed his china, and tore up Mr Partridge's sheets, and threw the Matisse into his water-jug; Mr Sanders had nothing to break except his windows, but they found the manuscript at which he had been working for the Newdigate Prize Poem, and had great fun with that. Sir Alastair Digby-Vane-Trumpington felt quite ill with excitement, and was supported to bed by Lumsden of Strathdrummond. It was half-past eleven. Soon the evening would come to an end. But there was still a treat to come.

*

Paul Pennyfeather was reading for the Church. It was his third year of uneventful residence at Scone. He had come there after a creditable career at a small public school of ecclesiastical temper on the South Downs, where he had edited the magazine, been President of the Debating Society, and had, as his report said, 'exercised a wholesome influence for good' in the House in which he was head boy. At home he lived in Onslow Square with his guardian, a prosperous solicitor who was proud of his progress and abysmally bored by his company. Both his parents had died in India at the time when he won the essay prize at his preparatory school. For two years he had lived within his allowance, aided by two valuable scholarships. He smoked three ounces of tobacco a week – John Cotton, Medium – and drank a pint and a half of beer a day, the half at luncheon and the pint at dinner, a meal he invariably ate in Hall. He had four friends, three of whom had been at school with him. None of the Bollinger Club had ever heard of Paul Pennyfeather, and he, oddly enough, had not heard of them.

Little suspecting the incalculable consequences that the evening was to have for him, he bicycled happily back from a meeting of the League of Nations Union. There had been a most interesting paper about plebiscites in Poland. He thought of smoking a pipe and reading another chapter of the *Forsyte Saga* before going to bed. He knocked at the gate, was admitted, put away his bicycle, and diffidently, as always, made his way across the quad towards his rooms. What a lot of people there seemed to be about! Paul had no particular objection to drunkenness – he had read a rather daring paper to the Thomas More Society on the subject – but he was consumedly shy of drunkards.

Out of the night Lumsden of Strathdrummond swayed across his path like a druidical rocking-stone. Paul tried to pass.

Now it so happened that the tie of Paul's old school bore a marked resemblance to the pale blue and white of the Bollinger Club. The difference of a quarter of an inch in the width of the stripes was not one that Lumsden of Strathdrummond was likely to appreciate.

'Here's an awful man wearing the Boller tie,' said the Laird. It is not for nothing that since pre-Christian times his family had exercised chieftainship over unchartered miles of barren moorland.

Mr Sniggs was looking rather apprehensively at Mr Postlethwaite.

'They appear to have caught somebody,' he said. 'I hope they don't do him any serious harm.'

'Dear me, can it be Lord Rending? I think I ought to intervene.'

'No, Sniggs,' said Mr Postlethwaite, laying a hand on his impetuous colleague's arm. 'No, no, no. It would be unwise. We have the prestige of the senior common-room to consider. In their present state they might not prove amenable to discipline. We must at all costs avoid an *outrage*.'

At length the crowd parted, and Mr Sniggs gave a sigh of relief.

'But it's quite all right. It isn't Rending. It's Pennyfeather – someone of no importance.'

'Well, that saves a great deal of trouble. I am glad, Sniggs; I am, really. What a lot of clothes the young man appears to have lost!'

*

Next morning there was a lovely College meeting.

'Two hundred and thirty pounds,' murmured the Domestic Bursar ecstatically, '*not* counting the damage! That means five evenings, with what we have already collected. Five evenings of Founder's port!'

'The case of Pennyfeather,' the Master was saying, 'seems to be quite a different matter altogether. He ran the whole length of the quadrangle, you say, *without his trousers*. It is unseemly. It is more: it is indecent. In fact, I am almost prepared to say that it is flagrantly indecent. It is *not* the conduct we expect of a scholar.'

'Perhaps if we fined him really heavily?' suggested the Junior Dean.

'I very much doubt whether he could pay. I understand he is not well off. *Without trousers*, indeed! And at that time of night! I think we should do far better to get rid of him altogether. That sort of young man does the College no good.'

*

Two hours later, while Paul was packing his three suits in his little leather trunk, the Domestic Bursar sent a message that he wished to see him.

'Ah, Mr Pennyfeather,' he said, 'I have examined your rooms and noticed two slight burns, one on the window-sill and the other on the chimneypiece, no doubt from cigarette ends. I am charging you five-and-sixpence for each of them on your battels. That is all, thank you.'

As he crossed the quad Paul met Mr Sniggs.

'Just off?' said the Junior Dean brightly.

'Yes, sir,' said Paul.

And a little farther on he met the Chaplain.

'Oh, Pennyfeather, before you go, surely you have my copy of Dean Stanley's *Eastern Church*?'

'Yes. I left it on your table.'

'Thank you. Well, good-bye, my dear boy. I suppose that after that reprehensible affair last night you will have to think of some other profession. Well, you may congratulate yourself that you discovered your unfitness for the priesthood before it was too late. If a parson does a thing of that sort, you know, all the world knows. And so many do, alas! What do you propose doing?'

'I don't really know yet.'

'There is always commerce, of course. Perhaps you may be able to bring to the great world of business some of the ideals you have learned at Scone. But it won't be easy, you know. It is a thing to be lived down with courage. What did Dr Johnson say about fortitude? . . . Dear, dear! *no trousers!*'

At the gates Paul tipped the porter.

'Well, good-bye, Blackall,' he said. 'I don't suppose I shall see you again for some time.'

'No, sir, and very sorry I am to hear about it. I expect you'll be becoming a schoolmaster, sir. That's what most of the gentlemen does, sir, that gets sent down for indecent behaviour.'

'God damn and blast them all to hell,' said Paul meekly to himself as he drove to the station, and then he felt rather ashamed, because he rarely swore.

PART ONE

CHAPTER 1
Vocation

'SENT down for indecent behaviour, eh?' said Paul Pennyfeather's guardian. 'Well, thank God your poor father has been spared this disgrace. That's all I can say.'

There was a hush in Onslow Square, unbroken except by Paul's guardian's daughter's gramophone playing Gilbert and Sullivan in her little pink boudoir at the top of the stairs.

'My daughter must know nothing of this,' continued Paul's guardian.

There was another pause.

'Well,' he resumed, 'you know the terms of your father's will. He left the sum of five thousand pounds, the interest of which was to be devoted to your education and the sum to be absolutely yours on your twenty-first birthday. That, if I am right, falls in eleven months' time. In the event of your education being finished before that time, he left me with complete discretion to withhold this allowance should I not consider your course of life satisfactory. I do not think that I should be fulfilling the trust which your poor father placed in me if, in the present circumstances, I continued any allowance. Moreover, you will be the first to realize how impossible it would be for me to ask you to share the same home with my daughter.'

'But what is to happen to me?' said Paul.

'I think you ought to find some work,' said his guardian thoughtfully. 'Nothing like it for taking the mind off nasty subjects.'

'But what kind of work?'

'Just work, good healthy toil. You have led too sheltered a life, Paul. Perhaps I am to blame. It will do you the world of good to face facts a bit – look at life in the raw, you know. See things steadily and see them whole, eh?' And Paul's guardian lit another cigar.

'Have I no legal right to any money at all?' asked Paul.

'None whatever, my dear boy,' said his guardian quite cheerfully. . . .

That spring Paul's guardian's daughter had two new evening frocks and, thus glorified, became engaged to a well-conducted young man in the Office of Works.

*

'Sent down for indecent behaviour, eh?' said Mr Levy, of Church and Gargoyle, scholastic agents. 'Well, I don't think we'll say anything about that. In fact, officially, mind, you haven't told me. We call that sort of thing "Education discontinued for personal reasons", you understand.' He picked up the telephone. 'Mr Samson, have we any "education discontinued" posts, male, on hand? . . . Right! . . . Bring it up, will you? I think,' he added, turning again to Paul, 'we have just the thing for you.'

A young man brought in a slip of paper.

'What about that?'

Paul read it:

Private and Confidential Notice of Vacancy.

Augustus Fagan, Esquire, Ph.D., Llanabba Castle, N. Wales, requires immediately Junior assistant master to teach Classics and English to University Standard with subsidiary Mathematics, German and French. Experience essential; first-class games essential.

Status of School: *School.*

Salary offered: £120 *resident post.*

Reply promptly but carefully to Dr Fagan ('Esq., Ph.D.,' on envelope), enclosing copies of testimonials and photographs, if considered advisable, mentioning that you have heard of the vacancy through us.

'Might have been made for you,' said Mr Levy.

'But I don't know a word of German, I've had no experience, I've got no testimonials, and I can't play cricket.'

'It doesn't do to be too modest,' said Mr Levy. 'It's wonderful what one can teach when one tries. Why, only last term we sent a man who had never been in a laboratory in his life as senior

Science Master to one of our leading public schools. He came wanting to do private coaching in music. He's doing very well, I believe. Besides, Dr Fagan can't expect *all* that for the salary he's offering. Between ourselves, Llanabba hasn't a good name in the profession. We class schools, you see, into four grades: Leading School, First-rate School, Good School, and School. Frankly,' said Mr Levy, 'school is pretty bad. I think you'll find it a very suitable post. So far as I know, there are only two other candidates, and one of them is totally deaf, poor fellow.'

*

Next day Paul went to Church and Gargoyle to interview Dr Fagan. He had not long to wait. Dr Fagan was already there interviewing the other candidates. After a few minutes Mr Levy led Paul into the room, introduced him, and left them together.

'A most exhausting interview,' said Dr Fagan. 'I am sure he was a very nice young man, but I could not make him understand a word I said. Can *you* hear me quite clearly?'

'Perfectly, thank you.'

'Good; then let us get to business.'

Paul eyed him shyly across the table. He was very tall and very old and very well dressed; he had sunken eyes and rather long white hair over jet black eyebrows. His head was very long, and swayed lightly as he spoke; his voice had a thousand modulations, as though at some remote time he had taken lessons in elocution; the backs of his hands were hairy, and his fingers were crooked like claws.

'I understand you have had no previous experience?'

'No, sir, I am afraid not.'

'Well, of course, that is in many ways an advantage. One too easily acquires the professional tone and loses vision. But of course we must be practical. I am offering a salary of one hundred and twenty pounds, but only to a man with experience. I have a letter here from a young man who holds a diploma in forestry. He wants an extra ten pounds a year on the strength of it, but it is vision I need, Mr Pennyfeather, not diplomas.

I understand, too, that you left your University rather suddenly. Now – why was that?'

This was the question that Paul had been dreading, and, true to his training, he had resolved upon honesty.

'I was sent down, sir, for indecent behaviour.'

'Indeed, indeed? Well, I shall not ask for details. I have been in the scholastic profession long enough to know that nobody enters it unless he has some very good reason which he is anxious to conceal. But, again to be practical, Mr Pennyfeather, I can hardly pay one hundred and twenty pounds to anyone who has been sent down for indecent behaviour. Suppose that we fix your salary at ninety pounds a year to begin with? I have to return to Llanabba to-night. There are six more weeks of term, you see, and I have lost a master rather suddenly. I shall expect you to-morrow evening. There is an excellent train from Euston that leaves at about ten. I think you will like your work,' he continued dreamily, 'you will find that my school is built upon an ideal – an ideal of service and fellowship. Many of the boys come from the very best families. Little Lord Tangent has come to us this term, the Earl of Circumference's son, you know. Such a nice little chap, erratic, of course, like all his family, but he has *tone*.' Dr Fagan gave a long sigh. 'I wish I could say the same for my staff. Between ourselves, Pennyfeather, I think I shall have to get rid of Grimes fairly soon. He is *not* out of the top drawer, and boys notice these things. Now, your predecessor was a thoroughly agreeable young man. I was sorry to lose him. But he used to wake up my daughters coming back on his motor bicycle at all hours of the night. He used to borrow money from the boys, too, quite large sums, and the parents objected. I had to get rid of him.... Still, I was very sorry. *He* had tone.'

Dr Fagan rose, put on his hat at a jaunty angle, and drew on a glove.

'Good-bye, my dear Pennyfeather. I think, in fact I know, that we are going to work well together. I can always tell these things.'

'Good-bye, sir,' said Paul....

'Five per cent of ninety pounds is four pounds ten shillings,' said Mr Levy cheerfully. 'You can pay now or on receipt of your first term's salary. If you pay now there is a reduction of 15 per cent. That would be three pounds six shillings and sixpence.'

'I'll pay you when I get my wages,' said Paul.

'Just as you please,' said Mr Levy. 'Only too glad to have been of use to you.'

CHAPTER 2
Llanabba Castle

LLANABBA CASTLE presents two quite different aspects, according as you approach it from the Bangor or the coast road. From the back it looks very much like any other large country house, with a great many windows and a terrace, and a chain of glass-houses and the roofs of innumerable nondescript kitchen buildings, disappearing into the trees. But from the front – and that is how it is approached from Llanabba station – it is formidably feudal; one drives past at least a mile of machicolated wall before reaching the gates; these are towered and turreted and decorated with heraldic animals and a workable portcullis. Beyond them at the end of the avenue stands the Castle, a model of medieval impregnability.

The explanation of this rather striking contrast is simple enough. At the time of the cotton famine in the sixties Llanabba House was the property of a prosperous Lancashire millowner. His wife could not bear to think of their men starving; in fact, she and her daughters organized a little bazaar in their aid, though without any very substantial results. Her husband had read the Liberal economists and could not think of paying without due return. Accordingly 'enlightened self-interest' found a way. An encampment of mill-hands was settled in the park, and they were put to work walling the grounds and facing the house with great blocks of stone from a neighbouring quarry. At the end of the American war they returned to their mills, and Llanabba House became Llanabba Castle after a great deal of work had been done very cheaply.

Driving up from the station in a little closed taxi, Paul saw little of all this. It was almost dark in the avenue and quite dark inside the house.

'I am Mr Pennyfeather,' he said to the butler. 'I have come here as a master.'

'Yes,' said the butler, 'I know all about you. This way.'

They went down a number of passages, unlit and smelling obscurely of all the ghastly smells of school, until they reached a brightly lighted door.

'In there. That's the Common Room.' Without more ado, the butler made off into the darkness.

Paul looked round. It was not a very big room. Even he felt that, and all his life he had been accustomed to living in constricted spaces.

'I wonder how many people live here,' he thought, and with a sick thrust of apprehension counted sixteen pipes in a rack at the side of the chimneypiece. Two gowns hung on a hook behind the door. In a corner were some golf clubs, a walking-stick, an umbrella, and two miniature rifles. Over the chimney-piece was a green baize notice-board covered with lists; there was a typewriter on the table. In a bookcase were a number of very old textbooks and some new exercise-books. There were also a bicycle pump, two armchairs, a straight chair, half a bottle of invalid port, a boxing-glove, a bowler hat, yesterday's *Daily News*, and a packet of pipe-cleaners.

Paul sat down disconsolately on the straight chair.

Presently there was a knock at the door, and a small boy came in.

'Oh!' he said, looking at Paul intently.

'Hullo!' said Paul.

'I was looking for Captain Grimes,' said the little boy.

'Oh!' said Paul.

The child continued to look at Paul with a penetrating, impersonal interest.

'I suppose you're the new master?' he said.

'Yes,' said Paul. 'I'm called Pennyfeather.'

The little boy gave a shrill laugh. 'I think that's terribly funny,' he said, and went away.

Presently the door opened again, and two more boys looked in. They stood and giggled for a time and then made off.

In the course of the next half hour six or seven boys appeared on various pretexts and stared at Paul.

Then a bell rang, and there was a terrific noise of whistling and scampering. The door opened, and a very short man of about thirty came into the Common Room. He had made a great deal of noise in coming because he had an artificial leg. He had a short red moustache, and was slightly bald.

'Hullo!' he said.

'Hullo!' said Paul.

'I'm Captain Grimes,' said the newcomer, and 'Come in, you,' he added to someone outside.

Another boy came in.

'What do you mean,' said Grimes, 'by whistling when I told you to stop?'

'Everyone else was whistling,' said the boy.

'What's that got to do with it?' said Grimes.

'I should think it had a lot to do with it,' said the boy.

'Well, just you do a hundred lines, and next time, remember, I shall beat you,' said Grimes, 'with this,' said Grimes, waving the walking-stick.

'That wouldn't hurt much,' said the boy, and went out.

'There's no discipline in the place,' said Grimes, and then he went out too.

'I wonder whether I'm going to enjoy being a schoolmaster,' thought Paul.

Quite soon another and older man came into the room.

'Hullo!' he said to Paul.

'Hullo!' said Paul.

'I'm Prendergast,' said the newcomer. 'Have some port?'

'Thank you, I'd love to.'

'Well, there's only one glass.'

'Oh, well, it doesn't matter, then.'

'You might get your tooth-glass from your bedroom.'

'I don't know where that is.'

'Oh, well, never mind; we'll have some another night. I suppose you're the new master?'

'Yes.'

'You'll hate it here. I know. I've been here ten years. Grimes only came this term. He hates it already. Have you seen Grimes?'

'Yes, I think so.'

'He isn't a gentleman. Do you smoke?'

'Yes.'

'A pipe, I mean.'

'Yes.'

'Those are my pipes. Remind me to show them to you after dinner.'

At this moment the butler appeared with a message that Dr Fagan wished to see Mr Pennyfeather.

Dr Fagan's part of the Castle was more palatial. He stood at the end of a long room with his back to a rococo marble chimneypiece; he wore a velvet dinner-jacket.

'Settling in?' he asked.

'Yes,' said Paul.

Sitting before the fire, with a glass bottle of sweets in her lap, was a brightly dressed woman in early middle age.

'That,' said Dr Fagan with some disgust, 'is my daughter.'

'Pleased to meet you,' said Miss Fagan. 'Now what I always tells the young chaps as comes here is, "Don't let the dad over-work you." He's a regular Tartar, is Dad, but then you know what scholars are – inhuman. Ain't you,' said Miss Fagan, turning on her father with sudden ferocity – 'ain't you inhuman?'

'At times, my dear, I am grateful for what little detachment I have achieved. But here,' he added, 'is my other daughter.'

Silently, except for a scarcely perceptible jingling of keys, another woman had entered the room. She was younger than her sister, but far less gay.

'How do you do?' she said. 'I do hope you have brought some soap with you. I asked my father to tell you, but he so often forgets these things. Masters are not supplied with soap or with boot polish or with washing over two shillings and sixpence weekly. Do you take sugar in your tea?'

'Yes, usually.'

'I will make a note of that and have two extra lumps put out for you. Don't let the boys get them, though.'

'I have put you in charge of the fifth form for the rest of this term,' said Dr Fagan. 'You will find them delightful boys, quite delightful. Clutterbuck wants watching, by the way, a very delicate little chap. I have also put you in charge of the games, the carpentering class, and the fire drill. And I forgot, do you teach music?'

'No, I'm afraid not.'

'Unfortunate, most unfortunate. I understood from Mr Levy that you did. I have arranged for you to take Beste-Chetwynde in organ lessons twice a week. Well, you must do the best you can. There goes the bell for dinner. I won't detain you. Oh, one other thing. Not a word to the boys, please, about the reasons for your leaving Oxford! We schoolmasters must temper discretion with deceit. There, I fancy I have said something for you to think about. Good night.'

'Tootle-oo,' said the elder Miss Fagan.

CHAPTER 3
Captain Grimes

PAUL had very little difficulty in finding the dining-hall. He was guided there by the smell of cooking and the sound of voices. It was a large, panelled room, far from disagreeable, with fifty or sixty boys of ages ranging from ten to eighteen settled along four long tables. The smaller ones wore Eton suits, the elder ones dinner-jackets.

He was led to a place at the head of one of the tables. The boys on either side of him stood up very politely until he sat down. One of them was the boy who had whistled at Captain Grimes. Paul thought he rather liked him.

'I'm called Beste-Chetwynde,' he said.

'I've got to teach you the organ, I believe.'

'Yes, it's great fun: we play in the village church. Do you play terribly well?'

Paul felt this was not a moment for candour, and so, 'tempering discretion with deceit', he said, 'Yes, remarkably well.'

'I say, do you really, or are you rotting?'

'Indeed, I'm not. I used to give lessons to the Master of Scone.'

'Well, you won't be able to teach me much,' said Beste-Chetwynde cheerfully. 'I only do it to get off gym. I say, they haven't given you a napkin. These servants are too awful. Philbrick,' he shouted to the butler, 'why haven't you given Mr Pennyfeather a napkin?'

'Forgot,' said Philbrick, 'and it's too late because Miss Fagan's locked the linen up.'

'Nonsense!' said Beste-Chetwynde; 'go and get one at once. That man's all right, really,' he added, 'only he wants watching.'

In a few minutes Philbrick returned with the napkin.

'It seems to me that you're a remarkably intelligent boy,' said Paul.

'Captain Grimes doesn't think so. He says I'm half-witted. I'm glad you're not like Captain Grimes. He's so common, don't you think?'

'You mustn't talk about the other masters like that in front of me.'

'Well that's what we all think about him, anyway. What's more, he wears combinations. I saw it in his washing-book one day when I was fetching him his hat. I think combinations are rather awful, don't you?'

There was a commotion at the end of the hall.

'I expect that's Clutterbuck being sick,' said Beste-Chetwynde. 'He's awfully sick when we have mutton.'

The boy on Paul's other side now spoke for the first time.

'Mr Prendergast wears a wig,' he said, and then became very confused and subsided into a giggle.

'That's Briggs,' said Beste-Chetwynde, 'only everyone calls him Brolly, because of the shop, you know.'

'They're silly rotters,' said Briggs.

All this was a great deal easier than Paul had expected; it didn't seem so very hard to get on with boys, after all.

After a time they all stood up, and amid considerable noise Mr Prendergast said grace. Someone called out 'Prendy!' very loudly just by Paul's ear.

'*. . . per Christum Dominum nostrum. Amen*,' said Mr Prendergast. 'Beste-Chetwynde, was that you who made that noise?'

'Me, sir? No, sir.'

'Pennyfeather, did Beste-Chetwynde make that noise?'

'No, I don't think so,' said Paul, and Beste-Chetwynde gave him a friendly look, because, as a matter of fact, he had.

Captain Grimes linked arms with him outside the dining-hall.

'Filthy meal, isn't it, old boy?' he said.

'Pretty bad,' said Paul.

'Prendy's on duty to-night. I'm off to the pub. How about you?'

'All right,' said Paul.

'Prendy's not so bad in his way,' said Grimes, 'but he can't keep order. Of course, you know he wears a wig. Very hard for a man with a wig to keep order. I've got a false leg, but that's different. Boys respect that. Think I lost it in the war. Actually,' said the Captain, 'and strictly between ourselves, mind, I was run over by a tram in Stoke-on-Trent when I was one-over-the-eight. Still, it doesn't do to let that out to everyone. Funny thing, but I feel I can trust you. I think we're going to be pals.'

'I hope so,' said Paul.

'I've been feeling the need of a pal for some time. The bloke before you wasn't bad – a bit stand-offish, though. He had a motor-bike, you see. The daughters of the house didn't care for him. Have you met Miss Fagan?'

'I've met two.'

'They're both bitches,' said Grimes, and added moodily, 'I'm engaged to be married to Flossie.'

'Good God! Which is she?'

'The elder. The boys call them Flossie and Dingy. We haven't told the old boy yet. I'm waiting till I land in the soup again. Then I shall play that as my last card. I generally get into the soup sooner or later. Here's the pub. Not such a bad little place in its way. Clutterbuck's father makes all the beer round here. Not bad stuff, either. Two pints, please, Mrs Roberts!'

In the farther corner sat Philbrick, talking volubly in Welsh to a shady-looking old man.

'Damned cheek his coming in here!' said Grimes.

Mrs Roberts brought them their beer. Grimes took a long draught and sighed happily.

'This looks like being the first end of term I've seen for two years,' he said dreamily. 'Funny thing, I can always get on all right for about six weeks, and then I land in the soup. I don't believe I was ever meant by Nature to be a schoolmaster. Temperament,' said Grimes, with a far-away look in his eyes – 'that's been my trouble, temperament and sex.'

'Is it quite easy to get another job after – after you've been in the soup?' asked Paul.

'Not at first, it isn't, but there're ways. Besides, you see, I'm a public school man. That means everything. There's a blessed equity in the English social system,' said Grimes, 'that ensures the public school man against starvation. One goes through four or five years of perfect hell at an age when life is bound to be hell, anyway, and after that the social system never lets one down.

'Not that I stood four or five years of it, mind; I got the push soon after my sixteenth birthday. But my housemaster was a public school man. He knew the system. "Grimes," he said, "I can't keep you in the House after what has happened. I have the other boys to consider. But I don't want to be too hard on you. I want you to start again." So he sat down there and then and wrote me a letter of recommendation to any future employer, a corking good letter, too. I've got it still. It's been very useful at one time or another. That's the public school system all over. They may kick you out, but they never let you down.

'I subscribed a guinea to the War Memorial Fund. I felt I owed it to them. I was really sorry,' said Grimes, 'that that cheque never got through.

'After that I went into business. Uncle of mine had a brush factory at Edmonton. Doing pretty well before the war. That put the lid on the brush trade for me. You're too young to have been in the war, I suppose? Those were days, old boy. We shan't see the like of them again. I don't suppose I was really sober for more than a few hours for the whole of that war. Then I got into the soup again, pretty badly that time. Happened over in France. They said, "Now, Grimes, you've got to behave like a gentleman. We don't want a court-martial in this regiment. We're going to leave you alone for half an hour. There's your revolver. You know what to do. Good-bye, old man," they said quite affectionately.

'Well, I sat there for some time looking at that revolver. I put it up to my head twice, but each time I brought it down again. "Public school men don't end like this," I said to myself. It was a long half hour, but luckily they had left a decanter of whisky in there with me. They'd all had a few, I think. That's what made them all so solemn. There wasn't much whisky left when they came back, and, what with that and the strain of the situation, I could only laugh when they came in. Silly thing to do, but they looked so surprised, seeing me there alive and drunk.

' "The man's a cad," said the colonel, but even then I couldn't stop laughing, so they put me under arrest and called a court-martial.

'I must say I felt pretty low next day. A major came over from another battalion to try my case. He came to see me first, and bless me if it wasn't a cove I'd known at school.

' "God bless my soul," he said, "if it isn't Grimes of Podger's! What's all this nonsense about a court-martial?" So I told him. "H'm," he said, "pretty bad. Still, it's out of the question to shoot an old Harrovian. I'll see what I can do about it." And next day I was sent to Ireland on a pretty cushy job connected with postal service. That saw me out as far as the war was concerned. You can't get into the soup in Ireland, do what you like. I don't know if all this bores you?'

'Not at all,' said Paul. 'I think it's most encouraging.'

'I've been in the soup pretty often since then, but never quite so badly. Someone always turns up and says, "I can't see a public school man down and out. Let me put you on your feet again." I should think,' said Grimes, 'I've been put on my feet more often than any living man.'

Philbrick came across the bar parlour towards them.

'Feeling lonely?' he said. 'I've been talking to the station-master here, and if either of you wants an introduction to a young lady – '

'Certainly not,' said Paul.

'Oh, all right,' said Philbrick, making off.

'Women are an enigma,' said Grimes, 'as far as Grimes is concerned.'

CHAPTER 4
Mr Prendergast

PAUL was awakened next morning by a loud bang on his door, and Beste-Chetwynde looked in. He was wearing a very expensive-looking Charvet dressing-gown.

'Good morning, sir,' he said. 'I thought I'd come and tell you, as you wouldn't know: there's only one bathroom for the masters. If you want to get there before Mr Prendergast, you ought to go now. Captain Grimes doesn't wash much,' he added, and then disappeared.

Paul went to the bath and was rewarded some minutes later by hearing the shuffling of slippers down the passage and the door furiously rattled.

As he was dressing Philbrick appeared.

'Oh, I forgot to call you. Breakfast is in ten minutes.'

After breakfast Paul went up to the Common Room. Mr Prendergast was there polishing his pipes, one by one, with a chamois leather. He looked reproachfully at Paul.

'We must come to some arrangement about the bathroom,' he said. 'Grimes very rarely has a bath. I have one before breakfast.'

'So do I,' said Paul defiantly.

'Then I suppose I shall have to find some other time,' said Mr Prendergast, and he gave a deep sigh as he returned his attention to his pipes. 'After ten years, too,' he added, 'but everything's like that. I might have known you'd want the bath. It was so easy when there was only Grimes and that other young man. He was never down in time for breakfast. Oh dear! oh dear! I can see that things are going to be very difficult.'

'But surely we could both have one?'

'No, no, that's out of the question. It's all part of the same thing. Everything has been like this since I left the ministry.'

Paul made no answer, and Mr Prendergast went on breathing and rubbing.

'I expect you wonder how I came to be here?'

'No, no,' said Paul soothingly. 'I think it's very natural.'

'It's not natural at all; it's most unnatural. If things had happened a little differently I should be a rector with my own little house and bathroom. I might even have been a rural dean, only' – and Mr Prendergast dropped his voice to a whisper – 'only I had *Doubts*.

'I don't know why I'm telling you all this, nobody else knows. I somehow feel you'll understand.

'Ten years ago I was a clergyman of the Church of England. I had just been presented to a living in Worthing. It was such an attractive church, not old, but *very* beautifully decorated, six candles on the altar, Reservation in the Lady Chapel, and an excellent heating apparatus which burned coke in a little shed by the sacristy door, no graveyard, just a hedge of golden privet between the church and the rectory.

'As soon as I moved in my mother came to keep house for me. She bought some chintz, out of her own money, for the drawing-room curtains. She used to be "at home" once a week to the ladies of the congregation. One of them, the dentist's wife, gave me a set of the *Encyclopaedia Britannica* for my study. It was all very pleasant until my *Doubts* began.'

'Were they as bad as all that?' asked Paul.

'They were insuperable,' said Mr Prendergast; 'that is why I am here now. But I expect I am boring you?'

'No, do go on. That's to say, unless you find it painful to think about.'

'I think about it all the time. It happened like this, quite suddenly. We had been there about three months, and my mother had made great friends with some people called Bundle – rather a curious name. I think he was an insurance agent until he retired. Mrs Bundle used very kindly to ask us in to supper on Sundays after Evensong. They were pleasant informal gatherings, and I used quite to look forward to them. I can see them now as they sat there on this particular evening; there was my mother and Mr and Mrs Bundle, and their son, rather a spotty boy, I remember, who used to go in to Brighton College by train every day, and Mrs Bundle's mother, a Mrs Crump, rather deaf, but a very good Churchwoman, and Mrs Aber – that was the name of the dentist's wife who gave me the *Encyclopaedia Britannica* – and old Major Ending, the people's warden. I had preached two sermons that day besides taking the children's Bible-class in the afternoon, and I had rather dropped out of the conversation. They were all talking away quite happily about the preparations that were being made on the pier for the summer season, when suddenly, for no reason at all, my *Doubts* began.' He paused, and Paul felt constrained to offer some expression of sympathy.

'What a terrible thing!' he said.

'Yes, I've not known an hour's real happiness since. You see, it wasn't the ordinary sort of Doubt about Cain's wife or the Old Testament miracles or the consecration of Archbishop Parker. I'd been taught how to explain all those while I was at college.

No, it was something deeper than all that. *I couldn't understand why God had made the world at all.* There was my mother and the Bundles and Mrs Crump talking away quite unconcernedly while I sat there wrestling with this sudden assault of doubt. You see how fundamental that is. Once granted the first step, I can see that everything else follows – Tower of Babel, Babylonian captivity, Incarnation, Church, bishops, incense, everything – but what I couldn't see, and what I can't see now, is, *why* did it all begin?

'I asked my bishop; he didn't know. He said that he didn't think the point really arose as far as my practical duties as a parish priest were concerned. I discussed it with my mother. At first she was inclined to regard it as a passing phase. But it didn't pass, so finally she agreed with me that the only honourable thing to do was to resign my living; she never really recovered from the shock, poor old lady. It was a great blow after she had bought the chintz and got so friendly with the Bundles.'

A bell began ringing down a distant passage.

'Well, well, we must go to prayers, and I haven't finished my pipes.' He took his gown from the peg behind the door and slipped it over his shoulders.

'Perhaps one day I shall see Light,' he said, 'and then I shall go back to the ministry. Meanwhile –'

Clutterbuck ran past the door, whistling hideously.

'That's a nasty little boy,' said Mr Prendergast, 'if ever there was one.'

CHAPTER 5
Discipline

PRAYERS were held downstairs in the main hall of the Castle. The boys stood ranged along the panelled walls, each holding in his hands a little pile of books. Grimes sat on one of the chairs beside the baronial chimneypiece.

'Morning,' he said to Paul; 'only just down, I'm afraid. Do I smell of drink?'

'Yes,' said Paul.

'Comes of missing breakfast. Prendy been telling you about his Doubts?'

'Yes,' said Paul.

'Funny thing,' said Grimes, 'but I've never been worried in that way. I don't pretend to be a particularly pious sort of chap, but I've never had any Doubts. When you've been in the soup as often as I have, it gives you a sort of feeling that everything's for the best, really. You know, God's in His heaven; all's right with the world. I can't quite explain it, but I don't believe one can ever be unhappy for long provided one does just exactly what one wants to and when one wants to. The last chap who put me on my feet said I was "singularly in harmony with the primitive promptings of humanity". I've remembered that phrase because somehow it seemed to fit me. Here comes the old man. This is where we stand up.'

As the bell stopped ringing Dr Fagan swept into the hall, the robes of a Doctor of Philosophy swelling and billowing about him. He wore an orchid in his buttonhole.

'Good morning, gentlemen,' he said.

'Good morning, sir,' chorused the boys.

The Doctor advanced to the table at the end of the room, picked up a Bible, and opening it at random, read a chapter of blood-curdling military history without any evident relish. From that he plunged into the Lord's prayer, which the boys took up in a quiet chatter. Prendergast's voice led them in tones that testified to his ecclesiastical past.

Then the Doctor glanced at a sheet of notes he held in his hand. 'Boys,' he said, 'I have some announcements to make. The Fagan cross-country running challenge cup will not be competed for this year on account of the floods.'

'I expect the old boy has popped it,' said Grimes in Paul's ear.

'Nor will the Llanabba Essay Prize.'

'On account of the floods,' said Grimes.

'I have received my account for the telephone,' proceeded Dr Fagan, 'and I find that during the past quarter there have been no less than twenty-three trunk calls to London, none of which was sent by me or by members of my family. I look to the prefects to stop this, unless of course they are themselves responsible, in which case I must urge them in my own interests to make use of the village post-office, to which they have access.

'I think that is everything, isn't it, Mr Prendergast?'

'*Cigars*,' said Mr Prendergast in a stage whisper.

'Ah yes, cigars. Boys, I have been deeply distressed to learn that several cigar ends have been found – where have they been found?'

'*Boiler-room.*'

'In the boiler-room. I regard this as reprehensible. What boy has been smoking cigars in the boiler-room?'

There was a prolonged silence, during which the Doctor's eye travelled down the line of boys.

'I will give the culprit until luncheon to give himself up. If I do not hear from him by then the whole school will be heavily punished.'

'Damn!' said Grimes. 'I gave those cigars to Clutterbuck. I hope the little beast has the sense to keep quiet.'

'Go to your classes,' said the Doctor.

The boys filed out.

'I should think, by the look of them, they were exceedingly cheap cigars,' added Mr Prendergast sadly. 'They were a pale yellow colour.'

'That makes it worse,' said the Doctor. 'To think of any boy under my charge smoking pale yellow cigars in a boiler-room! It is *not* a gentlemanly fault.'

The masters went upstairs.

'That's your little mob in there,' said Grimes; 'you let them out at eleven.'

'But what am I to teach them?' said Paul in sudden panic.

'Oh, I shouldn't try to *teach* them anything, not just yet, anyway. Just keep them quiet.'

'Now that's a thing I've never learned to do,' sighed Mr Prendergast.

Paul watched him amble into his classroom at the end of the passage, where a burst of applause greeted his arrival. Dumb with terror he went into his own classroom.

Ten boys sat before him, their hands folded, their eyes bright with expectation.

'Good morning, sir,' said the one nearest him.

'Good morning,' said Paul.

'Good morning, sir,' said the next.

'Good morning,' said Paul.

'Good morning, sir,' said the next.

'Oh, shut up,' said Paul.

At this the boy took out a handkerchief and began to cry quietly.

'Oh, sir,' came a chorus of reproach, 'you've hurt his feelings. He's very sensitive; it's his Welsh blood, you know; it makes people very emotional. Say "Good morning" to him, sir, or he won't be happy all day. After all, it is a good morning, isn't it, sir?'

'Silence!' shouted Paul above the uproar, and for a few moments things were quieter.

'Please, sir,' said a small voice – Paul turned and saw a grave-looking youth holding up his hand – 'please, sir, perhaps he's been smoking cigars and doesn't feel well.'

'Silence!' said Paul again.

The ten boys stopped talking and sat perfectly still staring at him. He felt himself getting hot and red under their scrutiny.

'I suppose the first thing I ought to do is to get your names clear. What is your name?' he asked, turning to the first boy.

'Tangent, sir.'

'And yours?'

'Tangent, sir,' said the next boy. Paul's heart sank.

'But you can't both be called Tangent.'

'No, sir, *I'm* Tangent. He's just trying to be funny.'

'I like that. *Me* trying to be funny! Please, sir, I'm Tangent, sir; really I am.'

'If it comes to that,' said Clutterbuck from the back of the room, 'there is only one Tangent here, and that is me. Anyone else can jolly well go to blazes.'

Paul felt desperate.

'Well, is there anyone who isn't Tangent?'

Four or five voices instantly arose.

'I'm not, sir; I'm not Tangent. I wouldn't be called Tangent, not on the end of a barge pole.'

In a few seconds the room had become divided into two parties: those who were Tangent and those who were not. Blows were already being exchanged, when the door opened and Grimes came in. There was a slight hush.

'I thought you might want this,' he said, handing Paul a walking-stick. 'And if you take my advice, you'll set them something to do.'

He went out; and Paul, firmly grasping the walking-stick, faced his form.

'Listen,' he said. 'I don't care a damn what any of you are called, but if there's another word from anyone I shall keep you all in this afternoon.'

'You can't keep me in,' said Clutterbuck; 'I'm going for a walk with Captain Grimes.'

'Then I shall very nearly kill you with this stick. Meanwhile you will all write an essay on "Self-indulgence". There will be a prize of half a crown for the longest essay, irrespective of any possible merit.'

From then onwards all was silence until break. Paul, still holding his stick, gazed despondently out of the window. Now and then there rose from below the shrill voices of the servants scolding each other in Welsh. By the time the bell rang Clutterbuck had covered sixteen pages, and was awarded the half-crown.

'Did you find those boys difficult to manage?' asked Mr Prendergast, filling his pipe.

'Not at all,' said Paul.

'Ah, you're lucky. I find all boys utterly intractable. I don't know why it is. Of course my wig has a lot to do with it. Have you noticed that I wear a wig?'

'No, no, of course not.'

'Well, the boys did as soon as they saw it. It was a great mistake my ever getting one. I thought when I left Worthing that I looked too old to get a job easily. I was only forty-one. It was very expensive, even though I chose the cheapest quality. Perhaps that's why it looks so like a wig. I don't know. I knew from the first that it was a mistake, but once they had seen it, it was too late to go back. They make all sorts of jokes about it.'

'I expect they'd laugh at something else if it wasn't that.'

'Yes, no doubt they would. I daresay it's a good thing to localize their ridicule as far as possible. Oh dear! oh dear! If it wasn't for my pipes, I don't know how I should manage to keep on. What made you come here?'

'I was sent down from Scone for indecent behaviour.'

'Oh yes, like Grimes?'

'No,' said Paul firmly, 'not like Grimes.'

'Oh, well, it's all much the same really. And there's the bell. Oh dear! oh dear! I believe that loathsome little man's taken my gown.'

*

Two days later Beste-Chetwynde pulled out the *vox humana* and played *Pop goes the Weasel.*

'D'you know, sir, you've made rather a hit with the fifth form?'

He and Paul were seated in the organ-loft of the village church. It was their second music-lesson.

'For goodness' sake, leave the organ alone. How d'you mean "hit"?'

'Well, Clutterbuck was in the matron's room this morning. He'd just got a tin of pineapple chunks. Tangent said, "Are you going to take that into Hall?" and he said, "No, I'm going to eat them in Mr Pennyfeather's hour." "Oh no, you're not," said Tangent. "Sweets and biscuits are one thing, but pineapple chunks are going too far. It's little stinkers like you," he said, "who turn decent masters savage."'

'Do you think that's so very complimentary?'

'I think it's one of the most complimentary things I ever heard said about a master,' said Beste-Chetwynde; 'would you like me to try that hymn again?'

'No,' said Paul decisively.

'Well, then, I'll tell you another thing,' said Beste-Chetwynde. 'You know that man Philbrick. Well, I think there's something odd about him.'

'I've no doubt of it.'

'It's not just that he's such a bad butler. The servants are always ghastly here. But I don't believe he's a butler at all.'

'I don't quite see what else he *can* be.'

'Well, have you ever known a butler with a diamond tie-pin?'

'No, I don't think I have.'

'Well, Philbrick's got one, and a diamond ring too. He showed them to Brolly. Colossal great diamonds, Brolly says. Philbrick said he used to have bushels of diamonds and emeralds before the war, and that he used to eat off gold plate. We believe that he's a Russian prince in exile.'

'Generally speaking, Russians are not shy about using their titles, are they? Besides, he looks very English.'

'Yes, we thought of that, but Brolly said lots of Russians came to school in England before the war. And now I *am* going to play the organ,' said Beste-Chetwynde. 'After all, my mother does pay five guineas a term extra for me to learn.'

CHAPTER 6
Conduct

SITTING over the Common Room fire that afternoon waiting for the bell for tea, Paul found himself reflecting that on the whole the last week had not been quite as awful as he had expected. As Beste-Chetwynde had told him, he was a distinct success with his form; after the first day an understanding had been established between them. It was tacitly agreed that when Paul wished to read or to write letters he was allowed to do so undisturbed while he left them to employ the time as they thought best; when Paul took it upon him to talk to them about their lessons they remained silent, and when he set them work to do some of it was done. It had rained steadily, so that there had been no games. No punishments, no reprisals, no exertion, and in the evenings the confessions of Grimes, any one of which would have glowed with outstanding shamelessness from the appendix to a treatise in psycho-analysis.

Mr Prendergast came in with the post.

'A letter for you, two for Grimes, nothing for me,' he said. 'No one ever writes to me. There was a time when I used to get five or six letters a day, not counting circulars. My mother used to file them for me to answer – one heap of charity appeals, another for personal letters, another for marriages and funerals, another for baptisms and churchings, and another for anonymous abuse. I wonder why it is the clergy always get so many letters of that sort, sometimes from quite educated people. I remember my father had great trouble in that way once, and he was forced to call in the police because they became so threatening. And, do you know, it was the curate's wife who had sent them – such a quiet little woman. There's your letter. Grimes' look like bills. I can't think why shops give that man credit at all. I always pay cash, or at least I should if I ever bought anything. But d'you know that, except for my tobacco and the *Daily News* and occasionally a little port when it's very cold, I don't think I've bought anything for two years. The last thing I bought was that walking-stick. I got it at Shanklin, and Grimes uses it for beating the boys with. I hadn't really meant to buy one, but I was there for the day – two years this August – and I went into the tobacconist's to buy some tobacco. He hadn't the sort I wanted, and I felt I couldn't go out without getting something, so I bought that. It cost one-and-six,' he added wistfully, 'so I had no tea.'

Paul took his letter. It had been forwarded from Onslow Square. On the flap were embossed the arms of Scone College. It was from one of his four friends.

Scone College, J.C.R.,
Oxford.

My dear Pennyfeather, it ran,

I need hardly tell you how distressed I was when I heard of your disastrous misfortune. It seems to me that a real injustice has been done to you. I have not heard the full facts of the case, but I was confirmed in my opinion by a very curious incident last evening. I was just going to bed when Digby-Vane-Trumpington came into my rooms without knocking. He was smoking a cigar. I had never spoken to him before, as you know, and was very much surprised at his visit. He said: 'I'm told you are a friend of Pennyfeather's.' I said I was, and he said: 'Well, I gather I've rather got him into a mess'; I said: 'Yes,' and he said: 'Well, will you apologize to him for me when you write?' I said I would. Then he said: 'Look here, I'm told he's rather poor. I thought of sending him some money – £20 for sort of damages, you know. It's all I can spare at the moment. Wouldn't it be a useful thing to do?' I fairly let him have it, I can tell you, and told him just what I thought of him for making such an insulting suggestion. I asked him how he dared treat a gentleman like that just because he wasn't in his awful set. He seemed rather taken aback and said: 'Well all my *friends spend all their time trying to get money out of me,' and went off.*

I bicycled over to St Magnus's at Little Bechley and took some rubbings of the brasses there. I wished you had been with me.

Yours,
Arthur Potts.

PS. – *I understand you are thinking of taking up educational work. It seems to me that the great problem of education is to train the moral perceptions, not merely to discipline the appetites. I cannot help thinking that it is in greater fastidiousness rather than in greater self-control that the future progress of the race lies. I shall be interested to hear what your experience has been over the matter. The chaplain does not agree with me in this. He says great sensibility usually leads to enervation of will. Let me know what you think.*

'What do you think about that?' asked Paul, handing Mr Prendergast the letter.

'Well,' he said after studying it carefully, 'I think your friend is wrong about sensibility. It doesn't do to rely on one's own feelings, does it, not in anything?'

'No, I mean about the money.'

'Good gracious, Pennyfeather! I hope you are in no doubt about that. Accept it at once, of course.'

'It's a temptation.'

'My dear boy, it would be a sin to refuse. Twenty pounds! Why, it takes me half a term to earn that.'

The bell rang for tea. In the dining-hall Paul gave the letter to Grimes.

'Shall I take the twenty pounds?' he asked.

'Take it? My God! I should think you would.'

'Well, I'm not sure,' said Paul.

He thought about it all through afternoon school, all the time he was dressing for dinner, and all through dinner. It was a severe struggle, but his early training was victorious.

'If I take that money,' he said to himself, 'I shall never know whether I have acted rightly or not. It would always be on my mind. If I refuse, I shall be sure of having done right. I shall look upon my self-denial with exquisite self-approval. By refusing I can convince myself that, in spite of the unbelievable things that have been happening to me during the last ten days, I am still the same Paul Pennyfeather I have respected so long. It is a test-case of the durability of my ideals.'

He tried to explain something of what he felt to Grimes as they sat in Mrs Roberts' bar parlour that evening.

'I'm afraid you'll find my attitude rather difficult to understand,' he said. 'I suppose it's largely a matter of upbringing. There is every reason why I should take this money. Digby-Vane-Trumpington is exceedingly rich; and if he keeps it, it will undoubtedly be spent on betting or on some deplorable debauch. Owing to his party I have suffered irreparable harm. My whole future is shattered, and I have directly lost one hundred and twenty pounds a year in scholarships and two hundred and fifty pounds a year allowance from my guardian. By any ordinary process of thought, the money is justly mine. But,' said Paul Pennyfeather, 'there is my honour. For generations the British bourgeoisie have spoken of themselves as gentlemen, and by that they have meant, among other things, a self-respecting scorn of irregular perquisites. It is the quality that distinguishes the gentleman from both the artist and the aristocrat. Now I am a gentleman. I can't help it: it's born in me. I just can't take that money.'

'Well, I'm a gentleman too, old boy,' said Grimes, 'and I was afraid you might feel like that, so I did my best for you and saved you from yourself.'

'What d'you mean by that?'

'Dear old boy, don't be angry, but immediately after tea I sent off a wire to your friend Potts: *Tell Trumpington send money quick*, and signed it "*Pennyfeather*". I don't mind lending you the bob till it comes, either.'

'Grimes, you wretch!' said Paul, but, in spite of himself, he felt a great wave of satisfaction surge up within him. 'We must have another drink on that.'

'Good for you,' said Grimes, 'and it's on me this round.'

'To the durability of ideals!' said Paul as he got his pint.

'My word, what a mouthful!' said Grimes; 'I can't say that. Cheerioh!'

*

Two days later came another letter from Arthur Potts:

Dear Pennyfeather,

I enclose Trumpington's cheque for £20. I am glad that my dealings with him are at an end. I cannot pretend to understand your attitude in this matter, but no doubt you are the best judge.

Stiggins is reading a paper to the O.S.C.U. on 'Sex Repression and Religious Experience'. *Everyone expects rather a row, because you know how keen Walton is on the mystical element, which I think Stiggins is inclined to discount.*

Yours,
Arthur Potts.

There is a most interesting article in the 'Educational Review' *on the new methods that are being tried at the Innesborough High School to induce co-ordination of the senses. They put small objects into the children's mouths and make them draw the shapes in red chalk. Have you tried this with your boys? I must say I envy you your opportunities. Are your colleagues enlightened?*

'This same Potts,' said Grimes as he read the letter, 'would appear to be something of a stinker. Still, we've got the doings. How about a binge?'

'Yes,' said Paul, 'I think we ought to do something about one. I should like to ask Prendy too.'

'Why, of course. It's just what Prendy needs. He's been looking awfully down in the mouth lately. Why shouldn't we all go over to the Metropole at Cwmpryddyg for dinner one night? We shall have to wait until the old boy goes away, otherwise he'll notice that there's no one on duty.'

Later in the day Paul suggested the plan to Mr Prendergast.

'Really, Pennyfeather,' he said, 'I think that's uncommonly kind of you. I hardly know what to say. Of course, I should love it. I can't remember when I dined at an hotel last. Certainly not since the war. It *will* be a treat. My dear boy. I'm quite overcome.'

And, much to Paul's embarrassment, a tear welled-up in each of Mr Prendergast's eyes, and coursed down his cheeks.

CHAPTER 7
Philbrick

THAT morning just before luncheon the weather began to show signs of clearing, and by half-past one the sun was shining. The Doctor made one of his rare visits to the school dining-hall. At his entry everybody stopped eating and laid down his knife and fork.

'Boys,' said the Doctor, regarding them benignly, 'I have an announcement to make. Clutterbuck, will you kindly stop eating while I am addressing the school. The boys' manners need correcting, Mr Prendergast. I look to the prefects to see to this. Boys, the chief sporting event of the year will take place in the playing-fields to-morrow. I refer to the Annual School Sports, unfortunately postponed last year owing to the General Strike. Mr Pennyfeather, who, as you know, is himself a distinguished athlete, will be in charge of all arrangements. The preliminary heats will be run off to-day. All boys must compete in all events. The Countess of Circumference has kindly consented to present the prizes. Mr Prendergast will act as referee, and Captain Grimes as timekeeper. I shall myself be present to-morrow to watch the final competitions. That is all, thank you. Mr Pennyfeather, perhaps you will favour me with an interview when you have finished your luncheon?'

'Good God!' murmured Paul.

'I won the long-jump at the last sports,' said Briggs, 'but everyone said that it was because I had spiked shoes. Do you wear spiked shoes, sir?'

'Invariably,' said Paul.

'Everyone said it was taking an unfair advantage. You see, we never know beforehand when there's going to be sports, so we don't have time to get ready.'

'My mamma's coming down to see me to-morrow,' said Beste-Chetwynde; 'just my luck! Now I shall have to stay here all the afternoon.'

After luncheon Paul went to the morning-room, where he found the Doctor pacing up and down in evident high excitement.

'Ah, come in, Pennyfeather! I am just making the arrangements for to-morrow's fête. Florence, will you get on to the Clutterbucks on the telephone and ask them to come over, and the Hope-Brownes. I think the Warringtons are too far away, but you might ask them, and of course the Vicar and old Major Sidebotham. The more guests the better, Florence!

'And, Diana, you must arrange the tea. Sandwiches, *foie gras* sandwiches – last time, you remember, the liver sausage you bought made Lady Bunway ill – and cakes, plenty of cakes, with coloured sugar! You had better take the car into Llandudno and get them there.

'Philbrick, there must be champagne-cup, and will you help the men putting up the marquee. And flags, Diana! There must be flags left over from last time.'

'I made them into dusters,' said Dingy.

'Well, we must buy more. No expense must be spared. Pennyfeather, I want you to get the results of the first heats out by four o'clock. Then you can telephone them to the printers, and we shall have the programmes by to-morrow. Tell them that fifty will be enough; they must be decorated with the school colours and crest in gold. And there must be flowers, Diana, banks of flowers,' said the Doctor with an expansive gesture. 'The prizes shall stand among banks of flowers. Do you think there ought to be a bouquet for Lady Circumference?'

'No,' said Dingy.

'Nonsense!' said the Doctor. 'Of course there must be a bouquet. It is rarely that the scholarly calm of Llanabba gives place to festival, but when it does taste and dignity shall go unhampered. It shall be an enormous bouquet, redolent of hospitality. You are to produce the most expensive bouquet that Wales can offer; do you understand? Flowers, youth, wisdom, the glitter of jewels, music,' said the Doctor, his imagination soaring to dizzy heights under the stimulus of the words, 'music! There must be a band.'

'I never heard of such a thing,' said Dingy. 'A band indeed! You'll be having fireworks next.'

'*And fireworks*,' said the Doctor, 'and do you think it would be a good thing to buy Mr Prendergast a new tie? I noticed how shabby he looked this morning.'

'No,' said Dingy with finality, 'that is going too far. Flowers and fireworks are one thing, but I insist on drawing a line somewhere. It would be sinful to buy Mr Prendergast a tie.'

'Perhaps you are right,' said the Doctor. 'But there shall be music. I understand that the Llanabba Silver Band was third at the North Wales Eisteddfod last month. Will you get on to them, Florence? I think Mr Davies at the station is the bandmaster. Can the Clutterbucks come?'

'Yes,' said Flossie, 'six of them.'

'Admirable! And then there is the Press. We must ring up the *Flint and Denbigh Herald* and get them to send a photographer. That means whisky. Will you see to that, Philbrick? I remember at one of our sports I omitted to offer whisky to the Press, and the result was a *most* unfortunate photograph. Boys do get into such indelicate positions during the obstacle race, don't they?

'Then there are the prizes. I think you had better take Grimes into Llandudno with you to help with the prizes. I don't think there is any need for undue extravagance with the prizes. It gives boys a wrong idea of sport. I wonder whether Lady Circumference would think it odd if we asked her to present parsley crowns. Perhaps she would. Utility, economy, and apparent durability are the qualities to be sought for, I think.

'And, Pennyfeather, I hope you will see that they are distributed fairly evenly about the school. It doesn't do to let any boy win more than two events; I leave you to arrange that. I think it would be only right if little Lord Tangent won something, and Beste-Chetwynde – yes, his mother is coming down, too.

'I am afraid all this has been thrown upon your shoulders rather suddenly. I only learned this morning that Lady Circumference proposed to visit us, and as Mrs Beste-Chetwynde was coming too, it seemed too good an opportunity to be missed. It is not often that the visits of two such important parents coincide. She is the Honourable Mrs Beste-Chetwynde, you know – sister-in-law of Lord Pastmaster – a very wealthy woman, South American. They always say that she poisoned her husband, but of course little Beste-Chetwynde doesn't know that. It never came into court, but there was a great deal of talk about it at the time. Perhaps you remember the case?'

'No,' said Paul.

'Powdered glass,' said Flossie shrilly, 'in his coffee.'

'Turkish coffee,' said Dingy.

'To work!' said the Doctor; 'we have a lot to see to.'

*

It was raining again by the time that Paul and Mr Prendergast reached the playing-fields. The boys were waiting for them in bleak little groups, shivering at the unaccustomed austerity of bare knees and open necks. Clutterbuck had fallen down in the mud and was crying quietly behind a tree.

'How shall we divide them?' said Paul.

'I don't know,' said Mr Prendergast. 'Frankly, I deplore the whole business.'

Philbrick appeared in an overcoat and a bowler hat.

'Miss Fagan says she's very sorry, but she's burnt the hurdles and the jumping posts for firewood. She thinks she can hire some in Llandudno for to-morrow. The Doctor says you must do the best you can till then. I've got to help the gardeners put up the blasted tent.'

'I think that, if anything, sports are rather worse than concerts,' said Mr Prendergast. 'They at least happen indoors. Oh dear! oh dear! How wet I am getting. I should have got my boots mended if I'd known this was going to happen.'

'Please, sir,' said Beste-Chetwynde, 'we're all getting rather cold. Can we start?'

'Yes, I suppose so,' said Paul. 'What do you want to do?'

'Well, we ought to divide up into heats and then run a race.'

'All right! Get into four groups.'

This took some time. They tried to induce Mr Prendergast to run too.

'The first race will be a mile. Prendy, will you look after them? I want to see if Philbrick and I can fix up anything for the jumping.'

'But what am I to do?' said Mr Prendergast.

'Just make each group run to the Castle and back and take the names of the first two in each heat. It's quite simple.'

'I'll try,' he said sadly.

Paul and Philbrick went into the pavilion together.

'Me, a butler,' said Philbrick, 'made to put up tents like a blinking Arab!'

'Well, it's a change,' said Paul.

'It's a change for me to be a butler,' said Philbrick. 'I wasn't made to be anyone's servant.'

'No, I suppose not.'

'I expect you wonder how it is that I come to be here?' said Philbrick.

'No,' said Paul firmly, 'nothing of the kind. I don't in the least want to know anything about you; d'you hear?'

'I'll tell you,' said Philbrick; 'it was like this –'

'I don't want to hear your loathsome confessions; can't you understand?'

'It isn't a loathsome confession,' said Philbrick. 'It's a story of love. I think it is without exception the most beautiful story I know.

'I daresay you have heard of Sir Solomon Philbrick?'

'No,' said Paul.

'What, never heard of old Solly Philbrick?'

'No; why?'

'Because that's me. And I can tell you this. It's a pretty well-known name across the river. You've only to say Solly Philbrick, of the "Lamb and Flag", anywhere south of Waterloo Bridge to see what fame is. Try it.'

'I will one day.'

'Mind you, when I say *Sir* Solomon Philbrick, that's only a bit of fun, see? That's what the boys call me. Plain Mr Solomon Philbrick I am, really, just like you or him,' with a jerk of the thumb towards the playing-fields, from which Mr Prendergast's voice could be heard crying weakly: 'Oh, do get into line, you beastly boys,' 'but *Sir* Solomon's what they call me. Out of respect, see?'

'When I say, "Are you ready? Go!" I want you to go,' Mr Prendergast could be heard saying. 'Are you ready? Go! Oh, why *don't* you go?' And his voice became drowned in shrill cries of protest.

'Mind you,' went on Philbrick, 'I haven't always been in the position that I am now. I was brought up rough, damned rough. Ever heard speak of "Chick" Philbrick?'

'No, I'm afraid not.'

'No, I suppose he was before your time. Useful little boxer, though. Not first-class, on account of his drinking so much *and* being short in the arm. Still, he used to earn five pound a night at the Lambeth Stadium. Always popular with the boys, he was, even when he was so full, he couldn't hardly fight. He was my dad, a good-hearted sort of fellow but rough, as I was telling you; he used to knock my poor mother about something awful. Got jugged for it twice, but my! he took it out of her when he got out. There aren't many left like him nowadays, what with education and whisky the price it is.

' "Chick" was all for getting me on in the sporting world, and before I left school I was earning a few shillings a week holding the sponge at the Stadium on Saturday nights. It was there I met Toby Cruttwell. Perhaps you ain't heard of him, neither?'

'No, I am terribly afraid I haven't. I'm not very well up in sporting characters.'

'Sporting! What, Toby Cruttwell a sporting character! You make me laugh. Toby Cruttwell,' said Philbrick with renewed emphasis, 'what brought off the Buller diamond robbery of 1912, and the Amalgamated Steel Trust robbery of 1910, and the Isle of Wight burglaries in 1914? He wasn't no sporting character, Toby wasn't. Sporting character! D'you know what he done to Alf Larrigan, what tried to put it over on one of his girls? I'll tell you. Toby had a doctor in tow at the time, name of Peterfield; lives in Harley Street, with a swell lot of patients. Well, Toby knew a thing about him. He'd done in one of Toby's girls what went to him because she was going to have a kid. Well, Toby knew that, so he had to do what Toby told him, see?

'Toby didn't kill Alf; that wasn't his way. Toby never killed no one except a lot of blinking Turks the time they gave him the V.C. But he got hold of him and took him to Dr Peterfield, and –' Philbrick's voice sank to a whisper.

'Second heat, get ready. Now, if you don't go when I say "Go", I shall disqualify you all; d'you hear? Are you ready? *Go!*'

'... He hadn't no use for girls after that. Ha, ha, ha! Sporting character's good. Well, me and Toby worked together for five years. I was with him in the Steel Trust and the Buller diamonds, and we cleared a nice little profit. Toby took 75 per cent, him being the older man, but even with that I did pretty well. Just before the war we split. He stuck to safe-cracking, and I settled down comfortable at the "Lamb and Flag", Camberwell Green. A very fine house that was before the war, and it's the best in the locality now, though I says it. Things aren't quite so easy as they was, but I can't complain. I've got the Picture House next to it, too. Just mention my name there any day you like to have a free seat.'

'That's very kind of you.'

'You're welcome. Well, then there was the war. Toby got the V.C. in the Dardanelles and turned respectable. He's in Parliament now – Major Cruttwell, M.P., Conservative member for some potty town on the South Coast. My old woman ran the pub for me. Didn't tell you I was married, did I? Pretty enough bit of goods when we was spliced, but she ran to fat. Women do in the public-house business. After the war things were a bit slow, and then my old woman kicked the bucket. I didn't think I'd mind much, her having got so fat and all, nor I didn't not at first, but after a time, when the excitement of the funeral had died down and things were going on just the same as usual, I began to get restless. You know how things get, and I took to reading the papers. Before that my old woman used to read out the bits she'd like, and sometimes I'd listen and sometimes I wouldn't, but anyhow they weren't the things that interested me. She never took no interest in crime, not unless it was a murder. But I took to reading the police news, and I took to dropping in at the pictures whenever they sent me a crook film. I didn't sleep so well, neither, and I used to lie awake thinking of old times. Of course I could have married again: in my position I could have married pretty well who I liked; but it wasn't that I wanted.

'Then one Saturday night I came into the bar. I generally drop in on Saturday evenings and smoke a cigar and stand a round of drinks. It sets the right tone. I wear a buttonhole in the summer, too, and a diamond ring. Well, I was in the saloon when who did I see in the corner but Jimmy Drage – cove I used to know when I was working with Toby Cruttwell. I never see a man look more discouraged.

'"Hullo, Jimmy!" I says. "We don't see each other as often as we used. How are things with you?" I says it cordial, but careful like, because I didn't know what Jimmy was up to.

'"Pretty bad," said Jimmy. "Just fooled a job."

'"What sort of job?" I says. "Nobbling," he says, meaning kidnapping.

'"It was like this," he says. "You know a toff called Lord Utteridge?"

'"The bloke what had them electric burglar alarms," I says, "Utteridge House, Belgrave Square?"

'"That's the blinking bastard. Well, he's got a son – nasty little kid about twelve, just going off to college for the first time. I'd had my eye on him," Jimmy said, "for a long time, him being the only son and his father so rich, so when I'd finished the last job I was on I had a go at him. Everything went as easy as drinking," Jimmy said. There was a garage just round the corner behind Belgrave Square where he used to go every morning to watch them messing about with cars. Crazy about cars the kid was. Jimmy comes in one day with his motor-bike and side-car and asks for some petrol. He comes up and looks at it in the way he had.

'"That bike's no good," he says. "No good?" says Jimmy. "I wouldn't sell it not for a hundred quid, I wouldn't. This bike," he says, "won the Grand Prix at Boulogne." "Nonsense!" the kid says; "it wouldn't do thirty, not downhill." "Well, just you see," Jimmy says. "Come for a run? I bet you I'll do eighty on the road." In he got, and away they went till they got to a place Jimmy knew. Then Jimmy shuts him up safe and writes to the father. The kid was happy as blazes taking down the engine of Jimmy's bike. It's never been the same since, Jimmy told me, but then it wasn't much to talk of before. Everything had gone through splendid till Jimmy got his answer from Lord Utteridge. Would you believe it, that unnatural father wouldn't stump up, him that owns ships and coal mines enough to buy the blinking Bank of England. Said he was much obliged to Jimmy for the trouble he had taken, that the dearest wish of his life had been gratified and the one barrier to his complete happiness removed, but that, as the matter had been taken up without his instructions, he did not feel called upon to make any payment in respect of it, and remained his sincerely, Utteridge.

'That was a nasty one for Jimmy. He wrote once or twice after that, but got no answer, so by the time the kid had spread bits of the bike all over the room Jimmy let him go.

' "Did you try pulling out 'is teeth and sending them to his pa?" I asks.

' "No," says Jimmy, "I didn't do that."

' "Did you make the kid write pathetic, asking to be let out?"

' "No," says Jimmy, "I didn't do that."

' "Did you cut off one of his fingers and put it in the letter-box?"

' "No," he says.

' "Well, man alive," I says, "you don't deserve to succeed, you just don't know your job."

' "Oh, cut that out," he says; "it's easy to talk. You've been out of the business ten years. You don't know what things are like nowadays."

'Well, that rather set me thinking. As I say, I'd been getting restless doing nothing but just pottering round the pub all day. "Look here," I says, "I bet you I can bring off a job like that any day with any kid you like to mention." "Done!" says Jimmy. So he opens a newspaper. "The first toff we find what's got a' only son," he says. "Right!" says I. Well, about the first thing we found was a picture of Lady Circumference with her only son, Lord Tangent, at Warwick Races. "There's your man," says Jimmy. And that's what brought me here.'

'But, good gracious,' said Paul, 'why have you told me this monstrous story? I shall certainly inform the police. I never heard of such a thing.'

'That's all right,' said Philbrick. 'The job's off. Jimmy's won his bet. All this was before I met Dina, see?'

'Dina?'

'Miss Diana. Dina I calls her, after a song I heard. The moment I saw that girl I knew the game was up. My heart just stood still. There's a song about that, too. That girl,' said Philbrick, 'could bring a man up from the depths of hell itself.'

'You feel as strongly as that about her?'

'I'd go through fire and water for that girl. She's not happy here. I don't think her dad treats her proper. Sometimes,' said Philbrick, 'I think she's only marrying me to get away from here.'

'Good Heavens! Are you going to get married?'

'We fixed it up last Thursday. We've been going together for some time. It's bad for a girl being shut away like that, never seeing a man. She was in a state she'd have gone with anybody until I come along, just housekeeping day in, day out. The only pleasure she ever got was cutting down the bills and dismissing the servants. Most of them leave before their month is up, anyway, they're that hungry. She's got a head on her shoulders, she has. Real business woman, just what I need at the "Lamb".

'Then she heard me on the phone one day giving instructions to our manager at the Picture Theatre. That made her think a bit. A prince in disguise, as you might say. It was she who actually suggested our getting married. I shouldn't have had the face to, not while I was butler. What I'd meant to do was to hire a car one day and come down with my diamond ring and buttonhole and pop the question. But there wasn't any need for that. Love's a wonderful thing.'

Philbrick stopped speaking and was evidently deeply moved by his recital. The door of the pavilion opened, and Mr Prendergast came in.

'Well,' asked Paul, 'how are the sports going?'

'Not very well,' said Mr Prendergast; 'in fact, they've gone.'

'All over?'

'Yes. You see, none of the boys came back from the first race. They just disappeared behind the trees at the top of the drive. I expect they've gone to change. I don't blame them, I'm sure. It's terribly cold. Still, it was discouraging launching heat after heat and none coming back. Like sending troops into battle, you know.'

'The best thing for us to do is to go back and change too.'

'Yes, I suppose so. Oh, what a day!'

Grimes was in the Common Room.

'Just back from the gay metropolis of Llandudno,' he said. 'Shopping with Dingy is not a seemly occupation for a public school man. How did the heats go?'

'There weren't any,' said Paul.

'Quite right,' said Grimes: 'you leave this to me. I've been in the trade some time. These things are best done over the fire. We can make out the results in peace. We'd better hurry. The old boy wants them sent to be printed this evening.'

And taking a sheet of paper and a small stub of pencil, Grimes made out the programme.

'How about that?' he said.

'Clutterbuck seems to have done pretty well,' said Paul.

'Yes, he's a splendid little athlete,' said Grimes. 'Now just you telephone that through to the printers, and they'll get it done to-night. I wonder if we ought to have a hurdle race?'

'No,' said Mr Prendergast.

CHAPTER 8
The Sports

HAPPILY enough, it did not rain next day, and after morning school everybody dressed up to the nines. Dr Fagan appeared in a pale grey morning coat and sponge-bag trousers, looking more than ever *jeune premier*; there was a spring in his step and a pronounced sprightliness of bearing that Paul had not observed before. Flossie wore a violet frock of knitted wool made for her during the preceding autumn by her sister. It was the colour of indelible ink on blotting paper, and was ornamented at the waist with flowers of emerald green and pink. Her hat, also home-made, was the outcome of many winter evenings of ungrudged labour. All the trimmings of all her previous hats had gone to its adornment. Dingy wore a little steel brooch made in the shape of a bull-dog. Grimes wore a stiff evening collar of celluloid.

'Had to do something to celebrate the occasion,' he said, 'so I put on a "choker". Phew, though, it's tight. Have you seen my fiancée's latest creation? Ascot ain't in it. Let's get down to Mrs Roberts for a quick one before the happy throng rolls up.'

'I wish I could, but I've got to go round the ground with the Doctor.'

'Righto, old boy! See you later. Here comes Prendy in his coat of many colours.'

Mr Prendergast wore a blazer of faded stripes, which smelt strongly of camphor.

'I think Dr Fagan encourages a certain amount of display on these occasions,' he said. 'I used to keep wicket for my college, you know, but I was too short-sighted to be much good. Still, I am entitled to the blazer,' he said with a note of defiance in his voice, 'and it is more appropriate to a sporting occasion than a stiff collar.'

'Good old Prendy!' said Grimes. 'Nothing like a change of clothes to bring out latent pep. I felt like that my first week in khaki. Well, so long. Me for Mrs Roberts. Why don't you come too, Prendy?'

'D'you know,' said Mr Prendergast, 'I think I will.'

Paul watched them disappear down the drive in amazement. Then he went off to find the Doctor.

'Frankly,' said the Doctor, 'I am at a loss to understand my own emotions. I can think of no entertainment that fills me with greater detestation than a display of competitive athletics, none – except possibly folk-dancing. If there are two women in the world whose company I abominate – and there are very many more than two – they are Mrs Beste-Chetwynde and Lady Circumference. I have, moreover, had an extremely difficult encounter with my butler, who – will you believe it? – waited at luncheon in a mustard-coloured suit of plus-fours and a diamond tie-pin, and when I reprimanded him, attempted to tell me some ridiculous story about his being the proprietor of a circus or swimming-bath or some such concern. And yet,' said the Doctor, 'I am filled with a wholly delightful exhilaration. I can't understand it. It is not as though this was the first occasion of the kind. During the fourteen years that I have been at Llanabba there have been six sports days and two concerts, all of them, in one way or another, utterly disastrous. Once Lady Bunyan was taken ill; another time it was the matter of the press photographers and the obstacle race; another time some quite unimportant parents brought a dog with them which bit two of the boys very severely and one of the masters, who swore terribly in front of everyone. I could hardly blame him, but of course he had to go. Then there was the concert when the boys refused to sing "God Save the King" because of the pudding they had had for luncheon. One way and another, I have been consistently unfortunate in my efforts at festivity. And yet I look forward to each new fiasco with the utmost relish. Perhaps, Pennyfeather, you will bring luck to Llanabba; in fact, I feel confident you have already done so. Look at the sun!'

Picking their way carefully among the dry patches in the waterlogged drive, they reached the playing-fields. Here the haphazard organization of the last twenty-four hours seemed to have been fairly successful. A large marquee was already in position, and Philbrick – still in plus-fours – and three gardeners were at work putting up a smaller tent.

'That's for the Llanabba Silver Band,' said the Doctor. 'Philbrick, I required you to take off those loathsome garments.'

'They were new when I bought them,' said Philbrick, 'and they cost eight pounds fifteen. Anyhow, I can't do two things at once, can I? If I go back to change, who's going to manage all this, I'd like to know?'

'All right! Finish what you are doing first. Let us just review the arrangements. The marquee is for the visitors' tea. That is Diana's province. I expect we shall find her at work.'

Sure enough, there was Dingy helping two servants to arrange plates of highly-coloured cakes down a trestle table. Two other servants in the background were cutting sandwiches. Dingy, too, was obviously enjoying herself.

'Jane, Emily, remember that that butter has to do for three loaves. Spread it thoroughly, but don't waste it, and cut the crusts as thin as possible. Father, will you see to it that the boys who come in with their parents come in *alone*? You remember last time how Briggs brought in four boys with him, and they ate all the jam sandwiches before Colonel Loder had had any. Mr Pennyfeather, the champagne-cup is *not* for the masters. In fact, I expect you will find yourselves too much occupied helping the visitors to have any tea until they have left the tent. You had better tell Captain Grimes that, too. I am sure Mr Prendergast would not think of pushing himself forward.'

Outside the marquee were assembled several seats and tubs of palms and flowering shrubs. 'All this must be set in order,' said the Doctor; 'our guests may arrive in less than an hour.' He passed on. 'The cars shall turn aside from the drive here and come right into the ground. It will give a pleasant background to the photographs, and, Pennyfeather, if you would with tact direct the photographer so that more prominence was given to Mrs Beste-Chetwynde's Hispano Suiza than to Lady Circumference's little motor car, I think it would be all to the good. All these things count, you know.'

'Nothing seems to have been done about marking out the ground,' said Paul.

'No,' said the Doctor, turning his attention to the field for the first time, 'nothing. Well, you must do the best you can. They can't do everything.'

'I wonder if any hurdles have come?'

'They were ordered,' said the Doctor. 'I am certain of it. Philbrick, have any hurdles come?'

'Yes,' said Philbrick with a low chuckle.

'Why, pray, do you laugh at the mention of hurdles?'

'Just you look at them!' said Philbrick. 'They're behind the tea-house there.'

Paul and the Doctor went to look and found a pile of spiked iron railings in sections heaped up at the back of the marquee. They were each about five feet high and were painted green with gilt spikes.

'It seems to me that they have sent the wrong sort,' said the Doctor.

'Yes.'

'Well, we must do the best we can. What other things ought there to be?'

'Weight, hammer, javelin, long-jump pit, high-jump posts, low hurdles, eggs, spoons, and greasy pole,' said Philbrick.

'Previously competed for,' said the Doctor imperturbably. 'What else?'

'Somewhere to run,' suggested Paul.

'Why, God bless my soul, they've got the whole park! How did you manage yesterday for the heats?'

'We judged the distance by eye.'

'Then that is what we shall have to do to-day. Really, my dear Pennyfeather, it is quite unlike you to fabricate difficulties in this way. I am afraid you are getting unnerved. Let them go on racing until it is time for tea; and remember,' he added sagely, 'the longer the race the more time it takes. I leave the details to you. I am concerned with *style*. I wish, for instance, we had a starting pistol.'

'Would this be any use?' said Philbrick, producing an enormous service revolver. 'Only take care; it's loaded.'

'The very thing,' said the Doctor. 'Only fire into the ground, mind. We must do everything we can to avoid an accident. Do you always carry that about with you?'

'Only when I'm wearing my diamonds,' said Philbrick.

'Well, I hope that is not often. Good gracious! Who are these extraordinary-looking people?'

Ten men of revolting appearance were approaching from the drive. They were low of brow, crafty of eye, and crooked of limb. They advanced huddled together with the loping tread of wolves, peering about them furtively as they came, as though in constant terror of ambush; they slavered at their mouths, which hung loosely over their receding chins, while each clutched under his ape-like arm a burden of curious and unaccountable shape. On seeing the Doctor they halted and edged back, those behind squinting and moulting over their companions' shoulders.

'Crikey!' said Philbrick. 'Loonies! This is where I shoot.'

'I refuse to believe the evidence of my eyes,' said the Doctor. 'These creatures simply do not exist.'

After brief preliminary shuffling and nudging, an elderly man emerged from the back of the group. He had a rough black beard and wore on his uneven shoulders a druidical wreath of brass mistletoe-berries.

'Why, it's my friend the stationmaster!' said Philbrick.

'We are the silver band the Lord bless and keep you,' said the stationmaster in one breath, 'the band that no one could beat whatever but two indeed in the Eisteddfod that for all North Wales was look you.'

'I see,' said the Doctor; 'I see. That's splendid. Well, will you please go into your tent, the little tent over there.'

'To march about you would not like us?' suggested the stationmaster; 'we have a fine yellow flag look you that embroidered for us was in silks.'

'No, no. Into the tent!'

The stationmaster went back to consult with his fellow-musicians. There was a baying and growling and yapping as of the jungle at moonrise, and presently he came forward again with an obsequious, sidelong shuffle.

'Three pounds you pay us would you said indeed to at the sports play.'

'Yes, yes, that's right, three pounds. Into the tent!'

'Nothing whatever we can play without the money first,' said the stationmaster firmly.

'How would it be,' said Philbrick, 'if I gave him a clout on the ear?'

'No, no, I beg you to do nothing of the kind. You have not lived in Wales as long as I have.' He took a note-case from his pocket, the sight of which seemed to galvanize the musicians into life; they crowded round, twitching and chattering. The Doctor took out three pound notes and gave them to the stationmaster. 'There you are, Davies!' he said. 'Now take your men into the tent. They are on no account to emerge until after tea; do you understand?'

The band slunk away, and Paul and the Doctor turned back towards the Castle.

'The Welsh character is an interesting study,' said Dr Fagan. 'I have often considered writing a little monograph on the subject, but I was afraid it might make me unpopular in the village. The ignorant speak of them as Celts, which is of course wholly erroneous. They are of pure Iberian stock – the aboriginal inhabitants of Europe who survive only in Portugal and the Basque district. Celts readily intermarry with their neighbours and absorb them. From the earliest times the Welsh have been looked upon as an unclean people. It is thus that they have preserved their racial integrity. Their sons and daughters rarely mate with human-kind except their own blood relations. In Wales there was no need for legislation to prevent the conquering people intermarrying with the conquered. In Ireland that was necessary, for there intermarriage was a political matter. In Wales it was moral. I hope, by the way, you have no Welsh blood?'

'None whatever,' said Paul.

'I was sure you had not, but one cannot be too careful. I once spoke of this subject to the sixth form and learned later that one of them had a Welsh grandmother. I am afraid it hurt his feelings terribly, poor little chap. She came from Pembrokeshire, too, which is of course quite a different matter. I often think,' he continued, 'that we can trace almost all the disasters of English history to the influence of Wales. Think of Edward of Caernarvon, the first Prince of Wales, a perverse life, Pennyfeather, and an unseemly death, then the Tudors and the dissolution of the Church, then Lloyd George, the temperance movement, Nonconformity, and lust stalking hand in hand through the country, wasting and ravaging. But perhaps you think I exaggerate? I have a certain rhetorical tendency, I admit.'

'No, no,' said Paul.

'The Welsh,' said the Doctor, 'are the only nation in the world that has produced no graphic or plastic art, no architecture, no drama. They just sing,' he said with disgust, 'sing and blow down wind instruments of plated silver. They are deceitful because they cannot discern truth from falsehood, depraved because they cannot discern the consequences of their indulgence. Let us consider,' he continued, 'the etymological derivations of the Welsh language. . . .'

But here he was interrupted by a breathless little boy who panted down the drive to meet them. 'Please, sir, Lord and Lady Circumference have arrived sir. They're in the library with Miss Florence. She asked me to tell you.'

'The sports will start in ten minutes,' said the Doctor. 'Run and tell the other boys to change and go at once to the playing-fields. I will talk to you about the Welsh again. It is a matter to which I have given some thought, and I can see that you are sincerely interested. Come in with me and see the Circumferences.'

Flossie was talking to them in the library.

'Yes, isn't it a sweet colour?' she was saying. 'I do like something bright myself. Diana made it for me; she does knit a treat, does Diana, but of course I chose the colour, you know, because, you see, Diana's taste is all for wishy-washy greys and browns. Mournful, you know. Well, here's the dad. Lady Circumference was just saying how much she likes my frock what you said was vulgar, so there!'

A stout elderly woman dressed in a tweed coat and skirt and jaunty Tyrolean hat advanced to the Doctor. 'Hullo!' she said in a deep bass voice, 'how are you? Sorry if we're late. Circumference ran over a fool of a boy. I've just been chaffing your daughter here about her frock. Wish I was young enough to wear that kind of thing. Older I get the more I like colour. We're both pretty long in the tooth, eh?' She gave Dr Fagan a hearty shake of the hand, that obviously caused him acute pain. Then she turned to Paul.

'So you're the Doctor's hired assassin, eh? Well, I hope you keep a firm hand on my toad of a son. How's he doin'?'

'Quite well,' said Paul.

'Nonsense!' said Lady Circumference. 'The boy's a dunderhead. If he wasn't he wouldn't be here. He wants beatin' and hittin' and knockin' about generally, and then he'll be no good. That grass is shockin' bad on the terrace, Doctor; you ought to sand it down and re-sow it, but you'll have to take that cedar down if you ever want it to grow properly at the side. I hate cuttin' down a tree – like losin' a tooth – but you have to choose, tree or grass; you can't keep 'em both. What d'you pay your head man?'

As she was talking Lord Circumference emerged from the shadows and shook Paul's hand. He had a long fair moustache and large watery eyes which reminded Paul a little of Mr Prendergast.

'How do you do?' he said.

'How do you do?' said Paul.

'Fond of sport, eh?' he said. 'I mean these sort of sports?'

'Oh, yes,' said Paul. 'I think they're so good for the boys.'

'Do you? Do you think that,' said Lord Circumference very earnestly: 'you think they're good for the boys?'

'Yes,' said Paul; 'don't you?'

'Me? Yes, oh yes. I think so, too. Very good for the boys.'

'So useful in the case of a war or anything,' said Paul.

'Do you think so? D'you really and truly think so? That there's going to be another war, I mean?'

'Yes, I'm sure of it; aren't you?'

'Yes, of course. I'm sure of it too. And that awful bread, and people coming on to one's own land and telling one what one's to do with one's own butter and milk, and commandeering one's horses! Oh, yes all over again! My wife shot her hunters rather than let them go to the army. And girls in breeches on all the farms! All over again! Who do you think it will be this time?'

'The Americans,' said Paul stoutly.

'No, indeed, I hope not. We had German prisoners on two of the farms. That wasn't so bad, but if they start putting Americans on my land, I'll just refuse to stand it. My daughter brought an American down to luncheon the other day, and, do you know . . . ?'

'Dig it and dung it,' said Lady Circumference. 'Only it's got to be dug deep, mind. Now how did your calceolarias do last year?'

'I really have no idea,' said the Doctor. 'Flossie, how did our calceolarias do?'

'Lovely,' said Flossie.

'I don't believe a word of it,' said Lady Circumference. 'Nobody's calceolarias did well last year.'

'Shall we adjourn to the playing-fields?' said the Doctor. 'I expect they are all waiting for us.'

Talking cheerfully, the party crossed the hall and went down the steps.

'Your drive's awful wet,' said Lady Circumference. 'I expect there's a blocked pipe somewhere. Sure it ain't sewage?'

'I was never any use at short distances,' Lord Circumference was saying. 'I was always a slow starter, but I was once eighteenth in the Crick at Rugby. We didn't take sports so seriously at the 'Varsity when I was up: everybody rode. What college were you at?'

'Scone.'

'Scone, were you? Ever come across a young nephew of my wife's called Alastair Digby-Vane-Trumpington?'

'I just met him,' said Paul.

'That's very interesting, Greta. Mr Pennyfoot knows Alastair.'

'Does he? Well, that boy's doing no good for himself. Got fined twenty pounds the other day, his mother told me. Seemed proud of it. If my brother had been alive he'd have licked all that out of the young cub. It takes a man to bring up a man.'

'Yes,' said Lord Circumference meekly.

'Who else do you know at Oxford? Do you know Freddy French-Wise?'

'No.'

'Or Tom Obblethwaite or that youngest Castleton boy?'

'No, I'm afraid not. I had a great friend called Potts.'

'*Potts!*' said Lady Circumference, and left it at that.

All the school and several local visitors were assembled in the field. Grimes stood by himself, looking depressed. Mr Prendergast, flushed and unusually vivacious, was talking to the Vicar. As the headmaster's party came into sight the Llanabba Silver Band struck up *Men of Harlech.*

'Shockin' noise,' commented Lady Circumference graciously.

The head prefect came forward and presented her with a programme, be-ribboned and embossed in gold. Another prefect set a chair for her. She sat down with the Doctor next to her and Lord Circumference on the other side of him.

'Pennyfeather,' cried the Doctor above the band, 'start them racing.'

Philbrick gave Paul a megaphone. 'I found this in the pavilion,' he said. 'I thought it might be useful.'

'Who's that extraordinary man?' asked Lady Circumference.

'He is the boxing coach and swimming professional,' said the Doctor. 'A finely developed figure, don't you think?'

'First race,' said Paul through the megaphone, 'under sixteen. Quarter-mile!' He read out Grimes' list of starters.

'What's Tangent doin' in this race?' said Lady Circumference. 'The boy can't run an inch.'

The silver band stopped playing.

'The course,' said Paul, 'starts from the pavilion, goes round that clump of elms . . . '

'Beeches,' corrected Lady Circumference loudly.

' . . . and ends in front of the bandstand. Starter, Mr Prendergast; timekeeper, Captain Grimes.'

'I shall say, "Are you ready? one, two, three!" and then fire,' said Mr Prendergast. 'Are you ready? One' – there was a terrific report. 'Oh dear! I'm sorry' – but the race had begun. Clearly Tangent was not going to win; he was sitting on the grass crying because he had been wounded in the foot by Mr Prendergast's bullet. Philbrick carried him, wailing dismally, into the refreshment tent, where Dingy helped him off with his shoe. His heel was slightly grazed. Dingy gave him a large slice of cake, and he hobbled out surrounded by a sympathetic crowd.

'That won't hurt him,' said Lady Circumference, 'but I think someone ought to remove the pistol from that old man before he does anything serious.'

'I knew that was going to happen,' said Lord Circumference.

'A most unfortunate beginning,' said the Doctor.

'Am I going to die?' said Tangent, his mouth full of cake.

'For God's sake, look after Prendy,' said Grimes in Paul's ear. 'The man's as tight as a lord, and on one whisky, too.'

'First blood to me!' said Mr Prendergast gleefully.

'The last race will be run again,' said Paul down the megaphone. 'Starter, Mr Philbrick; timekeeper, Mr Prendergast.'

'On your marks! Get set.' Bang went the pistol, this time without disaster. The six little boys scampered off through the mud, disappeared behind the beeches and returned rather more slowly. Captain Grimes and Mr Prendergast held up a piece of tape.

'Well run, sir!' shouted Colonel Sidebotham. 'Jolly good race.'

'Capital,' said Mr Prendergast, and dropping his end of the tape, he sauntered over to the Colonel. 'I can see you are a fine judge of a race, sir. So was I once. So's Grimes. A capital fellow, Grimes; a bounder, you know, but a capital fellow. Bounders can be capital fellows; don't you agree, Colonel Slidebottom? In fact, I'd go further and say that capital fellows *are* bounders. What d'you say to that? I wish you'd stop pulling at my arm, Pennyfeather. Colonel Shybottom and I are just having a most interesting conversation about bounders.'

The silver band struck up again, and Mr Prendergast began a little jig, saying: 'Capital fellow!' and snapping his fingers. Paul led him to the refreshment tent.

'Dingy wants you to help her in there,' he said firmly, 'and, for God's sake, don't come out until you feel better.'

'I never felt better in my life,' said Mr Prendergast indignantly. 'Capital fellow! capital fellow!'

'It is not my affair, of course,' said Colonel Sidebotham, 'but if you ask me I should say that man had been drinking.'

'He was talking very excitedly to me,' said the Vicar, 'about some apparatus for warming a church in Worthing and about the Apostolic Claims of the Church of Abyssinia. I confess I could not follow him clearly. He seems deeply interested in Church matters. Are you quite sure he is right in the head? I have noticed again and again since I have been in the Church that lay interest in ecclesiastical matters is often a prelude to insanity.'

'Drink, pure and simple,' said the Colonel. 'I wonder where he got it? I could do with a spot of whisky.'

'Quarter-mile open!' said Paul through his megaphone.

Presently the Clutterbucks arrived. Both the parents were stout. They brought with them two small children, a governess, and an elder son. They debouched from the car one by one, stretching their limbs in evident relief.

'This is Sam,' said Mr Clutterbuck, 'just down from Cambridge. He's joined me in the business, and we've brought the nippers along for a treat. Don't mind, do you, Doc? And last, but not least, my wife.'

Dr Fagan greeted them with genial condescension and found them seats.

'I am afraid you have missed all the jumping events,' he said. 'But I have a list of the results here. You will see that Percy has done extremely well.'

'Didn't know the little beggar had it in him. See that, Martha? Percy's won the high-jump and the long-jump and the hurdles. How's your young hopeful been doing, Lady Circumference?'

'My boy has been injured in the foot,' said Lady Circumference coldly.

'Dear me! Not badly, I hope? Did he twist his ankle in the jumping?'

'No,' said Lady Circumference, 'he was shot at by one of the assistant masters. But it is kind of you to inquire.'

'Three Miles Open!' announced Paul. 'The course of six laps will be run as before.'

'On your marks! Get set.' Bang went Philbrick's revolver. Off trotted the boys on another race.

'Father,' said Flossie, 'don't you think it's time for the tea interval?'

'Nothing can be done before Mrs Beste-Chetwynde arrives,' said the Doctor.

Round and round the muddy track trotted the athletes while the silver band played sacred music unceasingly.

'Last lap!' announced Paul.

The school and the visitors crowded about the tape to cheer the winner. Amid loud applause Clutterbuck breasted the tape well ahead of the others.

'Well run! Oh, good, jolly good, sir!' cried Colonel Sidebotham.

'Good old Percy! That's the stuff,' said Mr Clutterbuck.

'Well run, Percy!' chorused the two little Clutterbucks, prompted by their governess.

'That boy cheated,' said Lady Circumference. 'He only went round five times. I counted.'

'I think unpleasantness so mars the afternoon,' said the Vicar.

'How dare you suggest such a thing?' asked Mrs Clutterbuck. 'I appeal to the referee. Percy ran the full course, didn't he?'

'Clutterbuck wins,' said Captain Grimes.

'Fiddlesticks!' said Lady Circumference. 'He deliberately lagged behind and joined the others as they went behind the beeches. The little toad!'

'Really, Greta,' said Lord Circumference, 'I think we ought to abide by the referee's decision.'

'Well, they can't expect me to give away the prizes, then. Nothing would induce me to give that boy a prize.'

'Do you understand, madam, that you are bringing a serious accusation against my son's honour?'

'Serious accusation fiddlesticks! What he wants is a jolly good hidin'.'

'No doubt you judge other people's sons by your own. Let me tell you, Lady Circumference . . . '

'Don't attempt to browbeat me, sir. I know a cheat when I see one.'

At this stage of the discussion the Doctor left Mrs Hope-Browne's side, where he had been remarking upon her son's progress in geometry, and joined the group round the winning-post.

'If there is a disputed decision,' he said genially, 'they shall race again.'

'Percy has won already,' said Mr Clutterbuck. 'He has been adjudged the winner.'

'Splendid! splendid! A promising little athlete. I congratulate you, Clutterbuck.'

'But he only ran five laps,' said Lady Circumference.

'Then clearly he has won the five furlongs race, a very exacting length.'

'But the other boys,' said Lady Circumference, almost beside herself with rage, 'have run six lengths.'

'Then they,' said the Doctor imperturbably, 'are first, second, third, fourth, and fifth respectively in the Three Miles. Clearly there has been some confusion. Diana, I think we might now serve tea.'

Things were not easy, but there was fortunately a distraction, for as he spoke an enormous limousine of dove-grey and silver stole soundlessly on to the field.

'But what could be more opportune? Here is Mrs Beste-Chetwynde.'

Three light skips brought him to the side of the car, but the footman was there before him. The door opened, and from the cushions within emerged a tall young man in a clinging dove-grey overcoat. After him, like the first breath of spring in the Champs-Élysées, came Mrs Beste-Chetwynde – two lizard-skin feet, silk legs, chinchilla body, a tight little black hat, pinned with platinum and diamonds, and the high invariable voice that may be heard in any Ritz Hotel from New York to Budapest.

'I hope you don't mind my bringing Chokey, Dr Fagan?' she said. 'He's just crazy about sport.'

'I sure am that,' said Chokey.

'Dear Mrs Beste-Chetwynde!' said Dr Fagan; 'dear, dear, Mrs Beste-Chetwynde!' He pressed her glove, and for the moment was at a loss for words of welcome, for 'Chokey', though graceful of bearing and irreproachably dressed, was a Negro.

CHAPTER 9
The Sports – continued

THE refreshment tent looked very nice. The long table across the centre was covered with a white cloth. Bowls of flowers were ranged down it at regular intervals, and between them plates of sandwiches and cakes and jugs of lemonade and champagne-cup. Behind it against a background of palms stood the four Welsh housemaids in clean caps and aprons pouring out tea. Behind them again sat Mr Prendergast, a glass of champagne-cup in his hand, his wig slightly awry. He rose unsteadily to his feet at the approach of the guests, made a little bow, and then sat down again rather suddenly.

'Will you take round the *foie gras* sandwiches, Mr Penny-feather?' said Dingy. 'They are not for the boys or Captain Grimes.'

'One for little me!' said Flossie as he passed her.

Philbrick, evidently regarding himself as one of the guests, was engaged in a heated discussion on greyhound-racing with Sam Clutterbuck.

'What price the coon?' he asked as Paul gave him a sandwich.

'It does my heart good to see old Prendy enjoying himself,' said Grimes. 'Pity he shot that kid, though.'

'There's not much the matter with him to see the way he's eating his tea. I say, this is rather a poor afternoon, isn't it?'

'Circulate, old boy, circulate. Things aren't going too smoothly.'

Nor indeed were they. The sudden ebullition of ill-feeling over the Three-mile race, though checked by the arrival of Mrs Beste-Chetwynde, was by no means forgotten. There were two distinctly hostile camps in the tea-tent. On one side stood the Circumferences, Tangent, the Vicar, Colonel Sidebotham, and the Hope-Brownes; on the other the seven Clutterbucks, Philbrick, Flossie, and two or three parents who had been snubbed already that afternoon by Lady Circumference. No one spoke of the race, but outraged sportsmanship glinted perilously in every eye. Several parents, intent on their tea, crowded round Dingy and the table. Eminently aloof from all these stood Chokey and Mrs Beste-Chetwynde. Clearly the social balance was delicately poised, and the issue depended upon them. With or without her nigger, Mrs Beste-Chetwynde was a woman of vital importance.

'Why, Dr Fagan,' she was saying, 'it is too disappointing that we've missed the sports. We had just the slowest journey, stopping all the time to see the churches. You can't move Chokey once he's seen an old church. He's just crazy about culture, aren't you, darling?'

'I sure am that,' said Chokey.

'Are you interested in music?' said the Doctor tactfully.

'Well, just you hear that, Baby,' said Chokey; 'am *I* interested in music? I should say I am.'

'He plays just too divinely,' said Mrs Beste-Chetwynde.

'Has he heard my new records, would you say?'

'No, darling, I don't expect he has.'

'Well, just you hear *them*, sir, and then you'll know – am I interested in music.'

'Now, darling, don't get discouraged. I'll take you over and introduce you to Lady Circumference. It's his inferiority complex, the angel. He's just crazy to meet the aristocracy, aren't you, my sweet?'

'I sure am that,' said Chokey.

'I think it's an insult bringing a nigger here,' said Mrs Clutterbuck. 'It's an insult to our own women.'

'Niggers are all right,' said Philbrick. 'Where I draw a line is a Chink, nasty inhuman things. I had a pal bumped off by a Chink once. Throat cut horrible, it was, from ear to ear.'

'Good gracious!' said the Clutterbuck governess; 'was that in the Boxer rising?'

'No,' said Philbrick cheerfully. 'Saturday night in the Edgware Road. Might have happened to any of us.'

'What did the gentleman say?' asked the children.

'Never you mind, my dears. Run and have some more of the green cake.'

They ran off obediently, but the little boy was later heard whispering to his sister as she knelt at her prayers, 'cut horrible from ear to ear', so that until quite late in her life Miss Clutterbuck would feel a little faint when she saw a bus that was going to the Edgware Road.

'I've got a friend lives in Savannah,' said Sam, 'and he's told me a thing or two about niggers. Of course it's hardly a thing to talk about before the ladies, but, to put it bluntly, *they have uncontrollable passions*. See what I mean?'

'What a terrible thing!' said Grimes.

'You can't blame 'em, mind; it's just their nature. Animal, you know. Still, what I do say is, since they're like that, the less we see of them the better.'

'Quite,' said Mr Clutterbuck.

'I had such a curious conversation just now,' Lord Circumference was saying to Paul, 'with your bandmaster over there. He asked me whether I should like to meet his sister-in-law; and when I said, "Yes, I should be delighted to," he said that it would cost a pound normally, but that he'd let me have special terms. What *can* he have meant, Mr Pennyfoot?'

''Pon my soul,' Colonel Sidebotham was saying to the Vicar, 'I don't like the look of that nigger. I saw enough of Fuzzy-Wuzzy in the Soudan – devilish good enemy and devilish bad friend. I'm going across to talk to Mrs Clutterbuck. Between ourselves, I think Lady C. went a bit far. I didn't see the race myself, but there are limits. . . . '

'Rain ain't doin' the turnip crop any good,' Lady Circumference was saying.

'No, indeed,' said Mrs Beste-Chetwynde. 'Are you in England for long?'

'Why, I live in England, of course,' said Lady Circumference.

'My dear, how divine! But don't you find it just too expensive?'

This was one of Lady Circumference's favourite topics, but somehow she did not feel disposed to enlarge on it to Mrs Beste-Chetwynde with the same gusto as when she was talking to Mrs Sidebotham and the Vicar's wife. She never felt quite at ease with people richer than herself.

'Well, we all feel the wind a bit since the war,' she said briefly. 'How's Bobby Pastmaster?'

'Dotty,' said Mrs Beste-Chetwynde, 'terribly dotty, and he and Chokey don't get on. You'll like Chokey. He's just crazy about England, too. We've been around all the cathedrals, and now we're going to start on the country houses. We were thinking of running over to see you at Castle Tangent one afternoon.'

'That would be delightful, but I'm afraid we are in London at present. Which did you like best of the cathedrals, Mr Chokey?'

'Chokey's not really his name, you know. The angel's called "Mr Sebastian Cholmondley". '

'Well,' said Mr Cholmondley, 'they were all fine, just fine. When I saw the cathedrals my heart just rose up and sang within me. I sure am crazy about culture. You folk think because we're coloured we don't care about nothing but jazz. Why, I'd give all the jazz in the world for just one little stone from one of your cathedrals.'

'It's quite true. He would.'

'Well, that's most interesting, Mr Cholmondley. I used to live just outside Salisbury when I was a girl, but, little as I like jazz, I never felt quite as strongly as that about it.'

'Salisbury is full of historical interest, Lady Circumference, but in my opinion York Minster is the more refined.'

'Oh, you angel!' said Mrs Beste-Chetwynde. 'I could eat you up every bit.'

'And is this your first visit to an English school?' asked the Doctor.

'I should say not. Will you tell the Doctor the schools I've seen?'

'He's been to them all, even the quite new ones. In fact, he liked the new ones best.'

'They were more spacious. Have you ever seen Oxford?'

'Yes; in fact, I was educated there.'

'Were you, now? I've seen Oxford and Cambridge and Eton and Harrow. That's me all over. That's what I like, see? *I* appreciate art. There's plenty coloured people come over here and don't see nothing but a few night clubs. I read Shakespeare,' said Chokey, '*Hamlet*, *Macbeth*, *King Lear*. Ever read them?'

'Yes,' said the Doctor; 'as a matter of fact, I have.'

'My race,' said Chokey, 'is essentially an artistic race. We have the child's love of song and colour and the child's natural good taste. All you white folks despise the poor coloured man. . . . '

'No, no,' said the Doctor.

'Let him say his piece, the darling,' said Mrs Beste-Chetwynde. 'Isn't he divine!'

'You folks all think the coloured man hasn't got a soul. Anything's good enough for the poor coloured man. Beat him; put him in chains; load him with burdens. . . . ' Here Paul observed a responsive glitter in Lady Circumference's eye. 'But all the time that poor coloured man has a soul same as you have. Don't he breathe the same as you? Don't he eat and drink? Don't he love Shakespeare and cathedrals and the paintings of the old masters same as you? Isn't he just asking for your love and help to raise him from the servitude into which your forefathers plunged him? Oh, say, white folks, why don't you stretch out a helping hand to the poor coloured man, that's as good as you are, if you'll only let him be?'

'My sweet,' said Mrs Beste-Chetwynde, 'you mustn't get discouraged. They're all friends here.'

'Is that so?' said Chokey. 'Should I sing them a song?'

'No, don't do that, darling. Have some tea.'

'I had a friend in Paris,' said the Clutterbuck governess, 'whose sister knew a girl who married one of the black soldiers during the war, and you wouldn't believe what he did to her. Joan and Peter, run and see if Daddy wants some more tea. He tied her up with a razor strop and left her on the stone floor for the night without food or covering. And then it was over a year before she could get a divorce.'

'Used to cut off the tent ropes,' Colonel Sidebotham was saying, 'and then knife the poor beggars through the canvas.'

'You can see 'em in Shaftesbury Avenue and Charing Cross Road any night of the week,' Sam Clutterbuck was saying. 'The women just hanging on to 'em.'

'The mistake was ever giving them their freedom,' said the Vicar. 'They were far happier and better looked after before.'

'It's queer,' said Flossie, 'that a woman with as much money as Mrs Beste-Chetwynde should wear such *dull* clothes.'

'That ring didn't cost less than five hundred,' said Philbrick.

'Let's go and talk to the Vicar about God,' said Mrs Beste-Chetwynde. 'Chokey thinks religion is just divine.'

'My race is a very spiritual one,' said Chokey.

'The band has been playing *Men of Harlech* for over half an hour,' said the Doctor. 'Diana, do go and tell them to try something else.'

'I sometimes think I'm getting rather bored with coloured people,' Mrs Beste-Chetwynde said to Lady Circumference. 'Are you?'

'I have never had the opportunity.'

'I daresay you'd be good with them. They take a lot of living up to; they *are* so earnest. Who's that dear, dim, drunk little man?'

'That is the person who shot my son.'

'My dear, how too shattering for you. Not dead, I hope? Chokey shot a man at a party the other night. He gets gay at times, you know. It's only when he's on his best behaviour that he's so class-conscious. I must go and rescue the Vicar.'

The stationmaster came into the tent, crab-like and obsequious.

'Well, my good man?' said the Doctor.

'The young lady I have been telling that no other tunes can we play whatever with the lady smoking at her cigarette look you.'

'God bless my soul. Why not?'

'The other tunes are all holy tunes look you. Blasphemy it would be to play the songs of Sion while the lady at a cigarette smokes whatever. *Men of Harlech* is good music look you.'

'This is most unfortunate. I can hardly ask Mrs Beste-Chetwynde to stop smoking. Frankly I regard this as impertinence.'

'But no man can you ask against his Maker to blaspheme whatever unless him to pay more you were. Three pounds for the music is good and one for blasphemy look you.'

Dr Fagan gave him another pound. The stationmaster retired, and in a few minutes the silver band began a singularly emotional rendering of *In Thy courts no more are needed Sun by day and Moon by night.*

CHAPTER 10
Post Mortem

AS the last car drove away the Doctor and his daughters and Paul and Grimes walked up the drive together towards the Castle.

'Frankly the day has been rather a disappointment to me,' said the Doctor. 'Nothing seemed to go quite right in spite of all our preparations.'

'And expense,' said Dingy.

'I am sorry, too, that Mr Prendergast should have had that unfortunate disagreement with Mrs Beste-Chetwynde's coloured friend. In all the ten years during which we have worked together I have never known Mr Prendergast so self-assertive. It was *not* becoming of him. Nor was it Philbrick's place to join in. I was seriously alarmed. They seemed so angry, and all about some minor point of ecclesiastical architecture.'

'Mr Cholmondley was very sensitive,' said Flossie.

'Yes, he seemed to think that Mr Prendergast's insistence on the late development of the rood-screen was in some way connected with colour-prejudice. I wonder why that was? To my mind it showed a very confused line of thought. Still, it would have been more seemly if Mr Prendergast had let the matter drop, and what could Philbrick know of the matter?'

'Philbrick is not an ordinary butler,' said Dingy.

'No, indeed not,' said the Doctor. 'I heartily deplore his jewellery.'

'I didn't like Lady Circumference's speech,' said Flossie. 'Did you?'

'I did not,' said the Doctor; 'nor, I think, did Mrs Clutterbuck. I thought her reference to the Five Furlong race positively brutal. I was glad Clutterbuck had done so well in the jumping yesterday.'

'She rather wanders from the point, doesn't she?' said Dingy. 'All that about hunting, I mean.'

'I don't think Lady Circumference is conscious of any definite divisions in the various branches of sport. I have often observed in women of her type a tendency to regard all athletics as inferior forms of foxhunting. It is *not* logical. Besides, she was nettled at some remark of Mr Cholmondley's about cruelty to animals. As you say, it was irrelevant and rather unfortunate. I also resented the reference to the Liberal Party. Mr Clutterbuck has stood three times, you know. Taken as a whole, it was *not* a happy speech. I was quite glad when I saw her drive away.'

'What a pretty car Mrs Beste-Chetwynde has got!' said Flossie, 'but how ostentatious of her to bring a footman.'

'I can forgive the footman,' said Dingy, 'but I can't forgive Mr Cholmondley. He asked me whether I had ever heard of a writer called Thomas Hardy.'

'He asked *me* to go to Reigate with him for the weekend,' said Flossie, '. . . in rather a sweet way, too.'

'Florence, I trust you refused?'

'Oh, yes,' said Flossie sadly, 'I refused.'

They went on up the drive in silence. Presently Dingy asked: 'What are we going to do about those fireworks you insisted on buying? Everyone has gone away.'

'I don't feel in a mood for fireworks,' said the Doctor. 'Perhaps another time, but not now.'

*

Back in the Common Room, Paul and Grimes subsided moodily into the two easy-chairs. The fire, unattended since luncheon, had sunk to a handful of warm ashes.

'Well, old boy,' said Grimes, 'so that's over.'

'Yes,' said Paul.

'All the gay throng melted away?'

'Yes,' said Paul.

'Back to the daily round and cloistral calm?'

'Yes,' said Paul.

'As a beano,' said Grimes, 'I have known better.'

'Yes,' said Paul.

'Lady C.'s hardly what you might call bonhommous.'

'Hardly.'

'Old Prendy made rather an ass of himself?'

'Yes.'

'Hullo, old boy! You sound a bit flat. Feeling the strain of the social vortex, a bit giddy after the gay whirl, eh?'

'I say, Grimes,' said Paul, 'what d'you suppose the relationship is between Mrs Beste-Chetwynde and that nigger?'

'Well, I don't suppose she trots with him just for the uplift of his conversation; do you?'

'No, I suppose not.'

'In fact, I don't mind diagnosing a simple case of good old sex.'

'Yes, I suppose you're right.'

'I'm sure of it. Great Scott, what's that noise?'

It was Mr Prendergast.

'Prendy, old man,' said Grimes, 'you've let down the morale of the Common Room a pretty good wallop.'

'Damn the Common Room!' said Mr Prendergast. 'What does the Common Room know about rood-screens?'

'That's all right, old boy. We're all friends here. What you say about rood-screens goes.'

'They'll be questioning the efficacy of infant baptism next. The Church has never countenanced lay opinion on spiritual matters. Now if it were a question of food and drink,' said Mr Prendergast, 'if it were a question of drink – But not infant baptism. Just drink.' And he sat down.

'A sad case, brother,' said Grimes, 'truly a sad case. Prendy, do you realize that in two minutes the bell will go for Prep. and you're on duty?'

'Ding, dong, dell! Pussy's in the well.'

'Prendy, that's irrelevant.'

'I know several songs about bells. Funeral bells, wedding-bells, sacring bells, sheep-bells, fire-bells, door-bells, dumb-bells, and just plain bells.'

Paul and Grimes looked at each other sadly.

'It seems to me,' said Paul, 'that one of us will have to take Prep. for him to-night.'

'No, no, old boy; that'll be all right,' said Grimes. 'You and I are off to Mrs Roberts. Prendy gives me a thirst.'

'But we can't leave him like this.'

'He'll be all right. The little beasts can't make any more noise than they do usually.'

'You don't think the old man will find him?'

'Not a chance.'

The bell rang. Mr Prendergast jumped to his feet, straightened his wig and steadied himself gravely against the chimneypiece.

'There's a good chap,' said Grimes gently. 'Just you trot down the passage to the little boys and have a good nap.'

Singing quietly to himself, Mr Prendergast sauntered down the passage.

'I hope he's none the worse for this,' said Grimes. 'You know, I feel quite fatherly towards old Prendy. He did give it to that blackamoor about Church architecture, bless him.'

Arm in arm they went down the main avenue towards the inn.

'Mrs Beste-Chetwynde asked me to call on her in London,' said Paul.

'Did she? Well, just you go. I've never been much of a one for society and the smart set myself, but if you like that sort of thing, Mrs Beste-Chetwynde is the goods all right. Never open a paper but there's a photograph of her at some place or other.'

'Does she photograph well?' asked Paul. 'I should rather think that she would.'

Grimes looked at him narrowly. 'Fair to middling. Why the sudden interest?'

'Oh, I don't know. I was just wondering.'

At Mrs Roberts' they found the Llanabba Silver Band chattering acrimoniously over the division of the spoils.

'All the afternoon the band I have led in *Men of Harlech* and sacred music too look you and they will not give me a penny more than themselves whatever. The college gentleman whatever if it is right I ask,' said the stationmaster, 'me with a sister-in-law to support too look you.'

'Now don't bother, old boy,' said Grimes, 'because, if you do, I'll tell your pals about the extra pound you got out of the Doctor.'

The discussion was resumed in Welsh, but it was clear that the stationmaster was slowly giving way.

'That's settled him all right. Take my tip, old boy; never get mixed up in a Welsh wrangle. It doesn't end in blows, like an Irish one, but goes on for ever. They'll still be discussing that three pounds at the end of term; just you see.'

'Has Mr Beste-Chetwynde been dead long?' asked Paul.

'I shouldn't say so; why?'

'I was just wondering.'

They sat for some time smoking in silence.

'If Beste-Chetwynde is fifteen,' said Paul, 'that doesn't necessarily make her more than thirty-one, does it?'

'Old boy,' said Grimes, 'you're in love.'

'Nonsense!'

'Smitten?' said Grimes.

'No, no.'

'The tender passion?'

'No.'

'Cupid's jolly little darts?'

'No.'

'Spring fancies, love's young dream?'

'Nonsense!'

'Not even a quickening of the pulse?'

'No.'

'A sweet despair?'

'Certainly not.'

'A trembling hope?'

'No.'

'A *frisson*? a *Je ne sais quoi*?'

'Nothing of the sort.'

'Liar!' said Grimes.

There was another long pause. 'Grimes,' said Paul at length, 'I wonder if you can be right?'

'Sure of it, old boy. Just you go in and win. Here's to the happy pair! May all your troubles be little ones.'

In a state of mind totally new to him, Paul accompanied Grimes back to the Castle. Prep. was over. Mr Prendergast was leaning against the fireplace with a contented smile on his face.

'Hullo, Prendy, old wine-skin! How are things with you?'

'Admirable,' said Mr Prendergast. 'I have never known them better. I have just caned twenty-three boys.'

CHAPTER 11

Philbrick – continued

NEXT day Mr Prendergast's self-confidence had evaporated.

'Head hurting?' asked Grimes.

'Well, as a matter of fact, it is rather.'

'Eyes tired? Thirsty?'

'Yes, a little.'

'Poor old Prendy! Don't I know? Still, it was worth it, wasn't it?'

'I don't remember very clearly all that happened, but I walked back to the Castle with Philbrick, and he told me all about his life. It appears he is really a rich man and not a butler at all.'

'I know,' said Paul and Grimes simultaneously.

'You both knew? Well, it came as a great surprise to me, although I must admit I had noticed a certain superiority in his manner. But I find almost everyone like that. Did he tell you his whole story – about his shooting the Portuguese Count and everything?'

'No, he didn't tell me *that*,' said Paul.

'Shooting a Portuguese Count? Are you sure you've got hold of the right end of the stick, old boy?'

'Yes, yes, I'm sure of it. It impressed me very much. You see Philbrick is really Sir Solomon Philbrick, the shipowner.'

'The novelist, you mean,' said Grimes.

'The retired burglar,' said Paul.

The three masters looked at each other.

'Old boys, it seems to me someone's been pulling our legs.'

'Well, this is the story that he told me,' continued Mr Prendergast. 'It all started from our argument about Church architecture with the black man. Apparently Philbrick has a large house in Carlton House Terrace.'

'Camberwell Green.'

'Cheyne Walk.'

'Well, I'm telling you what he told me. He has a house in Carlton House Terrace. I remember the address well because a sister of Mrs Crump's was once governess in a house in the same row, and he used to live there with an actress who, I regret to say, was not his wife. I forget her name, but I know it is a particularly famous one. He was sitting in the Athenaeum Club one day when the Archbishop of Canterbury approached him and said that the Government were anxious to make him a peer, but that it was impossible while he lived a life of such open irregularity. Philbrick turned down the offer. He is a Roman Catholic, I forgot to tell you. But all that doesn't really explain why he is here. It only shows how important he is. His ships weigh *hundreds* and *hundreds* of tons, he told me.

'Well, one evening he and his play-actress were giving a party, and they were playing baccarat. There was a Portuguese Count there – a very dark man from the Legation, Philbrick said. The game rapidly became a personal contest between these two. Philbrick won over and over again until the Count had no more money left and had signed many IOU's. Finally, very late in the night, he took from the Countess's hand – she was sitting beside him with haggard eyes watching him play – an enormous emerald. As big as a golf ball, Philbrick said.

' "This has been an heirloom of my family since the first crusade," said the Portuguese Count. "It is the one thing which I had hoped to leave to my poor, poor little son." And he tossed it on to the table.

' "I will wager against it my new four-funnel, turbine-driven liner called *The Queen of Arcady*," said Philbrick.

' "That's not enough," said the Portuguese Countess.

' "And my steam-yacht *Swallow* and four tugs and a coaling-barge," said Philbrick. All the party rose to applaud his reckless bid.

'The hand was played. Philbrick had won. With a low bow he returned the emerald to the Portuguese Countess. "For your son!" he said. Again the guests applauded, but the Portuguese Count was livid with rage. "You have insulted my honour," he said. "In Portugal we have only one way of dealing with such an occurrence."

'There and then they went out into Hyde Park, which was quite close. They faced each other and fired: it was just dawn. At the feet of the Achilles statue Philbrick shot the Portuguese Count dead. They left him with his smoking revolver in his hand. The Portuguese Countess kissed Philbrick's hand as she entered her car. "No one will ever know," she said. "It will be taken for suicide. It is a secret between us."

'But Philbrick was a changed man. The actress was driven from his house. He fell into a melancholy and paced up and down his deserted home at night, overpowered by his sense of guilt. The Portuguese Countess rang him up, but he told her it was the wrong number. Finally he went to a priest and confessed. He was told that for three years he must give up his house and wealth and live among the lowest of the low. That,' said Mr Prendergast simply, 'is why he is here. Wasn't that the story he told you?'

'No, it wasn't,' said Paul.

'Not the shade of a likeness,' said Grimes. 'He told me all about himself one evening at Mrs Roberts'. It was like this:

'Mr Philbrick, senior, was a slightly eccentric sort of a cove. He made a big pile out of diamond mines while he was quite young and settled in the country and devoted his declining years to literature. He had two kids: Philbrick and a daughter called Gracie. From the start Philbrick was the apple of the old chap's eye, while he couldn't stick Miss Gracie at any price. Philbrick could spout Shakespeare and *Hamlet* and things by the yard before Gracie could read "The cat sat on the mat." When he was eight he had a sonnet printed in the local paper. After that Gracie wasn't in it anywhere. She lived with the servants like Cinderella, Philbrick said, while he, sensible little beggar, had the best of everything and quoted classics and flowery language to the old boy upstairs. After he left Cambridge he settled down in London and wrote away like blazes. The old man just loved that; he had all Philbrick's books bound in blue leather and put in a separate bookcase with a bust of Philbrick on top. Poor old Gracie found things a bit thin, so she ran off with a young chap in the motor trade who didn't know one end of a book from the other, or of a car for that matter, as it turned out. When the old boy popped off he left Philbrick everything, except a few books to Gracie. The young man had only married her because he thought the old boy was bound to leave her something, so he hopped it. That didn't worry Philbrick. He lived for his art, he said. He just moved into a bigger house and went on writing away fifteen to the dozen. Gracie tried to get some money out of him more than once, but he was so busy writing books, he couldn't bother about her. At last she became a cook in a house at Southgate. Next year she died. That didn't worry Philbrick at first. Then after a week or so he noticed an odd thing. There was always a smell of cooking all over the house, in his study, in his bedroom, everywhere. He had an architect in who said he couldn't notice any smell, and rebuilt the kitchen and put in all sorts of ventilators. Still, the smell got worse. It used to hang about his clothes so that he didn't dare go out, a horrible fatty smell. He tried going abroad, but the whole of Paris reeked of English cooking. That was bad enough, but after a time plates began rattling round his bed when he tried to sleep at nights and behind his chair as he wrote his books. He used to wake up in the night and hear the frizzling of fried fish and the singing of kettles. Then he knew what it was: it was Gracie haunting him. He went to the Society for Psychical Research, and they got through a conversation to Gracie. He asked how he could make reparation. She said that he must live among servants for a year and write a book about them that would improve their lot. He tried to go the whole hog at first and started as *chef*, but of course that wasn't really in his line, and the family he was with got so ill, he had to leave. So he came here. He says the book is most moving, and that he'll read me bits of it some day. Not quite the same story as Prendy's.'

'No, it's not. By the way, did he say anything about marrying Dingy?'

'Not a word. He said that as soon as the smell of cooking wore off he was going to be the happiest man in the world. Apparently he's engaged to a female poet in Chelsea. He's not the sort of cove I'd have chosen for a brother-in-law. But then Flossie isn't really the sort of wife I'd have chosen. These things happen, old boy.'

Paul told them about the 'Lamb and Flag' at Camberwell Green and about Toby Cruttwell. 'D'you think that story is true, or yours, or Prendy's?' he asked.

'No,' said Mr Prendergast.

CHAPTER 12
The Agony of Captain Grimes

TWO days later Beste-Chetwynde and Paul were in the organ-loft of the Llanabba Parish Church.

'I don't think I played that terribly well, do you, sir?'

'No.'

'Shall I stop for a bit?'

'I wish you would.'

'Tangent's foot has swollen up and turned black,' said Beste-Chetwynde with relish.

'Poor little brute!' said Paul.

'I had a letter from my mamma this morning,' Beste-Chetwynde went on. 'There's a message for you in it. Shall I read you what she says?'

He took out a letter written on the thickest possible paper. 'The first part is all about racing and a row she's had with Chokey. Apparently he doesn't like the way she's rebuilt our house in the country. I think it was time she dropped that man, don't you?'

'What does she say about me?' asked Paul.

'She says: "*By the way, dear boy, I must tell you that the spelling in your last letters has been* just too shattering *for words. You know how terribly anxious I am for you to get on and go to Oxford, and everything, and I have been thinking, don't you think it might be a good thing if we were to have a tutor next holidays? Would you think it* too *boring? Some one young who would fit in. I thought, would that good-looking young master you said you liked care to come? How much ought I to pay him? I never know these things. I don't mean the drunk one, tho' he was sweet too.*" I think that must be you, don't you?' said Beste-Chetwynde; 'it can hardly be Captain Grimes.'

'Well, I must think that over,' said Paul. 'It sounds rather a good idea.'

'Well, yes,' said Beste-Chetwynde doubtfully, 'it might be all right, only there mustn't be too much of the schoolmaster about it. That man Prendergast beat me the other evening.'

'And there'll be no organ lessons, either,' said Paul.

Grimes did not receive the news as enthusiastically as Paul had hoped; he was sitting over the Common Room fire despondently biting his nails.

'Good, old boy! That's splendid,' he said abstractedly. 'I'm glad; I am really.'

'Well, you don't sound exactly gay.'

'No, I'm not. Fact is, I'm in the soup again.'

'Badly?'

'Up to the neck.'

'My dear chap, I *am* sorry. What are you going to do about it?'

'I've done the only thing: I've announced my engagement.'

'That'll please Flossie.'

'Oh, yes, she's as pleased as hell about it, damn her nasty little eyes.'

'What did the old man say?'

'Baffled him a bit, old boy. He's just thinking things out at the moment. Well, I expect everything'll be all right.'

'I don't see why it shouldn't be.'

'Well, there *is* a reason. I don't think I told you before, but fact is, I'm married already.'

That evening Paul received a summons from the Doctor. He wore a double-breasted dinner-jacket, which he smoothed uneasily over his hips at Paul's approach. He looked worried and old.

'Pennyfeather,' he said, 'I have this morning received a severe shock, two shocks in fact. The first was disagreeable, but not wholly unexpected. Your colleague, Captain Grimes, has been convicted before me, on evidence that leaves no possibility of his innocence, of a crime – I might almost call it a course of action – which I can neither understand nor excuse. I daresay I need not particularize. However, that is all a minor question. I have quite frequently met with similar cases during a long experience in our profession. But what has disturbed and grieved me more than I can moderately express is the information that he is engaged to be married to my elder daughter. That, Pennyfeather, I had not expected. In the circumstances it seemed a humiliation I might reasonably have been spared. I tell you all this, Pennyfeather, because in our brief acquaintance I have learned to trust and respect you.'

The Doctor sighed, drew from his pocket a handkerchief of *crêpe de chine*, blew his nose with every accent of emotion, and resumed:

'He is *not* the son-in-law I should readily have chosen. I could have forgiven him his wooden leg, his slavish poverty, his moral turpitude, and his abominable features; I could even have forgiven him his incredible vocabulary, if only he had been a *gentleman*. I hope you do not think me a snob. You may have discerned in me a certain prejudice against the lower orders. It is quite true. I *do* feel deeply on the subject. You see, I married one of them. But that, unfortunately, is neither here nor there. What I really wished to say to you was this: I have spoken to the unhappy young woman my daughter, and find that she has no particular inclination towards Grimes. Indeed, I do not think that any daughter of mine could fall as low as that. But she is, for some reason, uncontrollably eager to be married to somebody fairly soon. Now, I should be quite prepared to offer a partnership in Llanabba to a son-in-law of whom I approved. The income of the school is normally not less than three thousand a year – that is with the help of dear Diana's housekeeping – and my junior partner would start at an income of a thousand, and of course succeed to a larger share upon my death. It is a prospect that many young men would find inviting. And I was wondering, Pennyfeather, whether by any chance, looking at the matter from a business-like point of view, without prejudice, you understand, fair and square, taking things as they are for what they are worth, facing facts, whether possibly *you*... I wonder if I make myself plain?'

'No,' said Paul. 'No, sir, I'm afraid it would be impossible. I hope I don't appear rude, but – no, really I'm afraid...'

'That's all right, my dear boy. Not another word! I quite understand. I was afraid that would be your answer. Well, it must be Grimes, then. I don't think it would be any use approaching Mr Prendergast.'

'It was very kind of you to suggest it, sir.'

'Not at all, not at all. The wedding shall take place a week to-day. You might tell Grimes that if you see him. I don't want to have more to do with him than I can help. I wonder whether it would be a good thing to give a small party?' For a moment a light sprang up in Dr Fagan's eyes and then died out. 'No, no, there will be no party. The sports were not encouraging. Poor little Lord Tangent is still laid up, I hear.'

Paul returned to the Common Room with the Doctor's message.

'Hell!' said Grimes. 'I still hoped it might fall through.'

'What d'you want for a wedding present?' Paul asked.

Grimes brightened. 'What about that binge you promised me and Prendy?'

'All right!' said Paul. 'We'll have it tomorrow.'

*

The Hotel Metropole, Cwmpryddyg, is by far the grandest hotel in the north of Wales. It is situated on a high and healthy eminence overlooking the strip of water that railway companies have gallantly compared to the Bay of Naples. It was built in the ample days preceding the war, with a lavish expenditure on looking-glass and marble. To-day its shows signs of wear, for it has never been quite as popular as its pioneers hoped. There are cracks in the cement on the main terrace, the winter garden is draughty, and one comes disconcertingly upon derelict bath-chairs in the Moorish Court. Besides this, none of the fountains ever play, the string band that used to perform nightly in the ballroom has given place to a very expensive wireless set which one of the waiters knows how to operate, there is never any notepaper in the writing-room, and the sheets are not long enough for the beds. Philbrick pointed out these defects to Paul as he sat with Grimes and Mr Prendergast drinking cocktails in the Palm Court before dinner.

'And it isn't as though it was really cheap,' he said. Philbrick had become quite genial during the last few days. 'Still, one can't expect much in Wales, and it is something. I can't live without some kind of luxury for long. I'm not staying this evening, or I'd ask you fellows to dine with me.'

'Philbrick, old boy,' said Grimes, 'me and my pals here have been wanting a word with you for some time. How about those yarns you spun about your being a shipowner and a novelist and a burglar?'

'Since you mention it,' said Philbrick with dignity, 'they were untrue. One day you shall know my full story. It is stranger than any fiction. Meanwhile I have to be back at the Castle. Good night.'

'He certainly seems quite a swell here,' said Grimes as they watched him disappear into the night escorted with every obsequy by the manager and the head-waiter. 'I daresay he *could* tell a story if he wanted to.'

'I believe it's their keys,' said Mr Prendergast suddenly. It was the first time that he had spoken. For twenty minutes he had been sitting very upright in his gilt chair and very alert, his eyes unusually bright, darting this way and that in his eagerness to miss nothing of the gay scene about him.

'What's their keys, Prendy?'

'Why, the things they get given at the counter. I thought for a long time it was money.'

'Is that what's been worrying you? Bless your heart, I thought it was the young lady in the office you were after.'

'Oh, Grimes!' said Mr Prendergast, and he blushed warmly and gave a little giggle.

Paul led his guests into the dining-room.

'I haven't taught French for nothing all these years,' said Grimes, studying the menu. 'I'll start with some jolly old *huîtres*.'

Mr Prendergast ate a grape-fruit with some difficulty. 'What a big orange!' he said when he had finished it. 'They do things on a large scale here.'

The soup came in little aluminium bowls. 'What price the ancestral silver?' said Grimes. The Manchester merchants on the spree who sat all round them began to look a little askance at Paul's table.

'Someone's doing himself well on bubbly,' said Grimes as a waiter advanced staggering under the weight of an ice-pail from which emerged a Jeroboam of champagne. 'Good egg! It's coming to us.'

'With Sir Solomon Philbrick's compliments to Captain Grimes and congratulations on his approaching marriage, sir.'

Grimes took the waiter by the sleeve. 'See here, old boy, this Sir Solomon Philbrick – know him well?'

'He's here quite frequently, sir.'

'Spends a lot of money, eh?'

'He doesn't entertain at all, but he always has the best of everything himself, sir.'

'Does he pay his bill?'

'I really couldn't say, I'm afraid, sir. Would you be requiring anything else?'

'All right, old boy! Don't get sniffy. Only he's a pal of mine, see?'

'Really, Grimes,' said Mr Prendergast, 'I am afraid you made him quite annoyed with your questions, and that stout man over there is staring at us in the most marked way.'

'I've got a toast to propose. Prendy, fill up your glass. Here's to Trumpington, whoever he is, who gave us the money for this binge!'

'And here's to Philbrick,' said Paul, 'whoever *he* is!'

'And here's to Miss Fagan,' said Mr Prendergast, 'with our warmest hopes for her future happiness!'

'Amen,' said Grimes.

After the soup the worst sort of sole. Mr Prendergast made a little joke about soles and souls. Clearly the dinner-party was being a great success.

'You know,' said Grimes, 'look at it how you will, marriage is rather a grim thought.'

'The three reasons for it given in the Prayer-book have always seemed to me quite inadequate,' agreed Mr Prendergast. 'I have never had the smallest difficulty about the avoidance of fornication, and the other two advantages seem to me nothing short of disastrous.'

'My first marriage,' said Grimes, 'didn't make much odds either way. It was in Ireland. I was tight at the time, and so was everyone else. God knows what became of Mrs Grimes. It seems to me, though, that with Flossie I'm in for a pretty solemn solemnization. It's not what I should have chosen for myself, not by a long chalk. Still, as things are, I suppose it's the best thing that could have happened. I think I've about run through the schoolmastering profession. I don't mind telling you I might have found it pretty hard to get another job. There are limits. Now I'm set up for life, and no more worry about testimonials. That's something. In fact, that's all there is to be said. But there have been moments in the last twenty-four hours, I don't mind telling you, when I've gone cold all over at the thought of what I was in for.'

'I don't want to say anything discouraging,' said Mr Prendergast, 'but I've known Flossie for nearly ten years now, and –'

'There isn't anything you can tell me about Flossie that I don't know already. I almost wish it was Dingy. I suppose it's too late now to change. Oh dear!' said Grimes despondently, gazing into his glass. 'Oh, Lord! oh, Lord! That I should come to this!'

'Cheer up, Grimes. It isn't like you to be as depressed as this,' said Paul.

'Old friends,' said Grimes – and his voice was charged with emotion – 'you see a man standing face to face with retribution. Respect him even if you cannot understand. Those that live by the flesh shall perish by the flesh. I am a very sinful man, and I am past my first youth. Who shall pity me in that dark declivity to which my steps inevitably seem to tend? I have boasted in my youth and held my head high and gone on my way careless of consequence, but ever behind me, unseen, stood stark Justice with his two-edged sword.'

More food was brought them. Mr Prendergast ate with a hearty appetite.

'Oh, why did nobody warn me?' cried Grimes in his agony. 'I should have been told. They should have told me in so many words. They should have warned me about Flossie, not about the fires of hell. I've risked them, and I don't mind risking them again, but they should have told me about marriage. They should have told me that at the end of that gay journey and flower-strewn path were the hideous lights of home and the voices of children. I should have been warned of the great lavender-scented bed that was laid out for me, of the wistaria at the windows, of all the intimacy and confidence of family life. But I daresay I shouldn't have listened. Our life is lived between two homes. We emerge for a little into the light, and then the front door closes. The chintz curtains shut out the sun, and the hearth glows with the fire of home, while upstairs, above our heads, are enacted again the awful accidents of adolescence. There's a home and family waiting for every one of us. We can't escape, try how we may. It's the seed of life we carry about with us like our skeletons, each one of us unconsciously pregnant with desirable villa residences. There's no escape. As individuals we simply do not exist. We are just potential home-builders, beavers, and ants. How do we come into being? What is birth?'

'I've often wondered,' said Mr Prendergast.

'What is this impulse of two people to build their beastly home? It's you and me, unborn, asserting our presence. All we are is a manifestation of the impulse of family life, and if by chance we have escaped the itch ourselves, Nature forces it upon us another way. Flossie's got that itch enough for two. I just haven't. I'm one of the blind alleys off the main road of procreation, but it doesn't matter. Nature always wins. Oh, Lord! oh, Lord! Why didn't I die in that first awful home? Why did I ever hope I could escape?'

Captain Grimes continued his lament for some time in deep bitterness of heart. Presently he became silent and stared at his glass.

'I wonder,' said Mr Prendergast, 'I wonder whether I could have just a little more of this very excellent pheasant?'

'Anyway,' said Grimes, 'there shan't be any children; I'll see to that.'

'It has always been a mystery to me why people marry,' said Mr Prendergast. 'I can't see the smallest reason for it. Quite happy, normal people. Now I can understand it in Grimes' case. He has everything to gain by the arrangement, but what does Flossie expect to gain? And yet she seems more enthusiastic about it than Grimes. It has been the tragedy of my life that whenever I start thinking about any quite simple subject I invariably feel myself confronted by some flat contradiction of this sort. Have you ever thought about marriage – in the abstract, I mean, of course?'

'Not very much, I'm afraid.'

'I don't believe,' said Mr Prendergast, 'that people would ever fall in love or want to be married if they hadn't been told about it. It's like abroad: no one would want to go there if they hadn't been told it existed. Don't you agree?'

'I don't think you can be quite right,' said Paul; 'you see, animals fall in love quite a lot, don't they?'

'Do they?' said Mr Prendergast. 'I didn't know that. What an extraordinary thing! But then I had an aunt whose cat used to put its paw up to its mouth when it yawned. It's wonderful what animals can be taught. There is a sea-lion at the circus, I saw in the paper, who juggles with an umbrella and two oranges.'

'I know what I'll do,' said Grimes. 'I'll get a motor bicycle.'

This seemed to cheer him up a little. He took another glass of wine and smiled wanly. 'I'm afraid I've not been following all you chaps have said. I was thinking. What were we talking about?'

'Prendy was telling me about a sea-lion who juggled with an umbrella and two oranges.'

'Why, that's nothing. I can juggle with a whacking great bottle and a lump of ice and two knives. Look!'

'Grimes, don't! Everyone is looking at you.'

The head-waiter came over to remonstrate. 'Please remember where you are, sir,' he said.

'I know where I am well enough,' said Grimes. 'I'm in the hotel my pal Sir Solomon Philbrick is talking of buying, and I tell you this, old boy: if he does, the first person to lose his job will be you. See?'

Nevertheless he stopped juggling, and Mr Prendergast ate two *pêches Melba* undisturbed.

'The black cloud has passed,' said Grimes. 'Grimes is now going to enjoy his evening.'

CHAPTER 13

The Passing of a Public School Man

SIX days later the school was given a half-holiday, and soon after luncheon the bigamous union of Captain Edgar Grimes and Miss Florence Selina Fagan was celebrated at the Llanabba Parish Church. A slight injury to his hand prevented Paul from playing the organ. He walked down the church with Mr Prendergast, who, greatly to his dismay, had been instructed by Dr Fagan to give away the bride.

'I do not intend to be present,' said the Doctor. 'The whole business is exceedingly painful to me.' Everybody else, however, was there except little Lord Tangent, whose foot was being amputated at a local nursing-home. The boys for the most part welcomed the event as a pleasant variation to the rather irregular routine of their day. Clutterbuck alone seemed disposed to sulk.

'I don't suppose that their children will be terribly attractive,' said Beste-Chetwynde.

There were few wedding presents. The boys had subscribed a shilling each and had bought at a shop in Llandudno a silver-plated teapot, coyly suggestive of *art nouveau*. The Doctor gave them a cheque for twenty-five pounds. Mr Prendergast gave Grimes a walking-stick – 'because he was always borrowing mine' – and Dingy, rather generously, two photograph frames, a calendar, and a tray of Benares brassware. Paul was the best man.

The service passed off without a hitch, for Grimes' Irish wife did not turn up to forbid the banns. Flossie wore a frock of a rather noticeable velveteen and a hat with two pink feathers to match.

'I was so pleased when I found he didn't want me to wear white,' she said, 'though, of course, it might have been dyed afterwards.'

Both bride and bridegroom spoke up well in the responses, and afterwards the Vicar delivered a very moving address on the subject of Home and Conjugal Love.

'How beautiful it is,' he said, 'to see two young people in the hope of youth setting out with the Church's blessing to face life together; how much more beautiful to see them when they have grown to full manhood and womanhood coming together and saying, "Our experience of life has taught us that *one* is not enough."'

The boys lined the path from the church door to the lych-gate, and the head prefect said: 'Three cheers for Captain and Mrs Grimes!'

Then they returned to the Castle. The honeymoon had been postponed until the end of term, ten days later, and the arrangements for the first days of their married life were a little meagre. 'You must do the best you can,' the Doctor had said. 'I suppose you will wish to share the same bedroom. I think there would be no objection to your both moving into the large room in the West Tower. It is a little damp, but I daresay Diana will arrange for a fire to be lighted there. You may use the morning-room in the evenings, and Captain Grimes will, of course, have his meals at my table in the dining-room, not with the boys. I do not wish to find him sitting about in the drawing-room, nor, of course, in my library. He had better keep his books and gown in the Common Room, as before. Next term I will consider some other arrangement. Perhaps I could hand over one of the lodges to you or fit up some sort of sitting-room in the tower. I was not prepared for a domestic upheaval.'

Diana, who was really coming out of the business rather creditably, put a bowl of flowers in their bedroom, and lit a fire of reckless proportions, in which she consumed the remains of a desk and two of the boys' play-boxes.

That evening, while Mr Prendergast was taking Prep. at the end of the passage, Grimes visited Paul in the Common Room. He looked rather uncomfortable in his evening clothes.

'Well, dinner's over,' he said. 'The old man does himself pretty well.'

'How are you feeling?'

'Not too well, old boy. The first days are always a strain, they say, even in the most romantic marriages. My father-in-law is *not* what you might call easy. Needs thawing gently, you know. I suppose as a married man I oughtn't to go down to Mrs Roberts'?'

'I think it might seem odd on the first evening, don't you?'

'Flossie's playing the piano; Dingy's making up the accounts; the old man's gone off to the library. Don't you think we've time for a quick one?'

Arm in arm they went down the familiar road.

'Drinks are on me to-night,' said Grimes.

The silver band were still sitting with their heads together discussing the division of their earnings.

'They tell me that married this afternoon you were?' said the stationmaster.

'That's right,' said Grimes.

'And my sister-in-law never at all you would meet whatever,' he continued reproachfully.

'Look here, old boy,' said Grimes, 'just you shut up. You're not being tactful. See? Just you keep quiet, and I'll give you all some nice beer.'

When Mrs Roberts shut her doors for the night, Paul and Grimes turned back up the hill. A light was burning in the West Tower.

'There she is, waiting for me,' said Grimes. 'Now it might be a very romantic sight to some chaps, a light burning in a tower window. I knew a poem about a thing like that once. Forget it now, though. I was no end of a one for poetry when I was a kid – love and all that. Castle towers came in quite a lot. Funny how one grows out of that sort of thing.'

Inside the Castle he turned off down the main corridor.

'Well, so long, old boy! This is the way I go now. See you in the morning.' The baize door swung to behind him, and Paul went up to bed.

*

Paul saw little of Grimes during the next few days. They met at prayers and on the way to and from their classrooms, but the baize door that separated the school from the Doctor's wing was also separating them. Mr Prendergast, now in unchallenged possession of the other easy-chair, was smoking away one evening when he suddenly said:

'You know, I miss Grimes. I didn't think I should, but I do. With all his faults, he was a very cheery person. I think I was beginning to get on better with him.'

'He doesn't look as cheery as he did,' said Paul. 'I don't believe that life "above stairs" is suiting him very well.'

As it happened, Grimes chose that evening to visit them.

'D'you chaps mind if I come in for a bit?' he asked with unwonted diffidence. They rose to welcome him. 'Sure you don't mind? I won't stay long.'

'My dear man, we were just saying how much we missed you. Come and sit down.'

'Won't you have some of my tobacco?' said Prendergast.

'Thanks, Prendy! I just had to come in and have a chat. I've been feeling pretty fed up lately. Married life is *not* all beer and skittles, I don't mind telling you. It's not Flossie, mind; she's been hardly any trouble at all. In a way I've got quite to like her. She likes me, anyway, and that's the great thing. The Doctor's my trouble. He never lets me alone, that man. It gets on my nerves. Always laughing at me in a nasty kind of way and making me feel small. You know the way Lady Circumference talks to the Clutterbucks – like that. I tell you I simply dread going into meals in that dining-room. He's got a sort of air as though he always knew exactly what I was going to say before I said it, and as if it was always a little worse than he'd expected. Flossie says he treats *her* that way sometimes. He does it to me the whole time, damn him.'

'I don't expect he means it,' said Paul, 'and anyway I shouldn't bother about it.'

'That's the point. I'm beginning to feel he's quite right. I suppose I am a pretty coarse sort of chap. I don't know anything about art, and I haven't met any grand people, and I don't go to a good tailor, and all that. I'm not what he calls "out of the top drawer". I never pretended I was, but the thing is that up till now it hasn't worried me. I don't think I was a conceited sort of chap, but I felt as good as anyone else, and I didn't care what people thought as long as I had my fun. And I *did* have fun, too, and, what's more, I enjoyed it. But now I've lived with that man for a week, I feel quite different. I feel half ashamed of myself all the time. And I've come to recognize that supercilious look he gives me in other people's eyes as well.'

'Ah, how well I know that feeling!' sighed Mr Prendergast.

'I used to think I was popular among the boys, but you know I'm not, and at Mrs Roberts' they only pretend to like me in the hope I'd stand 'em drinks. I did, too, but they never gave me one back. I thought it was just because they were Welsh, but I see now it was because they despised me. I don't blame them. God knows I despise myself. You know, I used to use French phrases a certain amount – things like *savoir faire* and *Je ne sais quoi.* I never thought about it, but I suppose I haven't got much of an accent. How could I? I've never been in France except for that war. Well, every time I say one of them now the Doctor gives a sort of wince as if he's bitten on a bad tooth. I have to think the whole time now before I say anything, to see if there's any French in it or any of the expressions he doesn't think refined. Then when I do say anything my voice sounds so funny that I get in a muddle and he winces again. Old boy, it's been hell this last week, and it's worrying me. I'm getting an inferiority complex. Dingy's like that. She just never speaks now. He's always making little jokes about Flossie's clothes, too, but I don't think the old girl sees what he's driving at. That man'll have me crazy before the term's over.'

'Well, there's only a week more,' was all that Paul could say to comfort him.

*

Next morning at prayers Grimes handed Paul a letter. 'Irony,' he said.

Paul opened it and read:

John Clutterbuck & Sons,
Wholesale Brewers and Wine Merchants.

My Dear Grimes,

The other day at the sports you asked whether there was by any chance a job open for you at the brewery. I don't know if you were serious in this, but if you were a post has just fallen vacant which I feel might suit you. I should be glad to offer it to any friend who has been so kind to Percy. We employ a certain number of travellers to go round to various inns and hotels to sample the beer and see that it has not been diluted or in any way adulterated. Our junior traveller, who was a friend of mine from Cambridge, has just developed D.T.s and has had to be suspended. The salary is two hundred a year with car and travelling expenses. Would this attract you at all? If so, will you let me know during the next few days.

Yours sincerely,
Sam Clutterbuck.

'Just look at that,' said Grimes. 'God's own job and mine for the asking! If that had come ten days ago my whole life might have been different.'

'You don't think of taking it now?'

'Too late, old boy, too late. The saddest words in the English language.'

In 'break' Grimes said to Paul: 'Look here, I've decided to take Sam Clutterbuck's job, and be damned to the Fagans!' His eyes shone with excitement. 'I shan't say a word to them. I shall just go off. They can do what they like about it. I don't care.'

'Splendid!' said Paul. 'It's much the best thing you can do.'

'I'm going this very afternoon,' said Grimes.

An hour later, at the end of morning school, they met again. 'I've been thinking over that letter,' said Grimes. 'I see it all now. It's just a joke.'

'Nonsense!' said Paul. 'I'm sure it isn't. Go and see the Clutterbucks right away.'

'No, no, they don't mean it seriously. They've heard about my marriage from Percy, and they're just pulling my leg. It was too good to be true. Why should they offer *me* a job like that, even if such a wonderful job exists?'

'My dear Grimes, I'm perfectly certain it was a genuine offer. Anyway, there's nothing to lose by going to see them.'

'No, no, it's too late, old boy. Things like that don't happen.' And he disappeared beyond the baize door.

*

Next day there was fresh trouble at Llanabba. Two men in stout boots, bowler hats, and thick grey overcoats presented themselves at the Castle with a warrant for Philbrick's arrest. Search was made for him, but it was suddenly discovered that he had already left by the morning train for Holyhead. The boys crowded round the detectives with interest and a good deal of disappointment. They were not, they thought, particularly impressive figures as they stood in the hall fingering their hats and drinking whisky and calling Dingy 'miss'.

'We've been after 'im for some time now,' said the first detective. 'Ain't we, Bill?'

'Pretty near six months. It's too bad, his getting away like this. They're getting rather restless at H.Q. about our travelling expenses.'

'Is it a very serious case?' asked Mr Prendergast. The entire school were by this time assembled in the hall. 'Not shooting or anything like that?'

'No, there ain't been no bloodshed up to date, sir. I oughtn't to tell about it, really, but seeing as you've all been mixed up in it to some extent, I don't mind telling you that I think he'll get off on a plea of insanity. Loopy, you know.'

'What's he been up to?'

'False pretences and impersonation, sir. There's five charges against him in different parts of the country, mostly at hotels. He represents himself as a rich man, stays there for some time living like a lord, cashes a big cheque and then goes off. Calls 'isself Sir Solomon Philbrick. Funny thing is, I think he really believes his tale 'isself. I've come across several cases like that one time or another. There was a bloke in Somerset what thought 'e was Bishop of Bath and Wells and confirmed a whole lot of kids – very reverent, too.'

'Well, anyway,' said Dingy, 'he went without his wages from here.'

'I always felt there was something untrustworthy about that man,' said Mr Prendergast.

'Lucky devil!' said Grimes despondently.

*

'I'm worried about Grimes,' said Mr Prendergast that evening. 'I never saw a man more changed. He used to be so self-confident and self-assertive. He came in here quite timidly just now and asked me whether I believed that Divine retribution took place in this world or the next. I began to talk to him about it, but I could see he wasn't listening. He sighed once or twice and then went out without a word while I was still speaking.'

'Beste-Chetwynde tells me he has kept in the whole of the third form because the blackboard fell down in his classroom this morning. He was convinced they had arranged it on purpose.'

'Yes, they often do.'

'But in this case, they hadn't. Beste-Chetwynde said they were quite frightened at the way he spoke to them. Just like an actor, Beste-Chetwynde said.'

'Poor Grimes! I think he is seriously unnerved. It will be a relief when the holidays come.'

But Captain Grimes' holiday came sooner than Mr Prendergast expected, and in a way which few people could have foreseen. Three days later he did not appear at morning prayers, and Flossie, red-eyed, admitted that he had not come in from the village the night before. Mr Davies, the stationmaster, confessed to seeing him earlier in the evening in a state of depression. Just before luncheon a youth presented himself at the Castle with a little pile of clothes he had found on the seashore. They were identified without difficulty as having belonged to the Captain. In the breast pocket of the jacket was an envelope addressed to the Doctor, and in it a slip of paper inscribed with the words: 'THOSE THAT LIVE BY THE FLESH SHALL PERISH BY THE FLESH.'

As far as was possible this intelligence was kept from the boys.

Flossie, though severely shocked at this untimely curtailment of her married life, was firm in her resolution not to wear mourning. 'I don't think my husband would have expected it of me,' she said.

In these distressing circumstances the boys began packing their boxes to go away for the Easter holidays.

END OF PART ONE

PART TWO

CHAPTER 1
King's Thursday

MARGOT BESTE-CHETWYNDE had two houses in England – one in London and the other in Hampshire. Her London house, built in the reign of William and Mary, was, by universal consent, the most beautiful building between Bond Street and Park Lane, but opinion was divided on the subject of her country house. This was very new indeed; in fact, it was scarcely finished when Paul went to stay there at the beginning of the Easter holidays. No single act in Mrs Beste-Chetwynde's eventful and in many ways disgraceful career had excited quite so much hostile comment as the building, or rather the rebuilding, of this remarkable house.

It was called King's Thursday, and stood on the place which since the reign of Bloody Mary had been the seat of the Earls of Pastmaster. For three centuries the poverty and inertia of this noble family had preserved its home unmodified by any of the succeeding fashions that fell upon domestic architecture. No wing had been added, no window filled in; no portico, façade, terrace, orangery, tower, or battlement marred its timbered front. In the craze for coal-gas and indoor sanitation, King's Thursday had slept unscathed by plumber or engineer. The estate carpenter, an office hereditary in the family of the original joiner who had panelled the halls and carved the great staircase, did such restorations as became necessary from time to time for the maintenance of the fabric, working with the same tools and with the traditional methods, so that in a few years his work became indistinguishable from that of his grandsires. Rushlights still flickered in the bedrooms long after all Lord Pastmaster's neighbours were blazing away electricity, and in the last fifty years Hampshire had gradually become proud of

King's Thursday. From having been considered rather a blot on the progressive county, King's Thursday gradually became the Mecca of week-end parties. 'I thought we might go over to tea at the Pastmasters',' hostesses would say after luncheon on Sundays. 'You really must see their house. Quite unspoilt, my dear. Professor Franks, who was here last week, said it was recognized as the finest piece of domestic Tudor in England.'

It was impossible to ring the Pastmasters up, but they were always at home and unaffectedly delighted to see their neighbours, and after tea Lord Pastmaster would lead the new-comers on a tour round the house, along the great galleries and into the bedrooms, and would point out the priest-hole and the closet where the third Earl imprisoned his wife for wishing to rebuild a smoking chimney. 'That chimney still smokes when the wind's in the east,' he would say, 'but we haven't rebuilt it yet.'

Later they would drive away in their big motor cars to their modernized manors, and as they sat in their hot baths before dinner the more impressionable visitors might reflect how they seemed to have been privileged to step for an hour and a half out of their own century into the leisurely, prosaic life of the English Renaissance, and how they had talked at tea of field-sports and the reform of the Prayer-book just as the very-great-grandparents of their host might have talked in the same chairs and before the same fire three hundred years before, when their own ancestors, perhaps, slept on straw or among the aromatic merchandise of some Hanse ghetto.

But the time came when King's Thursday had to be sold. It had been built in an age when twenty servants were not an unduly extravagant establishment, and it was scarcely possible to live there with fewer. But servants, the Beste-Chetwyndes found, were less responsive than their masters to the charms of Tudor simplicity; the bedrooms originally ordained for them among the maze of rafters that supported the arches of uneven stone roofs were unsuited to modern requirements, and only the dirtiest and most tipsy of cooks could be induced to inhabit the enormous stone-flagged kitchen or turn the spits at the open fire. Housemaids tended to melt away under the recurring strain of trotting in the bleak hour before breakfast up and down the narrow servants' staircases and along the interminable passages with jugs of warm water for the morning baths. Modern democracy called for lifts and labour-saving devices, for hot-water taps and cold-water taps and (horrible innovation!) drinking water taps, for gas-rings, and electric ovens.

With rather less reluctance than might have been expected, Lord Pastmaster made up his mind to sell the house; to tell the truth, he could never quite see what all the fuss was about; he supposed it was very historic, and all that, but his own taste lay towards the green shutters and semi-tropical vegetation of a villa on the French Riviera, in which, if his critics had only realized it, he was fulfilling the traditional character of his family far better than by struggling on at King's Thursday. But the County was slow to observe this, and something very like consternation was felt, not only in the Great Houses, but in the bungalows and the villas for miles about, while in the neighbouring rectories antiquarian clergymen devised folk-tales of the disasters that should come to crops and herds when there was no longer a Beste-Chetwynde at King's Thursday. Mr Jack Spire in the *London Hercules* wrote eloquently on the *Save King's Thursday Fund*, urging that it should be preserved for the nation, but only a very small amount was collected of the very large sum which Lord Pastmaster was sensible enough to demand, and the theory that it was to be transplanted and re-erected in Cincinnati found wide acceptance.

Thus the news that Lord Pastmaster's rich sister-in-law had bought the family seat was received with the utmost delight by her new neighbours and by Mr Jack Spire, and all sections of the London Press which noticed the sale. *Teneat Bene Beste-Chetwynde*, the motto carved over the chimneypiece in the great hall, was quoted exultantly on all sides, for very little was known about Margot Beste-Chetwynde in Hampshire, and the illustrated papers were always pleased to take any occasion to embellish their pages with her latest portrait; the reporter to whom she remarked, 'I can't think of anything more bourgeois and awful than timbered Tudor architecture,' did not take in what she meant or include the statement in his 'story'.

King's Thursday had been empty for two years when Margot Beste-Chetwynde bought it. She had been there once before, during her engagement.

'It's worse than I thought, far worse,' she said as she drove up the main avenue which the loyal villagers had decorated with the flags of the sometime allied nations in honour of her arrival. 'Liberty's new building cannot be compared with it,' she said, and stirred impatiently in the car, as she remembered, how many years ago, the romantic young heiress who had walked entranced among the cut yews, and had been wooed, how phlegmatically, in the odour of honeysuckle.

Mr Jack Spire was busily saving St Sepulchre's, Egg Street (where Dr Johnson is said once to have attended Matins), when Margot Beste-Chetwynde's decision to rebuild King's Thursday became public. He said, very seriously: 'Well, we did what we could,' and thought no more about it.

Not so the neighbours, who as the work of demolition proceeded, with the aid of all that was most pulverizing in modern machinery, became increasingly enraged, and, in their eagerness to preserve for the county a little of the great manor, even resorted to predatory expeditions, from which they would return with lumps of carved stonework for their rock gardens, until the contractors were forced to maintain an extra watchman at night. The panelling went to South Kensington, where it has come in for a great deal of admiration from the Indian students. Within nine months of Mrs Beste-Chetwynde's taking possession the new architect was at work on his plans.

It was Otto Friedrich Silenus' first important commission. 'Something clean and square,' had been Mrs Beste-Chetwynde's instructions, and then she had disappeared on one of her mysterious world-tours, saying as she left: 'Please see that it is finished by the spring.'

Professor Silenus – for that was the title by which this extraordinary young man chose to be called – was a 'find' of

Mrs Beste-Chetwynde's. He was not yet very famous anywhere, though all who met him carried away deep and diverse impressions of his genius. He had first attracted Mrs Beste-Chetwynde's attention with the rejected design for a chewing-gum factory which had been produced in a progressive Hungarian quarterly. His only other completed work was the *décor* for a cinema-film of great length and complexity of plot – a complexity rendered the more inextricable by the producer's austere elimination of all human characters, a fact which had proved fatal to its commercial success. He was starving resignedly in a bed-sitting-room in Bloomsbury, despite the untiring efforts of his parents to find him – they were very rich in Hamburg – when he was offered the commission of rebuilding King's Thursday. 'Something clean and square' – he pondered for three hungry days upon the aesthetic implications of these instructions and then began his designs.

'The problem of architecture as I see it,' he told a journalist who had come to report on the progress of his surprising creation of ferro-concrete and aluminium, 'is the problem of all art – the elimination of the human element from the consideration of form. The only perfect building must be the factory, because that is built to house machines, not men. I do not think it is possible for domestic architecture to be beautiful, but I am doing my best. All ill comes from man,' he said gloomily; 'please tell your readers that. Man is never beautiful, he is never happy except when he becomes the channel for the distribution of mechanical forces.'

The journalist looked doubtful. 'Now, Professor,' he said, 'tell me this. Is it a fact that you have refused to take any fee for the work you are doing, if you don't mind my asking?'

'It is not,' said Professor Silenus.

'Peer's Sister-in-Law Mansion Builder on Future of Architecture,' thought the journalist happily. 'Will machines live in houses? Amazing forecast of Professor-Architect.'

Professor Silenus watched the reporter disappear down the drive and then, taking a biscuit from his pocket, began to munch.

'I suppose there ought to be a staircase,' he said gloomily. 'Why can't the creatures stay in one place? Up and down, in and out, round and round! Why can't they sit still and work? Do dynamos require staircases? Do monkeys require houses? What an immature, self-destructive, antiquated mischief is man! How obscure and gross his prancing and chattering on his little stage of evolution! How loathsome and beyond words boring all the thoughts and self-approval of his biological by-product! this half-formed, ill-conditioned body! this erratic, maladjusted mechanism of his soul: on one side the harmonious instincts and balanced responses of the animal, on the other the inflexible purpose of the engine, and between them man, equally alien from the *being* of Nature and the *doing* of the machine, the vile *becoming*!'

Two hours later the foreman in charge of the concrete-mixer came to consult with the Professor. He had not moved from where the journalist had left him; his fawn-like eyes were fixed and inexpressive, and the hand which had held the biscuit still rose and fell to and from his mouth with a regular motion, while his empty jaws champed rhythmically; otherwise he was wholly immobile.

CHAPTER 2
Interlude in Belgravia

ARTHUR POTTS knew all about King's Thursday and Professor Silenus.

On the day of Paul's arrival in London he rang up his old friend and arranged to dine with him at the Queen's Restaurant in Sloane Square. It seemed quite natural that they should be again seated at the table where they had discussed so many subjects of public importance, Budgets and birth control and Byzantine mosaics. For the first time since the disturbing evening of the Bollinger dinner he felt at ease. Llanabba Castle, with its sham castellations and preposterous inhabitants, had sunk into the oblivion that waits upon even the most lurid of nightmares. Here were sweet corn and pimentoes, and white Burgundy, and the grave eyes of Arthur Potts, and there on the peg over his head hung the black hat he had bought in St James's that afternoon. For an evening at least the shadow that has flitted about this narrative under the name of Paul Pennyfeather materialized into the solid figure of an intelligent, well-educated, well-conducted young man, a man who could be trusted to use his vote at a general election with discretion and proper detachment, whose opinion on a ballet or a critical essay was rather better than most people's, who could order a dinner without embarrassment and in a creditable French accent, who could be trusted to see to luggage at foreign railway-stations and might be expected to acquit himself with decision and decorum in all the emergencies of civilized life. This was the Paul Pennyfeather who had been developing in the placid years which preceded this story. In fact, the whole of this book is really an account of the mysterious disappearance of Paul Pennyfeather, so that readers must not complain if the shadow which took his name does not amply fill the important part of hero for which he was originally cast.

'I saw some of Otto Silenus' work at Munich,' said Potts. 'I think that he's a man worth watching. He was in Moscow at one time and in the Bauhaus at Dessau. He can't be more than twenty-five now. There were some photographs of King's Thursday in a paper the other day. It looked extraordinarily interesting. It's said to be the only really *imaginative* building since the French Revolution. He's got right away from Corbusier, anyway.'

'If people realized,' said Paul, 'Corbusier is a pure nineteenth-century, Manchester school utilitarian, and that's why they like him.'

Then Paul told Potts about the death of Grimes and the doubts of Mr Prendergast, and Potts told Paul about rather an interesting job he had got under the League of Nations and how he had decided not to take his Schools in consequence and of the unenlightened attitude adopted in the matter by Potts' father.

For an evening Paul became a real person again, but next day he woke up leaving himself disembodied somewhere between Sloane Square and Onslow Square. He had to meet Beste-Chetwynde and catch a morning train to King's Thursday, and there his extraordinary adventures began anew. From the point of view of this story Paul's second disappearance is necessary, because, as the reader will probably have discerned already, Paul Pennyfeather would never have made a hero, and the only interest about him arises from the unusual series of events of which his shadow was witness.

CHAPTER 3
Pervigilium Veneris

'I'M looking forward to seeing our new house,' said Beste-Chetwynde as they drove out from the station. 'Mamma says it may be rather a surprise.'

The lodges and gates had been left undisturbed, and the lodge-keeper's wife, white-aproned as Mrs Noah, bobbed at the car as it turned into the avenue. The temperate April sunlight fell through the budding chestnuts and revealed between their trunks green glimpses of parkland and the distant radiance of a lake. 'English spring,' thought Paul. 'In the dreaming ancestral beauty of the English country.' Surely, he thought, these great chestnuts in the morning sun stood for something enduring and serene in a world that had lost its reason and would so stand when the chaos and confusion were forgotten? And surely it was the spirit of William Morris that whispered to him in Margot Beste-Chetwynde's motor car about seed-time and harvest, the superb succession of the seasons, the harmonious interdependence of rich and poor, of dignity, innocence, and tradition? But at a turn in the drive the cadence of his thoughts was abruptly transected. They had come into sight of the house.

'Golly!' said Beste-Chetwynde. 'Mamma has done herself proud this time.'

The car stopped. Paul and Beste-Chetwynde got out, stretched themselves, and were led across a floor of bottle-green glass into the dining-room, where Mrs Beste-Chetwynde was already seated at the vulcanite table beginning her luncheon.

'My dears,' she cried, extending a hand to each of them, 'how divine to see you! I have been waiting for this to go straight to bed.'

She was a thousand times more beautiful than all Paul's feverish recollections of her. He watched her, transported.

'Darling boy, how are you?' she said. 'Do you know you're beginning to look rather lovely in a coltish kind of way. Don't you think so, Otto?'

Paul had noticed nothing in the room except Mrs Beste-Chetwynde; he now saw that there was a young man sitting beside her, with very fair hair and large glasses, behind which his eyes lay like slim fish in an aquarium; they woke from their slumber, flashed iridescent in the light, and darted towards little Beste-Chetwynde.

'His head is too big, and his hands are too small,' said Professor Silenus. 'But his skin is pretty.'

'How would it be if I made Mr Pennyfeather a cocktail?' Beste-Chetwynde asked.

'Yes, Peter, dear, do. He makes them rather well. You can't think what a week I've had, moving in and taking the neighbours round the house and the Press photographers. Otto's house doesn't seem to be a great success with the county, does it, Otto? What was it Lady Vanburgh said?'

'Was that the woman like Napoleon the Great?'

'Yes, darling.'

'She said she understood that the drains were satisfactory, but that, of course, they were underground. I asked her if she wished to make use of them, and said that I did, and went away. But, as a matter of fact, she was quite right. They are the only tolerable part of the house. How glad I shall be when the mosaics are finished and I can go!'

'Don't you like it?' asked Peter Beste-Chetwynde over the cocktail-shaker. 'I think it's so good. It was rather Chokey's taste before.'

'I hate and detest every bit of it,' said Professor Silenus gravely. 'Nothing I have ever done has caused me so much disgust.' With a deep sigh he rose from the table and walked from the room, the fork with which he had been eating still held in his hand.

'Otto has real genius,' said Mrs Beste-Chetwynde. 'You must be sweet to him, Peter. There's a whole lot of people coming down to-morrow for the week-end, and, my dear, that Maltravers has invited himself again. You wouldn't like him for a stepfather, would you, darling?'

'No,' said Peter. 'If you must marry again do choose someone young and quiet.'

'Peter, you're an angel. I will. But now I'm going to bed. I had to wait to see you both. Show Mr Pennyfeather the way about, darling.'

The aluminium lift shot up, and Paul came down to earth.

'That's an odd thing to ask me in a totally strange house,' said Peter Beste-Chetwynde. 'Anyway, let's have some luncheon.'

It was three days before Paul next saw Mrs Beste-Chetwynde.

*

'Don't you think that she's the most wonderful woman in the world?' said Paul.

'Wonderful? In what way?'

He and Professor Silenus were standing on the terrace after dinner. The half-finished mosaics at their feet were covered with planks and sacking; the great colonnade of black glass pillars shone in the moonlight; beyond the polished aluminium balustrade the park stretched silent and illimitable.

'The most beautiful and the most free. She almost seems like the creature of a different species. Don't you feel that?'

'No,' said the Professor after a few moments' consideration. 'I can't say that I do. If you compare her with other women of her age you will see that the particulars in which she differs from them are infinitesimal compared with the points of similarity.

A few millimetres here and a few millimetres there, such variations are inevitable in the human reproductive system; but in all her essential functions – her digestion, for example – she conforms to type.'

'You might say that about anybody.'

'Yes, I do. But it's Margot's variations that I dislike so much. They are small, but obtrusive, like the teeth of a saw. Otherwise I might marry her.'

'Why do you think she would marry you?'

'Because, as I said, all her essential functions are normal. Anyway, she asked me to twice. The first time I said I would think it over, and the second time I refused. I'm sure I was right. She would interrupt me terribly. Besides, she's getting old. In ten years she will be almost worn out.'

Professor Silenus looked at his watch – a platinum disc from Cartier, the gift of Mrs Beste-Chetwynde. 'Quarter to ten,' he said. 'I must go to bed.' He threw the end of his cigar clear of the terrace in a glowing parabola. 'What do you take to make you sleep?'

'I sleep quite easily,' said Paul, 'except on trains.'

'You're lucky. Margot takes veronal. I haven't been to sleep for over a year. That's why I go to bed early. One needs more rest if one doesn't sleep.'

That night as Paul marked his place in *The Golden Bough*, and, switching off his light, turned over to sleep, he thought of the young man a few bedrooms away, lying motionless in the darkness, his hands at his sides, his legs stretched out, his eyes closed, and his brain turning and turning regularly all the night through, drawing in more and more power, storing it away like honey in its intricate cells and galleries, till the atmosphere about it became exhausted and vitiated and only the brain remained turning in the darkness.

So Margot Beste-Chetwynde wanted to marry Otto Silenus, and in another corner of this extraordinary house she lay in a drugged trance, her lovely body cool and fragrant and scarcely stirring beneath the bedclothes; and outside in the park a thousand creatures were asleep, and beyond that, again, were

Arthur Potts, and Mr Prendergast, and the Llanabba station-master. Quite soon Paul fell asleep. Downstairs Peter Beste-Chetwynde mixed himself another brandy and soda and turned a page in Havelock Ellis, which, next to *The Wind in the Willows*, was his favourite book.

*

The aluminium blinds shot up, and the sun poured in through the vita-glass, filling the room with beneficent rays. Another day had begun at King's Thursday.

From his bathroom window Paul looked down on to the terrace. The coverings had been removed, revealing the half-finished pavement of silver and scarlet. Professor Silenus was already out there directing two workmen with the aid of a chart.

The week-end party arrived at various times in the course of the day, but Mrs Beste-Chetwynde kept to her room while Peter received them in the prettiest way possible. Paul never learned all their names, nor was he ever sure how many of them there were. He supposed about eight or nine, but as they all wore so many different clothes of identically the same kind, and spoke in the same voice, and appeared so irregularly at meals, there may have been several more or several less.

The first to come were The Hon. Miles Malpractice and David Lennox, the photographer. They emerged with little shrieks from an Edwardian electric brougham and made straight for the nearest looking-glass.

In a minute the panotrope was playing, David and Miles were dancing, and Peter was making cocktails. The party had begun. Throughout the afternoon new guests arrived, drifting in vaguely or running in with cries of welcome just as they thought suited them best.

Pamela Popham, square-jawed and resolute as a big-game huntress, stared round the room through her spectacles, drank three cocktails, said: 'My God!' twice, cut two or three of her friends, and stalked off to bed.

'Tell Olivia I've arrived when she comes,' she said to Peter.

After dinner they went to a whist drive and dance in the village hall. By half-past two the house was quiet; at half-past three Lord Parakeet arrived, slightly drunk and in evening clothes, having 'just escaped less than one second ago' from Alastair Trumpington's twenty-first birthday party in London.

'Alastair was with me some of the way,' he said, 'but I think he must have fallen out.'

The party, or some of it, reassembled in pyjamas to welcome him. Parakeet walked round bird-like and gay, pointing his thin white nose and making rude little jokes at everyone in turn in a shrill, emasculate voice. At four the house was again at rest.

*

Only one of the guests appeared to be at all ill at ease: Sir Humphrey Maltravers, the Minister of Transportation. He arrived early in the day with a very large car and two very small suitcases, and from the first showed himself as a discordant element in the gay little party by noticing the absence of their hostess.

'Margot? No, I haven't seen her at all. I don't believe she's terribly well,' said one of them, 'or perhaps she's lost somewhere in the house. Peter will know.'

Paul found him seated alone in the garden after luncheon, smoking a large cigar, his big red hands folded before him, a soft hat tilted over his eyes, his big red face both defiant and disconsolate. He bore a preternatural resemblance to his caricatures in the evening papers, Paul thought.

'Hullo, young man!' he said. 'Where's everybody?'

'I think Peter's taking them on a tour round the house. It's much more elaborate than it looks from outside. Would you care to join them?'

'No, thank you, not for me. I came here for a rest. These young people tire me. I have enough of the House during the week.' Paul laughed politely. 'It's the devil of a session. You keen on politics at all?'

'Hardly at all,' Paul said.

'Sensible fellow! I can't think why I keep on at it. It's a dog's life, and there's no money in it, either. If I'd stayed at the Bar I'd have been a rich man by now.

'Rest, rest and riches,' he said – 'it's only after forty one begins to value things of that kind. And half one's life, perhaps, is lived after forty. Solemn thought that. Bear it in mind, young man, and it will save you from most of the worst mistakes. If everyone at twenty realized that half his life was to be lived after forty…

'Mrs Beste-Chetwynde's cooking and Mrs Beste-Chetwynde's garden,' said Sir Humphrey meditatively. 'What could be desired more except our fair hostess herself? Have you known her long?'

'Only a few weeks,' said Paul.

'There's no one like her,' said Sir Humphrey. He drew a deep breath of smoke. Beyond the yew hedges the panotrope could be faintly heard. 'What did she want to build this house for?' he asked. 'It all comes of this set she's got into. It's not doing her any good. Damned awkward position to be in – a rich woman without a husband! Bound to get herself talked about. What Margot ought to do is to marry – someone who would stabilize her position, someone,' said Sir Humphrey, 'with a position in public life.'

And then, without any apparent connexion of thought, he began talking about himself. '"Aim high" has been my motto,' said Sir Humphrey, 'all through my life. You probably won't get what you want, but you may get something; aim low, and you get nothing at all. It's like throwing a stone at a cat. When I was a kid that used to be great sport in our yard; I daresay you were throwing cricket-balls when you were that age, but it's the same thing. If you throw straight at it, you fall short; aim above, and with luck you score. Every kid knows that. I'll tell you the story of my life.'

Why was it, Paul wondered, that everyone he met seemed to specialize in this form of autobiography? He supposed he must have a sympathetic air. Sir Humphrey told of his early life: of a family of nine living in two rooms, of a father who drank and a mother who had fits, of a sister who went on the streets, of a brother who went to prison, of another brother who was born a deaf-mute. He told of scholarships and polytechnics, of rebuffs and encouragements, of a University career of brilliant success and unexampled privations.

'I used to do proof-reading for the Holywell Press,' he said; 'then I learned shorthand and took down the University sermons for the local papers.'

As he spoke the clipped yews seemed to grow grey with the soot of the slums, and the panotrope in the distance took on the gay regularity of a barrel-organ heard up a tenement staircase.

'We were a pretty hot lot at Scone in my time,' he said, naming several high officers of state with easy familiarity, 'but none of them had so far to go as I had.'

Paul listened patiently, as was his habit. Sir Humphrey's words flowed easily, because, as a matter of fact, he was rehearsing a series of articles he had dictated the evening before for publication in a Sunday newspaper. He told Paul about his first briefs and his first general election, the historic Liberal campaign of 1906, and of the strenuous days just before the formation of the Coalition.

'I've nothing to be ashamed of,' said Sir Humphrey. 'I've gone farther than most people. I suppose that, if I keep on, I may one day lead the party. But all this winter I've been feeling that I've got as far as I shall ever get. I've got to the time when I should like to go into the other House and give up work and perhaps keep a racehorse or two' – and his eyes took on the far-away look of a popular actress describing the cottage of her dreams – 'and a yacht and a villa at Monte. The others can do that when they like, and they know it. It's not till you get to my age that you really feel the disadvantage of having been born poor.'

On Sunday evening Sir Humphrey suggested a 'hand of cards'. The idea was received without enthusiasm.

'Wouldn't that be rather *fast*?' said Miles. 'It is Sunday. I think cards are divine, particularly the kings. Such *naughty* old faces! But if I start playing for money, I always lose my temper and cry. Ask Pamela; she's so brave and manly.'

'Let's all play billiards and make a Real House Party of it,' said David, 'or shall we have a Country House Rag?'

'Oh I do feel such a *rip*,' said Miles when he was at last persuaded to play. Sir Humphrey won. Parakeet lost thirty pounds, and opening his pocket book, paid him in ten-pound notes.

'How he did cheat!' said Olivia on the way to bed.

'Did he, darling? Well, let's *jolly well* not pay him,' said Miles.

'It never occurred to me to do such a thing. Why, I couldn't afford to possibly.'

Peter tossed Sir Humphrey double or quits, and won.

'After all, I am host,' he explained.

'When I was your age,' said Sir Humphrey to Miles, 'we used to sit up all night sometimes playing poker. Heavy money, too.'

'Oh, you wicked old thing!' said Miles.

Early on Monday morning the Minister of Transportation's Daimler disappeared down the drive. 'I rather think he expected to see Mamma,' said Peter. 'I told him what was the matter with her.'

'You shouldn't have done that,' said Paul.

'No, it didn't go down awfully well. He said that he didn't know what things were coming to and that even in the slums such things were not spoken about by children of my age. What a lot he ate! I did my best to make him feel at home, too, by talking about trains.'

'I thought he was a very sensible old man,' said Professor Silenus. 'He was the only person who didn't think it necessary to say something polite about the house. Besides, he told me about a new method of concrete construction they're trying at one of the Government Superannuation Homes.'

Peter and Paul went back to their cylindrical study and began another spelling-lesson.

*

As the last of the guests departed Mrs Beste-Chetwynde reappeared from her little bout of veronal, fresh and exquisite as a seventeenth-century lyric. The meadow of green glass seemed to burst into flower under her feet as she passed from the lift to the cocktail table.

'You poor angels!' she said. 'Did you have the hell of a time with Maltravers? And all those people? I quite forget who asked to come this week-end. I gave up inviting people long ago,' she said, turning to Paul, 'but it didn't make a bit of difference.' She gazed into the opalescent depths of her *absinthe frappée*. 'More and more I feel the need of a husband, but Peter is horribly fastidious.'

'Well, your men are all so awful,' said Peter.

'I sometimes think of marrying old Maltravers,' said Mrs Beste-Chetwynde, 'just to get my own back, only "Margot Maltravers" does sound a little too much, don't you think? And if they give him a peerage, he's bound to choose something quite awful. . . . '

In the whole of Paul's life no one had ever been quite so sweet to him as Margot Beste-Chetwynde was during the next few days. Up and down the shining lift shafts, in and out of the rooms, and along the labyrinthine corridors of the great house he moved in a golden mist. Each morning as he dressed a bird seemed to be singing in his heart, and as he lay down to sleep he would pillow his head against a hand about which still hung a delicate fragrance of Margot Beste-Chetwynde's almost unprocurable scent.

'Paul, dear,' she said one day as hand in hand, after a rather fearful encounter with a swan, they reached the shelter of the lake house, 'I can't bear to think of you going back to that awful school. Do, please, write and tell Dr Fagan that you won't.'

The lake house was an eighteenth-century pavilion, built on a little mound above the water. They stood there for a full minute still hand in hand on the crumbling steps.

'I don't quite see what else I could do,' said Paul.

'Darling, *I* could find you a job.'

'What sort of job, Margot?' Paul's eyes followed the swan gliding serenely across the lake; he did not dare to look at her.

'Well, Paul, you might stay and protect me from swans, mightn't you?' Margot paused and then, releasing her hand, took a cigarette-case from her pocket. Paul struck a match. 'My dear, what an unsteady hand! I'm afraid you're drinking too many of Peter's cocktails. That child has a lot to learn yet about the use of vodka. But seriously I'm sure I can find you a better job. It's absurd your going back to Wales. I still manage a great deal of my father's business, you know, or perhaps you didn't. It was mostly in South America in – in places of entertainment, cabarets and hotels and theatres, you know, and things like that. I'm sure I could find you a job helping in that, if you think you'd like it.'

Paul thought of this gravely. 'Oughtn't I to know Spanish?' he said. It seemed quite a sensible question, but Margot threw away her cigarette with a little laugh and said: 'It's time to go and change. You are being difficult this evening, aren't you?'

Paul thought about this conversation as he lay in his bath – a sunk bath of malachite – and all the time while he dressed and as he tied his tie he trembled from head to foot like one of the wire toys which street vendors dangle from trays.

At dinner Margot talked about matters of daily interest, about some jewels she was having reset, and how they had come back all wrong; and how all the wiring of her London house was being overhauled because of the fear of fire; and how the man she had left in charge of her villa at Cannes had made a fortune at the Casino and given her notice, and she was afraid she might have to go out there to arrange about it; and how the Society for the Preservation of Ancient Buildings was demanding a guarantee that she would not demolish her castle in Ireland; and how her cook seemed to be going off his head that night, the dinner was so dull; and how Bobby Pastmaster was trying to borrow money from her again, on the grounds that she had misled him when she bought his house and that if he had known she was going to pull it down he would have made her pay more. 'Which is not logical of Bobby,' she said. 'The less I valued this house, the less I ought to have paid, surely? Still, I'd better send him something, otherwise he'll go and marry, and I think it may be nice for Peter to have the title when he grows up.'

Later, when they were alone, she said: 'People talk a great deal of nonsense about being rich. Of course it is a bore in some ways, and it means endless work, but I wouldn't be poor, or even moderately well-off, for all the ease in the world. Would you be happy if you were rich, do you think?'

'Well, it depends how I got the money,' said Paul.

'I don't see how that comes in.'

'No, I don't quite mean that. What I mean is that I think there's only one thing that could make me really happy, and if I got that I should be rich too, but it wouldn't matter being rich, you see, because, however rich I was, and I hadn't got what would make me happy, I shouldn't be happy, you see.'

'My precious, that's rather obscure,' said Margot, 'but I think it may mean something rather sweet.' He looked up at her, and her eyes met his unfalteringly. 'If it does, I'm glad,' she added.

'Margot, darling, beloved, please, will you marry me?' Paul was on his knees by her chair, his hands on hers.

'Well, that's rather what I've been wanting to discuss with you all day.' But surely there was a tremor in her voice?

'Does that mean that possibly you might, Margot? Is there a chance that you will?'

'I don't see why not. Of course we must ask Peter about it, and there are other things we ought to discuss first,' and then, quite suddenly, 'Paul, dear, dear creature, come here.'

*

They found Peter in the dining-room eating a peach at the sideboard.

'Hullo, you two!' he said.

'Peter, we've something to tell you,' said Margot. 'Paul says he wants me to marry him.'

'Splendid!' said Peter. 'I *am* glad. Is that what you've been doing in the library?'

'Then you don't mind?' said Paul.

'Mind? It's what I've been trying to arrange all this week. As a matter of fact, that's why I brought you here at all. I think it's altogether admirable,' he said, taking another peach.

'You're the first man he's said that about, Paul. I think it's rather a good omen.'

'Oh, Margot, let's get married at once.'

'My dear, I haven't said that I'm going to yet. I'll tell you in the morning.'

'No, tell me now, Margot. You do like me a little, don't you? Please marry me just terribly soon.'

'I'll tell you in the morning. There're several things I must think about first. Let's go back to the library.'

*

That night Paul found it unusually difficult to sleep. Long after he had shut his book and turned out the light he lay awake, his eyes open, his thoughts racing uncontrollably. As in the first night of his visit, he felt the sleepless, involved genius of the house heavy about his head. He and Margot and Peter and Sir Humphrey Maltravers were just insignificant incidents in the life of the house: this new-born monster to whose birth ageless and forgotten cultures had been in travail. For half an hour he lay looking into the darkness until gradually his thoughts began to separate themselves from himself, and he knew he was falling asleep. Suddenly he was roused to consciousness by the sound of his door opening gently. He could see nothing, but he heard the rustle of silk as someone came into the room. Then the door shut again.

'Paul, are you asleep?'

'Margot!'

'Hush, dear! Don't turn on the light. Where are you?' The silk rustled again as though falling to the ground. 'It's best to make sure, isn't it, darling, before we decide anything? It may be just an idea of yours that you're in love with me. And, you see, Paul, I like you so very much, it would be a pity to make a mistake, wouldn't it?'

But happily there was no mistake, and next day Paul and Margot announced their engagement.

CHAPTER 4
Resurrection

CROSSING the hall one afternoon a few days later, Paul met a short man with a long red beard stumping along behind the footman towards Margot's study.

'Good Lord!' he said.

'Not a word, old boy!' said the bearded man as he passed on.

A few minutes later Paul was joined by Peter. 'I say, Paul,' he said, 'who do you think's talking to Mamma?'

'I know,' said Paul. 'It's a very curious thing.'

'I somehow never felt he was dead,' said Peter. 'I told Clutterbuck that to try and cheer him up.'

'Did it?'

'Not very much,' Peter admitted. 'My argument was that if he'd really gone out to sea he would have left his wooden leg behind with his clothes, but Clutterbuck said he was very sensitive about his leg. I wonder what he's come to see Mamma about?'

A little later they ambushed him in the drive, and Grimes told them. 'Forgive the beaver,' he said, 'but it's rather important at the moment.'

'In the soup again?' asked Paul.

'Well, not exactly, but things have been rather low lately. The police are after me. That suicide didn't go down well. I was afraid it wouldn't. They began to fuss a bit about no body being found and about my game leg. And then my other wife turned up, and that set them thinking. Hence the vegetation. Clever of you two to spot me.'

They led him back to the house, and Peter mixed him a formidable cocktail, the principal ingredients of which were absinthe and vodka.

'It's the old story,' said Grimes. 'Grimes has fallen on his feet again. By the way, old boy, I have to congratulate you, haven't I? You've done pretty well for yourself, too.' His eye travelled appreciatively over the glass floor, and the pneumatic rubber furniture, and the porcelain ceiling, and the leather-hung walls. 'It's not everyone's taste,' he said, 'but I think you'll be comfortable. Funny thing, I never expected to see you when I came down here.'

'What we want to know,' said Peter, 'is what brought you down to see Mamma at all.'

'Just good fortune,' said Grimes. 'It was like this. After I left Llanabba I was rather at a loose end. I'd borrowed a fiver from Philbrick just before he left, and that got me to London, but for a week or so things were rather thin. I was sitting in a pub one day in Shaftesbury Avenue, feeling my beard rather warm and knowing I only had about five bob left in the world, when I noticed a chap staring at me pretty hard in the other corner of the bar. He came over after a bit and said: "Captain Grimes, I think?" That rather put the wind up me. "No, no, old boy," I said, "quite wrong, rotten shot. Poor old Grimes is dead, drowned. Davy Jones' locker, old boy!" And I made to leave. Of course it wasn't a very sensible thing to say, because, if I hadn't been Grimes, it was a hundred to one against my knowing Grimes was dead, if you see what I mean. "Pity," he said, "because I heard old Grimes was down on his luck, and I had a job I thought might suit him. Have a drink, anyway." Then I realized who he was. He was an awful stout fellow called Bill, who'd been quartered with me in Ireland. "Bill," I said, "I thought you were a bobby." "That's all right, old boy," said Bill. Well, it appeared that this Bill had gone off to the Argentine after the war and had got taken on as manager of a . . .' – Grimes stopped as though suddenly reminded of something – 'a place of entertainment. Sort of night club, you know. Well, he'd done rather well in that job, and had been put in charge of a whole chain of places of entertainment all along the coast. They're a syndicate owned in England. He'd come back on leave to look for a couple of chaps to go out with him and help. "The Dagos are no use at the job," he said, "not dispassionate enough." Had to be chaps who could control themselves where women were concerned. That's what made him think of me. But it was a pure act of God, our meeting.

'Well, apparently the syndicate was first founded by young Beste-Chetwynde's grandpapa, and Mrs Beste-Chetwynde still takes an interest in it, so I was sent down to interview her and see if she agreed to the appointment. It never occurred to me it was the same Mrs Beste-Chetwynde who came down to the sports the day Prendy got so tight. Only shows how small the world is, doesn't it?'

'Did Mamma give you the job?' asked Peter.

'She did, and fifty pounds advance on my wages, and some jolly sound advice. It's been a good day for Grimes. Heard from the old man lately, by the way?'

'Yes,' said Paul, 'I got a letter this morning,' and he showed it to Grimes:

Llanabba Castle,
North Wales.

My dear Pennyfeather,

Thank you for your letter and the enclosed cheque! I need hardly tell you that it is a real disappointment to me to hear that you are not returning to us next term. I had looked forward to a long and mutually profitable connexion. However my daughters and I join in wishing you every happiness in your married life. I hope you will use your new influence to keep Peter at the school. He is a boy for whom I have great hopes. I look to him as one of my prefects in the future.

The holidays so far have afforded me little rest. My daughters and I have been much worried by the insistence of a young Irish woman of most disagreeable appearance and bearing who claims to be the widow of poor Captain Grimes. She has got hold of some papers which seem to support her claim. The police, too, are continually here asking impertinent questions about the number of suits of clothes my unfortunate son-in-law possessed.

Besides this, I have had a letter from Mr Prendergast stating that he too wishes to resign his post. Apparently he has been reading a series of articles by a popular bishop and has discovered that there is a species of person called a 'Modern Churchman' who draws the full salary of a beneficed clergyman and need not commit himself to any religious belief. This seems to be a comfort to him, but it adds to my own inconvenience.

Indeed, I hardly think that I have the heart to keep on at Llanabba. I have had an offer from a cinema company, the managing director of which, oddly enough, is called Sir Solomon Philbrick, who wish to buy the Castle. They say that its combination of medieval and Georgian architecture is a unique advantage. My daughter Diana is anxious to start a nursing-home or an hotel. So you see that things are not easy.

Yours sincerely,
Augustus Fagan.

There was another surprise in store for Paul that day. Hardly had Grimes left the house when a tall young man with a black hat and thoughtful eyes presented himself at the front door and asked for Mr Pennyfeather. It was Potts.

'My dear fellow,' said Paul, 'I am glad to see you.'

'I saw your engagement in *The Times*,' said Potts, 'and as I was in the neighbourhood, I wondered if you'd let me see the house.'

Paul and Peter led him all over it and explained its intricacies. He admired the luminous ceiling in Mrs Beste-Chetwynde's study and the india-rubber fungi in the recessed conservatory and the little drawing-room, of which the floor was a large kaleidoscope, set in motion by an electric button. They took him up in the lift to the top of the great pyramidal tower, from which he could look down on the roofs and domes of glass and aluminium which glittered like Chanel diamonds in the afternoon sun. But it was not this that he had come to see. As soon as he and Paul were alone he said, as though casually: 'Who was that little man I met coming down the drive?'

'I think he was something to do with the Society for the Preservation of Ancient Buildings,' said Paul. 'Why?'

'Are you sure?' asked Potts in evident disappointment. 'How maddening! I've been on a false scent again.'

'Are you doing Divorce Court shadowings, Potts?'

'No, no, it's all to do with the League of Nations,' said Potts vaguely, and he called attention to the tank of octopuses which was so prominent a feature of the room in which they were standing.

Margot invited Potts to stay to dinner. He tried hard to make a good impression on Professor Silenus, but in this he was not successful. In fact, it was probably Potts' visit which finally drove the Professor from the house. At any rate, he left early the next morning without troubling to pack or remove his luggage. Two days later, when they were all out, he arrived in a car and took away his mathematical instruments, and some time after that again appeared to fetch two clean handkerchiefs and a change of underclothes. That was the last time he was seen at King's Thursday. When Margot and Paul went up to London they had his luggage packed and left downstairs for him, in case he should come again, but there it stayed, none of the male servants finding anything in it that he would care to wear. Long afterwards Margot saw the head gardener's son going to church in a *batik* tie of Professor Silenus' period. It was the last relic of a great genius, for before that King's Thursday had been again rebuilt.

CHAPTER 5

The Latin-American Entertainment Co., Ltd

AT the end of April Peter returned to Llanabba, Dr Fagan having announced that the sale of the Castle had not been effected, and Margot and Paul went up to London to make arrangements for the wedding, which, contrary to all reasonable expectation, Margot decided was to take place in church with all the barbaric concomitants of bridesmaids, Mendelssohn, and Mumm. But before the wedding she had a good deal of South American business to see to.

'My first honeymoon was rather a bore,' she said, 'so I'm not taking any chances with this one. I must get everything settled before we start, and then we're going to have the three best months of your life.'

The work seemed to consist chiefly of interviewing young women for jobs in cabarets and as dancing partners. With some reluctance Margot allowed Paul to be present one morning as she saw a new batch. The room in which she conducted her business was the Sports Room, which had been decorated for her, in her absence, by little Davy Lennox, the society photographer. Two stuffed buffaloes stood one on each side of the door. The carpet was of grass-green marked out with white lines, and the walls were hung with netting. The lights were in glass footballs, and the furniture was ingeniously designed of bats and polo-sticks and golf-clubs. Athletic groups of the early nineties and a painting of a prize ram hung on the walls.

'It's terribly common,' said Margot, 'but it rather impresses the young ladies, which is a good thing. Some of them tend to be rather mannery if they aren't kept in order.'

Paul sat in the corner – on a chair made in the shape of an inflated Channel swimmer – enraptured at her business ability. All her vagueness had left her; she sat upright at the table, which was covered with Balmoral tartan, her pen poised over an inkpot, which was set in a stuffed grouse, the very embodiment of the Feminist movement. One by one the girls were shown in.

'Name?' said Margot.

'Pompilia de la Conradine.'

Margot wrote it down.

'Real name?'

'Bessy Brown.'

'Age?'

'Twenty-two.'

'Real age?'

'Twenty-two.'

'Experience?'

'I was at Mrs Rosenbaum's, in Jermyn Street, for two years, mum.'

'Well, Bessy, I'll see what I can do for you. Why did you leave Mrs Rosenbaum's?'

'She said the gentlemen liked a change.'

'I'll just ask her.' Margot took up the telephone, which was held by a boxing-glove. 'Is that Mrs Rosenbaum? This is Latin-American Entertainments, Ltd speaking. Can you tell me about Miss de la Conradine? . . . Oh, that was the reason she left you? Thank you so much! I rather thought that might be it.' She rang off. 'Sorry, Bessy; nothing for you just at present.'

She pressed the bell, which was in the eye of a salmon trout, and another young lady was shown in.

'Name?'

'Jane Grimes.'

'Who sent you to me?'

'The gentleman at Cardiff. He gave me this to give you.' She produced a crumpled envelope and handed it across the table. Margot read the note. 'Yes, I see. So you're new to the business, Jane?'

'Like a babe unborn, mum.'

'But you married?'

'Yes, mum, but it was in the war, and he was very drunk.'

'Where's your husband?'

'Dead, so they do say.'

'That's excellent, Jane. You're just the sort we want. How soon can you sail?'

'How soon would you be wanting me to?'

'Well, there's a vacancy in Rio I'm filling at the end of the week. I'm sending out two very nice girls. Would you like to be going with them?'

'Yes, mum, very pleased, I'm sure.'

'D'you want any money in advance?'

'Well, I could do with a bit to send my dad if you could spare it.'

Margot took some notes from a drawer, counted them, and made out the receipt.

'Sign this, will you? I've got your address. I'll send you your tickets in a day or so. How are you off for clothes?'

'Well, I've got a fine silk dress, but it's at Cardiff with the other things. The gentleman said I'd be getting some new clothes, perhaps.'

'Yes, quite right. I'll make a note of that. The arrangement we generally make is that our agent chooses the clothes and you pay for them out of your salary in instalments.'

Mrs Grimes went out, and another girl took her place.

By luncheon-time Margot Beste-Chetwynde was tired. 'Thank heavens, that's the last of them,' she said. 'Were you terribly bored, my angel?'

'Margot, you're wonderful. You ought to have been an empress.'

'Don't say that you were a Christian slave, dearest.'

'It never occurred to me,' said Paul.

'There's a young man just like your friend Potts on the other side of the street,' said Margot at the window. 'And my dear, he's picked up the last of those poor girls, the one who wanted to take her children and her brother with her.'

'Then it can't be Potts,' said Paul lazily. 'I say, Margot, there was one thing I couldn't understand. Why was it that the less experience those chorus-girls had, the more you seemed to want them? You offered much higher wages to the ones who said they'd never had a job before.'

'Did I, darling? I expect it was because I feel so absurdly happy.'

At the time this seemed quite a reasonable explanation, but, thinking the matter over, Paul had to admit to himself that there had been nothing noticeably light-hearted in Margot's conduct of her business.

'Let's have luncheon out to-day,' said Margot. 'I'm tired of this house.'

They walked across Berkeley Square together in the sunshine. A footman in livery stood on the steps of one of the houses. A hatter's van, emblazoned with the royal arms, trotted past them on Hay Hill, two cockaded figures upright upon the box. A very great lady, bolstered up in an old-fashioned landaulette, bowed to Margot with an inclination she had surely learned in the Court of the Prince Consort. All Mayfair seemed to throb with the heart of Mr Arlen.

Philbrick sat at the next table at the *Maison Basque* eating the bitter little strawberries which are so cheap in Provence and so very expensive in Dover Street.

'Do come and see me some time,' he said. 'I'm living up the street at Batts'.'

'I hear you're buying Llanabba,' said Paul.

'Well, I thought of it,' said Philbrick. 'But I'm afraid it's too far away, really.'

'The police came for you soon after you left,' said Paul.

'They're bound to get me some time,' said Philbrick. 'But thanks for the tip all the same! By the way, you might warn your fiancée that they'll be after her soon, if she's not careful. That League of Nations Committee is getting busy at last.'

'I haven't the least idea what you mean,' said Paul, and returned to his table.

'Obviously the poor man's dotty,' said Margot when he told her of the conversation.

CHAPTER 6

A Hitch in the Wedding Preparations

MEANWHILE half the shops in London were engaged on the wedding preparations. Paul asked Potts to be his best man, but a letter from Geneva declined the invitation. In other circumstances this might have caused him embarrassment, but during the past fortnight Paul had received so many letters and invitations from people he barely remembered meeting that his only difficulty in filling his place was the fear of offending any of his affectionate new friends. Eventually he chose Sir Alastair Digby-Vane-Trumpington, because he felt that, however indirectly, he owed him a great deal of his present good fortune. Sir Alastair readily accepted, at the same time borrowing the money for a new tall hat, his only one having come to grief a few nights earlier.

A letter from Onslow Square, which Paul left unanswered, plainly intimated that Paul's guardian's daughter would take it as a personal slight, and as a severe blow to her social advancement, if she were not chosen as one of the bridesmaids.

For some reason or other, Paul's marriage seemed to inspire the public as being particularly romantic. Perhaps they admired the enterprise and gallantry with which Margot, after ten years of widowhood, voluntarily exposed herself to a repetition of the hundred and one horrors of a fashionable wedding, or perhaps Paul's sudden elevation from schoolmaster to millionaire struck a still vibrant chord of optimism in each of them, so that they said to themselves over their ledgers and typewriters: 'It may be me next time.' Whatever the reason, the wedding was certainly an unparalleled success among the lower orders. Inflamed by the popular Press, a large crowd assembled outside St Margaret's on the eve of the ceremony equipped, as for a first night, with collapsible chairs, sandwiches, and spirit stoves, while by half-past two, in spite of heavy rain, it had swollen to such dimensions that the police were forced to make several baton-charges and many guests were crushed almost to death in their attempts to reach the doors, and the route down which Margot had to drive was lined as for a funeral with weeping and hysterical women.

Society was less certain in its approval, and Lady Circumference, for one, sighed for the early nineties, when Edward Prince of Wales, at the head of *ton*, might have given authoritative condemnation to this ostentatious second marriage.

'It's maddenin' Tangent having died just at this time,' she said. 'People may think that that's my reason for refusin'. I can't imagine that *anyone* will go.'

'I hear your nephew Alastair Trumpington is the best man,' said Lady Vanburgh.

'You seem to be as well informed as my chiropodist,' said Lady Circumference with unusual felicity, and all Lowndes Square shook at her departure.

In the unconverted mewses of Mayfair and the upper rooms of Shepherd's Market and North Audley Street, where fashionable bachelors lurk disconsolately on their evenings at home, there was open lamentation at the prey that had been allowed to slip through their elegantly gloved fingers, while more than one popular dancing man inquired anxiously at his bank to learn whether his month's remittance had been paid in as usual. But Margot remained loyal to all her old obligations, and invitations to her wedding-reception were accepted by whole bevies of young men who made it their boast that they never went out except to a square meal, while little Davy Lennox, who for three years had never been known to give anyone a 'complimentary sitting', took two eloquent photographs of the back of her head and one of the reflection of her hands in a bowl of ink.

Ten days before the wedding Paul moved into rooms at the Ritz, and Margot devoted herself seriously to shopping. Five or six times a day messengers appeared at his suite bringing little by-products of her activity – now a platinum cigarette-case, now a dressing-gown, now a tie-pin or a pair of links – while Paul, with unaccustomed prodigality, bought two new ties, three pairs of shoes, an umbrella, and a set of Proust. Margot had fixed his personal allowance at two thousand a year.

Far away in the Adriatic feverish preparations were being made to make Mrs Beste-Chetwynde's villa at Corfu ready for the first weeks of her honeymoon, and the great bed, carved with pineapples, that had once belonged to Napoleon III, was laid out for her reception with fragrant linen and pillows of unexampled softness. All this the newspapers retailed with uncontrolled profusion, and many a young reporter was handsomely commended for the luxuriance of his adjectives.

However, there was a hitch.

Three days before the date fixed for the wedding Paul was sitting in the Ritz opening his morning's post, when Margot rang him up.

'Darling, rather a tiresome thing's happened,' she said. 'You know those girls we sent to Rio the other day? Well, they're stuck at Marseilles, for some reason or other. I can't quite make out why. I think it's something to do with their passports. I've just had a very odd cable from my agent there. He's giving up the job. It's such a bore all this happening just now. I do so want to get everything fixed before Thursday. I wonder if you could be an angel and go over and see to it for me? It's probably only a matter of giving the right man a few hundred francs. If you fly you'll be back in plenty of time. I'd go myself, only you know, don't you, darling, I simply haven't one minute to spare.'

Paul did not have to travel alone. Potts was at Croydon, enveloped in an ulster and carrying in his hand a little attaché case.

'League of Nations business,' he said, and was twice sick during the flight.

At Paris Paul was obliged to charter a special aeroplane. Potts saw him off.

'Why are you going to Marseilles?' he asked. 'I thought you were going to be married.'

'I'm only going there for an hour or two, to see some people on business,' said Paul.

How like Potts, he thought, to suppose that a little journey like this was going to upset his marriage. Paul was beginning to feel cosmopolitan, the Ritz to-day, Marseilles to-morrow, Corfu next day, and afterwards the whole world stood open to him like one great hotel, his way lined for him with bows and orchids. How pathetically insular poor Potts was, he thought, for all his talk of internationalism.

It was late evening when Paul arrived at Marseilles. He dined at Basso's in the covered balcony off bouillabaisse and Meursault at a table from which he could see a thousand lights reflected in the still water. Paul felt very much of a man of the world as he paid his bill, calculated the correct tip, and sat back in the open cab on his way to the old part of the town.

'They'll probably be at *Alice's*, in the Rue de Reynarde,' Margot had said. 'Anyway, you oughtn't to have any difficulty in finding them if you mention my name.'

At the corner of the Rue Ventomargy the carriage stopped. The way was too narrow and too crowded for traffic. Paul paid the driver. '*Merci, Monsieur! Gardez bien votre chapeau*,' he said as he drove off. Wondering what the expression could mean, Paul set off with less certain steps down the cobbled alley. The houses overhung perilously on each side, gaily alight from cellar to garret; between them swung lanterns; a shallow gutter ran down the centre of the path. The scene could scarcely have been more sinister had it been built at Hollywood itself for some orgiastic incident of the Reign of Terror. Such a street in England, Paul reflected, would have been saved long ago by Mr Spire and preserved under a public trust for the sale of brass toasting forks, picture postcards, and 'Devonshire teas'. Here the trade was of a different sort. It did not require very much worldly wisdom to inform him of the character of the quarter he was now in. Had he not, guide-book in hand, traversed the forsaken streets of Pompeii?

No wonder, Paul reflected, that Margot had been so anxious to rescue her protégées from this place of temptation and danger.

A Negro sailor, hideously drunk, addressed Paul in no language known to man, and invited him to have a drink. He hurried on. How typical of Margot that, in all her whirl of luxury, she should still have time to care for the poor girls she had unwittingly exposed to such perils.

Deaf to the polyglot invitations that arose on all sides, Paul pressed on his way. A young lady snatched his hat from his head; he caught a glimpse of her bare leg in a lighted doorway; then she appeared at a window, beckoning him to come in and retrieve it.

All the street seemed to be laughing at him. He hesitated; and then, forsaking, in a moment of panic, both his black hat and his self-possession, he turned and fled for the broad streets and the tram lines where, he knew at heart, was his spiritual home.

*

By daylight the old town had lost most of its terrors. Washing hung out between the houses, the gutters ran with fresh water and the streets were crowded with old women carrying baskets of fish. *Chez Alice* showed no sign of life, and Paul was forced to ring and ring before a tousled old concierge presented himself.

'*Avez-vous les jeunes filles de Madame Beste-Chetwynde?*' Paul asked, acutely conscious of the absurdity of the question.

'Sure, step right along, Mister,' said the concierge; 'she wired us you was coming.'

Mrs Grimes and her two friends were not yet dressed, but they received Paul with enthusiasm in dressing-gowns which might have satisfied the taste for colour of the elder Miss Fagan. They explained the difficulty of the passports, which, Paul thought, was clearly due to some misapprehension by the authorities of their jobs in Rio. They didn't know any French, and of course they had explained things wrong.

He spent an arduous morning at consulates and police bureaux. Things were more difficult than he had thought, and the officials received him either with marked coldness or with incomprehensible winks and innuendo.

Things had been easier six months ago, they said, but now, with the League of Nations – And they shrugged their shoulders despairingly. Perhaps it might be arranged once more, but Madame Beste-Chetwynde must really understand that there were forms that must be respected. Eventually the young ladies were signed on as stewardesses.

'And if they should not go farther with me than Rio,' said the captain, 'well, I have a sufficient staff already. You say there are posts waiting for them there? No doubt their employers will be able to arrange things there with the authorities.'

But it cost Paul several thousand francs to complete the arrangements. 'What an absurd thing the League of Nations seems to be!' said Paul. 'They seem to make it harder to get about instead of easier.' And this, to his surprise, the officials took to be a capital joke.

Paul saw the young ladies to their ship, and all three kissed him good-bye. As he walked back along the quay he met Potts.

'Just arrived by the morning train,' he said. Paul felt strongly inclined to tell him his opinion of the League of Nations, but remembering Potts' prolixity in argument and the urgency of his own departure, he decided to leave his criticisms for another time. He stopped long enough in Marseilles to cable to Margot, 'Everything arranged satisfactorily. Returning this afternoon. All my love,' and then left for Paris by air, feeling that at last he had done something to help.

*

At ten o'clock on his wedding morning Paul returned to the Ritz. It was raining hard, and he felt tired, unshaven and generally woebegone. A number of newspaper reporters were waiting for him outside his suite, but he told them that he could see no one. Inside he found Peter Beste-Chetwynde, incredibly smart in his first morning-coat.

'They've let me come up from Llanabba for the day,' he said. 'To tell you the truth, I'm rather pleased with myself in these clothes. I bought you a buttonhole in case you'd forgotten. I say, Paul, you're looking tired.'

'I am, rather. Turn on the bath for me like an angel.'

When he had had his bath and shaved he felt better. Peter had ordered a bottle of champagne and was a little tipsy. He walked round the room, glass in hand, talking gaily, and every now and then pausing to look at himself in the mirror. 'Pretty smart,' he said, 'particularly the tie; don't you think so, Paul? I think I shall go back to the school like this. That would make them see what a superior person I am. I hope you notice that I gave you the grander buttonhole? I can't tell you what Llanabba is like this term, Paul. Do try and persuade Mamma to take me away. Clutterbuck has left, and Tangent is dead, and the three new masters are quite awful. One is like your friend Potts, only he stutters, and Brolly says he's got a glass eye. He's called Mr Makepeace. Then there's another one with red hair who keeps beating everyone all the time, and the other's rather sweet, really, only he has fits. I don't think the Doctor cares for any of them much. Flossie's been looking rather discouraged all the time. I wonder if Mamma could get her a job in South America? I'm glad you're wearing a waistcoat like that. I nearly did, but I thought perhaps I was a bit young. What do you think? We had a reporter down at the school the other day wanting to know particulars about you. Brolly told a splendid story about how you used to go out swimming in the evenings and swim for hours and hours in the dark composing elegiac verses, and then he spoilt it by saying you had webbed feet and a prehensile tail, which made the chap think he was having his leg pulled. I say, am I terribly in the way?'

As Paul dressed his feelings of well-being began to return. He could not help feeling that he too looked rather smart. Presently Alastair Digby-Vane-Trumpington came in, and drank some champagne.

'This wedding of ours is about the most advertised thing that's happened for a generation,' he said. 'D'you know, the *Sunday Mail* has given me fifty pounds to put my name to an article describing my sensations as best man. I'm afraid every one will know it's not me, though; it's too jolly well written. I've had a marvellous letter from Aunt Greta about it, too. Have you seen the presents? The Argentine Chargé d'Affaires has given you the works of Longfellow bound in padded green leather, and the Master of Scone has sent those pewter plates he used to have in his hall.'

Paul fastened the gardenia in his buttonhole, and they went down to luncheon. There were several people in the restaurant obviously dressed for a wedding, and it gave Paul some satisfaction to notice that he was the centre of interest of the whole room. The *maître d'hôtel* offered his graceful good wishes as he led them to their table. Peter, earlier in the morning, had ordered the luncheon.

'I doubt if we shall have time to eat it all,' he said, 'but fortunately the best things all come at the beginning.'

As he was peeling his second gull's egg, Paul was called away to the telephone.

'Darling,' said Margot's voice, 'how are you? I've been so anxious all the time you were away. I had an awful feeling something was going to stop you coming back. Are you all right, dearest? Yes, I'm terribly well. I'm at home having luncheon in my bedroom and feeling, my dear, I can't tell you how virginal, really and truly completely débutante. I hope you'll like my frock. It's Boulanger, darling, do you mind? Good-bye, my sweet. Don't let Peter get too drunk, will you?'

Paul went back to the dining-room.

'I've eaten your eggs,' said Peter. 'I just couldn't help it.'

By two o'clock they had finished their luncheon. Mrs Beste-Chetwynde's second-best Hispano Suiza was waiting in Arlington Street.

'You must just have one more drink with me before we go,' said the best man; 'there's heaps of time.'

'I think perhaps it would be a mistake if I did,' said Peter.

Paul and his best man refilled their glasses with brandy.

'It is a funny thing,' said Alastair Digby-Vane-Trumpington. 'No one could have guessed that when I had the Boller blind in my rooms it was going to end like this.'

Paul turned the liqueur round in his glass, inhaled its rich bouquet for a second, and then held it before him.

'To Fortune,' he said, 'a much-maligned lady!'

*

'Which of you gentlemen is Mr Paul Pennyfeather?'

Paul put down his glass and turned to find an elderly man of military appearance standing beside him.

'I am,' he said. 'But I'm afraid that, if you're from the Press, I really haven't time . . . '

'I'm Inspector Bruce, of Scotland Yard,' said the stranger. 'Will you be so good as to speak to me for a minute outside?'

'Really, officer,' said Paul, 'I'm in a great hurry. I suppose it's about the men to guard the presents. You should have come to me earlier.'

'It's not about presents, and I couldn't have come earlier. The warrant for your arrest has only this minute been issued.'

'Look here,' said Alastair Digby-Vane-Trumpington, 'don't be an ass. You've got the wrong man. They'll laugh at you like blazes over this at Scotland Yard. This is the Mr Pennyfeather who's being married to-day.'

'I don't know anything about that,' said Inspector Bruce. 'All I know is, there's a warrant out for his arrest, and that anything he says may be used as evidence against him. And as for you, young man, I shouldn't attempt to obstruct an officer of the law, not if I was you.'

'It's all some ghastly mistake,' said Paul. 'I suppose I must go with this man. Try and get on to Margot and explain to her.'

Sir Alastair's amiable pink face gaped blank astonishment. 'Good God,' he said, 'how damned funny! At least it would be at any other time.' But Peter, deadly white, had left the restaurant.

END OF PART TWO

PART THREE

CHAPTER 1
Stone Walls do not a Prison Make

PAUL's trial, which took place some weeks later at the Old Bailey, was a bitter disappointment to the public, the news editors, and the jury and counsel concerned. The arrest at the Ritz, the announcement at St Margaret's that the wedding was postponed, Margot's flight to Corfu, the refusal of bail, the meals sent in to Paul on covered dishes from Boulestin's, had been 'front-page stories' every day. After all this, Paul's conviction and sentence were a lame conclusion. At first he pleaded guilty on all charges, despite the entreaties of his counsel, but eventually he was galvanized into some show of defence by the warning of the presiding judge that the law allowed punishment with the cat-o'-nine-tails for offences of this sort. Even then things were very flat. Potts as chief witness for the prosecution was unshakeable and was later warmly commended by the court; no evidence, except of previous good conduct, was offered by the defence; Margot Beste-Chetwynde's name was not mentioned, though the judge in passing sentence remarked that 'no one could be ignorant of the callous insolence with which, on the very eve of arrest for this most infamous of crimes, the accused had been preparing to join his name with one honoured in his country's history, and to drag down to his own pitiable depths of depravity a lady of beauty, rank, and stainless reputation. The just censure of society,' remarked the judge, 'is accorded to those so inconstant and intemperate that they must take their pleasures in the unholy market of humanity that still sullies the fame of our civilization; but for the traders themselves, these human vampires who prey upon the degradation of their species, society has reserved the right of ruthless suppression.' So Paul was sent off to prison, and the papers headed the column they reserve for home events of minor importance with 'Prison for Ex-Society Bridegroom. Judge on Human Vampires', and there, as far as the public were concerned, the matter ended.

Before this happened, however, a conversation took place which deserves the attention of all interested in the confused series of events of which Paul had become a part. One day, while he was waiting for trial, he was visited in his cell by Peter Beste-Chetwynde.

'Hullo!' he said.

'Hullo, Paul!' said Peter. 'Mamma asked me to come in to see you. She wants to know if you are getting the food all right she's ordered for you. I hope you like it, because I chose most of it myself. I thought you wouldn't want anything very heavy.'

'It's splendid,' said Paul. 'How's Margot?'

'Well, that's rather what I've come to tell you, Paul. Margot's gone away.'

'Where to?'

'She's gone off alone to Corfu. I made her, though she wanted to stay and see your trial. You can imagine what a time we've had with reporters and people. You don't think it awful of her, do you? And listen, there's something else. Can that policeman hear? It's this. You remember that awful old man Maltravers. Well, you've probably seen, he's Home Secretary now. He's been round to see Mamma in the most impossible Oppenheim kind of way, and said that if she'd marry him he could get you out. Of course, he's obviously been reading books. But Mamma thinks it's probably true, and she wants to know how you feel about it. She rather feels the whole thing's rather her fault, really, and, short of going to prison herself, she'll do anything to help. You can't imagine Mamma in prison, can you? Well, would you rather get out now and her marry Maltravers? or wait until you do get out and marry her yourself? She was rather definite about it.'

Paul thought of Professor Silenus' 'In ten years she will be worn out,' but he said:

'I'd rather she waited if you think she possibly can.'

'I thought you'd say that, Paul. I'm so glad. Mamma said: "I won't say I don't know how I shall ever be able to make up to him for all this, because I think he knows I can." Those were her words. I don't suppose you will get more than a year or so, will you?'

'Good Lord, I hope not,' said Paul.

His sentence of seven years' penal servitude was rather a blow. 'In ten years she will be worn out,' he thought as he drove in the prison van to Blackstone Gaol.

*

On his first day there Paul met quite a number of people, some of whom he knew already. The first person was a warder with a low brow and distinctly menacing manner. He wrote Paul's name in the 'Body Receipt Book' with some difficulty and then conducted him to a cell. He had evidently been reading the papers.

'Rather different from the Ritz Hotel, eh?' he said. 'We don't like your kind 'ere, see? And we knows 'ow to treat 'em. You won't find nothing like the Ritz 'ere, you dirty White Slaver.'

But there he was wrong, because the next person Paul met was Philbrick. His prison clothes were ill-fitting, and his chin was unshaven, but he still wore an indefinable air of the grand manner.

'Thought I'd be seeing you soon,' he said. 'They've put me on to reception bath cleaner, me being an old hand. I've been saving the best suit I could find for you. Not a louse on it, hardly.' He threw a little pile of clothes, stamped with the broad arrow, on to the bench.

The warder returned with another, apparently his superior officer. Together they made a careful inventory of all Paul's possessions.

'Shoes, brown, one pair; socks, fancy, one pair; suspenders, black silk, one pair,' read out the warder in a sing-song voice. 'Never saw a bloke with so much clothes.'

There were several checks due to difficulties of spelling, and it was some time before the list was finished.

'Cigarette-case, white metal, containing two cigarettes; watch, white metal; tie-pin, fancy' – it had cost Margot considerably more than the warder earned in a year, had he only known – 'studs, bone, one pair; cuff links, fancy, one pair.' The officers looked doubtfully at Paul's gold cigar piercer, the gift of the best man. 'What's this 'ere?'

'It's for cigars,' said Paul.

'Not so much lip!' said the warder, banging him on the top of his head with the pair of shoes he happened to be holding. 'Put it down as "instrument". That's the lot,' he said, 'unless you've got false teeth. You're allowed to keep them, only we must make a note of it.'

'No,' said Paul.

'Truss or other surgical appliance?'

'No,' said Paul.

'All right! You can go to the bath.'

Paul sat for the regulation ten minutes in the regulation nine inches of warm water – which smelt reassuringly of disinfectant – and then put on his prison clothes. The loss of his personal possessions gave him a curiously agreeable sense of irresponsibility.

'You look a treat,' said Philbrick.

Next he saw the Medical Officer, who sat at a table covered with official forms.

'Name?' said the Doctor.

'Pennyfeather.'

'Have you at any time been detained in a mental home or similar institution? If so, give particulars.'

'I was at Scone College, Oxford, for two years,' said Paul.

The Doctor looked up for the first time. 'Don't you dare to make jokes here, my man,' he said, 'or I'll soon have you in the strait-jacket in less than no time.'

'Sorry,' said Paul.

'Don't speak to the Medical Officer unless to answer a question,' said the warder at his elbow.

'Sorry,' said Paul, unconsciously, and was banged on the head.

'Suffering from consumption or any contagious disease?' asked the M.D.

'Not that I know of,' said Paul.

'That's all,' said the Doctor. 'I have certified you as capable of undergoing the usual descriptions of punishment as specified below, to wit, restraint of handcuffs, leg-chains, cross-irons, body-belt, canvas dress, close confinement, No. 1 diet, No. 2 diet, birch-rod, and cat-o'-nine-tails. Any complaint?'

'But must I have all these at once?' asked Paul, rather dismayed.

'You will if you ask impertinent questions. Look after that man, officer; he's obviously a troublesome character.'

'Come 'ere, you,' said the warder. They went up a passage and down two flights of iron steps. Long galleries with iron railings stretched out in each direction, giving access to innumerable doors. Wire-netting was stretched between the landings. 'So don't you try no monkey-tricks. Suicide isn't allowed in this prison. See?' said the warder. 'This is your cell. Keep it clean, or you'll know the reason why, and this is your number.' He buttoned a yellow badge on to Paul's coat.

'Like a flag-day,' said Paul.

'Shut up, you ——,' remarked the warder, and locked the door.

'I suppose I shall learn to respect these people in time,' thought Paul. 'They all seem so much less awe-inspiring than anyone I ever met.'

His next visit was from the Schoolmaster. The door was unlocked, and a seedy-looking young man in a tweed suit came into the cell.

'Can you read and write, D.4.12?' asked the newcomer.

'Yes,' said Paul.

'Public or secondary education?'

'Public,' said Paul. His school had been rather sensitive on this subject.

'What was your standard when you left school?'

'Well, I don't quite know. I don't think we had standards.'

The Schoolmaster marked him down as 'Memory defective' on a form and went out. Presently he returned with a book.

'You must do your best with that for the next four weeks,' he said. 'I'll try and get you into one of the morning classes. You won't find it difficult, if you can read fairly easily. You see, it begins there,' he said helpfully, showing Paul the first page.

It was an English Grammar published in 1872.

'*A syllable is a single sound made by one simple effort of the voice*,' Paul read.

'Thank you,' he said; 'I'm sure I shall find it useful.'

'You can change it after four weeks if you can't get on with it,' said the Schoolmaster. 'But I should stick to it, if you can.'

Again the door was locked.

Next came the Chaplain. 'Here is your Bible and a book of devotion. The Bible stays in the cell always. You can change the book of devotion any week if you wish to. Are you Church of England? Services are voluntary – that is to say, you must either attend all or none.' The Chaplain spoke in a nervous and hurried manner. He was new to his job, and he had already visited fifty prisoners that day, one of whom had delayed him for a long time with descriptions of a vision he had seen the night before.

'Hullo, Prendy!' said Paul.

Mr Prendergast looked at him nervously. 'I didn't recognize you,' he said. 'People look so much alike in those clothes. This is most disturbing, Pennyfeather. As soon as I saw you'd been convicted I was afraid they might send you here. Oh dear! oh dear! It makes everything still more difficult!'

'What's the matter, Prendy? Doubts again?'

'No, no, discipline, my old trouble. I've only been at the job a week. I was very lucky to get it. My bishop said he thought there was more opening for a Modern Churchman in this kind of work than in the parishes. The Governor is very modern too. But criminals are just as bad as boys, I find. They pretend to make confessions and tell me the most dreadful things just to see what I'll say, and in chapel they laugh so much that the warders spend all their time correcting them. It makes the services seem so irreverent. Several of them got put on No. 1 diet this morning for singing the wrong words to one of the hymns, and of course that only makes me more unpopular. Please, Pennyfeather, if you don't mind, you mustn't call me Prendy, and if anyone passes the cell will you stand up when you're talking to me. You're supposed to, you see, and the Chief Warder has said some very severe things to me about maintaining discipline.'

At this moment the face of the warder appeared at the peephole in the door.

'I trust you realize the enormity of your offence and the justice of your punishment?' said Mr Prendergast in a loud voice. 'Pray for penitence.'

A warder came into the cell.

'Sorry to disturb you, sir, but I've got to take this one to see the Governor. There's D.4.18 down the way been asking for you for days. I said I'd tell you, only, if you'll forgive my saying so, I shouldn't be too soft with 'im, sir. We know 'im of old. 'E's a sly old devil, begging your pardon, sir, and 'e's only religious when 'e thinks it'll pay.'

'I think that I am the person to decide that, officer,' said Mr Prendergast with some dignity. 'You may take D.4.12 to the Governor.'

Sir Wilfred Lucas-Dockery had not been intended by nature or education for the Governor of a prison; his appointment was the idea of a Labour Home Secretary who had been impressed by an appendix on the theory of penology which he had contributed to a report on the treatment of 'Conscientious Objectors'. Up to that time Sir Wilfred had held the Chair of Sociology at a Midland university; only his intimate friends and a few specially favoured pupils knew that behind his mild and professional exterior he concealed an ardent ambition to serve in the public life of his generation. He stood twice for Parliament, but so diffidently that his candidature passed almost unnoticed. Colonel MacAdder, his predecessor in office, a veteran of numberless unrecorded campaigns on the Afghan frontier, had said to him on his retirement: 'Good luck, Sir Wilfred! If I may give you a piece of advice, it's this. Don't bother about the lower warders or the prisoners. Give hell to the man immediately below you, and you can rely on him to pass it on with interest. If you make a prison bad enough, people'll take jolly good care to keep out of it. That's been my policy all through, and I'm proud of it' (a policy which soon became quite famous in the society of Cheltenham Spa).

Sir Wilfred, however, had his own ideas. 'You must understand,' he said to Paul, 'that it is my aim to establish personal contact with each of the men under my care. I want you to take a pride in your prison and in your work here. So far as possible, I like the prisoners to carry on with their avocations in civilized life. What's this man's profession, officer?'

'White Slave traffic, sir.'

'Ah yes. Well, I'm afraid you won't have much opportunity for that here. What else have you done?'

'I was nearly a clergyman once,' said Paul.

'Indeed? Well, I hope in time, if I find enough men with the same intention, to get together a theological class. You've no doubt met the Chaplain, a very broad-minded man. Still for the present we are only at the beginning. The Government regulations are rather uncompromising. For the first four weeks you will have to observe the solitary confinement ordained by law. After that we will find you something more creative. We don't want you to feel that your personality is being stamped out. Have you any experience of art leather work?'

'No, sir.'

'Well, I might put you into the Arts and Crafts Workshop. I came to the conclusion many years ago that almost all crime is due to the repressed desire for aesthetic expression. At last we have the opportunity for testing it. Are you an extrovert or an introvert?'

'I'm afraid I'm not sure, sir.'

'So few people are. I'm trying to induce the Home Office to install an official psycho-analyst. Do you read the *New Nation*, I wonder? There is rather a flattering article this week about our prison called *The Lucas-Dockery Experiments*. I like the prisoners to know these things. It gives them corporate pride. I may give you one small example of the work we are doing that affects your own case. Up till now all offences connected with prostitution have been put into the sexual category. Now I hold that an offence of your kind is essentially acquisitive and shall grade it accordingly. It does not, of course, make any difference as far as your conditions of imprisonment are concerned – the routine of penal servitude is prescribed by Standing Orders – but you see what a difference it makes to the annual statistics.'

'The human touch,' said Sir Wilfred after Paul had been led from the room. 'I'm sure it makes all the difference. You could see with that unfortunate man just now what a difference it made to him to think that, far from being a mere nameless slave, he has now become part of a great revolution in statistics.'

'Yes, sir,' said the Chief Warder, 'and, by the way, there are two more attempted suicides being brought up to-morrow. You must really be more strict with them, sir. Those sharp tools you've issued to the Arts and Crafts School is just putting temptation in the men's way.'

*

Paul was once more locked in, and for the first time had the opportunity of examining his cell. There was little to interest him. Besides his Bible, his book of devotion – *Prayers on Various Occasions of Illness, Uncertainty, and Loss, by the Rev. Septimus Bead, M.A., Edinburgh*, 1863 – and his English Grammar, there was a little glazed pint pot, a knife and spoon, a slate and slate-pencil, a salt-jar, a metal water-can, two earthenware vessels, some cleaning materials, a plank bed upright against the wall, a roll of bedding, a stool, and a table. A printed notice informed him that he was not to look out of the window. Three printed cards on the wall contained a list of other punishable offences, which seemed to include every human activity, some Church of England prayers, and an explanation of the 'system of progressive stages'. There was also a typewritten 'Thought for the Day', one of Sir Wilfred Lucas-Dockery's little innovations. The message for the first day of Paul's imprisonment was: '*SENSE OF SIN IS SENSE OF WASTE, the Editor of the "Sunday Express"*.'

Paul studied the system of progressive stages with interest. After four weeks, he read, he would be allowed to join in associated labour, to take half an hour's exercise on Sundays, to wear a stripe on his arm, if illiterate to have school instruction, to take one work of fiction from the library weekly, and, if special application were made to the Governor, to exhibit four photographs of his relatives or of approved friends; after eight weeks, provided that his conduct was perfectly satisfactory, he might receive a visit of twenty minutes' duration and write and receive a letter. Six weeks later he might receive another visit and another letter and another library book weekly.

Would Davy Lennox's picture of the back of Margot's head be accepted as the photograph of an approved friend, he wondered?

After a time his door was unlocked again and opened a few inches. A hand thrust in a tin, and a voice said, 'Pint pot quick!' Paul's mug was filled with cocoa, and the door was again locked. The tin contained bread, bacon, and beans. That was the last interruption for fourteen hours. Paul fell into a reverie. It was the first time he had been really alone for months. How very refreshing it was, he reflected.

*

The next four weeks of solitary confinement were among the happiest of Paul's life. The physical comforts were certainly meagre, but at the Ritz Paul had learned to appreciate the inadequacy of purely physical comfort. It was so exhilarating, he found, never to have to make any decision on any subject, to be wholly relieved from the smallest consideration of time, meals, or clothes, to have no anxiety ever about what kind of impression he was making; in fact, to be free. At some rather chilly time in the early morning a bell would ring, and the warder would say, 'Slops outside!'; he would rise, roll up his bedding, and dress; there was no need to shave, no hesitation about what tie he should wear, none of the fidgeting with studs and collars and links that so distracts the waking moments of civilized man. He felt like the happy people in the advertisements for shaving soap who seem to have achieved very simply that peace of mind so distant and so desirable in the early morning. For about an hour he stitched away at a mail-bag, until his door was again unlocked to admit a hand with a lump of bread and a large ladle of porridge. After breakfast he gave a cursory polish to the furniture and crockery of his cell and did some more sewing until the bell rang for chapel. For a quarter of an hour or twenty minutes he heard Mr Prendergast blaspheming against the beauties of sixteenth-century diction. This was certainly a bore, and so was the next hour during which he had to march round the prison square, where between concentric paths of worn asphalt a few melancholy cabbages showed their heads. Some of the men during this period used to fall out under the pretence of tying a shoe-lace and take furtive bites at the leaves of the vegetables. If observed they were severely punished. Paul never felt any temptation to do this. After that the day was unbroken save for luncheon, supper, and the Governor's inspection. The heap of sacking which every day he was to turn into mail-bags was supposed by law to keep him busy for nine hours. The prisoners in the cells on either side of him, who were not quite in their right minds, the warder told Paul, found some difficulty in finishing their task before lights out. Paul found that with the least exertion he had finished long before supper, and spent the evenings in meditation and in writing up on his slate the thoughts which had occurred to him during the day.

CHAPTER 2
The Lucas-Dockery Experiments

SIR WILFRED LUCAS-DOCKERY, as has already been suggested, combined ambition, scholarship, and genuine optimism in a degree rarely found in his office. He looked forward to a time when the Lucas-Dockery experiments should be recognized as the beginning of a new epoch in penology, and he rehearsed in his mind sentences from the social histories of the future which would contain such verdicts as '*One of the few important events of this Labour Government's brief tenure of power was the appointment as Governor of Blackstone Gaol of Sir Wilfred Lucas-Dockery. The administration of this intrepid and far-seeing official is justly regarded as the foundation of the present system of criminal treatment. In fact, it may safely be said that no single man occupies so high a place in the history of the social reform of his century, etc.*' His eminent qualities, however, did not keep him from many severe differences of opinion with the Chief Warder. He was sitting in his study one day working at a memorandum for the Prison Commissioners – one of the neglected series of memoranda whose publication after his retirement indicated Sir Wilfred's claim to be the pioneer of artificial sunlight in prisons – when the Chief Warder interrupted him.

'A bad report from the Bookbinding Shop, sir. The instructor says that a practice is growing among the men of eating the paste issued to them for their work. They say it is preferable to their porridge. We shall either have to put on another warder to supervise the bookbinding or introduce something into the paste which will make it unpalatable.'

'Has the paste any nutritive value?' asked Sir Wilfred.

'I couldn't say, sir.'

'Weigh the men in the Bookbinding Shop, and then report to me any increase in weight. How many times must I ask you to ascertain *all* the facts before reporting on any case?'

'Very good, sir! And there's a petition from D.4.12. He's finished his four weeks' solitary, and he wants to know if he can keep at it for another four.'

'I disapprove of cellular labour. It makes a man introvert. Who is D.4.12?'

'Long sentence, sir, waiting transference to Egdon.'

'I'll see D.4.12 myself.'

'Very good, sir!'

Paul was led in.

'I understand you wish to continue cellular labour instead of availing yourself of the privilege of working in association. Why is that?'

'I find it so much more interesting, sir,' said Paul.

'It's a most irregular suggestion,' said the Chief Warder. 'Privileges can only be forfeited by a breach of the regulations witnessed and attested by two officers. Standing Orders are most emphatic on the subject.'

'I wonder whether you have narcissistic tendencies?' said the Governor. 'The Home Office has not as yet come to any decision about my application for a staff psycho-analyst.'

'Put him in the observation cell,' said the Chief Warder. 'That brings out any insanity. I've known several cases of men you could hardly have told were mad – just eccentric, you know – who've been put on observation, and after a few days they've been raving lunatics. Colonel MacAdder was a great believer in the observation cells.'

'Did you lead a very lonely life before conviction? Perhaps you were a shepherd or a lighthouse-keeper, or something of the kind?'

'No, sir.'

'Most curious. Well, I will consider your case and give you my answer later.'

Paul was led back to his cell, and next day was again summoned before the Governor.

'I have considered your application,' said Sir Wilfred, 'with the most minute care. In fact, I have decided to include it in my forthcoming work on the criminal mind. Perhaps you would like to hear what I have written about you?'

Case R., he read:

A young man of respectable family and some education. No previous criminal record. Committed to seven years' penal servitude for traffic in prostitution. Upon completing his first four weeks R. petitioned for extension of cellular labour. Treatment as prescribed by Standing Orders: either (a) *detention in observation cell for the Medical Officer to satisfy himself about the state of the prisoner's mind, or* (b) *compulsory work in association with other prisoners unless privilege forfeited by misdemeanour.*

Treatment by Sir Wilfred Lucas-Dockery. – I decided that R. was suffering from misanthropic tendencies induced by a sense of his own inferiority in the presence of others. R.'s crime was the result of an attempt to assert individuality at the expense of community. (Cf. Cases D, G, and I.)

Accordingly I attempted to break down his social inhibitions by a series of progressive steps. In the first stage he exercised for half an hour in the company of one other prisoner. Conversation was allowed during this period upon approved topics, history, philosophy, public events, etc., the prisoners being chosen among those whose crimes would tend as little as possible to aggravate and encourage R.'s.

'I have not yet thought out the other stages of your treatment,' said Sir Wilfred, 'but you can see that individual attention is being paid to your reclamation. It may cause you some gratification to realize that, thanks to my report, you may in time become a case of scientific interest throughout the world. Sir Wilfred Lucas-Dockery's treatment of Case R. may haply become a precedent for generations yet unborn. That is something to lift you above the soul-destroying monotony of routine, is it not?'

Paul was led away.

'The men in the kitchen have lodged a complaint that they cannot work with C.2.9,' said the Chief Warder. 'They say he has an infectious skin disease all over his hands.'

'I can't be worried with things like that,' said the Governor irritably. 'I am trying to decide upon Case R.'s – I mean D.4.12's – third stage of reclamation.'

*

Case R. of the Lucas-Dockery experiments began on the new *régime* that afternoon.

'Come out,' said the warder, unlocking his cell, 'and bring your 'at.'

The parade ground, empty of its revolving squads, looked particularly desolate.

'Stand there and don't move till I come back,' said the warder.

Presently he returned with a little bony figure in prison dress.

'This 'ere's your pal,' he said, 'this 'ere's the path you've got to walk on. Neither of you is to touch the other or any part of 'is clothing. Nothing is to be passed from one to the other.

You are to keep at a distance of one yard and talk of 'istory, philosophy, or kindred subjects. When I rings the bell you stops talking, see? Your pace is to be neither quicker nor slower than average walking-pace. Them's the Governor's instructions, and Gawd 'elp yer if yer does anything wrong. Now walk.'

'This is a silly dodge,' said the little man. 'I've been in six prisons, and I never seen nothing to touch it. Most irregular. You doesn't know where you are these days. This blinking prison is going to the dogs. Look at the Chaplain. Wears a wig!'

'Are you here for long?' asked Paul politely.

'Not this time. They couldn't get a proper charge against me. "Six months for loitering with intent." They'd been watching me for weeks, but I wasn't going to let them have a chance this time. Now six months is a very decent little sentence, if you take my meaning. One picks up with old friends, and you like it all the more when you comes out. I never minds six months. What's more, I'm known here, so I always gets made "landing cleaner". I expect you've seen me hand often enough coming round with the grub. The warders know me, see, so they always keeps the job open for me if they hears I'm coming back. If you're nice to 'em the first two or three times you're 'ere, they'll probably do the same for you.'

'Is it a very good job?'

'Well, not as jobs go, but it's a nice start. The best job of all is Reception-cleaner. One doesn't get that for years, unless you've special recommendations. You see, you has all the people coming in fresh from outside, and you hears all the news and gets tobacco sometimes and racing tips. Did you see the cleaner when you came in? Know who he is?'

'Yes,' said Paul, 'as a matter of fact, I do. He's called Philbrick.'

'No, no, old man, you've got the wrong chap. I mean a big stout man. Talks a lot about hotels and restaurants.'

'Yes, that's the man I mean.'

'Why, don't you know who that is? That's the Governor's brother: Sir Solomon Lucas-Dockery. Told me so hisself. 'Ere for arson. Burnt a castle in Wales. You can see he's a toff.'

CHAPTER 3
The Death of a Modern Churchman

SOME days later Paul entered on another phase of his reclamation. When he came into the prison-square for his afternoon exercise he found that his companion's place had been taken by a burly man of formidable aspect. He had red hair and beard, and red-rimmed eyes, and vast red hands which twirled convulsively at his sides. He turned his ox-like eyes on Paul and gave a slight snarl of welcome.

'Your new pal,' said the warder. 'Get on with it.'

'How do you do?' said Paul politely. 'Are you here for long?'

'Life,' said the other. 'But it doesn't matter much. I look daily for the Second Coming.'

They marched on in silence.

'Do you think that this is a good plan of the Governor's?' asked Paul.

'Yes,' said his companion. They walked on in silence, once round, twice round, three times round.

'Talk, you two,' shouted the warder. 'That's your instructions. Talk.'

'It makes a change,' said the big man.

'What are you here for?' asked Paul. 'You don't mind my asking, do you?'

'It's all in the Bible,' said the big man. 'You should read about it there. Figuratively, you know,' he added. 'It wouldn't be plain to you, I don't suppose, not like it is to me.'

'It's not an easy book to understand, is it?'

'It's not understanding that's needed. It's vision. Do you ever have visions?'

'No, I'm afraid I don't.'

'Nor does the Chaplain. He's no Christian. It was a vision brought me here, an angel clothed in flame, with a crown of flame on his head, crying "Kill and spare not. The Kingdom is at hand." Would you like to hear about it? I'll tell you. I'm a carpenter by profession, or at least I was, you understand.' He spoke with a curious blend of cockney and Biblical English. 'Not a joiner – a cabinet-maker. Well, one day I was just sweeping out the shop before shutting up when the angel of the Lord came in. I didn't know who it was at first. "Just in time," I said. "What can I do for you?" Then I noticed that all about him there was a red flame and a circle of flame over his head, same as I've been telling you. Then he told me how the Lord had numbered His elect and the day of tribulation was at hand. "Kill and spare not," he says. I'd not been sleeping well for some time before this. I'd been worrying about my soul and whether I was saved. Well, all that night I thought of what the angel had told me. I didn't see his meaning, not at first, same as you wouldn't. Then it all came to me in a flash. Unworthy that I am, I am the Lord's appointed,' said the carpenter. 'I am the sword of Israel; I am the lion of the Lord's elect.'

'And did you kill anybody?' asked Paul.

'Unworthy that I am, I smote the Philistine; in the name of the Lord of hosts, I struck off his head. It was for a sign of Israel. And now I am gone into captivity, and the mirth is turned into weeping, but the Lord shall deliver me in His appointed time. Woe unto the Philistine in that day! woe unto the uncircumcised! It were better that a stone were hanged about his neck and he were cast into the depths of the sea.'

The warder rang his bell. 'Inside, you two!' he shouted.

'Any complaints?' asked the Governor on his rounds.

'Yes, sir,' said Paul.

The Governor looked at him intently. 'Are you the man I put under special treatment?'

'Yes, sir.'

'Then it's ridiculous to complain. What is it?'

'I have reason to believe that the man I have to take exercise with is a dangerous lunatic.'

'Complaints by one prisoner about another can only be considered when substantiated by the evidence of a warder or of two other prisoners,' said the Chief Warder.

'Quite right,' said the Governor. 'I never heard a more ridiculous complaint. All crime is a form of insanity. I myself chose the prisoner with whom you exercise. I chose him for his peculiar suitability. Let me hear no more on this subject, please.'

That afternoon Paul spent another disquieting half-hour on the square.

'I've had another vision,' said the mystical homicide. 'But I don't yet know quite what it portends. No doubt I shall be told.'

'Was it a very beautiful vision?' asked Paul.

'No words can describe the splendour of it. It was all crimson and wet like blood. I saw the whole prison as if it were carved of ruby, hard and glittering, and the warders and the prisoners creeping in and out like little red ladybirds. And then as I watched all the ruby became soft and wet, like a great sponge soaked in wine, and it was dripping and melting into a great lake of scarlet. Then I woke up. I don't know the meaning of it yet, but I feel that the hand of the Lord is hanging over this prison. D'you ever feel like that, as though it were built in the jaws of a beast? I sometimes dream of a great red tunnel like the throat of a beast and men running down it, sometimes one by one and sometimes in great crowds, running down the throat of the beast, and the breath of the beast is like the blast of a furnace. D'you ever feel like that?'

'I'm afraid not,' said Paul. 'Have they given you an interesting library book?'

'*Lady Almina's Secret*,' said the lion of the Lord's elect. 'Pretty soft stuff, old-fashioned, too. But I keep reading the Bible. There's a lot of killing in that.'

'Dear me, you seem to think about killing a great deal.'

'I do. It's my mission, you see,' said the big man simply.

*

Sir Wilfred Lucas-Dockery felt very much like Solomon at ten o'clock every morning of the week except Sunday. It was then that he sat in judgment upon the cases of misconduct among the prisoners that were brought to his notice. From his chair Colonel MacAdder had delivered sentence in undeviating accordance with the spirit and the letter of the Standing Orders

Concerning the Government of Her Majesty's Prisons, dispensing automatic justice like a slot machine: in went the offence; out came the punishment. Not so Wilfred Lucas-Dockery. Never, he felt, was his mind more alert or resourceful or his vast accumulation of knowledge more available than at his little court of summary justice. 'No one knows what to expect,' complained warders and prisoners alike.

'Justice,' said Sir Wilfred, 'is the capacity for regarding each case as an entirely new problem.' After a few months of his administration, Sir Wilfred was able to point with some pride to a marked diminution in the number of cases brought before him.

One morning, soon after Paul began on his special *régime* of reclamation, his companion was called up before the Governor.

'God bless my soul!' said Sir Wilfred; 'that's the man I put on special treatment. What is he here for?'

'I was on night duty last night between the hours of 8 p.m. and 4 a.m.,' testified the warder in a sing-song voice, 'when my attention was attracted by sounds of agitation coming from the prisoner's cell. Upon going to the observation hole I observed the prisoner pacing up and down his cell in a state of high excitement. In one hand he held his Bible, and in the other a piece of wood which he had broken from his stool. His eyes were staring; he was breathing heavily, and at times muttering verses of the Bible. I remonstrated with the prisoner when he addressed me in terms prejudicial to good discipline.'

'What are the words complained of?' asked the Chief Warder.

'He called me a Moabite, an abomination of Moab, a wash-pot, an unclean thing, an uncircumcised Moabite, an idolater, and a whore of Babylon, sir.'

'I see. What do you advise, officer?'

'A clear case of insubordination, sir,' said the Chief Warder. 'Try him on No. 1 diet for a bit.'

But when he asked the Chief Warder's opinion, Sir Wilfred was not really seeking advice. He liked to emphasize in his own mind, and perhaps that of the prisoner, the difference between the official view and his own.

'What would you say was the most significant part of the evidence?' he asked.

The Chief Warder considered. 'I think whore of Babylon, on the whole, sir.'

Sir Wilfred smiled as a conjurer may who has forced the right card.

'Now I,' he said, 'am of a different opinion. It may surprise you, but I should say that the *significant* thing about this case was the fact that the prisoner held a piece of the stool.'

'Destruction of prison property,' said the Chief Warder. 'Yes, that's pretty bad.'

'Now what was your profession before conviction?' asked the Governor, turning to the prisoner.

'Carpenter, sir.'

'*I knew it*,' said the Governor triumphantly. 'We have another case of the frustrated creative urge. Now listen, my man. It is very wrong of you to insult the officer, who is clearly none of the things you mentioned. He symbolizes the just disapproval of society and is, like all the prison staff, a member of the Church of England. But I understand your difficulty. You have been used to creative craftsmanship, have you not, and you find prison life deprives you of the means of self-expression, and your energies find vent in these foolish outbursts? I will see to it that a bench and a set of carpenter's tools are provided for you. The first thing you shall do is to mend the piece of furniture you so wantonly destroyed. After that we will find other work for you in your old trade. You may go. Get to the cause of the trouble,' Sir Wilfred added when the prisoner was led away; 'your Standing Orders may repress the symptoms; they do not probe to the underlying cause.'

*

Two days later the prison was in a state of intense excitement. Something had happened. Paul woke as the bell rang at the usual time, but it was nearly half an hour before the doors were unlocked. He heard the warder's 'Slops outside!' getting nearer and nearer, interjected with an occasional 'Don't ask questions,' 'Mind your own business,' or a sinister 'You'll know soon enough,' in reply to the prisoners' questions. They, too, had sensed something unusual. Perhaps it was an outbreak of some disease – spotted fever, Paul thought, or a national disaster in the world outside – a war or revolution. In their enforced silence the nerves of all the men were tightened to an acuteness of perception. Paul read wholesale massacres in the warder's face.

'Anything wrong?' he asked.

'I should bleeding well say there was,' said the warder, 'and the next man as asks me a question is going to cop it hot.'

Paul began scrubbing out his cell. Dissatisfied curiosity contended in his thoughts with irritation at this interruption of routine. Two warders passed his door talking.

'I don't say I'm not sorry for the poor bird. All I says is, it was time the Governor had a lesson.'

'It might have been one of us,' said the other warder in a hushed voice.

Breakfast arrived. As the hand appeared at his door Paul whispered: 'What's happened?'

'Why, ain't you 'eard? There's been a murder, shocking bloodthirsty.'

'Get on there,' roared the warder in charge of the landing.

So the Governor had been murdered, thought Paul; he had been a mischievous old bore. Still, it was very disturbing, for the news of a murder which was barely noticed in the gay world of trams and tubes and boxing-matches caused an electric terror in this community of silent men. The interval between breakfast and chapel seemed interminable. At last the bell went. The doors were opened again. They marched in silence to the chapel. As it happened, Philbrick was in the next seat to Paul. The warders sat on raised seats, watchful for any attempt at conversation. The hymn was the recognized time for the exchange of gossip. Paul waited for it impatiently. Clearly it was not the Governor who had been murdered. He stood on the chancel steps, Prayer-book in hand. Mr Prendergast was nowhere to be seen. The

Governor conducted the service. The Medical Officer read the lessons, stumbling heavily over the longer words. Where was Mr Prendergast?

At last the hymn was announced. The organ struck up, played with great feeling by a prisoner who until his conviction had been assistant organist at a Welsh cathedral. All over the chapel the men filled their chests for a burst of conversation.

'O God, our help in ages past,' sang Paul.
  'Where's Prendergast to-day?'
'What, ain't you 'eard? 'e's been done in.'
  'And our eternal home.'

'Old Prendy went to see a chap
  What said he'd seen a ghost;
Well, he was dippy, and he'd got
  A mallet and a saw.'

'Who let the madman have the things?'
  'The Governor; who d'you think?
He asked to be a carpenter,
  He sawed off Prendy's head.

'A pal of mine what lives next door,
  'E 'eard it 'appening;
The warder must 'ave 'eard it too,
  'E didn't interfere.'

'Time, like an ever-rolling stream,
  Bears all its sons away.'
'Poor Prendy 'ollered fit to kill
  For nearly 'alf an hour.

'Damned lucky it was Prendergast,
  Might 'ave been you or me!
The warder says – and I agree –
  It serves the Governor right.'

'*Amen.*'

From all points of view it was lucky that the madman had chosen Mr Prendergast for attack. Some people even suggested that the choice had been made in a more responsible quarter. The death of a prisoner or warder would have called for a Home Office inquiry which might seriously have discouraged the Lucas-Dockery reforms and also reflected some discredit upon the administration of the Chief Warder. Mr Prendergast's death passed almost unnoticed. His assassin was removed to Broadmoor, and the life of the prison went on smoothly. It was observed, however, that the Chief Warder seemed to have more influence with his superior than he had before. Sir Wilfred concentrated his attention upon the statistics, and the life of the prison was equitably conducted under the Standing Orders. It was quite like it had been in old MacAdder's day, the warders observed. But Paul did not reap the benefits of this happy reversion to tradition, because some few days later he was removed with a band of others to the Convict Settlement at Egdon Heath.

CHAPTER 4
Nor Iron Bars a Cage

THE granite walls of Egdon Heath Penal Settlement are visible, when there is no mist, from the main road, and it is not uncommon for cars to stop there a few moments while the occupants stand up and stare happily about them. They are looking for convicts, and as often as not they are rewarded by seeing move across the heath before them a black group of men chained together and uniformly dressed, with a mounted and armed warder riding at their side. They give an appearance of industry which on investigation is quite illusionary, for so much of the day at Egdon is taken up with marching to and from the quarries, in issuing and counting tools, in guarding and chaining and releasing the workmen, that there is very little work done. But there is usually something to be seen from the road, enough, anyway, to be imagined from the very aspect of the building to send the trippers off to their teas with their consciences agreeably unquiet at the memory of small dishonesties in railway trains, inaccurate income tax returns, and the hundred and one minor infractions of law that are inevitable in civilized life.

Paul arrived from Blackstone late one afternoon in early autumn with two warders and six other long-sentence prisoners. The journey had been spent in an ordinary third-class railway carriage, where the two warders smoked black tobacco in cheap little wooden pipes and were inclined towards conversation.

'You'll find a lot of improvements since you were here last,' said one of them. 'There's two coloured-glass windows in the chapel presented by the last Governor's widow. Lovely they are, St Peter and St Paul in prison being released by an angel. Some of the Low Church prisoners don't like them, though.

'We had a lecture last week, too, but it wasn't very popular – "The Work of the League of Nations", given by a young chap of the name of Potts. Still, it makes a change. I hear you've been having a lot of changes at Blackstone.'

'I should just about think we have,' said one of the convicts, and proceeded to give a somewhat exaggerated account of the death of Mr Prendergast.

Presently one of the warders, observing that Paul seemed shy of joining in the conversation, handed him a daily paper. 'Like to look at this, sonny?' he said. 'It's the last you'll see for some time.'

There was very little in it to interest Paul, whose only information from the outside world during the last six weeks had come from Sir Wilfred Lucas-Dockery's weekly bulletins (for one of the first discoveries of his captivity was that interest in 'news' does not spring from genuine curiosity, but from the desire for completeness. During his long years of freedom he had scarcely allowed a day to pass without reading fairly fully from at least two newspapers, always pressing on with a series of events which never came to an end. Once the series was broken he had little desire to resume it), but he was deeply moved to discover on one of the middle plates an obscure but recognizable photograph of Margot and Peter. 'The Honourable Mrs Beste-Chetwynde,' it said below, 'and her son, Peter, who succeeds his uncle as Earl of Pastmaster.' In the next column was an announcement of the death of Lord Pastmaster and a brief survey of his uneventful life. At the end it said, 'It is understood that Mrs Beste-Chetwynde and the young Earl, who have been spending the last few months at their villa in Corfu, will return to England in a few days. Mrs Beste-Chetwynde has for many years been a prominent hostess in the fashionable world and is regarded as one of the most beautiful women in Society. Her son's succession to the earldom recalls the sensation caused in May of this year by the announcement of her engagement to Mr Paul Pennyfeather and the dramatic arrest of the bridegroom at a leading West End hotel a few hours before the wedding ceremony. The new Lord Pastmaster is sixteen years old, and has up till now been educated privately.'

Paul sat back in the carriage for a long time looking at the photograph, while his companions played several hands of poker in reckless disregard of Standing Orders. In his six weeks of solitude and grave consideration he had failed to make up his mind about Margot Beste-Chetwynde; it was torn and distracted by two conflicting methods of thought. On one side was the dead weight of precept, inherited from generations of schoolmasters and divines. According to these, the problem was difficult but not insoluble. He had 'done the right thing' in shielding the woman: so much was clear, but Margot had not quite filled the place assigned to her, for in this case she was grossly culpable, and he was shielding her, not from misfortune nor injustice, but from the consequence of her crimes; he felt a flush about his knees as Boy Scout honour whispered that Margot had got him into a row and ought jolly well to own up and face the music. As he sat over his post-bags he had wrestled with this argument without achieving any satisfactory result except a growing conviction that there was something radically inapplicable about this whole code of ready-made honour that is the still small voice, trained to command, of the

Englishman all the world over. On the other hand was the undeniable cogency of Peter Beste-Chetwynde's 'You can't see Mamma in prison, can you?' The more Paul considered this, the more he perceived it to be the statement of a natural law. He appreciated the assumption of comprehension with which Peter had delivered it. As he studied Margot's photograph, dubiously transmitted as it was, he was strengthened in his belief that there was, in fact, and should be, one law for her and another for himself, and that the raw little exertions of nineteenth-century Radicals were essentially base and trivial and misdirected. It was not simply that Margot had been very rich or that he had been in love with her. It was just that he saw the *impossibility* of Margot in prison; the bare connexion of vocables associating the ideas was obscene. Margot dressed in prison uniform, hustled down corridors by wardresses – all like the younger Miss Fagan – visited by philanthropic old ladies with devotional pamphlets, set to work in the laundry washing the other prisoners' clothes – these things were *impossible*, and if the preposterous processes of law had condemned her, then the woman that they actually caught and pinned down would not have been Margot, but some quite other person of the same name and somewhat similar appearance. It was impossible to imprison the Margot who had committed the crime. If some one had to suffer that the public might be discouraged from providing poor Mrs Grimes with the only employment for which civilization had prepared her, then it had better be Paul than that other woman with Margot's name, for anyone who has been to an English public school will always feel comparatively at home in prison. It is the people brought up in the gay intimacy of the slums, Paul learned, who find prison so soul-destroying.

How lovely Margot was, Paul reflected, even in this absurd photograph, this grey-and-black smudge of ink! Even the most hardened criminal there – he was serving his third sentence for blackmail – laid down his cards for a moment and remarked upon how the whole carriage seemed to be flooded with the delectable savour of the Champs-Élysées in early June. 'Funny,' he said. 'I thought I smelt scent.' And that set them off talking about women.

*

Paul found another old friend at Egdon Heath Prison: a short, thick-set, cheerful figure who stumped along in front of him on the way to chapel, making a good deal of noise with an artificial leg. 'Here we are again, old boy!' he remarked during one of the responses. 'I'm in the soup as per usual.'

'Didn't you like the job?' Paul asked.

'Top hole,' said Grimes, 'but the hell of a thing happened. Tell you later.'

That morning, complete with pickaxes, field-telephone, and two armed and mounted warders, Paul and a little squad of fellow-criminals were led to the quarries. Grimes was in the party.

'I've been here a fortnight,' said Grimes as soon as they got an opportunity of talking, 'and it seems too long already. I've always been a sociable chap, and I don't like it. Three years is too long, old boy. Still, we'll have God's own beano when I get out. I've been thinking about that day and night.'

'I suppose it was bigamy?' said Paul.

'The same. I ought to have stayed abroad. I was arrested as soon as I landed. You see, Mrs Grimes turned up at the shop, so off Grimes went. There are various sorts of hell, but that young woman can beat up a pretty lively one of her own.'

A warder passed them by, and they moved apart, banging industriously at the sandstone cliff before them.

'I'm not sure it wasn't worth it, though,' said Grimes, 'to see poor old Flossie in the box and my sometime father-in-law. I hear the old man's shut down the school. Grimes gave the place a bad name. See anything of old Prendy ever?'

'He was murdered the other day.'

'Poor old Prendy! He wasn't cut out for the happy life, was he? D'you know, I think I shall give up schoolmastering for good when I get out. It doesn't lead anywhere.'

'It seems to have led us both to the same place.'

'Yes, rather a coincidence, isn't it? Damn, here's that policeman again.'

Soon they were marched back to the prison. Except for the work in the quarries, life at Egdon was almost the same as at Blackstone.

'Slops outside', chapel, privacy.

After a week, however, Paul became conscious of an alien influence at work. His first intimation of this came from the Chaplain.

'Your library books,' he said one day, popping cheerfully in Paul's cell and handing him two new novels, still in their wrappers, and bearing inside them the label of a Piccadilly bookseller. 'If you don't like them I have several for you to choose from.' He showed him rather coyly the pile of gaily-bound volumes he carried under his arm. 'I thought you'd like the new Virginia Woolf. It's only been out two days.'

'Thank you, sir,' said Paul politely. Clearly the library of his new prison was run on a much more enterprising and extravagant plan than at Blackstone.

'Or there's this book on Theatrical Design,' said the Chaplain, showing him a large illustrated volume that could hardly have cost less than three guineas. 'Perhaps we might stretch a point and give you that as well as your "education work".'

'Thank you, sir,' said Paul.

'Let me know if you want a change,' said the Chaplain. 'And, by the way, you're allowed to write a letter now, you know. If, by any chance, you're writing to Mrs Beste-Chetwynde, do mention that you think the library good. She's presenting a new pulpit to the chapel in carved alabaster,' he added irrelevantly, and popped out again to give Grimes a copy of Smiles' *Self-Help*, out of which some unreceptive reader in the remote past had torn the last hundred and eight pages.

'People may think as they like about well-thumbed favourites,' thought Paul, 'but there is something incomparably thrilling in first opening a brand-new book. Why should the Chaplain want me to mention the library to Margot?' he wondered.

That evening at supper Paul noticed without surprise that there were several small pieces of coal in his dripping: that kind of thing did happen now and then; but he was somewhat disconcerted, when he attempted to scrape them out, to find that they were quite soft. Prison food was often rather odd; it was a mistake to complain; but still . . . He examined his dripping more closely. It had a pinkish tinge that should not have been there and was unusually firm and sticky under his knife. He tasted it dubiously. It was *pâté de foie gras*.

From then onwards there was seldom a day on which some small meteorite of this kind did not mysteriously fall from the outside world. One day he returned from the heath to find his cell heavy with scent in the half-dark, for the lights were rarely lit until some time after sundown, and the window was very small. His table was filled with a large bunch of winter roses, which had cost three shillings each that morning in Bond Street. (Prisoners at Egdon are allowed to keep flowers in their cells, and often risk severe reprimand by stooping to pick pimpernels and periwinkles on their way from work.)

On another occasion the prison-doctor, trotting on his daily round of inspection, paused at Paul's cell, examined his name on the card hanging inside his door, looked hard at him and said, 'You need a tonic.' He trotted on without more ado, but next day a huge medicine-bottle was placed in Paul's cell. 'You're to take two glasses with each meal,' said the warder, 'and I hopes you like it.' Paul could not quite decide whether the warder's tone was friendly or not, but he liked the medicine, for it was brown sherry.

On another occasion great indignation was aroused in the cell next door to him, whose occupant – an aged burglar – was inadvertently given Paul's ration of caviare. He was speedily appeased by the substitution for it of an unusually large lump of cold bacon, but not before the warder in charge had suffered considerable alarm at the possibility of a complaint to the Governor.

'I'm not one to make a fuss really,' said the old burglar, 'but I will be treated fair. Why, you only had to look at the stuff they give to me to see that it was bad, let alone taste it. And on bacon night, too! You take my tip,' he said to Paul as they found themselves alone in the quarries one day, 'and keep your eyes open. You're a new one, and they might easily try and put a thing like that over on you. Don't eat it; that's putting you in the wrong. Keep it and show it to the Governor. They ain't got no right to try on a thing like that, and they knows it.'

Presently a letter came from Margot. It was not a long one.

Dear Paul, it said,

It is so difficult writing to you because, you know, I never can write letters, and it's so particularly hard with you because the policemen read it and cross it all out if they don't like it, and I can't really think of anything they will like. Peter and I are back at King's Thursday. It was divine at Corfu, except for an English Doctor who was a bore and would call so often. Do you know, I don't really like this house terribly, and I am having it redone. Do you mind? Peter has become an earl – did you know? – and is rather sweet about it, and very self-conscious, which you wouldn't expect, really, would you, knowing Peter? I'm going to come and see you some time – may I? – when I can get away, but Bobby P.'s death has made such a lot of things to see to. I do hope you're getting enough food and books and things, or will they cross that out? Love, Margot. I was cut by Lady Circumference, my dear, at Newmarket, a real point-blank Tranby Croft cut. Poor Maltravers says if I'm not careful I shall find myself socially ostracized. Don't you think that will be marvellous? I may be wrong, but, d'you know, I rather believe poor little Alastair Trumpington's going to fall in love with me. What shall I do?

*

Eventually Margot came herself.

It was the first time they had met since the morning in June when she had sent him off to rescue her distressed protégées in Marseilles. The meeting took place in a small room set aside for visitors. Margot sat at one end of the table, Paul at the other, with a warder between them.

'I must ask you both to put your hands on the table in front of you,' said the warder.

'Like Up Jenkins,' said Margot faintly, laying her exquisitely manicured hands with the gloves beside her bag. Paul for the first time noticed how coarse and ill-kept his hands had become. For a moment neither spoke.

'Do I look awful?' Paul said at last. 'I haven't seen a looking-glass for some time.'

'Well, perhaps just a little *mal soigné*, darling. Don't they let you shave at all?'

'No discussion of the prison *régime* is permitted. Prisoners are allowed to make a plain statement of their state of health but must on no account make complaints or comments upon their general condition.'

'Oh dear!' said Margot; 'this is going to be very difficult. What are we to say to each other? I'm almost sorry I came. You are glad I came, aren't you?'

'Don't mind me, mum, if you wants to talk personal,' said the warder kindly. 'I only has to stop conspiracy. Nothing I hears ever goes any farther, and I hears a good deal, I can tell you. They carry on awful, some of the women, what with crying and fainting and hysterics generally. Why, one of them,' he said with relish, 'had an epileptic fit not long ago.'

'I think it's more than likely I shall have a fit,' said Margot. 'I've never felt so shy in my life. Paul, *do* say something, please.'

'How's Alastair?' said Paul.

'Rather sweet, really. He's always at King's Thursday now. I like him.'

Another pause.

'Do you know,' said Margot, 'it's an odd thing, but I do believe that after all these years I'm beginning to be regarded as no longer a respectable woman. I told you when I wrote, didn't I, that Lady Circumference cut me the other day? Of course she's just a thoroughly bad-mannered old woman, but there have been a whole lot of things rather like that lately. Don't you think it's rather awful?'

'You won't mind much, will you?' said Paul. 'They're awful old bores, anyway.'

'Yes, but I don't like *them* dropping *me*. Of course, I don't mind, really, but I think it's just a pity, particularly for Peter. It's not just Lady Circumference, but Lady Vanburgh and Fanny Simpleforth and the Stayles and all those people. It's a pity it should happen just when Peter's beginning to be a little class-conscious, anyway. It'll give him all the wrong ideas, don't you think?'

'How's business?' asked Paul abruptly.

'Paul, you mustn't be nasty to me,' said Margot in a low voice. 'I don't think you'd say that if you knew quite how I was feeling.'

'I'm sorry, Margot. As a matter of fact, I just wanted to know.'

'I'm selling out. A Swiss firm was making things difficult. But I don't think that business has anything to do with the – the ostracism, as Maltravers would say. I believe it's all because I'm beginning to grow old.'

'I never heard anything so ridiculous. Why, all those people are about eighty, and anyway, you aren't at all.'

'I was afraid you wouldn't understand,' said Margot, and there was another pause.

'Ten minutes more,' said the warder.

'Things haven't turned out quite as we expected them to, have they?' said Margot.

They talked about some parties Margot had been to and the books Paul was reading. At last Margot said: 'Paul, I'm going. I simply can't stand another moment of this.'

'It was nice of you to come,' said Paul.

'I've decided something rather important,' said Margot, 'just this minute. I am going to be married quite soon to Maltravers. I'm sorry, but I am.'

'I suppose it's because I look so awful?' said Paul.

'No, it's just everything. It's that, too, in a way, but not the way you mean, Paul. It's simply something that's going to happen. Do you understand at all, dear? It may help you, too, in a way, but I don't want you to think that that's the reason, either. It's just how things are going to happen. Oh dear! How difficult it is to say anything.'

'If you should want to kiss good-bye,' said the gaoler, 'not being husband and wife, it's not usual. Still, I don't mind stretching a point for once...'

'Oh, God!' said Margot, and left the room without looking back.

Paul returned to his cell. His supper had already been served out to him, a small pie from which protruded the feet of two pigeons; there was even a table-napkin wrapped round it. But Paul had very little appetite, for he was greatly pained at how little he was pained by the events of the afternoon.

CHAPTER 5
The Passing of a Public School Man

A DAY or two later Paul found himself next to Grimes in the quarry. When the warder was out of earshot Grimes said: 'Old boy, I can't stand this much longer. It just ain't good enough.'

'I don't see any way out,' said Paul. 'Anyway, it's quite bearable. I'd as soon be here as at Llanabba.'

'Not so Grimes,' said Grimes. 'He just languishes in captivity, like the lark. It's all right for you – you like reading and thinking and all that. Well, I'm different, you know. I like drink and a bit of fun, and chatting now and then to my pals. I'm a sociable chap. It's turning me into a giddy machine, this life, and there's an awful chaplain, who gives me the pip, who keeps butting in in a breezy kind of way and asking if I feel I'm "right with God". Of course I'm not, and I tell him so. I can stand most sorts of misfortune, old boy, but I can't stand repression. That was what broke me up at Llanabba, and it's what's going to break me up here, if I don't look out for myself. It seems to me it's time Grimes flitted off to another clime.'

'No one has ever succeeded in escaping from this prison,' said Paul.

'Well, just you watch next time there's a fog!'

As luck would have it, there was a fog next day, a heavy impenetrable white mist which came up quite suddenly while they were at work, enveloping men and quarry in the way that mists do on Egdon Heath.

'Close up there,' said the warder in charge. 'Stop work and close up. Look out there, you idiot!' for Grimes had stumbled over the field-telephone. 'If you've broken it you'll come up before the Governor to-morrow.'

'Hold this horse,' said the other warder, handing the reins to Grimes.

He stooped and began to collect the chains on which the men were strung for their march home. Grimes seemed to be having some difficulty with the horse, which was plunging and rearing farther away from the squad. 'Can't you even hold a horse?' said the warder. Suddenly Grimes, with remarkable agility considering his leg, was seen to be in the saddle riding away into the heath.

'Come back,' roared the warder, 'come back, or I'll fire.' He put his rifle to his shoulder and fired into the fog. 'He'll come back all right,' he said. 'No one ever gets away for long. He'll get solitary confinement and No. 1 diet for this, poor fish.'

No one seemed to be much disturbed by the incident, even when it was found that the field-telephone was disconnected.

'He hasn't a hope,' said the warder. 'They often do that, just put down their tools sudden and cut and run. But they can't get away in those clothes and with no money. We shall warn all the farms to-night. Sometimes they stays out hiding for several days, but back they comes when they're hungry, or else they get arrested the moment they shows up in a village. I reckon it's just nerves makes them try it.'

That evening the horse came back, but there was no sign of Grimes. Special patrols were sent out with bloodhounds straining at their leashes; the farms and villages on the heath were warned, and the anxious inhabitants barred their doors closely and more pertinently forbade their children to leave the house on any pretext whatever; the roads were watched for miles, and all cars were stopped and searched, to the intense annoyance of many law-abiding citizens. But Grimes did not turn up. Bets were slyly made among the prisoners as to the day of his recovery; but days passed, and the rations of bread changed hands, but still there was no Grimes.

A week later at morning-service the Chaplain prayed for his soul: the Governor crossed his name off the Body Receipt Book and notified the Home Secretary, the Right Honourable Sir Humphrey Maltravers, that Grimes was dead.

'I'm afraid it was a terrible end,' said the Chaplain to Paul.

'Did they find the body?'

'No, that is the worst thing about it. The hounds followed his scent as far as Egdon Mire; there it ended. A shepherd who knows the paths through the bog found his hat floating on the surface at the most treacherous part. I'm afraid there is no doubt that he died a very horrible death.'

'Poor old Grimes!' said Paul. 'And he was an old Harrovian, too.'

But later, thinking things over as he ate peacefully, one by one, the oysters that had been provided as a 'relish' for his supper, Paul knew that Grimes was not dead. Lord Tangent was dead; Mr Prendergast was dead; the time would even come for Paul Pennyfeather; but Grimes, Paul at last realized, was of the immortals. He was a life force. Sentenced to death in Flanders, he popped up in Wales; drowned in Wales, he emerged in South America; engulfed in the dark mystery of Egdon Mire, he would rise again somewhere at some time, shaking from his limbs the musty integuments of the tomb. Surely he had followed in the Bacchic train of distant Arcady, and played on the reeds of myth by forgotten streams, and taught the childish satyrs the art of love? Had he not suffered unscathed the fearful dooms of all the offended gods, of all the histories, fire, brimstone, and yawning earthquakes, plague, and pestilence? Had he not stood, like the Pompeiian sentry, while the Citadels of the Plain fell to ruin about his ears? Had he not, like some grease-caked Channel-swimmer, breasted the waves of the Deluge? Had he not moved unseen when the darkness covered the waters?

'I often wonder whether I am blameless in the matter,' said the Chaplain. 'It is awful to think of someone under my care having come to so terrible an end. I tried to console him and reconcile him with his life, but things are so difficult; there are so many men to see. Poor fellow! To think of him alone out there in the bog, with no one to help him!'

CHAPTER 6
The Passing of Paul Pennyfeather

A FEW days later Paul was summoned to the Governor's room.

'I have an order here from the Home Secretary granting leave for you to go into a private nursing-home for the removal of your appendix. You will start under escort, in plain clothes, this morning.'

'But, sir,' said Paul, 'I don't want to have my appendix removed. In fact, it was done years ago when I was still at school.'

'Nonsense!' said the Governor. 'I've got an order here from the Home Secretary especially requiring that it shall be done. Officer, take this man away and give him his clothes for the journey.'

Paul was led away. The clothes in which he had been tried had been sent with him from Blackstone. The warder took them out of a locker, unfolded them and handed them to Paul. 'Shoes, socks, trousers, waistcoat, coat, shirt, collar, tie, and hat,' he said. 'Will you sign for them? The jewellery stays here.' He collected the watch, links, tie-pin, note-case, and the other odds and ends that had been in Paul's pockets and put them back in the locker. 'We can't do anything about your hair,' said the warder, 'but you're allowed a shave.'

Half an hour later Paul emerged from his cell, looking for all the world like a normal civilized man, such as you might see daily in any tube-railway.

'Feels funny, don't it?' said the warder who let him out. 'Here's your escort.'

Another normal civilized man, such as you might see daily in any tube-railway, confronted Paul.

'Time we started, if you're quite ready,' he said. Robbed of their uniforms, it seemed natural that they should treat each other with normal consideration. Indeed, Paul thought he detected a certain deference in the man's tone.

'It's very odd,' said Paul in the van that took them to the station; 'it's no good arguing with the Governor, but he's made some ridiculous mistake. I've had my appendix out already.'

'Not half,' said the warder with a wink, 'but don't go talking about it so loud. The driver's not in on this.'

A first-class carriage had been reserved for them in the train. As they drew out of Egdon Station the warder said: 'Well, that's the last you'll see of the old place for some time. Solemn thought, death, ain't it?' And he gave another shattering wink.

They had luncheon in their carriage, Paul feeling a little too shy of his closely-cropped head to venture hatless into the restaurant car. After luncheon they smoked cigars. The warder paid from a fat note-case. 'Oh, I nearly forgot,' he said. 'Here's your will for you to sign, in case anything should happen.' He produced a long blue paper and handed it to Paul. *The Last Will and Testament of Paul Pennyfeather* was handsomely engrossed at the top. Below, it was stated, with the usual legal periphrases, that he left all he possessed to Margot Beste-Chetwynde. Two witnesses had already signed below the vacant space. 'I'm sure this is all very irregular,' said Paul signing; 'I wish you'd tell me what all this means.'

'I don't know nothing,' said the warder. 'The young gentleman give me the will.'

'What young gentleman?'

'How should I know?' said the warder. 'The young gentleman what's arranged everything. Very sensible to make a will. You never know with an operation what may happen, do you? I had an aunt died having gallstones taken out, and she hadn't made a will. Very awkward it was, her not being married properly, you see. Fine healthy woman, too, to look at her. Don't you get worried, Mr Pennyfeather; everything will be done strictly according to regulations.'

'Where are we going? At least you must know that.'

For answer the warder took a printed card from his pocket.

Cliff Place, Worthing, he read. *High-class Nursing and Private Sanatorium. Electric thermal treatment under medical supervision. Augustus Fagan, M.D., Proprietor.* 'Approved by the Home Secretary,' said the warder. 'Nothing to complain of.'

Later in the afternoon they arrived. A car was waiting to take them to Cliff Place.

'This ends my responsibility,' said the warder. 'From now on the doctor's in charge.'

*

Like all Dr Fagan's enterprises, Cliff Place was conceived on a large scale. The house stood alone on the seashore some miles from the town, and was approached by a long drive. In detail, however, it showed some signs of neglect. The veranda was deep in driven leaves; two of the windows were broken. Paul's escort rang the bell at the front door, and Dingy, dressed as a nurse, opened it to them.

'The servants have all gone,' she said. 'I suppose this is the appendicitis case. Come in.' She showed no signs of recognizing Paul as she led him upstairs. 'This is your room. The Home Office regulations insisted that it should be on an upper storey with barred windows. We have had to put the bars in specially. They will be charged for in the bill. The surgeon will be here in a few minutes.'

As she went out she locked the door. Paul sat down on the bed and waited. Below his window the sea beat on the shingle. A small steam-yacht lay at anchor some distance out to sea. The grey horizon faded indistinctly into the grey sky.

Presently steps approached, and his door opened. In came Dr Fagan, Sir Alastair Digby-Vane-Trumpington, and an elderly little man with a drooping red moustache, evidently much the worse for drink.

'Sorry we're late,' said Sir Alastair, 'but I've had an awful day with this man trying to keep him sober. He gave me the slip just as we were starting. I was afraid at first that he was too tight to be moved, but I think he can just carry on. Have you got the papers made out?'

No one paid much attention to Paul.

'Here they are,' said Dr Fagan. 'This is the statement you are to forward to the Home Secretary, and a duplicate for the Governor of the prison. Shall I read them to you?'

''Sh'all right!' said the surgeon.

'They merely state that you operated on the patient for appendicitis, but that he died under the anaesthetic without regaining consciousness.'

'Poor ole chap!' said the surgeon. 'Poor, poor l'il girl!' And two tears of sympathy welled up in his eyes. 'I daresay the world had been very hard on her. It's a hard world for women.'

'That's all right,' said Sir Alastair. 'Don't worry. You did all that was humanly possible.'

'That's the truth,' said the surgeon, 'and I don't care who knows it.'

'This is the ordinary certificate of death,' said Dr Fagan. 'Will you be so good as to sign it there?'

'Oh, death, where is thy sting-a-ling-a-ling?' said the surgeon, and with these words and a laboured effort of the pen he terminated the legal life of Paul Pennyfeather.

'Splendid!' said Sir Alastair. 'Now here's your money. If I were you I should run off and have a drink while the pubs are still open.'

'D'you know, I think I will,' said the surgeon, and left the sanatorium.

There was a hush for nearly a minute after he had left the room. The presence of death, even in its coldest and most legal form, seemed to cause an air of solemnity. It was broken at length by the arrival of Flossie, splendidly attired in magenta and green.

'Why, here you all are!' she said with genuine delight. 'And Mr Pennyfeather, too, to be sure! Quite a little party!'

She had said the right thing. The word 'party' seemed to strike a responsive note in Dr Fagan.

'Let us go down to supper,' he said. 'I'm sure we all have a great deal to be thankful for.'

*

After supper Dr Fagan made a little speech. 'I think this an important evening for most of us,' he said, 'most of all for my dear friend and sometime colleague Paul Pennyfeather, in whose death to-night we are all to some extent participants. For myself as well as for him it is the beginning of a new phase of life. Frankly, this nursing-home has not been a success. A time must come to every man when he begins to doubt his vocation. You may think me almost an old man, but I do not feel too old to start lightheartedly on a new manner of life. This evening's events have made this possible for me. I think,' he said, glancing at his daughters, 'that it is time I was alone. But this is not the hour to review the plans of my future. When you get to my age, if you have been at all observant of the people you have met and the accidents which have happened to you, you cannot help being struck with an amazing cohesiveness of events. How promiscuously we who are here this evening have been thrown together! How enduring and endearing the memories that from now onwards will unite us! I think we should drink a toast – to Fortune, a much-maligned lady.'

Once before Paul had drunk the same toast. This time there was no calamity. They drank silently, and Alastair rose from the table.

'It's time Paul and I were going,' he said.

They walked down to the beach together. A boat was waiting for them.

'That's Margot's yacht,' said Alastair. 'It's to take you to her house at Corfu until you've decided about things. Good-bye. Good luck!'

'Aren't you coming any farther?' asked Paul.

'No, I've got to drive back to King's Thursday. Margot will be anxious to know how things have gone off.'

Paul got into the boat and was rowed away. Sir Alastair, like Sir Bedivere, watched him out of sight.

CHAPTER 7
Resurrection

THREE weeks later Paul sat on the veranda of Margot's villa, with his evening *apéritif* before him, watching the sunset on the Albanian hills across the water change, with the crude brilliance of a German picture-postcard, from green to violet. He looked at his watch, which had that morning arrived from England. It was half-past six.

Below him in the harbour a ship had come in from Greece and was unloading her cargo. The little boats hung round her like flies, plying their trade of olive-wood souvenirs and forged francs. There were two hours before dinner. Paul rose and descended the arcaded street into the square, drawing his scarf tight about his throat; the evenings began to get cold about this time. It was odd being dead. That morning Margot had sent him a bunch of Press cuttings about himself, most of them headed 'Wedding Sensation Echo' or 'Death of Society Bridegroom Convict'. With them were his tie-pin and the rest of his possessions which had been sent to her from Egdon. He felt the need of the bustle at the cafés and the quayside to convince him fully of his existence. He stopped at a stall and bought some Turkish delight. It was odd being dead.

Suddenly he was aware of a familiar figure approaching him across the square.

'Hullo!' said Paul.

'Hullo!' said Otto Silenus. He was carrying on his shoulder a shapeless knapsack of canvas.

'Why don't you give that to one of the boys? They'll take it for a few drachmas.'

'I have no money. Will you pay him?'

'Yes.'

'All right! Then that will be best. I suppose you are staying with Margot?'

'I'm staying at her house. She's in England.'

'That's a pity. I hoped I should find her here. Still I will stay for a little, I think. Will there be room for me?'

'I suppose so. I'm all alone here.'

'I have changed my mind. I think, after all, I will marry Margot.'

'I'm afraid it's too late.'

'Too late?'

'Yes, she married someone else.'

'I never thought of that. Oh well, it doesn't matter really. Whom did she marry? That sensible Maltravers?'

'Yes, he's changed his name now. He's called Viscount Metroland.'

'What a funny name!'

They walked up the hill together. 'I've just been to Greece to see the buildings there,' said Professor Silenus.

'Did you like them?'

'They are unspeakably ugly. But there were some nice goats. I thought they sent you to prison.'

'Yes, they did, but I got out.'

'Yes, you must have, I suppose. Wasn't it nice?'

'Not terribly.'

'Funny! I thought it would suit you so well. You never can tell with people, can you, what's going to suit them?'

Margot's servants did not seem surprised at the arrival of another guest.

'I think I shall stay here a long time,' said Professor Silenus after dinner. 'I have no money left. Are you going soon?'

'Yes, I'm going back to Oxford again to learn theology.'

'That will be a good thing. You used not to have a moustache, used you?' he asked after a time.

'No,' said Paul. 'I'm just growing one now. I don't want people to recognize me when I go back to England.'

'I think it's uglier,' said Professor Silenus. 'Well, I must go to bed.'

'Have you slept any better lately?'

'Twice since I saw you. It's about my average. Good night.'

Ten minutes later he came back on to the terrace, wearing silk pyjamas and a tattered old canvas dressing-gown.

'Can you lend me a nail file?' he asked.

'There's one on my dressing-table.'

'Thank you.' But he did not go. Instead he walked to the parapet and leant out, looking across the sea. 'It's a good thing for you to be a clergyman,' he said at last. 'People get ideas about a thing they call life. It sets them all wrong. I think it's poets that are responsible chiefly. Shall I tell you about life?'

'Yes, do,' said Paul politely.

'Well, it's like the big wheel at Luna Park. Have you seen the big wheel?'

'No, I'm afraid not.'

'You pay five francs and go into a room with tiers of seats all round, and in the centre the floor is made of a great disc of polished wood that revolves quickly. At first you sit down and watch the others. They are all trying to sit in the wheel, and they keep getting flung off, and that makes them laugh, and you laugh too. It's great fun.'

'I don't think that sounds very much like life,' said Paul rather sadly.

'Oh, but it is, though. You see, the nearer you can get to the hub of the wheel the slower it is moving and the easier it is to stay on. There's generally someone in the centre who stands up and sometimes does a sort of dance. Often he's paid by the management, though, or, at any rate, he's allowed in free. Of course at the very centre there's a point completely at rest, if one could only find it: I'm not sure I am not very near that point myself. Of course the professional men get in the way. Lots of people just enjoy scrambling on and being whisked off and scrambling on again. How they all shriek and giggle! Then there are others, like Margot, who sit as far out as they can and hold on for dear life and enjoy that. But the whole point about the wheel is that you needn't get on it at all, if you don't want to. People get hold of ideas about life, and that makes them think they've got to join in the game, even if they don't enjoy it. It doesn't suit everyone.

'People don't see that when they say "life" they mean two different things. They can mean simply existence, with its physiological implications of growth and organic change. They can't escape that – even by death, but because that's inevitable they think the other idea of life is too – the scrambling and excitement and bumps and the effort to get to the middle, and when we do get to the middle, it's just as if we never started. It's so odd.

'Now you're a person who was clearly meant to stay in the seats and sit still and if you get bored watch the others. Somehow you got on to the wheel, and you got thrown off again at once with a hard bump. It's all right for Margot, who can cling on, and for me, at the centre, but you're static. Instead of this absurd division into sexes they ought to class people as static and dynamic. There's a real distinction there, though I can't tell you how it comes. I think we're probably two quite different species spiritually.

'I used that idea of the wheel in a cinema-film once. I think it rather sounds like it, don't you? What was it I came back for?'

'A nail file.'

'Oh yes, of course. I know of no more utterly boring and futile occupation than generalizing about life. Did you take in what I was saying?'

'Yes, I think so.'

'I think I shall have my meals alone in future. Will you tell the servants? It makes me feel quite ill to talk so much. Good night.'

'Good night,' said Paul.

*

Some months later Paul returned to Scone College after the absence of little more than a year. His death, though depriving him of his certificates, left him his knowledge. He sat successfully for Smalls and Matriculation and entered his old college once more, wearing a commoner's gown and a heavy cavalry moustache. This and his natural diffidence formed a complete disguise. Nobody recognized him. After much doubt and deliberation he retained the name of Pennyfeather, explaining to the Chaplain that he had, he believed, had a distant cousin at Scone a short time ago.

'He came to a very sad end,' said the Chaplain, 'a wild young man.'

'He was a *very* distant cousin,' said Paul hastily.

'Yes, yes, I am sure he was. There is no resemblance between you. He was a thoroughly degenerate type, I am afraid.'

Paul's scout also remembered the name.

'There used to be another Mr Pennyfeather on this staircase once,' he said, 'a very queer gentleman indeed. Would you believe it, sir, he used to take off all his clothes and go out and dance in the quad at night. Nice quiet gentleman, too, he was, except for his dancing. He must have been a little queer in his head, I suppose. I don't know what became of him. They say he died in prison.' Then he proceeded to tell Paul about an Annamese student who had attempted to buy one of the Senior Tutor's daughters.

On the second Sunday of term the Chaplain asked Paul to breakfast. 'It's a sad thing,' he said, 'the way that the 'Varsity breakfast – "brekker" we used to call it in my day – is dying out. People haven't time for it. Always off to lectures at nine o'clock, except on Sundays. Have another kidney, won't you?'

There was another don present, called Mr Sniggs, who addressed the Chaplain rather superciliously, Paul thought, as 'Padre'.

There was also an undergraduate from another college, a theological student called Stubbs, a grave young man with a quiet voice and with carefully formed opinions. He had a little argument with Mr Sniggs about the plans for rebuilding the Bodleian. Paul supported him.

Next day Paul found Stubbs' card on his table, the corner turned up. Paul went to Hertford to call on Stubbs, but found him out. He left his card, the corner turned up. Two days later a little note came from Hertford:

Dear Pennyfeather,

I wonder if you would care to come to tea next Tuesday, to meet the College Secretary of the League of Nations Union and the Chaplain of the Oxford prison. It would be so nice if you could.

Paul went and ate honey buns and anchovy toast. He liked the ugly, subdued little College, and he liked Stubbs.

As term went on Paul and Stubbs took to going for walks together, over Mesopotamia to Old Marston and Beckley. One afternoon, quite lighthearted at the fresh weather, and their long walk, and their tea, Stubbs signed *Randall Cantuar* in the visitors' book.

Paul rejoined the League of Nations Union and the O.S.C.U. On one occasion he and Stubbs and some other friends went to the prison to visit the criminals there and sing part-songs to them.

'It opens the mind,' said Stubbs, 'to see all sides of life. How those unfortunate men appreciated our singing!'

One day in Blackwell's bookshop Paul found a stout volume, which, the assistant told him, was rapidly becoming a best-seller. It was called *Mother Wales*, by *Augustus Fagan*. Paul bought it and took it back with him. Stubbs had already read it.

'Most illuminating,' he said. 'The hospital statistics are terrible. Do you think it would be a good idea to organize a joint debate with Jesus on the subject?' The book was dedicated '*To my wife, a wedding present*'. It was eloquently written. When he had read it Paul put it on his shelves next to Dean Stanley's *Eastern Church*.

One other incident recalled momentarily Paul's past life.

One day at the beginning of his second year, as Paul and Stubbs were bicycling down the High from one lecture to another, they nearly ran into an open Rolls-Royce that swung out of Oriel Street at a dangerous speed. In the back, a heavy fur rug over his knees, sat Philbrick. He turned round as he passed and waved a gloved hand to Paul over the hood.

'Hullo!' he said; 'hullo! How are you! Come and look me up one day. I'm living on the river – Skindle's.'

Then the car disappeared down the High Street, and Paul went on to the lecture.

'Who was your opulent friend?' asked Stubbs, rather impressed.

'Arnold Bennett,' said Paul.

'I thought I knew his face,' said Stubbs.

Then the lecturer came in, arranged his papers, and began a lucid exposition of the heresies of the second century. There was a bishop of Bithynia, Paul learned, who had denied the Divinity of Christ, the immortality of the soul, the existence of good, the legality of marriage, and the validity of the Sacrament of Extreme Unction. How right they had been to condemn him!

EPILOGUE

IT was Paul's third year of uneventful residence at Scone. Stubbs finished his cocoa, knocked out his pipe and rose to go. 'I must be off to my digs,' he said. 'You're lucky staying in college. It's a long ride back to Walton Street on a night like this.'

'D'you want to take Von Hugel?' asked Paul.

'No, not to-night. May I leave it till to-morrow?'

Stubbs picked up his scholar's gown and wrapped it round his shoulders. 'That was an interesting paper to-night about the Polish plebiscites.'

'Yes, wasn't it?' said Paul.

Outside there was a confused roaring and breaking of glass.

'The Bollinger seem to be enjoying themselves,' said Paul. 'Whose rooms are they in this time?'

'Pastmaster's, I think. That young man seems to be going a bit fast for his age.'

'Well, I hope he enjoys it,' said Paul. 'Good night.'

'Good night, Paul,' said Stubbs.

Paul put the chocolate biscuits back in the cupboard, refilled his pipe, and settled down in his chair.

Presently he heard footsteps and a knock at his door.

'Come in,' he said, looking round.

Peter Pastmaster came into the room. He was dressed in the bottle-green and white evening coat of the Bollinger Club. His face was flushed and his dark hair slightly disordered.

'May I come in?'

'Yes, do.'

'Have you got a drink?'

'You seem to have had a good many already.'

'I've had the Boller in my rooms. Noisy lot. Oh, hell! I must have a drink.'

'There's some whisky in the cupboard. You're drinking rather a lot these days, aren't you, Peter?'

Peter said nothing, but helped himself to some whisky and soda.

'Feeling a bit ill,' he said. Then, after a pause, 'Paul, why have you been cutting me all this time?'

'I don't know. I didn't think there was much to be gained by our knowing each other.'

'Not angry about anything?'

'No, why should I be?'

'Oh, I don't know.' Peter turned his glass in his hand, staring at it intently. 'I've been rather angry with you, you know.'

'Why?'

'Oh, I don't know – about Margot and the man Maltravers and everything.'

'I don't think I was much to blame.'

'No, I suppose not, only you were part of it all.'

'How's Margot?'

'She's all right – *Margot Metroland*. D'you mind if I take another drink?'

'I suppose not.'

'Viscountess Metroland,' said Peter. 'What a name! What a man! Still, she's got Alastair all the time. Metroland doesn't mind. He's got what he wanted. I don't see much of them really. What do you do all the time, Paul?'

'I'm going to be ordained soon.'

'Wish I didn't feel so damned ill. What were we saying? Oh yes, about Metroland. You know, Paul, I think it was a mistake you ever got mixed up with us; don't you? We're different somehow. Don't quite know how. Don't think that's rude, do you, Paul?'

'No, I know exactly what you mean. You're dynamic, and I'm static.'

'Is that it? Expect you're right. Funny thing you used to teach me once; d'you remember? Llanabba – Latin sentences, *Quominus* and *Quin*, and the organ; d'you remember?'

'Yes, I remember,' said Paul.

'Funny how things happen. You used to teach me the organ; d'you remember?'

'Yes, I remember,' said Paul.

'And then Margot Metroland wanted to marry you; d'you remember?'

'Yes,' said Paul.

'And then you went to prison, and Alastair – that's Margot Metroland's young man – and Metroland – that's her husband – got you out; d'you remember?'

'Yes,' said Paul, 'I remember.'

'And here we are talking to one another like this, up here, after all that! Funny, isn't it?'

'Yes, it is rather.'

'Paul, do you remember a thing you said once at the Ritz – Alastair was there – that's Margot Metroland's young man, you know – d'you remember? I was rather tight then too. You said, "Fortune, a much-maligned lady." D'you remember that?'

'Yes,' said Paul, 'I remember.'

'Good old Paul! I knew you would. Let's drink to that now; shall we? How did it go? Damn, I've forgotten it. Never mind. I wish I didn't feel so ill.'

'You drink too much, Peter.'

'Oh, damn, what else is there to do? You going to be a clergyman, Paul?'

'Yes.'

'Damned funny that. You know you ought never to have got mixed up with me and Metroland. May I have another drink?'

'Time you went to bed, Peter, don't you think?'

'Yes, I suppose it is. Didn't mind my coming in, did you? After all, you used to teach me the organ; d'you remember? Thanks for the whisky!'

So Peter went out, and Paul settled down again in his chair. So the ascetic Ebionites used to turn towards Jerusalem when they prayed. Paul made a note of it. Quite right to suppress them. Then he turned out the light and went into his bedroom to sleep.

VILE BODIES

With Love to
Bryan and Diana Guinness

'Well in *our* country,' said Alice, still panting a little, 'you'd generally get to somewhere else – if you ran very fast for a long time, as we've been doing.'

'A slow sort of country!' said the Queen. 'Now, here, you see, it takes all the running you can do, to keep in the same place. If you want to get somewhere else, you must run at least twice as fast as that!'

'If I wasn't real,' Alice said – half laughing through her tears, it all seemed so ridiculous – 'I shouldn't be able to cry.'

'I hope you don't suppose those are real tears?' Tweedledum interrupted in a tone of great contempt.

—*Through the Looking-Glass*

CHAPTER 1

IT was clearly going to be a bad crossing.

With Asiatic resignation Father Rothschild S.J. put down his suitcase in the corner of the bar and went on deck. (It was a small suitcase of imitation crocodile hide. The initials stamped on it in Gothic characters were not Father Rothschild's, for he had borrowed it that morning from the *valet-de-chambre* of his hotel. It contained some rudimentary underclothes, six important new books in six languages, a false beard and a school atlas and gazetteer heavily annotated.) Standing on the deck Father Rothschild leant his elbows on the rail, rested his chin in his hands and surveyed the procession of passengers coming up the gangway, each face eloquent of polite misgiving.

Very few of them were unknown to the Jesuit, for it was his happy knack to remember everything that could possibly be learned about everyone who could possibly be of any importance. His tongue protruded very slightly and, had they not all been so concerned with luggage and the weather, someone might have observed in him a peculiar resemblance to those plaster reproductions of the gargoyles of Notre Dame which may be seen in the shop windows of artists' colourmen tinted the colour of 'Old Ivory', peering intently from among stencil outfits and plasticine and tubes of water-colour paint. High above his head swung Mrs Melrose Ape's travel-worn Packard car, bearing the dust of three continents, against the darkening sky, and up the companion-way at the head of her angels strode Mrs Melrose Ape, the woman evangelist.

'Faith.'

'Here, Mrs Ape.'

'Charity.'

'Here, Mrs Ape.'

'Fortitude.'

'Here, Mrs Ape.'

'Chastity.... Where is Chastity?'

'Chastity didn't feel well, Mrs Ape. She went below.'

'That girl's more trouble than she's worth. Whenever there's any packing to be done, Chastity doesn't feel well. Are all the rest here – Humility, Prudence, Divine Discontent, Mercy, Justice and Creative Endeavour?'

'Creative Endeavour lost her wings, Mrs Ape. She got talking to a gentleman in the train.... Oh, there she is.'

'Got 'em?' asked Mrs Ape.

Too breathless to speak, Creative Endeavour nodded. (Each of the angels carried her wings in a little black box like a violin case.)

'Right,' said Mrs Ape, 'and just you hold on to 'em tight and not so much talking to gentlemen in trains. You're angels, not a panto, see?'

The angels crowded together disconsolately. It was awful when Mrs Ape was like this. My, how they would pinch Chastity and Creative Endeavour when they got them alone in their nightshirts. It was bad enough their going to be so sick without that they had Mrs Ape pitching into them too.

Seeing their discomfort, Mrs Ape softened and smiled. She was nothing if not 'magnetic'.

'Well, girls,' she said, 'I must be getting along. They say it's going to be rough, but don't you believe it. If you have peace in your hearts your stomach will look after itself, and remember if you *do* feel queer – *sing*. There's nothing like it.'

'Good-bye, Mrs Ape, and thank you,' said the angels; they bobbed prettily, turned about and trooped aft to the second-class part of the ship. Mrs Ape watched them benignly, then, squaring her shoulders and looking (except that she had really no beard to speak of) every inch a sailor, strode resolutely forrard to the first-class bar.

*

Other prominent people were embarking, all very unhappy about the weather; to avert the terrors of sea-sickness they had indulged in every kind of civilized witchcraft, but they were lacking in faith.

Miss Runcible was there, and Miles Malpractice, and all the Younger Set. They had spent a jolly morning strapping each other's tummies with sticking plaster (how Miss Runcible had wriggled).

The Right Honourable Walter Outrage, M.P., last week's Prime Minister, was there. Before breakfast that morning (which had suffered in consequence) Mr Outrage had taken twice the maximum dose of a patent preparation of chloral, and losing heart later had finished the bottle in the train. He moved in an uneasy trance, closely escorted by the most public-looking detective sergeants. These men had been with Mr Outrage in Paris, and what they did not know about his goings on was not worth knowing, at least from a novelist's point of view. (When they spoke about him to each other they called him 'the Right Honourable Rape', but that was more by way of being a pun about his name than a criticism of the conduct of his love affairs, in which, if the truth were known, he displayed a notable diffidence and the liability to panic.)

*

Lady Throbbing and Mrs Blackwater, those twin sisters whose portrait by Millais auctioned recently at Christie's made a record in rock-bottom prices, were sitting on one of the teak benches eating apples and drinking what Lady Throbbing, with late Victorian *chic*, called 'a bottle of pop', and Mrs Blackwater, more exotically, called '*champagne*', pronouncing it as though it were French.

'Surely, Kitty, that is Mr Outrage, last week's Prime Minister.'

'Nonsense, Fanny, where?'

'Just in front of the two men with bowler hats, next to the clergyman.'

'It is certainly like his photographs. How strange he looks.'

'Just like poor Throbbing... all that last year.'

'... And none of us even suspected... until they found the bottles under the board in his dressing-room... and we all used to think it was drink...'

'I don't think one finds *quite* the same class as Prime Minister nowadays, do you think?'

'They say that only *one* person *has* any influence with Mr Outrage...'

'At the Japanese Embassy...'

'Of course, dear, not so loud. But tell me, Fanny, seriously, do you think really and truly Mr Outrage has IT?'

'He has a very nice figure for a man of his age.'

'Yes, but *his* age, and the bull-like type is so often disappointing. Another glass? You will be grateful for it when the ship begins to move.'

'I quite thought we *were* moving.'

'How absurd you are, Fanny, and yet I can't help laughing.'

So arm in arm and shaken by little giggles the two tipsy old ladies went down to their cabin.

Of the other passengers, some had filled their ears with cotton-wool, others wore smoked glasses, while several ate dry captain's biscuits from paper bags, as Red Indians are said to eat snake's flesh to make them cunning. Mrs Hoop repeated feverishly over and over again a formula she had learned from a yogi in New York City. A few 'good sailors', whose luggage bore the labels of many voyages, strode aggressively about smoking small, foul pipes and trying to get up a four of bridge.

Two minutes before the advertised time of departure, while the first admonitory whistling and shouting was going on, a young man came on board carrying his bag. There was nothing particularly remarkable about his appearance. He looked exactly as young men like him do look; he was carrying his own bag, which was disagreeably heavy, because he had no money left in francs and very little left in anything else. He had been two months in Paris writing a book and was coming home because, in the course of his correspondence, he had got engaged to be married. His name was Adam Fenwick-Symes.

Father Rothschild smiled at him in a kindly manner.

'I doubt whether you remember me,' he said. 'We met at Oxford five years ago at luncheon with the Dean of Balliol. I shall be interested to read your book when it appears – an autobiography, I understand. And may I be one of the first to congratulate you on your engagement? I am afraid you will find your father-in-law a little eccentric – and forgetful. He had a nasty attack of bronchitis this winter. It's a draughty house – far too big for these days. Well, I must go below now. It is going to be rough and I am a bad sailor. We meet at Lady Metroland's on the twelfth, if not, as I hope, before.'

Before Adam had time to reply the Jesuit disappeared. Suddenly the head popped back.

'There is an extremely dangerous and disagreeable woman on board – a Mrs Ape.'

Then he was gone again, and almost at once the boat began to slip away from the quay towards the mouth of the harbour.

Sometimes the ship pitched and sometimes she rolled and sometimes she stood quite still and shivered all over, poised above an abyss of dark water; then she would go swooping down like a scenic railway train into a windless hollow and up again with a rush into the gale; sometimes she would burrow her path, with convulsive nosings and scramblings like a terrier in a rabbit hole; and sometimes she would drop dead like a lift. It was this last movement that caused the most havoc among the passengers.

'Oh,' said the Bright Young People, 'Oh, oh oh.'

'It's just exactly like being inside a cocktail shaker,' said Miles Malpractice. 'Darling, your face – eau de Nil.'

'Too, too sick-making,' said Miss Runcible, with one of her rare flashes of accuracy.

*

Kitty Blackwater and Fanny Throbbing lay one above the other in their bunks rigid from wig to toe.

'I wonder, do you think the *champagne*...?'

'Kitty.'

'Yes, Fanny, dear.'

'Kitty, I think, in fact, I am sure I have some sal volatile.... Kitty, I thought that perhaps as you are nearer... it would really hardly be safe for me to try and descend... I might break a leg.'

'Not after *champagne*, Fanny, do you think?'

'But I need it. Of course, dear, *if it's too much trouble*?'

'Nothing is too much trouble, darling, you know that. But now I come to think of it, I remember, quite clearly, for a fact, that you did *not* pack the sal volatile.'

'Oh, Kitty, oh, Kitty, please... you would be sorry for this if I died... oh.'

'But I saw the sal volatile on your dressing-table after your luggage had gone down, dear. I remember thinking, I must take that down to Fanny, and then, dear, I got confused over the tips, so you see...'

'I... put... it... in... myself.... Next to my brushes... you... beast.'

'Oh, Fanny...'

'Oh... Oh... Oh.'

*

To Father Rothschild no passage was worse than any other. He thought of the sufferings of the saints, the mutability of human nature, the Four Last Things, and between whiles repeated snatches of the penitential psalms.

*

The Leader of his Majesty's Opposition lay sunk in a rather glorious coma, made splendid by dreams of Oriental imagery – of painted paper houses; of golden dragons and gardens of almond blossom; of golden limbs and almond eyes, humble and caressing; of very small golden feet among almond blossoms; of little painted cups full of golden tea; of a golden voice singing behind a painted paper screen; of humble, caressing little golden hands and eyes shaped like almonds and the colour of night.

Outside his door two very limp detective sergeants had deserted their posts.

'The bloke as could make trouble on a ship like this 'ere deserves to get away with it,' they said.

The ship creaked in every plate, doors slammed, trunks fell about, the wind howled; the screw, now out of the water, now in, raced and churned, shaking down hat-boxes like ripe apples; but above all the roar and clatter there rose from the second-class ladies' saloon the despairing voices of Mrs Ape's angels, in frequently broken unison, singing, singing, wildly, desperately, as though their hearts would break in the effort and their minds lose their reason, Mrs Ape's famous hymn, *There ain't no flies on the Lamb of God.*

*

The Captain and the Chief Officer sat on the bridge engrossed in a crossword puzzle.

'Looks like we may get some heavy weather if the wind gets up,' he said. 'Shouldn't wonder if there wasn't a bit of a sea running to-night.'

'Well, we can't always have it quiet like this,' said the Chief Officer. 'Word of eighteen letters meaning carnivorous mammal. Search me if I know how they do think of these things.'

*

Adam Fenwick-Symes sat among the good sailors in the smoking-room drinking his third Irish whiskey and wondering how soon he would feel definitely ill. Already there was a vague depression gathering at the top of his head. There were thirty-five minutes more, probably longer with the head wind keeping them back.

Opposite him sat a much-travelled and chatty journalist telling him smutty stories. From time to time Adam interposed some more or less appropriate comment, 'No, I say that's a good one', or, 'I must remember that', or just 'Ha, Ha, Ha', but his mind was not really in a receptive condition.

Up went the ship, up, up, up, paused and then plunged down with a sidelong slither. Adam caught at his glass and saved it. Then shut his eyes.

'Now I'll tell you a drawing-room one,' said the journalist.

Behind them a game of cards was in progress among the commercial gents. At first they had rather a jolly time about it, saying, 'What ho, she bumps', or 'Steady, the Buffs', when the cards and glasses and ash-tray were thrown on to the floor, but in the last ten minutes they were growing notably quieter. It was rather a nasty kind of hush.

'... And forty aces and two-fifty for the rubber. Shall we cut again or stay as we are?'

'How about knocking off for a bit? Makes me tired – table moving about all the time.'

'Why, Arthur, you ain't feeling ill, surely?'

' 'Course I ain't feeling ill, only tired.'

'Well, of course, if Arthur's feeling ill ...'

'Who'd have thought of old Arthur feeling ill?'

'I ain't feeling ill, I tell you. Just tired. But if you boys want to go on I'm not the one to spoil a game.'

'Good old Arthur. 'Course he ain't feeling ill. Look out for the cards, Bill, up she goes again.'

'What about one all round? Same again?'

'Same again.'

'Good luck, Arthur.' 'Good luck.' 'Here's fun.' 'Down she goes.'

'Whose deal? You dealt last, didn't you, Mr Henderson?'

'Yes, Arthur's deal.'

'Your deal, Arthur. Cheer up, old scout.'

'Don't you go doing that. It isn't right to hit a chap on the back like that.'

'Look out with the cards, Arthur.'

'Well, what d'you expect, being hit on the back like that. Makes me tired.'

'Here, I got fifteen cards.'

'I wonder if you've heard this one,' said the journalist. 'There was a man lived at Aberdeen, and he was terribly keen on fishing, so when he married, he married a woman with worms. That's rich, eh? You see he was keen on fishing, see, and she had worms, see, he lived in Aberdeen. That's a good one, that is.'

'D'you know, I think I shall go on deck for a minute. A bit stuffy in here, don't you think?'

'You can't do that. The sea's coming right over it all the time. Not feeling queer, are you?'

'No, of course I'm not feeling queer. I only thought a little fresh air.... Christ, why don't the damn thing stop?'

'Steady, old boy. I wouldn't go trying to walk about, not if I were you. Much better stay just where you are. What you want is a spot of whisky.'

'Not feeling ill, you know. Just stuffy.'

'That's all right, old boy. Trust Auntie.'

The bridge party was not being a success.

'Hullo, Mr Henderson. What's that spade?'

'That's the ace, that is.'

'I can see it's the ace. What I mean you didn't ought to have trumped that last trick not if you had a spade.'

'What d'you mean, didn't ought to have trumped it? Trumps led.'

'No, they did *not.* Arthur led a spade.'

'He led a trump, didn't you, Arthur?'

'Arthur led a spade.'

'He couldn't have led a spade because for why he put a heart on my king of spades when I thought he had the queen. He hasn't got no spades.'

'What d'you mean, not got no spades? I got the queen.'

'Arthur, old man, you *must* be feeling queer.'

'No, I ain't, I tell you, just tired. You'd be tired if you'd been hit on the back same as I was... anyway I'm fed up with this game... there go the cards again.'

This time no one troubled to pick them up. Presently Mr Henderson said, 'Funny thing, don't know why I feel all swimmy of a sudden. Must have ate something that wasn't quite right. You never can tell with foreign foods – all messed up like they do.'

'Now you mention it, I don't feel too spry myself. Damn bad ventilation on these Channel boats.'

'That's what it is. Ventilation. You said it.'

'You know I'm funny. I never feel sea-sick, mind, but I often find going on boats doesn't agree with me.'

'I'm like that, too.'

'Ventilation . . . a disgrace.'

'Lord, I shall be glad when we get to Dover. Home, sweet home, eh?'

Adam held on very tightly to the brass-bound edge of the table and felt a little better. He was *not* going to be sick, and that was that; not with that gargoyle of a man opposite anyway. They *must* be in sight of land soon.

*

It was at this time, when things were at their lowest, that Mrs Ape reappeared in the smoking-room. She stood for a second or two in the entrance balanced between swinging door and swinging door-post; then, as the ship momentarily righted herself, she strode to the bar, her feet well apart, her hands in the pockets of her tweed coat.

'Double rum,' she said and smiled magnetically at the miserable little collection of men seated about the room. 'Why, boys,' she said, 'but you're looking terrible put out over something. What's it all about? Is it your souls that's wrong or is it that the ship won't keep still? Rough? 'Course it's rough. But let me ask you this. If you're put out this way over just an hour's sea-sickness' ('Not seasick, ventilation,' said Mr Henderson mechanically), 'what are you going to be like when you make the mighty big journey that's waiting for us all? Are you right with God?' said Mrs Ape. 'Are you prepared for death?'

'Oh, am I not?' said Arthur. 'I 'aven't thought of nothing else for the last half-hour.'

'Now, boys, I'll tell you what we're going to do. We're going to sing a song together, you and me.' ('Oh, God,' said Adam.) 'You may not know it, but you are. You'll feel better for it body *and* soul. It's a song of Hope. You don't hear much about Hope these days, do you? Plenty about Faith, plenty about Charity. They've forgotten all about Hope. There's only one great evil in the world to-day. Despair. I know all about England, and I tell you straight, boys, I've got the goods for you. Hope's what you want and Hope's what I got. Here, steward, hand round these leaflets. There's the song on the back. Now all together . . . sing. Five bob for you, steward, if you can shout me down. Splendid, all together, boys.'

In a rich, very audible voice Mrs Ape led the singing. Her arms rose, fell and fluttered with the rhythm of the song. The bar steward was hers already – inaccurate sometimes in his reading of the words, but with a sustained power in the low notes that defied competition. The journalist joined in next and Arthur set up a little hum. Soon they were all at it, singing like blazes, and it is undoubtedly true that they felt the better for it.

*

Father Rothschild heard it and turned his face to the wall.

*

Kitty Blackwater heard it.

'Fanny.'

'Well.'

'Fanny, dear, do you hear singing?'

'Yes, dear, thank you.'

'Fanny, dear, I hope they aren't holding a *service*. I mean, dear, it sounds so like a hymn. Do you think, possibly, we are *in danger*? Fanny, are we going to be wrecked?'

'I should be neither surprised nor sorry.'

'Darling, how can you? . . . We should have heard it, shouldn't we, if we had actually *hit* anything? . . . Fanny, dear, if you like I will have a look for your sal volatile.'

'I hardly think that would be any help, dear, since you *saw* it on my dressing-table.'

'I may have been mistaken.'

'You *said* you *saw* it.'

*

The Captain heard it. 'All the time I been at sea,' he said, 'I never could stand for missionaries.'

'Word of six letters beginning with ZB,' said the Chief Officer, 'meaning "used in astronomic calculation".'

'Z can't be right,' said the Captain after a few minutes' thought.

*

The Bright Young People heard it. 'So like one's first parties,' said Miss Runcible, 'being sick with other people singing.'

*

Mrs Hoop heard it. 'Well,' she thought, 'I'm through with theosophy after this journey. Reckon I'll give the Catholics the once over.'

*

Aft, in the second-class saloon, where the screw was doing its worst, the angels heard it. It was some time since they had given up singing.

'Her again,' said Divine Discontent.

*

Mr Outrage alone lay happily undisturbed, his mind absorbed in lovely dream sequences of a world of little cooing voices, so caressing, so humble; and dark eyes, night-coloured, the shape of almonds over painted paper screens; little golden bodies, so flexible, so firm, so surprising in the positions they assumed.

*

They were still singing in the smoking-room when, in very little more than her usual time, the ship came into the harbour at Dover. Then Mrs Ape, as was her invariable rule, took round the hat and collected nearly two pounds, not counting her own five shillings which she got back from the bar steward.

'Salvation doesn't do them the same good if they think it's free,' was her favourite axiom.

CHAPTER 2

'HAVE you anything to declare?'

'Wings.'

'Have you wore them?'

'Sure.'

'That's all right, then.'

'Divine Discontent gets all the smiles all the time,' complained Fortitude to Prudence. 'Golly, but it's good to be on dry land.'

Unsteadily, but with renewed hope, the passengers had disembarked.

Father Rothschild fluttered a diplomatic *laissez-passer* and disappeared in the large car that had been sent to meet him. The others were jostling one another with their luggage, trying to attract the Customs officers and longing for a cup of tea.

'I got half a dozen of the best stowed away,' confided the journalist. 'They're generally pretty easy after a bad crossing.' And sure enough he was soon settled in the corner of a first-class carriage (for the paper was, of course, paying his expenses) with his luggage safely chalked in the van.

It was some time before Adam could get attended to.

'I've nothing but some very old clothes and some books,' he said.

But here he showed himself deficient in tact, for the man's casual air disappeared in a flash.

'Books, eh?' he said. 'And what sort of books, may I ask?'

'Look for yourself.'

'Thank *you*, that's what I mean to do. *Books*, indeed.'

Adam wearily unstrapped and unlocked his suitcase.

'Yes,' said the Customs officer menacingly, as though his worst suspicions had been confirmed, 'I should just about say you had got some books.'

One by one he took the books out and piled them on the counter. A copy of Dante excited his especial disgust.

'French, eh?' he said. 'I guessed as much, and pretty dirty, too, I shouldn't wonder. Now just you wait while I look up these here *books*' – how he said it! – 'in my list. Particularly against books the Home Secretary is. If we can't stamp out literature in the country, we can at least stop its being brought in from outside. That's what he said the other day in Parliament, and I says "Hear, hear. . . . " Hullo, hullo, what's this, may I ask?'

Gingerly, as though it might at any moment explode, he produced and laid on the counter a large pile of typescript.

'That's a book, too,' said Adam. 'One I've just written. It is my memoirs.'

'Ho, it is, is it? Well, I'll take that along, too, to the chief. You better come too.'

'But I've got to catch the train.'

'You come along. There's worse things than missing trains,' he hinted darkly.

They went together into an inner office, the walls of which were lined with contraband pornography and strange instruments, whose purpose Adam could not guess. From the next room came the shrieks and yells of poor Miss Runcible, who had been mistaken for a well-known jewel smuggler, and was being stripped to the skin by two terrific wardresses.

'Now then, what's this about books?' said the chief.

With the help of a printed list (which began 'Aristotle, Works of (Illustrated)' they went through Adam's books, laboriously, one at a time, spelling out the titles.

Miss Runcible came through the office, working hard with lipstick and compact.

'Adam, darling, I never saw you on the boat,' she said. 'My dear, I can't *tell* you the *things* that have been happening to me in there. The way they looked . . . too, too shaming. Positively surgical, my dear, and *such* wicked old women, just like *Dowagers*, my dear. As soon as I get to London I shall just ring up every Cabinet Minister and *all* the newspapers and give them all the most shy-making details.'

The chief was at this time engrossed in Adam's memoirs, giving vent at intervals to a sinister chuckling sound that was partly triumphant and partly derisive, but in the main genuinely appreciative.

'Coo, Bert,' he said. 'Look at this; that's rich, ain't it?'

Presently he collected the sheets, tied them together and put them on one side.

'Well, see here,' he said. 'You can take these books on architecture and the dictionary, and I don't mind stretching a point for once and letting you have the history books, too. But this book on Economics comes under Subversive Propaganda. That you leaves behind. And this here *Purgatorio* doesn't look right to me, so that stays behind, pending inquiries. But as for this autobiography, that's just downright dirt, and we burns that straight away, see.'

'But, good heavens, there isn't a word in the book – you must be misinterpreting it.'

'Not so much of it. I knows dirt when I sees it or I shouldn't be where I am to-day.'

'But do you realize that my whole livelihood depends on this book?'

'And *my* livelihood depends on stopping works like this coming into the country. Now 'ook it quick if you don't want a police-court case.'

'Adam, angel, don't fuss or we shall miss the train.'

Miss Runcible took his arm and led him back to the station and told him all about a lovely party that was going to happen that night.

*

'*Queer*, who felt queer?'

'You did, Arthur.'

'No I never . . . just tired.'

'It certainly was stuffy in there just for a bit.'

'Wonderful how that old girl cheered things up. Got a meeting next week in the Albert Hall.'

'Shouldn't be surprised if I didn't go. What do you say, Mr Henderson?'

'She got a troupe of angels, so she said. All dressed up in white with wings, lovely. Not a bad-looker herself, if it comes to that.'

'What did you put in the plate, Arthur?'

'Half-crown.'

'So did I. Funny thing, I ain't never give a half-crown like that before. She kind of draws it out of you, damned if she doesn't.'

'You won't get away from the Albert Hall not without putting your hand in your pocket.'

'No, but I'd like to see those angels dressed up, eh, Mr Henderson?'

*

'Fanny, surely that is Agatha Runcible, poor Viola Chasm's daughter?'

'I wonder Viola allows her to go about like that. If she were my daughter . . . '

'*Your* daughter, Fanny. . . . '

'Kitty, that was not kind.'

'My dear, I only meant . . . have you, by the way, heard of her lately?'

'The last we heard was worse than anything, Kitty. She has left Buenos Aires. I am afraid she has severed her connection with Lady Metroland altogether. They think that she is in some kind of touring company.'

'Darling, I'm sorry. I should never have mentioned it, but whenever I see Agatha Runcible I can't help thinking . . . girls seem to know so much nowadays. We had to learn everything for ourselves, didn't we, Fanny, and it took so long. If I'd had Agatha Runcible's chances . . . Who is the young man with her?'

'I don't know, and frankly, I don't think, do you? . . . He has that self-contained look.'

'He has very nice eyes. And he moves well.'

'I dare say when it came to the point . . . Still, as I say, if I had had Agatha Runcible's advantages . . . '

'What are you looking for, darling?'

'Why, darling, such an extraordinary thing. Here is the sal volatile next to my brushes all the time.'

'Fanny, how awful of me, if I'd only known...'

'I dare say there must have been another bottle you saw on the dressing-table, sweetest. Perhaps the maid put it there. You never know at the Lotti, do you?'

'Fanny, forgive me....'

'But, dearest, what is there to forgive? After all, you *did see* another bottle, didn't you, Kitty darling?'

'Why, look, there's Miles.'

'Miles?'

'Your son, darling. My nephew, you know.'

'*Miles*. Do you know, Kitty, I believe it is. He never comes to see me now, the naughty boy.'

'My dear, he looks terribly *tapette*.'

'Darling, I know. It is a great grief to me. Only I try not to think about it too much – he had so little chance with poor Throbbing what he was.'

'The sins of the fathers, Fanny...'

*

Somewhere not far from Maidstone Mr Outrage became fully conscious. Opposite him in the carriage the two detectives slept, their bowler hats jammed forwards on their foreheads, their mouths open, their huge red hands lying limply in their laps. Rain beat on the windows; the carriage was intensely cold and smelt of stale tobacco. Inside there were advertisements of horrible picturesque ruins; outside in the rain were hoardings advertising patent medicines and dog biscuits. 'Every Molassine dog cake wags a tail,' Mr Outrage read, and the train repeated over and over again, 'Right Honourable gent, Right Honourable gent, Right Honourable gentleman, Right Honourable gent...'

*

Adam got into the carriage with the Younger Set. They still looked a bit queer, but they cheered up wonderfully when they heard about Miss Runcible's outrageous treatment at the hands of the Customs officers.

'*Well*,' they said, '*Well!* how too, too shaming, Agatha, darling,' they said. 'How devastating, how unpoliceman-like, how goat-like, how sick-making, how too, too awful.' And then they began talking about Archie Schwert's party that night.

'Who's Archie Schwert?' asked Adam.

'Oh, he's someone new since you went away. The *most* bogus man. Miles discovered him, and since then he's been climbing and climbing and *climbing*, my dear, till he hardly knows us. He's rather sweet, really, only too terribly common, poor darling. He lives at the Ritz, and I think that's rather grand, don't you?'

'Is he giving his party there?'

'My dear, of course not. In Edward Throbbing's house. He's Miles' brother, you know, only he's frightfully dim and political, and doesn't know anybody. He got ill and went to Kenya or somewhere and left his perfectly sheepish house in Hertford Street, so we've all gone to live there. You'd better come, too. The caretakers didn't like it a bit at first, but we gave them drinks and things, and now they're simply thrilled to the marrow about it and spend all their time cutting out "bits", my dear, from the papers about our goings on.

'One awful thing is we haven't got a car. Miles broke it, Edward's, I mean, and we simply can't afford to get it mended, so I think we shall have to move soon. Everything's getting rather broken up, too, and dirty, if you know what I mean. Because, you see, there aren't any servants, only the butler and his wife, and they are always tight now. So demoralizing. Mary Mouse has been a perfect angel, and sent us great hampers of caviare and things.... She's paying for Archie's party to-night, of course.'

'Do you know, I rather think I'm going to be sick again?'

'Oh, Miles!'

(Oh, Bright Young People!)

*

Packed all together in a second-class carriage, the angels were late in recovering their good humour.

'She's taken Prudence off in her car again,' said Divine Discontent, who once, for one delirious fortnight, had been Mrs Ape's favourite girl. 'Can't see what she sees in her. What's London like, Fortitude? I never been there but once.'

'Just exactly heaven. Shops and all.'

'What are the men like, Fortitude?'

'Say, don't you never think of nothing but *men*, Chastity?'

'I should say I do. I was only asking.'

'Well, they ain't much to look at, not after the shops. But they has their uses.'

'Say, did you hear that? You're a cute one, Fortitude. Did you hear what Fortitude said? She said "they have their uses".'

'What, shops?'

'No, silly, men.'

'*Men*. That's a good one, I should say.'

Presently the train arrived at Victoria, and all these passengers were scattered all over London.

*

Adam left his bag at Shepheard's Hotel, and drove straight to Henrietta Street to see his publishers. It was nearly closing time, so that most of the staff had packed up and gone home, but by good fortune Mr Sam Benfleet, the junior director with whom Adam always did his business, was still in his room correcting proofs for one of his women novelists. He was a competent young man, with a restrained elegance of appearance (the stenographer always trembled slightly when she brought him his cup of tea).

'No, she can't print that,' he kept saying, endorsing one after another of the printer's protests. 'No, damn it, she can't print *that*. She'll have us all in prison.' For it was one of his most exacting duties to 'ginger up' the more reticent of the manuscripts submitted and 'tone down' the more 'outspoken' until he had reduced them all to the acceptable moral standard of his day.

He greeted Adam with the utmost cordiality.

'Well, well, Adam, how are you? This is nice. Sit down. Have a cigarette. What a day to arrive in London. Did you have a good crossing?'

'Not too good.'

'I say, I *am* sorry. Nothing so beastly as a beastly crossing, is there? Why don't you come round to dinner at Wimpole Street to-night? I've got some rather nice Americans coming. Where are you staying?'

'At "Shepheard's" – Lottie Crump's.'

'Well, that's always fun. I've been trying to get an autobiography out of Lottie for ten years. And that reminds me. You're bringing us your manuscript, aren't you? Old Rampole was asking about it only the other day. It's a week overdue, you know. I hope you'll like the preliminary notices we've sent out. We've fixed the day of publication for the second week in December, so as to give it a fortnight's run before Johnnie Hoop's autobiography. That's going to be a seller. Sails a bit near the wind in places. We had to cut out some things – you know what old Rampole is. Johnnie didn't like it a bit. But I'm looking forward terribly to reading yours.'

'Well, Sam, rather an awful thing happened about that…'

'I say, I hope you're not going to say it's not finished. The date on the contract, you know…'

'Oh, it's finished all right. Burnt.'

'Burnt?'

'Burnt.'

'What an awful thing. I hope you are insured.'

Adam explained the circumstances of the destruction of his autobiography. There was a longish pause while Sam Benfleet thought.

'What worries me is how are we going to make that sound convincing to old Rampole.'

'I should think it sounded convincing enough.'

'You don't know old Rampole. It's sometimes very difficult for me, Adam, working under him. Now if I had my own way I'd say, "Take your own time. Start again. Don't worry…" But there's old Rampole. He's a devil for contracts, you know, and you did *say*, didn't you . . . ? It's all very difficult. You know, I wish it hadn't happened.'

'So do I, oddly enough,' said Adam.

'There's another difficulty. You've had an advance already, haven't you? Fifty pounds, wasn't it? Well, you know, *that* makes things very difficult. Old Rampole never likes big advances like that to young authors. You know I hate to say it, but I can't help feeling that the best thing would be for you to repay the advance – plus interest, of course, old Rampole would insist on that – and cancel the contract. Then if you ever thought of rewriting the book, well, of course, we should be delighted to consider it. I suppose that – well, I mean, it *would* be quite *convenient*, and all that, to repay the advance?'

'Not only inconvenient, but impossible,' said Adam in no particular manner.

There was another pause.

'Deuced awkward,' said Sam Benfleet. 'It's a shame the way the Customs House officers are allowed to take the law into their own hands. Quite ignorant men, too. Liberty of the subject, I mean, and all that. I tell you what we'll do. We'll start a correspondence about it in the *New Statesman*. . . . It is all so deuced awkward. But I think I can see a way out. I suppose you could get the book rewritten in time for the Spring List? Well, we'll cancel the contract and forget all about the advance. No, no, my dear fellow, don't thank me. If only I was alone here I'd be doing that kind of thing all day. Now instead we'll have a new contract. It won't be quite so good as the last, I'm afraid. Old Rampole wouldn't stand for that. I'll tell you what, we'll give you our standard first-novel contract. I've got a printed form here. It won't take a minute to fill up. Just sign here.'

'May I just see the terms?'

'Of course, my dear fellow. They look a bit hard at first, I know, but it's our usual form. We made a very special case for you, you know. It's very simple. No royalty on the first two thousand, then a royalty of two and a half per cent, rising to five per cent on the tenth thousand. We retain serial, cinema, dramatic, American, Colonial and translation rights, of course. And, of course, an option on your next twelve books on the same terms. It's a very straightforward arrangement really. Doesn't leave room for any of the disputes which embitter the relations of author and publisher. Most of our authors are working on a contract like that.... Splendid. Now don't you bother any more about that advance. I understand *perfectly*, and I'll square old Rampole somehow, even if it comes out of my director's fees.'

'Square old Rampole,' repeated Mr Benfleet thoughtfully as Adam went downstairs. It was fortunate, he reflected, that none of the authors ever came across the senior partner, that benign old gentleman, who once a week drove up to board meetings from the country, whose chief interest in the business was confined to the progress of a little book of his own about bee-keeping, which they had published twenty years ago and, though he did not know it, allowed long ago to drop out of print. He often wondered in his uneasy moments what he would find to say when Rampole died.

*

It was about now that Adam remembered that he was engaged to be married. The name of his young lady was Nina Blount. So he went into a tube station to a telephone-box, which smelt rather nasty, and rang her up.

'Hullo.'

'Hullo.'

'May I speak to Miss Blount, please?'

'I'll just see if she's in,' said Miss Blount's voice. 'Who's speaking, please?' She was always rather snobbish about this fiction of having someone to answer the telephone.

'Mr Fenwick-Symes.'

'Oh.'

'Adam, you know.... How are you, Nina?'

'Well, I've got rather a pain just at present.'

'Poor Nina. Shall I come round and see you?'

'No, don't do that, darling, because I'm just going to have a bath. Why don't we dine together?'

'Well, I asked Agatha Runcible to dinner.'

'Why?'

'She'd just had all her clothes taken off by some sailors.'

'Yes, I know, it's all in the evening paper to-night.... Well, I'll tell you what. Let's meet at Archie Schwert's party. Are you going?'

'I rather said I would.'

'That's all right, then. Don't dress up. No one will, except Archie.'

'Oh, I say. Nina, there's one thing – I don't think I shall be able to marry you after all.'

'Oh, *Adam*, you are a bore. Why not?'

'They burnt my book.'

'Beasts. Who did?'

'I'll tell you about it to-night.'

'Yes, *do*. Good-bye, darling.'

'Good-bye, my sweet.'

He hung up the receiver and left the telephone-box. People had crowded into the Underground station for shelter from the rain, and were shaking their umbrellas and reading their evening papers. Adam could see the headlines over their shoulders.

PEER'S DAUGHTER'S DOVER ORDEAL

SERIOUS ALLEGATIONS BY SOCIETY BEAUTY

HON. A. RUNCIBLE SAYS

'TOO SHAMING'

'Poor pretty,' said an indignant old woman at his elbow. 'Disgraceful, I calls it. And such a good sweet face. I see her picture in the papers only yesterday. Nasty prying minds. That's what they got. And her poor father and all. Look, Jane, there's a piece about him, too. "Interviewed at the Carlton Club this evening, Lord Chasm", that's her dad, "refused to make a definite statement. 'The matter shall not be allowed to rest here,' he said." *And* quite right, too, I says. You know I feels about that girl just as though it was me own daughter. Seeing her picture so often and our Sarah having done the back stairs, Tuesdays, at them flats where her aunt used to live – the one as had that 'orrible divorce last year.'

Adam bought a paper. He had just ten shillings left in the world. It was too wet to walk, so he took a very crowded tube train to Dover Street and hurried across in the rain to Shepheard's Hotel (which, for the purposes of the narrative, may be assumed to stand at the corner of Hay Hill).

CHAPTER 3

LOTTIE CRUMP, proprietress of Shepheard's Hotel, Dover Street, attended invariably by two Cairn terriers, is a happy reminder to us that the splendours of the Edwardian era were not entirely confined to Lady Anchorage or Mrs Blackwater. She is a fine figure of a woman, singularly unscathed by any sort of misfortune and superbly oblivious of those changes in the social order which agitate the more observant *grandes dames* of her period. When the war broke out she took down the signed photograph of the Kaiser and, with some solemnity, hung it in the men-servants' lavatory; it was her one combative action; since then she has had her worries – income-tax forms and drink restrictions and young men whose fathers she used to know, who give her bad cheques, but these have been soon forgotten; one can go to Shepheard's parched with modernity any day, if Lottie likes one's face, and still draw up, cool and uncontaminated, great, healing draughts from the well of Edwardian certainty.

Shepheard's has a plain, neatly pointed brick front and large, plain doorway. Inside it is like a country house. Lottie is a great one for sales, and likes, whenever one of the great houses of her day is being sold up, to take away something for old times' sake. There is a good deal too much furniture at Shepheard's, some of it rare, some of it hideous beyond description; there is plenty of red plush and red morocco and innumerable wedding presents of the 'eighties; in particular many of those massive, mechanical devices covered with crests and monograms, and associated in some way with cigars. It is the sort of house in which one expects to find croquet mallets and polo sticks in the bathroom, and children's toys at the bottom of one's chest of drawers, and an estate map and an archery target – exuding straw – and a bicycle and one of those walking-sticks which turn into saws, somewhere in passages, between baize doors, smelling of damp. (As a matter of fact, all you are likely to find in your room at Lottie's is an empty champagne bottle or two and a crumpled camisole.)

The servants, like the furniture, are old and have seen aristocratic service. Doge, the head waiter, who is hard of hearing, partially blind, and tortured with gout, was once a Rothschild's butler. He had, in fact, on more than one occasion in Father Rothschild's youth, dandled him on his knee, when he came with his father (at one time the fifteenth richest man in the world) to visit his still richer cousins, but it would be unlike him to pretend that he ever really liked the embryo Jesuit who was 'too clever by half', given to asking extraordinary questions, and endowed with a penetrating acumen in the detection of falsehood and exaggeration.

Besides Doge, there are innumerable old housemaids always trotting about with cans of hot water and clean towels. There is also a young Italian who does most of the work and gets horribly insulted by Lottie, who once caught him powdering his nose, and will not let him forget it. Indeed, it is one of the few facts in Lottie's recent experience that seems always accessible.

Lottie's parlour, in which most of the life of Shepheard's centres, contains a comprehensive collection of signed photographs. Most of the male members of the royal families of Europe are represented (except the ex-Emperor of Germany, who has not been reinstated, although there was a distinct return of sentiment towards him on the occasion of his second marriage). There are photographs of young men on horses riding in steeple-chases, of elderly men leading in the winners of 'classic' races, of horses alone and of young men alone, dressed in tight, white collars or in the uniform of the Brigade of Guards. There are caricatures by 'Spy', the photographs cut from illustrated papers, many of them with brief obituary notices 'killed in action'. There are photographs of yachts in full sail and of elderly men in yachting caps; there are some funny pictures of the earliest kind of motor-car. There are very few writers or painters and no actors, for Lottie is true to the sound old snobbery of pound sterling and strawberry leaves.

Lottie was standing in the hall abusing the Italian waiter when Adam arrived.

'Well,' she said, 'you are a stranger. Come along in. We were just thinking about having a little drink. You'll find a lot of your friends here.'

She led Adam into the parlour, where they found several men, none of whom Adam had ever seen before.

'You all know Lord Thingummy, don't you?' said Lottie.

'Mr Symes,' said Adam.

'Yes, dear, that's what I said. Bless you, I knew you before you were born. How's your father? Not dead, is he?'

'Yes, I'm afraid he is.'

'Well, I never. I could tell you some things about him. Now let me introduce you – that's Mr What's-his-name, you remember him, don't you? And over there in the corner, that's the Major, and there's Mr What-d'you-call-him, and that's an American, and there's the King of Ruritania.'

'Alas, no longer,' said a sad, bearded man.

'Poor chap,' said Lottie Crump, who always had a weak spot for royalty, even when deposed. 'It's a shame. They gave him the boot after the war. Hasn't got a penny. Not that he ever did have much. His wife's locked up in a looney house, too.'

'Poor Maria Christina. It is true how Mrs Crump says. Her brains, they are quite gone out. All the time she thinks everyone is a bomb.'

'It's perfectly true, poor old girl,' said Lottie with relish. 'I drove the King down Saturday to see her...(I won't have him travelling third class). It fair brought tears to my eyes. Kept skipping about all the time, she did, dodging. Thought they were throwing things at her.'

'It is one strange thing, too,' said the King. 'All my family they have bombs thrown at them, but the Queen, never. My poor Uncle Joseph he blow all to bits one night at the opera, and my sister she find three bombs in her bed. But my wife, never. But one day her maid is brushing her hair before dinner, and she said, "Madam", she said, "the cook has had lesson from the cook at the French Legation" – the food at my home was not what you call *chic*. One day it was mutton hot, then mutton cold, then the same mutton hot again, but less nicer, not *chic*, you understand me – "he has had lesson from the French cook", the maid say, "and he has made one big bomb as a surprise for your dinner-party to-night for the Swedish Minister." Then the poor Queen say "Oh", like so, and since then always her poor brains has was all nohow.'

The ex-King of Ruritania sighed heavily and lit a cigar.

'Well,' said Lottie, brushing aside a tear, 'what about a little drink? Here, you over there, your Honour Judge What's-your-name, how about a drink for the gentlemen?'

The American, who, like all the listeners, had been profoundly moved by the ex-King's recitation, roused himself to bow and say, 'I shall esteem it a great honour if His Majesty and yourself, Mrs Crump, and these other good gentlemen . . . '

'That's the way,' said Lottie. 'Hi, there, where's my Fairy Prince? Powdering hisself again, I suppose. Come here, Nancy, and put away the beauty cream.'

In came the waiter.

'Bottle of wine,' said Lottie, 'with Judge Thingummy there.' (Unless specified in detail, all drinks are champagne in Lottie's parlour. There is also a mysterious game played with dice which always ends with someone giving a bottle of wine to everyone in the room, but Lottie has an equitable soul and she generally sees to it, in making up the bills, that the richest people pay for everything.)

After the third or fourth bottle of wine Lottie said, 'Who d'you think we've got dining upstairs to-night? *Prime Minister*.'

'Me, I have never liked Prime Ministers. They talk and talk and then they talk more. "Sir, you must sign that." "Sir, you must go here and there." "Sir, you must do up that button before you give audience to the black plenipotentiary from Liberia." Pah! After the war my people give me the bird, yes, but they throw my Prime Minister out of the window, bump right bang on the floor. Ha, ha.'

'He ain't alone either,' said Lottie with a terrific wink.

'What, Sir James Brown?' said the Major, shocked in spite of himself, 'I don't believe it.'

'No, name of Outrage.'

'He's not Prime Minister.'

'Yes he is. I saw it in the paper.'

'No, he's not. He went out of office last week.'

'Well I never. How they keep changing. I've no patience with it. Doge. Doge. What's the Prime Minister's name?'

'Beg pardon, mum.'

'What's the name of the Prime Minister?'

'Not to-night, I don't think, mum, not as I've been informed anyway.'

'What's the name of the Prime Minister, you stupid old man?'

'Oh, I beg your pardon, mum. I didn't quite hear you. Sir James Brown, mum, Bart. A very nice gentleman, so I've been told. Conservative, I've heard said. Gloucestershire they come from, I think.'

'There, what did I say?' said Lottie triumphantly.

'It is one very extraordinary thing, your British Constitution,' said the ex-King of Ruritania. 'All the time when I was young they taught me nothing but British Constitution. My tutor had been a master at your Eton school. And now when I come to England always there is a different Prime Minister and no one knows which is which.'

'Oh, sir,' said the Major, 'that's because of the Liberal Party.'

'Liberals? Yes. We, too, had Liberals. I tell you something now, I had a gold fountain-pen. My godfather, the good Archduke of Austria, give me one gold fountain-pen with eagles on him. I loved my gold fountain-pen.' Tears stood in the King's eyes. Champagne was a rare luxury to him now. 'I loved very well my pen with the little eagles. And one day there was a Liberal Minister. A Count Tampen, one man, Mrs Crump, of exceedingly evilness. He come to talk to me and he stood at my little escritoire and he thump and talk too much about somethings I not understand, and when he go – where was my gold fountain-pen with eagles – gone too.'

'Poor old King,' said Lottie. 'I tell you what. You have another drink.'

'... Esteem it a great honour,' said the American, 'if your Majesty and these gentlemen and Mrs Crump...'

'Doge, tell my little love-bird to come hopping in... you there, Judge wants another bottle of wine.'

'... Should honour it a great esteem... esteem it a great honour if Mrs Majesty and these gentlemen and His Crump...'

'That's all right, Judge. Another bottle coming.'

'... Should esteem it a great Crump if his honour and these Majesties and Mrs Gentlemen...'

'Yes, yes, that's all right, Judge. Don't let him fall down, boys. Bless me, how these Americans do drink.'

'... I should Crump it a great Majesty if Mrs Esteem...'

And his Honour Judge Skimp of the Federal High Court began to laugh rather a lot. (It must be remembered in all these people's favour that none of them had yet dined.)

Now there was a very bland, natty, moustachioed young man sitting there who had been drinking away quietly in the corner without talking to anyone except for an occasional 'Cheerioh' to Judge Skimp. Suddenly he got up and said:

'Bet-you-can't-do-this.'

He put three halfpennies on the table, moved them about very deliberately for a bit, and then looked up with an expression of pride. 'Only touched each half-penny five times, and changed their positions twice,' he said. 'Do-it-again if you like.'

'Well, isn't he a clever boy?' said Lottie. 'Wherever did they teach you that?'

'Chap-in-a-train showed me,' he said.

'It didn't look very hard,' said Adam.

'Just-you-try. Bet-you-anything-you-like you can't do it.'

'How much will you bet?' Lottie loved this kind of thing.

'Anything-you-like. Five hundred pounds.'

'Go on,' said Lottie. 'You do it. He's got lots of money.'

'All right,' said Adam.

He took the halfpennies and moved them about just as the young man had done. When he finished he said, 'How's that?'

'Well I'm jiggered,' said the young man. 'Never saw anyone do it like that before. I've won a lot of money this week with that trick. Here you are.' And he took out a note-case and gave Adam a five-hundred-pound note. Then he sat down in his corner again.

'Well,' said Lottie with approval, 'that's sporting. Give the boys a drink for that.'

So they all had another drink.

Presently the young man stood up again.

'Toss you double-or-quits,' he said. 'Best-out-of-three.'

'All right,' said Adam.

They tossed twice and Adam won both times.

'Well I'm jiggered,' said the young man, handing over another note. 'You are a lucky chap.'

'He's got pots of money,' said Lottie. 'A thousand pounds is nothing to him.'

She liked to feel like that about all her guests. Actually in this young man's case she was wrong. He happened to have all that money in his pocket because he had just sold out his few remaining securities to buy a new motor-car. So next day he bought a second-hand motor-bicycle instead.

Adam felt a little dizzy, so he had another drink.

'D'you mind if I telephone?' he said.

He rang up Nina Blount.

'Is that Nina?'

'Adam, dear, you're tight already.'

'How d'you know?'

'I can hear it. What is it? I'm just going out to dinner.'

'I just rang up to say that it's all right about our getting married. I've got a thousand pounds.'

'Oh, good. How?'

'I'll tell you when we meet. Where are you dining?'

'Ritz, Archie. Darling, I *am* glad about our getting married.'

'So am I. But don't let's get intense about it.'

'I wasn't, and anyway you're tight.'

He went back to the parlour. Miss Runcible had arrived and was standing in the hall very much dressed up.

'Who's that tart?' asked Lottie.

'That's not a tart, Lottie, that's Agatha Runcible.'

'Looks like a tart. How do you do, my dear, come in. We're just thinking of having a little drink. You know everyone here, of course, don't you? That's the King with the beard.... No, dearie, the King of Ruritania. You didn't mind my taking you for a tart, did you, dear? You look so like one, got up like that. Of course, I can see you aren't now.'

'*My dear*,' said Miss Runcible, 'if you'd seen me this afternoon...' and she began to tell Lottie Crump about the Customs House.

'What would you do if you suddenly got a thousand pounds?' Adam asked.

'A thousand *pound*,' said the King, his eyes growing dreamy at this absurd vision. 'Well, first I should buy a house and a motor-car and a yacht and a new pair of gloves, and then I would start one little newspaper in my country to say that I must come back and be the King, and then I don't know what I do, but have such fun and grandness again.'

'But you can't do all that with a thousand pounds, you know, sir.'

'No... can't I not?... not with thousand pound.... Oh, well, then I think I buy a gold pen with eagles on him like the Liberals stole.'

'I know what I'd do,' said the Major. 'I'd put it on a horse.'

'What horse?'

'I can tell you a likely outsider for the November Handicap. Horse named Indian Runner. It's at twenty to one at present, and the odds are likely to lengthen. Now if you were to put a thousand on him to win and he won, why you'd be rich, wouldn't you?'

'Yes, so I would. How marvellous. D'you know, I think I'll do that. It's a *very* good idea. How can I do it?'

'Just you give me the thousand and I'll arrange it.'

'I say, that's awfully nice of you.'

'Not at all.'

'No, really, I think that's frightfully nice of you. Look, here's the money. Have a drink, won't you?'

'No, you have one with me.'

'I said it first.'

'Let's both have one, then.'

'Wait a minute though, I must go and telephone about this.'

He rang up the Ritz and got on to Nina.

'Darling, you do telephone a lot, don't you?'

'Nina, I've something very important to say.'

'Yes, darling.'

'Nina, have you heard of a horse called Indian Runner?'

'Yes, I think so. Why?'

'What sort of a horse is it?'

'My dear, quite the worst sort of horse. Mary Mouse's mother owns it.'

'Not a good horse?'

'No.'

'Not likely to win the November Handicap, I mean.'

'Quite sure not to. I don't suppose it'll run even. Why?'

'I say, Nina, d'you know I don't think we shall be able to get married after all.'

'Why not, my sweet?'

'You see, I've put my thousand pounds on Indian Runner.'

'That was silly. Can't you get it back?'

'I gave it to a Major.'

'What sort of a Major?'

'Rather a drunk one. I don't know his name.'

'Well, I should try and catch him. I must go back and eat now. Good-bye.'

But when he got back to Lottie's parlour the Major was gone.

'What Major?' said Lottie, when he asked about him. 'I never saw a Major.'

'The one you introduced me to in the corner.'

'How d'you know he's a Major?'

'You said he was.'

'My dear boy, I've never seen him before. Now I come to think of it, he did look like a Major, didn't he? But this sweet little girlie here is telling me a story. Go on, my dear. I can hardly bear to hear it, it's so wicked.'

While Miss Runcible finished her story (which began to sound each time she told it more and more like the most lubricous kind of anti-Turkish propaganda) the ex-King of Ruritania told Adam about a Major *he* had known, who had come from Prussia to reorganize the Ruritanian Army. He had disappeared south, taking with him all the mess plate of the Royal Guard, and the Lord Chamberlain's wife, and a valuable pair of candle-sticks from the Chapel Royal.

By the time Miss Runcible had finished, Lottie was in a high state of indignation.

'The very idea of it,' she said. 'The dirty hounds. And I used to know your poor father, too, before you were born *or* thought of. I'll talk to the Prime Minister about this,' she said, taking up the telephone. 'Give me Outrage,' she said to the exchange boy. 'He's up in number twelve with a Japanese.'

'Outrage isn't Prime Minister, Lottie.'

'Of course he is. Didn't Doge say so. . . . Hullo, is that Outrage? This is Lottie. A fine chap you are, I don't think. Tearing the clothes off the back of a poor innocent girl.'

Lottie prattled on.

Mr Outrage had finished dinner, and, as matter of fact, the phrasing of this accusation was not wholly inappropriate to his mood. It was some minutes before he began to realize that all this talk was only about Miss Runcible. By that time Lottie's flow of invective had come to an end, but she finished finely.

'Outrage your name, and Outrage your nature,' she said, banging down the receiver. 'And that's what I think of *him*. Now how about a little drink?'

But her party was breaking up. The Major was gone. Judge Skimp was sleeping, his fine white hair in an ashtray. Adam and Miss Runcible were talking about where they would dine. Soon only the King remained. He gave her his arm with a grace he had acquired many years ago; far away in his sunny little palace, under a great chandelier which scattered with stars of light like stones from a broken necklace, a crimson carpet woven with a pattern of crowned ciphers.

So Lottie and the King went in to dinner together.

Upstairs in No. 12, which is a suite of notable grandeur, Mr Outrage was sliding back down the path of self-confidence he had so laboriously climbed. He really would have brought matters to a crisis if it had not been for that telephone, he told himself, but now the Baroness was saying she was sure he was busy, must be wanting her to go: would he order her car.

It was so difficult. For a European the implications of an invitation to dinner *tête-à-tête* in a private room at Shepheard's were definitely clear. Her acceptance on the first night of his return to England had thrown him into a flutter of expectation. But all through dinner she had been so self-possessed, so supremely social. Yet, surely, just before the telephone rang, surely then, when they left the table and moved to the fire, there had been *something* in the atmosphere. But you never know with Orientals. He clutched his knees and said in a voice which sounded very extraordinary to him, must she go, it was lovely after a fortnight, and then, desperately, he had thought of her in Paris such a lot. (Oh, for words, words! That massed treasury of speech that was his to squander at will, to send bowling and spinning in golden pieces over the floor of the House of Commons; that glorious largesse of vocables he cast far and wide, in ringing handfuls about his constituency!)

The little Baroness Yoshiwara, her golden hands clasped in the lap of her golden Paquin frock, sat where she had been sent, more puzzled than Mr Outrage, waiting for orders. What did the clever Englishman want? If he was busy with his telephone, why did he not send her away; tell her another time to come: if he wanted to be loved, why did he not tell her to come over to him? Why did he not pick her out of her red plush chair and sit her on his knee? Was she, perhaps, looking ugly to-night? She had thought not. It was so hard to know what these Occidentals wanted.

Then the telephone rang again.

'Will you hold on a minute? Father Rothschild wants to speak to you,' said a voice. '... Is that you, Outrage? Will you be good enough to come round and see me as soon as you can? There are several things which I must discuss with you.'

'Really, Rothschild... I don't see why I should. I have a guest.'

'The baroness had better return immediately. The waiter who brought you your coffee has a brother at the Japanese Embassy.'

'Good God, has he? But why don't you go and worry Brown? He's P.M., you know, not me.'

'You will be in office to-morrow.... As soon as possible, please, at my usual address.'

'Oh, all right.'

'Why, of course.'

CHAPTER 4

AT Archie Schwert's party the fifteenth Marquess of Vanburgh, Earl Vanburgh de Brendon, Baron Brendon, Lord of the Five Isles and Hereditary Grand Falconer to the Kingdom of Connaught, said to the eighth Earl of Balcairn, Viscount Erdinge, Baron Cairn of Balcairn, Red Knight of Lancaster, Count of the Holy Roman Empire and Chenonceaux Herald to the Duchy of Aquitaine, 'Hullo,' he said. 'Isn't this a repulsive party? What are you going to say about it?' for they were both of them, as it happened, gossip writers for the daily papers.

'I've just telephoned my story through,' said Lord Balcairn. 'And now I'm going, thank God.'

'I can't think of what to say,' said Lord Vanburgh. 'My editress said yesterday she was tired of seeing the same names over and over again – and here they are again, all of them. There's Nina Blount's engagement being broken off, but she's not got any publicity value to speak of. Agatha Runcible's usually worth a couple of paragraphs, but they're featuring her as a front-page news story to-morrow over this Customs House business.'

'I made rather a good thing over Edward Throbbing being in a log shanty in Canada which he built himself with the help of one Red Indian. I thought that was fairly good because, you see, I could contrast that with Miles being dressed as a Red Indian to-night, don't you think so, or don't you?'

'I say, that's rather good, may I use it?'

'Well, you can have the shanty, but the Red Indian's mine.'

'Where is he actually?'

'Heaven knows. Government House at Ottawa, I think.'

'Who's that awful-looking woman? I'm sure she's famous in some way. It's not Mrs Melrose Ape, is it? I heard she was coming.'

'Who?'

'That one. Making up to Nina.'

'Good lord, no. She's no one. Mrs Panrast she's called now.'

'She seems to know you.'

'Yes, I've known her all my life. As a matter of fact, she's my mother.'

'My dear, how too shaming. D'you mind if I put that in?'

'I'd sooner you didn't. The family can't bear her. She's been divorced twice since then, you know.'

'My dear, of course not, I quite understand.'

Five minutes later he was busy at the telephone, dictating his story. '...Orchid stop, new paragraph. One of the most striking women in the room was Mrs Panrast – P-A-N-R-A-S-T, no, T for telephone, you know – former Countess of Balcairn. She dresses with that severely masculine chic, italics, which American women know so well how to assume, stop. Her son, comma, the present Earl, comma, was with her, stop. Lord Balcairn is one of the few young men about town...'

'...the Hon. Miles Malpractice was dressed as a Red Indian. He is at present living in the house of his brother, Lord Throbbing, at which yesterday's party was held. His choice of costume was particularly – what shall I say? hullo, yes – was particularly piquant, italics, since the latest reports of Lord Throbbing say that he is living in a log shack in Canada which he built with his own hands, aided by one Red Indian servant, stop....'

*

You see, that was the kind of party Archie Schwert's party was.

*

Miss Mouse (in a very enterprising frock by Cheruit) sat on a chair with her eyes popping out of her head. She never *could* get used to so much excitement, never. To-night she had brought a little friend with her – a Miss Brown – because it was so much more fun if one had someone to talk to. It was too thrilling to see all that dull money her father had amassed, metamorphosed in this way into so much glitter and noise and so many bored young faces. Archie Schwert, as he passed, champagne bottle in hand, paused to say, 'How are you, Mary darling? Quite all right?'

'That's Archie Schwert,' said Miss Mouse to Miss Brown. 'Isn't he too clever?'

'Is he?' said Miss Brown, who would have liked a drink, but didn't know how quite to set about it. 'You *are* lucky to know such amusing people, Mary darling. I never see anyone.'

'Wasn't the invitation clever? Johnnie Hoop wrote it.'

'Well, yes, I suppose it was. But you know, was it dreadful of me, I hadn't heard of any of the names.'*

'My dear, of course you have,' said Miss Mouse, feeling somewhere in her depths – those unplumbed places in Miss Mouse's soul – a tiny, most unaccustomed flicker of superiority; for she had gone through that invitation word by word in papa's library some days ago and knew all about it.

She almost wished in this new mood of exaltation that she had come to the party in fancy dress. It was called a Savage party, that is to say that Johnnie Hoop had written on the invitation that they were to come dressed as savages. Numbers of them had done so; Johnnie himself in a mask and black gloves represented the Maharanee of Pukkapore, somewhat to the annoyance of the Maharajah, who happened to drop in. The real aristocracy, the younger members of those two or three great brewing families which rule London, had done nothing about it. They had come on from a dance and stood in a little group by themselves, aloof, amused but not amusing. Pit-a-pat went the heart of Miss Mouse. How she longed to tear down her dazzling frock to her hips and dance like a Bacchante before them all. One day she would surprise them all, thought Miss Mouse.

*

There was a famous actor making jokes (but it was not so much what he said as the way he said it that made the people laugh who did laugh). 'I've come to the party as a wild widower,' he

* Perhaps it should be explained – there were at this time three sorts of formal invitation card; there was the nice sensible copy-book hand sort with a name and *At Home* and a date and time and address; then there was the sort that came from Chelsea, *Noel and Audrey are having a little whoopee on Saturday evening; do please come and bring a bottle too, if you can*; and finally there was the sort that Johnnie Hoop used to adapt from *Blast* and Marinetti's *Futurist Manifesto*. These had two columns of close print; in one was a list of all the things Johnnie hated, and in the other all the things he thought he liked. Most of the parties which Miss Mouse financed had invitations written by Johnnie Hoop.

said. They were that kind of joke – but, of course, he made a droll face when he said it.

Miss Runcible had changed into Hawaiian costume and was the life and soul of the evening.

She had heard someone say something about an Independent Labour Party, and was furious that she had not been asked.

There were two men with a lot of explosive powder taking photographs in another room. Their flashes and bangs had rather a disquieting effect on the party, causing a feeling of tension, because everyone looked negligent and said what a bore the papers were, and how *too* like Archie to let the photographers come, but most of them, as a matter of fact, wanted dreadfully to be photographed and the others were frozen with unaffected terror that they might be taken unawares and then their mamas would know where they had been when they said they were at the Bicesters' dance, and then there would be a row again, which was so *exhausting*, if nothing else.

There were Adam and Nina getting rather sentimental.

'D'you know,' she said, pulling out a lump, 'I'd quite made up my mind that your hair was dark?' Archie Schwert, pausing with a bottle of champagne, said, 'Don't be so sadistic, Nina.'

'Go away, hog's rump,' said Adam, in Cockney, adding, in softer tones, 'Are you disappointed?'

'Well, no, but it's rather disconcerting getting engaged to someone with dark hair and finding it's fair.'

'Anyway, we aren't engaged any more, are we – or are we?'

'I'm not sure that we're not. How much money *have* you, Adam?'

'Literally, none, my dear. Poor Agatha had to pay for dinner as it was, and God knows what I'm going to do about Lottie Crump's bill.'

'Of course, you know – Adam, don't fall asleep – there's always papa. I believe he's really much richer than he looks. He might give us some money until your books start paying.'

'You know, if I wrote a book a month I should be free of that contract in a year . . . I hadn't thought of that before. I don't at all see why I shouldn't do that, do you? . . . or do you?'

'Of course not, darling. I'll tell you what. We'll go down and see papa to-morrow, shall we?'

'Yes, that would be divine, darling.'

'Adam, don't go to sleep.'

'Sorry, darling, what I meant was that that would be divine.'

And he went to sleep for a little, with his head in her lap.

'Pretty as a picture,' said Archie, in Cockney, passing with a bottle of champagne in his hand.

'Wake up, Adam,' said Nina, pulling out more hair. 'It's time to go.'

'That would be divine.... I say, have I been asleep?'

'Yes, for hours and hours. You looked rather sweet.'

'And you sat there.... I say, Nina, you are getting sentimental.... Where are we going?'

There were about a dozen people left at the party; that hard kernel of gaiety that never breaks. It was about three o'clock.

'Let's go to Lottie Crump's and have a drink,' said Adam.

So they all got into two taxicabs and drove across Berkeley Square to Dover Street. But at Shepheard's the night porter said that Mrs Crump had just gone to bed. He thought that Judge Skimp was still up with some friends; would they like to join him? They went up to Judge Skimp's suite, but there had been a disaster there with a chandelier that one of his young ladies had tried to swing on. They were bathing her forehead with champagne; two of them were asleep.

So Adam's party went out again into the rain.

'Of course, there's always the Ritz,' said Archie. 'I believe the night porter can usually get one a drink.' But he said it in the sort of voice that made all the others say, no, the Ritz was too, too boring at that time of night.

They went to Agatha Runcible's house, which was quite near, but she found that she'd lost her latchkey, so that was no good. Soon someone would say the fatal words, 'Well, I think it's time for me to go to bed. Can I give anyone a lift to Knightsbridge?' and the party would be over.

But instead a little breathless voice said, 'Why don't you come to *my* house?'

It was Miss Brown.

So they all got into taxicabs again and drove rather a long way to Miss Brown's house. She turned on the lights in a sombre dining-room and gave them glasses of whisky and soda. (She turned out to be rather a good hostess, though over-zealous.) Then Miles said he wanted something to eat, so they all went downstairs into a huge kitchen lined with every shape of pot and pan and found some eggs and some bacon and Miss Brown cooked them. Then they had some more whisky upstairs and Adam fell asleep again. Presently Vanburgh said, 'D'you mind if I use the telephone? I must just send the rest of my story to the paper.' Miss Brown took him to a study that looked almost like an office, and he dictated the rest of his column, and then he came back and had some more whisky.

It was a lovely evening for Miss Brown. Flushed with successful hospitality, she trotted from guest to guest, offering here a box of matches, there a cigar, there a fruit from the enormous gilt dishes on the sideboard. To think that all these brilliant people, whom she had heard so much about, with what envy, from Miss Mouse, should be here in papa's dining-room, calling her 'my dear' and 'darling'. And when at last they said they really had to go, Miss Runcible said, 'well, *I* can't go, because I've lost my latchkey. D'you mind awfully if I sleep here?'

Miss Brown, her heart in her mouth, but in the most natural way possible, said, 'Of course not, Agatha darling, that would be divine.'

And then Miss Runcible said, 'How too divine of you, darling.'

Rapture!

*

At half-past nine the next morning the Brown family came down to breakfast in the dining-room.

There were four quiet girls (of whom the Miss Brown who had given the party was the youngest), their brother who worked in the motor shop and had had to get off early. They were seated at the table when their mama came down.

'Now, children,' she said, 'do try to remember to talk to your father at breakfast. He was quite hurt yesterday. He feels out of things. It's so easy to bring him into the conversation if you take a little trouble, and he does so enjoy hearing about everything.'

'Yes, Mama,' they said. 'We do try, you know.'

'And what was the Bicesters' dance like, Jane?' she said, pouring out some coffee. 'Did you have a good time?'

'It was just too divine,' said the youngest Miss Brown.

'It was *what*, Jane?'

'I mean it was *lovely*, Mama.'

'So I should think. You girls are very lucky nowadays. There were not nearly so many dances when I was your age. Perhaps two a week in the season, you know, but *none* before Christmas ever.'

'Mama.'

'Yes, Jane.'

'Mama. I asked a girl to stay the night.'

'Yes, dear. When? We're rather full up, you know.'

'Last night, Mama.'

'What an extraordinary thing to do. Did she accept?'

'Yes, she's here now.'

'*Well*. . . . Ambrose, will you tell Mrs Sparrow to put on another egg?'

'I'm very sorry, my lady, Mrs Sparrow can't understand it, but there *are* no eggs this morning. She thinks there must have been burglars.'

'Nonsense, Ambrose, who ever heard of burglars coming into a house to steal eggs?'

'The shells were all over the floor, my lady.'

'I see. That's all, thank you, Ambrose. Well, Jane, has your guest eaten all our eggs too?'

'Well, I'm afraid she has . . . at least . . . I mean . . .'

At this moment Agatha Runcible came down to breakfast. She was not looking her best really in the morning light.

'Good morning, all,' she said in Cockney. 'I've found the right room at last. D'you know, I popped into a study or something. There was a sweet old boy sitting at a desk. He *did* look surprised to see me. Was it your papa?'

'This is Mama,' said Jane.

'How are you?' said Miss Runcible. 'I say, I think it's quite too sweet of you to let me come down to breakfast like this.' (It must be remembered that she was still in Hawaiian costume.) 'Are you sure you're not *furious* with me? All this is really much more embarrassing for *me*, isn't it, don't you think... or don't you?'

'Do you take tea or coffee?' at last Jane's mother managed to say. 'Jane, dear, give your friend some breakfast.' For in the course of a long public life she had formed the opinion that a judicious offer of food eased most social situations.

Then Jane's father came in.

'Martha, the most extraordinary thing!... I think I must be losing my reason. I was in my study just now going over that speech for this afternoon, when suddenly the door opened and in came a sort of dancing Hottentot woman half-naked. It just said, "Oh, how shy-making", and then disappeared, and... oh...' For he had suddenly caught sight of Miss Runcible '...oh...how do you do?...How...?'

'I don't think you have met my husband before.'

'Only for a second,' said Miss Runcible.

'I hope you slept well,' said Jane's father desperately. 'Martha never told me we had a guest. Forgive me if I appeared inhospitable...I – er...Oh, why doesn't somebody else say something?'

Miss Runcible, too, was feeling the strain. She picked up the morning paper.

'Here's something terribly funny,' she said, by way of making conversation. 'Shall I read it to you?'

'"*Midnight Orgies at No.* 10." My dear, isn't that divine? Listen, "*What must be the most extraordinary party of the little season took place in the small hours of this morning at No.* 10 *Downing Street. At about* 4 *a.m. the policemen who are always posted outside the Prime Minister's residence were surprised to witness*" – Isn't this too amusing – "*the arrival of a fleet of taxis, from which emerged a gay throng in exotic fancy dress*" – How I should have loved to have seen it. Can't you imagine what they were like? – "*the hostess of what was described by one of the guests as the brightest party the Bright Young People have yet given, was no other than Miss Jane Brown, the youngest of the Prime Minister's four lovely daughters, The Honourable Agatha*..." Why, what an extraordinary thing.... Oh, my God!'

Suddenly light came flooding in on Miss Runcible's mind as once when, in her débutante days, she had gone behind the scenes at a charity matinée, and returning had stepped through the wrong door and found herself in a blaze of flood-lights on the stage in the middle of the last act of *Othello*. 'Oh, my God!' she said, looking round the Brown breakfast table. 'Isn't that just too bad of Vanburgh. He's always doing that kind of thing. It really would serve him right if we complained, and he lost his job, don't you think so, Sir James... or... don't you?'

Miss Runcible paused and met the eyes of the Brown family once more.

'Oh, dear,' she said, 'this really is all too bogus.'

Then she turned round and, trailing garlands of equatorial flowers, fled out of the room and out of the house to the huge delight and profit of the crowd of reporters and Press photographers who were already massed round the historic front door.

CHAPTER 5

ADAM woke up feeling terribly ill. He rang his bell once or twice, but nobody came. Later he woke up again and rang the bell. The Italian waiter appeared, undulating slightly in the doorway. Adam ordered breakfast. Lottie came in and sat on his bed.

'Had a nice breakfast, dear?' she said.

'Not yet,' said Adam. 'I've only just woken up.'

'That's right,' said Lottie. 'Nothing like a nice breakfast. There was a young lady for you on the 'phone, but I can't remember what it was she said at the minute. We've all been upside down this morning. Such a fuss. Had the police in, we have, ever since I don't know what time, drinking up my wine and asking questions and putting their noses where they're not wanted. All because Flossie must needs go and swing on the chandelier. She never had any sense, Flossie. Well, she's learned her lesson now, poor girl. Whoever heard of such a thing – swinging on a chandelier. Poor Judge What's-his-name is in a terrible state about it. I said to him it's not so much the price of the chandelier, I said. What money can make, money can mend, I said, and that's the truth, isn't it, dear? But what I mind, I said, is having a death in the house and all the fuss. It doesn't do *anyone* any good having people killing theirselves in a house like Flossie did. Now what may *you* want, my Italian queen?' said Lottie as the waiter came in with a tray, the smell of kippers contending with *nuit de Noël* rather disagreeably.

'Gentleman's breakfast,' said the waiter.

'And how many *more* breakfasts do you think he wants, I should like to know? He's had his breakfast hours ago while you were powdering your nose downstairs, haven't you, dear?'

'No,' said Adam, 'as a matter of fact, no.'

'There, do you hear what the gentleman says? *He* doesn't want two breakfasts. Don't stand there wiggling your behind at me. Take it away quick or I'll catch you such a smack. . . . That's just the way – once you get the police in everyone gets all upset. There's that boy brings you two breakfasts and I dare say there's some poor fellow along the passage somewhere who hasn't had any breakfast at all. You can't get anywhere without a nice breakfast. Half the young fellows as come here now don't have anything except a *cachet Faivre* and some orange juice. It's not right,' said Lottie, 'and I've spoken to that boy about using scent twenty times if I've spoken once.'

The waiter's head appeared, and with it another wave of *nuit de Noël.*

'If you please, madam, the inspectors want to speak to you downstairs, madam.'

'All right, my little bird of paradise, I'll be there.'

Lottie trotted away and the waiter came sidling back bearing his tray of kippers and leering at Adam with a horrible intimacy.

'Turn on my bath, will you, please,' said Adam.

'Alas, there is a gentleman asleep in the bath. Shall I wake him?'

'No, it doesn't matter.'

'Will that be all, sir?'

'Yes, thank you.'

The waiter stood about fingering the brass knobs at the end of the bed, smiling ingratiatingly. Then he produced from under his coat a gardenia, slightly browned at the edges. (He had found it in an evening coat he had just been brushing.)

'Would the signor perhaps like a buttonhole?'...Madame Crump was so severe...it was nice sometimes to be able to have a talk with the gentlemen...

'No,' said Adam. 'Go away.' For he had a headache.

The waiter sighed deeply, and walked with pettish steps to the door; sighed again and took the gardenia to the gentleman in the bathroom.

Adam ate some breakfast. No kipper, he reflected, is ever as good as it smells; how this too earthly contact with flesh and bone spoiled the first happy exhilaration; if only one could live, as Jehovah was said to have done, on the savour of burnt offerings. He lay back for a little in his bed thinking about the smells of food, of the greasy horror of fried fish and the deeply moving smell that came from it; of the intoxicating breath of bakeries and the dullness of buns.... He planned dinners of enchanting aromatic foods that should be carried under the nose, snuffed and thrown to the dogs...endless dinners, in which one could alternate flavour with flavour from sunset to dawn without satiety, while one breathed great draughts of the bouquet of old brandy.... Oh for the wings of a dove, thought Adam, wandering a little from the point as he fell asleep again (everyone is liable to this ninetyish feeling in the early morning after a party).

*

Presently the telephone by Adam's bed began ringing.

'Hullo, yes.'

'Lady to speak to you.... Hullo, is that you, Adam?'

'Is that Nina?'

'How are you, my darling?'

'*Oh, Nina....*'

'My poor sweet, I feel like that, too. Listen, angel. You haven't forgotten that you're going to see my papa to-day, have you... or have you? I've just sent him a wire to say that you're going to lunch with him. D'you know where he lives?'

'But you're coming too?'

'Well, no. I don't think I will, if you don't mind.... I've got rather a pain.'

'My dear, if you *knew* what a pain I've got....'

'Yes, but that's different, darling. Anyway, there's no object in our both going.'

'But what am I to say?'

'*Darling*, don't be tiresome. You know perfectly well. Just ask him for some money.'

'Will he like that?'

'Yes, darling, of course he will. Why will you go *on*? I've got to get up now. Good-bye. Take care of yourself.... Ring me up when you get back and tell me what papa said. By the way, have you seen the paper this morning? – there's something so funny about last night. *Too* bad of Van. Good-bye.'

While Adam was dressing, he realized that he did not know where he was to go. He rang up again. 'By the way, Nina, where does your papa live?'

'Didn't I tell you? It's a house called Doubting, and it's all falling down really. You go to Aylesbury by train and then take a taxi. They're the most expensive taxis in the world, too.... Have you got any money?'

Adam looked on the dressing-table: 'About seven shillings,' he said.

'My dear, that's not enough. You'll have to make poor papa pay for the taxi.'

'Will he like that?'

'Yes, of course, he's an angel.'

'I wish you'd come too, Nina.'

'Darling, I told you. I've got such a pain.'

Downstairs, as Lottie had said, everything was upside down. That is to say that there were policemen and reporters teeming in every corner of the hotel, each with a bottle of champagne and a glass. Lottie, Doge, Judge Skimp, the Inspector, four plain-clothes men and the body were in Judge Skimp's suite.

'What is *not* clear to me, sir,' said the Inspector, 'is what *prompted* the young lady to swing on the chandelier. Not wishing to cause offence, sir, and begging your pardon, was she . . . ?'

'Yes,' said Judge Skimp, 'she was.'

'*Exactly*,' said the Inspector. 'A clear case of misadventure, eh, Mrs Crump? There'll have to be an inquest, of course, but I think probably I shall be able to arrange things so that there is no mention of your name in the case, sir . . . well, that's very kind of you, Mrs Crump, perhaps just one more glass.'

'Lottie,' said Adam, 'can you lend me some money?'

'Money, dear? Of course. Doge, have you got any money?'

'I was asleep at the time myself, mum, and was not even made aware of the occurrence until I was called this morning. Being slightly deaf, the sound of the disaster . . . '

'Judge What's-your-name, got any money?'

'I should take it as a great privilege if I could be of any assistance . . . '

'That's right, give some to young Thingummy here. That all you want, deary? Don't run away. We're just thinking of having a little drink. . . . No, not that wine, dear, it's what we keep for the police. I've just ordered a better bottle if my young butterfly would bring it along.'

Adam had a glass of champagne, hoping it would make him feel a little better. It made him feel much worse.

Then he went to Marylebone. It was Armistice Day, and they were selling artificial poppies in the streets. As he reached the station it struck eleven and for two minutes all over the country everyone was quiet and serious. Then he went to Aylesbury, reading on the way Balcairn's account of Archie Schwert's party. He was pleased to see himself described as 'the brilliant young novelist', and wondered whether Nina's papa read gossip paragraphs, and supposed not. The two women opposite him in the carriage obviously did.

'I no sooner opened the paper,' said one, 'than I was on the phone *at once* to all the ladies of the committee, and we'd sent off a wire to our Member before one o'clock. We know how to make things hum at the Bois. I've got a copy of what we sent. Look. *Members of the Committee of the Ladies' Conservative Association at Chesham Bois wish to express their extreme displeasure at reports in this morning's paper of midnight party at No. 10. They call upon Captain Crutwell* – that's our Member; such a nice stamp of man – *strenuously to withhold support to Prime Minister.* It cost nearly four shillings, but, as I said at the time, it was not a moment to spoil the ship for a ha'p'orth of tar. Don't you agree, Mrs Ithewaite?'

'I do, indeed, Mrs Orraway-Smith. It is clearly a case in which a mandate from the constituencies is required. I'll talk to our chairwoman at Wendover.'

'Yes, do, Mrs Ithewaite. It is in a case like this that the woman's vote can count.'

'If it's a choice between my moral judgment and the nationalization of banking, I prefer nationalization, if you see what I mean.'

'Exactly what I think. Such a terrible example to the lower classes, *apart from everything.*'

'That's what I mean. There's our Agnes, now. How can I stop her having young men in the kitchen when she knows that Sir James Brown has parties like that at all hours of the night. . . .'

They were both wearing hats like nothing on earth, which bobbed and nodded as they spoke.

*

At Aylesbury Adam got into a Ford taxi and asked to be taken to a house called Doubting.

'Doubting 'All?'

'Well, I suppose so. Is it falling down?'

'Could do with a lick of paint,' said the driver, a spotty youth. 'Name of Blount?'

'That's it.'

'Long way from here Doubting 'All is. Cost you fifteen bob.'

'All right.'

'If you're a commercial, I can tell you straight it ain't no use going to 'im. Young feller asked me the way there this morning. Driving a Morris. Wanted to sell him a vacuum cleaner. Old boy 'ad answered an advertisement asking for a demonstration. When he got there the old boy wouldn't even look at it. Can you beat that?'

'No, I'm not trying to sell him anything – at least not exactly.'

'Personal visit, perhaps.'

'Yes.'

'Ah.'

Satisfied that his passenger was in earnest about the journey, the taxi-driver put on some coats – for it was raining – got out of his seat and cranked up the engine. Presently they started.

They drove for a mile or two past bungalows and villas and timbered public houses to a village in which every house seemed to be a garage and filling station. Here they left the main road and Adam's discomfort became acute.

At last they came to twin octagonal lodges and some heraldic gate-posts and large wrought-iron gates, behind which could be seen a broad sweep of ill-kept drive.

'Doubting 'All,' said the driver.

He blew his horn once or twice, but no lodge-keeper's wife, aproned and apple-cheeked, appeared to bob them in. He got out and shook the gates reproachfully.

'Chained-and-locked,' he said. 'Try another way.'

They drove on for another mile; on the side of the Hall the road was bordered by dripping trees and a dilapidated stone wall; presently they reached some cottages and a white gate. This they opened and turned into a rough track, separated from the park by low iron railings. There were sheep grazing on either side. One of them had strayed into the drive. It fled before them in a frenzied trot, stopping and looking round over its dirty tail and then plunging on again until its agitation brought it to the side of the path, where they overtook it and passed it.

The track led to some stables, then behind rows of hot-houses, among potting-sheds and heaps of drenched leaves, past nondescript outbuildings that had once been laundry and bakery and brewhouse and a huge kennel where once someone had kept a bear, until suddenly it turned by a clump of holly and elms and laurel bushes into an open space that had once been laid with gravel. A lofty Palladian façade stretched before them and in front of it an equestrian statue pointed a baton imperiously down the main drive.

' 'Ere y'are,' said the driver.

Adam paid him and went up the steps to the front door. He rang the bell and waited. Nothing happened. Presently he rang again. At this moment the door opened.

'Don't ring twice,' said a very angry old man. 'What do you want?'

'Is Mr Blount in?'

'There's no Mr Blount here. This is Colonel Blount's house.'

'I'm sorry.... I think the Colonel is expecting me to luncheon.'

'Nonsense. I'm Colonel Blount,' and he shut the door.

The Ford had disappeared. It was still raining hard. Adam rang again.

'Yes,' said Colonel Blount, appearing instantly.

'I wonder if you'd let me telephone to the station for a taxi?'

'Not on the telephone.... It's raining. Why don't you come in? It's absurd to walk to the station in this. Have you come about the vacuum cleaner?'

'No.'

'Funny, I've been expecting a man all the morning to show me a vacuum cleaner. Come in, do. Won't you stay to luncheon?'

'I should love to.'

'Splendid. I get very little company nowadays. You must forgive me for opening the door to you myself. My butler is in bed to-day. He suffers terribly in his feet when it is wet. Both my footmen were killed in the war.... Put your hat and coat here. I hope you haven't got wet.... I'm sorry you didn't bring the vacuum cleaner... but never mind. How are you?' he said, suddenly holding out his hand.

They shook hands and Colonel Blount led the way down a long corridor, lined with marble busts on yellow marble pedestals, to a large room full of furniture, with a fire burning in a fine rococo fireplace. There was a large leather-topped walnut writing-table under a window opening on to a terrace. Colonel Blount picked up a telegram and read it.

'I'd quite forgotten,' he said in some confusion. 'I'm afraid you'll think me very discourteous, but it is, after all, impossible for me to ask you to luncheon. I have a guest coming on very intimate family business. You understand, don't you?... To tell you the truth, it's some young rascal who wants to marry my daughter. I must see him alone to discuss settlements.'

'Well, I want to marry your daughter, too,' said Adam.

'What an extraordinary coincidence. Are you sure you do?'

'Perhaps the telegram may be about me. What does it say?'

'"*Engaged to marry Adam Symes. Expect him luncheon. Nina.*" Are you Adam Symes?'

'Yes.'

'My dear boy, why didn't you say so before, instead of going on about a vacuum cleaner? How are you?'

They shook hands again.

'If you don't mind,' said Colonel Blount, 'we will keep our business until after luncheon. I'm afraid everything is looking very bare at present. You must come down and see the gardens in the summer. We had some lovely hydrangeas last year. I don't think I shall live here another winter. Too big for an old man. I was looking at some of the houses they're putting up outside Aylesbury. Did you see them coming along? Nice little red houses. Bathroom and everything. Quite cheap, too, and near the cinematographs. I hope you are fond of the cinematograph too? The Rector and I go a great deal. I hope you'll like the Rector. Common little man rather. But he's got a motor-car, useful that. How long are you staying?'

'I promised Nina I'd be back to-night.'

'That's a pity. They change the film at the Electra Palace. We might have gone.'

An elderly woman servant came in to announce luncheon. 'What is at the Electra Palace, do you know, Mrs Florin?'

'Greta Garbo in *Venetian Kisses*, I think, sir.'

'I don't really think I like Greta Garbo. I've tried to,' said Colonel Blount, 'but I just don't.'

They went in to luncheon in a huge dining-room dark with family portraits.

'If you don't mind,' said Colonel Blount, 'I prefer not to talk at meals.'

He propped a morocco-bound volume of *Punch* before his plate against a vast silver urn, from which grew a small castor-oil plant.

'Give Mr Symes a book,' he said.

Mrs Florin put another volume of *Punch* beside Adam.

'If you come across anything really funny read it to me,' said Colonel Blount.

Then they had luncheon.

They were nearly an hour over luncheon. Course followed course in disconcerting abundance while Colonel Blount ate and ate, turning the leaves of his book and chuckling frequently. They ate hare soup and boiled turbot and stewed sweetbreads and black Bradenham ham with Madeira sauce and roast pheasant and a rum omelette and toasted cheese and fruit. First they drank sherry, then claret, then port. Then Colonel Blount shut his book with a broad sweep of his arm rather as the headmaster of Adam's private school used to shut the Bible after evening prayers, folded his napkin carefully and stuffed it into a massive silver ring, muttered some words of grace and finally stood up, saying:

'Well, I don't know about you, but I'm going to have a little nap,' and trotted out of the room.

'There's a fire in the library, sir,' said Mrs Florin. 'I'll bring you your coffee there. The Colonel doesn't have coffee, he finds it interferes with his afternoon sleep. What time would you like your afternoon tea, sir?'

'I ought really to be getting back to London. How long will it be before the Colonel comes down, do you think?'

'Well, it all depends, sir. Not usually till about five or half-past. Then he reads until dinner at seven and after dinner gets the Rector to drive him in to the pictures. A sedentary life, as you might say.'

She led Adam into the library and put a silver coffee-pot at his elbow.

'I'll bring you tea at four,' she said.

Adam sat in front of the fire in a deep armchair. Outside the rain beat on the double windows. There were several magazines in the library – mostly cheap weeklies devoted to the cinema. There was a stuffed owl and a case of early British remains, bone pins and bits of pottery and a skull, which had been dug up in the park many years ago and catalogued by Nina's governess. There was a cabinet containing the relics of Nina's various collecting fevers – some butterflies and a beetle or two, some fossils and some birds' eggs and a few postage stamps. There were some bookcases of superbly unreadable books, a gun, a butterfly net, an alpenstock in the corner. There were catalogues of agricultural machines and acetylene plants, lawn mowers, 'sports requisites'. There was a fire screen worked with a coat of arms. The chimney-piece was hung with the embroidered saddle-cloths of Colonel Blount's regiment of Lancers. There was an engraving of all the members of the Royal Yacht Squadron, with a little plan in the corner, marked to show who was who. There were many other things of equal interest besides, but before Adam had noticed any more he was fast asleep.

Mrs Florin woke him at four. The coffee had disappeared and its place was taken by a silver tray with a lace cloth on it. There was a silver tea-pot, and a silver kettle with a little spirit-lamp underneath, and a silver cream jug and a covered silver dish full of muffins. There was also hot buttered toast and honey and gentleman's relish and a chocolate cake, a cherry cake, a seed cake and a fruit cake and some tomato sandwiches and pepper and salt and currant bread and butter.

'Would you care for a lightly boiled egg, sir? The Colonel generally has one if he's awake.'

'No, thank you,' said Adam. He felt a thousand times better for his rest. When Nina and he were married, he thought, they would often come down there for the day after a really serious party. For the first time he noticed an obese liver-and-white spaniel, which was waking up, too, on the hearthrug.

'Please not to give her muffins,' said Mrs Florin, 'it's the one thing she's not supposed to have, and the Colonel will give them to her. He loves that dog,' she added with a burst of confidence. 'Takes her to the pictures with him of an evening. Not that she can appreciate them really like a human can.'

Adam gave her – the spaniel, not Mrs Florin – a gentle prod with his foot and a lump of sugar. She licked his shoe with evident cordiality. Adam was not above feeling flattered by friendliness in dogs.

He had finished his tea and was filling his pipe when Colonel Blount came into the library.

'Who the devil are you?' said his host.

'Adam Symes,' said Adam.

'Never heard of you. How did you get in? Who gave you tea? What do you want?'

'You asked me to luncheon,' said Adam. 'I came about being married to Nina.'

'My dear boy, of course. How absurd of me. I've such a bad memory for names. It comes of seeing so few people. How are you?'

They shook hands again.

'So you're the young man who's engaged to Nina,' said the Colonel, eyeing him for the first time in the way prospective sons-in-laws are supposed to be eyed. 'Now what in the world do you want to get married for? I shouldn't, you know, really I shouldn't. Are you rich?'

'No, not at present, I'm afraid, that's rather what I wanted to talk about.'

'How much money have you got?'

'Well, sir, actually at the moment I haven't got any at all.'

'When did you last have any?'

'I had a thousand pounds last night, but I gave it all to a drunk Major.'

'Why did you do that?'

'Well, I hoped he'd put it on Indian Runner for the November Handicap.'

'Never heard of the horse. Didn't he?'

'I don't think he can have.'

'When will you next have some money?'

'When I've written some books.'

'How many books?'

'Twelve.'

'How much will you have then?'

'Probably fifty pounds advance on my thirteenth book.'

'And how long will it take you to write twelve books?'

'About a year.'

'How long would it take most people?'

'About twenty years. Of course, put like that I do see that it sounds rather hopeless . . . but, you see, Nina and I hoped that you, that is, that perhaps for the next year until I get my twelve books written, that you might help us . . .'

'How could I help you? I've never written a book in my life.'

'No, we thought you might give us some money.'

'You thought that, did you?'

'Yes, that's what we thought . . .'

Colonel Blount looked at him gravely for some time. Then he said, 'I think that an admirable idea. I don't see any reason at all why I shouldn't. How much do you want?'

'That's really terribly good of you, sir. . . . Well, you know, just enough to live on quietly for a bit. I hardly know . . .'

'Well, would a thousand pounds be any help?'

'Yes, it would indeed. We shall both be terribly grateful.'

'Not at all, my dear boy. Not at all. What did you say your name was?'

'Adam Symes.'

Colonel Blount went to the table and wrote out a cheque. 'There you are,' he said. 'Now don't go giving that away to another drunk major.'

'Really, sir! I don't know how to thank you. Nina . . . '

'Not another word. Now I expect that you will want to be off to London again. We'll send Mrs Florin across to the Rectory and make the Rector drive you to the station. Useful having a neighbour with a motor-car. They charge fivepence on the buses from here to Aylesbury. *Robbers.*'

*

It does not befall many young men to be given a thousand pounds by a complete stranger twice on successive evenings. Adam laughed aloud in the Rector's car as they drove to the station. The Rector, who had been in the middle of writing a sermon and resented with daily increasing feeling Colonel Blount's neighbourly appropriation of his car and himself, kept his eyes fixed on the streaming windscreen, pretending not to notice. Adam laughed all the way to Aylesbury, sitting and holding his knees and shaking all over. The Rector could hardly bring himself to say good night when they parted in the station yard.

There was half an hour to wait for a train and the leaking roof and wet railway lines had a sobering effect on Adam. He bought an evening paper. On the front page was an exquisitely funny photograph of Miss Runcible in Hawaiian costume tumbling down the steps of No. 10 Downing Street. The Government had fallen that afternoon, he read, being defeated on a motion rising from the answer to a question about the treatment of Miss Runcible by Customs House officers. It was generally held in Parliamentary circles that the deciding factor in this reverse had been the revolt of the Liberals and the Nonconformist members at the revelations of the life that was led at No. 10 Downing Street, during Sir James Brown's tenancy. The *Evening Mail* had a leading article, which drew a fine analogy between Public and Domestic Purity, between sobriety in the family and in the State.

There was another small paragraph which interested Adam.

TRAGEDY IN WEST-END HOTEL

The death occurred early this morning at a private hotel in Dover Street of Miss Florence Ducane, described as being of independent means, following an accident in which Miss Ducane fell from a chandelier which she was attempting to mend. The inquest will be held to-morrow, which will be followed by the cremation at Golders Green. Miss Ducane, who was formerly connected with the stage, was well known in business circles.

Which only showed, thought Adam, how much better Lottie Crump knew the business of avoiding undesirable publicity than Sir James Brown.

*

When Adam reached London the rain had stopped, but there was a thin fog drifting in belts before a damp wind. The station was crowded with office workers hurrying with attaché-cases and evening papers to catch their evening trains home, coughing and sneezing as they went. They still wore their poppies. Adam went to a telephone-box and rang up Nina. She had left a message for him that she was having cocktails at Margot Metroland's house. He drove to Shepheard's.

'Lottie,' he said, 'I've got a thousand pounds.'

'Have you, now,' said Lottie indifferently. She lived on the assumption that everyone she knew always had several thousand pounds. It was to her as though he had said, 'Lottie, I have a tall hat.'

'Can you lend me some money till to-morrow till I cash the cheque?'

'What a boy you are for borrowing. Just like your poor father. Here, you in the corner, lend Mr What-d'you-call-him some money.'

A tall Guardsman shook his retreating forehead and twirled his moustaches.

'No good coming to me, Lottie,' he said in a voice trained to command.

'Mean hound,' said Lottie. 'Where's that American?'

Judge Skimp, who, since his experiences that morning, had become profoundly Anglophile, produced two ten-pound notes. 'I shall be only too proud and honoured . . . ' he said.

'Good old Judge Thingummy,' said Lottie. 'That's the way.'

Adam hurried out into the hall as another bottle of champagne popped festively in the parlour.

'Doge, ring up the Daimler Hire Company and order a car in my name. Tell it to go round to Lady Metroland's – Pastmaster House, Hill Street,' he said. Then he put on his hat and walked down Hay Hill, swinging an umbrella and laughing again, only more quietly, to himself.

At Lady Metroland's he kept on his coat and waited in the hall.

'Will you please tell Miss Blount I've called for her? No, I won't go up.'

He looked at the hats on the table. Clearly there was quite a party. Two or three silk hats of people who had dressed early, the rest soft and black like his own. Then he began to dance again, jigging to himself in simple high spirits.

In a minute Nina came down the broad Adam staircase.

'Darling, why didn't you come up? It's so rude. Margot is longing to see you.'

'I'm so sorry, Nina. I couldn't face a party. I'm so excited.'

'Why, what's happened?'

'Everything. I'll tell you in the car.'

'Car?'

'Yes, it'll be here in a minute. We're going down to the country for dinner. I can't tell you how clever I've been.'

'But what have you done, darling? Do stop dancing about.'

'Can't stop. You've no idea how clever I am.'

'Adam. Are you tight again?'

'Look out of the window and see if you can see a Daimler waiting.'

'Adam, what *have* you been doing? I will be told.'

'Look,' said Adam, producing the cheque. 'Whatcher think of that?' he added in Cockney.

'*My dear*, a thousand pounds. Did papa give you that?'

'I earned it,' said Adam. 'Oh, I earned it. You should have seen the luncheon I ate and the jokes I read. I'm going to be married to-morrow. Oh, Nina, would Margot hate it if I sang in her hall?'

'She'd simply loathe it, darling, and so should I. I'm going to take care of that cheque. You remember what happened the last time you were given a thousand pounds.'

'That's what your papa said.'

'Did you tell him that?'

'I told him everything – and he gave me a thousand pounds.'

'... Poor Adam ...' said Nina suddenly.

'Why did you say that?'

'I don't know.... I believe this is your car....'

'Nina, why did you say "Poor Adam"?'

'... Did I? ... Oh, I don't know.... Oh, I do adore you so.'

'I'm going to be married to-morrow. Are you?'

'Yes, I expect so, dear.'

The chauffeur got rather bored while they tried to decide where they would dine. At every place he suggested they gave a little wail of dismay. 'But that's sure to be full of awful people we know,' they said. Maidenhead, Thame, Brighton, he suggested. Finally they decided to go to Arundel.

'It'll be nearly nine before we get there,' the chauffeur said. 'Now there's a very nice hotel at Bray....'

But they went to Arundel.

'We'll be married to-morrow,' said Adam in the car. 'And we won't ask anybody to the wedding at all. And we'll go abroad at once, and just not come back till I've written all those books. Nina, isn't it divine? Where shall we go?'

'Anywhere you like, only rather warm, don't you think?'

'I don't believe you really think we are going to be married, Nina, do you, or do you?'

'I don't know ... it's only that I don't believe that really divine things like that ever do happen.... I don't know why.... Oh, I do like you so much to-night. If only you *knew* how sweet you looked skipping about in Margot's hall all by yourself. I'd been watching you for hours before I came down.'

'I shall send the car back,' said Adam, as they drove through Pulborough. 'We can go home by train.'

'If there is a train.'

'There's bound to be,' said Adam. But this raised a question in both their minds that had been unobtrusively agitating them throughout the journey. Neither said any more on the subject, but there was a distinct air of constraint in the Daimler from Pulborough onwards.

This question was settled when they reached the hotel at Arundel.

'We want dinner,' said Adam, 'and a room for the night.'

'*Darling*, am I going to be seduced?'

'I'm afraid you are. Do you mind terribly?'

'Not as much as all that,' said Nina, and added in Cockney. 'Charmed, I'm sure.'

Everyone had finished dinner. They dined alone in a corner of the coffee-room, while the other waiters laid the tables for breakfast, looking at them resentfully. It was the dreariest kind of English dinner. After dinner the lounge was awful; there were some golfers in dinner-jackets playing bridge, and two old ladies. Adam and Nina went across the stable-yard to the tap-room and sat until closing-time in a warm haze of tobacco smoke listening to the intermittent gossip of the townspeople. They sat hand-in-hand, unembarrassed; after the first minute no one noticed them. Just before closing time Adam stood a round of drinks. They said:

'Good health, sir. Best respects, madam,' and the barman said, 'Come along, please. Finish your drinks, please,' in a peculiar sing-song tone.

There was a clock chiming as they crossed the yard and a slightly drunk farmer trying to start up his car. Then they went up an oak staircase lined with blunderbusses and coaching prints to their room.

They had no luggage (the chambermaid remarked on this next day to the young man who worked at the wireless shop, saying that that was the worst of being in a main-road hotel. You got all sorts).

Adam undressed very quickly and got into bed; Nina more slowly arranging her clothes on the chair and fingering the ornaments on the chimney-piece with less than her usual self-possession. At last she put out the light.

'Do you know,' she said, trembling slightly as she got into bed, 'this is the first time this has happened to me?'

'It's great fun,' said Adam, 'I promise you.'

'I'm sure it is,' said Nina seriously, 'I wasn't saying anything against it. I was only saying that it hadn't happened before . . . Oh, Adam. . . . '

*

'And you said that really divine things didn't happen,' said Adam in the middle of the night.

'I don't think that this is at all divine,' said Nina. 'It's given me a pain. And – my dear, that reminds me. I've something terribly important to say to you in the morning.'

'What?'

'Not now, darling. Let's go to sleep for a little, don't you think?'

Before Nina was properly awake Adam dressed and went out into the rain to get a shave. He came back bringing two tooth-brushes and a bright red celluloid comb. Nina sat up in bed and combed her hair. She put Adam's coat over her back.

'My dear, you look exactly like *La Vie Parisienne*,' said Adam, turning round from brushing his teeth.

Then she threw off the coat and jumped out of bed, and he told her that she looked like a fashion drawing without the clothes. Nina was rather pleased about that, but she said that it was cold and that she still had a pain, only not so bad as it was. Then she dressed and they went downstairs.

Everyone else had had breakfast and the waiters were laying the tables for luncheon.

'By the way,' said Adam. 'You said there was something you wanted to say.'

'Oh, yes, so there is. My dear, something quite awful.'

'Do tell me.'

'Well, it's about that cheque papa gave you. I'm afraid it won't help us as much as you thought.'

'But, darling, it's a thousand pounds, isn't it?'

'Just look at it, my sweet.' She took it out of her bag and handed it across the table.

'I don't see anything wrong with it,' said Adam.

'Not the signature?'

'Why, good lord, the old idiot's signed it "Charlie Chaplin."'

'That's what I mean, darling.'

'But can't we get him to alter it? He must be dotty. I'll go down and see him again to-day.'

'I shouldn't do that, dear . . . don't you see. . . . Of course, he's very old, and . . . I dare say you may have made things sound a little odd . . . don't you think, dear, *he* must have thought *you* a little dotty? . . . I mean . . . perhaps . . . that cheque was a kind of joke.'

'Well I'm damned . . . this really is a bore. When everything seemed to be going so well, too. When did you notice the signature, Nina?'

'As soon as you showed it to me, at Margot's. Only you looked so happy I didn't like to say anything. . . . You did look happy, you know, Adam, and so sweet. I think I really fell in love with you for the first time when I saw you dancing all alone in the hall.'

'Well I'm damned,' said Adam again. 'The old devil.'

'Anyway, you've had some fun out of it, haven't you . . . or haven't you?'

'Haven't *you*?'

'My dear, I never hated anything so much in my life . . . still, as long as you enjoyed it that's something.'

'I say, Nina,' said Adam after some time, 'we shan't be able to get married after all.'

'No, I'm afraid not.'

'It *is* a bore, isn't it?'

Later he said, 'I expect that parson thought I was dotty too.'

And later, 'As a matter of fact, it's rather a good joke, don't you think?'

'I think it's divine.'

In the train Nina said: 'It's awful to think that I shall probably never, as long as I live, see you dancing like that again all by yourself.'

CHAPTER 6

THAT evening Lady Metroland gave a party for Mrs Melrose Ape. Adam found the telegram of invitation waiting for him on his return to Shepheard's. (Lottie had already used the prepaid reply to do some betting with. Someone had given her a tip for the November Handicap and she wanted to 'make her little flutter' before she forgot the name.) He also found an invitation to luncheon from Simon Balcairn.

The food at Shepheard's tends to be mostly game-pie – quite black inside and full of beaks and shot and inexplicable vertebrae – so Adam was quite pleased to lunch with Simon Balcairn, though he knew there must be some slightly sinister motive behind this sudden hospitality.

They lunched *Chez Espinosa*, the second most expensive restaurant in London; it was full of oilcloth and Lalique glass, and the sort of people who liked that sort of thing went there continually and said how awful it was.

'I hope you don't mind coming to this awful restaurant,' said Balcairn. 'The truth is that I get meals free if I mention them occasionally in my page. Not drinks, unfortunately. Who's here, Alphonse?' he asked the *maître d'hôtel.*

Alphonse handed him the typewritten slip that was always kept for gossip writers.

'H'm, yes. Quite a good list this morning, Alphonse. I'll do what I can about it.'

'Thank you, sir. A table for two? A cocktail?'

'No, I don't think I want a cocktail. I really haven't time. Will you have one, Adam? They aren't very good here.'

'No, thanks,' said Adam.

'Sure?' said Balcairn, already making for their table.

When they were being helped to caviare he looked at the wine list.

'The lager is rather good,' he said. 'What would you like to drink?'

'Whatever you're having.... I think some lager would be lovely.'

'Two small bottles of lager, please.... Are you sure you really like that better than anything?'

'Yes, really, thank you.'

Simon Balcairn looked about him gloomily, occasionally adding a new name to his list. (It is so depressing to be in a profession in which literally all conversation is 'shop'.)

Presently he said, with a deadly air of carelessness:

'Margot Metroland's got a party to-night, hasn't she? Are you going?'

'I think probably. I usually like Margot's parties, don't you?'

'Yes.... Adam, I'll tell you a very odd thing. She hasn't sent me an invitation to this one.'

'I expect she will. I only got mine this morning.'

'... Yes... who's that woman just come in in the fur coat? I know her so well by sight.'

'Isn't it Lady Everyman?'

'Yes, of course.' Another name was added to the list. Balcairn paused in utmost gloom and ate some salad. 'The thing is... she told Agatha Runcible she wasn't *going* to ask me.'

'Why not?'

'Apparently she's in a rage about something I said about something she said about Miles.'

'People do take things so seriously,' said Adam encouragingly.

'It means ruin for me,' said Lord Balcairn. 'Isn't that Pamela Popham?'

'I haven't the least idea.'

'I'm sure it is... I must look up the spelling in the stud book when I get back. I got into awful trouble about spelling the other day.... Ruin.... She's asked Vanburgh.'

'Well, he's some sort of cousin, isn't he?'

'It's so damned unfair. All my cousins are in lunatic asylums or else they live in the country and do indelicate things with wild animals... except my mamma, and that's worse.... They were furious at the office about Van getting that Downing Street "scoop". If I miss this party I may as well leave Fleet Street for good... I may as well put my head into a gas-oven and have done with it.... I'm sure if Margot knew how much it meant to me she wouldn't mind my coming.'

Great tears stood in his eyes threatening to overflow.

'All this last week,' he said, 'I've been reduced to making up my page from the Court Circular and Debrett.... No one ever asks me anywhere now....'

'I'll tell you what,' said Adam, 'I know Margot pretty well. If you like I'll ring her up and ask if I may bring you.'

'Will you? Will you, Adam? If only you really would. Let's go and do it at once. We've no time for coffee or liqueurs. Quick, we can telephone from my office... yes, that black hat and my umbrella, no, I've lost the number... there, no, there, oh do hurry.... Yes, a taxi...'

They were out in the street and into a taxi before Adam had time to say any more. Soon they were embedded in a traffic block in the Strand, and after a time they reached Balcairn's office in Fleet Street.

They went up to a tiny room with 'Social' written on the glass of the door. Its interior seemed not to justify its name. There was one chair, a typewriter, a telephone, some books of reference and a considerable litter of photographs. Balcairn's immediate superior sat in the one chair.

'Hullo,' she said. 'So you're back. Where you been?'

'Espinosa. Here's the list.'

The social editress read it through. 'Can't have Kitty Blackwater,' she said. 'Had her yesterday. Others'll do. Write 'em down to a couple of paragraphs. Suppose you didn't notice what they were wearing?'

'Yes,' said Balcairn eagerly. 'All of them.'

'Well, you won't have room to use it. We got to keep everything down for Lady M.'s party. I've cut out the D. of Devonshire altogether. By the way, the photograph you used yesterday wasn't the present Countess of Everyman. It's an old one of the Dowager. We had 'em both on the phone about it, going on something awful. That's *you* again. Got your invite for to-night?'

'Not yet.'

'You better get it quick. I got to have a first-hand story before we go to press, see? By the way, know anything about this? Lady R.'s maid sent it in to-day.' She picked up a slip of paper: '"Rumoured engagement broken off between Adam Fenwick-Symes, only son of the late Professor Oliver Fenwick-Symes, and Nina Blount, of Doubting Hall, Aylesbury". Never heard of either. Ain't even been announced, so far as I'm aware of.'

'You'd better ask him. This is Adam Symes.'

'Hullo, no offence meant, I'm sure.... What about it?'

'It is neither announced nor broken off.'

'N.B.G. in fact, eh? Then *that* goes *there*.' She put the slip into the wastepaper basket. 'That girl's sent us a lot of bad stuff lately. Well, I'm off for a bit of lunch. I'll be over at the Garden Club if anything urgent turns up. So long.'

The editress went out, banging the door labelled 'Social', and whistled as she went down the passage.

'You see how they treat me,' said Lord Balcairn. 'They were all over me when I first arrived. I do so wish I were dead.'

'Don't cry,' said Adam, 'it's too shy-making.'

'I can't help it... oh, do come in.'

The door marked 'Social' opened and a small boy came in.

'Lord Circumference's butler downstairs with some engagements and a divorce.'

'Tell him to leave them.'

'Very good, my lord.'

'That's the only person in this office who's ever polite to me,' said Balcairn as the messenger disappeared. 'I wish I had something to leave him in my will.... Do ring up Margot. Then I shall at any rate know the worst.... Come in.'

'Gentleman of the name of General Strapper downstairs. Wants to see you very particular.'

'What about?'

'Couldn't say, my lord, but he's got a whip. Seems very put out about something.'

'Tell him the social editor is having luncheon.... Do ring up Margot.'

Adam said, 'Margot, may I bring someone with me to-night?'

'Well, Adam, I really don't think you can. I can't imagine how everyone's going to get in as it is. I'm terribly sorry, who is it?'

'Simon Balcairn. He's particularly anxious to come.'

'I dare say he is. I'm rather against that young man. He's written things about me in the papers.'

'*Please*, Margot.'

'Certainly not. I won't have him inside my house. I've only asked Van on the strictest understanding that he doesn't write anything about it. I don't wish to have anything more to do with Simon Balcairn.'

'My dear, how *rich* you sound.'

'I feel my full income when that young man is mentioned. Good-bye. See you to-night.'

'You needn't tell me,' said Balcairn, 'I know what she's said... it's no good, is it?'

'I'm afraid not.'

'Done for...' said Balcairn. '... End of the tether....' He turned over some slips of paper listlessly. 'Would it interest you to hear that Agatha and Archie are engaged?'

'I don't believe it.'

'Neither do I. One of our people has just sent it in. Half of what they send us is lies, and the other half libel... they sent us a long story about Miles and Pamela Popham having spent last night at Arundel.... But we couldn't use it even if it were true, which it obviously isn't, knowing Miles. Thank you for doing what you could... good-bye.'

Downstairs in the outer office there was an altercation in progress. A large man of military appearance was shaking and stamping in front of a middle-aged woman. Adam recognized the social editress.

'Answer me, yes or no,' the big man was saying. 'Are you or are you not responsible for this damnable lie about my daughter?'

(He had read in Simon Balcairn's column that his daughter had been seen at a night club. To anyone better acquainted with Miss Strapper's habits of life the paragraph was particularly reticent.)

'Yes or no,' cried the General, 'or I'll shake the life out of you.'

'No.'

'Then who is? Let me get hold of the cad who wrote it. Where is he?' roared the General.

'Upstairs,' the social editress managed to say.

'More trouble for Simon,' thought Adam.

*

Adam went to pick Nina up at her flat. They had arranged to go to a cinema together. She said, 'You're much later than you said. It's so boring to be late for a talkie.'

He said, 'Talkies are boring, anyhow.'

They treated each other quite differently after their night's experiences. Adam was inclined to be egotistical and despondent; Nina was rather grown-up and disillusioned and distinctly cross. Adam began to say that as far as he could see he would have to live on at Shepheard's now for the rest of his life, or at any rate for the rest of Lottie's life, as it wouldn't be fair to leave without paying the bill.

Then Nina said, 'Do be amusing, Adam. I can't bear you when you're not amusing.'

Then Adam began to tell her about Simon Balcairn and Margot's party. He described how he had seen Simon being horse-whipped in the middle of the office.

Nina said, 'Yes, that's amusing. Go on like that.'

The story of Simon's whipping lasted them all the way to the cinema. They were very late for the film Nina wanted to see, and that set them back again. They didn't speak for a long time. Then Nina said *à propos* of the film, 'All this fuss about sleeping together. For physical pleasure I'd sooner go to my dentist any day.'

Adam said, 'You'll enjoy it more next time.'

Nina said, '*Next time*,' and told him that he took too much for granted.

Adam said that that was a phrase which only prostitutes used.

Then they started a real quarrel which lasted all through the film and all the way to Nina's flat and all the time she was cutting up a lemon and making a cocktail, until Adam said that if she didn't stop going on he would ravish her there and then on her own hearth-rug.

Then Nina went on.

But by the time that Adam went to dress she had climbed down enough to admit that perhaps love was a thing one could grow to be fond of after a time, like smoking a pipe. Still she maintained that it made one feel very ill at first, and she doubted if it was worth it.

Then they began to argue at the top of the lift about whether acquired tastes were ever worth acquiring. Adam said it was imitation, and that it was natural to man to be imitative, so that acquired tastes were natural.

But the presence of the lift boy stopped that argument coming to a solution as the other had done.

*

'My, ain't this classy,' said Divine Discontent.

'It's all right,' said Chastity in a worldly voice. 'Nothing to make a song and dance about.'

'Who's making a song and dance? I just said it was classy – and it *is* classy, ain't it?'

'I suppose everything's classy to *some* people.'

'Now you two,' said Temperance, who had been put in charge of the angels for the evening, 'don't you start anything in here, not with your wings on. Mrs Ape won't stand for scrapping in wings, and you know it.'

'Who's starting anything?'

'Well, you are then.'

'Oh, it's no use talking to Chastity. She's too high and mighty to be an angel now. Went out for a drive with Mrs Panrast in a Rolls-Royce,' said Fortitude. 'I saw her. I was *so* sorry it rained all the time, or it might have been quite enjoyable, mightn't it, Chastity?'

'Well, you ought to be glad. Leaves the *men* for you, Fortitude. Only they don't seem to want to take advantage, do they?'

Then they talked about men for some time. Divine Discontent thought the second footman had nice eyes.

'And he knows it,' said Temperance.

They were all having supper together in what was still called the schoolroom in Lady Metroland's house. From the window they could see the guests arriving for the party. In spite of the rain quite a large crowd had collected on either side of the awning to criticize the cloaks with appreciative 'oohs' and 'ahs' or contemptuous sniffs. Cars and taxis drove up in close succession. Lady Circumference splashed up the street in goloshes, wearing a high fender of diamonds under a tartan umbrella. The Bright Young People came popping all together, out of someone's electric brougham like a litter of pigs, and ran squealing up the steps. Some 'gate-crashers' who had made the mistake of coming in Victorian fancy dress were detected and repulsed. They hurried home to change for a second assault. No one wanted to miss Mrs Ape's *début*.

But the angels were rather uneasy. They had been dressed ever since seven o'clock in their white shifts, gold sashes and wings. It was now past ten, and the strain was beginning to tell, for it was impossible to sit back comfortably in wings.

'Oh, I wish they'd hurry up so we could get it over,' said Creative Endeavour. 'Mrs Ape said we could have some champagne afterwards if we sang nice.'

'I don't mind betting *she's* doing herself pretty well, down there.'

'*Chastity!*'

'Oh, *all* right.'

Then the footman with the nice eyes came to clear the table. He gave them a friendly wink as he shut the door. 'Pretty creatures,' he thought. 'Blooming shame that they're so religious . . . wasting the best years of their lives.'

(There had been a grave debate in the servants' hall about the exact status of angels. Even Mr Blenkinsop, the butler, had been uncertain. 'Angels are certainly not guests,' he had said, 'and I don't think they are deputations. Nor they ain't governesses either, nor clergy not strictly speaking; they're not entertainers, because entertainers *dine* nowadays, the more's the pity.'

'I believe they're decorators,' said Mrs Blouse, 'or else charitable workers.'

'Charitable workers are governesses, Mrs Blouse. There is nothing to be gained by multiplying social distinctions indefinitely. Decorators are either guests or workmen.'

After further discussion the conclusion was reached that angels were nurses, and that became the official ruling of the household. But the second footman was of the opinion that they were just 'young persons', pure and simple, 'and very nice too', for nurses cannot, except in very rare cases, be winked at, and clearly angels could.)

'What we want to know, Chastity,' said Creative Endeavour, 'is how you come to take up with Mrs Panrast at all.'

'Yes,' said the Angels, 'yes. It's not like *you*, Chastity, to go riding in a motor-car with a woman.' They fluttered their feathers in a menacing way. 'Let's third-degree her,' said Humility with rather nasty relish.

(There was a system of impromptu jurisdiction among the Angels which began with innuendo, went on to cross-examination, pinches and slaps and ended, as a rule, in tears and kisses.)

Faced by this circle of spiteful and haloed faces, Chastity began to lose her air of superiority.

'Why shouldn't I ride with a friend,' she asked plaintively, 'without all you girls pitching on me like this?'

'*Friend?*' said Creative Endeavour. 'You never saw her before to-day,' and she gave her a nasty pinch just above the elbow.

'*Ooooh!*' said Chastity. '*Ooh, please*... beast.'

Then they all pinched her all over, but precisely and judiciously, so as not to disturb her wings or halo, for this was no orgy (sometimes in their bedroom, they gave way, but not here, in Lady Metroland's schoolroom, before an important first night).

'Ooh,' said Chastity. '*Ooh, ow, ooh, ow. Please,* beasts, swine, cads... *please*... ooh... well, if you must know, I thought she *was* a man.'

'Thought she was a *man*, Chastity? That doesn't sound right to me.'

'Well, she looks like a man and – and she *goes on* like a man. I saw her sitting at a table in a tea-shop. She hadn't got a hat on, and I couldn't see her skirt... ooh... how can I tell you if you keep pinching... and she smiled and so, well, I went and had some tea with her, and she said would I go out with her in her motor-car, and I said yes and, ooh, I wish I hadn't now.'

'What did she say in the motor-car, Chastity?'

'I forget – nothing much.'

'Oh, what.' 'Do tell us.' 'We'll never pinch you again if you tell us.' 'I'm sorry if I hurt you, Chastity, do tell *me*.' 'You'd *better* tell us.'

'No, I can't, *really* – I don't remember, I tell you.'

'Give her another little nip, girls.'

'Ooh, ooh, ooh, *stop*. I'll tell you.'

Their heads were close together and they were so deeply engrossed in the story that they did not hear Mrs Ape's entry.

'Smut again,' said a terrible voice. 'Girls, I'm sick ashamed of you.'

Mrs Ape looked magnificent in a gown of heavy gold brocade embroidered with texts.

'I'm sick ashamed of you,' repeated Mrs Ape, 'and you've made Chastity cry again, just before the big act. If you must bully someone, *why* choose Chastity? You all know by this time that crying always gives her a red nose. How do *I* look, I should like to know, standing up in front of a lot of angels with red noses? You don't ever think of nothing but your own pleasures, do you? *Sluts.*' This last word was spoken with a depth of expression that set the angels trembling. 'There'll be no champagne for anyone to-night, see. And if you don't sing perfectly, I'll give the whole lot of you a good hiding, see. Now, come on, now, and for the love of the Lamb, Chastity, *do something to your nose.* They'll think it's a temperance meeting to see you like that.'

It was a brilliant scene into which the disconsolate angels trooped two minutes later. Margot Metroland shook hands with each of them as they came to the foot of the staircase, appraising them, one by one, with an expert eye.

'You don't look happy, my dear,' she found time to say to Chastity, as she led them across the ballroom to their platform, banked in orchids at the far end. 'If you feel you want a change, let me know later, and I can get you a job in South America. *I mean it.*'

'Oh, thank you,' said Chastity, 'but I could never leave Mrs Ape.'

'Well, think it over, child. You're far too pretty a girl to waste your time singing hymns. Tell that other girl, the red-headed one, that I can probably find a place for her, too.'

'What, Humility? Don't you have nothing to do with her. She's a fiend.'

'Well, some men like rough stuff, but I don't want anyone who makes trouble with the other girls.'

'She makes trouble all right. Look at that bruise.'

'My dear!'

Margot Metroland and Mrs Ape led the angels up the steps between the orchids and stood them at the back of the platform facing the room. Chastity stood next to Creative Endeavour.

'Please, Chastity, I'm sorry if we hurt you,' said Creative Endeavour. '*I* didn't pinch hard, did I?'

'Yes,' said Chastity. 'Like hell you did.'

A slightly sticky hand tried to take hers, but she clenched her fist. She would go to South America and work for Lady Metroland . . . and she wouldn't say anything about it to Humility either. She glared straight in front of her, saw Mrs Panrast and dropped her eyes.

*

The ballroom was filled with little gilt chairs and the chairs with people. Lord Vanburgh, conveniently seated near the door, through which he could slip away to the telephone, was taking them all in. They were almost all, in some way or another, notable. The motives for Margot Metroland's second marriage* had been mixed, but entirely worldly; chief among them had been the desire to re-establish her somewhat shaken social position, and her party that night testified to her success, for while many people can entertain the Prime Minister and the Duchess of Stayle and Lady Circumference, and anybody can, and often against her will does, entertain Miles Malpractice and Agatha Runcible, it is only a very confident hostess who will invite both these sets together at the same time, differing as they do upon almost all questions of principle and deportment. Standing near Vanburgh, by the door, was a figure who seemed in himself to typify the change that had come over Pastmaster House when Margot Beste-Chetwynd became Lady Metroland; an unobtrusive man of rather less than average height, whose black beard, falling in tight burnished curls, nearly concealed the order of St Michael and St George which he wore round his neck; he wore a large signet ring on the little finger of his left hand outside his white glove; there was an orchid in his buttonhole. His eyes, youthful but grave, wandered among the crowd; occasionally he bowed with grace and decision. Several people were asking about him.

'See the beaver with the medal,' said Humility to Faith.

'Who is that *very* important young man?' asked Mrs Blackwater of Lady Throbbing.

* See *Decline and Fall.*

'I don't know, dear. He bowed to *you.*'

'He bowed to *you*, dear.'

'How very nice . . . I wasn't quite sure. . . . He reminds me a little of dear Prince Anrep.'

'It's so nice in these days, isn't it, dearest, to see someone who really looks . . . don't you think?'

'You mean the beard?'

'*The beard among other things*, darling.'

*

Father Rothschild was conspiring with Mr Outrage and Lord Metroland. He stopped short in the middle of his sentence.

'Forgive me,' he said, 'but there are spies everywhere. That man with the beard, do you know him?'

Lord Metroland thought vaguely he had something to do with the Foreign Office; Mr Outrage seemed to remember having seen him before.

'*Exactly*,' said Father Rothschild. 'I think it would be better if we continued our conversation in private. I have been watching him. *He is bowing across the room to empty places and to people whose backs are turned to him.*' The Great Men withdrew to Lord Metroland's study. Father Rothschild closed the door silently and looked behind the curtains.

'Shall I lock the door?' asked Lord Metroland.

'No,' said the Jesuit. 'A lock does not prevent a spy from hearing; but it does hinder us, inside, from catching the spy.'

'Well, I should never have thought of that,' said Mr Outrage in frank admiration.

*

'How pretty Nina Blount is,' said Lady Throbbing, busy from the front row with her lorgnette, 'but don't you think, a little changed; almost as though . . .'

'You notice everything, darling.'

'When you get to our age, dear, there is so little left, but I do believe Miss Blount must have had an *experience* . . . she's sitting next to Miles. You know I heard from Edward to-night. He's on his way back. It will be a great blow for Miles because he's been living in Edward's house all this time. To tell you the truth I'm a little glad because from what I hear from Anne Opalthorpe, who lives opposite, the things that go on . . . he's got a friend staying there now. Such an odd man . . . a dirt-track racer. But then it's no use attempting to disguise the fact, *is* there. . . . There's Mrs Panrast . . . yes, dear, of course you know her, she used to be Eleanor Balcairn . . . now *why* does dear Margot ask anyone like that, do you think? . . . it is not as though Margot was so innocent . . . and there's Lord Monomark . . . yes, the man who owns those *amusing* papers . . . they say that he and Margot, but *before* her marriage, of course (her second marriage, I mean), but you never know, do you, how things *crop* up again? . . . I wonder where Peter Pastmaster is? . . . he never stays to Margot's parties . . . he was at dinner, of course, and, my dear, *how* he drank. . . . He can't be more than twenty-one. . . . Oh, so that is Mrs Ape. What a coarse face . . . no dear, of course she can't hear . . . she looks like a *procureuse* . . . but perhaps I shouldn't say that *here*, should I?'

*

Adam came and sat next to Nina.

'Hullo,' they said to each other.

'My dear, do look at Mary Mouse's new young man,' said Nina.

Adam looked and saw that Mary was sitting next to the Maharajah of Pukkapore.

'I call that a pretty pair,' he said.

'Oh, how bored I feel,' said Nina.

*

Mr Benfleet was there talking to two poets. They said ' . . . and I wrote to tell William that I didn't write the review, but it was true that Tony did read me the review over the telephone when I was very sleepy before he sent it in. I thought it was best to tell him the truth because he would hear it from Tony anyway. Only I said I advised him not to publish it just as I had advised

William not to publish the book in the first place. Well, Tony rang up Michael and told him that I'd said that William thought Michael had written the review because of the review I had written of Michael's book last November, though, as a matter of fact, it was Tony himself who wrote it. . . .'

'Too bad,' said Mr Benfleet. 'Too bad.'

'. . . But is that any reason, even if I had written it, why Michael should tell Tony that I had stolen five pounds from William?'

'Certainly not,' said Mr Benfleet. 'Too bad.'

'Of course, they're *simply* not *gentlemen*, either of them. That's all it is, only one's shy of saying it nowadays.'

Mr Benfleet shook his head sadly and sympathetically.

*

Then Mrs Melrose Ape stood up to speak. A hush fell in the ballroom beginning at the back and spreading among the gilt chairs until only Mrs Blackwater's voice was heard exquisitely articulating some details of Lady Metroland's past. Then she, too, was silent and Mrs Ape began her oration about Hope.

'Brothers and Sisters,' she said in a hoarse, stirring voice. Then she paused and allowed her eyes, renowned throughout three continents for their magnetism, to travel among the gilded chairs. (It was one of her favourite openings.) '*Just you look at yourselves*,' she said.

Magically, self-doubt began to spread in the audience. Mrs Panrast stirred uncomfortably; had that silly little girl been talking, she wondered.

'Darling,' whispered Miss Runcible, 'is my nose awful?'

Nina thought how once, only twenty-four hours ago, she had been in love. Mr Benfleet thought should he have made it three per cent on the tenth thousand. The gate-crashers wondered whether it would not have been better to have stayed at home. (Once in Kansas City Mrs Ape had got no further than these opening words; there had been a tornado of emotion and all the seats in the hall had been broken to splinters. It was there that Humility had joined the Angels.) There were a thousand things in Lady Throbbing's past.... Every heart found something to bemoan.

'She's got 'em again,' whispered Creative Endeavour. 'Got 'em stiff.'

Lord Vanburgh slipped from the room to telephone through some racy paragraphs about fashionable piety.

Mary Mouse shed two little tears and felt for the brown, bejewelled hand of the Maharajah.

But suddenly on that silence vibrant with self-accusation broke the organ voice of England, the hunting-cry of the *ancien régime*. Lady Circumference gave a resounding snort of disapproval:

'What a damned impudent woman,' she said.

Adam and Nina and Miss Runcible began to giggle, and Margot Metroland for the first time in her many parties was glad to realize that the guest of the evening was going to be a failure. It had been an awkward moment.

*

In the study Father Rothschild and Mr Outrage were plotting with enthusiasm. Lord Metroland was smoking a cigar and wondering how soon he could get away. He wanted to hear Mrs Ape and to have another look at those Angels. There was one with red hair.... Besides, all this statesmanship and foreign policy had always bored him. In his years in the Commons he had always liked a good scrap, and often thought a little wistfully of those orgies of competitive dissimulation in which he had risen to eminence. Even now, when some straightforward, easily intelligible subject was under discussion, such as poor people's wages or public art, he enjoyed from time to time making a sonorous speech to the Upper House. But this sort of thing was not at all in his line.

Suddenly Father Rothschild turned out the light.

'There's someone coming down the passage,' he said. 'Quick, get behind the curtains.'

'Really, Rothschild...' said Mr Outrage.

'I say...' said Lord Metroland.

'*Quick*,' said Father Rothschild.

The three statesmen hid themselves. Lord Metroland, still smoking, his head thrown back and his cigar erect. They heard the door open. The light was turned on. A match was struck. Then came the slight tinkle of the telephone as someone lifted the receiver.

'Central ten thousand,' said a slightly muffled voice.

'*Now*,' said Father Rothschild, and stepped through the curtain.

The bearded stranger who had excited his suspicions was standing at the table smoking one of Lord Metroland's cigars and holding the telephone.

'Oh, hullo,' he said, 'I didn't know you were here. Just thought I'd use the telephone. So sorry. Won't disturb you. Jolly party, isn't it? Good-bye.'

'Stay exactly where you are,' said Father Rothschild, 'and take off that beard.'

'Damned if I do,' said the stranger crossly. 'It's no use talking to me as though I were one of your choir boys . . . you old *bully*.'

'Take off that beard,' said Father Rothschild.

'Take off that beard,' said Lord Metroland and the Prime Minister, emerging suddenly from behind the curtain.

This concurrence of Church and State, coming so unexpectedly after an evening of prolonged embarrassment, was too much for Simon.

'Oh, all right,' he said, 'if you *will* make such a *thing* about it . . . it hurts too frightfully, if you knew . . . it ought to be soaked in hot water . . . ooh . . . ow.'

He gave some tugs at the black curls, and bit by bit they came away.

'*There*,' he said. 'Now I should go and make Lady Throbbing take off her wig. . . . I should have a really jolly evening while you're about it, if I were you.'

'I seem to have over-estimated the gravity of the situation,' said Father Rothschild.

'Who is it, after all this?' said Mr Outrage. 'Where are those detectives? What does it all mean?'

'That,' said Father Rothschild bitterly, 'is Mr *Chatterbox*.'

'Never heard of him. I don't believe there is such a person.... *Chatterbox*, indeed... you make us hide behind a curtain and then you tell us that some young man in a false beard is called Chatterbox. Really, Rothschild...'

'Lord Balcairn,' said Lord Metroland, 'will you kindly leave my house immediately?'

'*Is* this young man called Chatterbox or is he not?... Upon my soul, I believe you're all crazy.'

'Oh yes, I'm going,' said Simon. 'You didn't think I was going to go back to the party like this, did you? – or did you?' Indeed, he looked very odd with little patches of black hair still adhering to parts of his chin and cheeks.

'Lord Monomark is here this evening. I shall certainly inform him of your behaviour...'

'He writes for the papers,' Father Rothschild tried to explain to the Prime Minister.

'Well, damn it, so do I, but I don't wear a false beard and call myself Chatterbox.... I simply do not understand what has happened.... Where are those detectives?... Will no one explain?... *You treat me like a child*,' he said. It was all like one of those Cabinet meetings, when they all talked about something he didn't understand and paid no attention to him.

Father Rothschild led him away, and attempted with almost humiliating patience and tact to make clear to him some of the complexities of modern journalism.

'I don't believe a word of it,' the Prime Minister kept saying. 'It's all humbug. You're keeping something back.... *Chatterbox*, indeed.'

Simon Balcairn was given his hat and coat and shown to the door. The crowd round the awning had dispersed. It was still raining. He walked back to his little flat in Bourdon Street. The rain washed a few of the remaining locks from his face; it dripped down his collar.

They were washing a car outside his front door; he crept between it and his dustbin, fitted his latchkey in the lock and went upstairs. His flat was like *Chez Espinosa* – all oilcloth and Lalique glass; there were some enterprising photographs by David Lennox, a gramophone (on the instalment system) and numberless cards of invitation on the mantelpiece. His bath towel was where he had left it on his bed.

Simon went to the ice box in the kitchen and chipped off some ice. Then he made himself a cocktail. Then he went to the telephone.

'Central ten thousand . . .' he said. . . . Give me Mrs Brace. Hullo, this is Balcairn.'

'Well . . . gotcher story?'

'Oh yes, I've got my story, only this isn't gossip, it's news – front page. You'll have to fill up the Chatterbox page on Espinosa's.'

'Hell!'

'Wait till you see the story. . . . Hullo, give me news, will you. . . . This is Balcairn. Put on one of the boys to take this down, will you? . . . ready? All right.'

At his glass-topped table, sipping his cocktail, Simon Balcairn dictated his last story.

'*Scenes of wild religious enthusiasm, comma, reminiscent of a negro camp-meeting in Southern America, comma, broke out in the heart of Mayfair yesterday evening at the party given for the famous American Revivalist Mrs Ape by the Viscountess Metroland, formerly the Hon. Mrs Beste-Chetwynd, at her historic mansion, Pastmaster House, stop. The magnificent ballroom can never have enshrined a more brilliant assembly* . . .'

It was his swan-song. Lie after monstrous lie bubbled up in his brain.

'. . . *The Hon. Agatha Runcible joined Mrs Ape among the orchids and led the singing, tears coursing down her face* . . .'

Excitement spread at the *Excess* office. The machines were stopped. The night staff of reporters, slightly tipsy, as always at that hour, stood over the stenographer as he typed. The compositors snatched the sheets of copy as they came. The sub-editors began ruthlessly cutting and scrapping; they suppressed important political announcements, garbled the evidence at a murder trial, reduced the dramatic criticism to one caustic paragraph, to make room for Simon's story.

It came through 'hot and strong, as nice as mother makes it', as one of them remarked.

'Little Lord Fauntleroy's on a good thing at last,' said another.

'What-ho,' said a third appreciatively.

'*... barely had Lady Everyman finished before the Countess of Throbbing rose to confess her sins, and in a voice broken with emotion disclosed the hitherto unverified details of the parentage of the present Earl....*'

'Tell Mr Edwardes to look up photographs of all three of 'em,' said the assistant news editor.

'*... The Marquess of Vanburgh, shaken by sobs of contrition.... Mrs Panrast, singing feverishly.... Lady Anchorage with downcast eyes...*'

'*... The Archbishop of Canterbury, who up to now had remained unmoved by the general emotion, then testified that at Eton in the 'eighties he and Sir James Brown ...*'

'*... the Duchess of Stayle next threw down her emerald and diamond tiara, crying "a Guilt Offering", an example which was quickly followed by the Countess of Circumference and Lady Brown, until a veritable rain of precious stones fell on to the parquet flooring, heirlooms of priceless value rolling among Tecla pearls and Chanel diamonds. A blank cheque fluttered from the hands of the Maharajah of Pukkapore ...*'

It made over two columns, and when Simon finally rang off, after receiving the congratulations of his colleagues, he was for the first time in his journalistic experience perfectly happy about his work. He finished the watery dregs of the cocktail shaker and went into the kitchen. He shut the door and the window and opened the door of the gas oven. Inside it was very black and dirty and smelled of meat. He spread a sheet of newspaper on the lowest tray and lay down, resting his head on it. Then he noticed that by some mischance he had chosen Vanburgh's gossip-page in the *Morning Despatch*. He put in another sheet. (There were crumbs on the floor.) Then he turned on the gas. It came surprisingly with a loud roar; the wind of it stirred his hair and the remaining particles of his beard. At first he held his breath. Then he thought that was silly and gave a sniff. The sniff made him cough, and coughing made him breathe, and breathing made him feel very ill; but soon he fell into a coma and presently died.

So the last Earl of Balcairn went, as they say, to his fathers (who had fallen in many lands and for many causes, as the eccentricities of British Foreign Policy and their own wandering natures had directed them; at Acre and Agincourt and Killiecrankie, in Egypt and America. One had been picked white by fishes as the tides rolled him among the tree-tops of a submarine forest; some had grown black and unfit for consideration under tropical suns; while many of them lay in marble tombs of extravagant design).

*

At Pastmaster House, Lady Metroland and Lord Monomark were talking about him. Lord Monomark was roaring with boyish laughter.

'That's a great lad,' he said. 'Came in a false beard, did he? That's peppy. What'd you say his name was? I'll raise him tomorrow first thing.'

And he turned to give Simon's name to an attendant secretary.

And when Lady Metroland began to expostulate, he shut her up rather discourteously.

'Shucks, Margot,' he said. 'You know better than to get on a high horse with me.'

CHAPTER 7

THEN Adam became Mr Chatterbox. He and Nina were lunching at Espinosa's and quarrelling half-heartedly when a business-like, Eton-cropped woman came across to their table, whom Adam recognized as the social editress of the *Daily Excess*.

'See here,' she said, 'weren't you over at the office with Balcairn the day he did himself in?'

'Yes.'

'Well, a pretty mess he's let us in for. Sixty-two writs for libel up to date and more coming in. And that's not the worst. Left me to do his job and mine. I was wondering if you could tell me the names of any of these people and anything about them.'

Adam pointed out a few well-worn faces.

'Yes, they ain't no good. They're on the black list. You see, Monomark was in an awful way about Balcairn's story of Lady Metroland's party, and he's sent down a chit that none of the people who are bringing actions against the paper can be mentioned again. Well, I ask you, what's one to do? It's just bricks without straw. Why, we can't even mention the Prime Minister or the Archbishop of Canterbury. I suppose you don't know of anyone who'd care to take on the job? They'd have to be a pretty good mutt, if they would.'

'What do they pay?'

'Ten pounds a week and expenses. Know anyone?'

'I'd do it myself for that.'

'*You*?' The social editress looked at him sceptically. 'Would you be any good?'

'I'll try for a week or two.'

'That's about as long as anyone sticks it. All right, come back to the office with me when you've finished lunch. You can't cause more trouble than Balcairn, any how, and he looked the goods at first.'

'Now we can get married,' said Nina.

*

Meanwhile the libel actions against the authors, printers and publishers of Simon Balcairn's last story practically paralysed the judicial system of the country. The old brigade, led by Mrs Blackwater, threw themselves with relish into an orgy of litigation such as they had not seen since the war (one of the younger counsel causing Lady Throbbing particular delight. . . . 'I do think, when you get to my age, dear, there is something *sympathique* about a wig, don't you? . . . '). The younger generation for the most part allowed their cases to be settled out of court and later gave a very delightful party on the proceeds in a captive dirigible. Miss Runcible, less well advised, filled two albums with Press cuttings portraying her various appearances at the Law Courts, sometimes as plaintiff, sometimes as witness, sometimes (in a hat borrowed from Miss Mouse) as part of the queue of 'fashionably dressed women waiting for admission', once as an intruder being removed by an usher from the Press gallery, and finally as prisoner being sentenced to a fine of ten pounds or seven days' imprisonment for contempt of court.

The proceedings were considerably complicated by the behaviour of Mrs Ape, who gave an interview in which she fully confirmed Simon Balcairn's story. She also caused her Press agent to wire a further account to all parts of the world. She then left the country with her angels, having received a sudden call to ginger up the religious life of Oberammergau.

At intervals letters arrived from Buenos Aires in which Chastity and Divine Discontent spoke rather critically of Latin American entertainment.

'They didn't know when they was well off,' said Mrs Ape.

'It don't sound much different from us,' said Creative Endeavour wistfully.

'They won't be dead five minutes before *they* see the difference,' said Mrs Ape.

Edward Throbbing and two secretaries returned to Hertford Street somewhat inopportunely for Miles and his dirt-track racer, who were obliged to move into Shepheard's. Miles said that the thing he resented about his brother's return was not so much the inconvenience as the expense. For some weeks Throbbing suffered from the successive discoveries by his secretaries of curious and compromising things in all parts of the house; his butler, too, seemed changed. He hiccoughed heavily while serving dinner to two Secretaries of State, complained of spiders in his bath and the sound of musical instruments, and finally had 'the horrors', ran mildly amok in the pantry with the kitchen poker, and had to be taken away in a van. Long after these immediate causes of distress had been removed, the life of Throbbing's secretaries was periodically disturbed by ambiguous telephone calls and the visits of menacing young men who wanted new suits or tickets to America, or a fiver to go on with.

But all these events, though of wide general interest, are of necessity a closed book to the readers of Mr Chatterbox's page.

Lord Monomark's black list had made a devastating change in the personnel of the *Daily Excess* gossip. In a single day Mr Chatterbox's readers found themselves plunged into a murky underworld of nonentities. They were shown photographs of the misshapen daughters of backwoods peers carrying buckets of meal to their fathers' chickens; they learned of the engagement of the younger sister of the Bishop of Chertsey and of a dinner party given in Elm Park Gardens by the widow of a High Commissioner to some of the friends she had made in their colony. There were details of the blameless home life of women novelists, photographed with their spaniels before rose-covered cottages; stories of undergraduate 'rags' and regimental reunion dinners; anecdotes from Harley Street and the Inns of Court; snaps and snippets about cocktail parties given in basement flats by spotty announcers at the B.B.C., of tea dances in Gloucester Terrace and jokes made at High Table by dons.

Urged on by the taunts of the social editress, Adam brought new enterprise and humanity into this sorry column. He started a series of 'Notable Invalids', which was, from the first, wildly successful. He began chattily. '*At a dinner party the other evening my neighbour and I began to compile a list of the most popular deaf peeresses. First, of course, came old Lady — . . .*'

Next day he followed it up with a page about deaf peers and statesmen; then about the one-legged, blind and bald. Postcards of appreciation poured in from all over the country.

'*I have read your column for many years now,*' wrote a correspondent from Bude, '*but this is the first time I have really enjoyed it. I have myself been deaf for a long time, and it is a great comfort to me to know that my affliction is shared by so many famous men and women. Thank you, Mr Chatterbox, and good luck to you.*'

Another wrote: '*Ever since childhood I have been cursed with abnormally large ears which have been a source of ridicule to me and a serious handicap in my career (I am a chub fuddler). I should be so glad to know whether any great people have suffered in the same way.*'

Finally, he ransacked the lunatic asylums and mental houses of the country, and for nearly a week ran an extremely popular series under the heading 'Titled Eccentrics'.

'*It is not generally known that the Earl of —, who lives in strict retirement, has the unusual foible of wearing costume of the Napoleonic Period. So great, indeed, is his detestation of modern dress that on one occasion . . .*'

'*Lord —, whose public appearances are regrettably rare nowadays, is a close student of comparative religions. There is an amusing story of how, when lunching with the then Dean of Westminster, Lord — startled his host by proclaiming that so far from being of divine ordinance, the Ten Commandments were, in point of fact, composed by himself and delivered by him to Moses on Sinai. . . .*'

'*Lady —, whose imitations of animal sounds are so lifelike that she can seldom be persuaded to converse in any other way, . . .*'

And so on.

Besides this, arguing that people did not really mind *whom* they read about provided that a kind of vicarious inquisitiveness into the lives of others was satisfied, Adam began to invent people.

He invented a sculptor called Provna, the son of a Polish nobleman, who lived in a top-floor studio in Grosvenor House. Most of his work (which was all in private hands) was constructed in cork, vulcanite and steel. The Metropolitan Museum at New York, Mr Chatterbox learned, had been negotiating for some time to purchase a specimen, but so far had been unable to outbid the collectors.

Such is the power of the Press, that soon after this a steady output of early Provnas began to travel from Warsaw to Bond Street and from Bond Street to California, while Mrs Hoop announced to her friends that Provna was at the moment at work on a bust of Johnny, which she intended to present to the nation (a statement which Adam was unable to record owing to the presence of Mrs Hoop's name on the black list, but which duly appeared, under a photograph of Johnny, in the Marquess of Vanburgh's rival column).

Encouraged by his success, Adam began gradually to introduce to his readers a brilliant and lovely company. He mentioned them casually at first in lists of genuine people. There was a popular young attaché at the Italian Embassy called Count Cincinnati. He was descended from the famous Roman Consul, Cincinnatus, and bore a plough as his crest. Count Cincinnati was held to be the best amateur 'cellist in London. Adam saw him one evening dancing at the Café de la Paix. A few evenings later Lord Vanburgh noticed him at Covent Garden, remarking that his collection of the original designs for the Russian ballet was unequalled in Europe. Two days later Adam sent him to Monte Carlo for a few days' rest, and Vanburgh hinted that there was more in this visit than met the eye, and mentioned the daughter of a well-known American hostess who was staying there at her aunt's villa.

There was a Captain Angus Stuart-Kerr, too, whose rare appearances in England were a delight to his friends; unlike most big-game hunters, he was an expert and indefatigable dancer. Much to Adam's disgust he found Captain Stuart-Kerr taken up by an unknown gossip-writer in a twopenny illustrated weekly, who saw him at a point-to-point meeting, and remarked that he was well known as the hardest rider in the Hebrides. Adam put a stop to that next day.

'*Some people*,' he wrote, '*are under the impression that Captain Angus Stuart-Kerr, whom I mentioned on this page a short time ago, is a keen rider. Perhaps they are confusing him with Alastair Kerr-Stuart, of Inverauchty, a very distant cousin. Captain Stuart-Kerr never rides, and for a very interesting reason. There is an old Gaelic rhyme repeated among his clansmen which says in rough translation "the Laird rides well on two legs". Tradition has it that when the head of the house mounts a horse the clan will be dispersed.*'*

But Adam's most important creation was Mrs Andrew Quest. There was always some difficulty about introducing English

* This story, slightly expanded, found its way later into a volume of Highland Legends called *Tales from the Mist*, which has been approved to be read in elementary schools. This shows the difference between what is called a 'living' as opposed to a 'dead' folk tradition.

people into his column as his readers had a way of verifying his references in Debrett (as he knew to his cost, for one day, having referred to the engagement of the third and youngest daughter of a Welsh baronet, he received six postcards, eighteen telephone calls, a telegram and a personal visit of protest to inform him that there are two equally beautiful sisters still in the schoolroom. The social editress had been scathing about this). However, he put Imogen Quest down one day, quietly and decisively, as the most lovely and popular of the younger married set. And from the first she exhibited signs of a marked personality. Adam wisely eschewed any attempts at derivation, but his readers nodded to each other and speedily supplied her with an exalted if irregular origin. Everything else Adam showered upon her. She had slightly more than average height, and was very dark and slim, with large Laurencin eyes and the negligent grace of the trained athlete (she fenced with the sabre for half an hour every morning before breakfast). Even Provna, who was notoriously indifferent to conventional beauty, described her as 'justifying the century'.

Her clothes were incomparable, with just that suggestion of the haphazard which raised them high above the mere *chic* of the mannequin.

Her character was a lovely harmony of contending virtues – she was witty and tender-hearted, passionate and serene, sensual and temperate, impulsive and discreet.

Her set, the most intimate and brilliant in Europe, achieved a superb mean between those two poles of savagery Lady Circumference and Lady Metroland.

Soon Imogen Quest became a byword for social inaccessibility – the final goal for all climbers.

Adam went one day to a shop in Hanover Square to watch Nina buy some hats and was seriously incommoded by the heaps of bandboxes disposed on the chairs and dressing-tables ostentatiously addressed to Mrs Andrew Quest. He could hear her name spoken reverently in cocktail clubs, and casually let slip in such phrases as 'My dear, I never see Peter now. He spends all his time with Imogen Quest', or 'As Imogen would say...' or 'I think the Quests have got one like that. I must ask them where it came from'. And this knowledge on the intangible Quest set, moving among them in uncontrolled dignity of life, seemed to leaven and sweeten the lives of Mr Chatterbox's readers.

One day Imogen gave a party, the preparations for which occupied several paragraphs. On the following day Adam found his table deep in letters of complaint from gate-crashers who had found the house in Seamore Place untenanted.

Finally a message came down that Lord Monomark was interested in Mrs Quest; could Mr Chatterbox arrange a meeting. That day the Quests sailed for Jamaica.

Adam also attempted in an unobtrusive way to exercise some influence over the clothes of his readers. '*I noticed at the Café de la Paix yesterday evening*', he wrote, '*that two of the smartest men in the room were wearing black suède shoes with their evening clothes – one of them, who shall be nameless, was a Very Important Person indeed. I hear that this fashion, which comes, like so many others, from New York, is likely to become popular over here this season.*' A few days later he mentioned Captain Stuart-Kerr's appearance at the Embassy '*wearing, of course, the ultra-fashionable black suède shoes*'. In a week he was gratified to notice that Johnny Hoop and Archie Schwert had both followed Captain Stuart-Kerr's lead, while in a fortnight the big emporiums of ready-made clothes in Regent Street had transposed their tickets in the windows and arranged rows of black suède shoes on a silver step labelled 'For evening wear'.

His attempt to introduce a bottle-green bowler hat, however, was not successful; in fact, a 'well-known St James's Street hatter', when interviewed by an evening paper on the subject, said that he had never seen or heard of such a thing, and though he would not refuse to construct one if requested to by an old customer, he was of the opinion that no old customer of his would require a hat of that kind (though there was a sad case of an impoverished old beau who attempted to stain a grey hat with green ink, as once in years gone by he had been used to dye the carnation for his buttonhole).

As the days passed, Mr Chatterbox's page became almost wholly misleading. With sultanesque caprice Adam would tell his readers of inaccessible eating-houses which were now the centre of fashion; he drove them to dance in temperance hotels in Bloomsbury. In a paragraph headed 'Montparnasse in Belgravia', he announced that the buffet at Sloane Square tube station had become the haunt of the most modern artistic coterie (Mr Benfleet hurried there on his first free evening, but saw no one but Mrs Hoop and Lord Vanburgh and a plebeian toper with a celluloid collar).

As a last resort, on those hopeless afternoons when invention failed and that black misanthropy settled on him which waits alike on gossip writer and novelist, Adam sometimes found consolation in seizing upon some gentle and self-effacing citizen and transfiguring him with a blaze of notoriety.

He did this with a man called Ginger.

As part of his duties, which led him into many unusual places, Adam and Nina went up to Manchester for the November Handicap. Here they had the disheartening experience of seeing Indian Runner come in an easy winner and the totalisator paying out thirty-five to one. It was during the bottle-green bowler campaign, and Adam was searching in vain for any sign of his influence when, suddenly, among the crowd, he saw the genial red face of the drunk Major to whom he had entrusted his thousand pounds at Lottie's. It seemed odd that a man so bulky could be so elusive. Adam was not sure whether the Major saw him, but in some mysterious way Adam's pursuit coincided with the Major's complete disappearance. The crowd became very dense, brandishing flasks and sandwiches. When Adam reached the spot where the Major had stood he found two policemen arresting a pickpocket.

''Ere, who are you pushing?' asked the spectators.

'Have you seen a drunk Major anywhere?' asked Adam.

But no one could help him, and he returned disconsolately to Nina, whom he found in conversation with a young man with a curly red moustache.

The young man said he was fed up with racing, and Adam said he was too; so the young man said why didn't they come back to London in his bus, so Adam and Nina said they would. The bus turned out to be a very large, brand-new racing car, and they got to London in time for dinner. Nina explained that the young man used to play with her as a child, and that he had been doing something military in Ceylon for the last five years. The young man's name was Eddy Littlejohn, but over dinner he said, look here, would they call him Ginger; everyone else did. So they began to call him Ginger, and he said wouldn't it be a good idea if they had another bottle of fizz, and Nina and Adam said yes, it would, so they had a magnum and got very friendly.

'You know,' said Ginger, 'it was awful luck meeting you two to-day. I was getting awfully fed up with London. It's so damn slow. I came back meaning to have a good time, you know, paint the place a bit red, and all that. Well, the other day I was reading the paper, and there was a bit that said that the posh place to go to dance nowadays was the Casanova Hotel in Bloomsbury. Well, it seemed a bit rum to me – place I'd never heard of, you know – but, still, I'd been away for some time and places change and all that, so I put on my bib and tucker and toddled off, hoping for a bit of innocent amusement. Well, I mean to say, you never saw such a place. There were only about three people dancing, so I said, "Where's the bar?" And they said, "Bar!" And I said, "You know, for a drink." And they said, well, they could probably make me some coffee. And I said, "No, not coffee." And then they said they hadn't got a licence for what they called alcohol. Well, I mean to say, if that's the best London can do, give me Colombo. I wonder who writes things like that in the papers?'

'As a matter of fact, *I* do.'

'I say no, do you? You must be frightfully brainy. Did you write all that about the green bowlers?'

'Yes.'

'Well, I mean to say, whoever heard of a green bowler, I mean.... I tell you what, you know, I believe it was all a leg pull. You know, I think that's damn funny. Why, a whole lot of poor mutts may have gone and bought green bowlers.'

After this they went on to the Café de la Paix, where they met Johnny Hoop, who asked them all to the party in a few days' time in the captive balloon.

But Ginger was not to be had twice.

'Oh no, you know,' he said, 'not in a captive balloon. You're trying to pull the old leg again. Whoever heard of a party in a captive balloon? I mean to say, suppose one fell out, I mean?'

Adam telephoned his page through to the *Excess*, and soon after this a coloured singer appeared, paddling his black suède shoes in a pool of limelight, who excited Ginger's disapproval. He didn't mind niggers, Ginger said; remarking justly that niggers were all very well in their place, but, after all, one didn't come all the way from Colombo to London just to see niggers. So they left the Café de la Paix, and went to Lottie's, where Ginger became a little moody, saying that London wasn't home to him any more and that things were changed.

'You know,' said Ginger, 'all the time I've been out in Ceylon I've always said to myself, "As soon as the governor kicks the bucket, and I come in for the family doubloons and pieces of eight, I'm going to come back to England and have a real old bust." And now when it comes to the point there doesn't seem to be anything I much want to do.'

'How about a little drink?' said Lottie.

So Ginger had a drink, and then he and an American sang the Eton Boating Song several times. At the end of the evening he admitted that there was some life left in the jolly old capital of the Empire.

Next day Mr Chatterbox's readers learned that: '*Captain "Ginger" Littlejohn, as he is known to his intimates, was one of the well-known sporting figures at the November Handicap who favoured the new bottle-green bowler. Captain Littlejohn is one of the wealthiest and best-known bachelors in Society, and I have lately heard his name spoken of in connection with the marriage of the daughter of a famous ducal house. He came all the way to yesterday's races in his own motor omnibus, which he drives himself . . .'*

For some days Ginger's name figured largely on Adam's page, to his profound embarrassment. Several engagements were predicted for him, it was rumoured that he had signed a contract with a film company, that he had bought a small island in the Bristol Channel which he proposed to turn into a country club, and that his forthcoming novel about Singhalese life contained many very thinly disguised portraits of London celebrities.

But the green bowler joke had gone too far. Adam was sent for by Lord Monomark.

'Now see here, Symes,' said the great man, 'I like your page. It's peppy; it's got plenty of new names in it and it's got the intimate touch I like. I read it every day and so does my daughter. Keep on that way and you'll be all right. But *what's all this about bottle-green bowlers?*'

'Well, of course, sir, they're only worn by a limited number of people at present, but . . .'

'Have you got one? Show me a green bowler.'

'I don't wear one myself, I'm afraid.'

'Well, where d'you see 'em? I haven't seen one yet. My daughter hasn't seen one. Who does wear 'em? Where do they buy 'em? That's what I want to know. Now see here, Symes, I don't say that there ain't any such thing as a green bowler; there may be and again there mayn't. But from now on there are going to be no more bottle-green bowlers in my paper. See. And another thing. This Count Cincinnati. I don't say *he* doesn't exist. He may do and he mayn't. But the Italian Ambassador doesn't know anything about him and the Almanach de Gotha doesn't. So as far as my paper goes that's good enough for him. And I don't want any more about Espinosa's. They made out my bill wrong last night.

'Got those three things clear? Tabulate them in the mind – 1, 2, 3, that's the secret of memory. Tab-u-late. All right, then, run along now and tell the Home Secretary he can come right in. You'll find him waiting in the passage – ugly little man with pince-nez.'

CHAPTER 8

TWO nights later Adam and Nina took Ginger to the party in the captive dirigible. It was not a really good evening. The long drive in Ginger's car to the degraded suburb where the airship was moored chilled and depressed them, dissipating the gaiety which had flickered rather spasmodically over Ginger's dinner.

The airship seemed to fill the whole field, tethered a few feet from the ground by innumerable cables over which they stumbled painfully on the way to the steps. These had been covered by a socially minded caterer with a strip of red carpet.

Inside, the saloons were narrow and hot, communicating with each other by spiral staircases and metal alleys. There were protrusions at every corner, and Miss Runcible had made herself a mass of bruises in the first half-hour. There was a band and a bar and all the same faces. It was the first time that a party was given in an airship.

Adam went aloft to a kind of terrace. Acres of inflated silk blotted out the sky, stirring just perceptibly in the breeze. The lights of other cars arriving lit up the uneven grass. A few louts had collected round the gates to jeer. There were two people making love to each other near him on the terrace, reclining on cushions. There was also a young woman he did not know, holding one of the stays and breathing heavily; evidently she felt unwell. One of the lovers lit a cigar and Adam observed that they were Mary Mouse and the Maharajah of Pukkapore.

Presently Nina joined him. 'It seems such a waste,' she said, thinking of Mary and the Maharajah, 'that two very rich people like that should fall in love with each other.'

'Nina,' said Adam, 'let's get married soon, don't you think?'

'Yes, it's a bore not being married.'

The young woman who felt ill passed by them, walking shakily, to try and find her coat and her young man to take her home.

'. . . I don't know if it sounds absurd,' said Adam, 'but I do feel that a marriage ought to *go on* – for quite a long time, I mean. D'you feel that too, at all?'

'Yes, it's one of the things about a marriage!'

'I'm glad you feel that. I didn't quite know if you did. Otherwise it's all rather bogus, isn't it?'

'I think you ought to go and see papa again,' said Nina. 'It's never any good writing. Go and tell him that you've got a job and are terribly rich and that we're going to be married before Christmas!'

'All right. I'll do that.'

'...D'you remember last month we arranged for you to go and see him the first time?...just like this...it was at Archie Schwert's party...'

'Oh, Nina, *what a lot of parties.*'

(...Masked parties, Savage parties, Victorian parties, Greek parties, Wild West parties, Russian parties, Circus parties, parties where one had to dress as somebody else, almost naked parties in St John's Wood, parties in flats and studios and houses and ships and hotels and night clubs, in windmills and swimming-baths, tea parties at school where one ate muffins and meringues and tinned crab, parties at Oxford where one drank brown sherry and smoked Turkish cigarettes, dull dances in London and comic dances in Scotland and disgusting dances in Paris – all that succession and repetition of massed humanity.... Those vile bodies...)

He leant his forehead, to cool it, on Nina's arm and kissed her in the hollow of her forearm.

'I *know,* darling,' she said, and put her hand on his hair.

Ginger came strutting jauntily by, his hands clasped under his coat-tails.

'Hullo, you two,' he said. 'Pretty good show this, what.'

'Are you enjoying yourself, Ginger?'

'*Rather.* I say, I've met an awful good chap called Miles. Regular topper. You know, *pally.* That's what I like about a really decent party – you meet such topping fellows. I mean some chaps it takes absolutely years to know, but a chap like Miles I feel is a pal straight away.'

Presently cars began to drive away again. Miss Runcible said that she had heard of a divine night club near Leicester Square somewhere where you could get a drink at any hour of the night. It was called the St Christopher's Social Club.

So they all went there in Ginger's car.

On the way Ginger said, 'That cove Miles, you know, he's awfully *queer* . . .'

St Christopher's Social Club took some time to find.

It was a little door at the side of a shop, and the man who opened it held his foot against it and peeped round.

They paid ten shillings each and signed false names in the visitors' book. Then they went downstairs to a very hot room full of cigarette smoke; there were unsteady tables with bamboo legs round the walls and there were some people in shirt sleeves dancing on a shiny linoleum floor.

There was a woman in a yellow beaded frock playing a piano and another in red playing the fiddle.

They ordered some whisky. The waiter said he was sorry, but he couldn't oblige, not that night he couldn't. The police had just rung up to say that they were going to make a raid any minute. If they liked they could have some nice kippers.

Miss Runcible said that kippers were not very drunk-making and that the whole club seemed bogus to her.

Ginger said well, anyway they had better have some kippers now they were there. Then he asked Nina to dance and she said no. Then he asked Miss Runcible and she said no, too.

Then they ate kippers.

Presently one of the men in shirt sleeves (who had clearly had a lot to drink before the St Christopher's Social Club knew about the police) came up to their table and said to Adam:

'You don't know me. I'm Gilmour. I don't want to start a row in front of ladies, but when I see a howling cad I like to tell him so.'

Adam said, 'Why do you spit when you talk?'

Gilmour said, 'That is a very unfortunate physical disability, and it shows what a howling cad you are that you mention it.'

Then Ginger said, 'Same to you, old boy, with knobs on.'

Then Gilmour said, 'Hullo, Ginger, old scout.'

And Ginger said, 'Why, it's Bill. You mustn't mind Bill. Awfully stout chap. Met him on the boat.'

Gilmour said, 'Any pal of Ginger's is a pal of mine.'

So Adam and Gilmour shook hands.

Gilmour said, 'This is a pretty low joint, anyhow. You chaps come round to my place and have a drink.'

So they went to Gilmour's place.

Gilmour's place was a bed-sitting-room in Ryder Street.

So they sat on the bed in Gilmour's place and drank whisky while Gilmour was sick next door.

And Ginger said, 'There's nowhere like London, really you know.'

*

That same evening while Adam and Nina sat on the deck of the dirigible a party of quite a different sort was being given at Anchorage House. This last survivor of the noble town houses of London was, in its time, of dominating and august dimensions, and even now, when it had become a mere 'picturesque bit' lurking in a ravine between concrete skyscrapers, its pillared façade, standing back from the street and obscured by railings and some wisps of foliage, had grace and dignity and other-worldliness enough to cause a flutter or two in Mrs Hoop's heart as she drove into the forecourt.

'Can't you just see the *ghosts*?' she said to Lady Circumference on the stairs. 'Pitt and Fox and Burke and Lady Hamilton and Beau Brummel and Dr Johnson' (a concurrence of celebrities, it may be remarked, at which something memorable might surely have occurred). 'Can't you just *see* them – in their buckled shoes?'

Lady Circumference raised her lorgnette and surveyed the stream of guests debouching from the cloak-rooms like City workers from the Underground. She saw Mr Outrage and Lord Metroland in consultation about the Censorship Bill (a statesmanlike and much-needed measure which empowered a committee of five atheists to destroy all books, pictures and films they considered undesirable, without any nonsense about defence or appeal). She saw both Archbishops, the Duke and Duchess of Stayle, Lord Vanburgh and Lady Metroland, Lady Throbbing and Edward Throbbing and Mrs Blackwater, Mrs Mouse and Lord Monomark and a superb Levantine, and behind and about them a great concourse of pious and honourable people (many of whom made the Anchorage House reception the one outing of the year), their women-folk well gowned in rich and durable stuffs, their men-folk ablaze with orders; people who had represented their country in foreign places and sent their sons to die for her in battle, people of decent and temperate life, uncultured, unaffected, unembarrassed, unassuming, unambitious people, of independent judgment and marked eccentricities, kind people who cared for animals and the deserving poor, brave and rather unreasonable people, that fine phalanx of the passing order, approaching, as one day at the Last Trump they hoped to meet their Maker, with decorous and frank cordiality to shake Lady Anchorage by the hand at the top of her staircase. Lady Circumference saw all this and sniffed the exhalation of her own herd. But she saw no ghosts.

'That's all my eye,' she said.

But Mrs Hoop ascended step by step in a confused but very glorious dream of eighteenth-century elegance.

*

The Presence of Royalty was heavy as thunder in the drawing-room.

The Baroness Yoshiwara and the Prime Minister met once more.

'I tried to see you twice this week,' she said, 'but always you were busy. We are leaving London. Perhaps you heard? My husband has been moved to Washington. It was his wish to go . . . '

'No. I say, Baroness . . . I had no idea. That's very bad news. We shall all miss you terribly.'

'I thought perhaps I would come to make my adieux. One day next week.'

'Why, yes, of course, that would be delightful. You must both come to dine. I'll get my secretary to fix something up to-morrow.'

'It has been nice being in London... you were kind.'

'Not a bit. I don't know what London could be without our guests from abroad.'

'Oh, twenty damns to your great pig-face,' said the Baroness suddenly and turned away.

Mr Outrage watched her bewildered. Finally he said, 'For East is East and West is West and never the twain shall meet' (which was a poor conclusion for a former Foreign Secretary).

Edward Throbbing stood talking to the eldest daughter of the Duchess of Stayle. She was some inches taller than he and inclined slightly so that, in the general murmur of conversation, she should not miss any of his colonial experiences. She wore a frock such as only duchesses can obtain for their elder daughters, a garment curiously puckered and puffed up and enriched with old lace at improbable places, from which her pale beauty emerged as though from a clumsily tied parcel. Neither powder, rouge nor lipstick had played any part in her toilet, and her colourless hair was worn long and bound across her forehead in a broad fillet. Long pearl drops hung from her ears and she wore a tight little collar of pearls round her throat. It was generally understood that now Edward Throbbing was back these two would become engaged to be married.

Lady Ursula was acquiescent if unenthusiastic. When she thought about marriage at all, which was rarely (for her chief interests were a girls' club in Canning Town and a younger brother at school), she thought what a pity it was that one had to be so ill to have children. Her married friends spoke of this almost with relish and her mother with awe.

An innate dilatoriness of character rather than any doubt of the ultimate issue kept Edward from verbal proposal. He had decided to arrange everything before Christmas and that was enough. He had no doubt that a suitable occasion would soon be devised for him. It was clearly suitable that he should marry before he was thirty. Now and then when he was with Ursula he felt a slight quickening of possessive impulse towards her fragility and distance; occasionally when he read some rather lubricous novel or saw much love-making on the stage he would translate the characters in his mind and put Lady Ursula, often incongruously, in the place of the heroine. He had no doubt that he was in love. Perhaps he would propose this very evening and get it over. It was up to Lady Ursula to engineer an occasion. Meanwhile he kept the conversation on to the subject of labour problems in Montreal, about which his information was extensive and accurate.

'He's a nice, steady boy,' said the Duchess, 'and it's a comfort, nowadays, to see two young people so genuinely fond of each other. Of course, nothing is actually arranged yet, but I was talking to Fanny Throbbing yesterday, and apparently Edward has already spoken to her on the subject. I think that everything will be settled before Christmas. Of course, there's not a great deal of money, but one's learnt not to expect that nowadays, and Mr Outrage speaks very highly of his ability. Quite one of the coming men in the party.'

'Well,' said Lady Circumference, 'you know your own business, but if you ask me I shouldn't care to see a daughter of mine marry into that family. Bad hats every one of them. Look at the father and the sister, and from all I hear the brother is rotten all through.'

'I don't say it's a match I should have chosen myself. There's certainly a bad strain in the Malpractices . . . but you know how headstrong children are nowadays, and they seem so fond of each other . . . and there seem so few young men about. At least I never seem to see any.'

'Young toads, the whole lot of them,' said Lady Circumference.

'And these *terrible* parties which I'm told they give. I don't know what I should have done if Ursula had ever wanted to go to them ... the poor Chasms. ...'

'If I were Viola Chasm I'd give that girl a thunderin' good hidin'.'

*

The topic of the Younger Generation spread through the company like a yawn. Royalty remarked on their absence and those happy mothers who had even one docile daughter in tow swelled with pride and commiseration.

'I'm told that they're having another of their parties,' said Mrs Mouse, 'in an aeroplane this time.'

'In an aeroplane? How very extraordinary.'

'Of course, I never hear a word from Mary, but her maid told my maid ...'

'What I always wonder, Kitty dear, is what they actually *do* at these parties of theirs. I mean, *do* they ... ?'

'My dear, from all I hear, I think they do.'

'Oh, to be young again, Kitty. When I think, my dear, of all the trouble and exertion which we had to go through to be even moderately bad ... those passages in the early morning and mama sleeping next door.'

'And yet, my dear, I doubt very much whether they really *appreciate* it all as much as we should ... young people take things so much for granted. *Si la jeunesse savait.*'

'*Si la vieillesse pouvait*, Kitty.'

*

Later that evening Mr Outrage stood almost alone in the supper-room drinking a glass of champagne. Another episode in his life was closed, another of those tantalizing glimpses of felicity capriciously withdrawn. Poor Mr Outrage, thought Mr Outrage; poor, poor old Outrage, always just on the verge of revelation, of some sublime and transfiguring experience; always frustrated. ... Just Prime Minister, nothing more, bullied by his colleagues, a source of income to low caricaturists. Was

Mr Outrage an immortal soul, thought Mr Outrage; had he wings, was he free and unconfined, was he born for eternity? He sipped his champagne, fingered his ribbon of the Order of Merit, and resigned himself to the dust.

Presently he was joined by Lord Metroland and Father Rothschild.

'Margot's left – gone on to some party in an airship. I've been talking to Lady Anchorage for nearly an hour about the younger generation.'

'Everyone seems to have been talking about the younger generation to-night. The most boring subject I know.'

'Well, after all, what does all this stand for if there's going to be no one to carry it on?'

'All what?' Mr Outrage looked round the supper-room, deserted save for two footmen who leant against the walls looking as waxen as the clumps of flowers sent up that morning from hothouses in the country. 'What does all what stand for?'

'All this business of government.'

'As far as I'm concerned it stands for a damned lot of hard work and precious little in return. If those young people can find a way to get on without it, good luck to them.'

'I see what Metroland means,' said Father Rothschild.

'Blessed if I do. Anyway I've got no children myself, and I'm thankful for it. I don't understand them, and I don't want to. They had a chance after the war that no generation has ever had. There was a whole civilization to be saved and remade – and all they seem to do is to play the fool. Mind you, I'm all in favour of them having a fling. I dare say that Victorian ideas *were* a bit strait-laced. Saving your cloth, Rothschild, it's only human nature to run a bit loose when one's young. But there's something wanton about these young people today. That step-son of yours, Metroland, and that girl of poor old Chasm's and young Throbbing's brother.'

'Don't you think,' said Father Rothschild gently, 'that perhaps it is all in some way historical? I don't think people ever *want* to lose their faith either in religion or anything else. I know very few young people, but it seems to me that they are all possessed with an almost fatal hunger for permanence. I think all these divorces show that. People aren't content just to muddle along nowadays.... And this word "bogus" they all use.... They won't make the best of a bad job nowadays. My private schoolmaster used to say, "If a thing's worth doing at all, it's worth doing well." My Church has taught that in different words for several centuries. But these young people have got hold of another end of the stick, and for all we know it may be the right one. They say, "If a thing's not worth doing well, it's not worth doing at all." It makes everything very difficult for them.'

'Good heavens, I should think it did. What a darned silly principle. I mean to say, if one didn't do anything that wasn't worth doing well – why, what *would* one do? I've always maintained that success in this world depends on knowing exactly how little effort each job is worth... distribution of energy.... And, I suppose, most people would admit that I was a pretty successful man.'

'Yes, I suppose they would, Outrage,' said Father Rothschild, looking at him rather quizzically.

But that self-accusing voice in the Prime Minister's heart was silent. There was nothing like a little argument for settling the mind. Everything became so simple as soon as it was put into words.

'And anyway, what do you mean by "historical"?'

'Well, it's like this war that's coming....'

'*What war?*' said the Prime Minister sharply. 'No one has said anything to me about a war. I really think I should have been told. I'll be damned,' he said defiantly, 'if they shall have a war without consulting me. What's a Cabinet for if there's not more mutual confidence than that? What do they want a war for, anyway?'

'That's the whole point. No one talks about it, and no one wants it. No one talks about it *because* no one wants it. They're all afraid to breathe a word about it.'

'Well, hang it all, if no one wants it, who's going to make them have it?'

'Wars don't start nowadays because people want them. We long for peace, and fill our newspapers with conferences about disarmament and arbitration, but there is a radical instability in our whole world-order, and soon we shall all be walking into the jaws of destruction again, protesting our pacific intentions.'

'Well, you seem to know all about it,' said Mr Outrage, 'and I think I should have been told sooner. This will have to mean a coalition with that old wind-bag Brown, I suppose.'

'Anyhow,' said Lord Metroland, 'I don't see how all that explains why my stepson should drink like a fish and go about everywhere with a negress.'

'I think they're connected, you know,' said Father Rothschild. 'But it's all very difficult.'

Then they separated.

Father Rothschild pulled on a pair of overall trousers in the forecourt and, mounting his motor-cycle, disappeared into the night, for he had many people to see and much business to transact before he went to bed.

Lord Metroland left the house in some depression. Margot had taken the car, but it was scarcely five minutes' walk to Hill Street. He took a vast cigar from his case, lit it and sank his chin in the astrakhan collar of his coat, conforming almost exactly to the popular conception of a highly enviable man. But his heart was heavy. What a lot of nonsense Rothschild had talked. At least he hoped it was nonsense.

By ill-fortune he arrived on the doorstep to find Peter Pastmaster fumbling with the lock, and they entered together. Lord Metroland noticed a tall hat on the table by the door. 'Young Trumpington's, I suppose,' he thought. His stepson did not once look at him, but made straight for the stairs, walking unsteadily, his hat on the back of his head, his umbrella still in his hand.

'Good night, Peter,' said Lord Metroland.

'Oh, go to hell,' said his stepson thickly, then, turning on the stairs, he added, 'I'm going abroad to-morrow for a few weeks. Will you tell my mother?'

'Have a good time,' said Lord Metroland. 'You'll find it just as cold everywhere, I'm afraid. Would you care to take the yacht? No one's using it.'

'Oh, go to hell.'

Lord Metroland went into the study to finish his cigar. It would be awkward if he met young Trumpington on the stairs. He sat down in a very comfortable chair.... A radical instability, Rothschild had said, radical instability.... He looked round his study and saw shelves of books – the *Dictionary of National Biography*, the *Encyclopædia Britannica* in an early and very bulky edition, *Who's Who*, Debrett, Burke, Whitaker, several volumes of Hansard, some Blue Books and Atlases – a safe in the corner painted green with a brass handle, his writing-table, his secretary's table, some very comfortable chairs and some very business-like chairs, a tray with decanters and a plate of sandwiches, his evening mail laid out on the table... radical instability, indeed. How like poor old Outrage to let himself get taken in by that charlatan of a Jesuit.

He heard the front door open and shut behind Alastair Trumpington.

Then he rose and went quietly upstairs, leaving his cigar smouldering in the ash-tray, filling the study with fragrant smoke.

A quarter of a mile away the Duchess of Stayle went, as she always did, to say good night to her eldest daughter. She crossed the room and drew up the window a few inches, for it was a cold and raw night. Then she went over to the bed and smoothed the pillow.

'Good night, dear child,' she said. 'I thought you looked sweet to-night.'

Lady Ursula wore a white cambric night-gown with a little yoke collar and long sleeves. Her hair hung in two plaits.

'Mama,' she said. 'Edward proposed to me to-night.'

'*Darling*. What a funny girl you are. Why didn't you tell me before? You weren't frightened, were you? You know that your father and I are delighted at anything that makes our little girl happy.'

'Well, I said I wouldn't marry him... I'm sorry.'

'But, my dear, it's nothing to be sorry about. Leave it to your old mother. I'll put it all right for you in the morning.'

'But, Mama, I don't want to marry him. I didn't know until it actually came to the point. I'd always meant to marry him, as you know. But, somehow, when he actually asked me... I just couldn't.'

'There, dear child, you mustn't worry any more. You know perfectly well, don't you, that your father and I would not let you do anything you didn't want. It's a matter that only you can decide. After all, it's your life and your happiness at stake, not ours, isn't it, Ursula?... But I *think* you'd better marry Edward.'

'But, Mama, I don't want to... I couldn't... it would kill me!'

'Now, now, my pet mustn't worry her head about it any more. You know your father and I only want *your* happiness, dear one. No one is going to make my darling girl do anything she doesn't want to.... Papa shall see Edward in the morning and make everything all right... dear Lady Anchorage was only saying to-night what a lovely bride you will make.'

'But, Mama...'

'Not another word, dear child. It's very late and you've got to look your best for Edward to-morrow, haven't you, love?'

The Duchess closed the door softly and went to her own room. Her husband was in his dressing-room.

'Andrew.'

'What is it, dear? I'm saying my prayers.'

'Edward proposed to Ursula to-night.'

'Ah!'

'Aren't you glad?'

'I told you, dear, I'm trying to say my prayers.'

'It's a real joy to see the dear children so happy.'

CHAPTER 9

AT luncheon-time next day Adam rang up Nina.

'Nina, darling, are you awake?'

'Well, I wasn't...'

'Listen, do you really want me to go and see your papa to-day?'

'Did we say you were going to?'

'Yes.'

'Why?'

'To say could we be married now I had a job.'

'I remember... yes, go and see him, darling. It would be nice to be married.'

'But, listen, what about my page?'

'What page, angel?'

'My page in the *Excess*... my job, you know.'

'Oh... well, look... Ginger and I will write that for you.'

'Wouldn't that be a bore?'

'I think it would be divine. I know just the sort of things you say.... I expect Ginger does too by now, the poor angel... how he did enjoy himself last night.... I'm going to sleep now... such a pain... good-bye, my sweet.'

Adam had some luncheon. Agatha Runcible was at the next table with Archie Schwert. She said they were all going to some motor races next day. Would Adam and Nina come, too. Adam said yes. Then he went to Aylesbury.

There were two women on the other side of the carriage, and they, too, were talking about the Younger Generation.

'... and it's a very good position, too, for a boy of that age, and I've told him and his father told him. "You ought to think yourself lucky", I've said, "to get a good position like that in these days, particularly when it's so hard to get a position at all of any kind *or* sort." And there's Mrs Hemingway with her son next door who left school eighteen months ago, and there he is kicking his heels about the house all day and doing nothing, and taking a correspondence course in civil engineering. "It's a very good position", I told him, "and, of course, you can't expect *work* to be interesting, though no doubt after a time you get used to it just as your father's done, and would probably miss it if you hadn't it to do" – you know how Alfred gets on his holidays, doesn't know what to do with himself half the time, just looks at the sea and says, "Well, this *is* a change", and then starts wondering how things are at the office. Well, I told Bob that, but it's no good, and all he wants to do is to go into the motor business; well, as I said to him, the motor business is all right for them that have influence, but what could Bob hope to do throwing up a good job, too, and with nothing to fall back on supposing things did go wrong. But, no, Bob is all for motors, and, of course, you know it doesn't really do having him living at home. He and his father don't get on. You can't have two men in a house together and both wanting the bath at the same time, and I suppose it's only natural that Bob should feel he ought to have his own way a bit more now that he's earning his own money. But, then, what is he to do? He can't go and live on his own with his present salary, and I shouldn't be any too pleased to see him doing it even if he could afford it – you know what it is with young people, how easy it is to get into mischief when they're left to themselves. And there are a great many of Bob's friends now that I don't really approve of, not to have in and out of the house, you know the way they do come. He meets them at the hockey club he goes to Saturdays. And they're most of them earning more money than he is, or, at any rate, they seem to have more to throw about, and it isn't good for a boy being about with those that have more money than him. It only makes him discontented. And I did think at one time that perhaps Bob was thinking of Betty Rylands, you know Mrs Rylands' girl at the Laurels, such nice people, and they used to play tennis together and people remarked how much they were about, but now he never seems to pay any attention to her, it's all his hockey friends, and I said one Saturday, "Wouldn't you like to ask Betty over to tea?" and he said, "Well, you can if you like", and she came looking ever so sweet, and, would you believe it, Bob went out and didn't come in at all until supper-time. Well, you can't expect any girl to put up with that, and now she's practically engaged to that young Anderson boy who's in the wireless business.'

'Well, and there's our Lily now. You know how she would go in for being a manicurist. Her father didn't like it, and for a long time he wouldn't have it at all. He said it was just an excuse for holding hands, but, anyway, I said, "If that's what the girl wants to do, and if she can make good money doing it, I think you ought to be able to trust your own daughter better than to stand in her way." I'm a modern, you see. "We're not living in the Victorian Age", I told him. Well, she's in a very nice job. Bond Street – and they treat her very fair, and we've no complaints on that score, but now there's this man she's met there – he's old enough to be her father – well, middle-aged anyway – but very smart, you know, neat little grey moustache, absolute gentleman, with a Morris Oxford saloon. And he comes and takes her out for drives Sundays, and sometimes he fetches her after work and takes her to the pictures, and always most polite and well spoken to me and my husband, just as you'd expect, seeing the sort of man he is, and he sent us all tickets for the theatre the other night. Very affable, calls me "Ma", if you please ... and, anyway, I *hope* there's no harm in it ...'

'Now our Bob ...'

They got out at Berkhamsted, and a man got in who wore a bright brown suit and spent his time doing sums, which never seemed to come right, in a little note-book with a stylographic pen. 'Has he given all to his daughters?' thought Adam.

He drove out to Doubting by a bus which took him as far as the village of petrol pumps. From there he walked down the lane to the park gates. To his surprise these stood open, and as he approached he narrowly missed being run down by a large and ramshackle car which swept in at a high speed; he caught a glimpse of two malignant female eyes which glared contemptuously at him from the small window at the back. Still more surprising was a large notice which hung on the central pier of the gates and said: 'NO ADMITTANCE EXCEPT ON BUSINESS'. As Adam walked up the drive two lorries thundered past him. Then a man appeared with a red flag.

'Hi! You can't go that way. They're shooting in front. Go round by the stables, whoever you are.'

Wondering vaguely what kind of sport this could be, Adam followed the side path indicated. He listened for sounds of firing, but hearing nothing except distant shouting and what seemed to be a string band, he concluded that the Colonel was having a poor day. It seemed odd, anyway, to go shooting in front of one's house with a string band, and automatically Adam began making up a paragraph about it:

'*Colonel Blount, father of the lovely Miss Nina Blount referred to above, rarely comes to London nowadays. He devotes himself instead to shooting on his estate in Buckinghamshire. The coverts, which are among the most richly stocked in the country, lie immediately in front of the house, and many amusing stories are related of visitors who have inadvertently found themselves in the line of fire.... Colonel Blount has the curious eccentricity of being unable to shoot his best except to the accompaniment of violin and 'cello. (Mr "Ginger" Littlejohn has the similar foible that he can only fish to the sound of the flageolet...)*'

He had not gone very far in his detour before he was again stopped, this time by a man dressed in a surplice, episcopal lawn sleeves and scarlet hood and gown; he was smoking a cigar.

'Here, what in hell do *you* want?' said the Bishop.

'I came to see Colonel Blount.'

'Well, you can't, son. They're just shooting him now.'

'Good heavens. What for?'

'Oh, nothing important. He's just one of the Wesleyans, you know – we're trying to polish off the whole crowd this afternoon while the weather's good.'

Adam found himself speechless before this cold-blooded bigotry.

'What d'you want to see the old geezer about, anyway?'

'Well, it hardly seems any good now. I came to tell him that I'd got a job on the *Excess*.'

'The devil you have. Why didn't you say so before? Always pleased to see gentlemen of the Press. Have a weed?' A large cigar-case appeared from the recesses of the episcopal bosom. 'I'm Bishop Philpotts, you know,' he said, slipping a voluminously clothed arm through Adam's. 'I dare say you'd like to come round to the front and see the fun. I should think they'd be just singing their last hymn now. It's been uphill work,' he confided as they walked round the side of the house, 'and there's been some damned bad management. Why, yesterday, they kept Miss La Touche waiting the whole afternoon, and then the light was so bad when they did shoot her that they made a complete mess of her – we had the machine out and ran over all the bits carefully last night after dinner – you never saw such rotten little scraps – quite unrecognizable half of them. We didn't dare show them to her husband – he'd be sick to death about it – so we just cut out a few shots to keep and threw away the rest. I say, you're not feeling queer, are you? You look all green suddenly. Find the weed a bit strong?'

'Was – was she a Wesleyan too?'

'My dear boy, she's playing lead . . . she's Selina, Countess of Huntingdon. . . . There, now you can see them at work.'

They had rounded the wing and were now in full view of the front of the house, where all was activity and animation. A dozen or so men and women in eighteenth-century costume were standing in a circle singing strongly, while in their centre stood a small man in a long clerical coat and a full white wig, conducting them. A string band was playing not far off, and round the singers clustered numerous men in shirt-sleeves bearing megaphones, cinematograph cameras, microphones, sheaves of paper and arc lamps. Not far away, waiting their turn to be useful, stood a coach and four, a detachment of soldiers and some scene shifters with the transept of Exeter Cathedral in sections of canvas and match-boarding.

'The Colonel's somewhere in that little crowd singing the hymn,' said the Bishop. 'He was crazy to be allowed to come on as a super, and as he's letting us the house dirt cheap Isaacs said he might. I don't believe he's ever been so happy in his life.'

As they approached the hymn stopped.

'All right,' said one of the men with megaphones. 'You can beat it. We'll shoot the duel now. I shall want two supers to carry the body. The rest of you are through for the afternoon.'

A man in a leather apron, worsted stockings and flaxen wig emerged from the retreating worshippers.

'Oh, please, Mr Isaacs,' he said, 'please may *I* carry the body?'

'All right, Colonel, if you want to. Run in and tell them in the wardrobe to give you a smock and a pitchfork.'

'Thank you so much,' said Colonel Blount, trotting off towards his house. Then he stopped. 'I suppose,' he said, 'I suppose it wouldn't be better for me to carry a sword?'

'No, pitchfork, and hurry up about it or I shan't let you carry the body at all; someone go and find Miss La Touche.'

The young lady whom Adam had seen in the motor-car came down the steps of the house in a feathered hat, riding-habit and braided cape. She carried a hunting-crop in her hand. Her face was painted very yellow.

'Do I or do I not have a horse in this scene, Mr Isaacs? I've been round to Bertie and he says all the horses are needed for the coach.'

'I'm sorry, Effie, you do *not* and it's no good taking on. We only got four horses and you know that, and you saw what it was like when we tried to move the coach with two. So you've just got to face it. You comes across the fields on foot.'

'Dirty Yid,' said Effie La Touche.

'The trouble about this film,' said the Bishop, 'is that we haven't enough capital. It's heart-breaking. Here we have a first-rate company, first-rate producer, first-rate scene, first-rate story and the whole thing being hung up for want of a few hundred pounds. How can he expect to get the best out of Miss La Touche if they won't give her a horse? No girl will stand for that sort of treatment. If I were Isaacs I'd scrap the whole coach sooner. It's no sense getting a star and not treating her right. Isaacs is putting everyone's back up the way he goes on. Wanted to do the whole of my cathedral scene with twenty-five supers. But you're here to give us a write-up, aren't you? I'll call Isaacs across and let him give you the dope. . . . *Isaacs*!'

'Yuh?'

'*Daily Excess* here.'

'Where?'

'Here.'

'I'll be right over.' He put on his coat, buttoned it tightly at the waist and strode across the lawn, extending a hand of welcome. Adam shook it and felt what seemed to be a handful of rings under his fingers. 'Pleased to meet you, Mister. Now just you ask me anything you want about this film because I'm just here to answer. Have you got my name? Have a card. That's the name of the company in the corner. Not the one that's scratched out. The one written above. *The Wonderfilm Company of Great Britain.* Now this film,' he said, in what seemed a well-practised little speech, 'of which you have just witnessed a mere fragment marks a stepping stone in the development of the British Film Industry. It is the most important All-Talkie super-religious film to be produced solely in this country by British artists and management and by British capital. It has been directed throughout regardless of difficulty and expense, and supervised by a staff of expert historians and theologians. Nothing has been omitted that would contribute to the meticulous accuracy of every detail. The life of that great social and religious reformer John Wesley is for the first time portrayed to a British public in all its humanity and tragedy.... Look here, I've got all this written out. I'll have them give you a copy before you go. Come and see the duel....

'That's Wesley and Whitefield just going to start. Of course, it's not them really. Two fencing instructors we got over from the gym at Aylesbury. That's what I mean when I say we spare no expense to get the details accurate. Ten bob each we're paying them for the afternoon.'

'But did Wesley and Whitefield fight a duel?'

'Well, it's not actually recorded, but it's known that they quarrelled and there was only one way of settling quarrels in those days. They're both in love with Selina, Countess of Huntingdon, you see. She comes to stop them, but arrives too late. Whitefield has escaped in the coach and Wesley is lying wounded. That's a scene that'll go over big. Then she takes him back to her home and nurses him back to health. I tell you, this is going to make film history. D'you know what the Wesleyan population of the British Isles is? Well nor do I, but I've been told and *you'd be surprised.* Well, every one of those is going to come and see this film and there's going to be discussions about it in all the chapels. We're recording extracts from Wesley's sermons and we're singing all his own hymns. I'm glad your paper's interested. You can tell them from me that we're on a big thing.... There's one thing though,' said Mr Isaacs, suddenly becoming confidential, 'which I shouldn't tell many people. But I think you'll understand because you've seen some of our work here and the sort of scale it's on, and you can imagine that expenses are pretty heavy. Why, I'm paying Miss La Touche alone over ten pounds a week. And the truth is – I don't mind telling you – we're beginning to feel the wind a bit. It's going to be a big success *when* and *if* it's finished. Now, suppose there was someone – yourself, for instance, or one of your friends – who had a little bit of loose capital he wanted to invest – a thousand pounds, say – well, I wouldn't mind selling him a half share. It's not a gamble, mind – it's a certain winner. If I cared to go into the open market with it, it would be snapped up before you could say knife. But I don't want to do that and I'll tell you why. This is a British company and I don't want to let any of those foreign speculators in on it, and once you let the shares get into the open market you can't tell who's buying them, see. Now why leave money idle bringing in four and a half or five per cent when you might be doubling it in six months?'

'I'm afraid it's no use coming to me for capital,' said Adam. 'Do you think I could possibly see Colonel Blount?'

'One of the things I hate in life,' said Mr Isaacs, 'is seeing anyone lose an opportunity. Now listen, I'll make you a fair offer. I can see you're interested in this film. Now I'll sell you the whole thing – film we've made up to date, artists' contracts, copyright of scenario, everything for five hundred quid. Then all you have to do is to finish it off and your fortune's made and I shall be cursing for not having held on longer. How about it?'

'It's very good of you, but really I don't think I can afford it at the moment.'

'Just as you like,' said Mr Isaacs airily. 'There's many who *can* who'd jump at the offer, only I thought I'd let you in on it first because I could see you were a smart kid.... Tell you what I'll do. I'll let you have it for four hundred. Can't say fairer than that, can I? And wouldn't do it for anyone but you.'

'I'm terribly sorry, Mr Isaacs, but I didn't come to buy your film. I came to see Colonel Blount.'

'Well, I shouldn't have thought you were the sort of chap to let an opportunity like that slip through your fingers. Now I'll give you one more chance and after that, mind, the offer is closed. I'll sell you it for three-fifty. Take it or leave it. That's my last word. Of course, you're not in any way obliged to buy,' said Mr Isaacs rather haughtily, 'but I assure you that you'll regret it from the bottom of your heart if you don't.'

'I'm sorry,' said Adam, 'I think it's a wonderfully generous offer, but the truth is I simply don't want to buy a film at all.'

'In that case,' said Mr Isaacs, 'I shall return to my business.'

Not till sunset did the Wonderfilm Company of Great Britain rest. Adam watched them from the lawn. He saw the two fencing instructors in long black coats and white neck bands lunging and parrying manfully until one of them fell; then the cameras stopped and his place was taken by the leading actor (who had been obliged through the exigencies of the wardrobe to lend his own coat). Whitefield took the place (and the wig) of the victor and fled to the coach. Effie La Touche appeared from the shrubbery still defiantly carrying her hunting-crop. Close-ups followed of Effie and Wesley and Effie and Wesley together. Then Colonel Blount and another super appeared as yokels and carried the wounded preacher back to the house. All this took a long time as the action was frequently held up by minor mishaps and once when the whole scene had been triumphantly enacted the chief cameraman found that he had forgotten to put in a new roll of film ('Can't think how I come to make a mistake like that, Mr Isaacs'). Finally the horses were taken out of the coach and mounted by grenadiers and a few shots taken of them plunging despairingly up the main drive.

'Part of Butcher Cumberland's army,' explained Mr Isaacs. 'It's always good to work in a little atmosphere like that. Gives more educational value. Besides we hire the horses by the day so we might as well get all we can out of them while they're here. If we don't use 'em in Wesley we can fit 'em in somewhere else. A hundred feet or so of galloping horses is always useful.'

When everything was over Adam managed to see Colonel Blount, but it was not a satisfactory interview.

'I'm afraid I've really got very little time to spare,' he said. 'To tell you the truth, I'm at work on a scenario of my own. They tell me you come from the *Excess* and want to write about the film. It's a glorious film, isn't it? Of course, you know, I have very little to do with it really. I have let them the house and have acted one or two small parts in the crowd. I don't have to pay for them though.'

'No, I should think not.'

'My dear boy, all the others have to. I knocked a little off the rent of the house, but I don't actually *pay*. In fact, you might almost say I was a professional already. You see, Mr Isaacs is the principal of the National Academy of Cinematographic Art. He's got a little office in Edgware Road, just one room, you know, to interview candidates in. Well, if he thinks that they're promising enough – he doesn't take anyone, mind, only a chosen few – he takes them on as pupils. As Mr Isaacs says, the best kind of training is practical work, so he produces a film straight away and pays the professionals out of the pupils' fees. It's really a very simple and sensible plan. All the characters in "John Wesley" are pupils, except Wesley himself and Whitefield and the Bishop and, of course, Miss La Touche – she's the wife of the man who looks after the Edgware Road office when Mr Isaacs is away. Even the cameramen are only learning. It makes everything so exciting, you know. This is the third film Mr Isaacs has produced. The first went wrong, through Mr Isaacs trusting one of the pupils to develop it. Of course, he made him pay damages – that's in the contract they all have to sign – but the film was ruined, and Mr Isaacs said it was disheartening – he nearly gave up the cinema altogether. But then a lot more pupils came along, so they produced another, which was *very* good indeed. Quite a revolution in Film Art, Mr Isaacs said, but that was boycotted through professional jealousy. None of the theatres would show it. But that's been made all right now. Mr Isaacs has got in with the ring, he says, and this is going to establish Wonderfilms as the leading company in the country. What's more, he's offered me a half share in it for five thousand pounds. It's wonderfully generous, when he might keep it all to himself, but he says that he must have someone who understands *acting* from the practical side on the board of directors. Funnily enough, my bank manager is very much against my going in for it. In fact, he's putting every obstacle in my way.... But I dare say Mr Isaacs would sooner you didn't put any of this into your paper.'

'What I really came about was your daughter, Nina.'

'Oh, she's not taking any part in the film at all. To tell you the truth, I very much doubt whether she has any real talent. It's funny how these things often skip a generation. My father, now, was a very bad actor indeed – though he always used to take a leading part when we had theatricals at Christmas. Upon my soul, he used to make himself look quite ridiculous sometimes. I remember once he did a skit of Henry Irving in "The Bells"...'

'I'm afraid you've forgotten me, sir, but I came here last month to see you about Nina. Well, she wanted me to tell you that I'm Mr Chatterbox now....'

'Chatterbox... no, my boy, I'm afraid I don't remember you. My memory's not what it was.... There's a Canon Chatterbox at Worcester I used to know... he was up at New College with me... unusual name.'

'Mr Chatterbox on the *Daily Excess*.'

'No, no, my dear boy, I assure you not. He was ordained just after I went down and was chaplain somewhere abroad – Bermuda, I think. Then he came home and went to Worcester. He was never on the *Daily Excess* in his life.'

'No, no, sir, *I'm* on the *Daily Excess*.'

'Well, you ought to know your own staff, certainly. He *may* have left Worcester and taken to journalism. A great many parsons do nowadays, I know. But I must say that he's the last fellow I should have expected it of. Awful stupid fellow. Besides, he must be at least seventy.... Well, well... who would have thought it. Good-bye, my boy, I've enjoyed our talk.'

'Oh, sir,' cried Adam, as Colonel Blount began to walk away. 'You don't understand – I want to marry Nina.'

'Well, it's no good coming here,' said the Colonel crossly. 'I told you, she's somewhere in London. She's got nothing to do with the film at all. You'll have to go and ask her about it. Anyway, I happen to know she's engaged already. There was a young ass of a chap down here about it the other day...the Rector said he was off his head. Laughed the whole time – bad sign that – still, Nina wants to marry him for some reason. So I'm afraid you're too late, my boy. I'm sorry... and, anyway, the Rector's behaved very badly about this film. Wouldn't lend his car. I suppose it's because of the Wesleyanism. Narrow-minded, that.... Well, good-bye. So nice of you to come. Remember me to Canon Chatterbox. I must look him up next time I come to London and pull his leg about it....Writing for the papers, indeed, at his age.'

And Colonel Blount retired victorious.

*

Late that evening Adam and Nina sat in the gallery of the Café de la Paix eating oysters.

'Well we won't bother any more about papa,' she said. 'We'll just get married at once.'

'We shall be terribly poor.'

'Well, we shan't be any poorer than we are now.... I think it will be divine....Besides, we'll be terribly economical. Miles says he's discovered a place near Tottenham Court Road where you can get oysters for three and six a dozen.'

'Wouldn't they be rather ill-making?'

'Well, Miles said the only odd thing about them is that they all taste a little different....I had lunch with Miles to-day. He rang up to find where you were. He wanted to sell Edward Throbbing's engagement to the *Excess*. But Van offered him five guineas for it, so he gave it to them.'

'I'm sorry we missed that. The editor will be furious. By the way, how did the gossip page go? Did you manage to fill it all right?'

'My dear, I think I did rather well. You see Van and Miles didn't know I was in the trade, so they talked about Edward's engagement a whole lot, so I went and put it in . . . was that very caddish? . . . and I wrote a lot about Edward and the girl he's to marry. I used to know her when I came out, and that took up half the page. So I just put in a few imaginary ones like you do, so then it was finished.'

'What did you say in the imaginary ones?'

'Oh, I don't know. I said I saw Count Cincinnati going into Espinosa's in a green bowler . . . things like that.'

'*You said that?*'

'Yes, wasn't it a good thing to say. . . . Angel, is anything wrong?'

'Oh, God.'

Adam dashed to the telephone.

'Central ten thousand . . . put me through to the night editor. . . . Look here, I've got to make a correction in the Chatterbox page . . . it's urgent.'

'Sorry, Symes. Last edition went to bed half an hour ago. Got everything made up early to-night.'

So Adam went back to finish his oysters.

'Bad tabulation there,' said Lord Monomark next morning, when he saw the paragraph.

*

So Miles Malpractice became Mr Chatterbox.

*

'Now we can't be married,' said Nina.

CHAPTER 10

ADAM and Miss Runcible and Miles and Archie Schwert went up to the motor races in Archie Schwert's car. It was a long and cold drive. Miss Runcible wore trousers and Miles touched up his eyelashes in the dining-room of the hotel where they stopped for luncheon. So they were asked to leave. At the next hotel they made Miss Runcible stay outside, and brought her cold lamb and pickles in the car. Archie thought it would be nice to have champagne, and worried the wine waiter about dates (a subject which had always been repugnant to him). They spent a long time over luncheon because it was warm there, and they drank Kümmel over the fire until Miss Runcible came in very angrily to fetch them out.

Then Archie said he was too sleepy to drive any more, so Adam changed places with him and lost the way, and they travelled miles in the wrong direction down a limitless by-pass road.

And then it began to be dark and the rain got worse. They stopped for dinner at another hotel, where everyone giggled at Miss Runcible's trousers in a dining-room hung with copper warming pans.

Presently they came to the town where the race was to be run. They drove to the hotel where the dirt-track racer was staying. It was built in the Gothic style of 1860, large, dark and called the Imperial.

They had wired him to book them rooms, but 'Bless you', said the woman at the counter marked 'Reception', 'all our rooms have been booked for the last six months. I couldn't fit you in anywhere, not if you was the Speed Kings themselves, I couldn't. I don't suppose you'll find anything in the town to-night. You might try at the Station Hotel. That's your only chance.'

At the Station Hotel they made Miss Runcible wait outside, but with no better success.

'I might put one of you on the sofa in the bar parlour, there's only a married couple in there at present and two little boys, or if you didn't mind sitting up all night, there's always the palm lounge.' As for a bed, that was out of the question. They might try at the 'Royal George', but she doubted very much whether they'd *like* that even if there was room, which she was pretty sure there was not.

Then Miss Runcible thought that she remembered that there were some friends of her father who lived quite near, so she found out their telephone number and rang them up, but they said no, they were sorry, but they had a completely full house and practically no servants, and that as far as they knew they had never heard of Lord Chasm. So that was no good.

Then they went to several more hotels, sinking through the various gradations of Old Established Family and Commercial, plain Commercial, High Class Board Residence pension terms, Working Girls' Hostel, plain Pub and Clean Beds: Gentlemen Only. All were full. At last, by the edge of a canal, they came to the 'Royal George'. The landlady stood at the door and rounded off an argument with an elderly little man in a bowler hat.

'First 'e takes off 'is boots in the saloon bar,' she said, enlisting the sympathy of her new audience, 'which is not the action of a gentleman.'

'They was wet,' said the little man; 'wet as 'ell.'

'Well, and who wants your wet boots on the counter, I should like to know. Then, if you please, he calls me a conspiring woman because I tells him to stop and put them on before he goes 'ome.'

'Want to go 'ome,' said the little man. ''Ome to my wife and kids. *Trying to keep a man from 'is wife.*'

'No one wants to keep you from your wife, you old silly. All I says is for Gawd's sake put on your boots before you go 'ome. What'll your wife think of you comin' 'ome without boots.'

'She won't mind 'ow I come 'ome. Why, bless you, I ain't been 'ome at all for five years. It's 'ard to be separated from a wife and kids by a conspiring woman trying to make yer put on yer boots.'

'My dear, she's quite right, you know,' said Miss Runcible. 'You'd far better put on your boots.'

'There, 'ear what the lady says. Lady says you've to put on your boots.'

The little man took his boots from the landlady, looked at Miss Runcible with a searching glance, and threw them into the canal. '*Lady*,' he said with feeling. '*Trousers*,' and then he paddled off in his socks into the darkness.

'There ain't no 'arm in 'im really,' said the landlady, 'only he do get a bit wild when he's 'ad the drink. Wasting good boots like that.... I expect he'll spend the night in the lock-up.'

'Won't he get back to his wife, poor sweet?'

'Lor' bless you, no. She lives in London.'

At this stage Archie Schwert, whose humanitarian interests were narrower than Miss Runcible's, lost interest in the discussion.

'The thing we want to know is, can you let us have beds for the night?'

The landlady looked at him suspiciously.

'Bed or beds?'

'Beds.'

'Might do.' She looked from the car to Miss Runcible's trousers and back to the car again, weighing them against each other. 'Cost you a quid each,' she said at last.

'Can you find room for us all?'

'Well,' she said, 'which of you's with the young lady?'

'I'm afraid I'm all alone,' said Miss Runcible. 'Isn't it too shaming?'

'Never you mind, dearie, luck'll turn one day. Well, now, how can we all fit in? There's one room empty. I can sleep with our Sarah, and that leaves a bed for the gentlemen – then if the young lady wouldn't mind coming in with me and Sarah... '

'If you don't think it rude, I think I'd sooner have the empty bed,' said Miss Runcible, rather faintly. 'You see,' she added, with tact, 'I snore so terribly.'

'Bless you, so does our Sarah. *We* don't mind... still, if you'd *rather*...'

'Really, I think I should,' said Miss Runcible.

'Well then, I could put Mr Titchcock on the floor, couldn't I?'

'Yes,' said Miles, 'just you put Mr Titchcock on the floor.'

'And if the other gentleman don't mind going on the landing.... Well, we'll manage somehow, see if we don't.'

So they all drank some gin together in the back parlour and they woke Mr Titchcock up and made him help with the luggage and they gave him some gin, too, and he said it was all the same to him whether he slept on the floor or in bed, and he was very pleased to be of any service to anyone and didn't mind if he did have another drop just as a night-cap, as they might say; and at last they all went to bed, very tired, but fairly contented, and oh, how they were bitten by bugs all that night.

Adam had secured one of the bedrooms. He awoke early to find rain beating on the window. He looked out and saw a grey sky, some kind of factory and the canal from whose shallow waters rose little islands of scrap-iron and bottles; a derelict perambulator lay partially submerged under the opposite bank. In his room stood a chest of drawers full of horrible fragments of stuff, a washhand stand with a highly coloured basin, an empty jug and an old toothbrush. There was also a rotund female bust covered in shiny red material, and chopped off short, as in primitive martyrdoms, at neck, waist and elbows; a thing known as a dressmaker's 'dummy' (there had been one of these in Adam's home which they used to call 'Jemima' – one day he stabbed 'Jemima' with a chisel and scattered stuffing over the nursery floor and was punished. A more enlightened age would have seen a complex in this action and worried accordingly. Anyway he was made to sweep up all the stuffing himself).

Adam was very thirsty, but there was a light green moss in the bottom of the water bottle that repelled him. He got into bed again and found someone's handkerchief (presumably Mr Titchcock's) under the pillow.

He woke again a little later to find Miss Runcible dressed in pyjamas and a fur coat sitting on his bed.

'Darling,' she said, 'there's no looking-glass in my room and no bath anywhere, and I trod on someone cold and soft asleep in the passage, and I've been awake all night killing bugs with drops of face lotion, and everything smells, and I feel so low I could die.'

'For heaven's sake let's go away,' said Adam.

So they woke Miles and Archie Schwert, and ten minutes later they all stole out of the 'Royal George' carrying their suitcases.

'I wonder, do you think we ought to leave some money?' asked Adam, but the others all said no.

'Well, perhaps we ought to pay for the gin,' said Miss Runcible.

So they left five shillings on the bar and drove away to the 'Imperial'.

It was still very early, but everyone seemed to be awake, running in and out of the lifts carrying crash helmets and overalls. Miles' friend, they were told, had been out before dawn, presumably at his garage. Adam met some reporters whom he used to see about the *Excess* office. They told him that it was anyone's race, and that the place to see the fun was Headlong Corner, where there had been three deaths the year before, and it was worse this year, because they'd been putting down wet tar. It was nothing more or less than a death trap, the reporters said. Then they went away to interview some more drivers. All teams were confident of victory, they said.

Meanwhile Miss Runcible discovered an empty bathroom, and came down half an hour later all painted up and wearing a skirt and feeling quite herself again and ready for anything. So they went in to breakfast.

The dining-room was very full indeed. There were Speed Kings of all nationalities, unimposing men mostly with small moustaches and apprehensive eyes; they were reading the forecasts in the morning papers and eating what might (and in some cases did) prove to be their last meal on earth. There were a great number of journalists making the best of an 'out-of-town' job; there were a troop of nondescript 'fans', knowledgeable young men with bright jumpers tucked inside their belted trousers, old public-school ties, check tweeds, loose mouths and scarcely discernible Cockney accents; there were R.A.C. officials and A.A. officials, and the representatives of oil firms and tyre manufacturers. There was one disconsolate family who had come to the town for the christening of a niece. (No one had warned them that there was a motor race on; their hotel bill *was* a shock.)

'Very better-making,' said Miss Runcible with approval as she ate her haddock.

Scraps of highly technical conversation rose on all sides of them.

'... Changed the whole engine over after they'd been scrutineered. Anyone else would have been disqualified...'

'... just cruising round at fifty...'

'... stung by a bee just as he was taking the corner, missed the tree by inches and landed up in the Town Hall. There was a Riley coming up behind, spun round twice, climbed the bank, turned right over and caught fire...'

'... local overheating at the valve-heads. It's no sense putting a supercharger in that engine at all...'

'... Headlong Corner's jam. All you want to do is to brake right down to forty or forty-five at the white cottage, then rev up opposite the pub and get straight away in second on the near side of the road. A child could do it. It's that double bend just after the railway bridge where you'll get the funny stuff.'

'... kept flagging him down from the pits. I tell you that bunch don't want him to win.'

'... She wouldn't tell me her name, but she said she'd meet me at the same place to-night and gave me a sprig of white heather for the car. I lost it, like a fool. She said she'd look out for it too...'

'... Only offers a twenty pound bonus this year...'

'... lapped at seventy-five...'

'... Burst his gasket and blew out his cylinder heads...'

'... Broke both arms and cracked his skull in two places...'

'... Tailwag...'

'... Speed-wobble...'

'... Merc...'

'... Mag...'

'... crash...'

When they finished breakfast Miss Runcible and Adam and Archie Schwert and Miles went to the garage to look for their Speed King. They found him hard at work listening to his engine. A corner of the garage had been roped off and the floor strewn with sand as though for a boxing match.

Outside this ring clustered a group of predatory little boys with autograph albums and leaking fountain pens, and inside, surrounded by attendants, stood the essential parts of a motor-car. The engine was running and the whole machine shook with fruitless exertion. Clouds of dark smoke came from it, and a shattering roar which reverberated from concrete floor and corrugated iron roof into every corner of the building so that speech and thought became insupportable and all the senses were numbed. At frequent intervals this high and heart-breaking note was varied by sharp detonations, and it was these apparently which were causing anxiety, for at each report Miles' friend, who clearly could not have been unduly sensitive to noise, gave a little wince and looked significantly at his head mechanic.

Apart from the obvious imperfection of its sound, the car gave the impression to an uninstructed observer of being singularly unfinished. In fact, it was obviously still under construction. It had only three wheels; the fourth being in the hands of a young man in overalls, who, in the intervals of tossing back from his eyes a curtain of yellow hair, was beating it with a hammer. It also had no seats, and another mechanic was screwing down slabs of lead ballast in the place where one would have expected to find them. It had no bonnet; that was in the hands of a sign painter, who was drawing a black number 13 in a white circle. There was a similar number on the back, and a mechanic was engaged in fixing another number board over one of the headlights. There was a mechanic, too, making a windscreen of wire gauze, and a mechanic lying flat doing something to the back axle with a tin of grate polish and a rag. Two more mechanics were helping Miles' friend to listen to the bangs. 'As if we couldn't have heard them from Berkeley Square,' said Miss Runcible.

The truth is that motor-cars offer a very happy illustration of the metaphysical distinction between 'being' and 'becoming'. Some cars, mere vehicles with no purpose above bare locomotion, mechanical drudges such as Lady Metroland's Hispano Suiza, or Mrs Mouse's Rolls-Royce, or Lady Circumference's 1912 Daimler, or the 'general reader's' Austin Seven, these have definite 'being' just as much as their occupants. They are bought all screwed up and numbered and painted, and there they stay through various declensions of ownership, brightened now and then with a lick of paint or temporarily rejuvenated by the addition of some minor organ, but still maintaining their essential identity to the scrap heap.

Not so the *real* cars, that become masters of men; those vital creations of metal who exist solely for their own propulsion through space, for whom their drivers, clinging precariously at the steering-wheel, are as important as his stenographer to a stockbroker. These are in perpetual flux; a vortex of combining and disintegrating units; like the confluence of traffic at some spot where many roads meet, streams of mechanism come together, mingle and separate again.

Miles' friend, even had it been possible in the uproar, seemed indisposed to talk. He waved abstractedly and went on with his listening. Presently he came across and shouted:

'Sorry I can't spare a moment. I'll see you in the pits. I've got you some brassards.'

'My dear, what *can* that be?'

He handed them each a strip of white linen, terminating in tape.

'For your arms,' he shouted. 'You can't get into the pits without them.'

'My dear, what bliss! Fancy their having pits.'

Then they tied on their brassards. Miss Runcible's said, 'SPARE DRIVER'; Adam's, 'DEPOT STAFF'; Miles', 'SPARE MECHANIC' and Archie's, 'OWNER'S REPRESENTATIVE'.

Up till now the little boys round the rope had been sceptical of the importance of Miss Runcible and her friends, but as soon as they saw these badges of rank they pressed forward with their autograph books. Archie signed them all with the utmost complaisance, and even drew a slightly unsuitable picture in one of them. Then they drove away in Archie's car.

The race was not due to start until noon, but any indecision which they may have felt about the employment of the next few hours was settled for them by the local police, who were engaged in directing all traffic, irrespective of its particular inclinations, on the road to the course. No pains had been spared about this point of organization; several days before, the Chief Constable had issued a little route map which was to be memorized by all constables on point duty, and so well had they learned their lesson that from early that morning until late in the afternoon no vehicle approaching the town from any direction escaped being drawn into that broad circuit marked by the arrows and dotted line A-B which led to the temporary car park behind the Grand Stand. (Many doctors, thus diverted, spent an enjoyable day without apparent prejudice to their patients.)

The advance of the spectators had already assumed the form of a slow and unbroken stream. Some came on foot from the railway station, carrying sandwiches and camp stools; some on tandem bicycles; some in 'runabouts' or motor-cycle side-car combinations, but most were in modestly priced motor-cars. Their clothes and demeanour proclaimed them as belonging to the middle rank; a few brought portable wireless sets with them and other evidence of gaiety, but the general air of the procession was one of sobriety and purpose. This was no Derby day holiday-making; they had not snatched a day from office to squander it among gypsies and roundabouts and thimble-and-pea men. They were there for the race. As they crawled along on bottom gear in a fog of exhaust gas, they discussed the technicalities of motor-car design and the possibilities of bloodshed, and studied their maps of the course to pick out the most dangerous corners.

The detour planned by the Chief Constable was a long one, lined with bungalows and converted railway carriages. Banners floated over it between the telegraph posts, mostly advertising the *Morning Despatch*, which was organizing the race and paying for the victor's trophy – a silver gilt figure of odious design, symbolizing Fame embracing Speed. (This at the moment was under careful guard in the steward's room, for the year before it had been stolen on the eve of the race by the official timekeeper, who pawned it for a ridiculously small sum in Manchester, and was subsequently deprived of his position and sent to gaol.) Other advertisements proclaimed the superiorities of various sorts of petrol and sparking plugs, while some said '£100 FOR LOSS OF LIMB. INSURE TO-DAY'. There was also an elderly man walking among the motor-cars with a blue and white banner inscribed, 'WITHOUT SHEDDING OF BLOOD IS NO REMISSION OF SIN', while a smartly dressed young man was doing a brisk trade in bogus tickets for the Grand Stand.

Adam sat in the back of the car with Miles, who was clearly put out about his friend's lack of cordiality. 'What I can't make out,' he said, 'is why we came to this beastly place at all. I suppose I ought to be thinking of something to write for the *Excess*. I *know* this is just going to be the most dreary day we've ever spent.'

Adam felt inclined to agree. Suddenly he became aware that someone was trying to attract his attention.

'There's an awful man shouting "Hi" at you,' said Miles. 'My dear, *your friends*.'

Adam turned and saw not three yards away, separated from him by a young woman riding a push-bicycle in khaki shorts, her companion, who bore a knapsack on his shoulders, and a small boy selling programmes, the long-sought figure of the drunk Major. He looked sober enough this morning, dressed in a bowler hat and Burberry, and he was waving frantically to Adam from the dicky of a coupé car.

'Hi!' cried the drunk Major. 'Hi! I've been looking for you everywhere.'

'I've been looking for you,' shouted Adam. 'I want some money.'

'Can't hear – what do you want?'

'Money.'

'It's no good – these infernal things make too much noise. What's your name? Lottie had forgotten.'

'Adam Symes.'

'Can't hear.'

The line of traffic, creeping forward yard by yard, had at last reached the point B on the Chief Constable's map, where the dotted lines diverged. A policeman stood at the crossing directing the cars right and left, some to the parking place behind the Grand Stand, others to the mound above the pits. Archie turned off to the left. The drunk Major's car accelerated and swept away to the right.

'*I must know your name*,' he cried. All the drivers seemed to choose this moment to sound their horns; the woman cyclist at Adam's elbow rang her bell; the male cyclist tooted a little horn like a Paris taxi, and the programme boy yelled in his ear, 'Official programme – map of the course – all the drivers.'

'Adam Symes,' he shouted desperately, but the Major threw up his hands in despair and he disappeared in the crowd.

'*The way you pick people up*...' said Miles, startled into admiration.

'The pits' turned out to be a line of booths, built of wood and corrugated iron immediately opposite the Grand Stand. Many of the cars had already arrived and stood at their 'pits', surrounded by a knot of mechanics and spectators; they seemed to be already under repair. Busy officials hurried up and down, making entries in their lists. Over their heads a vast loud speaker was relaying the music of a military band.

The Grand Stand was still fairly empty, but the rest of the course was already lined with people. It stretched up and down hill for a circle of thirteen or fourteen miles, and those who were fortunate enough to own cottages or public houses at the more dangerous corners had covered their roofs with unstable wooden forms, and were selling tickets like very expensive hot cakes. A grass-covered hill rose up sharply behind the pits. On this had been erected a hoarding where a troop of Boy Scouts were preparing to score the laps, passing the time contentedly with ginger beer, toffee and rough-and-tumble fights. Behind the hoarding was a barbed-wire fence, and behind that again a crowd of spectators and several refreshment tents. A wooden bridge, advertising the *Morning Despatch,* had been built on the road. At various points officials might be seen attempting to understand each other over a field telephone. Sometimes the band would stop and a voice would announce, 'Will Mr So-and-So kindly report at once to the timekeeper's office'; then the band would go on.

Miss Runcible and her party found their way to the pit numbered 13 and sat on the matchboard counter smoking and signing autograph books. An official bore down on them.

'No smoking in the pits, please.'

'My dear, I'm terribly sorry. I didn't know.'

There were six open churns behind Miss Runcible, four containing petrol and two water. She threw her cigarette over her shoulder, and by a beneficent attention of Providence which was quite rare in her career it fell into the water. Had it fallen into the petrol it would probably have been all up with Miss Runcible.

Presently No. 13 appeared. Miles' friend and his mechanic, wearing overalls, crash-helmets and goggles, jumped out, opened the bonnet and began to reconstruct it again.

'They didn't ought to have a No. 13 at all,' said the mechanic. 'It isn't fair.'

Miss Runcible lit another cigarette.

'No smoking in the pits, *please*,' said the official.

'My dear, how *awful* of me. I quite forgot.'

(This time it fell in the mechanic's luncheon basket and lay smouldering quietly on a leg of chicken until it had burnt itself out.)

Miles' friend began filling up his petrol tank with the help of a very large funnel.

'Listen,' he said. 'You're not allowed to hand me anything direct, but if Edwards holds up his left hand as we come past the pits, that means we shall be stopping next lap for petrol. So what you've got to do is to fill up a couple of cans and put them on the shelf with the funnel for Edwards to take. If Edwards holds up his right hand . . .' elaborate instructions followed.

'You're in charge of the depôt,' he said to Archie. 'D'you think you've got all the signals clear? The race may depend on them, remember.'

'What does it mean if I wave the blue flag?'

'That you want me to stop.'

'Why should I want you to stop?'

'Well, you might see something wrong – leaking tank or anything like that, or the officials might want the number plate cleaned.'

'I think perhaps I won't do anything much about the blue flag. It seems rather too bogus for me.'

Miss Runcible lit another cigarette.

'Will you kindly leave the pits if you wish to smoke?' said the official.

'What a damned rude man,' said Miss Runcible. 'Let's go up to that divine tent and get a drink.'

They climbed the hill past the Boy Scouts, found a gate in the wire fence, and eventually reached the refreshment tent. Here an atmosphere of greater geniality prevailed. A profusion of men in plus-fours were having 'quick ones' before the start. There was no nonsense about not smoking. There was a middle-aged woman sitting on the grass with a bottle of stout and a baby.

'Home from home,' said Miss Runcible.

Suddenly the military band stopped and a voice said, 'Five minutes to twelve. All drivers and mechanics on the other side of the track, please.'

There was a hush all over the course, and the refreshment tent began to empty quickly.

'Darling, we shall miss the start.'

'Still, a drink *would* be nice.'

So they went into the tent.

'Four whiskies, please,' said Archie Schwert.

'You'll miss the start,' said the barmaid.

'What a pig that man was,' said Miss Runcible. 'Even if we weren't supposed to smoke, he might at least have asked us politely.'

'My dear, it was only you.'

'Well, I think that made it worse.'

'Lor', Miss,' said the barmaid. 'You surely ain't going to miss the start?'

'It's the one thing I want to see more than anything... my dear, I believe they're off already.'

The sudden roar of sixty high-power engines rose from below. 'They *have* started... how too shaming.' They went to the door of the tent. Part of the road was visible over the heads of the spectators, and they caught a glimpse of the cars running all jammed together like pigs being driven through a gate; one by one they shook themselves free and disappeared round the bend with a high shriek of acceleration.

'They'll be round again in quarter of an hour,' said Archie. 'Let's have another drink.'

'Who was ahead?' asked the barmaid anxiously.

'I couldn't see for certain,' said Miss Runcible, 'but I'm fairly sure it was No. 13.'

'*My!*'

The refreshment tent soon began to fill up again. The general opinion seemed to be that it was going to be a close race between No. 13 and No. 28, a red Omega car, driven by Marino, the Italian 'ace'.

'Dirtiest driver I ever seen,' said one man with relish. 'Why, over at Belfast 'e was just tipping 'em all into the ditches, just like winking.'

'There's one thing you *can* be sure of. They won't *both* finish.'

'It's sheer murder the way that Marino drives – a fair treat to see 'im.'

'He's a one all right – a real artist and no mistake about it.'

Adam and Miss Runcible and Archie and Miles went back to their pit.

'After all,' said Miss Runcible, 'the poor sweet may be wanting all sorts of things and signalling away like mad, and no one there to pay any attention to him – so discouraging.'

By this time the cars were fairly evenly spread out over the course. They flashed by intermittently with dazzling speed and a shriek; one or two drew into their pits and the drivers leapt out, trembling like leaves, to tinker with the works. One had already come to grief – a large German whose tyre had burst – punctured, some said, by a hireling of Marino's. It had left the road and shot up a tree like a cat chased by a dog. Two little American cars had failed to start; their team worked desperately at them amid derisive comments from the crowd. Suddenly two cars appeared coming down the straight, running abreast within two feet of each other.

'It's No. 13,' cried Miss Runcible, really excited at last. 'And there's that Italian devil just beside it. Come on, thirteen! Come on!' she cried, dancing in the pit and waving a flag she found at hand. 'Come on. Oh! Well done, thirteen.'

The cars were gone in a flash and succeeded by others.

'Agatha, darling, you shouldn't have waved the blue flag.'

'My dear, how awful. Why not?'

'Well, that means that he's to stop next lap.'

'Good God. Did I wave a blue flag?'

'My dear, you know you did.'

'*How* shaming. What *am* I to say to him?'

'Let's all go away before he comes back.'

'D'you know, I think we'd better. He might be furious, mightn't he? Let's go to the tent and have another drink – don't you think, or don't you?'

So No. 13 pit was again deserted.

*

'What did I say?' said the mechanic. 'The moment I heard we'd drawn this blinkin' number I knew we was in for trouble.'

*

The first person they saw when they reached the refreshment tent was the drunk Major.

'Your boy friend again,' said Miles.

'Well, there you are,' said the Major. 'D'you know I've been chasing you all over London. What have you been doing with yourself all this time?'

'I've been staying at Lottie's.'

'Well, she said she'd never heard of you. You see, I don't mind admitting I'd had a few too many that night, and to tell you the truth I woke up with things all rather a blur. Well then I found a thousand pounds in my pocket, and it all came back to me. There'd been a cove at Lottie's who gave me a thousand pounds to put on Indian Runner. Well, as far as I knew, Indian Runner was no good. I didn't want to lose your money for you, but the devil of it was I didn't know you from Adam.' ('I think that's a perfect joke,' said Miss Runcible.) 'And apparently Lottie didn't either. You'd have thought it was easy enough to trace the sort of chap who deals out thousands of pounds to total strangers, but I couldn't find one fingerprint.'

'Do you mean,' said Adam, a sudden delirious hope rising in his heart, 'that you've still got my thousand?'

'Not so fast,' said the Major. 'I'm spinning this yarn. Well, on the day of the race I didn't know what to do. One half of me said, keep the thousand. The chap's bound to turn up some time, and it's his business to do his own punting – the other half said, put it on the favourite for him and give him a run for his money.'

'So you put it on the favourite?' Adam's heart felt like lead again.

'No, I didn't. In the end I said, well, the young chap must be frightfully rich. If he likes to throw away his money, it's none of my business, so I planked it all on Indian Runner for you.'

'You mean . . . '

'I mean I've got the nice little packet of thirty-five thou. waiting until you condescend to call for it.'

'Good heavens . . . look here, have a drink, won't you?'

'That's a thing I never refuse.'

'Archie, lend me some money until I get this fortune.'

'How much?'

'Enough to buy five bottles of champagne.'

'Yes, if you can get them.'

The barmaid had a case of champagne at the back of the tent. ('People often feel queer through watching the cars go by so fast – ladies especially,' she explained.) So they took a bottle each and sat on the side of the hill and drank to Adam's prosperity.

'Hullo, everybody,' said the loudspeaker, 'Car No. 28, the Italian Omega, driven by Captain Marino, has just completed the course in twelve minutes one second, lapping at an average speed of 78.3 miles per hour. This is the fastest time yet recorded.'

A burst of applause greeted this announcement, but Adam said, 'I've rather lost interest in this race.'

'Look here, old boy,' the Major said when they were well settled down, 'I'm in rather a hole. Makes me feel an awful ass, saying so, but the truth is I got my note-case pinched in the crowd. Of course, I've got plenty of small change to see me back to the hotel and they'll take a cheque of mine there, naturally, but the fact is I was keen to make a few bets with some chaps I hardly know. I wonder, old boy, could you possibly lend me a fiver? I can give it to you at the same time as I hand over the thirty-five thousand.'

'Why, of course,' said Adam. 'Archie, lend me a fiver, can you?'

'Awfully good of you,' said the Major, tucking the notes into his hip pocket. 'Would it be all the same if you made it a tenner while we're about it?'

'I'm sorry,' said Archie, with a touch of coldness. 'I've only just got enough to get home with.'

'That's all right, old boy, *I* understand. Not another word. . . . Well, here's to us all.'

'I was on the course at the November Handicap,' said Adam. 'I thought I saw you.'

'It would have saved a lot of fuss if we'd met, wouldn't it? Still, all's well that ends well.'

'What an *angelic* man your Major is,' said Miss Runcible.

When they had finished their champagne, the Major – now indisputably drunk – rose to go.

'Look here, old boy,' he said. 'I must be toddling along now. Got to see some chaps. Thanks no end for the binge. So jolly having met you all again. Bye-bye, little lady.'

'When shall we meet again?' said Adam.

'Any time, old boy. Tickled to death to see you any time you care to drop in. Always a pew and a drink for old friends. So long everybody.'

'But couldn't I come and see you soon? About the money, you know.'

'Sooner the better, old boy. Though I don't know what you mean about money.'

'My thirty-five thousand.'

'Why, yes, to be sure. Fancy my forgetting that. I tell you what. You roll along to-night to the Imperial and I'll give it to you then. Jolly glad to get it off my chest. Seven o'clock at the American bar – or a little before.'

'Let's go back and look at the motor-cars,' said Archie.

They went down the hill feeling buoyant and detached (as one should if one drinks a great deal before luncheon). When they reached the pits they decided they were hungry. It seemed too far to climb up to the dining tent, so they ate as much of the mechanic's lunch as Miss Runcible's cigarette had spared. Then a mishap happened to No. 13. It drew into the side uncertainly, with the mechanic holding the steering-wheel. A spanner, he told them, thrown from Marino's car as they were passing him under the railway bridge, had hit Miles' friend on the shoulder. The mechanic helped him get out, and supported him to the Red Cross tent. 'May as well scratch,' he said. 'He won't be good for anything more this afternoon. It's asking for trouble having a No. 13.' Miles went to help his friend, leaving Miss Runcible and Adam and Archie staring rather stupidly at their motor-car. Archie hiccoughed slightly as he ate the mechanic's apple.

Soon an official appeared.

'What happened here?' he said.

'Driver's just been murdered,' said Archie. 'Spanner under the railway bridge. Marino.'

'Well, are you going to scratch? Who's spare driver?'

'I don't know. Do you, Adam? I shouldn't be a bit surprised if they hadn't murdered the spare driver, too.'

'I'm spare driver,' said Miss Runcible. 'It's on my arm.'

'She's spare driver. Look, it's on her arm.'

'Well, do you want to scratch?'

'Don't you scratch, Agatha.'

'No, I don't want to scratch.'

'All right. What's your name?'

'Agatha. I'm the spare driver. It's on my arm.'

'I can see it is – all right, start off as soon as you like.'

'Agatha,' repeated Miss Runcible firmly as she climbed into the car. 'It's on my arm.'

'I say, Agatha,' said Adam. 'Are you sure you're all right?'

'It's on my arm,' said Miss Runcible severely.

'I mean, are you quite certain it's absolutely safe?'

'Not *absolutely* safe, Adam. Not if they throw spanners. But I'll go quite slowly at first until I'm used to it. Just you see. Coming too?'

'I'll stay and wave the flag,' said Adam.

'That's right. Good-bye . . . goodness, how too stiff-scaring. . . .'

The car shot out into the middle of the road, missed a collision by a foot, swung round and disappeared with a roar up the road.

'I say, Archie, is it all right being tight in a car, if it's on a race course? They won't run her in or anything?'

'No, no, that's all right. All tight on the race course.'

'Sure?'

'Sure.'

'All of them?'

'Absolutely everyone – tight as houses.'

'That's all right then. Let's go and have a drink.'

So they went up the hill again, through the Boy Scouts, to the refreshment tent.

It was not long before Miss Runcible was in the news.

'Hullo, everybody,' said the loudspeaker. 'No. 13, the English Plunket-Bowse, driven by Miss Agatha, came into collision at Headlong Corner with No. 28, the Italian Omega car, driven by Captain Marino. No. 13 righted itself and continued on the course. No. 28 overturned and has retired from the race.'

'Well done, Agatha,' said Archie.

A few minutes later:

'Hullo, everybody. No. 13, the English Plunket-Bowse, driven by Miss Agatha, has just completed the course in nine minutes forty-one seconds. This constitutes a record for the course.'

Patriotic cheers broke out on all sides, and Miss Runcible's health was widely drunk in the refreshment tent.

A few minutes later:

'Hullo, everybody; I have to contradict the announcement recently made that No. 13, the English Plunket-Bowse, driven by Miss Agatha, had established a record for the course. The stewards have now reported that No. 13 left the road just after the level crossing and cut across country for five miles, rejoining the track at the Red Lion corner. The lap has therefore been disallowed by the judges.'

A few minutes later:

'Hullo, everybody; No. 13, the English Plunket-Bowse car, driven by Miss Agatha, has retired from the race. It disappeared from the course some time ago, turning left instead of right at Church Corner, and was last seen proceeding south on the bye-road, apparently out of control.'

'My dear, that's lucky for me,' said Miles. 'A really good story my second day on the paper. This ought to do me good with the *Excess* – *very* rich-making,' and he hurried off to the post office tent – which was one of the amenities of the course – to despatch a long account of Miss Runcible's disaster.

Adam accompanied him and sent a wire to Nina: '*Drunk Major in refreshment tent not bogus thirty-five thousand married to-morrow everything perfect Agatha lost love Adam.*'

'That seems quite clear,' he said.

They went to the hospital tent after this – another amenity of the course – to see how Miles' friend was getting on. He seemed in some pain and showed anxiety about his car.

'I think it's very heartless of him,' said Adam. 'He ought to be worried about Agatha. It only shows . . . '

'Motor men *are* heartless,' said Miles, with a sigh.

Presently Captain Marino was borne in on a stretcher. He turned on his side with a deep groan and spat at Miles' friend as he went past him. He also spat at the doctor who came to bandage him and bit one of the V.A.D.'s.

They said Captain Marino was no gentleman in the hospital tent.

There was no chance of leaving the course before the end of the race, Archie was told, and the race would not be over for at least two hours. Round and round went the stream of cars. At intervals the Boy Scouts posted a large red R against one or other of the numbers, as engine trouble or collision or Headlong Corner took its toll. A long queue stretched along the top of the hill from the door of the luncheon tent. Then it began to rain.

There was nothing for it but to go back to the bar.

At dusk the last car completed its course. The silver gilt trophy was presented to the winner. The loudspeaker broadcast 'God Save the King', and a cheerful 'Goodbye, everybody'. The tail of the queue outside the dining tent were respectfully informed that no more luncheons could be served. The barmaids in the refreshment tent said, 'All glasses, ladies and gentlemen, please.' The motor ambulances began a final round of the track to pick up survivors. Then Adam and Miles and Archie Schwert went to look for their car.

Darkness fell during the drive back. It took an hour to reach the town. Adam and Miles and Archie Schwert did not talk much. The effects of their drinks had now entered on that secondary stage, vividly described in temperance hand-books, when the momentary illusion of well-being and exhilaration gives place to melancholy, indigestion and moral decay. Adam tried to concentrate his thoughts upon his sudden wealth, but they seemed unable to adhere to this high pinnacle, and as often as he impelled them up, slithered back helplessly to his present physical discomfort.

The sluggish procession in which they were moving led them eventually to the centre of the town and the soberly illuminated front of the Imperial Hotel. A torrential flow of wet and hungry motor enthusiasts swept and eddied about the revolving doors.

'I shall die if I don't eat something soon,' said Miles. 'Let's leave Agatha until we've had a meal.'

But the manager of the 'Imperial' was unimpressed by numbers or necessity and manfully upheld the integrity of British hotel-keeping. Tea, he explained, was served daily in the Palm Court, with orchestra on Thursdays and Sundays, between the hours of four and six. A *table d'hôte* dinner was served in the dining-room from seven-thirty until nine o'clock. An *à la carte* dinner was also served in the grill-room at the same time. It was now twenty minutes past six. If the gentlemen cared to return in an hour and ten minutes he would do his best to accommodate them, but he could not promise to reserve a table. Things were busy that day. There had been motor races in the neighbourhood, he explained.

The commissionaire was more helpful, and told them that there was a tea-shop restaurant called the Café Royal a little way down the High Street, next to the Cinema. He seemed, however, to have given the same advice to all comers, for the Café Royal was crowded and overflowing. Everyone was being thoroughly cross, but only the most sarcastic and overbearing were given tables, and only the gross and outrageous were given food. Adam and Miles and Archie Schwert then tried two more tea-shops, one kept by 'ladies' and called 'The Honest Injun', a workmen's dining-room and a fried-fish shop. Eventually they bought a bag of mixed biscuits at a co-operative store, which they ate in the Palm Court of the 'Imperial', maintaining a moody silence.

It was now after seven, and Adam remembered his appointment in the American bar. There, too, inevitably, was a dense crowd. Some of the 'Speed Kings' themselves had appeared, pink from their baths, wearing dinner jackets and stiff white shirts, each in his circle of admirers. Adam struggled to the bar.

'Have you seen a drunk Major in here anywhere?' he asked.

The barmaid sniffed. 'I should think not, indeed,' she said. 'And I shouldn't serve him if he *did* come in. I don't have people of that description in *my* bar. *The very idea.*'

'Well, perhaps he's not drunk now. But have you seen a stout, red-faced man, with a single eyeglass and a turned-up moustache?'

'Well, there *was* someone like that not so long ago. Are you a friend of his?'

'I want to see him badly.'

'Well, all I can say is I wish you'd try and look after him and don't bring him in here again. Going on something awful he was. Broke two glasses and got very quarrelsome with the other gentlemen. He had three or four pound notes in his hand. Kept waving them about and saying, "D'you know what? I met a mutt to-day. I owe him thirty-five thousand pounds and he lent me a fiver." Well, that's not the way to talk before strangers, is it? He went out ten minutes ago. I was glad to see the back of him, I can tell you.'

'Did he say that – about having met a mutt?'

'Didn't stop saying it the whole time he was in here – most monotonous.'

But as Adam left the bar he saw the Major coming out of the gentlemen's lavatory. He was walking very deliberately, and stared at Adam with a glazed and vacant eye.

'Hi!' cried Adam. 'Hi!'

'Cheerio,' said the drunk Major distantly.

'I say,' said Adam. 'What about my thirty-five thousand pounds?'

The drunk Major stopped and adjusted his monocle.

'Thirty-five thousand and five pounds,' he said. 'What about them?'

'Well, where are they?'

'They're safe enough. National and Provincial Union Bank of England, Limited. A perfectly sound and upright company. I'd trust them with more than that if I had it. I'd trust them with a million, old boy, honest I would. One of those fine old companies, you know. They don't make companies like that now. I'd trust that bank with my wife and kiddies.... You mustn't think I'd put your money into anything that wasn't straight, old boy. You ought to know me well enough for that....'

'No, of course not. It's terribly kind of you to have looked after it – you said you'd give me a cheque this evening. Don't you remember?'

The drunk Major looked at him craftily. 'Ah,' he said. 'That's another matter. I told *someone* I'd give him a cheque. But how am I to know it was you?... I've got to be careful, you know. Suppose you were just a crook dressed up. I don't say you are, mind, but supposing. Where'ld I be then? You have to look at both sides of a case like this.'

'Oh, God.... I've got two friends here who'll swear to you I'm Adam Symes. Will that do?'

'Might be a gang. Besides *I* don't know that the name of the chap who gave me the thousand *was* Adam what-d'you-call-it at all. Only your word for it. I'll tell you what,' said the Major, sitting down in a deep armchair, 'I'll sleep on it. Just forty winks. I'll let you know my decision when I wake up. Don't think me suspicious, old boy, but I've got to be careful... other chap's money, you know...' And he fell asleep.

Adam struggled through the crowd to the Palm Court, where he had left Miles and Archie. News of No. 13 had just come through. The car had been found piled up on the market cross of a large village about fifteen miles away (doing irreparable damage to a monument already scheduled for preservation by the Office of Works). But there was no sign of Miss Runcible.

'I suppose we ought to do something about it,' said Miles. 'This is the most miserable day I ever spent. Did you get your fortune?'

'The Major was too drunk to recognize me. He's just gone to sleep.'

'*Well.*'

'We must go to this beastly village and look for Agatha.'

'I can't leave my Major. He'll probably wake up soon and give the fortune to the first person he sees.'

'Let's just go and shake him until he gives us the fortune now,' said Miles.

But this was impracticable, for when they reached the chair where Adam had left him, the drunk Major was gone.

The hall porter remembered him going out quite clearly. He had pressed a pound into his hand, saying, 'Met-a-mutt-to-day', and taken a taxi to the station.

'D'you know,' said Adam, 'I don't believe that I'm ever going to get that fortune.'

'Well, I don't see that you've very much to complain of,' said Archie. 'You're no worse off than you were. *I've* lost a fiver and five bottles of champagne.'

'That's true,' said Adam, a little consoled.

*

They got into the car and drove through the rain to the village where the Plunket-Bowse had been found. There it stood, still smoking and partially recognizable, surrounded by admiring villagers. A constable in a water-proof cape was doing his best to preserve it intact from the raids of souvenir hunters who were collecting the smaller fragments.

No one seemed to have witnessed the disaster. The younger members of the community were all at the races, while the elders were engaged in their afternoon naps. One thought he had heard a crash.

Inquiries at the railway station, however, disclosed that a young lady, much dishevelled in appearance, and wearing some kind of band on her arm, had appeared in the booking office early that afternoon and asked where she was. On being told, she said, well, she wished she wasn't, because someone had left an enormous stone spanner in the middle of the road. She admitted feeling rather odd. The stationmaster had asked her if she would like to come in and sit down and offered to get her some brandy. She said, 'No, no more brandy', and bought a first-class ticket to London. She had left on the 3.25 train.

'So that's all right,' said Archie.

Then they left the village and presently found an hotel on the Great North Road, where they dined and spent the night. They reached London by luncheon-time next day, and learned that Miss Runcible had been found early that morning staring fixedly at a model engine in the central hall at Euston Station. In answer to some gentle questions, she replied that to the best of her knowledge she had no name, pointing to the brassard on her arm, as if in confirmation of this fact. She had come in a motor-car, she explained, which would not stop. It was full of bugs which she had tried to kill with drops of face lotion. One of them threw a spanner. There had been a stone thing in the way. They shouldn't put up symbols like that in the middle of the road, should they, or should they?

So they conveyed her to a nursing-home in Wimpole Street and kept her for some time in a darkened room.

CHAPTER 11

ADAM rang up Nina.

'Darling, I've been so happy about your telegram. Is it really true?'

'No, I'm afraid not.'

'The Major *is* bogus?'

'Yes.'

'You haven't got any money?'

'No.'

'We aren't going to be married to-day?'

'No.'

'I see.'

'Well?'

'I said, I see.'

'Is that all?'

'Yes, that's all, Adam.'

'I'm sorry.'

'I'm sorry, too. Good-bye.'

'Good-bye, Nina.'

Later Nina rang up Adam.

'Darling, is that you? I've got something rather awful to tell you.'

'Yes?'

'You'll be furious.'

'Well?'

'I'm engaged to be married.'

'Who to?'

'I hardly think I can tell you.'

'Who?'

'Adam, you won't be beastly about it, will you?'

'Who is it?'

'Ginger.'

'I don't believe it.'

'Well, I am. That's all there is to it.'

'You're going to marry Ginger?'

'Yes.'

'I see.'

'Well?'

'I said, I see.'

'Is that all?'

'Yes, that's all, Nina.'

'When shall I see you?'

'I don't want ever to see you again.'

'I see.'

'Well?'

'I said, I see.'

'Well, good-bye.'

'Good-bye.... I'm sorry, Adam.'

CHAPTER 12

TEN days later Adam bought some flowers at the corner of Wigmore Street and went to call on Miss Runcible at her nursing-home. He was shown first into the matron's room. She had numerous photographs in silver frames and a very nasty fox terrier. She smoked a cigarette in a greedy way, making slight sucking noises.

'Just taking a moment off in my den,' she explained. 'Down, Spot, down. But I can see you're fond of dogs,' she added, as Adam gave Spot a half-hearted pat on the head. 'So you want to see Miss Runcible? Well, I ought to warn you first that she must have no kind of excitement whatever. She's had a severe shock. Are you a relation, may I ask?'

'No, only a friend.'

'A very *special* friend, perhaps, eh?' said the matron archly. 'Never mind, I'll spare your blushes. Just you run up and see her. But not more than five minutes, mind, or you'll have me on your tracks.'

There was a reek of ether on the stairs which reminded Adam of the times when, waiting to take her to luncheon, he had sat on Nina's bed while she did her face. (She invariably made him turn his back until it was over, having a keen sense of modesty about this one part of her toilet, in curious contrast to some girls, who would die rather than be seen in their underclothes, and yet openly flaunt unpainted faces in front of anyone.)

It hurt Adam deeply to think much about Nina.

Outside Miss Runcible's door hung a very interesting chart which showed the fluctuations of her temperature and pulse and many other curious details of her progress. He studied this with pleasure until a nurse, carrying a tray of highly polished surgical instruments, gave him such a look that he felt obliged to turn away.

Miss Runcible lay in a high, narrow bed in a darkened room.

A nurse was crocheting at her side when Adam entered. She rose, dropping a few odds and ends from her lap, and said, 'There's someone come to see you, dear. Now remember you aren't to talk much.' She took the flowers from Adam's hand, said, 'Look, what lovelies. Aren't you a lucky girl?' and left the room with them. She returned a moment later carrying them in a jug of water. 'There, the thirsties,' she said. 'Don't they love to get back to the nice cool water?'

Then she went out again.

'Darling,' said a faint voice from the bed, 'I can't really see who it is. Would it be awful to draw the curtains?'

Adam crossed the room and let in the light of the grey December afternoon.

'My dear, how blind-making. There are some cocktail things in the wardrobe. Do make a big one. The nurses love them so. It's such a nice nursing-home this, Adam, only all the nurses are starved, and there's a breath-taking young man next door who keeps putting his head in and asking how I am. *He* fell out of an *aeroplane*, which is rather grand, don't you think?'

'How are you feeling, Agatha?'

'Well, rather odd, to tell you the truth.... How's Nina?'

'She's got engaged to be married – haven't you heard?'

'My dear, the nurses are interested in no one but Princess Elizabeth. Do tell me.'

'A young man called Ginger.'

'*Well?*'

'Don't you remember him? He came on with us after the airship party.'

'Not the one who was sick?'

'No, the other.'

'I don't remember...does Nina call him Ginger?'

'Yes.'

'Why?'

'He asked her to.'

'*Well!*'

'She used to play with him when they were children. So she's going to marry him.'

'My dear, isn't that rather sad-making for you?'

'I'm desperate about it. I'm thinking of committing suicide, like Simon.'

'Don't do that, darling...did Simon commit suicide?'

'My dear, you know he did. The night all those libel actions started.'

'Oh, *that* Simon. I thought you meant *Simon.*'

'Who's Simon?'

'The young man who fell out of the aeroplane. The nurses call him Simple Simon because it's affected his brains... but, Adam, I *am* sorry about Nina. I'll tell you what we'll do. As soon as I'm well again we'll make Mary Mouse give a lovely party to cheer you up.'

'Haven't you heard about Mary?'

'No, what?'

'She went off to Monte Carlo with the Maharajah of Pukkapore.'

'*My dear*, aren't the Mice furious?'

'She's just receiving religious instruction before her official reception as a royal concubine. Then they're going to India.'

'How people are *disappearing*, Adam. Did you get that money from the drunk Major?'

'No, he disappeared too.'

'D'you know, all that time when I was dotty I had the most awful dreams. I thought we were all driving round and round in a motor race and none of us could stop, and there was an enormous audience composed entirely of gossip writers and gate-crashers and Archie Schwert and people like that, all shouting at us at once to go faster, and car after car kept crashing until I was left all alone driving and driving – and then I used to crash and wake up.'

Then the door opened, and Miles came popping in.

'Agatha, Adam, my dears. The *time* I've had trying to get in. I can't tell you how bogus they were downstairs. First I said I was Lord Chasm, and that wasn't any good; and I said I was one of the doctors, and that wasn't any good; and I said I was your young man, and *that* wasn't any good; and I said I was a gossip writer, and they let me up at once and said I wasn't to excite you, but would I put a piece in my paper about their nursing-home. *How* are you, Aggie darling? I brought up some new records.'

'You are angelic. Do let's try them. There's a gramophone under the bed.'

'There's a whole lot more people coming to see you to-day. I saw them all at luncheon at Margot's. Johnny Hoop and

Van and Archie Schwert. I wonder if they'll all manage to get in.'

They got in.

So soon there was quite a party, and Simon appeared from next door in a very gay dressing-gown, and they played the new records and Miss Runcible moved her bandaged limbs under the bedclothes in negro rhythm.

Last of all, Nina came in looking quite lovely and very ill.

'Nina, I hear you're engaged.'

'Yes, it's very lucky. My papa has just put all his money into a cinema film and lost it all.'

'My dear, it doesn't matter at all. My papa lost all his twice. It doesn't make a bit of difference. That's just one of the things one has to learn about losing all one's money.... Is it true that you really call him Ginger?'

'Well, yes, only, Agatha, please don't be unkind about it.'

And the gramophone was playing the song which the black man sang at the Café de la Paix.

Then the nurse came in.

'Well, you are noisy ones, and no mistake,' she said. 'I don't know what the matron would say if she were here.'

'Have a chocolate, sister?'

'*Ooh, chocs!*'

Adam made another cocktail.

Miles sat on Miss Runcible's bed and took up the telephone and began dictating some paragraphs about the nursing-home.

'What it is to have a friend in the Press,' said the nurse.

Adam brought her a cocktail. 'Shall I?' she said. 'I hope you haven't made it too strong. Suppose it goes to my head. What would the patients think if their sister came in tiddly. Well, if you're *sure* it won't hurt me, thanks.'

'*... Yesterday I visited the Hon. Agatha Runcible comma Lord Chasm's lovely daughter comma at the Wimpole Street nursing-home where she is recovering from the effects of the motor accident recently* *described in this column stop Miss Runcible was entertaining quite a large party which included . . .*'

Adam, handing round cocktails, came to Nina.

'I thought we were never going to meet each other again.'

'We were obviously bound to, weren't we?'

'Agatha's looking better than I expected, isn't she? What an amusing nursing-home.'

'Nina, I must see you again. Come back to Lottie's this evening and have dinner with me.'

'No.'

'*Please.*'

'No. Ginger wouldn't like it.'

'Nina, you aren't in love with him?'

'No, I don't think so.'

'Are you in love with me?'

'I don't know . . . I was once.'

'Nina, I'm absolutely miserable not seeing you. Do come and dine with me to-night. What can be the harm in that?'

'My dear, I know exactly what it will mean.'

'Well, why not?'

'You see, Ginger's not like us really about that sort of thing. He'd be furious.'

'Well, what about me? Surely I have first claim?'

'Darling, don't *bully*. Besides, I used to play with Ginger as a child. His hair was a very pretty colour then.'

' *. . . Mr "Johnny" Hoop, whose memoirs are to be published next month, told me that he intends to devote his time to painting in future, and is going to Paris to study in the spring. He is to be taken into the studio of . . .*'

'For the last time, Nina . . .'

'Well, I suppose I must.'

'*Angel!*'

'I believe you knew I was going to.'

'*. . . Miss Nina Blount, whose engagement to Mr "Ginger" Littlejohn, the well-known polo player. . . . Mr Schwert . . .*'

'If only you were as rich as Ginger, Adam, or only half as rich. Or if only you had any money at all.'

'Well,' said the matron, appearing suddenly. 'Whoever heard of cocktails and a gramophone in a concussion case? Sister Briggs, pull down those curtains at once. Out you go, the whole lot of you. Why, I've known cases die with less.'

Indeed, Miss Runcible was already showing signs of strain. She was sitting bolt upright in bed, smiling deliriously, and bowing her bandaged head to imaginary visitors.

'*Darling*,' she said. 'How *too* divine . . . *how* are you? . . . and how are *you*? . . . how angelic of you all to come . . . only you must be careful not to fall out at the corners . . . ooh, just missed it. There goes that nasty Italian car . . . I wish I knew which thing was which in this car . . . darling, do try and drive more straight, my sweet, you were nearly into me then. . . . Faster . . . '

'That's all right, Miss Runcible, that's all right. You mustn't get excited,' said the matron. 'Sister Briggs, run for the ice-pack quickly.'

'All friends here,' said Miss Runcible, smiling radiantly. 'Faster. . . . Faster . . . it'll stop all right when the time comes . . . '

That evening Miss Runcible's temperature went rocketing up the chart in a way which aroused great interest throughout the nursing-home. Sister Briggs, over her evening cup of cocoa, said she would be sorry to lose that case. Such a nice bright girl – but terribly excitable.

At Shepheard's Hotel Lottie said to Adam:

'That chap's been in here again after you.'

'What chap, Lottie?'

'How do I know what chap? Same chap as before.'

'You never told me about a chap.'

'Didn't I, dear? Well, I meant to.'

'What did he want?'

'I don't know – something about money. Dun, I expect. Says he is coming back to-morrow.'

'Well, tell him I've gone to Manchester.'

'That's right, dear. . . . What about a glass of wine?'

*

Later that evening Nina said: 'You don't seem to be enjoying yourself very much to-night.'

'Sorry, am I being a bore?'

'I think I shall go home.'

'Yes.'

'Adam, darling, what's the matter?'

'I don't know. . . . Nina, do you ever feel that things simply can't go on much longer?'

'What d'you mean by things – us or everything?'

'Everything.'

'No – I wish I did.'

'I dare say you're right . . . what are you looking for?'

'Clothes.'

'Why?'

'Oh, Adam, what *do* you want . . . you're too impossible this evening.'

'Don't let's talk any more, Nina, d'you mind?'

Later he said : 'I'd give anything in the world for something different.'

'Different from me or different from everything?'

'Different from everything . . . only I've got nothing . . . what's the good of talking?'

'Oh, Adam, my dearest . . .'

'Yes?'

'Nothing.'

*

When Adam came down next morning Lottie was having her morning glass of champagne in the parlour.

'So your little bird's flown, has she? Sit down and have a glass of wine. That dun's been in again. I told him you was in Manchester.'

'Splendid.'

'Seemed rather shirty about it. Said he'd go and look for you.'

'Better still.'

Then something happened which Adam had been dreading for days. Lottie suddenly said:

'And that reminds me. What about my little bill?'

'Oh, yes,' said Adam, 'I've been meaning to ask for it. Have it made out and sent up to me some time, will you?'

'I've got it here. Bless you, what a lot you seem to have drunk.'

'Yes, I do, don't I? Are you sure some of this champagne wasn't the Judge's?'

'Well, it may have been,' admitted Lottie. 'We get a bit muddled with the books now and then.'

'Well, thank you so much, I'll send you down a cheque for this.'

'No, dear,' said Lottie. 'Suppose you write it down here. Here's the pen, here's the ink, and here's a blank cheque book.'

(Bills are delivered infrequently and irregularly at Lottie's, but when they come, there is no getting away from them.) Adam wrote out a cheque for seventy-eight pounds sixteen shillings.

'And twopence for the cheque,' said Lottie.

And twopence, Adam added.

'There's a dear,' said Lottie, blotting the cheque and locking it away in a drawer. 'Why, look who's turned up. If it isn't Mr Thingummy.'

It was Ginger.

'Good morning, Mrs Crump,' he said rather stiffly.

'Come and sit down and have a glass of wine, dear. Why, I knew you before you were born.'

'Hullo, Ginger,' said Adam.

'Look here, Symes,' said Ginger, looking in an embarrassed manner at the glass of champagne which had been put into his hand, 'I want to speak to you. Perhaps we can go somewhere where we shan't be disturbed.'

'Bless you, boys, I won't disturb you,' said Lottie. 'Just you have a nice talk. I've got lots to see to.'

She left the parlour, and soon her voice could be heard raised in anger against the Italian waiter.

'Well?' said Adam.

'Look here, Symes,' said Ginger, 'what I mean to say is, what I'm going to say may sound damned unpleasant, you know, and all that, but look here, you know, damn it, I mean *the better man won* – not that I mean I'm the *better* man. Wouldn't say that for a minute. And, anyway, Nina's a damn sight too good for either of us. It's just that I've been lucky. Awful rough luck on you, I mean, and all that, but still, when you come to think of it, after all, well, look here, damn it, I mean, d'you see what I mean?'

'Not quite,' said Adam gently. 'Now tell me again. Is it something about Nina?'

'Yes, it is,' said Ginger in a rush. 'Nina and I are engaged, and I'm not going to have you butting in or there'll be hell to pay.' He paused, rather taken aback at his own eloquence.

'What makes you think I'm butting in?'

'Well, hang it all, she dined with you last night, didn't she, and stayed out jolly late, too.'

'How do you know how late she stayed out?'

'Well, as a matter of fact, you see I wanted to speak to her about something rather important, so I rang her up once or twice and didn't get an answer until three o'clock.'

'I suppose you rang her up about every ten minutes?'

'Oh no, damn it, not as often as that,' said Ginger. 'No, no, not as often as that. I know it sounds rather unsporting and all that, but you see I wanted to speak to her, and, anyway, when I did get through, she just said she had a pain and didn't want to talk; *well, I mean to say.* After all, I mean, one is a gentleman. It isn't as though you were just a sort of friend of the family, is it? I mean, you were more or less engaged to her yourself, weren't you, at one time? Well, what would you have thought if I'd come butting in? You must look at it like that, from my point of view, too, mustn't you, I mean?'

'Well, I think that's rather what did happen.'

'Oh no, look here, Symes, I mean, damn it; you mustn't say things like that. D'you know all the time I was out East I had Nina's photograph over my bed, honest I did. I expect you think that's sentimental and all that, but what I mean is I didn't stop thinking of that girl once all the time I was away. Mind you, there were lots of other frightfully jolly girls out there, and I don't say I didn't sometimes get jolly pally with them, you know, tennis and gymkhana and all that sort of thing, I mean, and dancing in the evenings, but never anything serious, you know. Nina was the only girl I really thought of, and I'd sort of made up my mind when I came home to look her up, and if she'd have me . . . see what I mean? So you see it's awfully rough luck on me when someone comes butting in. You must see that, don't you?'

'Yes,' said Adam.

'And there's another thing, you know, sentiment and all that apart. I mean Nina's a girl who likes nice clothes and things, you know, comfort and all that. Well, I mean to say, of course, her father's a topping old boy, absolutely one of the best, but he's rather an ass about money, if you know what I mean. What I mean, Nina's going to be frightfully hard up, and all that, and I mean you haven't got an awful lot of money, have you?'

'I haven't any at all.'

'No, I mean, that's what I mean. *Awfully rough on you.* No one thinks the worse of you, respects you for it, I mean earning a living and all that. Heaps of fellows haven't any money nowadays. I could give you the names of dozens of stout fellows, absolute toppers, who simply haven't a bean. No, all I mean is, when it comes to marrying, then that does make a difference, doesn't it?'

'What you've been trying to say all this time is that you're not sure of Nina?'

'Oh, rot, my dear fellow, absolute bilge. Damn it, I'd trust Nina anywhere, of course I would. After all, damn it, what does being in love mean if you can't trust a person?'

('What, indeed?' thought Adam), and he said, 'Now, Ginger, tell the truth. What's Nina worth to you?'

'Good Lord, why what an extraordinary thing to ask; everything in the world of course. I'd go through fire and water for that girl.'

'Well, I'll sell her to you.'

'No, why, look here, good God, damn it, I mean ...'

'I'll sell my share in her for a hundred pounds.'

'You pretend to be fond of Nina and you talk about her like that! Why, hang it, it's not decent. Besides, a hundred pounds is the deuce of a lot. I mean, getting married is a damned expensive business, don't you know. And I'm just getting a couple of polo ponies over from Ireland. That's going to cost a hell of a lot, what with one thing and another.'

'A hundred down, and I leave Nina to you. I think it's cheap.'

'Fifty.'

'A hundred.'

'Seventy-five.'

'A hundred.'

'I'm damned if I'll pay more than seventy-five.'

'I'll take seventy-eight pounds sixteen and twopence. I can't go lower than that.'

'All right, I'll pay that. *You really will go away?*'

'I'll try, Ginger. Have a drink.'

'No, thank you ... this only shows what an escape Nina's had – poor little girl.'

'Good-bye, Ginger.'

'Good-bye, Symes.'

'Young Thingummy going?' said Lottie, appearing in the door. 'I was just thinking about a little drink.'

Adam went to the telephone-box.... 'Hullo, is that Nina?'

'Who's speaking, please? I don't think Miss Blount is in.'

'Mr Fenwick-Symes.'

'Oh, Adam. I was afraid it was Ginger. I woke up feeling I just couldn't bear him. He rang up last night just as I got in.'

'I know. Nina, darling, something awful's happened.'

'What?'

'Lottie presented me with her bill.'

'Darling, what *did* you do?'

'Well, I did something rather extraordinary.... My dear, I sold *you*.'

'Darling... *who to*?'

'Ginger. You fetched seventy-eight pounds sixteen and twopence.'

'*Well?*'

'And now I never am going to see you again.'

'Oh, but Adam, I think this is beastly of you; I don't want not to see you again.'

'I'm sorry.... Good-bye, Nina, darling.'

'Good-bye, Adam, my sweet. But I think you're rather a cad.'

*

Next day Lottie said to Adam, 'You know that chap I said came here asking for you?'

'The dun?'

'Well, he wasn't a dun. I've just remembered. He's a chap who used to come here quite a lot until he had a fight with a Canadian. He was here the night that silly Flossie killed herself on the chandelier.'

'Not the drunk Major.'

'He wasn't drunk yesterday. Not so as you'd notice anyway. Red-faced chap with an eyeglass. You ought to remember him, dear. He was the one made that bet for you on the November Handicap.'

'But I must get hold of him at once. What's his name?'

'Ah, that I couldn't tell you. I *did* know, but it's slipped my memory. He's gone to Manchester to look for you. Pity your missing him!'

Then Adam rang up Nina. 'Listen,' he said. 'Don't do anything sudden about Ginger. I may be able to buy you back. The drunk Major has turned up again.'

'But, darling, it's too late. Ginger and I got married this morning. I'm just packing for our honeymoon. We're going in an aeroplane.'

'Ginger wasn't taking any chances, was he? Darling, don't go.'

'No, I must. Ginger says he knows a "tophole little spot not far from Monte with a very decent nine-hole golf course".'

'*Well?*'

'*Yes, I know*... we shall only be away a few days. We're coming back to spend Christmas with Papa. Perhaps we shall be able to arrange something when we get back. I do hope so.'

'Good-bye.'

'Good-bye.'

*

Ginger looked out of the aeroplane: 'I say, Nina,' he shouted, 'when you were young did you ever have to learn a thing out of a poetry book about: "*This sceptre'd isle, this earth of majesty, this something or other Eden*"? D'you know what I mean? – "*this happy breed of men, this little world, this precious stone set in the silver sea....*

This blessed plot, this earth, this realm, this England
This nurse, this teeming womb of royal kings
Feared by their breed and famous by their birth..."

I forget how it goes on. Something about a stubborn Jew. But you know the thing I mean?'

'It comes in a play.'

'No, a blue poetry book.'

'I acted in it.'

'Well, they may have put it into a play since. It was in a blue poetry book when I learned it. Anyway, you know what I mean?'

'Yes, why?'

'Well, I mean to say, don't you feel somehow, up in the air like this and looking down and seeing everything underneath. I mean, don't you have a sort of feeling rather like that, if you see what I mean?'

Nina looked down and saw inclined at an odd angle a horizon of straggling red suburb; arterial roads dotted with little cars; factories, some of them working, others empty and decaying; a disused canal; some distant hills sown with bungalows; wireless masts and overhead power cables; men and women were indiscernible except as tiny spots; they were marrying and shopping and making money and having children. The scene lurched and tilted again as the aeroplane struck a current of air.

'I think I'm going to be sick,' said Nina.

'Poor little girl,' said Ginger. 'That's what the paper bags are for.'

*

There was rarely more than a quarter of a mile of the black road to be seen at one time. It unrolled like a length of cinema film. At the edges was confusion; a fog spinning past: '*Faster, faster,*' they shouted above the roar of the engine. The road rose suddenly and the white car soared up the sharp ascent without slackening speed. At the summit of the hill there was a corner. Two cars had crept up, one on each side, and were closing in. 'Faster,' cried Miss Runcible, 'faster.'

'Quietly, dear, quietly. You're disturbing everyone. You must lie quiet or you'll never get well. Everything's quite all right. There's nothing to worry about. Nothing at all.'

They were trying to make her lie down. How could one drive properly lying down?

Another frightful corner. The car leant over on two wheels, tugging outwards; it was drawn across the road until it was within a few inches of the bank. One ought to brake down at the corners, but one couldn't see them coming lying flat on one's back like this. The back wheels wouldn't hold the road at this speed. Skidding all over the place.

'*Faster. Faster.*'

The stab of a hypodermic needle.

'There's nothing to worry about, dear . . . *nothing at all . . . nothing.*'

CHAPTER 13

THE film had been finished, and everyone had gone away; Wesley and Whitefield, Bishop Philpotts and Miss La Touche, Mr Isaacs, and all his pupils from the National Academy of Cinematographic Art. The park lay deep in snow, a clean expanse of white, shadowless and unspotted save for tiny broad arrows stamped by the hungry birds. The bellringers were having their final practice, and the air was alive with pealing bells.

Inside the dining-room Florin and Mrs Florin and Ada, the fifteen-year-old housemaid, were arranging branches of holly above the frames of the family portraits. Florin held the basket, Mrs Florin held the steps and Ada put the decorations in their places. Colonel Blount was having his afternoon nap upstairs.

Florin had a secret. It was a white calico banner of great age lettered in red ribbon with the words 'WELCOME HOME'. He had always known where it was, just where to put his hand on it, at the top of the black trunk in the far attic behind the two hip baths and the 'cello case.

'The Colonel's mother made it,' he explained, 'when he first went away to school, and it was always hung out in the hall whenever he and Mister Eric came back for the holidays. It used to be the first thing he'd look for when he came into the house – even when he was a grown man home on leave. "Where's my banner?" he'd say. We'll have it up for Miss Nina – Mrs Littlejohn, I should say.'

Ada said should they put some holly in Captain and Mrs Littlejohn's bedroom.

Mrs Florin said, whoever heard of holly in a bedroom, and she wasn't sure but that it was unlucky to take it upstairs.

Ada said, 'Well, perhaps just a bit of mistletoe over the bed.'

Mrs Florin said Ada was too young to think about things like that, and she ought to be ashamed of herself.

Florin said would Ada stop arguing and answering back and come into the hall to put up the banner. One string went on the nose of the rhinoceros, he explained, the other round the giraffe.

Presently Colonel Blount came down.

'Should I light the fires in the big drawing-room?' asked Mrs Florin.

'Fires in the big drawing-room? No, why should you want to do that, Mrs Florin?'

'Because of Captain and Mrs Littlejohn – you haven't forgotten, have you, sir, that they're coming to stay this afternoon?'

'Captain and Mrs Fiddlesticks. Never heard of them. Who asked them to stay I should like to know? *I* didn't. Don't know who they are. Don't want them.... Besides, now I come to think of it, Miss Nina and her husband said they were coming down. I can't have the whole house turned into an hotel. If these people come, Florin, whoever they are, you tell them to go away. You understand? I won't have them, and I think it's very presumptuous of whoever asked them. It is not their place to invite guests here without consulting me.'

'Should I be lighting the fires in the big drawing-room for Miss Nina and her young gentleman, sir?'

'Yes, yes, certainly... and a fire in their bedroom, of course. And, Florin, I want you to come down to the cellar with me to look out some port... I've got the keys here.... I have a feeling I'm going to like Miss Nina's husband,' he confided on their way to the cellar. 'I hear very good reports of him – a decent, steady young fellow, and not at all badly off. Miss Nina said in her letter that he used to come over here as a little boy. D'you remember him, Florin? Blest if I do.... What's the name again?'

'Littlejohn, sir.'

'Yes. Littlejohn, to be sure. I had the name on the tip of my tongue only a minute ago. *Littlejohn.* I must remember that.'

'His father used to live over at Oakshott, sir. A very wealthy gentleman. Shipowners, I think they were. Young Mr Littlejohn used to go riding with Miss Nina, sir. Regular little monkey he was, sir, red-headed... a terrible one for cats.'

'Well, well, I dare say he's grown out of that. Mind the step, Florin, it's all broken away. Hold the lamp higher, can't you, man. Now, what did we come for? Port, yes, port. Now, there's some '96 somewhere, only a few bottles left. What does it say on this bin? I can't read. Bring the light over here.'

'We drank up the last of the '96, sir, when the film-acting gentlemen was here.'

'Did we, Florin, did we? We shouldn't have done that, you know.'

'Very particular about his wine, Mr Isaacs was. My instructions was to give them whatever they wanted.'

'Yes, but '96 port. . . . Well, well. Take up two bottles of the '04. Now, what else do we want? Claret – yes, *claret.* Claret, claret, claret, claret. Where do I keep the claret, Florin?'

*

Colonel Blount was just having tea – he had finished a brown boiled egg and was spreading a crumpet with honey – when Florin opened the library door and announced 'Captain and Mrs Littlejohn, sir.'

And Adam and Nina came in.

Colonel Blount put down his crumpet and rose to greet them.

'Well, Nina, it's a long time since you came to see your old father. So this is my son-in-law, eh? How do you do, my boy. Come and sit down, both of you. Florin will bring some more cups directly. . . . Well,' he said, giving Adam a searching glance, 'I can't say I should have recognized you. I used to know your father very well indeed at one time. Used to be a neighbour of mine over at where-was-it. I expect you've forgotten those days. You used to come over here to ride with Nina. You can't have been more than ten or eleven. . . . Funny, something gave me an idea you had red hair . . . '

'I expect you'd heard him called "Ginger",' said Nina, 'and that made you think of it.'

'Something of the kind, I dare say . . . extraordinary thing to call him "Ginger" when he's got ordinary fair hair . . . anyway, I'm very glad to see you, very glad. I'm afraid it'll be a very quiet week-end. We don't see many people here now. Florin says he's asked a Captain and Mrs Something-or-other to come and stay, damn his impudence, but I said I wouldn't see them. Why should I entertain Florin's friends? Servants seem to think after they've been with you some time they can do anything they like. There was poor old Lady Graybridge, now – they only found out after her death that her man had been letting lodgings all the time in the North Wing. She never could understand why none of the fruit ever came into the dining-room – the butler and his boarders were eating it all in the servants' hall. And after she was ill, and couldn't leave her room, he laid out a golf links in the park . . . shocking state of affairs. I don't believe Florin would do a thing like that – still, you never know. It's the thin edge of the wedge asking people down for the week-end.'

*

In the kitchen Florin said: '*That's* not the Mr Littlejohn I used to know.'

Mrs Florin said, 'It's the young gentleman that came here to luncheon last month.'

Ada said, 'He's very nice looking.'

Florin and Mrs Florin said, 'You be quiet, Ada. Have you taken the hot water up to their bedroom yet? Have you taken up their suitcases? Have you unpacked them? Did you brush the Colonel's evening suit? Do you expect Mr Florin and Mrs Florin to do *all* the work of the house? And look at your apron again, you wretched girl, if it isn't the second you've dirtied to-day.'

Florin added, 'Anyway, Miss Nina noticed the banner.'

*

In the library Colonel Blount said, 'I've got a treat for you to-night, anyway. The last two reels of my cinema film have just come back from being developed. I thought we'ld run through it to-night. We shall have to go across to the Rectory, because the Rector's got electric light, the lucky fellow. I told him to expect us. He didn't seem very pleased about it. Said he had to preach three sermons to-morrow, and be up at six for early service. That's not the Christmas spirit. Didn't want to bring the car round to fetch us either. It's only a matter of a quarter of a mile, no trouble to *him*, and how can we walk in the snow carrying all the apparatus? I said to him, "If you practised a little more Christianity yourself we might be more willing to subscribe to your foreign missions and Boy Scouts and organ funds." Had him there. Dammit, I put the man in his job myself – if I haven't a right to his car, who has?'

When they went up to change for dinner Nina said to Adam, 'I knew papa would never recognize you.'

Adam said, 'Look, someone's put mistletoe over our bed.'

'I think you gave the Florins rather a surprise.'

'My dear, what will the Rector say? He drove me to the station the first time I came. He thought I was mad.'

'... Poor Ginger. I wonder, are we treating him terribly badly? ... It seemed a direct act of fate that he should have been called up to join his regiment just at this moment.'

'I left him a cheque to pay for you.'

'Darling, you know it's a bad one.'

'No cheque is bad until it's refused by the bank. Tomorrow's Christmas, then Boxing Day, then Sunday. He can't pay it in until Monday, and anything may have happened by then. The drunk Major may have turned up. If the worst comes to the worst I can always send you back to him.'

'I expect it will end with that.... Darling, the honeymoon *was* hell... frightfully cold, and Ginger insisted on walking about on a terrace after dinner to see the moon on the Mediterranean – he played golf all day, and made friends with the other English people in the hotel. I can't tell you what it was like... too spirit-crushing, as poor Agatha used to say.'

'Did I tell you I went to Agatha's funeral? There was practically no one there except the Chasms and some aunts. I went with Van, rather tight, and got stared at. I think they felt I was partly responsible for the accident...'

'What about Miles?'

'He's had to leave the country, didn't you know?'

'Darling, I only came back from my honeymoon today. I haven't heard anything.... You know there seems to be none of us left now except you and me.'

'And Ginger.'

'Yes, and Ginger.'

*

The cinematograph exhibition that evening was not really a success.

The Rector arrived while they were finishing dinner, and was shown into the dining-room shaking the snow from the shoulders of his overcoat.

'Come in, Rector, come in. We shan't be many minutes now. Take a glass of port and sit down. You've met my daughter, haven't you? And this is my new son-in-law.'

'I think I've had the pleasure of meeting him before too.'

'Nonsense, first time he's been here since he was so high – long before your time.'

The Rector sipped his port and kept eyeing Adam over the top of his glass in a way which made Nina giggle. Then Adam giggled too, and the Rector's suspicions were confirmed. In this way relations were already on an uneasy basis before they reached the Rectory. The Colonel, however, was far too intent over the transport of his apparatus to notice anything.

'This is your first visit here?' said the Rector as he drove through the snow.

'I lived near here as a boy, you know,' said Adam.

'Ah... but you were down here the other day, were you not? The Colonel often forgets things....'

'No, no. I haven't been here for fifteen years.'

'*I see*,' said the Rector with sinister emphasis, and murmured under his breath, 'Remarkable... very sad and remarkable.'

The Rector's wife was disposed to make rather a party of it, and had arranged some coffee and chocolate biscuits in the drawing-room, but the Colonel soon put an end to any frivolity of this kind by plunging them all in darkness.

He took out the bulbs of their electric lights and fitted in the plug of his lantern. A bright beam shot across the drawing-room like a searchlight, picking out the Rector, who was whispering in his wife's ear the news of his discovery.

'... The same young man I told you of,' he was saying. 'Quite off his head, poor boy. He didn't even remember coming here before. One expects that sort of thing in a man of the Colonel's age, but for a young man like that... a very bad look-out for the next generation....'

The Colonel paused in his preparation.

'I say, Rector, I've just thought of something. I wish old Florin were here. He was in bed half the time they were taking the film. I know he'd love to see it. Could you be a good chap and run up in the car and fetch him?'

'No, really, Colonel, I hardly think that's necessary. I've just put the car away.'

'I won't start before you come back, if that's what you're thinking of. It'll take me some time to get everything fixed up. We'll wait for you. I promise you that.'

'My dear Colonel, it's snowing heavily – practically a blizzard. Surely it would be a mistaken kindness to drag an elderly man out of doors on a night like this in order to see a film which, I have no doubt, will soon be on view all over the country?'

'All right, Rector, just as you think best. I only thought after all it is Christmas... damn the thing; I got a nasty shock then.'

Adam and Nina and the Rector and his wife sat in the dark patiently. After a time the Colonel unrolled a silvered screen.

'Just help me take all these things off the chimneypiece, someone,' he said.

The Rector's wife scuttered to the preservation of her ornaments.

'Will it bear, do you think?' asked the Colonel, mounting precariously on the top of the piano, and exhibiting in his excitement an astonishing fund of latent vitality. 'Now hand up the screen to me, will you? That's splendid. You don't mind a couple of screws in your wall, do you, Rector? Quite small ones.'

Presently the screen was fixed and the lens directed so that it threw on to it a small square of light.

The audience sat down expectantly.

'*Now*,' said the Colonel, and set the machine in motion.

There was a whirring sound, and suddenly there appeared on the screen the spectacle of four uniformed horsemen galloping backwards down the drive.

'Hullo,' said the Colonel. 'Something wrong there... that's funny. I must have forgotten to rewind it.'

The horsemen disappeared, and there was a fresh whirring as the film was transferred to another spool.

'Now,' said the Colonel, and sure enough there appeared in small and clear letters the notice, 'THE WONDERFILM COMPANY OF GREAT BRITAIN PRESENTS'. This legend, vibrating a good deal, but without other variation, filled the screen for some time – ('Of course, I shall cut the captions a bit before it's shown commercially,' explained the Colonel) – until its place was taken by 'EFFIE LA TOUCHE IN'. This announcement was displayed for practically no time at all; indeed, they had scarcely had time to read it before it was whisked away obliquely. ('Damn,' said the Colonel. 'Skidded.') There followed another long pause, and then:

'A BRAND FROM THE BURNING: A FILM BASED ON THE LIFE OF JOHN WESLEY'

('*There*,' said the Colonel.)

'EIGHTEENTH-CENTURY ENGLAND'

*

There came in breathless succession four bewigged men in fancy costume, sitting round a card table. There were glasses, heaps of money and candles on the table. They were clearly gambling feverishly and drinking a lot. ('There's a song there, really,' said the Colonel, 'only I'm afraid I haven't got a talkie apparatus yet.') Then a highwayman holding up the coach which Adam had seen; then some beggars starving outside Doubting Church; then some ladies in fancy costume dancing a minuet. Sometimes the heads of the dancers would disappear above the top of the pictures; sometimes they would sink waist-deep as though in a quicksand; once Mr Isaacs appeared at the side in shirt-sleeves, waving them on. ('I'll have him out,' said the Colonel.)

'EPWORTH RECTORY, LINCOLNSHIRE (ENG.)'

('That's in case it's taken up in the States,' said the Colonel. 'I don't believe there is a Lincolnshire over there, but it's always courteous to put that in case.')

A corner of Doubting Hall appeared with clouds of smoke billowing from the windows. A clergyman was seen handing out a succession of children with feverish rapidity of action. ('It's on fire, you see,' said the Colonel. 'We did that quite simply, by burning some stuff Isaacs had. It did make a smell.')

So the film went on eventfully for about half an hour. One of its peculiarities was that whenever the story reached a point of dramatic and significant action, the film seemed to get faster and faster. Villagers trotted to church as though galvanized; lovers shot in and out of windows; horses flashed past like motor-cars; riots happened so quickly that they were hardly noticed. On the other hand, any scene of repose or inaction, a conversation in a garden between two clergymen, Mrs Wesley at her prayers, Lady Huntingdon asleep, etc., seemed prolonged almost unendurably. Even Colonel Blount suspected this imperfection.

'I think I might cut a bit there,' he said, after Wesley had sat uninterruptedly composing a pamphlet for four and a half minutes.

When the reel came to an end everyone stirred luxuriously.

'Well, that was very nice,' said the Rector's wife, 'very nice and instructive.'

'I really must congratulate you, Colonel. A production of absorbing interest. I had no idea Wesley's life was so full of adventure. I see I must read up my Lecky.'

'Too divine, Papa.'

'Thank you so much, sir, I enjoyed that immensely.'

'But, bless you, that isn't the end,' said the Colonel. 'There are four more reels yet.'

'Oh, that's good.' 'But how delightful.' 'Splendid.' 'Oh.'

But the full story was never shown. Just at the beginning of the second part – when Wesley in America was being rescued from Red Indians by Lady Huntingdon disguised as a cowboy – there occurred one of the mishaps from which the largest super-cinemas are not absolutely immune. There was a sudden crackling sound, a long blue spark, and the light was extinguished.

'Oh, dear,' said the Colonel, 'I wonder what's happened now. We were just getting to such an exciting place.' He bent all his energies on the apparatus, recklessly burning his fingers, while his audience sat in darkness. Presently the door opened and a housemaid appeared carrying a candle.

'If you please, mum,' she said, 'the light's gone out all over the house.'

The Rector hurried across to the door and tried the switch in the passage. He clicked it up and down several times; he tapped it like a barometer and shook it slightly.

'It looks as though the wires were fused,' he said.

'Really, Rector, how very inconvenient,' said the Colonel crossly. 'I can't possibly show the film without electric current. Surely there must be something you can do?'

'I am afraid it will be a job for an electrician; it will be scarcely possible to get one before Monday,' said the Rector with scarcely Christian calm. 'In fact it is clear to me that my wife and myself and my whole household will have to spend the entire Christmas week-end in darkness.'

'Well,' said the Colonel. 'I never expected this to happen. Of course, I know it's just as disappointing for you as it is for me. All the same . . .'

The housemaid brought in some candles and a bicycle lamp.

'There's only these in the house, sir,' she said, 'and the shops don't open till Monday.'

'I don't think in the circumstances my hospitality can be of much more use to you, can it, Colonel? Perhaps you would like me to ring up and get a taxi out from Aylesbury.'

'What's that? *Taxi?* Why, it's ridiculous to get a taxi out from Aylesbury to go a quarter of a mile!'

'I'm sure Mrs Littlejohn wouldn't like to walk all the way on a night like this?'

'Perhaps a taxi would be a good idea, Papa.'

'Of course, if you'ld care to take shelter here . . . it may clear up a little. But I think you'ld find it very wretched sitting here in the dark?'

'No, no, of course, order a taxi,' said the Colonel.

On the way back to the house he said, 'I'd half made up my mind to lend him some of our lamps for the week-end. I certainly shan't now. Fancy hiring a taxi seven miles to drive us a few hundred yards. On Christmas Eve, too. No wonder they find it hard to fill their churches when that's their idea of Christian fellowship. Just when I'd brought my film all that way to show them . . . '

Next morning Adam and Nina woke up under Ada's sprig of mistletoe to hear the bells ringing for Christmas across the snow. 'Come all to church, good people; good people come to church.' They had each hung up a stocking the evening before, and Adam had put a bottle of scent and a scent spray into Nina's, and she had put two ties and a new kind of safety-razor into his. Ada brought them their tea and wished them a happy Christmas. Nina had remembered to get a present for each of the Florins, but had forgotten Ada, so she gave her the bottle of scent.

'Darling,' said Adam, 'it cost twenty-five shillings – on Archie Schwert's account at Asprey.'

Later they put some crumbs of their bread and butter on the windowsill and a robin redbreast came to eat them. The whole day was like that.

Adam and Nina breakfasted alone in the dining-room. There was a row of silver plates kept hot by spirit lamps which held an omelette and devilled partridges and kedgeree and kidneys and sole and some rolls; there was also a ham and a tongue and some brawn and a dish of pickled herrings. Nina ate an apple and Adam ate some toast.

Colonel Blount came down at eleven wearing a grey tail coat. He wished them a very good morning and they exchanged gifts. Adam gave him a box of cigars; Nina gave him a large illustrated book about modern cinema production; he gave Nina a seed pearl brooch which had belonged to her mother, and he gave Adam a calendar with a coloured picture of a bulldog smoking a clay pipe and a thought from Longfellow for each day in the year.

At half-past eleven they all went to Matins.

'It will be a lesson to him in true Christian forgiveness,' said the Colonel (but he ostentatiously read his Bible throughout the sermon). After church they called in at two or three cottages. Florin had been round the day before distributing parcels of grocery. They were all pleased and interested to meet Miss Nina's husband. Many of them remembered him as a little boy, and remarked that he had grown out of all recognition. They reminded him with relish of many embarrassing episodes in Ginger's childhood, chiefly acts of destruction and cruelty to cats.

*

After luncheon they went down to see all the decorations in the servants' hall.

This was a yearly custom of some antiquity, and the Florins had prepared for it by hanging paper streamers from the gas brackets. Ada was having middle-day dinner with her parents who lived among the petrol pumps at Doubting village, so the Florins ate their turkey and plum pudding alone.

'I've seen as many as twenty-five sitting down to Christmas dinner at this table,' said Florin. 'Regular parties they used to have when the Colonel and Mr Eric were boys. Theatricals and all the house turned topsy-turvy, and every gentleman with his own valet.'

'Ah,' said Mrs Florin.

'Times is changed,' said Florin, picking a tooth.

'Ah,' said Mrs Florin.

Then the family came in from the dining-room.

The Colonel knocked on the door and said, 'May we come in, Mrs Florin?'

'That you may, sir, and welcome,' said Mrs Florin.

Then Adam and Nina and the Colonel admired the decorations and handed over their presents wrapped in tissue paper. Then the Colonel said, 'I think we should take a glass of wine together.'

Florin opened a bottle of sherry which he had brought up that morning and poured out the glasses, handing one first to Nina, then to Mrs Florin, then to the Colonel, then to Adam, and, finally, taking one for himself.

'My very best wishes to you, Mrs Florin,' said the Colonel, raising his glass, 'and to you, Florin. The years go by, and we none of us get any younger, but I hope and trust that there are many Christmases in store for us yet. Mrs Florin certainly doesn't look a day older than when she first came here. My best wishes to you both for another year of health and happiness.'

Mrs Florin said, 'Best respects, sir, and thank you, sir, and the same to you.'

Florin said, 'And a great pleasure it is to see Miss Nina – Mrs Littlejohn, I should say – with us once more at her old home, and her husband too, and I'm sure Mrs Florin and me wish them every happiness and prosperity in their married life together, and all I can say, if they can be as happy together as me and Mrs Florin has been, well, that's the best I can wish them.'

Then the family went away, and the house settled down to its afternoon nap.

*

After dinner that night Adam and the Colonel filled up their port glasses and turned their chairs towards the fire. Nina had gone into the drawing-room to smoke.

'You know,' said the Colonel, poking back a log with his foot, 'I'm very glad that Nina has married you, my boy. I've liked you from the moment I saw you. She's a headstrong girl – always was – but I knew that she'd make a sensible choice in the end. I foresee a very agreeable life ahead of you two young people.'

'I hope so, sir.'

'I'm sure of it, my boy. She's very nearly made several mistakes. There was an ass of a fellow here the other day wanting to marry her. A journalist. Awful silly fellow. He told me my old friend Canon Chatterbox was working on his paper. Well, I didn't like to contradict him – he ought to have known, after all – but I thought it was funny at the time, and then, d'you know, after he'd gone I was going through some old papers upstairs and I came on a cutting from the *Worcester Herald* describing his funeral. He died in 1912. Well, he must have been a muddle-headed sort of fellow to make a mistake like that, mustn't he? . . . Have some port?'

'Thank you.'

'Then there was another chap. Came here selling vacuum cleaners, if you please, and asked me to give him a thousand pounds! Impudent young cub. I soon sent him about his business. . . . But you're different, Littlejohn. Just the sort of son-in-law I'd have chosen for myself. Your marriage has been a great happiness to me, my boy.'

At this moment Nina came in to say that there were carol singers outside the drawing-room window.

'Bring 'em in,' said the Colonel. 'Bring 'em in. They come every year. And tell Florin to bring up the punch.'

Florin brought up the punch in a huge silver punch bowl and Nina brought in the waits. They stood against the sideboard, caps in hand, blinking in the gaslight, and very red about the nose and cheeks with the sudden warmth.

> '*Oh, tidings of comfort and joy*,' they sang, '*comfort and joy,*
> *Oh, tidings of comfort and joy.*'

They sang *Good King Wenceslas*, and *The First Noël*, and *Adeste Fideles*, and *While Shepherds Watched Their Flocks*. Then Florin ladled out the punch, seeing that the younger ones did not get the glasses intended for their elders, but that each, according to his capacity, got a little more, but not much more, than was good for him.

The Colonel tasted the punch and pronounced it excellent. He then asked the carol singers their names and where they came from, and finally gave their leader five shillings and sent them off into the snow.

'It's been just like this every year, as long as I can remember,' said the Colonel. 'We always had a party at Christmas when we were boys . . . acted some very amusing charades too . . . always a glass of sherry after luncheon in the servants' hall and carol singers in the evening. . . . Tell me,' he said, suddenly changing the subject, 'did you *really* like what you saw of my film yesterday?'

'It was the most divine film I ever saw, Papa.'

'I enjoyed it enormously, sir, really I did.'

'Did you? Did you? Well, I'm glad to hear that. I don't believe the Rector did – not properly. Of course, you only saw a bit of it, most disappointing. I didn't like to say so at the time, but I thought it most negligent of him to have his electric light in that sort of condition so that it wouldn't last out for one evening. Most inconsiderate to anyone who wants to show a film. But it's a glorious film, isn't it? You did think so?'

'I never enjoyed a film so much, honestly.'

'It makes a stepping stone in the development of the British film industry,' said the Colonel dreamily. 'It is the most important all-talkie super-religious film to be produced solely in this country by British artists and management and by British capital. It has been directed throughout regardless of difficulty and expense, and supervised by a staff of expert historians and theologians. Nothing has been omitted that would contribute to the meticulous accuracy of every detail. The life of that great social and religious reformer John Wesley is for the first time portrayed to a British public in all its humanity and tragedy . . . . I'm glad you realized all that, my boy, because, as a matter of fact, I had a proposal to make to you about it. I'm getting an old man and can't do everything, and I feel my services should be better spent in future as actor and producer, rather than on the commercial side. One needs someone young to manage that. Now what I thought was, that perhaps you would care to come in with me as business partner. I bought the whole thing from Isaacs and, as you're one of the family, I shouldn't mind selling you a half-share for, say, two thousand pounds. I know that that isn't much to you, and you'ld be humanly certain to double your money in a few months. What do you say to it?'

'*Well*...' said Adam.

But he was never called upon to answer, for just at that moment the door of the dining-room opened and the Rector came in.

'Hullo, Rector, come in. This is very neighbourly of you to come and call at this time of night. A happy Christmas to you.'

'Colonel Blount, I've got very terrible news. I had to come over and tell you...'

'I say, I am sorry. Nothing wrong at the Rectory, I hope?'

'Worse, far worse. My wife and I were sitting over the fire after dinner, and as we couldn't read – not having any light – we put on the wireless. They were having a very pretty carol service. Suddenly they stopped in the middle and a special news bulletin was read.... Colonel, the most terrible and unexpected thing – *War has been declared*.'

HAPPY ENDING

ON a splintered tree stump in the biggest battlefield in the history of the world, Adam sat down and read a letter from Nina. It had arrived early the day before, but in the intensive fighting which followed he had not had a spare minute in which to open it.

Doubting Hall,
Aylesbury.

Dearest Adam, – I wonder how you are. It is difficult to know what is happening quite because the papers say such odd things. Van has got a divine job making up all the war news, and he invented a lovely story about you the other day, how you'd saved hundreds of people's lives, and there's what they call a popular agitation saying why haven't you got the V.C., so probably you will have by now, isn't it amusing?

Ginger and I are very well. Ginger has a job in an office in Whitehall and wears a very grand sort of uniform, and, my dear, I'm going to have a baby, isn't it too awful? But Ginger has quite made up his mind it's his, and is as pleased as anything, so that's all right. He's quite forgiven you about last Christmas, and says anyway you're doing your bit now, and in war time one lets bygones be bygones.

Doubting is a hospital, did you know? Papa shows his film to the wounded and they adore it. I saw Mr Benfleet, and he said how awful it was when one had given all one's life in the cause of culture to see everything one's stood for swept away, but that he's doing very well with his 'Sword Unsheathed' series of war poets.

There's a new Government order that we have to sleep in gas masks because of the bombs, but no one does. They've put

Archie in prison as an undesirable alien, Ginger saw to that, he's terrific about spies. I'm sick such a lot because of this baby, but everyone says it's patriotic to have babies in war time. Why?

Lots of love, my angel, take care of your dear self.

N.

He put it back in its envelope and buttoned it into his breast-pocket. Then he took out a pipe, filled it and began to smoke. The scene all round him was one of unrelieved desolation; a great expanse of mud in which every visible object was burnt or broken. Sounds of firing thundered from beyond the horizon, and somewhere above the grey clouds there were aeroplanes. He had had no sleep for thirty-six hours. It was growing dark.

Presently he became aware of a figure approaching, painfully picking his way among the strands of barbed wire which strayed across the ground like drifting cobweb; a soldier clearly. As he came nearer Adam saw that he was levelling towards him a liquid-fire projector. Adam tightened his fingers about his Huxdane-Halley bomb (for the dissemination of leprosy germs), and in this posture of mutual suspicion they met. Through the dusk Adam recognized the uniform of an English staff officer. He put the bomb back in his pocket and saluted.

The newcomer lowered his liquid-fire projector and raised his gas mask. 'You're English, are you?' he said. 'Can't see a thing. Broken my damned monocle.'

'Why,' said Adam. 'You're the drunk Major.'

'I'm not drunk, damn you, sir,' said the drunk Major, 'and, what's more, I'm a General. What the deuce are *you* doing here?'

'Well,' said Adam. 'I've lost my platoon.'

'Lost your platoon. . . . I've lost my whole bloody division!'

'Is the battle over, sir?'

'I don't know, can't see a thing. It was going on all right last time I heard of it. My car's broken down somewhere over there. My driver went out to try and find someone to help and got lost, and I went out to look for him, and now

I've lost the car too. Damn difficult country to find one's way about in. No landmarks. . . . Funny meeting you. I owe you some money.'

'Thirty-five thousand pounds.'

'Thirty-five thousand and five. Looked for you everywhere before this scrap started. I can give you the money now if you like.'

'The pound's not worth much nowadays, is it?'

'About nothing. Still, I may as well give you a cheque. It'll buy you a couple of drinks and a newspaper. Talking of drinks, I've got a case of bubbly in the car if we could only find it. Salvaged it out of an R.A.F. mess that got bombed back at H.Q. Wish I could find that car.'

Eventually they did find it. A Daimler limousine sunk to the axles in mud.

'Get in and sit down,' said the General hospitably. 'I'll turn the light on in a second.'

Adam climbed in and found that it was not empty. In the corner, crumpled up in a French military great-coat was a young woman fast asleep.

'*Hullo*, I'd forgotten all about you,' said the General. 'I picked up this little lady on the road. I can't introduce you, because I don't know her name. Wake up, mademoiselle.'

The girl gave a little cry and opened two startled eyes.

'That's all right, little lady, nothing to be scared about – all friends here. *Parlez anglais?*'

'Sure,' said the girl.

'Well, what about a spot?' said the General, peeling the tinfoil from the top of a bottle. 'You'll find some glasses in the locker.'

The woebegone fragment of womanhood in the corner looked a little less terrified when she saw the wine. She recognized it as the symbol of international goodwill.

'Now perhaps our fair visitor will tell us her name,' said the General.

'I dunno,' she said.

'Oh, come, little one, you mustn't be shy.'

'I dunno. I been called a lot of things. I was called Chastity once. Then there was a lady at a party, and she sent me to Buenos Aires, and then when the war came she brought me back again, and I was with the soldiers training at Salisbury Plain. That was swell. They called me Bunny – I don't know why. Then they sent me over here and I was with the Canadians, what they called me wasn't nice, and then they left me behind when they retreated and I took up with some foreigners. They were nice too, though they *were* fighting against the English. Then *they* ran away, and the lorry I was in got stuck in the ditch, so I got in with some other foreigners who were on the same side as the English, and they were beasts, but I met an American doctor who had white hair, and he called me Emily because he said I reminded him of his daughter back home, so he took me to Paris and we had a lovely week till he took up with another girl in a night club, so he left me behind in Paris when he went back to the front, and I hadn't no money and they made a fuss about my passport, so they called me *numéro mille soixante dix-huit*, and they sent me and a lot of other girls off to the East to be with the soldiers there. At least they would have done only the ship got blown up, so I was rescued and the French sent me up here in a train with some different girls who were very unrefined. Then I was in a tin hut with the girls, and then yesterday they had friends and I was alone, so I went for a walk, and when I came back the hut was gone and the girls were gone, and there didn't seem anyone anywhere until you came in your car, and now I don't rightly know where I am. *My*, isn't war awful?'

The General opened another bottle of champagne.

'Well, you're as right as rain now, little lady,' he said, 'so let's see you smile and look happy. You mustn't sit there scowling, you know – far too pretty a little mouth for that. Let me take off that heavy coat. Look, I'll wrap it round your knees. There, now, isn't that better?... Fine, strong little legs, eh?...'

Adam did not embarrass them. The wine and the deep cushions and the accumulated fatigue of two days' fighting drew him away from them and, oblivious to all the happy emotion pulsing near him, he sank into sleep.

The windows of the stranded motor-car shone over the wasted expanse of the battlefield. Then the General pulled down the blinds, shutting out that sad scene.

'Cosier now, eh?' he said.

And Chastity in the prettiest way possible fingered the decorations on his uniform and asked him all about them.

And presently, like a circling typhoon, the sounds of battle began to return.

PUT OUT MORE FLAGS

Dedicatory Letter to

MAJOR RANDOLPH CHURCHILL

Fourth Hussars, Member of Parliament

Dear Randolph,

I am afraid that these pages may not be altogether acceptable to your ardent and sanguine nature. They deal, mostly, with a race of ghosts, the survivors of the world we both knew ten years ago, which you have outflown in the empyrean of strenuous politics, but where my imagination still fondly lingers. I find more food for thought in the follies of Basil Seal and Ambrose Silk, than in the sagacity of the higher command. These characters are no longer contemporary in sympathy; they were forgotten even before the war; but they lived on delightfully in holes and corners and, like everyone else, they have been disturbed in their habits by the rough intrusion of current history. Here they are in that odd, dead period before the Churchillian renaissance, which people called at the time the Great Bore War.

So please accept them with the sincere regards of
Your affectionate friend,

The Author

‘A man getting drunk at a farewell party
should strike a musical tone,
in order to strengthen his spirit...
and a drunk military man
should order gallons and put out more flags
in order to increase his military splendour.’

CHINESE SAGE
quoted and translated by Lin Yutang in
The Importance of Living

‘A little injustice in the heart
can be drowned by wine;
but a great injustice in the world
can be drowned only by the sword.’

EPIGRAMS OF CHANG CH’AO
quoted and translated by Lin Yutang in
The Importance of Living

CHAPTER 1
Autumn

1

IN the week which preceded the outbreak of the Second World War – days of surmise and apprehension which cannot, without irony, be called the last days of peace – and on the Sunday morning when all doubts were finally resolved and misconceptions corrected, three rich women thought first and mainly of Basil Seal. They were his sister, his mother and his mistress.

Barbara Sothill was at Malfrey; in recent years she had thought of her brother as seldom as circumstances allowed her, but on that historic September morning, as she walked to the village, he predominated over a multitude of worries.

She and Freddy had just heard the Prime Minister's speech, broadcast by wireless. 'It is an evil thing we are fighting,' he had said and as Barbara turned her back on the house where, for the most part, the eight years of her marriage had been spent, she felt personally challenged and threatened, as though, already, the mild, autumnal sky were dark with circling enemy and their shadows were trespassing on the sunlit lawns.

There was something female and voluptuous in the beauty of Malfrey; other lovely houses maintained a virginal modesty or a manly defiance, but Malfrey had no secret from the heavens; it had been built more than two hundred years ago in days of victory and ostentation and lay, spread out, sumptuously at ease, splendid, defenceless and provocative; a Cleopatra among houses; across the sea, Barbara felt, a small and envious mind, a meanly ascetic mind, a creature of the conifers, was plotting the destruction of her home. It was for Malfrey that she loved her prosaic and slightly absurd husband; for Malfrey, too, that she had abandoned Basil and with him the part of herself which, in the atrophy endemic to all fruitful marriages, she had let waste and die.

It was half a mile to the village down the lime avenue. Barbara walked because, just as she was getting into the car, Freddy had stopped her saying, 'No petrol now for gadding about.'

Freddy was in uniform, acutely uncomfortable in ten-year-old trousers. He had been to report at the yeomanry headquarters the day before, and was home for two nights collecting his kit, which, in the two years since he was last at camp, had been misused in charades and picnics and dispersed about the house in a dozen improbable places. His pistol, in particular, had been a trouble. He had had the whole household hunting it, saying fretfully, 'It's all very well, but I can get court-martialled for this,' until, at length, the nurserymaid found it at the back of the toy cupboard. Barbara was now on her way to look for his binoculars which she remembered vaguely having lent to the scoutmaster.

The road under the limes led straight to the village; the park gates of elaborately wrought iron swung on rusticated stone piers, and the two lodges formed a side of the village green; opposite them stood the church, on either side two inns, the vicarage, the shop and a row of grey cottages; three massive chestnuts grew from the roughly rectangular grass plot in the centre. It was a Beauty Spot, justly but reluctantly famous, too much frequented of late by walkers but still, through Freddy's local influence, free of charabancs; a bus stopped three times a day on weekdays, four times on Tuesdays when the market was held in the neighbouring town, and to accommodate passengers Freddy had that year placed an oak seat under the chestnuts.

It was here that Barbara's thoughts were brought up sharply by an unfamiliar spectacle; six dejected women sat in a row staring fixedly at the closed doors of the Sothill Arms. For a moment Barbara was puzzled; then she remembered. These were Birmingham women. Fifty families had arrived at Malfrey late on Friday evening, thirsty, hot, bewildered and resentful after a day in train and bus. Barbara had chosen the five saddest families for herself and dispersed the rest in the village and farms.

Punctually next day the head housemaid, a veteran of old Mrs Sothill's regime, had given notice of leaving. 'I don't know how we shall do without you,' said Barbara.

'It's my legs, madam. I'm not strong enough for the work. I could just manage as things were, but now with children all over the place . . . '

'You know we can't expect things to be easy in war time. We must expect to make sacrifices. This is our war work.'

But the woman was obdurate. 'There's my married sister at Bristol,' she said. 'Her husband was on the reserve. I ought to go and help her now he's called up.'

An hour later the remaining three housemaids had appeared with prim expressions of face.

'Edith and Olive and me have talked it over and we want to go and make aeroplanes. They say they are taking on girls at Brakemore's.'

'You'll find it terribly hard work, you know.'

'Oh, it's not the work, madam. It's the Birmingham women. The way they leave their rooms.'

'It's all very strange for them at first. We must do all we can to help. As soon as they settle down and get used to our ways . . . ' but she saw it was hopeless while she spoke.

'They say they want girls at Brakemore's,' said the maids.

In the kitchen Mrs Elphinstone was loyal. 'But I can't answer for the girls,' she said. 'They seem to think war is an excuse for a lark.'

It was the kitchen-maids, anyway, and not Mrs Elphinstone, thought Barbara, who had to cope with the extra meals . . .

Benson was sound. The Birmingham women caused *him* no trouble. But James would be leaving for the Army within a few weeks. It's going to be a difficult winter, thought Barbara.

These women, huddled on the green, were not Barbara's guests, but she saw on their faces the same look of frustration and defiance. Dutifully, rather than prudently, she approached the group and asked if they were comfortable. She spoke to them in general and each felt shy of answering; they looked away from her sullenly towards the locked inn. Oh dear, thought Barbara, I suppose they wonder what business it is of mine.

'I live up there,' she said, indicating the gates. 'I've been arranging your billets.'

'Oh, have you?' said one of the mothers. 'Then perhaps you can tell us how long we've got to stop.'

'That's right,' said another.

'D'you know,' said Barbara, 'I don't believe anyone has troubled to think about that. They've all been too busy getting you away.'

'They got no right to do it,' said the first mother. 'You can't keep us here compulsory.'

'But surely you don't *want* to have your children bombed, do you?'

'We won't stay where we're not wanted.'

'That's right,' said the yes-woman.

'But of *course* you're wanted.'

'Yes, like the stomach-ache.'

'That's right.'

For some minutes Barbara reasoned with the fugitives until she felt that her only achievement had been to transfer to herself all the odium which more properly belonged to Hitler. Then she went on her way to the scoutmaster's, where, before she could retrieve the binoculars, she had to listen to the story of the Birmingham schoolmistress, billeted on him, who refused to help wash up.

As she crossed the green on her homeward journey, the mothers looked away from her.

'I hope the children are enjoying themselves a little,' she said, determined not to be cut in her own village.

'They're down at the school. Teacher's making them play games.'

'The park's always open, you know, if any one of you care to go inside.'

'We had a park where we came from. With a band Sundays.'

'Well, I'm afraid I can't offer a band. But it's thought rather pretty, particularly down by the lake. Do take the children in if you feel like it.'

When she had left the chief mother said: 'What's she? Some kind of inspector, I suppose, with her airs and graces. The idea of inviting us into the park. You'd think the place belonged to her the way she goes on.'

Presently the two inns opened their doors and the scandalized village watched a procession of mothers assemble from cottage, farm and mansion and make for the bar parlours.

Luncheon decided him; Freddy went upstairs immediately he left the dining-room and changed into civilian clothes. 'Think I'll get my maid to put me into something loose,' he said in the voice he used for making jokes. It was this kind of joke Barbara had learned to recognize during her happy eight years in his company.

Freddy was large, masculine, prematurely bald and superficially cheerful; at heart he was misanthropic and gifted with that sly, sharp instinct for self-preservation that passes for wisdom among the rich; his indolence was qualified with enough basic bad temper to ensure the respect of those about him. He took in most people, but not his wife or his wife's family.

Not only did he have a special expression of face for making jokes; he had one for use when discussing his brother-in-law Basil. It should have conveyed lofty disapproval tempered by respect for Barbara's loyalty; in fact it suggested sulkiness and guilt.

The Seal children, for no reason that was apparent to the rest of the world, had always held the rest of the world in scorn. Freddy did not like Tony; he found him supercilious and effeminate, but he was prepared to concede to him certain superiorities; no one doubted that there was a brilliant career ahead of him in diplomacy. The time would come when they would all be very proud of Tony. But Basil from his earliest days had been a source of embarrassment and reproach. On his own terms Freddy might have been willing to welcome a black sheep in the

Seal family, someone who was 'never mentioned', to whom he might, every now and then, magnanimously unknown to anyone except Barbara, extend a helping hand; someone, even, in whom he might profess to see more good than the rest of the world. Such a kinsman might very considerably have redressed the balance of Freddy's self-esteem. But, as Freddy found as soon as he came to know the Seals intimately, Basil, so far from being never mentioned, formed the subject of nearly half their conversation. At that time they were ever ready to discuss with relish his latest outrage, ever hopeful of some splendid success for him in the immediate future, ever contemptuous of the disapproval of the rest of the world. And Basil himself regarded Freddy pitilessly, with eyes which, during his courtship and the first years of marriage, he had recognized in Barbara herself.

For there was a disconcerting resemblance between Basil and Barbara; she, too, was *farouche* in a softer and deadlier manner, and the charm which held him breathless, flashed in gross and acquisitive shape in Basil. Maternity and the tranquil splendour of Malfrey had wrought changes in her; it was very rarely, now, that the wild little animal in her came above ground; but it was there in its earth, and from time to time he was aware of it, peeping out after long absences; a pair of glowing eyes at the twist in the tunnel watching him as an enemy.

Barbara herself pretended to no illusions about Basil. Years of disappointment and betrayal had convinced her, in the reasoning part of her, that he was no good. They had played pirates together in the nursery and the game was over. Basil played pirates alone. She apostatized from her faith in him almost with formality, and yet, as a cult will survive centuries after its myths have been exposed and its sources of faith tainted, there was still deep in her that early piety, scarcely discernible now in a little residue of superstition, so that this morning when her world seemed rocking about her, she turned back to Basil. Thus, when earthquake strikes a modern city and the pavements gape, the sewers buckle up and the great buildings tremble and topple, men in bowler hats and natty, ready-made suitings, born of generations of literates and rationalists, will suddenly revert to the magic of the forest and cross their fingers to avert the avalanche of concrete.

Three times during luncheon Barbara had spoken of Basil and now, as she and Freddy walked arm in arm on the terrace, she said, 'I believe it's what he's been waiting for all these years.'

'Who, waiting for what?'

'Basil, for the war.'

'Oh... Well, I suppose in a way we all have really... the gardens are going to be a problem. I suppose we could get some of the men exemption on the grounds that they're engaged in agriculture, but it hardly seems playing the game.'

It was Freddy's last day at Malfrey and he did not want to spoil it by talking of Basil. It was true that the yeomanry were not ten miles away; it was true, also, that they were unlikely to move for a very long time; they had recently been mechanized, in the sense that they had had their horses removed; few of them had ever seen a tank; he would be back and forwards continually during the coming months; he meant to shoot the pheasants; but although this was no final leave taking he felt entitled to more sentiment than Barbara was showing.

'Freddy, don't be bloody.' She kicked him sharply on the ankle for she had found, early in married life, that Freddy liked her to swear and kick in private. 'You know exactly what I mean. Basil *needed* a war. He's not meant for peace.'

'That's true enough. The wonder is he's kept out of prison. If he'd been born in a different class he wouldn't have.'

Barbara suddenly chuckled. 'D'you remember how he took mother's emeralds, the time he went to Azania? But then you see that would never have happened if there'd been a war of our own for him to go to. He's always been mixed up in fighting.'

'If you call living in a gin palace in La Paz and seeing generals shoot one another... '

'And Spain.'

'Journalist and gun runner.'

'He's always been a soldier *manqué*.'

'Well, he hasn't done much about it. While he's been gadding about the rest of us have been training as territorials and yeomanry.'

'Darling, a fat lot of training you've done.'

'If there'd been more like us and fewer like Basil there'd never have been a war. You can't blame Ribbentrop for thinking us decadent when he saw people like Basil about. I don't suppose they'll have much use for him in the army. He's thirty-six. He might get some sort of job connected with censorship. He seems to know a lot of languages.'

'You'll see,' said Barbara. 'Basil will be covered with medals while your silly old yeomanry are still messing in a Trust House and waiting for your tanks.'

There were duck on the lake and she let Freddy talk about them. She led him down his favourite paths. There was a Gothic pavilion where by long habit Freddy often became amorous; he did become amorous. And all the time she thought of Basil. She thought of him in terms of the war books she had read. She saw him as Siegfried Sassoon, an infantry subaltern in a mud-bogged trench standing to at dawn, his eyes on his wrist watch, waiting for zero hour; she saw him as Compton Mackenzie, spider in a web of Balkan intrigue, undermining a monarchy among olive trees and sculptured marble; she saw him as T. E. Lawrence and Rupert Brooke.

Freddy, assuaged, reverted to sport. 'I won't ask any of the regiment over for the early shoots,' he said. 'But I don't see why we shouldn't let some of them have a bang at the cocks round about Christmas.'

2

LADY SEAL was at her home in London. She had taken fewer precautions against air raids than most of her friends. Her most valuable possession, her small Carpaccio, had been sent to safe keeping at Malfrey; the miniatures and Limoges enamels were at the bank; the Sèvres was packed in crates and put below stairs. Otherwise there was no change in her drawing-room.

The ponderous old curtains needed no unsightly strips of black paper to help them keep in the light.

The windows were open now on the balcony. Lady Seal sat in an elegant rosewood chair gazing out across the square. She had just heard the Prime Minister's speech. Her butler approached from the end of the room.

'Shall I remove the radio, my lady?'

'Yes, by all means. He spoke very well, very well indeed.'

'It's all very sad, my lady.'

'Very sad for the Germans, Anderson.'

It was quite true, thought Lady Seal; Neville Chamberlain had spoken surprisingly well. She had never liked him very much, neither him nor his brother – if anything she had preferred the brother, but they were uncomfortable, drab fellows both of them. However, he had spoken very creditably that morning, as though at last he were fully alive to his responsibilities. She would ask him to luncheon. But perhaps he would be busy; the most improbable people were busy in war time, she remembered.

Her mind went back to the other war, that until that morning had been The War. No one very near to her had fought. Christopher had been too old, Tony, just too young; her brother Edward had begun by commanding a brigade – they thought the world of him at the Staff College – but, inexplicably, his career had come to very little; he was still brigadier in 1918, at Dar-es-Salaam. But the war had been a sad time; so many friends in mourning and Christopher fretful about the coalition. It had been a bitter thing for them all, accepting Lloyd George, but Christopher had patriotically made the sacrifice with the rest of them; probably only she knew how much he had felt it. The worst time had been after the armistice, when peerages were sold like groceries and the peace terms were bungled. Christopher had always said they would have to pay for it in the long run.

The hideous, then unfamiliar shriek of the air-raid sirens sang out over London.

'That was the warning, my lady.'

'Yes, Anderson. I heard it.'

'Will you be coming downstairs?'

'No, not yet at any rate. Get all the servants down and see they are quiet.'

'Will you require your respirator, my lady?'

'I don't suppose so. From what Sir Joseph tells me the danger of gas is very slight. In any case I dare say this is only a practice. Leave it on the table.'

'Will that be all, my lady?'

'That's all. See that the maids don't get nervous.'

Lady Seal stepped on to the balcony and looked up into the clear sky. They'll get more than they bargain for if they try and attack *us*, she thought. High time that man was taught a lesson. He's made nothing but trouble for years. She returned to her chair thinking. Anyway *I* never made a fuss of that vulgar man von Ribbentrop. I wouldn't have him inside the house, even when that goose Emma Granchester was plaguing us all to be friendly to him. I hope she feels foolish this morning.

Lady Seal waited with composure for the bombardment to begin. She had told Anderson it was probably only a practice. That was what one told servants; otherwise they might panic – not Anderson but the maids. But in her heart Lady Seal was sure that the attack was coming; it would be just like the Germans, always blustering and showing off and pretending to be efficient. The history Lady Seal had learned in the schoolroom had been a simple tale of the maintenance of right against the superior forces of evil and the battle honours of her country rang musically in her ears – Crécy, Agincourt, Cadiz, Blenheim, Gibraltar, Inkerman, Ypres. England had fought many and various enemies with many and various allies, often on quite recondite pretexts, but always justly, chivalrously, and with ultimate success. Often, in Paris, Lady Seal had been proud that her people had never fallen to the habit of naming streets after their feats of arms; that was suitable enough for the short-lived and purely professional triumphs of the French, but to put those great manifestations of divine rectitude which were the victories of England to the use, for their postal addresses, of milliners and chiropodists, would have been a baseness to which even the radicals had not stooped. The steel engravings of her schoolroom lived before her eyes, like tableaux at a charity fête – Sydney at Zutphen, Wolfe at Quebec, Nelson at Trafalgar (Wellington, only, at Waterloo was excluded from the pageant by reason of the proximity of Blücher, pushing himself forward with typical Prussian effrontery to share the glory which the other had won) and to this tremendous assembly (not unlike in Lady Seal's mind those massed groups of wealth and respectability portrayed on the Squadron Lawn at Cowes and hung with their key plans in lobbies and billiard rooms) was added that morning a single new and rather improbable figure, Basil Seal.

The last war had cost her little; nothing, indeed, except a considerable holding of foreign investments and her brother Edward's reputation as a strategist. Now she had a son to offer her country. Tony had weak eyes and a career, Freddy was no blood of hers and was not cast in a heroic mould, but Basil, her wayward and graceless and grossly disappointing Basil, whose unaccountable taste for low company had led him into so many vexatious scrapes in the last ten years, whose wild oats refused to correspond with those of his Uncle Edward; Basil who had stolen her emeralds and made Mrs Lyne distressingly conspicuous; Basil, his peculiarities merged in the manhood of England, at last was entering on his inheritance. She must ask Jo about getting him a commission in a decent regiment.

At last, while she was still musing, the sirens sounded the All Clear.

Sir Joseph Mainwaring was lunching with Lady Seal that day. It was an arrangement made early in the preceding week before either of them knew that the day they were choosing was one which would be marked in the world's calendars until the end of history. He arrived punctually, as he always did; as he had done, times out of number, in the long years of their friendship.

Sir Joseph was not a church-going man except when he was staying at one of the very rare, very august houses where it was still the practice; on this Sunday morning, however, it would not have been fantastic to describe his spirit as inflamed by something nearly akin to religious awe. It *would* be fantastic to describe him as purged, and yet there had been something delicately purgative in the experiences of the morning and there was an unfamiliar buoyancy in his bearing as though he had been at somebody's Eno's. He felt ten years younger.

Lady Seal devoted to this old booby a deep, personal fondness which was rare among his numerous friends and a reliance which was incomprehensible but quite common.

'There's only ourselves, Jo,' she said as she greeted him. 'The Granchesters were coming but he had to go and see the King.'

'Nothing could have been more delightful. Yes, I think we shall all be busy again now. I don't know exactly what I shall be doing yet. I shall know better after I've been to Downing Street to-morrow morning. I imagine it will be some advisory capacity to the War Cabinet. It's nice to feel in the centre of things again, takes one back ten years. Stirring times, Cynthia, stirring times.'

'It's one of the things I wanted to see Emma Granchester about. There must be so many committees we ought to start. Last war it was Belgian refugees. I suppose it will be Poles this time. It's a great pity it isn't people who talk a language one knows.'

'No, no Belgians this time. It will be a different war in many ways. An economic war of attrition, that is how I see it. Of course we had to have all this A.R.P. and shelters and so on. The radicals were making copy out of it. But I think we can take it there won't be any air raids, not on London at any rate. Perhaps there may be an attempt on the sea-ports, but I was having a most interesting talk yesterday to Eddie Beste-Bingham at the Beefsteak; we've got a most valuable invention called R.D.F. That'll keep 'em off.'

'Dear Jo, you always know the most encouraging things. What is R.D.F.?'

'I'm not absolutely clear about that. It's very secret.'

'Poor Barbara has evacuees at Malfrey.'

'What a shocking business! Dear, dreaming Malfrey. Think of a Birmingham board school in that exquisite Grinling Gibbons saloon. It's all a lot of nonsense, Cynthia. You know I'm the last man to prophesy rashly, but I think we can take one thing as axiomatic. There will be no air attack on London. The Germans will never attempt the Maginot line. The French will hold on for ever, if needs be, and the German air-bases are too far away for them to be able to attack us. If they do, we'll R.D.F. them out of the skies.'

'Jo,' said Lady Seal, when they were alone with the coffee. 'I want to talk to you about Basil.'

How often in the last twenty years had Sir Joseph heard those heavy words, uttered with so many intonations in so wide a variety of moods, but always, without fail, the prelude, not, perhaps to boredom, but to a lowering of the interest and warmth of their converse! It was only in these maternal conferences that Cynthia Seal became less than the perfect companion, only then that, instead of giving, she demanded, as it were, a small sumptuary duty upon the riches of her friendship.

Had he been so minded Sir Joseph could have drawn a graph of the frequency and intensity of these discussions. There had been the steady rise from nursery through school to the university, when he had been called on to applaud each new phase of Basil's precocious development. In those days he had accepted Basil at his face value as an exceptionally brilliant and beautiful youth in danger of being spoiled. Then, towards the end of Basil's second year at Balliol, had come a series of small seismic disturbances, when Cynthia Seal was alternately mutely puzzled or eloquently distressed; then the first disaster, rapidly followed by Christopher's death. From then onwards for fifteen years the line had dipped and soared dizzily as Basil's iniquities rose on the crest or fell into the trough of notoriety, but with the passing years there had been a welcome decline in the mean level; it was at least six months since he had heard the boy's name.

'Ah,' he said. 'Basil, eh,' trying to divine from his hostess's manner whether he was required to be judicial, compassionate or congratulatory.

'You've so often been helpful in the past.'

'I've tried,' said Sir Joseph recalling momentarily his long record of failures on Basil's behalf. 'Plenty of good in the boy.'

'I feel so much happier about him since this morning, Jo. Sometimes, lately, I've begun to doubt whether we shall ever find the proper place for Basil. He's been a square peg in so many round holes. But this war seems to take the responsibility off our hands. There's room for everyone in war time, every *man*. It's always been Basil's *individuality* that's been wrong. You've said that often, Jo. In war time individuality doesn't matter any more. There are just *men*, aren't there?'

'Yes,' said Sir Joseph doubtfully. 'Yes. Basil's individuality has always been rather strong, you know. He must be thirty-five or thirty-six now. That's rather old for starting as a soldier.'

'Nonsense, Jo. Men of forty-five and fifty enlisted in the ranks in the last war and died as gallantly as anyone else. Now I want you to see the Lieutenant-Colonels of the foot guard regiments and see where he will fit in best . . .'

In her time Cynthia Seal had made many formidable demands on Basil's behalf. This, which she was now asking with such assumption of ease, seemed to Sir Joseph one of the most vexatious. But he was an old and loyal friend and a man of affairs, moreover, well practised, by a lifetime of public service, in the evasion of duty. 'Of course, my dear Cynthia, I can't promise any results. . . .'

3

ANGELA LYNE was returning by train from the South of France. It was the time when, normally, she went to Venice, but this year, with international politics tediously on every tongue, she had lingered at Cannes until and beyond the last moment. The French and Italians whom she met had said war was impossible; they said it with assurance before the Russian pact, with double assurance after it. The English said there would be war, but not immediately. Only the Americans knew what was coming, and exactly when. Now she was travelling in unwonted discomfort through a nation moving to action under the dour precepts, '*il faut en finir*' and '*nous gagnerons parce que nous sommes les plus forts*'.

It was a weary journey; the train was already eight hours late; the restaurant car had disappeared during the night at Avignon. Angela was obliged to share a two-berth sleeper with her maid and counted herself lucky to have got one at all; several of her acquaintances had stayed behind, waiting for things to get better; at the moment no reservations were guaranteed and the French seemed to have put off their politeness and packed it in moth-ball for the duration of hostilities.

Angela had a glass of Vichy water on the table before her. She sipped, gazing out at the passing landscape every mile of which gave some evidence of the changing life of the country; hunger and the bad night she had spent raised her a hair's breadth above reality and her mind, usually so swift and orderly, fell into pace with the train, now rocking in haste, now barely moving, seeming to grope its way from point to point.

A stranger passing the open door of her compartment might well have speculated on her nationality and place in the world and supposed her to be American, the buyer perhaps for some important New York dress shop whose present abstraction was due to the worries of war time transport for her 'collection'. She wore the livery of the highest fashion, but as one who dressed to inform rather than to attract: nothing which she wore, nothing it might be supposed in the pigskin jewel-case above her head, had been chosen by or for a man. Her smartness was individual; she was plainly not one of those who scrambled to buy the latest gadget in the few breathless weeks between its first appearance and the inundation of the cheap markets of the world with its imitations; her person was a record and criticism of succeeding fashions, written as it were, year after year, in one clear and characteristic fist. Had the curious fellow passenger stared longer – as he was free to do without offence, so absorbed was Angela in her own thoughts – he would have been checked in his hunt when he came to study his subject's face. All her properties – the luggage heaped above and around her, the set of her hair, her shoes, her finger-nails, the barely perceptible aura of scent that surrounded her, the Vichy water and the paper-bound volume of Balzac on the table before her – all these things spoke of what (had she been, as she seemed, American) she would have called her 'personality'. But the face was mute. It might have been carved in jade, it was so smooth and cool and conventionally removed from the human. A stranger might have watched her for mile after mile, as a spy or a lover or a newspaper reporter will loiter in the street before a closed house, and see no chink of light, hear no whisper of movement behind the shuttered façade, and in direct proportion to his discernment, he would have gone on his way down the corridor baffled and disturbed. Had he been told the bare facts about this seemingly cosmopolitan, passionless, barren, civilized woman, he might have despaired of ever again forming his judgment of a fellow being; for Angela Lyne was Scottish, the only child of a Glasgow millionaire – a jovial, rascally millionaire who had started life in a street gang – she was the wife of a dilettante architect, the mother of a single robust and unattractive son, the dead spit, it was said, of his grandfather, and her life had so foundered on passion that this golden daughter of fortune was rarely spoken of by her friends without the qualifying epithet of 'poor' Angela Lyne.

Only in one respect would the casual observer have hit upon the truth. Angela's appearance was not designed for man. It is sometimes disputed – and opinions are canvassed in popular papers to decide the question – whether woman alone on a desert island would concern herself with clothes; Angela, as far as she herself was concerned, disposed of the question finally. For seven years she had been on a desert island; her appearance had become a hobby and distraction, a pursuit entirely self-regarding and self-rewarding; she watched herself moving in the mirrors of the civilized world as a prisoner will watch the antics of a rat, whom he has domesticated to the dungeon. (In the case of her husband, grottoes took the place of fashion. He had six of them now, bought in various parts of Europe, some from Naples, some from Southern Germany, and painfully transported, stone by stone, to Hampshire.)

For seven years, ever since she was twenty-five and two years married to her dandy-aesthete, 'poor' Angela Lyne had been in love with Basil Seal. It was one of those affairs which, beginning lightheartedly as an adventure and accepted lightheartedly by their friends as an amusing scandal, seemed somehow petrified by a Gorgon glance and endowed with an intolerable permanence; as though in a world of capricious and fleeting alliances, the ironic Fates had decided to set up a standing, frightful example of the natural qualities of man and woman, of their basic aptitude to fuse together; a label on the packing case 'These chemicals are dangerous' – an admonitory notice, like the shattered motor-cars erected sometimes at dangerous turns in the road, so that the least censorious were chilled by the spectacle and recoiled saying, 'Really, you know, there's something rather squalid about those two.'

It was a relationship which their friends usually described as 'morbid', by which they meant that sensuality played a small part in it, for Basil was attracted only to very silly girls and it was by quite other bonds that he and Angela were fettered together.

Cedric Lyne pottering disconsolately in his baroque solitudes and watching with dismay the progress of his blustering son used to tell himself, with the minimum of discernment, that a béguine like that could not possibly last. For Angela there seemed no hope of release. Nothing, she felt in despair, would ever part them but death. Even the flavour of the Vichy water brought thoughts of Basil as she remembered the countless nights in the last seven years when she had sat late with him, while he got drunk and talked more and more wildly, and she sipping her water waited her turn to strike, hard and fierce, at his conceit, until as he got more drunk he became superior to her attacks and talked her down and eventually came stupidly away.

She turned to the window as the train slackened to walking pace, passing truck after truck of soldiers. '*Il faut en finir*', '*Nous gagnerons parce que nous sommes les plus forts*'. A hard-boiled people, the French. Two nights ago at Cannes, an American had been talking about the mutinous regiments decimated in the last war.

'It's a pity they haven't got anyone like old Pétain to command them this time,' he had said.

The villa at Cannes was shut now and the key was with the gardener. Perhaps she would never go back. This year she remembered it only as the place where she had waited in vain for Basil. He had telegraphed: 'International situation forbids joy riding.' She had sent him the money for his journey but there had been no answer. The gardener would make a good thing out of the vegetables. A hard-boiled people, the French; Angela wondered why that was thought to be a good thing; she had always had a revulsion from hard-boiled eggs, even at picnics in the nursery; hard-boiled; over-cooked; over-praised for their cooking. When people professed a love of France, they meant love of eating; the ancients located the deeper emotions in the bowels. She had heard a commercial traveller in the Channel packet welcome Dover and English food. 'I can't stomach that French messed-up stuff.' A commonplace criticism, thought Angela, that applied to French culture for the last two generations – 'messed-up stuff', stale ingredients from Spain and America and Russia and Germany, disguised in a sauce of white wine from Algeria. France died with her monarchy. You could not even eat well, now, except in the provinces. It all came back to eating. 'What's eating you?'... Basil claimed to have eaten a girl once in Africa; he had been eating Angela now for seven years. Like the Spartan boy and the fox... Spartans at Thermopylae, combing their hair before the battle; Angela had never understood that, because Alcibiades had cut off his hair in order to make himself acceptable. What did the Spartans think about hair really? Basil would have to cut his hair when he went into the army. Basil the Athenian would have to sit at the public tables of Sparta, clipped blue at the neck where before his dark hair had hung untidily to his collar. Basil in the pass at Thermopylae...

Angela's maid returned from gossiping with the conductor. 'He says he doesn't think the sleeping cars will go any farther than Dijon. We shall have to change into day coaches. Isn't it wicked, madam, when we've paid?'

'Well, we're at war now. I expect there'll be a lot to put up with.'

'Will Mr Seal be in the army?'

'I shouldn't be surprised.'

'He will look different, won't he, madam?'

'Very different.'

They were both silent, and in the silence Angela knew, by an intuition which defied any possible doubt, exactly what her maid was thinking. She was thinking: 'Supposing Mr Seal gets himself killed. Best thing really for all concerned.'

...Flaxman Greeks reclining in death among the rocks of Thermopylae; riddled scarecrows sprawling across the wire of no-man's land... Till death us do part... Through the haphazard trail of phrase and association, a single, unifying thought recurred, like the sentry posts at the side of the line, monotonously in Angela's mind. Death. 'Death the Friend' of the sixteenth-century woodcuts, who released the captive and bathed the wounds of the fallen; Death in frock coat and whiskers, the discreet undertaker, spreading his sable pall over all that was rotten and unsightly; Death the macabre paramour in whose embrace all earthly loves were forgotten; Death for Basil, that Angela might live again... that was what she was thinking as she sipped her Vichy water, but no one, seeing the calm and pensive mask of her face, could ever possibly have guessed.

4

RUPERT BROOKE, Old Bill, the Unknown Soldier – thus three fond women saw him, but Basil breakfasting late in Poppet Green's studio fell short and wide of all these ideals. He was not at his best that morning, both by reason of his heavy drinking with Poppet's friends the night before and the loss of face he was now suffering with Poppet in his attempts to explain his assertion that there would be no war. He had told them this the night before, not as a speculation, but as a fact known only to himself and half a dozen leading Germans; the Prussian military clique, he had told them, were allowing the Nazis to gamble just as long as their bluff was not called; he had had this, he said, direct from von Fritsch. The army had broken the Nazi Party in the July purge of 1936; they had let Hitler and Goering and Goebbels and Ribbentrop remain as puppets just as long as they proved valuable. The army, like all armies, was intensely pacifist; as soon as it became clear that Hitler was heading for war, he would be shot. Basil had expounded this theme not once but many times, over the table of the Charlotte Street restaurant, and because Poppet's friends did not know Basil, and were unused to people who claimed acquaintance with the great, Poppet had basked in vicarious esteem. Basil was little used to being heard with respect and was correspondingly resentful at being reproached with his own words.

'Well,' Poppet was saying crossly, from the gas stove. 'When do the army step in and shoot Hitler?'

She was a remarkably silly girl, and, as such, had commanded Basil's immediate attention when they met, three weeks earlier, with Ambrose Silk. With her Basil had spent the time he had promised to Angela at Cannes; on her he had spent the twenty pounds Angela had sent him for the journey. Even now when her fatuous face pouted in derision, she found a soft place in Basil's heart.

Evidence of her silliness abounded in the canvases, finished and unfinished, which crowded the studio. Eighty years ago her subjects would have been knights in armour, ladies in wimples and distress; fifty years ago 'nocturnes'; twenty years ago pierrots and willow trees; now, in 1939, they were bodiless heads, green horses and violet grass, sea-weed, shells and fungi, neatly executed, conventionally arranged in the manner of Dali. Her work in progress on the easel was an overlarge, accurate but buttercup-coloured head of the Aphrodite of Melos, poised against a background of bull's-eyes and barley-sugar.

'My dear,' Ambrose had said, 'you can positively hear her imagination *creaking*, as she does them, like a pair of old, old *corsets*, my dear, on a *harridan*.'

'They'll destroy London. What shall I do?' asked Poppet plaintively. 'Where can I go? It's the end of my painting. I've a good mind to follow Parsnip and Pimpernell' (two great poets of her acquaintance who had recently fled to New York).

'You'll be in more danger crossing the Atlantic than staying in London,' said Basil. 'There won't be any air raids on London.'

'For God's sake don't say that.' Even as she spoke the sirens wailed. Poppet stood paralysed with horror. 'Oh God,' she said. 'You've done it. They've come.'

'Faultless timing,' said Basil cheerfully. 'That's always been Hitler's strong point.'

Poppet began to dress in an ineffectual fever of reproach. 'You *said* there wouldn't be a war. You *said* the bombers would never come. Now we shall all be killed and you just sit there talking and talking.'

'You know I should have thought an air raid was just the thing for a surrealist; it ought to give you plenty of compositions – limbs and things lying about in odd places, you know.'

'I wish I'd never met you. I wish I'd been to church. I was brought up in a convent. I wanted to be a nun once. I wish I was a nun. I'm going to be killed. Oh, I wish I was a nun. Where's my gas-mask? I shall go mad if I don't find my gas-mask.'

Basil lay back on the divan and watched her with fascination. This was how he liked to see women behave in moments of alarm. He rejoiced, always, in the spectacle of women at a disadvantage: thus he would watch, in the asparagus season, a dribble of melted butter on a woman's chin, marring her beauty and making her ridiculous, while she would still talk and smile and turn her head, not knowing how she appeared to him.

'Now do make up your mind what you're frightened of,' he urged. 'If you're going to be bombed with high explosive, run down to the shelter; if you're going to be gassed, shut the skylight and stay up here. In any case I shouldn't bother about that respirator. If they use anything it'll be arsenical smoke and it's no use against that. You'll find arsenical smoke quite painless at first. You won't know you've been gassed for a couple of days; then it'll be too late. In fact for all we know we're being gassed at this moment. If they fly high enough and let the wind carry the stuff they may be twenty miles away. The symptoms, when they do appear, are rather revolting...'

But Poppet was gone, helter-skelter, downstairs, making little moaning noises as she went.

Basil dressed and, pausing only to paint in a ginger moustache across Poppet's head of Aphrodite, strolled out into the streets.

The normal emptiness of Sunday in South Kensington was made complete that morning by the air-raid scare. A man in a tin helmet shouted at Basil from the opposite pavement. 'Take cover, there. Yes, it's you I'm talking to.'

Basil crossed over to him and said in a low tone, 'M.I.13.'

'Eh?'

'M.I.13.'

'I don't quite twig.'

'But you *ought* to twig,' said Basil severely. 'Surely you realize that members of M.I.13 are free to go everywhere at all times?'

'Sorry, I'm sure,' said the warden. 'I was only took on yesterday. What a lark getting a raid second time on!' As he spoke the sirens sounded the All Clear. 'What a sell!' said the warden.

It seemed to Basil that this fellow was altogether too cheerful for a public servant in the first hours of war; the gas scare had been wasted on Poppet; in her panic she had barely listened; it was worthy of a more receptive audience. 'Cheer up,' he said. 'You may be breathing arsenical smoke at this moment. Watch your urine in a couple of days' time.'

'Coo. I say, what did you say you was?'

'M.I.13.'

'Is that to do with gas?'

'It's to do with almost everything. Good morning.'

He turned to walk on but the warden followed. 'Wouldn't we smell it or nothing?'

'No.'

'Or cough or anything?'

'No.'

'And you think they've dropped it, just in that minute and gone away leaving us all for dead?'

'My dear fellow, *I* don't think so. It's your job as a warden to find out.'

'Coo.'

That'll teach him to shout at me in the street, thought Basil.

After the All Clear various friends of Poppet's came together in her studio.

'I wasn't *the least* frightened. I was so surprised at my own courage I felt quite giddy.'

'I wasn't *frightened*, I just felt glum.'

'*I* felt positively glad. After all we've all said for years that the present order of things was doomed, haven't we? I mean it's always been the choice for *us* between a concentration camp and being blown up, hasn't it? I just sat thinking how much I preferred being blown up to being beaten with rubber truncheons.'

'*I* was frightened,' said Poppet.

'Dear Poppet, you always have the *healthiest* reactions. Erchman really did wonders for you.'

'Well, I'm not sure they *were* so healthy this time. D'you know, I found myself actually *praying*.'

'I say, did you? That's bad.'

'Better see Erchman again.'

'Unless he's in a concentration camp.'

'We shall all be in concentration camps.'

'If anyone so much as mentions concentration camps again,' said Ambrose Silk, 'I shall go frankly hay-wire.' ('He had an unhappy love affair in Munich,' one of Poppet's friends explained to another, 'then they found he was half Jewish and the Brown Shirt was shut away.') 'Let's look at Poppet's pictures and forget the war. Now *that*,' he said, pausing before the Aphrodite, '*that* I consider *good*. I consider it *good*, Poppet. The moustache... it shows you have crossed one of the artistic rubicons and feel strong enough to be facetious. Like those wonderfully dramatic old *chestnuts* in Parsnip's *Guernica Revisited.* You're growing up, Poppet, my dear.'

'I wonder if it's the effect of that old adventurer of hers.'

'Poor Basil, it's sad enough for him to be an *enfant terrible* at the age of thirty-six; but to be regarded by the younger generation as a kind of dilapidated Bulldog Drummond...'

Ambrose Silk was older than Poppet and her friends; he was, in fact, a contemporary of Basil's, with whom he had maintained a shadowy, mutually derisive acquaintance since they were undergraduates. In those days, the mid '20s at Oxford, when the last of the ex-service men had gone down and the first of the puritanical, politically minded had either not come up or, at any rate, had not made himself noticed, in those days of broad trousers and high-necked jumpers and cars parked nightly outside the Spread Eagle at Thame, there had been few sub-divisions; a certain spiritual extravagance in the quest for pleasure had been the sole common bond between friends who in subsequent years had drifted far apart, beyond hailing distance, on the wider seas. Ambrose, in those days, had ridden ridiculously and ignominiously in the Christ Church Grind, and Peter Pastmaster had gone to a Palais de Danse in Reading dressed as a woman. Alastair Digby-Vane-Trumpington, absorbed in immature experiments into the question of how far various lewd debutantes would go with him, still had time when tippling his port at Mickleham to hear, without disapproval, Ambrose's recitals of unrequited love for a rowing blue. Nowadays Ambrose saw few of his old friends except Basil. He fancied that he had been dropped and sometimes in moments of vainglory, to the right audience, represented himself as a martyr to Art; as one who made no concessions to Mammon. 'I can't come all the way with you,' he said once to Parsnip and Pimpernell when they explained that only by becoming proletarian (an expression to which they attached no pedantic suggestion of childbearing; they meant that he should employ himself in some ill-paid, unskilled labour of a mechanical kind) could he hope to be a valuable writer, 'I can't come all the way with you, dear Parsnip and Pimpernell. But at least you know I have never sold myself to the upper class.' In this mood he saw himself as a figure in a dream, walking down an endless fashionable street; every door stood open and the waiting footmen cried, 'Come in and join us; flatter our masters and we will feed you,' but Ambrose always marched straight ahead unheeding. 'I belong, hopelessly, to the age of the ivory tower,' he said.

It was his misfortune to be respected as a writer by almost everyone except those with whom he most consorted. Poppet and her friends looked on him as a survival from the Yellow Book. The more conscientiously he strove to put himself in the movement and to ally himself with the dour young proletarians of the new decade, the more antiquated did he seem to them. His very appearance, with the swagger and flash of the young Disraeli, made him a conspicuous figure among them. Basil with his natural shabbiness was less incongruous.

Ambrose knew this, and repeated the phrase 'old adventurer' with relish.

5

ALASTAIR and Sonia Trumpington changed house, on an average, once a year, ostensibly for motives of economy, and were now in Chester Street. Wherever they went they carried with them their own inalienable, inimitable disorder. Ten years ago, without any effort or desire on their part, merely by pleasing themselves in their own way, they had lived in the full blaze of fashionable notoriety; to-day without regret, without in fact being aware of the change, they formed a forgotten cove, where the wreckage of the roaring twenties, long tossed on the high seas, lay beached, dry and battered, barely worth the attention of the most assiduous beachcomber. Sonia would sometimes remark how odd it was that the papers nowadays never seemed to mention anyone one had ever heard of; they had been such a bore once, never leaving one alone.

Basil, when he was in England, was a constant visitor. It was really, Alastair said, in order to keep him from coming to stay that they had to live in such painfully cramped quarters.

Wherever they lived Basil developed a homing instinct towards them, an aptitude which, in their swift moves from house to house, often caused consternation to subsequent tenants, who, before he had had time to form new patterns of behaviour, would quite often wake in the night to hear Basil swarming up the drain pipes and looming tipsily in the bedroom window or, in the morning, to find him recumbent and insensible in the area. Now, on this catastrophic morning, Basil found himself orientated to them as surely as though he were in wine, and he arrived on their new doorstep without conscious thought of direction. He went upstairs immediately for, wherever they lived, it was always in Sonia's bedroom, as though it were the scene of an unending convalescence, that the heart of the household beat.

Basil had attended Sonia's levees (and there were three or four levees daily for, whenever she was at home, she was in bed) off and on for nearly ten years, since the days of her first, dazzling loveliness, when, almost alone among the chaste and daring brides of London, she had admitted mixed company to her bathroom. It was an innovation, or rather the revival of a more golden age, which, like everything Sonia did, was conceived without any desire for notoriety; she enjoyed company, she enjoyed her bath. There were usually three or four breathless and giddy young men, in those days, gulping Black Velvet in the steam, pretending to take their reception as a matter of common occurrence.

Basil saw little change in her beauty now and none in the rich confusion of letters, newspapers, half opened parcels and half empty bottles, puppies, flowers and fruit which surrounded the bed where she sat sewing (for it was one of the vagaries of her character to cover acres of silk, yearly, with exquisite embroidery).

'Darling Basil, have you come to be blown up with us? Where's your horrible girl friend?'

'She took fright.'

'She was a beast, darling, one of your very worst. Look at Peter. Isn't it all crazy?' Peter Pastmaster sat at the foot of her bed in uniform. Once, for reasons he had now forgotten, he had served, briefly, in the cavalry; the harvest of that early sowing had ripened, suddenly, overnight. 'Won't it be too ridiculous, starting all over again, lunching with young men on guard.'

'Not young, Sonia. You should see us. The average age of the subalterns is about forty, the colonel finished the last war as a brigadier, and our troopers are all either weather-beaten old commissionaires or fifteen-stone valets.'

Alastair came in from the bathroom. 'How's the art tart?' He opened bottles and began mixing stout and champagne in a deep jug. 'Blackers?' They had always drunk this sour and invigorating draught.

'Tell us all about the war,' said Sonia.

'Well –' Basil began.

'No, darling, I didn't mean that. Not *all*. Not about who's going to win or why we are fighting. Tell us what everyone is going to do about it. From what Margot tells me the last war was absolute heaven. Alastair wants to go for a soldier.'

'Conscription has rather taken the gilt off that particular gingerbread,' said Basil. 'Besides, this ain't going to be a soldier's war.'

'Poor Peter,' said Sonia, as though she was talking to one of the puppies. 'It isn't going to be your war, sweetheart.'

'Suits me,' said Peter.

'I expect Basil will have the most tremendous adventures. He always did in peace time. Goodness knows what he'll do in war.'

'There are too many people in on the racket,' said Basil.

'Poor sweet, I don't believe any of you are nearly as excited about it as I am.'

The name of the poet Parsnip, casually mentioned, reopened the great Parsnip-Pimpernell controversy which was torturing Poppet Green and her friends. It was a problem which, not unlike the Schleswig-Holstein question of the preceding century, seemed to admit of no logical solution, for, in simple terms, the postulates were self-contradictory. Parsnip and Pimpernell, as friends and collaborators, were inseparable; on that all agreed.

But Parsnip's art flourished best in England, even an embattled England, while Pimpernell's needed the peaceful and fecund soil of the United States. The complementary qualities which, many believed, made them together equal to one poet now threatened the dissolution of partnership.

'I don't say that Pimpernell is the *better* poet,' said Ambrose. 'All I say is that I *personally* find him the more nutritious; so I *personally* think they are right to go.'

'But I've always felt that Parsnip is so much more dependent on environment.'

'I know what you mean, Poppet, but I don't agree... Aren't you thinking only of *Guernica Revisited* and forgetting the Christopher Sequence... '

Thus the aesthetic wrangle might have run its familiar course, but there was in the studio that morning a cross, red-headed girl in spectacles from the London School of Economics; she believed in a People's Total War; an uncompromising girl whom none of them liked; a suspect of Trotskyism.

'What I don't see,' she said (and what this girl did not see was usually a very conspicuous embarrassment to Poppet's friends) – 'What I don't see is how these two can claim to be *Contemporary* if they run away from the biggest event in contemporary history. They were contemporary enough about Spain when no one threatened to come and bomb *them*.'

It was an awkward question; one that in military parlance was called 'a swift one'. At any moment, it was felt in the studio, this indecent girl would use the word 'escapism'; and, in the silence which followed her outburst, while everyone in turn meditated and rejected a possible retort, she did, in fact, produce the unforgivable charge. 'It's just sheer escapism,' she said.

The word startled the studio, like the cry of 'Cheat' in a card-room.

'That's a foul thing to say, Julia.'

'Well, what's the answer?'...

The answer, thought Ambrose, he knew an answer or two. There was plenty that he had learned from his new friends, that he could quote to them. He could say that the war in Spain was 'contemporary' because it was a class war; the present conflict, since Russia had declared herself neutral, was merely a phase in capitalist disintegration; that would have satisfied, or at least silenced, the red-headed girl. But that was not really the answer. He sought for comforting historical analogies, but every example which occurred to him was on the side of the red-head. She knew them too, he thought, and would quote them with all her post-graduate glibness – Socrates marching to the sea with Xenophon, Virgil sanctifying Roman military rule, Horace singing the sweetness of dying for one's country, the troubadours riding to war, Cervantes in the galleys at Lepanto, Milton working himself blind in the public service, even George IV, for whom Ambrose had a reverence which others devoted to Charles I, believed he had fought at Waterloo. All these, and a host of other courageous contemporary figures rose in Ambrose's mind. Cézanne had deserted in 1870, but Cézanne in the practical affairs of life was a singularly unattractive figure; moreover, he was a painter whom Ambrose found insufferably boring. There was no answer to be found on those lines.

'You're just sentimental,' said Poppet, 'like a spinster getting tearful at the sound of a military band.'

'Well, they have military bands in Russia, don't they? I expect plenty of spinsters get tearful in the Red Square when they march past Lenin's tomb.'

You can always stump them with Russia, thought Ambrose; they can always stump each other. It's the dead end of all discussion.

'The question is, would they write any better for being in danger,' said one.

'Would they help the People's Cause?' said another.

It was the old argument, gathering speed again after the rude girl's interruption. Ambrose gazed sadly at the jaundiced, mustachioed Aphrodite. What was he doing, he asked himself, in this galley?

Sonia was trying to telephone to Margot, to invite themselves all to luncheon.

'An odious man says that only official calls are being taken this morning.'

'Say you're M.I.13,' said Basil.

'I'm M.I.13.... What can that mean? Darling, I believe it's going to work... It *has* worked... Margot, this is Sonia... I'm dying to see you to...'

Aphrodite gazed back at him, blind, as though sculptured in butter; Parsnip and Pimpernell, Red Square and Brown House, thus the discussion raged. What was all this to do with him?

Art and Love had led him to this inhospitable room.

Love for a long succession of louts – rugger blues, all-in wrestlers, naval ratings; tender, hopeless love that had been rewarded at the best by an occasional episode of rough sensuality, followed, in sober light, with contempt, abuse and rapacity.

A pansy. An old queen. A habit of dress, a tone of voice, an elegant, humorous deportment that had been admired and imitated, a swift, epicene felicity of wit, the art of dazzling and confusing those he despised – these had been his, and now they were the current exchange of comedians; there were only a few restaurants, now, which he could frequent without fear of ridicule and there he was surrounded, as though by distorting mirrors, with gross reflections and caricatures of himself. Was it thus that the rich passions of Greece and Arabia and the Renaissance had worn themselves out? Did they simper when Leonardo passed and imitate with mincing grace the warriors of Sparta; was there a snigger across the sand outside the tents of Saladin? They burned the Knights Templar at the stake; their loves, at least, were monstrous and formidable, a thing to call down destruction from heaven, if man neglected his duty of cruelty and repression. Beddoes had died in solitude, by his own hand; Wilde had been driven into the shadows, tipsy and garrulous, but, to the end, a figure of tragedy looming big in his own twilight. But Ambrose, thought Ambrose, what of him? Born after his time, in an age which made a type of him, a figure of farce; like mothers-in-law and kippers, the century's contribution to the national store of comic objects; akin with the chorus boys who tittered under the lamps of Shaftesbury Avenue. And Hans, who at last, after so long a pilgrimage, had seemed to promise rest, Hans so simple and affectionate, like a sturdy young terrier, Hans lay in the unknown horrors of a Nazi concentration camp.

The huge, yellow face with scrawled moustaches offered Ambrose no comfort.

There was a young man of military age in the studio; he was due to be called up in the near future. 'I don't know what to do about it,' he said. 'Of course, I could always plead conscientious objections, but I haven't got a conscience. It would be a denial of everything we've stood for if I said I had a conscience.'

'No, Tom,' they said to comfort him. 'We know you haven't a conscience.'

'But then,' said the perplexed young man, 'if I haven't got a conscience, why in God's name should I mind so much saying that I have?'

'... Peter's here and Basil. We're all feeling very gay and warlike. May we come to luncheon? Basil says there's bound to be an enormous air raid to-night so it may be the last time we shall ever see each other.... What's that? Yes, I told you I'm (What am I, Basil?) I'm M.I.13. There's a ridiculous woman on the line saying is this a private call?)... Well, Margot, then we'll all come round to you. That'll be heaven... hello, *hello*, I do believe that damned woman has cut us off.'

Nature I loved, and next to Nature, Art. Nature in the raw is seldom mild; red in tooth and claw; matelots in Toulon smelling of wine and garlic, with tough brown necks, cigarettes stuck to the lower lip, lapsing into unintelligible, contemptuous argot.

Art: this was where Art had brought him, to this studio, to these coarse and tedious youngsters, to that preposterous yellow face among the boiled sweets.

It had been a primrose path in the days of Diaghilev; at Eton he had collected Lovat Frazer rhyme sheets; at Oxford he had recited *In Memoriam* through a megaphone to an accompaniment hummed on combs and tissue paper; in Paris he had frequented Jean Cocteau and Gertrude Stein; he had written and published his first book there, a study of Montparnasse Negroes that had been banned in England by Sir William Joynson-Hicks. That way the primrose path led gently downhill to the world of fashionable photographers, stage sets for Cochrane, Cedric Lyne and his Neapolitan grottoes.

He had made his decision then, turned aside from the primrose path, had deliberately chosen the austere and the heroic; it was the year of the American slump, a season of heroic decisions, when Paul had tried to enter a monastery and David had succeeded in throwing himself under a train. Ambrose had gone to Germany, lived in a workman's quarter, found Hans, begun a book, a grim, abstruse, interminable book, a penance for past frivolity; the unfinished manuscript lay somewhere in an old suitcase in Central Europe, and Hans was behind barbed wire; or worse, perhaps, had given in, as with his simple, easy-going acceptance of things was all too likely, was back among the Brown Shirts, a man with a mark against his name, never again to be trusted, but good enough for the firing line, good enough to be jostled into battle.

The red-headed girl was asking inconvenient questions again. 'But Tom,' she was saying. 'Surely if it was a good thing to share the life of the worker in a canned fruit factory, why isn't it a good thing to serve with him in the army?'

'Julia's just the type who used to go about distributing white feathers.'

'If it comes to that, why the hell not,' said Julia.

Ars longa, thought Ambrose, a short life but a grey one.

Alastair plugged his electric razor into the lamp on Sonia's writing table and shaved in the bedroom, so as not to miss what was going on. He had once in the past seen Peter in full-dress uniform at a Court Ball and had felt sorry for him because it meant that he could not come on afterwards to a night club; this was the first time he had seen him in khaki and he was jealous as a schoolboy. There was still a great deal of the schoolboy about Alastair; he enjoyed winter sports and sailing and squash racquets and the chaff round the bar at Bratts; he observed certain immature taboos of dress, such as wearing a bowler hat in London until after Goodwood week; he had a firm, personal sense of schoolboy honour. He felt these prejudices to be peculiar to himself; none of them made him at all censorious of anyone else; he accepted Basil's outrageous disregard for them without question. He kept his sense of honour as he might have kept an expensive and unusual pet; as, indeed, once, for a disastrous month, Sonia had kept a small kangaroo named Molly. He knew himself to be as eccentric, in his own way, as Ambrose Silk. For a year, at the age of twenty-one, he had been Margot Metroland's lover; it was an apprenticeship many of his friends had served; they had forgotten about it now, but at the time all their acquaintances knew about it; but never, even to Sonia, had Alastair alluded to the fact. Since marriage he had been unfaithful to Sonia for a week every year, during Bratts Club golf tournament at Le Touquet, usually with the wife of a fellow member. He did this without any scruple because he believed Bratts week to be in some way excluded from the normal life of loyalties and obligations; a Saturnalia when the laws did not run. At all other times he was a devoted husband.

Alastair had never come nearer to military service than in being senior private in the Corps at Eton; during the General Strike he had driven about the poorer quarters of London in a closed van to break up seditious meetings and had clubbed several unoffending citizens; that was his sole contribution to domestic politics, for he had lived, in spite of his many moves, in uncontested constituencies. But he had always held it as axiomatic that, should anything as preposterous and antiquated as a large-scale war occur, he would take a modest but vigorous part. He had no illusions about his abilities, but believed, justly, that he would make as good a target as anyone else for the King's enemies to shoot at. It came as a shock to him now to find his country at war and himself in pyjamas, spending his normal

Sunday noon with a jug of Black Velvet and some chance visitors. Peter's uniform added to his uneasiness. It was as though he had been taken in adultery at Christmas or found in mid-June on the steps of Bratts in a soft hat.

He studied Peter, with the rapt attention of a small boy, taking in every detail of his uniform, the riding boots, Sam Browne belt, the enamelled stars of rank, and felt disappointed but, in a way, relieved, that there was no sword; he could not have borne it if Peter had had a sword.

'I know I look awful,' Peter said. 'The adjutant left me in no doubt on that subject.'

'You look sweet,' said Sonia.

'I heard they had stopped wearing cross straps on the Sam Browne,' said Alastair.

'Yes, but technically *we* still carry swords.'

Technically. Peter *had* a sword, technically.

'Darling, do you think that if we went past Buckingham Palace the sentries will salute?'

'It's quite possible. I don't think Belisha has quite succeeded in putting it down yet.'

'We'll go there at once. I'll dress. Can't wait to see them.'

So they walked from Chester Street to Buckingham Palace; Sonia and Peter in front, Alastair and Basil a pace or two behind. The sentries saluted and Sonia pinched Peter as he acknowledged it. Alastair said to Basil:

'I suppose we'll be doing that soon.'

'They don't want volunteers in this war, Alastair. They'll call people up when they want them without any recruiting marches or popular songs. They haven't the equipment for the men in training now.'

'Who do you mean by "they"?'

'Hore-Belisha.'

'Who cares what *he* wants?' said Alastair. For him there was no 'they'. England was at war; he, Alastair Trumpington, was at war. It was not the business of any politician to tell him when or how he should fight. But he could not put this into words; not into words, anyway, which Basil would not make ridiculous, so he walked on in silence behind Peter's martial figure until Sonia decided to take a cab.

'I know what I want,' said Basil. 'I want to be one of those people one heard about in 1919; the hard-faced men who did well out of the war.'

6

ALTHOUGH it was common for Freddie Sothill, Sir Joseph Mainwaring and various others who from time to time were enlisted to help solve the recurrent problem of Basil's future, to speak of him in terms they normally reserved for the mining community of South Wales, as feckless and unemployable, the getting of jobs, of one kind and another, had, in fact, played a large part in his life, for it was the explanation and excuse of most of Basil's vagaries that he had never had any money of his own. Tony and Barbara by their father's will each enjoyed a reasonable fortune, but Sir Christopher Seal had died shortly after the first of Basil's major disgraces. If it were conceivable that one who held the office of Chief Whip for a quarter of a century could be shocked at any spectacle of human depravity, it might have been thought that shame hastened his end, so fast did one event follow upon the other. Be that as it may, it was on his deathbed that Sir Christopher, in true melodramatic style, disinherited his younger son, leaving his future entirely in his mother's hands.

Lady Seal's most devoted friend – and she had many – would not have credited her with more than human discretion, and some quite preternatural power would have been needed to deal with Basil's first steps in adult life. The system she decided on was, at the best, unimaginative and, like many such schemes, was suggested to her by Sir Joseph Mainwaring; it consisted, in his words, of 'giving the boy his bread and butter and letting him find the jam'. Removed from the realm of metaphor to plain English, this meant allowing Basil £400 a year, conditional on his good behaviour, and expecting him to supplement it by his own exertions if he wished for a more ample way of life.

The arrangement proved disastrous from the first. Four times in the last ten years Lady Seal had paid Basil's debts; once on condition of his living at home with her; once on condition of his living somewhere, anywhere, abroad; once on condition of his marrying; once on condition of refraining from his marriage. Twice he had been cut off with a penny; twice taken back to favour; once he had been set up in chambers in the Temple with an allowance of a thousand a year; several times a large lump sum of capital had been dangled before his eyes as the reward of his giving himself seriously to commerce; once he had been on the verge of becoming the recipient of a sisal farm in Kenya. Throughout all these changes of fortune Sir Joseph Mainwaring had acted the part of political agent to a recalcitrant stipendiary sultan, in a way which embittered every benevolence and minimized the value of every gift he brought. In the intervals of neglect and independence, Basil had fended for himself and had successively held all the jobs which were open to young men of his qualifications. He had never had much difficulty in getting jobs; the trouble had always been in keeping them, for he regarded a potential employer as his opponent in a game of skill. All Basil's resource and energy went into hoodwinking him into surrender; once he had received his confidence he lost interest. Thus English girls will put themselves to endless exertion to secure a husband and, once married, will think their labour at an end.

Basil had been leader writer on the *Daily Beast*, he had served in the personal entourage of Lord Monomark, he had sold champagne on commission, composed dialogue for the cinema and given the first of what was intended to be a series of talks for the B.B.C. Sinking lower in the social scale he had been press agent for a female contortionist and had once conducted a party of tourists to the Italian lakes (he dined out for some time on the story of that tour which had, after a crescendo of minor vexations, culminated in Basil making a bundle of all the tickets and all the passports and sinking them in Lake Garda. He had then travelled home alone by an early train, leaving fifty penniless Britons, none of whom spoke a word of any foreign language, to the care of whatever deity takes charge of forsaken strangers; for all Basil knew, they were still there).

From time to time he disappeared from the civilized area and returned with tales to which no one attached much credence – of having worked for the secret police in Bolivia and advised the Emperor of Azania on the modernization of his country. Basil was in the habit, as it were, of conducting his own campaigns, issuing his own ultimatums, disseminating his own propaganda, erecting about himself his own blackout; he was an obstreperous minority of one in a world of otiose civilians. He was used, in his own life, to a system of push, appeasement, agitation, and blackmail, which, except that it had no more distant aim than his own immediate amusement, ran parallel to Nazi diplomacy.

Like Nazi diplomacy it postulated for success a peace-loving, orderly and honourable world in which to operate. In the new, busy, secretive, chaotic world which developed during the first days of the war, Basil for the first time in his life felt himself at a disadvantage. It was like being in Latin America at a time of upheaval, and, instead of being an Englishman, being oneself a Latin American.

The end of September found Basil in a somewhat fretful mood. The air-raid scare seemed to be over for the time and those who had voluntarily fled from London were beginning to return, pretending that they had only been to the country to see that everything was all right there. The women and children of the poor, too, were flocking home to their evacuated streets. The newspapers said that the Poles were holding out; that their cavalry was penetrating deep into Germany; that the enemy was already short of motor oil; that Saarbrücken would fall to the French within a day or two; air-raid wardens roamed the remote hamlets of the kingdom, persecuting yokels who walked home from the inn with glowing pipes. Londoners who were slow to acquire the habit of the domestic hearth groped their way in darkness from one place of amusement to another, learning their destination by feeling the buttons on the commissionaires' uniforms; revolving, black glass doors gave access to a fairy land; it was as though, when children, they had been led blindfold into the room with the lighted Christmas tree. The casualty list of street accidents became formidable and there were terrifying tales of footpads who leaped on the shoulders of old gentlemen on the very steps of their clubs, or beat them to jelly on Hay Hill.

Everyone whom Basil met was busy getting a job. Some consciously or unconsciously had taken out an insurance policy against unemployment by joining some military unit in the past; there were those like Peter, who in early youth had gratified a parental whim by spending a few expensive years in the regular army, and those like Freddy who had gone into the yeomanry as they sat on the Bench and the county council as part of the normal obligations of rural life. These were now in uniform with their problems solved. In later months, as they sat idle in the Middle East, they were to think enviously of those who had made a more deliberate and judicious choice of service, but at the moment their minds were enviably at rest. The remainder were possessed with a passion to enrol in some form of public service, however uncongenial. Some formed ambulance parties and sat long hours at their posts waiting for air-raid victims; some became firemen, some minor civil servants. None of these honourable occupations made much appeal to Basil.

He was exactly the type of man who, if English life had run as it did in books of adventure, should at this turn in world affairs have been sent for. He should have been led to an obscure address in Maida Vale and there presented to a lean, scarred man with hard grey eyes; one of the men behind the scenes; one of the men whose names were unknown to the public and the newspapers, who passed unnoticed in the street, a name known only to the inner circle of the Cabinet and to the XXX heads of the secret police of the world . . . 'Sit down, Seal. We've followed your movements with interest ever since that affair in La Paz in '32. You're a rascal, but I'm inclined to think you're the kind of rascal the country needs at this moment. I take it you're game for anything?'

'I'm game.'

'That's what I expected you to say. These are your orders. You will go to Uxbridge aerodrome at 4.30 this afternoon where a man will meet you and give you your passport. You will travel under the name of Blenkinsop. You are a tobacco-grower from Latakia. A civil aeroplane will take you by various stages to Smyrna where you will register at the Miramar Hotel and await orders. Is that clear . . . ?'

It was clear, and Basil, whose life up to the present had been more like an adventure story than most people's, did half expect some such summons. None came. Instead he was invited to luncheon by Sir Joseph Mainwaring at the Travellers' Club.

Basil's luncheons at the Travellers' with Sir Joseph Mainwaring had for years formed a series of monuments in his downward path. There had been the luncheons of his four major debt settlements, the luncheon of his political candidature, the luncheons of his two respectable professions, the luncheon of the threatened divorce of Angela Lyne, the Luncheon of the Stolen Emeralds, the Luncheon of the Knuckledusters, the Luncheon of Freddy's Last Cheque – each would provide both theme and title for a work of popular fiction.

Hitherto these feasts had taken place *à deux* in a secluded corner. The Luncheon of the Commission in the Guards was altogether a more honourable affair and its purpose was to introduce Basil to the Lieutenant-Colonel of the Bombardiers – an officer whom Sir Joseph wrongly believed to have a liking for him.

The Lieutenant-Colonel did not know Sir Joseph well and was surprised and slightly alarmed by the invitation, for his distrust was based not, as might have been expected, on any just estimate of his capabilities, but, paradoxically, on the fear of him as a politician and man of affairs. All politicians were, to the Lieutenant-Colonel, not so much boobies as bogies. He saw them all, even Sir Joseph, as figures of Renaissance subtlety and intrigue. It was by being in with them that the great professional advances were achieved; but it was by falling foul of them that one fell into ignominy. For a simple soldier – and if ever anyone did, the Lieutenant-Colonel qualified for that honourable title – the only safe course was to avoid men like Sir Joseph. When met with, they should be treated with bluff and uncompromising reserve. Sir Joseph thus found himself, through his loyal friendship with Cynthia Seal, in the equivocal position of introducing, with a view to his advancement, a man for whom he had a deep-seated horror to a man who had something of the same emotion towards himself. It was not a concurrence which, on the face of it, seemed hopeful of good results.

Basil, like 'Lord Monmouth', 'never condescended to the artifice of the toilet', and the Lieutenant-Colonel studied him with distaste. Together the ill-assorted trio went to their table.

Soldier and statesman spread their napkins on their knees and in the interest of ordering their luncheon allowed a silence to fall between them into which Basil cheerfully plunged.

'We ought to do something about Liberia, Colonel,' he said.

The Colonel turned on him the outraged gaze with which a good regimental soldier always regards the discussion of war in its larger aspects.

'I expect those whose business it is have the question in hand,' he said.

'Don't you believe it,' said Basil. 'I don't expect they've given it a thought,' and for some twenty minutes he explained why and how Liberia should be immediately annexed.

The two elder men ate in silence. At length a chance reference to Russia gave Sir Joseph the chance to interpose an opinion.

'I always distrust prophecy in any form,' he said. 'But there is one thing of which I am certain. Russia will come in against us before the end of the year. That will put Italy and Japan on our side. Then it is simply a question of time before our blockade makes itself felt. All kinds of things that you and I have never heard of, like manganese and bauxite, will win the war for us.'

'And infantry.'

'*And* infantry.'

'Teach a man to march and shoot. Give him the right type of officer. Leave the rest to him.'

This seemed to Basil a suitable moment to introduce his own problems. 'What do you think is the right type of officer?'

'The officer-type.'

'It's an odd thing,' Basil began, 'that people always expect the upper class to be good leaders of men. That was all right in the old days when most of them were brought up with tenantry to look after. But now three-quarters of your officer-type live in towns. *I* haven't any tenantry.'

The Lieutenant-Colonel looked at Basil with detestation. 'No, no. I suppose not.'

'Well, have *you* any tenantry?'

'*I?* No. My brother sold the old place years ago.'

'Well, there you are.'

It was crystal-clear to Sir Joseph and faintly perceptible to Basil that the Lieutenant-Colonel did not take this well.

'Seal was for a time conservative candidate down in the West,' said Sir Joseph, anxious to remove one possible source of prejudice.

'Some pretty funny people have been calling themselves conservatives in the last year or two. Cause of half the trouble if you ask me.' Then, feeling he might have been impolite, he added graciously: 'No offence to you. Daresay you were all right. Don't know anything about you.'

Basil's political candidature was not an episode to be enlarged upon. Sir Joseph turned the conversation. 'Of course, the French will have to make some concessions to bring Italy in. Give up Jibuti or something like that.'

'Why the devil should they?' asked the Lieutenant-Colonel petulantly. 'Who wants Italy in?'

'To counterbalance Russia.'

'How? Why? Where? I don't see it at all.'

'Nor do I,' said Basil.

Threatened with support from so unwelcome a quarter, the Lieutenant-Colonel immediately abandoned his position. 'Oh, don't you?' he said. 'Well, I've no doubt Mainwaring knows best. His job to know these things.'

Warmed by these words Sir Joseph proceeded for the rest of luncheon to suggest some of the concessions which he thought France might reasonably make to Italy – Tunisia, French Somaliland, the Suez Canal. 'Corsica, Nice, Savoy?' asked Basil. Sir Joseph thought not.

Rather than ally himself with Basil the Lieutenant-Colonel listened to these proposals to dismember an ally in silence and fury. He had not wanted to come out to luncheon. It would be absurd to say that he was busy, but he was busier than he had ever been in his life before and he looked on the two hours or so which he allowed himself in the middle of the day as a time for general recuperation. He liked to spend them among people to whom he could relate all that he had done in the morning; to people who would appreciate the importance and rarity of such work; either that, or with a handsome woman. He left the Travellers' as early as he decently could and returned to his mess. His mind was painfully agitated by all he had heard and particularly by the presence of that seedy-looking young radical whose name he had not caught. That at least, he thought, he might have hoped to be spared at Sir Joseph's table.

'Well, Jo, is everything arranged?'

'Nothing is exactly *arranged* yet, Cynthia, but I've set the ball rolling.'

'I hope Basil made a good impression.'

'I hope he did, too. I'm afraid he said some rather unfortunate things.'

'Oh dear. Well, what is the next step?'

Sir Joseph would have liked to say that there was no next step in that direction; that the best Basil could hope for was oblivion; perhaps in a month or so, when the luncheon was forgotten . . . 'It's up to Basil now, Cynthia. I have introduced him. He must follow it up himself if he really wants to get into that regiment. But I have been wondering since you first mentioned the matter, do you really think it is quite suitable . . . '

'I'm told he could not do better,' said Lady Seal proudly.

'No, that is so. In one way he could not do better.'

'Then he shall follow up the introduction,' said that unimaginative mother.

The Lieutenant-Colonel was simmering quietly in his office; an officer – not a young officer but a mature reservist – had just been to see him without gloves, wearing suède shoes; the consequent outburst had been a great relief; the simmering was an expression of content, a kind of mental purr; it was a mood which his subordinates recognized as a good mood. He was feeling that as long as there was someone like himself at the head of the regiment, nothing much could go wrong with it (a feeling which, oddly enough, was shared by the delinquent officer). To the Lieutenant-Colonel, in this mood, it was announced that a civilian gentleman, Mr Seal, wanted to see him. The name was unfamiliar; so, for the moment, was Basil's appearance, for Angela had been at pains and expense to fit him up suitably for the interview. His hair was newly cut, he wore a stiff white collar, a bowler hat, a thin gold watch-chain and other marks of respectability, and he carried a new umbrella. Angela had also schooled him in the first words of his interview. 'I know you are very busy, Colonel, but I hoped you would spare me a few minutes to ask your advice . . . '

All this went fairly well. 'Want to go into the army?' said the Lieutenant-Colonel. 'Well, I suppose we must expect a lot of people coming in from outside nowadays. Lot of new battalions being formed, even in the Brigade. I presume you'll join the infantry. No point in going into the cavalry nowadays. All these machines. Might just as well be an engine driver and have done with it. There's a lot of damn fool talk about this being a mechanized war and an air war and a commercial war. All wars are infantry wars. Always have been.'

'Yes, it was infantry I was thinking of.'

'Quite right. I hear some of the line regiments are very short of officers. I don't imagine you want to go through the ranks, ha! ha! There's been a lot of nonsense about that lately. Not that it would do any harm to some of the young gentlemen I've seen about the place. But for a fellow of your age the thing to do is to join the Supplementary Reserve, put down the regiment you want to join – there are a number of line regiments who do very useful work in their way, and get the commanding officer to apply for you.'

'Exactly, sir, that's what I came to see you about. I was hoping that *you* –'

'That *I*. . . ?' Slowly to that slow mind there came the realization that Basil, this dissolute-looking young man who had so grossly upset his lunch interval the day before, this radical who had impugned the efficiency of the officer-type, was actually proposing to join the Bombardier Guards.

'I've always felt,' said Basil, 'that if I had to join the Foot Guards, I'd soonest join yours. You aren't as stuffy as the Grenadiers and you haven't got any of those bogus regional connections like the Scots and Irish and Welsh.'

Had there been no other cause of offence; had Basil come to him with the most prepossessing appearance, the most glittering sporting record, a manner in which deference to age was most perfectly allied with social equality, had he been lord of a thousand loyal tenants, had he been the nephew of the Colonel-in-Chief, the use by a civilian of such words as 'stuffy' and 'bogus' about the Brigade of Guards would have damned him utterly.

'So what I suggest,' Basil continued, 'is that I sign up for this Supplementary Reserve and put you down as my choice of regiment. Will that be O.K.?'

The Lieutenant-Colonel found his voice; it was not a voice of which he had full control; it might have been the voice of a man who had been suspended for a few seconds from a gibbet and then cut down. He fingered his collar as though, indeed, expecting to find the hangman's noose there. He said: 'That would *not* be O.K. We do not take our officers from the Supplementary Reserve.'

'Well, how *do* I join you?'

'I'm afraid I must have misled you in some way. I have no vacancy for you in the regiment. I'm looking for platoon commanders. As it is I've got six or seven ensigns of over thirty. Can you imagine yourself leading a platoon in action?'

'Well, as a matter of fact I can, but that's the last thing I want. In fact that's why I want to keep away from the line regiments. After all there is always a number of interesting staff jobs going for anyone in the Guards, isn't there? What I thought of doing was to sign up with you and then look round for something more interesting. I should be frightfully bored with regimental life, you know, but everyone tells me it's a great help to start in a decent regiment.'

The noose tightened about the Lieutenant-Colonel's throat. He could not speak. It was with a scarcely human croak and an eloquent gesture of the hand that he indicated that the interview was over.

In the office it quickly became known that he was in one of his bad moods again.

Basil went back to Angela.

'How did it go, darling?'

'Not well. Not well at all.'

'Oh dear, and you looked so particularly presentable.'

'Yes; it can't have been that. And I was tremendously polite. Said all the right things. I expect that old snake Jo Mainwaring has been making mischief again.'

7

'WHEN we say that Parsnip can't write in war time Europe, surely we mean that he can't write as he has written up till now? Mightn't it be better for him to stay here, even if it meant holding up production for a year or so, so that he can *develop*?'

'Oh, I don't think Parsnip and Pimpernell *can* develop. I mean an organ doesn't *develop*; it just goes on playing different pieces of music but remains the same. I feel Parsnip and Pimpernell have perfected themselves as an instrument.'

'Then suppose Parsnip were to develop and Pimpernell didn't. Or suppose they developed in different directions. What would happen then?'

'Yes, what would happen then?'

'Why does it take two to write a poem?' asked the red-headed girl.

'Now Julia, don't short-circuit the argument.'

'I should have thought poetry was a one-man job. Part-time work at that.'

'But Julia, you'll admit you don't know very much about poetry, dear.'

'That's exactly why I'm asking.'

'Don't pay any attention, Tom. She doesn't really want to know. She's only being tiresome.'

They were lunching at a restaurant in Charlotte Street; there were too many of them for the table; when you put out your hand for your glass and your neighbour at the same time put out his knife for the butter, he gave you a greasy cuff; too many for the menu; a single sheet of purple handwriting that was passed from hand to hand with indifference and indecision; too many for the waiter, who forgot their various orders; there were only six of them but it was too many for Ambrose. The talk was a series of assertions and interjections. Ambrose lived in and for conversation; he rejoiced in the whole intricate art of it – the timing and striking the proper juxtaposition of narrative and comment, the bursts of spontaneous parody, the allusion one would recognize and one would not, the changes of alliance, the betrayals, the diplomatic revolutions, the waxing and waning of dictatorships that could happen in an hour's session about a table. But could it happen? Was that, too, most exquisite and exacting of the arts, part of the buried world of Diaghilev?

For months, now, he had seen no one except Poppet Green and her friends, and now, since Angela Lyne's return, Basil had dropped out of the group as abruptly as he had entered it, leaving Ambrose strangely forlorn.

Why, he wondered, do real intellectuals always prefer the company of rakes to that of their fellows? Basil is a philistine and a crook; on occasions he can be a monumental bore; on occasions a grave embarrassment; he is a man for whom there will be no place in the coming workers' state; and yet, thought Ambrose, I hunger for his company. It is a curious thing, he thought, that every creed promises a paradise which will be absolutely uninhabitable for anyone of civilized taste. Nanny told me of a Heaven that was full of angels playing harps; the communists tell me of an earth full of leisured and contented factory hands. I don't see Basil getting past the gate of either. Religion is acceptable in its destructive phase; the desert monks carving up that humbug Hypatia; the anarchist gangs roasting the monks in Spain. Hellfire sermons in the chapels; soap-box orators screaming their envy of the rich. Hell is all right. The human mind is inspired enough when it comes to inventing horrors; it is when it tries to invent a Heaven that it shows itself cloddish. But Limbo is the place. In Limbo one has natural happiness without the beatific vision; no harps; no communal order; but wine and conversation and imperfect, various humanity. Limbo for the unbaptized, for the pious heathen, the sincere sceptic. Am I baptized into this modern world? At least I haven't taken a new name. All the rest of the left-wing writers have adopted plebeian monosyllables. Ambrose is irredeemably bourgeois. Parsnip often said so. Damn Parsnip, damn Pimpernell. Do these atrocious young people never discuss anything else?

They were disputing the bill now, and forgetting what he or she had eaten; passing the menu from hand to hand to verify the prices.

'When you've decided what it is, tell me.'

'Ambrose's bill is always the largest,' said the red-headed girl.

'Dear Julia, please don't tell me that I could have fed a worker's family for a week. I still feel definitely *peckish*, my dear. I am sure workers eat ever so much more.'

'D'you *know* the index figure for a family of four?'

'No,' said Ambrose wistfully, 'no, I don't know the index figure. Please don't tell me. It wouldn't surprise me in the least. I like to think of it as dramatically small.' (Why do I talk like this, nodding and fluttering my eyelids, as though with a repressed giggle; why can I not speak like a man? Mine is the brazen voice of Apuleius's ass, turning its own words to ridicule.)

The party left the restaurant and stood in an untidy group on the pavement, unable to make up their minds who was going with whom, in what direction, for what purpose. Ambrose bade them good-bye and hurried away, with his absurd, light step and his heavy heart. Two soldiers outside a public-house made rude noises as he passed. 'I'll tell your sergeant-major of you,' he said gaily, almost gallantly, and flounced down the street. I should like to be one of them, he thought. I should like to go with them and drink beer and make rude noises at passing aesthetes. What does world revolution hold in store for *me*? Will it make me any nearer them? Shall I walk differently, speak differently, be less bored with Poppet Green and her friends? Here is the war, offering a new deal for everyone; I alone bear the weight of my singularity.

He crossed Tottenham Court Road and Gower Street, walking without any particular object except to take the air. It was not until he was under its shadow and saw the vast bulk of London University insulting the autumnal sky, that he remembered that here was the Ministry of Information and that his publisher, Mr Geoffrey Bentley, was working there at the head of some newly-formed department. Ambrose decided to pay him a call.

It was far from easy to gain admission; only once in his life, when he had had an appointment in a cinema studio in the outer suburbs, had Ambrose met such formidable obstruction. All the secrets of all the services might have been hidden in that gross mass of masonry. Not until Mr Bentley had been summoned to the gate to identify him was Ambrose allowed to pass.

'We have to be very careful,' said Mr Bentley.

'Why?'

'Far too many people get in as it is. You've no conception how many. It adds terribly to our work.'

'What is your work, Geoffrey?'

'Well, mostly it consists of sending people who want to see me on to someone they don't want to see. I've never liked authors – except of course,' he added, 'my personal friends.

I'd no idea there were so many of them. I suppose, now I come to think of it, that explains why there are so many books. And I've never liked books – except, of course, books by personal friends.'

They rose in a lift and walked down a wide corridor, passing on the way Basil who was talking a foreign language which sounded like a series of expectorations to a sallow man in a tarboosh.

'That's *not* one of my personal friends,' said Mr Bentley bitterly.

'Does he work here?'

'I don't suppose so. No one works in the Near East department. They just lounge about talking.'

'The tradition of the bazaar.'

'The tradition of the Civil Service. This is my little room.'

They came to the door of what had once been a chemical laboratory, and entered. There was a white porcelain sink in the corner into which a tap dripped monotonously. In the centre of the oil-cloth floor stood a card table and two folding chairs. In his own office Mr Bentley sat under a ceiling painted by Angela Kauffmann, amid carefully chosen pieces of empire furniture. 'We have to rough it, you see,' he said. 'I brought those to make it look more human.'

'Those' were a pair of marble busts by Nollekens; they failed, in Ambrose's opinion, to add humanity to Mr Bentley's room.

'You don't like them? You remember them in Bedford Square.'

'I like them very much. I remember them well, but don't you think, dear Geoffrey, that here they are just a weeny bit macabre?'

'Yes,' said Mr Bentley sadly. 'Yes. I know what you mean. They're really here to annoy the civil servants.'

'Do they?'

'To a frenzy. Look at this.' He showed Ambrose a long typewritten memorandum which was headed *Furniture, Supplementary to Official Requirements, Undesirability of.* 'I sent back this.' He showed a still longer message headed *Art, Objets d', conducive to spiritual repose, Absence of in the quarters of advisory staff.* 'To-day I got this.' *Flowers, Framed Photographs and other minor ornaments, Massive marble and mahogany, Decorative features of, Distinction between.* 'Quite alliterative with rage, you see. There, for the moment, the matter rests, but as you see, it's uphill work to get anything done.'

'I suppose it would make no difference if you explained that Nollekens had inspired the greatest biography in the English language.'

'None, I should think.'

'What terrible people to work with. You are *brave*, Geoffrey. I couldn't do it.'

'But, bless my soul, Ambrose, isn't that what you came about?'

'No. I came to see you.'

'Yes, everyone comes to see me, but they all come hoping to be taken on in the Ministry. You'd better join now you're here.'

'No. No.'

'You might do worse, you know. We all abuse the old M. of I., but there are a number of quite human people here already, and we are gradually pushing more in every day. You might do much worse.'

'I don't want to do *anything*. I think this whole war's crazy.'

'You might write a book for us then. I'm getting out a very nice little series on "What We are Fighting For". I've signed up a retired admiral, a Church of England curate, an unemployed docker, a Negro solicitor from the Gold Coast, and a nose and throat specialist from Harley Street. The original idea was to have a symposium in one volume, but I've had to enlarge the idea a little. All our authors had such very different ideas it might have been a little confusing. We could fit you in very nicely. "I used to think war crazy." It's a new line.'

'But I *do* think war crazy *still*.'

'Yes,' said Mr Bentley, his momentary enthusiasm waning. 'I know what you mean.'

The door opened and a drab, precise little man entered. 'I beg your pardon,' he said coldly. 'I didn't expect to find *you* working.'

'This is Ambrose Silk. I expect you know his work.'

'No.'

'No? He is considering doing a book in our "Why We Are at War" series. This is Sir Philip Hesketh-Smithers, our departmental assistant director.'

'If you'll excuse me a minute, I came about a memorandum RQ/1082/B4. The director is very worried.'

'Was that *Documents, Confidential, destruction by fire of*?'

'No. No. Marble decorative features.'

'Massive marble and mahogany?'

'Yes. Mahogany has no application to your sub-department. That has reference to a *prie-dieu* in the religious department. The Church of England advisor has been hearing confessions there and the director is very concerned. No, it's these effigies.'

'You refer to my Nollekenses.'

'These great statues. They won't do, Bentley, you know, they really won't do.'

'Won't do for what?' said Mr Bentley bellicosely.

'They won't do for the departmental director. He says, very properly, that portraits of sentimental association ...'

'These are full of the tenderest association for me.'

'Of relatives ...'

'These are family portraits.'

'Really, Bentley. Surely that is George III?'

'A distant kinsman,' said Mr Bentley blandly, 'on my mother's side.'

'And Mrs Siddons?'

'A slightly closer kinswoman, on my father's side.'

'Oh,' said Sir Philip Hesketh-Smithers. 'Ah. I didn't realize ... I'll explain that to the director. But I'm sure,' he said suspiciously, 'that such a contingency was definitely excluded from the director's mind.'

'Flummoxed,' said Mr Bentley, as the door closed behind Sir Philip. 'Completely flummoxed. I'm glad you were there to see my little encounter. But you see what we have to contend with. And now to your affairs. I wonder where we can fit you in to our little household.'

'I don't want to be fitted in.'

'You would be a great asset. Perhaps the religious department. I don't think atheism is properly represented there.'

The head of Sir Philip Hesketh-Smithers appeared round the door. 'Could you tell me, please, *how* you are related to George III? Forgive my asking, but the director is bound to want to know.'

'The Duke of Clarence's natural daughter Henrietta married Gervase Wilbraham of Acton – at that time, I need not remind you, a rural district. His daughter Gertrude married my maternal grandfather who was, not that it matters, three times mayor of Chippenham. A man of substantial fortune, all, alas, now dissipated.... Flummoxed again, I think,' he added as the door closed.

'Was that true?'

'That my grandfather was mayor of Chippenham? Profoundly true.'

'About Henrietta?'

'It has always been believed in the family,' said Mr Bentley.

In another cell of that great hive Basil was explaining a plan for the annexation of Liberia. 'The German planters there outnumber the British by about fourteen to one. They're organized as a Nazi unit; they've been importing arms through Japan and they are simply waiting for the signal from Berlin to take over the government of the state. With Monrovia in enemy hands, with submarines based there, our West Coast trade route is cut. Then all the Germans have to do is to shut the Suez Canal, which they can do from Massawa whenever they like, and the Mediterranean is lost. Liberia is our one weak spot in West Africa. We've got to get in first. Don't you see?'

'Yes, yes, but I don't know why you come to me about it.'

'You'll have to handle all the preliminary propaganda there and the explanations in America afterwards.'

'But why *me*? This is the Near East Department. You ought to see Mr Pauling.'

'Mr Pauling sent me to you.'

'Did he? I wonder why. I'll ask him.' The unhappy official took up the telephone and after being successively connected with Films, the shadow cabinet of the Czecho-Slovaks and the A.R.P. section, said: 'Pauling. I have a man called Seal here. He says you sent him.'

'Yes.'

'Why?'

'Well, you sent me that frightful Turk this morning.'

'He was child's play to this.'

'Well, let it be a lesson to you not to send me any more Turks.'

'You wait and see what I send you . . . Yes,' turning to Basil, 'Pauling made a mistake. Your business is really his. It's a most interesting scheme. Wish I could do more for you. I'll tell you who, I think, would like to hear about it – Digby-Smith; he handles propaganda and subversive activities in enemy territory, and, as you say, Liberia is to all intents and purposes enemy territory.'

The door opened and there entered a beaming, bearded, hair-bunned figure in a long black robe; a gold cross swung from his neck; a brimless top-hat crowned his venerable head.

'I am the Archimandrite Antonios,' he said. 'I am coming in please?'

'Come in, Your Beatitude; please sit down.'

'I have been telling how I was expulsed from Sofia. They said I must be telling you.'

'You have been to our religious department?'

'I have been telling your office clergymen about my expulsing. The Bulgar peoples say it was for fornications, but it was for politics. They are not expulsing from Sofia for fornications unless there is politics too. So now I am the ally of the British peoples since the Bulgar peoples say it was for fornications.'

'Yes, yes, I quite understand, but that is not really the business of this department.'

'You are not dealing with the business of the Bulgar peoples?'

'Well, yes, but I think your case opens up a wider issue altogether. You must go and see Mr Pauling. I'll give you someone to show the way. He deals especially with cases like yours.'

'So? You have here a department of fornications?'

'Yes, you might call it that.'

'I find that good. In Sofia is not having any such department.'

His Beatitude was sent on his way. 'Now you want to see Digby-Smith, don't you?'

'Do I?'

'Yes, he'll be *most* interested in Liberia.'

Another messenger came; Basil was led away. In the corridor they were stopped by a small, scrubby man carrying a suitcase.

'Pardon me, can you put me right for the Near East?'

'There,' said Basil, 'in there. But you won't get much sense out of him.'

'Oh, he's bound to be interested in what I've got here. Everyone is. They're bombs. You could blow the roof off the whole of this building with what I got here,' said this lunatic. 'I've been carting 'em from room to room ever since the blinking war began and often I think it wouldn't be a bad plan if they did go off sudden.'

'Who sent you to the Near East?'

'Chap called Smith, Digby-Smith. Very interested in my bombs he was.'

'Have you been to Pauling, yet?'

'Pauling? Yes, I was with him yesterday. Very interested he was in my bombs. I tell you everyone is. It was him said I ought to show them to Digby-Smith.'

Mr Bentley talked at length about the difficulties and impossibilities of bureaucratic life. 'If it was not for the journalists and the civil servants,' he said, 'everything would be perfectly easy. They seem to think the whole Ministry exists for their convenience. Strictly, of course, I shouldn't have anything to do with the journalists – I deal with books here – but they always seem to shove them on to me when they get impatient. Not only journalists; there was a man here this morning with a suitcase full of bombs.'

'Geoffrey,' said Ambrose at length. 'Tell me, would you say I was pretty well known as a left wing writer?'

'Of course, my dear fellow, very well known.'

'As a *left* wing writer?'

'Of course, *very* left wing.'

'Well known, I mean, outside the left wing itself?'

'Yes, certainly. Why?'

'I was only wondering.'

They were now interrupted for some minutes by an American war correspondent who wanted Mr Bentley to verify the story of a Polish submarine which was said to have arrived at Scapa; to give him a pass to go there and see for himself; to provide him with a Polish interpreter; to explain why in hell that little runt Pappenhacker of the Hearst press had been told of this submarine and not himself.

'Oh dear,' said Mr Bentley. 'Why have they sent you to me?'

'It seems I'm registered with you and not with the press bureau.'

This proved to be true. As the author of *Nazi Destiny*, a work of popular history that had sold prodigiously on both sides of the Atlantic, this man had been entered as a 'man-of-letters' instead of as a journalist.

'You mustn't mind,' said Mr Bentley. 'In this country we think much more of men-of-letters than we do of journalists.'

'Does being a man-of-letters get me to Scapa?'

'Well, no.'

'Does it get me a Polish interpreter?'

'No.'

'To Hell with being a man-of-letters.'

'I'll get you transferred,' said Mr Bentley. 'The press bureau is the place for you.'

'There's a snooty young man at that bureau looks at me as if I was something the cat brought in,' complained the author of *Nazi Destiny*.

'He won't once you're registered with him. I wonder, since you're here, if you'd like to write a book for us.'

'No.'

'No? Well, I hope you get to Scapa all right . . . He won't, you know,' added Mr Bentley as the door closed. 'You may be absolutely confident that he'll never get there. Did you ever read his book? It was exceedingly silly. He said Hitler was secretly married to a Jewess. I don't know what he'd say if we let him go to Scapa.'

'What do you think he'll say if you don't?'

'Something very offensive, I've no doubt. But we shan't be responsible. At least, I wonder, shall we?'

'Geoffrey, when you say well known as a left wing writer, do you suppose that if the fascists got into power here, I should be on their black list?'

'Yes, certainly, my dear fellow.'

'They did frightful things to the Left Wing Intellectuals in Spain.'

'Yes.'

'And in Poland, now.'

'So the press department tell me.'

'I see.'

The Archimandrite dropped in for a few moments. He expressed great willingness to write a book about Axis intrigues in Sofia.

'You think you can help bring Bulgaria in on our side?' asked Mr Bentley.

'I am spitting in the face of the Bulgar peoples,' said His Beatitude.

'I believe he'd write a very good autobiography,' said Mr Bentley, when the prelate left them. 'In the days of peace I should have signed him up for one.'

'Geoffrey, you were serious when you said that I should be on the black list of Left Wing Intellectuals?'

'Quite serious. You're right at the top. You and Parsnip and Pimpernell.'

Ambrose winced at the mention of these two familiar names. '*They're* all right,' he said. '*They're* in the United States.'

Basil and Ambrose met as they left the Ministry. Together they loitered for a minute to watch a brisk little scene between the author of *Nazi Destiny* and the policeman on the gate; it appeared that in a fit of nervous irritation the American had torn up the slip of paper which had admitted him to the building; now they would not let him leave.

'I'm sorry for him in a way,' said Ambrose. 'It's not a place I'd care to spend the rest of the war in.'

'They wanted me to take a job there,' said Basil, lying.

'They wanted *me* to,' said Ambrose.

They walked together through the sombre streets of Bloomsbury. 'How's Poppet?' said Basil at length.

'She's cheered up wonderfully since you left. Painting away like a mowing machine.'

'I must look her up again sometime. I've been busy lately. Angela's back. Where are we going to?'

'I don't know. I've nowhere to go.'

'*I've* nowhere to go.'

An evening chill was beginning to breathe down the street.

'I nearly joined the Bombardier Guards a week or two ago,' said Basil.

'I once had a *great* friend who was a corporal in the Bombardiers.'

'We'd better go and see Sonia and Alastair.'

'I haven't been near them for years.'

'Come on.' Basil wanted someone to pay for the cab.

But when they reached the little house in Chester Street they found Sonia alone and packing. 'Alastair's gone off,' she said. 'He's joined the army – in the ranks. They said he was too old for a commission.'

'My dear, how very 1914.'

'I'm just off to join him. He's near Brookwood.'

'You'll be beautifully near the Necropolis,' said Ambrose. 'It's the most enjoyable place. Three public houses, my dear, inside the cemetery, right among the graves. I asked the barmaid if the funeral parties got very tipsy and she said, "No. It's when they come back to visit the graves. They seem to need something then." And did you know the Corps of Commissionaires have a special burial place. Perhaps if Alastair is a very good soldier they might make him an honorary member...' Ambrose chattered on. Sonia packed. Basil looked about for bottles. 'Nothing to drink.'

'All packed, darling. I'm sorry. We might go out somewhere.'

They went out later, when the packing was done, into the blackout to a bar. Other friends came to join them.

'No one seems interested in my scheme to annex Liberia.'

'Beasts.'

'No imagination. They won't take suggestions from outsiders. You know, Sonia, this war is developing into a kind of club enclosure on a racecourse. If you aren't wearing the right badge they won't let you in.'

'I think that's rather what Alastair felt.'

'It's going to be a long war. There's plenty of time. I shall wait until there's something amusing to do.'

'I don't believe it's going to be that kind of war.'

This is all that anyone talks about, thought Ambrose; jobs and the kind of war it is going to be. War in the air, war of attrition, tank war, war of nerves, war of propaganda, war of defence in depth, war of movement, people's war, total war, indivisible war, war infinite, war incomprehensible, war of essence without accidents or attributes, metaphysical war, war in time-space, war eternal... all war is nonsense, thought Ambrose. I don't care about their war. It's got nothing on me. But if, thought Ambrose, I was one of these people, if I were not a cosmopolitan, Jewish pansy, if I were not all that the Nazis mean when they talk about 'degenerates', if I were not a single, sane individual, if I were part of a herd, one of these people, normal and responsible for the welfare of my herd, Gawd strike me pink, thought Ambrose, I wouldn't sit around discussing what kind of war it was going to be. I'd make it my kind of war. I'd set about killing and stampeding the other herd as fast and as hard as I could. Lord love a duck, thought Ambrose, there wouldn't be any animals nosing about for suitable jobs in *my* herd.

'Bertie's hoping to help control petrol in the Shetland Isles.'

'Algernon's off to Syria on the most secret kind of mission.'

'Poor John hasn't got anything yet.'

Cor chase my Aunt Fanny round a mulberry bush, thought Ambrose, what a herd.

So the leaves fell and the blackout grew earlier and earlier, and autumn became winter.

CHAPTER 2
Winter

1

WINTER set in hard. Poland was defeated; east and west the prisoners rolled away to slavery. English infantry cut trees and dug trenches along the Belgian frontier. Parties of distinguished visitors went to the Maginot Line and returned, as though from a shrine, with souvenir-medals. Belisha was turned out; the radical papers began a clamour for his return and then suddenly shut up. Russia invaded Finland and the papers were full of tales of white-robed armies scouting through the forests. English soldiers on leave brought back reports of the skill and daring of Nazi patrols and of how much better the blackout was managed in Paris. A number of people were saying quietly and firmly that Chamberlain must go. The French said the English were not taking the war seriously, and the Ministry of Information said the French were taking it very seriously indeed. Sergeant instructors complained of the shortage of training stores. How could one teach the three rules of aiming without aiming discs?

The leaves fell in the avenue at Malfrey, and this year, where once there had been a dozen men to sweep them, there were now four and two boys. Freddy was engaged in what he called 'drawing in his horns a bit'. The Grinling Gibbons saloon and the drawing-rooms and galleries round it were shut up and shut off, carpets rolled, furniture sheeted, chandeliers bagged, windows shuttered and barred, hall and staircase stood empty and dark. Barbara lived in the little octagonal parlour which opened on the parterre; she moved the nursery over to the bedrooms next to hers; what had once been known as 'the bachelors' wing', in the Victorian days when bachelors were hardy fellows who could put up with collegiate and barrack simplicity, was given over to the evacuees. Freddy came over for the four good shoots which the estate provided; he made his guests stay out this year, one at the farm, three at the bailiff's house, two at the Sothill Arms. Now, at the end of the season, he had some of the regiment over to shoot off the cocks; bags were small and consisted mostly of hens.

When Freddy came on leave the central heating was lit; at other times an intense cold settled into the house; it was a system which had to be all or nothing; it would not warm Barbara's corner alone but had to circulate, ticking and guggling, through furlongs of piping, consuming cartloads of coke daily. 'Lucky we've got plenty of wood,' said Freddy; damp green logs were brought in from the park to smoke tepidly on the hearths. Barbara used to creep into the orangery to warm herself. 'Must keep the heat up there,' said Freddy. 'Got some very rare stuff in it. Man from Kew said some of the best in the country.' So Barbara had her writing table put there, and sat, absurdly, among tropical vegetation while outside, beyond the colonnade, the ground froze hard and the trees stood out white against the leaden sky.

Then, two days before Christmas, Freddy's regiment was moved to another part of the country. He had friends with a commodious house in the immediate neighbourhood, where he spent his week-ends, so the pipes were never heated and the chill in the house, instead of being a mere negation of warmth, became something positive and overwhelming. Soon after Christmas there was a great fall of snow and with the snow came Basil.

He came, as usual, unannounced. Barbara, embowered in palm and fern, looked up from her letter-writing to see him standing in the glass door. She ran to kiss him with a cry of delight. 'Darling, how very nice. Have you come to stay?'

'Yes, Mother said you were alone.'

'I don't know where we'll put you. Things are very odd here. You haven't brought anyone else, have you?' It was one of Freddy's chief complaints that Basil usually came not only uninvited but attended by undesirable friends.

'No, no one. There isn't anyone nowadays. I've come to write a book.'

'Oh, Basil. I am sorry. Is it as bad as that?'

There was much that needed no saying between brother and sister. For years now, whenever things were very bad with Basil, he had begun writing a book. It was as near surrender as he ever came and the fact that these books – two novels, a book of travel, a biography, a work of contemporary history – never got beyond the first ten thousand words was testimony to the resilience of his character.

'A book on strategy,' said Basil. 'I'm sick of trying to get ideas into the heads of the people in power. The only thing is to appeal over their heads to the thinking public. Chiefly, it is the case for the annexation of Liberia, but I shall touch on several other vital places as well. The difficulty will be to get it out in time to have any influence.'

'Mother said you were joining the Bombardier Guards.'

'Yes. Nothing came of it. They say they want younger men. It's a typical army paradox. They say we are too old now and that they will call us up in two years' time. I shall bring that out in my book. The only logical policy is to kill off the old first, while there's still some kick in them. I shan't deal only with strategy. I shall outline a general policy for the nation.'

'Well, it's very nice to see you, anyway. I've been lonely.'

'*I've* been lonely.'

'What's happened to everyone?'

'You mean Angela. She's gone home.'

'Home?'

'That house we used to call Cedric's Folly. It's hers really, of course. Cedric's gone back to the army. It's scarcely credible but apparently he was a dashing young subaltern once. So there was the house and the Lyne hooligan and the government moving in to make it a hospital, so Angela had to go back and see to things. It's full of beds and nurses and doctors waiting for air-raid victims and a woman in the village got appendicitis and she had to be taken forty miles to be operated on because she wasn't an air-raid victim and she died on the way. So Angela is carrying on a campaign about it and I should be surprised if she doesn't get something done. She seems to have made up her mind I ought to be killed. Mother's the same. It's funny. In the old days when from time to time there really were people gunning for me, no one cared a hoot. Now that I'm living in enforced safety and idleness, they seem to think it rather disgraceful.'

'No new girls?'

'There was one called Poppet Green. You wouldn't have liked her. I've been having a very dull time. Alastair is a private at Brookwood. I went down to see them. He and Sonia have got a horrible villa on a golf course where he goes whenever he's off duty. He says the worst thing about his training is the entertainments. They get detailed to go twice a week and the sergeant always picks on Alastair. He makes the same joke each time. "We'll send the playboy." Otherwise it's all very matey and soft, Alastair says. Peter has joined a very secret corps to go and fight in the Arctic. They had a long holiday doing winter sports in the Alps. I don't suppose you'd remember Ambrose Silk. He's starting a new magazine to keep culture alive.'

'Poor Basil. Well, I hope you don't have to write the book for long.' There was so much between brother and sister that did not need saying.

*

That evening Basil began his book; that is to say he lay on the rug before the column of smoke which rose from the grate of the octagonal parlour, and typed out a list of possible titles.

A Word to the Unwise.

Prolegomenon to Destruction.

Berlin or Cheltenham; the Choice for the General Staff.

Policy or Generalship; some questions put by a Civilian to vex the Professional Soldiers.

Policy or Professionalism.

The Gentle Art of Victory.

The Lost Art of Victory.

How to Win the War in Six Months; a simple lesson book for ambitious soldiers.

They all looked pretty good to him and looking at the list Basil was struck anew, as he had been constantly struck during the preceding four months, with surprise that anyone of his ability should be unemployed at a time like the present. It makes one despair of winning, he thought.

Barbara sat beside him reading. She heard him sigh and put out a sisterly hand to touch his hair. 'It's terribly cold,' she said. 'I wonder if it would be any good trying to black-out the orangery. Then we could sit there in the evenings.'

Suddenly there was a knock on the door and there entered a muffled, middle-aged woman; she wore fur gloves and carried an electric torch, dutifully dimmed with tissue paper; her nose was very red, her eyes were watering and she stamped snow off high rubber boots. It was Mrs Fremlin of the Hollies. Nothing but bad news would have brought her out on a night like this. 'I came straight in,' she said superfluously. 'Didn't want to stand waiting outside. Got some bad news. The Connollys are back.'

It was indeed bad news. In the few hours that he had been at Malfrey, Basil had heard a great deal about the Connollys.

'Oh God,' said Barbara. 'Where are they?'

'Here, outside in the lobby.'

Evacuation to Malfrey had followed much the same course as it had in other parts of the country and had not only kept Barbara, as billeting officer, constantly busy, but had transformed her, in four months, from one of the most popular women in the countryside into a figure of terror. When her car was seen approaching people fled through covered lines of retreat, through side doors and stable yards, into the snow, anywhere to avoid her persuasive, 'But surely you could manage *one* more. He's a boy this time and a very well-behaved little fellow,' for the urban authorities maintained a steady flow of refugees well in excess of the stream of returning malcontents. Few survived of the original party who had sat glumly on the village green on the first morning of war. Some had gone back immediately; others more reluctantly in response to ugly rumours of their husbands' goings on; one had turned out to be a fraud, who, herself childless, had kidnapped a baby from a waiting perambulator in order to secure her passage to safety, so impressed had she been by the propaganda of the local officials. It was mostly children now who assembled, less glumly, on the village green, and showed the agricultural community how another part of the world lived. They were tolerated now as one of the troubles of the time. Some had even endeared themselves to their hosts. But everyone, when evacuees were spoken of, implicitly excluded for all generalities the family of Connolly.

These had appeared as an act of God apparently without human agency; their names did not appear on any list; they carried no credentials; no one was responsible for them. They were found lurking under the seats of a carriage when the train was emptied on the evening of the first influx. They had been dragged out and stood on the platform where everyone denied knowledge of them, and since they could not be left there, they were included in the party that was being sent by bus to Malfrey village. From that moment they were on a list; they had been given official existence and their destiny was inextricably involved with that of Malfrey.

Nothing was ever discovered about the Connollys' parentage. When they could be threatened or cajoled into speaking of their antecedents they spoke, with distaste, of an 'Auntie'. To this woman, it seemed, the war had come as a God-sent release.

She had taken her dependants to the railway station, propelled them into the crowd of milling adolescence, and hastily covered her tracks by decamping from home. Enquiry by the police in the street where the Connollys professed to have lived produced no other information than that the woman had been there and was not there any longer. She owed a little for milk; otherwise she had left no memorial on that rather unimpressionable district.

There was Doris, ripely pubescent, aged by her own varied accounts anything from ten years to eighteen. An early and ingenious attempt to have her certified as an adult was frustrated by an inspecting doctor who put her at about fifteen. Doris had dark, black bobbed hair, a large mouth and dark pig's eyes. There was something of the Eskimo about her head, but her colouring was ruddy and her manner more vivacious than is common among that respectable race. Her figure was stocky, her bust prodigious, and her gait, derived from the cinematograph, was designed to be alluring.

Micky, her junior by the length of a rather stiff sentence for house-breaking, was of lighter build; a scrawny, scowling little boy; a child of few words and those, for the most part, foul.

Marlene was presumed to be a year younger. But for Micky's violent denials she might have been taken for his twin. She was the offspring of unusually prolonged coincident periods of liberty in the lives of her parents which the sociologist must deplore, for Marlene was simple. An appeal to have her certified imbecile was disallowed by the same inspecting doctor, who expressed an opinion that country life might work wonders with the child.

There the three had stood, on the eve of the war, in Malfrey Parish Hall, one leering, one lowering, and one drooling, as unprepossessing a family as could be found in the kingdom. Barbara took one look at them, looked again to see that her weary eyes were not playing tricks with her, and consigned them to the Mudges of Upper Lamstock, a tough farming family on a remote homestead.

Within a week Mr Mudge was at the Park, with the three children in the back of his milk truck. 'It's not for myself, Mrs Sothill; I'm out and about all day and in the evenings I'm sleepy, and being with animals so much I don't take on so. But it's my old woman. She *do* take on and she won't stand for it. She've locked herself in upstairs and she won't come down till they've gone, and when she do say that she means of it, Mrs Sothill. We're willing to do anything in reason to help the war, but these brats aren't to be borne and that's flat.'

'Oh dear, Mr Mudge, which of them is giving trouble?'

'Why it's all of 'em, m'am. There's the boy was the best of 'em at first though you can't understand what he do say, speaking as they do where he come from. Nasty, unfriendly ways he had but he didn't do much that you could call harm not till he'd seen me kill the goose. I took him out to watch to cheer him up like, and uncommon interested he was, and I thought I'll make a country lad of you yet. I gave him the head to play with and he seemed quite pleased. Then no sooner was I off down to the root field, then blessed if he didn't get hold of a knife and when I came back supper time there was six of my ducks dead and the old cat. Yes, mum, blessed if he hadn't had the head off of our old yellow cat. Then the little un, she's a dirty girl, begging your pardon, mum. It's not only her wetting the bed; she've wetted everywhere, chairs, floor and not only wetting, mum. Never seem to have been taught to be in a house where she comes from.'

'But doesn't the elder girl do anything to help?'

'If you ask me, mum, she's the worst of the lot. My old woman would stick it but for her, but it's that Doris makes her take on like she do. Soft about the men, she is, mum. Why she even comes making up to me and I'm getting on to be her grandfer. She won't leave our Willie alone not for a minute, and he's a bashful boy our Willie and he can't get on with the work, her always coming after him. So there it is, mum. I'm sorry not to oblige, but I've promised my old woman I won't come back with 'em and I dusn't go back on what I've said.'

Mr Mudge was the first of a succession of hosts. The longest that the Connollys stayed in any place was ten days; the shortest was an hour and a quarter. In six weeks they had become a legend far beyond the parish. When influential old men at the Turf in London put their heads together and said, 'The whole scheme has been a mistake. I was hearing last night some examples of the way some of the evacuees are behaving . . .' the chances were that the scandal originated with the Connollys. They were cited in the House of Commons; there were paragraphs about them in official reports.

Barbara tried separating them, but in their first night apart Doris climbed out of her window and was lost for two days, to be found in a barn eight miles away, stupefied with cider; she gave no coherent account of her adventure. On the same evening Micky bit the wife of the roadman on whom he was quartered, so that the district nurse had to be called in; while Marlene had a species of seizure which aroused unfulfilled hopes that she might be dead. Everyone agreed that the only place for the Connollys was 'an institution' and at last, just before Christmas, after formalities complicated by the obscurity of their origins, to an institution they were sent, and Malfrey settled back to entertain its guests with a Christmas tree and a conjurer, with an air of relief which could be sensed for miles around. It was as though the All Clear had sounded after a night of terror. And now the Connollys were back.

'What's happened, Mrs Fremlin? Surely the Home *can't* send them away.'

'It's been evacuated. All the children are being sent back to the places they came from. Malfrey was the only address they had for the Connollys, so here they are. The Welfare Woman brought them to the Parish Hall. I was there with the Guides so I said I'd bring them up to you.'

'They might have warned us.'

'I expect they thought that if we had time we should try and stop them coming.'

'How right they were. Have the Connollys been fed?'

'I think so. At any rate Marlene was terribly sick in the car.'

'I'm dying to see these Connollys,' said Basil.

'You shall,' said his sister grimly.

But they were not in the lobby where they had been left. Barbara rang the bell. 'Benson, you remember the Connolly children?'

'Vividly, madam.'

'They're back.'

'Here, madam?'

'Here. Somewhere in the house. You'd better institute a search.'

'Very good, madam. And when they are found, they will be going away immediately?'

'Not immediately. They'll have to stay here to-night. We'll find somewhere for them in the village to-morrow.'

Benson hesitated. 'It won't be easy, madam.'

'It won't be, Benson.'

He hesitated again; thought better of whatever he meant to say, and merely added: 'I will start the search, madam.'

'I know what that means,' said Barbara as the man left them. 'Benson is yellow.'

The Connollys were found at last and assembled. Doris had been in Barbara's bedroom trying out her make-up, Micky in the library tearing up a folio, Marlene grovelling under the pantry sink eating the remains of the dogs' dinners. When they were together again, in the lobby, Basil inspected them. Their appearance exceeded anything he had been led to expect. They were led away to the bachelors' wing and put together into a large bedroom.

'Shall we lock the door?'

'It would be no good. If they want to get out, they will.'

'Could I speak to you for a moment, madam?' said Benson.

When Barbara returned she said, 'Benson *is* yellow. He can't take it.'

'Wants to leave?'

'It's him or the Connollys, he says. I can't blame him. Freddy will never forgive me if I let him go.'

'Babs, you're blubbing.'

'Who wouldn't?' said Barbara, pulling out a handkerchief and weeping in earnest. 'I ask you, who wouldn't?'

'Don't be a chump,' said Basil, relapsing, as he often did with Barbara, into the language of the schoolroom. 'I'll fix it for you.'

'Swank. Chump yourself. Double chump.'

'Double chump with knobs on.'

'Darling Basil, it is nice to have you back. I do believe if anyone could fix it, you could.'

'Freddy couldn't, could he?'

'Freddy isn't here.'

'I'm cleverer than Freddy. Babs, say I'm cleverer than Freddy.'

'I'm cleverer than Freddy. Sucks to you.'

'Babs, say you love me more than Freddy.'

'You love me more than Freddy. Double sucks.'

'Say I, Barbara, love you, Basil, more than him, Freddy.'

'I won't. I don't... Beast, you're hurting.'

'Say it.'

'Basil, stop at once or I shall call Miss Penfold.'

They were back twenty years, in the schoolroom again. 'Miss Penfold, Miss Penfold, Basil's pulling my hair.'

They scuffled on the sofa. Suddenly a voice said, ''Ere, Mrs.' It was Doris. 'Mrs.'

Barbara stood up, panting and dishevelled. 'Well, Doris, what is it?'

'Marlene's queer again.'

'Oh dear. I'll come up. Run along.'

Doris looked languishingly at Basil. ''Aving a lark, eh?' she said. 'I like a lark.'

'Run along, Doris. You'll get cold.'

'I ain't cold. Pull my hair if you like, Mister.'

'I wouldn't dream of it,' said Basil.

'Dessay I shall. I dream a lot of funny things. Go on Mister, pull it. Hard. I don't mind.' She offered her bobbed head to Basil and then with a giggle ran out of the room.

'You see,' said Barbara. 'A problem child.'

When Marlene had been treated for her queerness, Barbara came back to say good night.

'I'll stay up a bit and work on this book.'

'All right, darling. Good night.' She bent over the back of the sofa and kissed the top of his head.

'Not blubbing any more?'

'No, not blubbing.'

He looked up at her and smiled. She smiled back; it was the same smile. They saw themselves, each in the other's eyes. There's no one like Basil, thought Barbara, seeing herself, no one like him, when he's nice.

2

NEXT morning Basil was called by Benson, who was the only manservant indoors since Freddy drew in his horns. (He had taken his valet with him to the yeomanry and supported him now, in a very much lower standard of comfort, at the King's expense.) Lying in bed and watching the man put out his clothes, Basil reflected that he still owed him a small sum of money from his last visit.

'Benson, what's this about your leaving?'

'I was cross last night, Mr Basil. I couldn't ever leave Malfrey and Mrs Sothill ought to know that. Not with the Captain away, too.'

'Mrs Sothill was very upset.'

'So was I, Mr Basil. You don't know what those Connollys are. They're not human.'

'We'll find a billet for them.'

'No one will take the Connollys in these parts. Not if they were given a hundred pounds.'

'I have an idea I owe you some money.'

'You do, Mr Basil. Twelve pound ten.'

'As much as that? Time I paid it back.'

'It is.'

'I will, Benson.'

'I hope so, sir, I'm sure.'

Basil went to his bath pondering. No one will take the Connollys in these parts. Not for a hundred pounds. Not for a hundred pounds.

*

Since the war began Barbara had taken to breakfasting downstairs in the mistaken belief that it caused less trouble. Instead of the wicker bed-table tray, a table had to be laid in the small dining-room, the fire had to be lit there two hours earlier, silver dishes had to be cleaned and the wicks trimmed under them. It was an innovation deplored by all.

Basil found her crouched over the fire with her cup of coffee; she turned her curly black head and smiled; both of them had the same devastating combination of dark hair and clear blue eyes. Narcissus greeted Narcissus from the watery depths as Basil kissed her.

'Spooney,' she said.

'I've squared Benson for you.'

'Darling, how clever of you.'

'I had to give the old boy a fiver.'

'Liar.'

'All right, don't believe me then.'

'I don't, knowing Benson and knowing you. I remember last time you stayed here I had to pay him over ten pounds that you'd borrowed.'

'You paid him?'

'Yes. I was afraid he'd ask Freddy.'

'The old double-crosser. Anyway he's staying.'

'Yes; thinking it over I knew he would. I don't know why I took it so hard last night. I think it was the shock of seeing the Connollys.'

'We must get them settled to-day.'

'It's hopeless. No one will take them.'

'You've got powers of coercion.'

'Yes, but I can't possibly use them.'

'*I* can,' said Basil. 'I shall enjoy it.'

After breakfast they moved from the little dining-room to the little parlour. The corridor, though it was one of the by-ways of the house, had a sumptuous cornice and a high, covered ceiling; the door cases were enriched with classic pediments in whose broken entablature stood busts of philosophers and composers. Other busts stood at regular intervals on marble pedestals. Everything in Malfrey was splendid and harmonious; everything except Doris who, that morning, lurked in their path rubbing herself on a pilaster like a cow on a stump.

'Hallo,' she said.

'Hallo, Doris. Where are Micky and Marlene?'

'Outside. They're all right. They've found the snow man the others made and they're mucking him up.'

'Run along and join them.'

'I want to stay here with you – and *him*.'

'I bet you do,' said Basil. 'No such luck. I'm going to find you a nice billet miles and miles away.'

'I want to stay with you.'

'You go and help muck up the snow man.'

'That's a kid's game. I'm not a kid. Mister, why wouldn't you pull my hair last night? Was it because you thought I had nits? I haven't any more. The nurse combed them all out at the institution and put oil on. That's why it's a bit greasy.'

'I don't pull girls' hair.'

'You do. I saw you. You pulled *hers*... he's your boy, isn't he?' she said, turning to Barbara.

'He's my brother, Doris.'

'Ah,' she said, her pig eyes dark with the wisdom of the slums, 'but you fancy him, don't you? I saw.'

'She really is an atrocious child,' said Barbara.

3

BASIL set about the problem of finding a home for the Connollys with zeal and method. He settled himself at a table with an ordnance map, the local newspaper and the little red leather-covered address book which had been one of old Mrs Sothill's legacies to Barbara; in this book were registered all her more well-to-do neighbours for a radius of twenty miles, the majority of whom were marked with the initials G.P.O. which stood for Garden Party Only. Barbara had done her best to keep this invaluable work of reference up to date, and had from time to time crossed out those who had died or left the district and added the names of newcomers.

Presently Basil said, 'What about the Harknesses of Old Mill House, North Grappling?'

'Middle-aged people. He retired from some sort of job abroad. I think she's musical. Why?'

'They're advertising for boarders.' He pushed the paper across to her, where she read in the *Accommodation* column: *Paying Guests accepted in lovely modernized fifteenth-century mill. Ideal surroundings for elderly or artistic people wishing to avoid war worries. All home produce. Secluded old-world gardens.* 6 *gns weekly. Highest references given and expected. Harkness, Old Mill House, North Grappling.*

'How about that for the Connollys?'

'Basil, you can't.'

'Can't I just? I'll get to work on them at once. Do they allow you extra petrol for your billeting work?'

'Yes, but . . .'

'That's grand. I'll take the Connollys over there this morning. D'you know, this is the first piece of serious war work I've done so far?'

Normally, whenever the car left the garage there was a stampede of evacuees to the running boards crying, 'Give us a ride.' This morning, however, seeing the three forbidding Connollys in the back seat, the other children fell back silently. They were not allowed by their mothers to play with the Connollys.

'Mister, why can't I sit in front with you?'

'You've got to keep the other two in order.'

'They'll be good.'

'That's what you think.'

'They'll be good if I tell them, Mister.'

'Then why aren't they?'

''Cos I tell 'em to be bad. In fun you know. Where are we going?'

'I'm finding a new home for you, Doris.'

'Away from you?'

'Far away from me.'

'Mister, listen. Micky ain't bad really nor Marlene isn't silly. Are you, Marlene?'

'Not very silly,' said Marlene.

'She can be clean if she wants to be, if I tell her. See here, Mister, play fair. You let us stay with you and I'll see the kids behave themselves.'

'And what about you, Doris?'

'I don't have to behave. I'm not a kid. Is it on?'

'It is not.'

'You going to take us away?'

'You bet I am.'

'Then just you wait and see what we give them where we're going.'

'I shan't wait and see,' said Basil, 'but I've no doubt I shall hear about it in good time.'

North Grappling was ten miles distant, a stone-built village of uneven stone tile roofs none of which was less than a century old. It lay off the main road in a fold of the hills; a stream ran through it following the line of its single street and crossing it under two old stone bridges. At the upper end of the street stood the church, which declared by its size and rich decoration that in the centuries since it was built, while the rest of the world was growing, North Grappling had shrunk; at the lower end, below the second bridge, stood Old Mill House. It was just such a home of ancient peace as a man might dream of who was forced to earn his living under a fiercer sky. Mr Harkness had in fact dreamed of it, year in, year out, as he toiled in his office at Singapore, or reclined after work on the club veranda, surrounded by gross vegetation and rude colours. He bought it from his father's legacy while on leave, when he was still a young man, meaning to retire there when the time came, and his years of waiting had been haunted by only one fear; that he would return to find the place 'developed', new red roofs among the grey and a tarmac road down the uneven street. But modernity spared North Grappling; he returned to find the place just as he had first come upon it, on a walking tour, late in the evening with the stones still warm from the afternoon sun and the scent of the gillyflowers sweet and fresh on the breeze.

This morning, half lost in snow, the stones which in summer seemed grey were a golden brown, and the pleached limes, which in their leaf hid the low front, now revealed the mullions and dripstones, the sundial above the long, centre window, and the stone hood of the door carved in the shape of a scallop shell. Basil stopped the car by the bridge.

'Jesus,' said Doris. 'You aren't going to leave us here.'

'Sit tight,' said Basil. 'You'll know soon enough.'

He threw a rug over the radiator of the car, opened the little iron gate and walked up the flagged path, grimly, a figure of doom. The low, winter sun cast his shadow before him, ominously, against the door which Mr Harkness had had painted apple green. The gnarled trunk of a wistaria rose from beside the door-jamb and twisted its naked length between the lines of the windows. Basil glanced once over his shoulder to see that his young passengers were invisible and then put his hand to the iron bell. He heard it ring melodiously not far away, and presently the door was opened by a maid dressed in apple green, with an apron of sprigged muslin and a starched white cap that was in effect part Dutch, part conventual, and wholly ludicrous. This figure of fancy led Basil up a step, down a step and into a living room, where he was left long enough to observe the decorations. The floor was covered in coarse rush matting and in places by bright Balkan rugs. On the walls were Thornton's flower prints (with the exception of his masterpiece, *The Night-Flowering Cereus*), samplers and old maps. The most prominent objects of furniture were a grand piano and a harp. There were also some tables and chairs of raw-looking beech. From an open hearth peat smoke billowed periodically into the room, causing Basil's eyes to water. It was just such a room as Basil had imagined from the advertisement and Mr and Mrs Harkness were just such a couple. Mrs Harkness wore a hand-woven woollen garment, her eyes were large and poetic, her nose was long and red with the frost, her hair nondescript in colour and haphazard in arrangement. Her husband had done all that a man can to disguise the effects of twenty years of club and bungalow life in the Far East. He had grown a little pointed beard; he wore a homespun suit of knickerbockers in the style of the pioneers of bicycling; he wore a cameo ring round his loose silk tie; yet there was something in his bearing which still suggested the dapper figure in white ducks who had stood his round of pink gins, evening after evening, to other dapper white figures, and had dined twice a year at Government House.

They entered from the garden door. Basil half expected Mr Harkness to say 'take a pew', and clap his hands for the gin. Instead they stood looking at him with enquiry and some slight distaste.

'My name is Seal. I came about your advertisement in the *Courier*.'

'Our advertisement. Ah yes,' said Mr Harkness vaguely. 'It was just an idea we had. We felt a little ashamed here, with so much space and beauty; the place is a little large for our requirements these days. We did think that perhaps if we heard of a few people like ourselves – the same simple tastes – we might, er, join forces as it were during the present difficult times. As a matter of fact we have one newcomer with us already. I don't think we *really* want to take anyone else, do we, Agnes?'

'It was just an idle thought,' said Mrs Harkness. 'A green thought in a green place.'

'This is not a Guest House, you know. We take in paying guests. Quite a different thing.'

Basil understood their difficulties with a keenness of perception that was rare to him. 'It's not for myself that I was enquiring,' he said.

'Ah, that's different. I daresay we might take in one or two more if they were, if they were *really*. . . '

Mrs Harkness helped him out. 'If we were sure they were the kind of people who would be happy here.'

'Exactly. It is essentially a *happy* house.'

It was like his housemaster at school. 'We are essentially a keen House, Seal. We may not win many cups but at least we try.'

'I can see it is,' he said gallantly.

'I expect you'd like to look round. It looks quite a little place from the road, but is surprisingly large, really, when you come to count up the rooms.'

A hundred years ago the pastures round North Grappling had all been corn-growing land and the mill had served a wide area. Long before the Harknesses' time it had fallen into disuse and, in the 'eighties, had been turned into a dwelling house by a disciple of William Morris. The stream had been diverted, the old mill pool drained and levelled and made into a sunken garden. The rooms that had held the grindstones and machinery, and the long lofts where the grain had been stored, had been tactfully floored and plastered and partitioned. Mrs Harkness pointed out all the features with maternal pride.

'Are your friends who were thinking of coming here artistic people?'

'No, I don't think you could call them that.'

'They don't write?'

'No, I don't think so.'

'I've always thought this would be an ideal place for someone who wanted to write. May I ask, what *are* your friends?'

'Well, I suppose you might call them evacuees.'

Mr and Mrs Harkness laughed pleasantly at the little joke. 'Townsfolk in search of sanctuary, eh?'

'Exactly.'

'Well, they will find it here, eh, Agnes?'

They were back in the living room. Mrs Harkness laid her hand on the gilded neck of the harp and looked out across the sunken garden with a dreamy look in her large grey eyes. Thus she had looked out across the Malaya golf course, dreaming of home.

'I like to think of this beautiful old house still being of use in the world. After all it was built for *use.* Hundreds of years ago it gave bread to the people. Then with the change of the times it was left forlorn and derelict. Then it became a home, but it was still out of the world, shut off from the life of the people. And now at last it comes into its own again. Fulfilling a *need.* You may think me fanciful,' she said, remote and whimsical, 'but in the last few weeks I feel sometimes I can see the old house smiling to itself and hear the old timbers whispering, "They thought we were no use. They thought we were old stick-in-the-muds. But they can't get on without us, all these busy go-ahead people. They come back to us when they're in trouble." '

'Agnes was always a poet,' said Mr Harkness. 'I have had to be the practical housewife. You saw our terms in the advertisement?'

'Yes.'

'They may have seemed to you a little heavy, but you must understand that our guests live exactly as we do ourselves. We live simply but we like our comfort. Fires,' he said, backing slightly from the belch of aromatic smoke which issued into the room as he spoke, 'the garden,' he said, indicating the frozen and buried enclosure outside the windows. 'In the summer we take our meals under the old mulberry tree. Music. Every week we have chamber music. There are certain *imponderabilia* at the Old Mill which, to be crude, have their market value. I *don't* think,' he said coyly, 'I *don't* think that in the circumstances' – and the circumstances Basil felt sure were meant to include a good fat slice of Mrs Harkness' poetic imagination – 'six guineas is too much to ask.'

The moment for which Basil had been waiting was come. This was the time for the grenade he had been nursing ever since he opened the little, wrought-iron gate and put his hand to the wrought-iron bell-pull. 'We pay eight shillings and sixpence a week,' he said. That was the safety pin; the lever flew up, the spring struck home; within the serrated metal shell the primer spat and, invisibly, flame crept up the finger's-length of fuse. Count seven slowly, then throw. One, two, three, four...

'Eight shillings and sixpence?' said Mr Harkness. 'I'm afraid there's been some misunderstanding.'

Five, six, *seven*. Here it comes. Bang! 'Perhaps I should have told you at once. I am the billeting officer. I've three children for you in the car outside.'

It was magnificent. It was war. Basil was something of a specialist in shocks. He could not recall a better.

After the first tremendous silence there were three stages of Harkness reaction; the indignant appeal to reason and justice, then the humble appeal to mercy, then the frigid and dignified acceptance of the inevitable.

First:

'I shall telephone to Mrs Sothill.... I shall go and see the County authorities.... I shall write to the Board of Education and the Lord Lieutenant. This is perfectly ridiculous; there must be a hundred cottagers who would be *glad* to take these children in.'

'Not *these* children,' said Basil. 'Besides, you know, this is a war for democracy. It looks awfully bad if the rich seem to be shirking their responsibilities.'

'*Rich*. It's only because we find it so hard to make both ends meet that we take paying guests at all.'

'Besides this is a *most* unsuitable place for children. They might fall into the stream and be drowned. There's no school within four miles...'

Secondly:

'We're not as young as we were. After living so long in the East the English winter is very difficult. Any additional burden...'

'Mr Seal, you've seen for yourself this lovely old house and the kind of life we live here. Don't you *feel* that there is something *different* here, something precious that could so easily be killed.'

'It's just this kind of influence these children need,' said Basil cheerfully. 'They're rather short on culture at the moment.'

Thirdly:

A hostility as cold as the winter hillside above the village. Basil led the Connollys up the flagged path, through the apple-green door, into the passage which smelled of peat smoke and pot-pourri. 'I'm afraid they haven't any luggage,' he said. 'This is Doris, this is Micky, and that – that is little Marlene. I expect after a day or two you'll wonder how you ever got on without them. We meet that over and over again in our work; people who are a little shy of children to begin with, and soon want to adopt them permanently. Good-bye, kids, have a good time. Good-bye, Mrs Harkness. We shall drop in from time to time just to see that everything is all right.'

And Basil drove back through the naked lanes with a deep interior warmth which defied the gathering blizzard.

That night there was an enormous fall of snow, telephone wires were down, the lane to North Grappling became impassable, and for eight days the Old Mill was cut off physically, as for so long it had been cut in spirit, from all contact with the modern world.

4

BARBARA and Basil sat in the orangery after luncheon. The smoke from Basil's cigar hung on the humid air, a blue line of cloud, motionless, breast high between the paved floor and the exotic foliage overhead. He was reading aloud to his sister.

'So much for the supply services,' he said, laying down the last sheet of manuscript. The book had prospered during the past week.

Barbara awoke, so gently that she might never have been asleep. 'Very good,' she said. 'First class.'

'It ought to wake them up,' said Basil.

'It ought,' said Barbara, on whom the work had so different an effect. Then she added irrelevantly, 'I hear they've dug the way through to North Grappling this morning.'

'There was providence in that fall of snow. It's let the Connollys and the Harknesses get properly to grips. Otherwise, I feel, one or other side might have despaired.'

'I dare say we shall hear something of the Harknesses shortly.'

And immediately, as though they were on the stage, Benson came to the door and announced that Mr Harkness was in the little parlour.

'I *must* see him,' said Barbara.

'Certainly not,' said Basil. 'This is my war effort,' and followed Benson into the house.

He had expected some change in Mr Harkness, but not so marked a change as he now saw. The man was barely recognizable. It was as though the crust of tropical respectability that had survived below the home-spun and tie-ring surface had been crushed to powder; the man was abject. The clothes were the same. It must be imagination which gave that trim beard a raffish look, imagination fired by the haunted look in the man's eyes.

Basil on his travels had once visited a prison in Transjordan where an ingenious system of punishment had been devised. The institution served the double purpose of penitentiary and lunatic asylum. One of the madmen was a tough old Arab of peculiar ferocity who could be subdued by one thing only – the steady gaze of the human eye. Bat an eyelid, and he was at you. Refractory convicts were taken to this man's cell and shut in with him for periods of anything up to forty-eight hours according to the gravity of their offences. Day and night the madman lurked in his corner with his eyes fixed, fascinated, on those of the delinquent. The heat of midday was his best opportunity; then even the wariest convict sometimes allowed his weary eyelids to droop and in that moment he was across the floor, tooth and nail, in a savage attack. Basil had seen a gigantic felon led out after a two days' session. There was something in Mr Harkness' eyes that brought the scene back vividly to him.

'I am afraid my sister's away,' said Basil.

Whatever hope had ever been in Mr Harkness' breast died when he saw his old enemy. 'You are Mrs Sothill's brother?'

'Yes; we are thought rather alike. I'm helping her here now that my brother-in-law's away. Is there anything I can do?'

'No,' he said brokenly. 'No. It doesn't matter. I'd hoped to see Mrs Sothill. When will she be back?'

'You can never tell,' said Basil. 'Most irresponsible in some ways. Goes off for months at a time. But this time she has me to watch out for her. Was it about your evacuees you wanted to see her? She was *very* glad to hear they had been happily settled. It meant she could go away with a clear conscience. That particular family had been something of an anxiety, if you understand me.'

Mr Harkness sat down uninvited. He sat on a gilt chair in that bright little room, like a figure of death. He seemed disposed neither to speak nor move.

'Mrs Harkness well?' said Basil affably.

'Prostrate.'

'And your paying guest?'

'She left this morning – as soon as the road was cleared. Our two maids went with her.'

'I hope Doris is making herself useful about the house.'

At the mention of that name Mr Harkness broke. He came clean. 'Mr Seal, I can't stand it. We neither of us can. We've come to the end. You must take those children away.'

'You surely wouldn't suggest sending them back to Birmingham to be bombed?'

This was an argument which Barbara often employed with good effect. As soon as Basil spoke he realized it was a false step. Suffering had purged Mr Harkness of all hypocrisy. For the first time something like a smile twisted his lips.

'There is nothing would delight me more,' he said.

'Tut, tut. You do yourself an injustice. Anyway it is against the law. I should like to help you. What can you suggest?'

'I thought of giving them weed-killer,' said Mr Harkness wistfully.

'Yes,' said Basil, 'that would be one way. Do you think Marlene could keep it down?'

'Or hanging.'

'Come, come, Mr Harkness, this is mere wishful thinking. We must be more practical.'

'Everything I've thought of has had Death in it; ours or theirs.'

'I'm sure there must be a way,' said Basil, and then, delicately, watching Mr Harkness while he spoke for any expression of distrust or resentment, he outlined a scheme which had come to him, vaguely, when he first saw the Connollys, and had grown more precise during the past week. 'The difficulty about billeting on the poor,' he said, 'is that the allowance barely covers what the children eat. Of course, where they are nice, affectionate children people are often glad enough to have them. But one wouldn't call the Connollys nice or affectionate' – Mr Harkness groaned. 'They are destructive, too. Well, I needn't tell you that. The fact is that it would be inflicting a very considerable hardship – a *financial* hardship – to put them in a cottage. Now if the meagre allowance paid by the Government were *supplemented* – do you follow me?'

'You mean I might *pay* someone to take them. Of course I will, anything – at least almost anything. How much shall I offer? How shall I set about it?'

'Leave it to me,' said Basil, suddenly dropping his urbane manner. 'What's it worth to you to have those children moved?'

Mr Harkness hesitated; with the quickening of hope came a stir of self-possession. One does not work in the East without acquiring a nose for a deal. 'I should think a pound a week would make all the difference to a poor family,' he said.

'How about a lump sum? People – poor people that is – will often be dazzled by the offer of a lump sum who wouldn't consider an allowance.'

'Twenty-five pounds.'

'Come, Mr Harkness, that's what you proposed paying over six months. The war is going to last longer than that.'

'Thirty. I can't go higher than thirty.'

He was not a rich man, Basil reflected; very likely thirty was all he could afford. 'I dare say I could find someone to take them for that,' he said. 'Of course, you realize that this is all highly irregular.'

'Oh, I realize that.' Did he? Basil wondered; perhaps he did. 'Will you fetch those children to-day?'

'To-day?'

'Without fail.' Mr Harkness seemed to be dictating terms now. 'The cheque will be waiting for you. I will make it out to bearer.'

*

'What a long time you've been,' said Barbara. 'Have you pacified him?'

'I've got to find a new home for the Connollys.'

'Basil, you've let him off!'

'He was so pathetic. I softened.'

'Basil, how very unlike you.'

'I must get to work with that address book again. We shall have to have the Connollys here for the night. I'll find them a new home in the morning.'

He drove over to North Grappling in the twilight. On either side of the lane the new-dug snow was heaped high, leaving a narrow, passable track. The three Connollys were standing outside the apple-green door waiting for him.

'The man with the beard said to give you this,' said Doris.

It was an envelope containing a cheque; nothing more. Neither Harkness appeared to see them off.

'Mister, am I glad to see you again?' said Doris.

'Jump in,' said Basil.

'May I come in front with you?'

'Yes, jump in.'

'Really? No kidding?'

'Come on, it's cold.' Doris got in beside Basil. 'You're here on sufferance.'

'What does that mean?'

'You can sit here as long as you behave yourself, and as long as Micky and Marlene do too. Understand?'

'Hear that, you brats?' said Doris with sudden authority. 'Behave, or I'll tan yer arses for yer. They'll be all right, Mister, if I tell 'em.'

They were all right.

'Doris, I think it's a very good game of yours making the kids be a nuisance, but we're going to play it my way in future. When you come to the house where I live you're to behave, always. See? I may take you to other houses from time to time. There you can usually be as bad as you like, but not until I give the word. See?'

'O.K. partner. Give us a cig.'

'I'm beginning to like you, Doris.'

'*I love you,*' said Doris with excruciating warmth, leaning back and blowing a cloud of smoke over the solemn children in the back. 'I love you more than anyone I ever seen.'

'Their week with the Harknesses seems to have had an extraordinary effect on the children,' said Barbara after dinner that night. 'I can't understand it.'

'Mr Harkness said there were *imponderabilia* at Mill House. Perhaps it's that.'

'Basil, you're up to something. I wish I knew what it was.'

Basil turned on her his innocent blue eyes, as blue as hers and as innocent; they held no hint of mischief. 'Just war work, Babs,' he said.

'Slimy snake.'

'I'm not.'

'Crawly spider.' They were back in the schoolroom, in the world where once they had played pirates. 'Artful monkey,' said Barbara, very fondly.

5

COMPANIES paraded at a quarter past eight; immediately after inspection men were fallen out for the company commander's orderly room; that gave time to sift out the genuine requests from the spurious, deal with minor offences, have the charge sheets made out properly and the names entered in the guard report of serious defaulters for the C.O.

'Private Tatton charged with losing by neglect one respirator, anti-gas, value 18*s.* 6*d.*'

Private Tatton fell into a rambling account of having left his respirator in the NAAFI and going back for it ten minutes later, having found it gone.

'Case remanded for the commanding officer.' Captain Mayfield could not give a punishment involving loss of pay.

'Case remanded for the commanding officer. About turn. As you were. I didn't say anything about saluting. About turn. Quick march.'

Captain Mayfield turned to the IN basket on his table.

'O.C.T.U. candidates,' said the company sergeant-major.

'Who have we got? The adjutant doesn't take nil returns.'

'Well, sir, there's Brodie.'

Brodie was a weedy solicitor who had appeared with the last draft.

'Really, sergeant-major, I can't see Brodie making much of an officer.'

'He's not much good in the company, sir, and he's a man of very superior education.'

'Well, put him down for one. What about Sergeant Harris?'

'Not suitable, sir.'

'He's a man of excellent character, fine disciplinarian, knows his stuff backwards, the men will follow him anywhere.'

'Yessir.'

'Well, what have you got against him?'

'Nothing against him, sir. But we can't get on without Sergeant Harris in the company football.'

'No. Well, who do you suggest?'

'There's our baronet, sir.' The sergeant-major said this with a smile. Alastair's position in the ranks was a slight embarrassment to Captain Mayfield but it was a good joke to the sergeant-major.

'Trumpington? All right, I'll see him and Brodie right away.'

The orderly brought them. The sergeant-major marched them in singly. 'Quick march. Halt. Salute. Brodie, sir.'

'Brodie. They want the names of two men from this company as O.C.T.U. candidates. I'm putting your name in. Of course the C.O. makes the decision. I don't say you *will* go to an O.C.T.U. I take it you would have no objection if the C.O. approves.'

'None, sir, if you really think I should make a good officer.'

'I don't suppose you'll make a *good* officer. They're very rare. But I dare say you'll make an officer of some kind.'

'Thank you, sir.'

'And as long as you're in my company you won't come into my office with a fountain pen sticking out of your pocket.'

'Sorry, sir.'

'Not so much talk,' said the sergeant-major.

'All right, that's all, sergeant-major.'

'About turn. Quick march. As you were. Swing the right arm forward as you step out.'

'I believe we'll have to give him a couple of stripes before we can get rid of him. I'll see the adjutant about that.'

Alastair was marched in. He had changed little since he joined the army. Perhaps there was a slight shifting of bulk from waist line to chest, but it was barely perceptible under the loose battle-dress.

Captain Mayfield addressed him in precisely the same words as he had used to Brodie.

'Yes, sir.'

'You don't want to take a commission?'

'No, sir.'

'That's very unusual, Trumpington. Any particular reason?'

'I believe a lot of people felt like that in the last war.'

'So I've heard. And a very wasteful business it was. Well if you won't, I can't make you. Afraid of responsibility, eh?'

Alastair made no answer. Captain Mayfield nodded and the sergeant-major marched him out.

'What d'you make of that?' asked Captain Mayfield.

'I've known men who think it's *safer* to stay in the ranks.'

'Shouldn't think that's the case with Trumpington. He's a volunteer, over age to have been called up.'

'Very rum, sir.'

'Very rum, sergeant-major.'

Alastair took his time about returning to his platoon. At this time of the morning they were doing P.T. It was the one part of the routine he really hated. He lurked behind the cookhouse until his watch told him that they would have finished. When he reported back the platoon were putting on their jackets, panting and sticky. He fell in and marched with them to the dining hut, where it was stuffy and fairly warm, to hear a lecture on hygiene from the medical officer. It dealt with the danger of flies; the medical officer described with appalling detail the journey of the fly from the latrine to the sugar basin; how its hairy feet carried the germs of dysentery; how it softened its food with contaminated saliva before it ate; how it excreted while it fed. This lecture always went down well. 'Of course,' he added rather lamely, 'this may not seem very important at the moment,' snow lay heavy on every side of them, 'but if we go to the East...'

When the lecture was finished the company fell out for twenty minutes; they smoked and ate chocolate and exchanged gossip, qualifying every noun, verb or adjective with the single, unvarying obscenity which punctuated all their speech like a hiccup; they stamped their feet and chafed their hands.

'What did the — company commander want?'

'He wanted to send me to a — O.C.T.U.,' said Alastair.

'Well some — are — lucky. When are you off?'

'I'm staying here.'

'Don't you want to be a — officer?'

'Not — likely,' said Alastair.

When people asked Alastair, as they quite often did, why he did not put in for a commission, he sometimes said, 'Snobbery. I don't want to meet the officers on social terms'; sometimes he said, 'Laziness. They work too hard in wartime'; sometimes he said, 'The whole thing's so crazy one might as well go the whole hog.' To Sonia he said, 'We've had a pretty easy life up to now. It's probably quite good for one to have a change sometimes.' That was the nearest he ever came to expressing the nebulous satisfaction which lay at the back of his mind. Sonia understood it, but left it undefined. Once, much later, she said to Basil, 'I believe I know what Alastair felt all that first winter of the war. It sounds awfully unlike him, but he was a much odder character than anyone knew. You remember that man who used to dress as an Arab and then went into the air force as a private because he thought the British Government had let the Arabs down. I forget his name but there were lots of books about him. Well, I believe Alastair felt like that. You see he'd never done anything for the country and though we were always broke we had lots of money really and lots of fun. I believe he thought that perhaps if we hadn't had so much fun perhaps there wouldn't have been any war. Though how he could blame himself for Hitler I never quite saw.... At least I do now in a way,' she added. 'He went into the ranks as a kind of penance or whatever it's called that religious people are always supposed to do.'

It was a penance whose austerities, such as they were, admitted of relaxation. After the stand-easy they fell in for platoon training. Alastair's platoon commander was away that morning. He was sitting on a Court of Enquiry. For three hours he and two other officers heard evidence, and recorded it at length, on the loss of a swill tub from H.Q. lines. At length it was clear either that there was a conspiracy of perjury on the part of all the witnesses, or that the tub had disappeared by some supernatural means independent of human agency; the Court therefore entered a verdict that no negligence was attributable to anyone in the matter and recommended that the loss be made good out of public funds. The President said, 'I don't expect the C.O. will approve that verdict. He'll send the papers back for fresh evidence to be taken.'

Meanwhile the platoon, left in charge of the sergeant, split up into sections and practised immediate action on the Bren gun.

'Gun fires two rounds and stops again. What do you look at now, Trumpington?'

'Gas regulator'... Off with the magazine. Press, pull back, press. 'Number Two gun clear.'

'What's he forgotten?'

A chorus, 'Butt strap.'

One man said, 'Barrel locking nut.' He had said it once, one splendid day, when asked a question, and he had been right when everyone else was stumped, and he had been commended. So now he always said it, like a gambler obstinately backing the same colour against a long run of bad luck; it was bound to turn up again one day.

The corporal ignored him. 'Quite right, he's forgotten the butt strap. Down again, Trumpington.'

It was Saturday. Work ended at twelve o'clock; as the platoon commander was away, they knocked off ten minutes earlier and got all the gear stowed so that as soon as the call was sounded off on the bugle they could run straight for their quarters. Alastair had his leave pass for reveille on Monday. He had no need to fetch luggage. He kept everything he needed at home. Sonia was waiting in the car outside the guardroom; they did not go away for week-ends but spent them mostly in bed, in the furnished house which they had taken nearby.

'I was pretty good with the Bren this morning,' said Alastair. 'Only one mistake.'

'Darling, you are clever.'

'And I managed to shirk P.T.'

They had packed up ten minutes early too; altogether it had been a very satisfactory morning. And now he could look forward to a day and a half of privacy and leisure.

'I've been shopping in Woking,' said Sonia, 'and I've got all kinds of delicious food and all the weekly papers. There's a film there we might go and see.'

'We might,' said Alastair doubtfully. 'It will probably be full of a lot of — soldiers.'

'Darling, I've never before heard words like that spoken. I thought they only came in print, in novels.'

Alastair had a bath and changed into tweeds. (It was chiefly in order that he might wear civilian clothes that he stayed indoors during week-ends; for that and the cold outside and the ubiquitous military.) Then he took a whisky and soda and watched Sonia cooking; they had fried eggs, sausages, bacon and cold plum pudding; after luncheon he lit a large cigar; it was snowing again, piling up round the steel-framed windows, shutting out the view of the golf course; there was a huge fire and at tea-time they toasted crumpets.

'There's all this evening, and all to-morrow,' said Sonia. 'Isn't it lovely. You know, Alastair, you and I always seem to manage to have fun, don't we, wherever we are.'

This was February 1940, in that strangely cosy interlude between peace and war, when there was leave every weekend and plenty to eat and drink and plenty to smoke, when France stood firm on the Maginot Line and the Finns stood firm in Finland, and everyone said what a cruel winter they must be having in Germany. During one of these week-ends Sonia conceived a child.

6

AS Mr Bentley had foretold, it was not long before Ambrose found himself enrolled on the staff of the Ministry of Information. He was in fact one of the reforms introduced at the first of the many purges. Questions had been asked about the Ministry in the House of Commons; the Press, hampered in so much else, was free to exploit its own grievances. Redress was promised and after a week of intrigue the new appointments were made. Sir Philip Hesketh-Smithers went to the folk-dancing department; Mr Pauling went to woodcuts and weaving; Mr Digby-Smith was given the Arctic circle; Mr Bentley himself, after a dizzy period in which, for a day, he directed a film about postmen, for another day filed press-cuttings from Istanbul, and for the rest of the week supervised the staff catering, found himself at length back beside his busts in charge of the men of letters. Thirty or forty officials retired thankfully into competitive commercial life, and forty or fifty new men and women appeared to take their place; among them, he never quite knew how, Ambrose. The Press, though sceptical of good results, congratulated the public upon maintaining a system of government in which the will of the people was given such speedy effect. *The lesson of the muddle at the Ministry of Information – for muddle there undoubtedly was – is not that such things occur under a democracy, but that they are susceptible to remedy,* they wrote; *the wind of democratic criticism has blown, clear and fresh, through the departments of the Ministry; charges have been frankly made and frankly answered. Our enemies may ponder this portent.*

Ambrose's post as sole representative of Atheism in the religious department was not, at this stage of the war, one of great importance. He was in no position, had he wished it, to introduce statuary into his quarters. He had for his use a single table and a single chair. He shared a room and a secretary with a fanatical young Roman Catholic layman who never tired of exposing discrepancies between *Mein Kampf* and the encyclical *Quadragesimo Anno*, a bland Nonconformist minister, and a Church of England clergyman who had been brought in to succeed the importer of the mahogany prie-dieu. 'We must re-orientate ourselves to Geneva,' this cleric said; 'the first false step was taken when the Lytton report was shelved.' He argued long and gently, the Roman Catholic argued long and fiercely, while the Nonconformist sat as a bemused umpire between them. Ambrose's task consisted in representing to British and colonial atheists that Nazism was at heart agnostic with a strong tinge of religious superstition; he envied the lot of his colleagues who had at their finger-tips long authentic summaries of suppressed Sunday Schools, persecuted monks, and pagan Nordic rites. His was uphill work; he served a small and critical public; but whenever he discovered in the pile of foreign newspapers which passed from desk to desk any reference to German church-going, he circulated it to the two or three magazines devoted to his cause. He counted up the number of times the word 'God' appeared in Hitler's speeches and found the sum impressive; he wrote a pointed little article to show that Jew-baiting was religious in origin. He did his best, but time lay heavy on his hands and, more and more, as the winter wore on, he found himself slipping away from his rancorous colleagues, to the more human companionship of Mr Bentley.

The great press of talent in search of occupation which had thronged the Ministry during its first weeks had now dropped to a mere handful; the door-keeper was schooled to detect and deter the job seekers. No one wanted another reorganization for some time to come. Mr Bentley's office became an enclave of culture in a barbaric world. It was here that the Ivory Tower was first discussed.

'Art for Art's sake, Geoffrey. Back to the lily and the lotus, away from these dusty young *immortelles*, these dandelions sprouting on the vacant lot.'

'A kind of new Yellow Book,' suggested Mr Bentley sympathetically.

Ambrose turned sharply from his contemplation of Mrs Siddons. '*Geoffrey*. How *can* you be so unkind?'

'My dear Ambrose . . .'

'That's just what they'll call it.'

'Who will?'

'Parsnip,' said Ambrose with venom, 'Pimpernell, Poppett and Tom. They'll say we're deserting the workers' cause.'

'I'm not aware that I ever joined it,' said Mr Bentley. 'I claim to be one of the very few living liberals.'

'We've allowed ourselves to be dominated by economists.'

'*I* haven't.'

'For years now we've allowed ourselves to think of nothing but concrete mixers and tractors.'

'*I* haven't,' said Mr Bentley crossly. 'I've thought a great deal about Nollekens.'

'Well,' said Ambrose, 'I've had enough. *Il faut en finir*,' and added, '*nous gagnerons parce que nous sommes les plus forts*.'

Later he said, 'I was never a party member.'

'Party?'

'Communist party. I was what they call in their horrible jargon a fellow traveller.'

'Ah.'

'Geoffrey, they do the most brutal things, don't they, to communists who try to leave the party?'

'So I've heard.'

'Geoffrey, you don't think they'd do that to fellow travellers, do you?'

'I don't expect so.'

'But they *might*?'

'Oh yes, they *might*.'

'Oh dear.'

Later he said, 'You know, Geoffrey, even in fascist countries they have underground organizations. Do you think the underground organizations would get hold of us?'

'Who?'

'The fellow travellers.'

'Really it's too ridiculous to talk like this of fellow travellers and the underground. It sounds like strap-hangers on the Bakerloo railway.'

'It's all very well for you to laugh. You were never one of them.'

'But my dear Ambrose, why should these political friends of yours mind so very much if you produce a purely artistic paper?'

'I heard of a 'cellist in America. He'd been a member of the party and he accepted an invitation to play at an anniversary breakfast of the Colonial Dames. It was during the Scottsboro' trials when feeling was running high. They tied him to a lamp-post and covered him with tar and set him on fire.'

'The Colonial Dames did?'

'No, no, the communists.'

After a long pause he said, 'But Russia's doing very badly in Finland.'

'Yes.'

'If only we knew what was going to happen.'

He returned pensively to the Religious Department.

'This is more in your line than mine,' said the Catholic representative, handing him a cutting from a Swiss paper.

It said that Storm Troopers had attended a requiem mass in Salzburg. Ambrose clipped it to a piece of paper and wrote 'Copies to *Free Thought*, the *Atheist Advertizer* and to *Godless Sunday at Home*'; then he placed it in his basket marked OUT. Two yards distant the Nonconformist minister was checking statistics about the popularity of beer-gardens among Nazi officials. The Church of England clergyman was making the most of some rather scrappy Dutch information about cruelty to animals in Bremen. There was no foundation here for an ivory tower, thought Ambrose, no cloud to garland its summit, and his thoughts began to soar lark-like into a tempera, fourteenth-century sky; into a heaven of flat, blank, blue and white clouds cross-hatched with gold leaf on their sunward edges; a vast altitude painted with shaving soap on a panel of lapis lazuli; he stood on a high, sugary pinnacle, on a new Tower of Babel;

like a muezzin calling his message to a world of domes and clouds; beneath him, between him and the absurd little figures bobbing and bending on their striped praying mats, lay fathoms of clear air where doves sported with the butterflies.

7

MOST of Mrs Sothill's Garden-Party-Only list were people of late middle age who, on retirement from work in the cities or abroad, had bought the smaller manor houses and the larger rectories; houses that once had been supported on the rent of a thousand acres and a dozen cottages now went with a paddock and a walled garden and their life subsisted on pensions and savings. To these modest landholders the rural character of the neighbourhood was a matter of particular jealousy; magnates like Freddy would eagerly sell off outlying farms for development. It was the G.P.O. list who suffered and protested. A narrow corner could not be widened or a tree lopped to clear the telegraph wires without its being noted and regretted in those sunny morning-rooms. These were benevolent, companionable people; their carefully limited families were 'out in the world' and came to them only for occasional visits. Their daughters had flats and jobs and lives of their own in London; their sons were self-supporting in the services and in business. The tribute of Empire flowed gently into the agricultural countryside, tithe barns were converted into village halls, the boy scouts had a new bell tent and the district nurse a motor-car; the old box pews were taken out of the churches, the galleries demolished, the Royal Arms and the Ten Commandments moved from behind the altar and replaced with screens of blue damask supported at the four corners with gilt Sarum angels; the lawns were close mown, fertilized and weeded, and from their splendid surface rose clumps of pampas grass and yucca; year in, year out, gloved hands grubbed in the rockeries, gloved hands snipped in the herbaceous border; baskets of bass stood beside trays of visiting cards on the hall tables. Now in the dead depths of winter, when ice stood thick on the lily ponds, and the kitchen gardens at night were a litter of sacking, these good people fed the birds daily with the crumbs from the dining-room table and saw to it that no old person in the village went short of coal.

It was this unfamiliar world that Basil contemplated in the leather-bound pages of Mrs Sothill's address book. He contemplated it as a marauder might look down from the hills into the fat pastures below; as Hannibal's infantry had looked down from the snow-line as the first elephants tried the etched footholds which led to the Lombardy plains below them and went lurching and trumpeting over the edge.

After the successful engagement at North Grappling, Basil took Doris into the nearest town and fed her liberally on fried fish and chipped potatoes; afterwards he took her to the cinema, allowed her to hold his hand in a fierce and sticky grasp throughout the length of two deeply sentimental films and brought her back to Malfrey in a state of entranced docility.

'You don't like blondes, do you?' she asked anxiously in the car.

'Yes, very much.'

'More than brunettes?'

'I'm not particular.'

'They say like goes to like. *She's* dark.'

'Who?'

'Her you call your sister.'

'Doris, you must get this idea out of your head. Mrs Sothill *is* my sister.'

'You aren't sweet on her.'

'Certainly not.'

'Then you *do* like blondes,' said Doris sadly.

Next day she disappeared alone into the village, returned mysteriously with a small parcel, and remained hidden all the morning in the bachelors' wing. Just before luncheon she appeared in the orangery with her head in a towel.

'I wanted you to see,' she said, and uncovered a damp mop of hair which was in part pale yellow, in part its original black, and in part mottled in every intervening shade.

'Good heavens, child,' said Barbara. 'What have you done?'

Doris looked only at Basil. 'D'you like it? I'll give it another go this afternoon.'

'I wouldn't,' said Basil. 'I'd leave it just as it is.'

'You like it?'

'I think it's fine.'

'Not too streaky?'

'Not a bit too streaky.'

If anything had been needed to complete the horror of Doris's appearance, that morning's work had done it.

Basil studied the address book with care. 'Finding a new home for the Connollys,' he said.

'Basil, we must do something to that poor child's head before we pass her on.'

'Not a bit of it. It suits her. What d'you know of the Graces of the Old Rectory, Adderford?'

'It's a pretty little house. He's a painter.'

'Bohemian?'

'Not the least. Very refined. Portraits of children in water-colour and pastel.'

'Pastel? He sounds suitable.'

'She's rather delicate I believe.'

'Perfect.'

The Connollys stayed two days at the Old Rectory and earned twenty pounds.

8

LONDON was full again. Those who had left in a hurry returned; those who had made arrangements to go after the first air raid remained. Margot Metroland shut her home and moved to the Ritz; opened her home and moved back; decided that after all she really preferred the Ritz and shut her home, this time, though she did not know it, for ever. No servant ever folded back the shutters from the long windows; they remained barred until late in the year when they were blown into Curzon Street; the furniture was still under dust sheets when it was splintered and burned.

*

Sir Joseph Mainwaring was appointed to a position of trust and dignity. He was often to be seen with Generals now and sometimes with an Admiral. 'Our first war aim,' he said, 'is to keep Italy out of the war until she is strong enough to come in on our side.' He summed up the situation at home by saying, 'One takes one's gas-mask to one's office but *not* to one's club.'

Lady Seal had not troubled him again about Basil. 'He's at Malfrey, helping Barbara with her evacuees,' she said. 'The army is very full just at present. Things will be much easier when we have had some casualties.'

Sir Joseph nodded but at heart he was sceptical. There were not going to be many casualties. Why, he had been talking to a very interesting fellow at the Beefsteak who knew a German Professor of History; this Professor was now in England; they thought a great deal of him at the Foreign Office; he said there were fifty million Germans ready to declare peace tomorrow on our own terms. It was just a question of outing those fellows in the government. Sir Joseph had seen many governments outed. It was quite easy in war time – they had outed Asquith quite easily and he was a far better fellow than Lloyd George who succeeded him. Then they outed Lloyd George and then they outed MacDonald. Christopher Seal knew how to do it. He'd soon out Hitler if he were alive and a German.

Poppet Green was in London with her friends.

'Ambrose has turned fascist,' she said.

'Not really?'

'He's working for the Government in the Ministry of Information and they've bribed him to start a new paper.'

'Is it a fascist paper?'

'You bet it is.'

'I heard it was to be called the *Ivory Tower*.'

'That's fascist if you like.'

'Escapist.'

'Trotskyist.'

'Ambrose never had the proletarian outlook. I can't think why we put up with him as we did. Parsnip always said . . .'

Peter Pastmaster came into Bratts wearing battle-dress and, on his shoulder, the name of a regiment to which he had not formerly belonged.

'Hullo. Why on earth are you dressed like that?'

Peter smirked as only a soldier can when he knows a secret. 'Oh, no particular reason.'

'Have they thrown you out of the regiment?'

'I'm seconded, temporarily, for special duty.'

'You're the sixth chap I've seen in disguise this morning.'

'That's the idea – security, you know.'

'What's it all about?'

'You'll hear in time, I expect,' said Peter with boundless smugness.

They went to the bar.

'Good morning, my lord,' said MacDougal, the barman. 'I see you're off to Finland too. Quite a number of our gentlemen are going to-night.'

Angela Lyne was back in London; the affairs of the hospital were in order, her son was at his private school, transported at the outbreak of war from the East coast to the middle of Dartmoor. She sat at the place she called 'home' listening to wireless news from Germany.

This place was a service flat and as smart and non-committal as herself, a set of five large rooms high up in the mansard floor of a brand new block in Grosvenor Square. The decorators had been at work there while she was in France; the style was what passes for Empire in the fashionable world. Next year, had there been no war, she would have had it done over again during August.

That morning she had spent an hour with her brokers giving precise, prudent directions for the disposition of her fortune; she had lunched alone, listening to the radio from Europe, after luncheon she had gone alone to the cinema in Curzon Street. It was darkening when she left the cinema and quite dark now outside, beyond the heavy crimson draperies which hung in a dozen opulent loops and folds, girded with gold cord, fringed with gold at the hem, over the new black shutters. Soon she would go out to dine with Margot at the Ritz. Peter was off somewhere and Margot was trying to get a party together for him.

She mixed herself a large cocktail; the principal ingredients were vodka and calvados; the decorators had left an electric shaker on the Pompeian side table. It was their habit to litter the houses where they worked with expensive trifles of this sort; parsimonious clients sent them back; the vaguer sort believed them to be presents for which they had forgotten to thank anyone, used them, broke them and paid for them a year later when the bills came in. Angela liked gadgets. She switched on the electric shaker and, when her drink was mixed, took the glass with her to the bathroom and drank it slowly in her bath.

Angela never drank cocktails except in private; there was something about them which bore, so faintly as to be discernible to no one but herself, a suggestion of good fellowship and good cheer; an infinitely small invitation to familiarity, derived perhaps from the days of prohibition when gin had ceased to be Hogarthian and had become chic; an aura of naughtiness, of felony compounded; a memory of her father's friends who sometimes had raised their glasses to her, of a man in a ship who had said '*à tes beaux yeux*'. And so Angela who hated human contact on any but her own terms never drank cocktails except in solitude. Lately all her days seemed to be spent alone.

Steam from the bath formed in a mist, and later in great beads of water, on the side of the glass. She finished her cocktail and felt the fumes rise inside her. She lay for a long time in the water, scarcely thinking, scarcely feeling anything except the warm water round her and the spirit within her. She called for her maid, from next door, to bring her a cigarette, smoked it slowly to the end, called for an ash tray and then for a towel. Presently she was ready to face the darkness, and the intense cold, and Margot Metroland's dinner party. She noticed in the last intense scrutiny before her mirrors that her mouth was beginning to droop a little at the corners. It was not the disappointed pout that she knew in so many of her friends; it was as the droop you sometimes saw in death masks, when the jaw had been set and the face had stiffened in lines which told those waiting round the bed that the will to live was gone.

At dinner she drank Vichy water and talked like a man. She said that France was no good any more and Peter used a phrase that was just coming into vogue, accusing her of being 'fifth column'. They went on to a dance at the Suivi. She danced and drank her Vichy water and talked sharply and well like a very clever man. She was wearing a new pair of earrings – an arrow set with a ruby point, the shaft a thin bar of emerald that seemed to transfix the lobe; she had designed them for herself and had called for them that morning on her way home from seeing her man of business. The girls in the party noticed Angela's earrings; they noticed everything about her clothes; she was the best-dressed woman there, as she usually was wherever she went.

She stayed to the end of the party and then returned to Grosvenor Square alone. Since the war there was no liftman on duty after midnight. She shut herself in, pressed the button for the mansard floor and rose to the empty, uncommunicative flat. There were no ashes to stir in the grate; illuminated glass coals glowed eternally in an elegant steel basket; the temperature of the rooms never varied, winter or summer, day or night. She mixed herself a large whisky and water and turned on the radio.

Tirelessly, all over the world, voices were speaking in their own and in foreign tongues. She listened and fidgeted with the knob; sometimes she got a burst of music, once a prayer. Presently she fetched another whisky and water.

Her maid lived out and had been told not to wait up. When she came in the morning she found Mrs Lyne in bed but awake; the clothes she had worn the evening before had been carefully hung up, not broadcast about the carpet as they used sometimes to be. 'I shan't be getting up this morning, Grainger,' she said. 'Bring the radio here and the newspapers.'

Later she had her bath, returned to bed, took two tablets of Dial and slept, gently, until it was time to fit the black, ply-wood screens into the window frames and hide them behind the velvet draperies.

9

'WHAT about Mr and Mrs Prettyman-Partridge of the Malt House, Grantley Green?'

Basil was choosing his objectives from the extreme quarters of the Malfrey billeting area. He had struck East and North. Grantley Green lay South where the land of spur and valley fell away and flattened out into a plain of cider orchards and market gardens.

'They're very old, I think,' said Barbara. 'I hardly know them. Come to think of it, I heard something about Mr Prettyman-Partridge the other day. I can't remember what.'

'Pretty house? Nice things in it?'

'As far as I remember.'

'People of regular habits? Fond of quiet?'

'Yes, I suppose so.'

'They'll do.'

Basil bent over the map tracing the road to Grantley Green which he would take next day.

He found the Malt House without difficulty. It had been a brewhouse in the seventeenth century and later was converted to a private house. It had a large, regular front of dressed stone, facing the village green. The curtains and the china in the window proclaimed that it was in 'good hands'. Basil noted the china with approval – large, black Wedgwood urns – valuable and vulnerable and no doubt well loved. When the door opened it disclosed a view straight through the house to a white lawn and a cedar tree laden with snow.

The door was opened by a large and lovely girl. She had fair curly hair and a fair skin, huge, pale blue eyes, a large, shy mouth. She was dressed in a tweed suit and woollen jumper as though for country exercise, but the soft, fur-lined boots showed that she was spending the morning at home. Everything about this girl was large and soft and round and ample. A dress shop might not have chosen her as a mannequin but she was not a fat girl; a more civilized age would have found her admirably proportioned; Boucher would have painted her half clothed in a flutter of blue and pink draperies, a butterfly hovering over a breast of white and rose.

'Miss Prettyman-Partridge?'

'No. Please don't say you've come to sell something. It's terribly cold standing here and if I ask you in I shall have to buy it.'

'I want to see Mr and Mrs Prettyman-Partridge.'

'They're dead. At least one is; the other sold us the house last summer. Is that all, please; I don't want to be rude but I must shut the door or freeze.'

So that was what Barbara had heard about the Malt House. 'May I come in?'

'Oh dear,' said this splendid girl, leading him into the room with the Wedgwood urns. 'Is it something to buy or forms to fill in or just a subscription? If it's the first two I can't help because my husband's away with the yeomanry; if it's a subscription I've got some money upstairs. I've been told to give the same as Mrs Andrews, the doctor's wife. If you haven't been to her yet, come back when you find what she's good for.'

Everything in the room was new; that is to say the paint was new and the carpets and the curtains, and the furniture had been newly put in position. There was a very large settee in front of the fireplace whose cushions, upholstered in *toile-de-jouy*, still bore the impress of that fine young woman; she had been lying there when Basil rang the bell. He knew that if he put his hand in the round concavity where her hip had rested, it would still be warm; and that further cushions had been tucked under her arm. The book she had been reading was on the lambskin hearth-rug. Basil could reconstruct the position, exactly, where she had been sprawling with the languor of extreme youth.

The girl seemed to sense an impertinence in Basil's scrutiny. 'Anyway,' she said. 'Why aren't you in khaki?'

'Work of national importance,' said Basil. 'I am the district billeting officer. I'm looking for a suitable home for three evacuated children.'

'Well, I hope you don't call this suitable. I ask you. I can't even look after Bill's sheepdog. I can't even look after myself very well. What should I do with three children?'

'These are rather exceptional children.'

'They'd have to be. Anyway I'm not having any, thank you. There was a funny little woman called Harkness came to call here yesterday. I do think people might let up on calling in war time, don't you? She told me the most gruesome things about some children that were sent to her. They had to bribe the man, literally bribe him with money, to get the brutes moved.'

'These are the same children.'

'Well, for God's sake, why pick on me?'

Her great eyes held him dazzled, like a rabbit before the headlights of a car. It was a delicious sensation. 'Well, actually, I picked on the Prettyman-Partridges... I don't even know your name.'

'I don't know yours.'

'Basil Seal.'

'Basil Seal?' There was a sudden interest in her voice. 'How very funny.'

'Why funny?'

'Only that I used to hear a lot about you once. Weren't you a friend of a girl called Mary Nichols?'

'Was I?' Was he? Mary Nichols? Mary Nichols?

'Well, she used to talk a lot about you. She was much older than me. I used to think her wonderful when I was sixteen. You met her in a ship coming from Copenhagen.'

'I dare say. I've been to Copenhagen.'

The girl was looking at him now with a keen and not wholly flattering attention. 'So you're Basil Seal,' she said. 'Well, I never...'

Four years ago in South Kensington, at Mary Nichols' home, there was a little back sitting-room on the first floor which was Mary's room. Here Mary entertained her girl friends to tea. Here she had come, day after day, to sit before the gas fire and eat Fuller's walnut cake and hear the details of Mary's Experience. 'But aren't you going to see him again?' she asked. 'No, it was something so beautiful, so complete in itself' – Mary had steeped herself in romantic literature since her Experience. 'I don't want to spoil it.' 'I don't think he sounds half good enough for you, darling.' 'He's absolutely *different.* You mustn't think of him as one of the young men one meets at dances...' The girl did not go to dances yet, and Mary knew it. Mary's tales of the young men she met at dances had been very moving, but not as moving as this tale of Basil Seal. The name had become graven on her mind.

And Basil, still standing, searched his memory. Mary Nichols? Copenhagen? No, it registered nothing. It was very consoling, he thought, the way in which an act of kindness, in the fullness of time, returns to bless the benefactor. One gives a jolly-up to a girl in a ship. She goes her way, he goes his. He forgets; he has so many benefactions of the kind to his credit. But she remembers and then one day, when it is least expected, Fate drops into his lap the ripe fruit of his reward, this luscious creature waiting for him, all unaware, in the Malt House, Grantley Green.

'Aren't you going to offer me a drink – on the strength of Mary Nichols?'

'I don't think there's anything in the house. Bill's away, you see. He's got some wine downstairs in the cellar, but the door's locked.'

'I expect we could open it.'

'Oh! I wouldn't do that. Bill would be furious.'

'Well, I don't suppose he'll be best pleased to come home on leave and find the Connolly family hacking up his home. By the way, you haven't seen them yet; they're outside in the car; I'll bring them in.'

'*Please* don't!' There was genuine distress and appeal in those blue cow-eyes.

'Well, take a look at them through the window.'

She went and looked. 'Good God,' said the girl. 'Mrs Harkness wasn't far wrong. I thought she was laying it on thick.'

'It cost her thirty pounds to get rid of them.'

'Oh, but I haven't got anything like that' – again the distress and appeal in her wide blue eyes. 'Bill makes me an allowance out of his pay. It comes in monthly. It's practically all I've got.'

'I'll take payment in kind,' said Basil.

'You mean the sherry?'

'I'd like a glass of sherry very much,' said Basil.

When they got to work with the crowbar on the cellar door, it was clear that this high-spirited girl thoroughly enjoyed herself. It was a pathetic little cellar; a poor man's treasury. Half a dozen bottles of hock, a bin of port, a dozen or two of claret. 'Mostly wedding presents,' explained the girl. Basil found some sherry and they took it up to the light.

'I've no maid now,' she explained. 'A woman comes in once a week.'

They found glasses in the pantry and a corkscrew in the dining-room.

'Is it any good?' she said anxiously, while Basil tasted the wine.

'Delicious.'

'I'm so glad. Bill knows about wine. I don't.'

So they began to talk about Bill, who was married in July to this lovely creature, who had a good job in an architect's office in the nearby town, had settled at Grantley Green in August, and in September had gone to join the yeomanry as a trooper....

Two hours later Basil left the Malt House and returned to his car. It was evidence of the compelling property of love that the Connolly children were still in their seats.

'Gawd, Mister, you haven't half been a time,' said Doris. 'We're fair froze. Do we get out here?'

'No.'

'We aren't going to muck up this house?'

'No, Doris, not this time. You're coming back with me.'

Doris sighed blissfully. 'I don't care how froze we are if we can come back with you,' she said.

When they returned to Malfrey, and Barbara once more found the children back in the bachelors' wing, her face fell. 'Oh, Basil,' she said. 'You've failed me.'

'Well not exactly. The Prettyman-Partridges are dead.'

'I knew there was something about them. But you've been a long time.'

'I met a friend. At least the friend of a friend. A very nice girl. I think you ought to do something about her.'

'What's her name?'

'D'you know, I never discovered. But her husband's called Bill. He joined Freddy's regiment as a trooper.'

'Who's she a friend of?'

'Mary Nichols.'

'I've never heard of her.'

'Old friend of mine. Honestly, Babs, you'll like this girl.'

'Well, ask her to dinner.' Barbara was not enthusiastic; she had known too many of Basil's girls.

'I have. The trouble is she hasn't got a car. D'you mind if I go and fetch her?'

'Darling, we simply haven't the petrol.'

'We can use the special allowance.'

'Darling, I *can't*. This has nothing to do with billeting.'

'Believe it or not Babs, it has.'

10

THE frost broke; the snow melted away; Colony Bog, Bagshot Heath, Chobham Common and all the little polygons of gorse and bush which lay between the high roads of Surrey, patches of rank land marked on the signposts W.D., marked on the maps as numbered training areas, reappeared from their brief period of comeliness.

'We can get on with the tactical training,' said the C.O.

For three weeks there were platoon schemes and company schemes. Captain Mayfield consumed his leisure devising ways of transforming into battlefields the few acres of close, soggy territory at his disposal. For the troops these schemes varied only according to the distance of the training area from camp, and the distance that had to be traversed before the cease-fire. Then for three days in succession the C.O. was seen to go out with the adjutant in the Humber Snipe, each carrying a map case. 'We're putting on a battalion exercise,' said Captain Mayfield. It was all one to his troops. 'It's our first battalion exercise. It's absolutely essential that every man in the company shall be in the picture all the time.'

Alastair was gradually learning the new languages. There was the simple tongue, the unchanging reiteration of obscenity, spoken by his fellow soldiers. That took little learning. There was also the language spoken by his officers, which from time to time was addressed to him. The first time that Captain Mayfield had asked him, 'Are you in the picture, Trumpington?' he supposed him to mean, was he personally conspicuous. He crouched at the time water-logged to the knees, in a ditch; he had, at the suggestion of Mr Smallwood – the platoon commander – ornamented his steel helmet with bracken. 'No, sir,' he had said, stoutly.

Captain Mayfield had seemed rather gratified than not by the confession. 'Put these men in the picture, Smallwood,' he said, and there had followed a tedious and barely credible narrative about the unprovoked aggression of Southland against Northland (who was not party to the Geneva gas protocol), about How support batteries, A.F.V.s and F.D.L.s.

Alastair learned, too, that all schemes ended in a 'shambles' which did not mean, as he feared, a slaughter, but a brief restoration of individual freedom of movement, when everyone wandered where he would, while Mr Smallwood blew his whistle and Captain Mayfield shouted, 'Mr Smallwood, will you kindly get your platoon to hell out of here and fall them in on the road.'

On the day of the battalion scheme they marched out of camp as a battalion. Alastair had been made mortar-man in Mr Smallwood's platoon. It was a gamble, the chances of which were hotly debated. At the moment there were no mortars and he was given instead a light and easily manageable counterfeit of wood which was slung on the back of his haversack, relieving him of a rifle. At present it was money for old rope, but a day would come, spoken of as 'when we get over 1098'; in that dire event he would be worse off than the riflemen. Two other men in the platoon had rashly put in to be anti-tank men; contrary to all expectations anti-tank rifles had suddenly arrived. One of these men had prudently gone sick on the eve of the exercise; the other went sick after it.

Water-bottles were filled, haversack rations were packed in mess-tins, and, on account of Northland's frank obduracy at Geneva, gas respirators frustrated the aim of the designers of the equipment to leave the man's chest unencumbered. Thus they marched out and after ten minutes at the command to march at ease, they began singing 'Roll out the Barrel', 'We'll hang out the Washing on the Siegfried Line', and 'The Quartermaster's Store'. Presently the order came back to march tactically. They knew all about that; it meant stumbling along in the ditch; singing stopped; the man with the anti-tank rifle swore monotonously. Then the order came back 'Gas'; they put on their respirators and the man with the anti-tank rifle suffered in silence.

'Gas clear. *Don't* put the respirators back in the haversacks. Leave them out a minute to dry.'

They marched eight miles or so and then turned off the main road into a lane and eventually halted. It was now eleven o'clock.

'This is the battalion assembly position,' announced Captain Mayfield. 'The C.O. has just gone forward with his recce group to make his recce.'

It was as though he were announcing to a crowd of pilgrims, 'This is the Vatican. The Pope has just gone into the Sistine Chapel.'

'It makes things much more interesting,' said Mr Smallwood rather apologetically, 'if you try and understand what is going on. Yes, carry on smoking.'

The company settled itself on the side of the road and began eating its haversack rations.

'I say, you know,' said Mr Smallwood. 'There'll be a halt for dinner.'

They ate, mostly in silence.

'Soon the C.O. will send for his O group,' announced Captain Mayfield.

Presently a runner appeared, not running but walking rather slowly, and led Captain Mayfield away.

'The C.O. *has* sent for his O group,' said Mr Smallwood. 'Captain Brown is now in command.'

Captain Brown announced, 'The C.O. has given out his orders. He is now establishing advanced Battalion H.Q. The company commanders are now making their recces. Soon *they* will send for *their* O groups.'

'Can't think what they want *us* here for at all,' said the man with the anti-tank rifle.

Three-quarters of an hour passed and then an orderly arrived with a written message for Captain Brown. He said to the three platoon commanders, 'You're to meet the company commander at the third E in "Bee Garden". I'm bringing the Company on to the B in Bee.'

Mr Smallwood and his orderly and his batman left platoon headquarters and drifted off uncertainly into the scrub.

'Get the company fallen in, sergeant-major.'

Captain Brown was not quite happy about his position; they tacked along behind him across the common; several times they halted while Captain Brown worried over the map. At last he said, 'This is the company assembly position. The company commander is now giving out orders to his O group.'

At this moment, just as the men were beginning to settle down, Captain Mayfield appeared. 'Where the hell are those platoon commanders?' he asked. 'And what is the company doing here? I said the B in Bee, this is the E in Garden.'

A discussion followed, inaudible to Alastair except for an occasional phrase, 'ring contour', 'track junction' and again and again 'well, the map's wrong.' Captain Brown seemed to get the better of the argument; at any rate Captain Mayfield went away in search of his O group and left the company in possession.

Half an hour passed. Captain Brown felt impelled to explain the delay.

'The platoon commanders are making their recces,' he said.

Presently the C.O. arrived. 'Is this C Company?' he asked.

'Yes, sir.'

'Well, what's happening? You ought to be on the start line by now.' Then since it was clearly no use attacking Captain Brown about that, he said in a way Captain Brown had learned to dread, 'I must have missed your sentries coming along. Just put me in the picture, will you, of your local defence.'

'Well, sir, we've just halted here ... '

The C.O. led Captain Brown away.

'He's getting a rocket,' said the anti-tank man. It was the first moment of satisfaction he had known that day.

Captain Brown came back looking shaken and began posting air look-outs and gas sentries with feverish activity. While he was in the middle of it the platoon orderlies came back to lead the platoons to assembly positions. Alastair advanced with the platoon another half mile. Then they halted. Mr Smallwood appeared and collected the section commanders round him. The C.O. was there too, listening to Mr Smallwood's orders. When they were finished he said, 'I don't think you mentioned the R.A.P., did you, Smallwood?'

'R.A.P. sir. No, sir, I'm afraid I don't know where it is.'

The C.O. led Mr Smallwood out of hearing of his platoon.

'Now *he's* getting a rocket,' said the anti-tank man with glee.

The section commanders came back to their men. Mr Smallwood's orders had been full of detail; start line, zero hour, boundaries inclusive and exclusive, objectives, supporting fire. 'It's like this,' said Corporal Deacon. 'They're over there and we're here. So then we go for un.'

Another half-hour passed. Captain Mayfield appeared. 'For Christ's sake, Smallwood, you ought to be half-way up the ridge by this time.'

'Oh,' said Mr Smallwood. 'Sorry. Come on. Forward.'

The platoon collected its equipment and toiled into action up the opposing slope. Major Bush, the second-in-command, appeared before them. They fired their blanks at him with enthusiasm. 'Got him,' said the man next to Alastair.

'You're coming under heavy fire,' said the Major. 'Most of you are casualties.'

'He's a casualty himself.'

'Well, what are you going to do, Smallwood?'

'Get down, sir.'

'Well *get* down.'

'Get down,' ordered Mr Smallwood.

'What are you going to do now?'

Mr Smallwood looked round desperately for inspiration. 'Put down smoke, sir.'

'Well, *put* down smoke.'

'Put down smoke,' said Mr Smallwood to Alastair.

The Major went on his way to confuse the platoon on their flank.

'Come on,' said Mr Smallwood. 'We've got to get up this infernal hill sometime. We might as well do it now.'

It was shorter than it looked; they were up in twenty minutes and at the summit there was a prolonged shambles. Bit by bit the whole battalion appeared from different quarters. C Company was collected and fallen in; then they were fallen out to eat their dinners. No one had any dinner left, so they lay on their backs and smoked.

Marching home the C.O. said, 'Not so bad for a first attempt.'

'Not so bad, Colonel,' said Major Bush.

'Bit slow off the mark.'

'A bit sticky.'

'Smallwood didn't do too well.'

'He was very slow off the mark.'

'Well, I think we learned some lessons. The men were interested. You could see that.'

It was dark by the time the battalion reached camp. They marched to attention passing the guard-room, split into companies, and halted on the company parade grounds.

'All rifles to be pulled through before supper,' said Captain Mayfield. 'Platoon sergeants collect empties. Foot inspection by platoons.' Then he dismissed the company.

Alastair had time to slip away to the telephone box and summon Sonia before Mr Mayfield came round the hut examining the feet with an electric torch. He pulled on a clean pair of socks, pushed his boots under his palliasse and put on a pair of shoes; then he was ready. Sonia was outside the guard-room, waiting for him in the car. 'Darling, you smell very sweaty,' she said. 'What have you been doing?'

'I put down smoke,' said Alastair proudly. 'The whole advance was held up until I put down smoke.'

'Darling, you *are* clever. I've got a tinned beefsteak and kidney pudding for dinner.'

After dinner Alastair settled in a chair. 'Don't let me go to sleep,' he said. 'I must be in by midnight.'

'I'll wake you.'

'I wonder if a real battle is much like that,' said Alastair just before he dropped off.

Peter Pastmaster's expedition never sailed. He resumed his former uniform and his former habits. His regiment was in barracks in London; his mother was still at the Ritz; most of his friends were still to be found round the bar at Bratts. With time on his hands and the prospect of action, for a few days imminent, now postponed, but always present as the basis of any future plans, Peter began to suffer from pangs of dynastic conscience. He was thirty-three years old. He might pop off any day. 'Mama,' he said, 'd'you think I ought to marry?'

'Who?'

'Anyone.'

'I don't see that you can say anyone *ought* to marry *anyone*.'

'Darling, don't confuse me. What I mean is, supposing I get killed.'

'I don't see a great deal in it for the poor girl,' said Margot.

'I mean I should like to have a son.'

'Well, then, you had better marry, darling. D'you know any girls?'

'I don't think I do.'

'I don't think I do either, come to think of it. I believe Emma Granchester's second girl is very pretty – try her. There are probably lots of others. I'll make enquiries.'

So Peter, little accustomed to their society, began, awkwardly at first, taking out a series of very young and very eligible girls; he quickly gained confidence; it was easy as falling off a log. Soon there were a dozen mothers who were old-fashioned enough to be pleasurably excited at the prospect of finding in their son-in-law all the Victorian excellences of an old title, a new fortune, and a shapely leg in blue overalls.

'Peter,' Margot said to him one day. 'D'you ever give yourself time from debutantes to see old friends? What's become of Angela? I never see her now.'

'I suppose she's gone back to the country.'

'Not with Basil?'

'No, not with Basil.'

But she was living still above the block of flats in Grosvenor Square. Below, layer upon layer of rich men and women came and went about their business, layer below layer down to street level; below that again, underground, the management were adapting the basement to serve as an air-raid shelter. Angela seldom went beyond her door, except once or twice a week to visit the cinema; she always went alone. She had taken to wearing spectacles of smoked glass; she wore them indoors, as well as out; she wore them in the subdued, concealed lighting of her drawing-room, as she sat hour after hour with the radio standing by the decanter and glass at her elbow; she wore them when she looked at herself in the mirror. Only Grainger, her maid, knew what was the matter with Mrs Lyne, and she only knew the shell of it. Grainger knew the number of bottles, empty and full, in the little pantry; she saw Mrs Lyne's face when the blackout was taken down in the morning. (She never had to wake Mrs Lyne nowadays; her eyes were always open when the maid came to call her; sometimes Mrs Lyne was up and sitting in her chair; sometimes she lay in bed, staring ahead, waiting to be called.) She knew the trays of food that came up from the restaurant and went back, as often as not, untasted. All this Grainger knew and, being a dull sensible girl, she kept her own counsel; but, being a dull and sensible girl, she was spared the knowledge of what went on in Mrs Lyne's mind.

So the snows vanished and the weeks of winter melted away with them; presently, oblivious of the hazards of war, the swallows returned to their ancestral building grounds.

CHAPTER 3
Spring

1

TWO events decided Basil to return to London. First, the yeomanry moved back to the country under canvas. Freddy telephoned to Barbara:

'Good news,' he said, 'we're coming home.'

'Freddy, how splendid,' said Barbara, her spirits falling a little. 'When?'

'I arrive to-morrow. I'm bringing Jack Cathcart; he's our second-in-command now. We're going to lay out a camp. We'll stay at Malfrey while we're doing it.'

'Lovely,' said Barbara.

'We'll be bringing servants, so we'll be self-supporting as far as that goes. There'll be a couple of sergeants. Benson can look after them. And I say, Barbara, what do you say to having the camp in the Park?'

'Oh, no, Freddy, for God's sake.'

'We could open up the saloon and have the mess there. I could live in. You'd have to have old Colonel Sproggin and probably Cathcart, too, but you wouldn't mind that, would you?'

'Please, Freddy, don't decide anything in a hurry.'

'Well, I have practically decided. See you to-morrow. I say, is Basil still with you?'

'Yes.'

'I can't see him getting on terribly well with Cathcart. Couldn't you give him a gentle hint?'

Barbara hung up sadly and went to make arrangements for Freddy's and Major Cathcart's reception.

Basil was at Grantley Green. He returned to Malfrey after dinner, to find Barbara still up.

'Darling, you've got to go away.'

'Yes, how did you know?'

'Freddy's coming home.'

'Oh, damn Freddy; who cares for him? *Bill's* coming home.'

'What does she say?'

'Believe it or not, she's as pleased as Punch.'

'Ungrateful beast,' said Barbara, and, after a pause, 'You never wrote that book either.'

'No, but we've had a lovely time, haven't we, Babs? Quite like the old days.'

'I suppose you'll want some money.'

'I could always do with some more, but as it happens I'm quite rich at the moment.'

'Basil, how?'

'One thing and another. I tell you what I will do before I go. I'll get the Connollys off your hands again. I'm afraid I've been neglecting them rather in the last few weeks.'

That led to the second deciding event.

On his way to and from Grantley Green, Basil had noticed a pretty stucco house standing in paddock and orchard, which seemed exactly suited to harbour the Connollys. He had asked Barbara about it, but she could tell him nothing. Basil was getting lax and, confident now in his methods, no longer bothered himself with much research before choosing his victims. The stucco house was marked down and next day he packed the Connollys into the car and drove over to do his business.

It was ten in the morning but he found the proprietor at breakfast. He did not appear to be quite the type that Basil was used to deal with. He was younger than the G.P.O. list. A game leg, stuck awkwardly askew, explained why he was not in uniform. He had got this injury in a motor race, he explained later to Basil. He had ginger hair and a ginger moustache and malevolent pinkish eyes. His name was Mr Todhunter.

He was eating kidneys and eggs and sausages and bacon and an overcooked chop; his teapot stood on the hob. He looked like a drawing by Leach for a book by Surtees.

'Well,' he said, cautious but affable. 'I know about you. You're Mrs Sothill's brother at Malfrey. I don't know Mrs Sothill but I know all about her. I don't know Captain Sothill but I know about him. What can I do for you?'

'I'm the billeting officer for this district,' said Basil.

'*Indeed.* I'm interested to meet you. Go on. You don't mind my eating, I'm sure.'

Feeling a little less confident than usual, Basil went through his now stereotyped preface. '... Getting harder to find billets, particularly since the anti-aircraft battery had come to South Grappling and put their men in the cottages there... important to stop the backwash to the towns... bad impression if the bigger houses seemed not to be doing their share... natural reluctance to employ compulsory powers but these powers *were* there, if necessary... three children who had caused some difficulty elsewhere...'

Mr Todhunter finished his breakfast, stood with his back to the fire and began to fill his pipe. 'And what if I don't want these hard cases of yours,' he said. 'What if I'd sooner pay the fine?'

Basil embarked on the second part of his recitation. '... official allowance barely covered cost of food... serious hardship to poor families... poor people valued their household gods even more than the rich... possible to find a cottage where a few pounds would make all the difference between dead loss and a small and welcome profit...'

Mr Todhunter heard him in silence. At last he said, 'So *that's* how you do it. Thank you. That was most instructive, very instructive indeed. I liked the bit about household gods.'

Basil began to realize that he was dealing with a fellow of broad and rather dangerous sympathies; someone like himself. 'In more cultured circles I say Lares et Penates.'

'Household gods is good enough. Household gods is very good indeed. What d'you generally count on raising?'

'Five pounds is the worst, thirty-five the best I've had so far.'

'So far? Do you hope to carry on long with this trade?'

'I don't see why not.'

'Don't you? Well I'll tell you something. D'you know who's billeting officer in this district? I am. Mrs Sothill's district ends at the main road. You're muscling in on my territory when you come past the crossing. Now what have you got to say for yourself?'

'D'you mean to say that Grantley Green is yours?'

'Certainly.'

'How damned funny.'

'Why funny?'

'I can't tell you,' said Basil. 'But it *is* – exquisitely funny.'

'So I'll ask you to keep to your own side of the road in future. Not that I'm ungrateful for your visit. It's given me some interesting ideas. I always felt there was money in this racket somehow, but I could never quite see my way to get it. Now I know. I'll remember about the household gods.'

'Wait a minute,' said Basil. 'It isn't quite as easy as all that, you know. It isn't just a matter of having the idea; you have to have the Connollys too. You don't understand it, and I don't understand it, but the fact remains that quite a number of otherwise sane human beings are perfectly ready to take children in; they like them; it makes them feel virtuous; they like the little pattering feet about the house – I know it sounds screwy but it's the truth. I've seen it again and again.'

'So have I,' said Mr Todhunter. 'There's no sense in it, but it's a fact – they make household gods of them.'

'Now the Connollys are something quite special; no one could make a household god of them. Come and have a look.'

He and Mr Todhunter went out into the circle of gravel in front of the porch where Basil had left the car.

'Doris,' he said. 'Come out and meet Mr Todhunter. Bring Micky and Marlene too.'

The three frightful children stood in a line to be inspected.

'Take that scarf off your head, Doris. Show him your hair.'

In spite of himself Mr Todhunter could not disguise the fact that he was profoundly moved. 'Yes,' he said. 'I give you that. They *are* special. If it's not a rude question, what did you pay for them?'

'I got them free. But I've put a lot of money into them since – fried fish and cinemas.'

'How did you get the girl's hair that way?'

'She did it herself,' said Basil, 'for love.'

'They certainly are special,' repeated Mr Todhunter with awe.

'You haven't seen anything yet. You should see them in action.'

'I can imagine it,' said Mr Todhunter. 'Well, what d'you want for them?'

'Five pounds a leg and that's cheap, because I'm thinking of closing down the business anyhow.'

Mr Todhunter was not a man to haggle when he was on a good thing. 'Done,' he said.

Basil addressed the Connollys. 'Well, children, this is your new headquarters.'

'Are we to muck 'em about?' asked Doris.

'That's up to Mr Todhunter. I'm handing you over to him now. You'll be working for him in future.'

'Ain't we never going to be with you again?' asked Doris.

'Never again, Doris. But you'll find you like Mr Todhunter just as much. He's very handsome, isn't he?'

'Not as handsome as you.'

'No, perhaps not, but he's got a fine little red moustache, hasn't he?'

'Yes, it's a lovely moustache,' Doris conceded; she looked from her old to her new master critically. 'But he's shorter than you.'

'Dammit, girl,' said Basil impatiently. 'Don't you realize there's a war on. We've all got to make sacrifices. There's many a little girl would be very grateful for Mr Todhunter. Look at his fine red nob.'

'Yes, it *is* red.'

Mr Todhunter tired of the comparison and stumped indoors to fetch his cheque book.

'Can't we muck his house up, just a bit?' said Micky wistfully.

'Yes, I don't see why not, just a bit.'

'Mister,' said Doris, near tears. 'Kiss me once before you go.'

'No. Mr Todhunter wouldn't like it. He's terribly jealous.'

'Is he?' she said lightening. 'I love jealous men.'

When Basil left her, her fervent, volatile affections were already plainly engaged with her new host. Marlene remained passive throughout the interview; she had few gifts, poor child, and those she was allowed to employ only on rare occasions. 'Mayn't I be sick here, Doris? Just once?'

'Not here, ducky. Wait till the gentleman billets you.'

'Will that be long?'

'No,' said Mr Todhunter decisively, 'not long.'

So the scourge of the Malfrey area moved South into the apple-growing country, and the market gardens; and all over the park at Malfrey, dispersed irregularly under the great elms, tents sprang up; and the yeomanry officers set up their mess in the Grinling Gibbons saloon; and Barbara had Colonel Sproggin and Major Cathcart to live in the house; and Freddy made an agreeable sum of money out of the arrangement; and Bill spent many blissful uxorious hours in the Malt House, Grantley Green (he was quite satisfied with the explanation he was given about the cellar door). And Basil returned to London.

2

HE decided to pay one of his rare, and usually rather brief, visits to his mother. He found her busy and optimistic, serving on half a dozen benevolent committees connected with comforts for the troops, seeing her friends regularly. The defeat of Finland had shocked her, but she found it a compensation that Russia was at last disclosed in its true light. She welcomed Basil to the house, heard his news of Barbara and gave him news of Tony. 'I want to have a little talk with you some time,' she said, after half an hour's gossip.

Basil, had he not been inured to his mother's euphemisms, might have supposed that a little talk was precisely what she had just had; but he knew what a little talk meant; it meant a discussion of his 'future'.

'Have you arranged anything for to-night?'

'No, mother, not yet.'

'Then we will dine in. Just the two of us.'

And that night after dinner she said, 'Basil, I never thought I should have to say this to you. I've been pleased, of course, that you were able to be of help to Barbara with her evacuees, but now that you have returned to London, I must tell you that I do not think it is *man's* work. At a time like this you ought to be *fighting*.'

'But mother, as far as I know, no one's fighting much at the moment.'

'Don't quibble, dear, you know what I mean.'

'Well, I went to see that colonel when you asked me to.'

'Yes. Sir Joseph explained that to me. They only want very young officers in the Guards. But he says that there are a number of other excellent regiments that offer a far better career. General Gordon was a Sapper, and I believe quite a number of the generals in this war were originally only gunners. I don't want you just lounging about London in uniform like your friend Peter Pastmaster. He seems to spend his whole time with girls. That goose Emma Granchester is seriously thinking of him for Molly. So is Etty Flintshire and so is poor Mrs Van Antrobus for *their* daughters. I don't know what they're thinking of. I knew his poor father. Margot led him a terrible dance. That was long before she married Metroland of course – before he was called Metroland, in fact. No,' said Lady Seal, abruptly checking herself in the flow of reminiscence. 'I want to see you doing something *important.* Now Sir Joseph has got me one of the forms you fill in to become an officer. It is called the Supplementary Reserve. Before you go to bed I want you to sign it. Then we'll see about getting it sent to the proper quarter. I'm sure that everything will be much easier now that that disgraceful Mr Belisha has been outed.'

'But you know, mother, I don't really fancy myself much as a subaltern.'

'No, dear,' said Lady Seal decisively, 'and if you had gone into the army when you left Oxford you would be a major by now. Promotion is very quick in war time because so many people get killed. I'm sure once you're in, they'll find great use for you. But you must begin somewhere. I remember Lord Kitchener told me that even he was once a subaltern.'

Thus it was that Basil found himself again in danger of being started on a career. 'Don't worry,' said Peter. 'No one ever gets taken off the Supplementary Reserve.' But Basil did worry. He had a rooted distrust of official forms. He felt that at any moment a telegram might summon him to present himself at some remote barracks, where he would spend the war, like Alastair's Mr Smallwood, teaching fieldcraft to thirty militiamen. It was not thus that he had welcomed the war as the ne'er-do-well's opportunity. He fretted about it for three days and then decided to pay a visit to the War Office.

He went there without any particular object in view, impelled by the belief that somewhere in that large organization was a goose who would lay eggs for him. In the first days of the war when he was seeking to interest the authorities in the annexation of Liberia, he had more than once sought an entrance. Perhaps, he felt now, he had pitched a little too high. The Chief of the Imperial General Staff was a busy man. This time he would advance humbly.

The maelstrom, which in early September had eddied round the vestibule of the building, seemed to have subsided very little. There was a similar – perhaps, he reflected sadly, an identical – crowd of officers of all ranks attempting to gain admission. Among them he saw a single civilian figure whom he recognized from his visit to the Ministry of Information.

'Hullo,' he said. 'Still hawking bombs?'

The little lunatic with the suitcase greeted him with great friendliness. 'They won't pay any attention. It's a most unsatisfactory office,' he said. 'They won't let me in. I was sent on here from the Admiralty.'

'Have you tried the Air Ministry?'

'Why, bless you, it was them sent me to the Ministry of Information. I've tried them all. I will say for the Ministry of Information they were uncommon civil. Not at all like they are here. At the M. of I. they were never too busy to see one. The only thing was, I felt I wasn't getting anywhere.'

'Come along,' said Basil. 'We'll get in.'

Veterans of the Ashanti and the Zulu campaigns guarded the entrance. Basil watched them stop a full general. 'If you'll fill in a form, sir, please, one of the boys will take you up to the department.' They were a match for anyone in uniform, but Basil and the bagman were a more uncertain quantity; a full general was just a full general, but a civilian might be anyone.

'Your passes, gentlemen, please.'

'That's all right, sergeant,' said Basil. 'I'll vouch for this man.'

'Yes, sir, but who are you, sir?'

'You ought to know by this time. M.I.13. We don't carry passes or give our names in my department.'

'Very good, sir; beg pardon, sir. D'you know the way or shall I send a boy up with you?'

'Of course I know my way,' said Basil sharply, 'and you might take a look at this man. He won't give his name or show a pass, but I expect you'll see him here often.'

'Very good, sir.'

The two civilians passed through the seething military into the calm of the corridors beyond.

'I'm sure I'm very obliged,' said the man with the suitcase; 'where shall I go now?'

'The whole place lies open to you,' said Basil. 'Take your time. Go where you like. I think if I were you I should start with the Chaplain General.'

'Where's he?'

'Up there,' said Basil vaguely. 'Up there and straight on.'

The little man thanked him gravely, trotted off down the corridor with the irregular, ill co-ordinated steps of the insane, and was lost to view up the bend in the staircase. Not wishing to compromise himself further by his act of charity, Basil took the opposing turning. A fine vista lay before him of twenty or more closed doors, any one of which might open upon prosperity and adventure. He strolled down the passage in a leisurely but purposeful manner; thus, he thought, an important agent might go to keep an appointment; thus, in fact, Soapy Sponge might have walked in the gallery of Jawleyford Court.

It was a vista full of potentiality but lacking, at the moment, in ornament – a vista of linoleum and sombre dado; the light came solely from the far end, so that a figure approaching appeared in silhouette, and in somewhat indistinct silhouette; a figure now approached and it was not until she was within a few yards of Basil that he realized that here was the enrichment which the austere architectural scheme demanded: a girl dressed in uniform with a lance-corporal's stripe on her arm – with a face of transparent, aethereal silliness which struck deep into Basil's heart. The classical image might have been sober fact, so swift and silent and piercing was the dart of pleasure. He turned in his tracks and followed the lance-corporal down the lane of linoleum which seemed, momentarily, as buoyant as the carpet of a cinema or theatre.

The lance-corporal led him a long way; she stopped from time to time to exchange greetings with passers-by, showing to all ranks from full general to second-class scout the same cheerful affection; she was clearly a popular girl in these parts. At length she turned into a door marked ADDIS; Basil followed her in. There was another lance-corporal – male – in the room.

This lance-corporal sat behind a typewriter; he had a white, pimply face, large spectacles and a cigarette in the corner of his mouth. He did not look up. The female lance-corporal smiled and said, 'So now you know where I live. Drop in any time you're passing.'

'What is ADDIS?' asked Basil.

'It's Colonel Plum.'

'What's Colonel Plum?'

'He's a perfect lamb. Go and take a peer at him if you like. He's in there.' She nodded towards a glass door marked KEEP OUT.

'Assistant Deputy Director Internal Security,' said the male lance-corporal without looking up from his typing.

'I think I'd like to come and work in this office,' said Basil.

'Yes, everyone says that. It was the same when I was in pensions.'

'I might take *his* job.'

'You're welcome,' said the male lance-corporal sourly. 'Suspects, suspects, suspects all day long, all with foreign names, none of them ever shot.'

A loud voice from beyond the glass door broke into the conversation. 'Susie, you slut, come here.'

'That's him, the angel. Just take a peer while the door's open. He's got the sweetest little moustache.'

Basil peered round the corner and caught a glimpse of a lean, military face and, as Susie had said, the sweetest little moustache. The colonel caught a glimpse of Basil.

'Who the devil's that?'

'I don't know,' said Susie lightly. 'He just followed me in.'

'Come here you,' said the Colonel. 'Who are you and what d'you want in my office?'

'Well,' said Basil, 'what the lance-corporal says is strictly true. I just followed her in. But since I'm here I can give you some valuable information.'

'If you can you're unique in this outfit. What is it?'

Until now the word 'Colonel' for Basil had connoted an elderly rock-gardener on Barbara's G.P.O. list. This formidable man of his own age was another kettle of fish. Here was a second Todhunter. What could he possibly tell him which would pass for valuable information?

'Can I speak freely before the lance-corporal?' he asked, playing for time.

'Yes, of course. She doesn't understand a word of any language.'

Inspiration came. 'There's a lunatic loose in the War Office,' Basil said.

'Of course there is. There are some hundreds of them. Is that all you came to tell me?'

'He's got a suitcase full of bombs.'

'Well I hope he finds his way to the Intelligence Branch. I don't suppose you know his name? No, well make out a card for him, Susie, with a serial number and index him under suspects. If his bombs go off we shall know where he is; if they don't it doesn't matter. These fellows usually do more harm to themselves than to anyone else. Run along, Susie, and shut the door. I want to talk to Mr Seal.'

Basil was shaken. When the door shut he said, 'Have we met before?'

'You bet we have. Jibuti 1936, St Jean de Luz 1937, Prague 1938. You wouldn't remember me. I wasn't dressed up like this then.'

'Were you a journalist?'

Vaguely at the back of Basil's mind was the recollection of an unobtrusive, discreet face among a hundred unobtrusive, discreet faces, that had passed in and out of his ken from time to time. During the past ten years he had usually managed to find himself, on one pretext or another, on the outer fringe of contemporary history; in that half-world there were numerous slightly sinister figures whose orbits crossed and recrossed, ubiquitous men and women camp-followers of diplomacy and the Press; among those shades he dimly remembered seeing Colonel Plum.

'Sometimes. We got drunk together once at the Bar Basque, the night you fought the United Press correspondent.'

'As far as I remember he won.'

'You bet he did. I took you back to your hotel. What are you doing now besides making passes at Susie?'

'I thought of doing counter-espionage.'

'Yes,' said Colonel Plum. 'Most people who come here seem to have thought of that. Hullo —' he added as a dull detonation shook the room slightly, 'that sounds as if your man has had a success with his bombs. That was a straight tip, anyway. I dare say you'd be no worse in the job than anyone else.'

Here it was at last, the scene that Basil had so often rehearsed, the scene, very slightly adapted by a later hand, in order to bring it up to date, from the adventure stories of his youth. Here was the lean, masterful man who had followed Basil's career saying, 'One day his country will have a use for him . . . '

'What are your contacts?'

What were his contacts? Alastair Digby-Vane-Trumpington, Angela Lyne, Margot Metroland, Peter Pastmaster, Barbara, the bride of Grantley Green, Mr Todhunter, Poppet Green – *Poppet Green*; there was his chicken.

'I know some very dangerous communists,' said Basil.

'I wonder if they're on our files. We'll look in a minute. We aren't doing much about communists at the moment. The politicians are shy of them for some reason. But we keep an eye on them, on the side, of course. I can't pay you much for communists.'

'As it happens,' said Basil with dignity, 'I came here to serve my country. I don't particularly want money.'

'The devil you don't? What *do* you want, then? You can't have Susie. I had the hell of a fight to get her away from the old brute in charge of pensions.'

'We can fight that out later. What I really want most at the moment is a uniform.'

'Good God! Why?'

'My mother is threatening to make me a platoon commander.'

Colonel Plum accepted this somewhat surprising statement with apparent understanding. 'Yes,' he said. 'There's a lot to be said for a uniform. For one thing you'll have to call me "sir" and if there's any funny stuff with the female staff I can take disciplinary action. For another thing it's the best possible disguise for a man of intelligence. No one ever suspects a soldier of taking a serious interest in the war. I think I can fix that.'

'What'll my rank be?'

'Second-Lieutenant, Crosse and Blackwell's regiment.'

'Crosse and Blackwell?'

'General Service List.'

'I say, can't you do anything better than that?'

'Not for watching communists. Catch a fascist for me and I'll think about making you a Captain of Marines.' At this moment the telephone bell rang. 'Yes, ADDIS speaking... oh, yes, the bomb... yes, we know all about that... the Chaplain General? I say that's bad... oh, only the Deputy Assistant Chaplain General and you think he'll recover. Well, what's all the fuss about?... Yes, we know all about the man in this branch. We've had him indexed a long time. He's nuts – yes, N for nuts, U for uncle, nuts, you've got it. No I don't want to see him. Lock him up. There must be plenty of padded cells in this building, I should imagine.'

News of the attempt to assassinate the Chaplain General reached the Religious Department of the Ministry of Information late in the afternoon, just when they were preparing to pack up for the day. It threw them into a fever of activity.

'Really,' said Ambrose pettishly. 'You fellows get all the fun. I shall be *most* embarrassed when I have to explain this to the editor of *The Godless Sunday at Home*.'

Lady Seal was greatly shocked.

'Poor man,' she said, 'I understand that his eyebrows have completely gone. It must have been Russians.'

3

FOR the third time since his return to London, Basil tried to put a call through to Angela Lyne. He listened to the repeated buzz, five, six, seven times, then hung up the receiver. Still away, he thought. I should have liked to show her my uniform.

Angela counted the rings, five, six, seven; then there was silence in the flat; silence except for the radio which said, '... dastardly attempt which has shocked the conscience of the civilized world. Messages of sympathy continue to pour into the Chaplain General's office from the religious leaders of four continents...'

She switched over to Germany where a rasping, contemptuous voice spoke of 'Churchill's attempt to make a second *Athenia* by bombing the military bishop'.

She switched on to France where a man of letters gave his impressions of a visit to the Maginot Line. Angela filled her glass from the bottle at her elbow. Her distrust of France was becoming an obsession with her now. It kept her awake at night and haunted her dreams by day; long, tedious dreams born of barbituric, dreams which had no element of fantasy or surprise, utterly real, drab dreams which, like waking life, held no promise of delight. She often spoke aloud to herself nowadays, living, as she did, so much alone; it was thus that lonely old women spoke, passing in the street with bags of rubbish in their hands, squatting, telling their rubbish. Angela was like an old woman squatting in a doorway picking over her day's gleaning of rubbish, talking to herself while she sorted the scraps of garbage. She had seen and heard old women like that, often, at the end of the day, in the side streets near the theatres.

Now she said to herself as loudly as though to someone sitting opposite on the white Empire day-bed, 'Maginot Line – Angela Lyne – both lines of least resistance' and laughed at her joke until the tears came and suddenly she found herself weeping in earnest.

Then she took a pull at herself. This wouldn't do at all. She had better go out to the cinema.

Peter Pastmaster was taking a girl out that evening. He looked very elegant and old-fashioned in his blue patrol jacket and tight overall trousers. He and the girl dined at a new restaurant in Jermyn Street.

She was Lady Mary Meadowes, Lord Granchester's second daughter. In his quest for a wife Peter had narrowed the field to three – Molly Meadowes; Sarah, Lord Flintshire's daughter; and Betty, daughter of the Duchess of Stayle. Since he was marrying for old-fashioned, dynastic reasons he proposed to make an old-fashioned, dynastic choice from among the survivors of the Whig oligarchy. He really could see very little difference between the three girls; in fact he sometimes caused offence by addressing them absent-mindedly by the wrong names. None of them carried a pound of superfluous flesh; they all had an enthusiasm for the works of Mr Ernest Hemingway; all had pet dogs of rather similar peculiarities. They had all found that the way to keep Peter amused was to get him to brag about his past iniquities.

During dinner he told Molly about the time when Basil Seal had stood for Parliament and he and Sonia and Alastair had done him dirt in his constituency. She laughed dutifully at the incident of Sonia throwing a potato at the mayor.

'Some of the papers got it wrong and said it was a bun,' he explained.

'What a lovely time you all seem to have had,' said Lady Mary wistfully.

'All past and done with,' said Peter primly.

'Is it? I *do* hope not.'

Peter looked at her with a new interest. Sarah and Betty had taken this tale as though it were one of highwaymen; something infinitely old-fashioned and picturesque.

Afterwards they walked to the cinema next door.

The vestibule was in darkness except for a faint blue light in the box office. Out of the darkness the voice of the commissionaire announced, 'No three and sixes. Plenty of room in the five and nines. Five and nines this way. Don't block up the gangway please.'

There was some kind of disturbance going on at the guichet. A woman was peering stupidly at the blue light and saying, 'I don't want five and nines. I want one three and sixpenny.'

'No three and sixes. Only five and nines.'

'But you don't understand. It isn't the price. The five and nines are too far away. I want to be *near*, in the three and sixpennies.'

'No three and sixes. Five and nines,' said the girl in the blue light.

'Come on, lady, make up your mind,' said a soldier, waiting.

'She's got a look of Mrs Cedric Lyne,' said Molly.

'Why,' said Peter, 'it *is* Angela. What on earth's the matter with her?'

She had now bought her ticket and moved away from the window, trying to read what was on it in the half-light and saying peevishly, 'I *told* them it was too far away. I can't see if I'm far away. I *said* three and sixpence.'

She held the ticket close up to her eyes, trying to read it; she did not notice the step, stumbled and sat down. Peter hurried forward.

'Angela, are you all right? Have you hurt yourself?'

'Perfectly all right,' said Angela, sitting quietly in the twilight. 'Not hurt at all, thank you.'

'Well for God's sake get up.'

Angela squinnied up at him from the step.

'*Peter*,' she said, 'I didn't recognize you. Too far away to recognize anyone in the five and ninepennies. *How* are you?'

'Angela, do get up.'

He held out his hand to help her up. She shook it cordially. 'How's Margot?' she said affably. 'Haven't seen her lately. I've been so busy. Well, that's not quite true. As a matter of fact I've not been altogether well.'

A crowd was beginning to assemble in the twilight. From the darkness beyond came the voice of the commissionaire, policemanlike, saying, 'What's going on here?'

'Pick her up, you coot,' said Molly Meadowes.

Peter got behind Angela, put his arms round her and picked her up. She was not heavy.

'Ups-a-daisy,' said Angela, making to sit down again.

Peter held her firm; he was glad of the darkness; this was no position for an officer of the Household Cavalry in uniform.

'A lady has fainted,' said Molly in a clear, authoritative voice. 'Please don't crowd round her,' and to the commissionaire, 'Call a cab.'

Angela was silent in the taxi.

'I say,' said Peter, 'I can't apologize enough for letting you in for this.'

'My dear man,' said Molly, 'don't be ridiculous. I'm thoroughly enjoying it.'

'I can't think what's the matter with her,' he said.

'Can't you?'

When they reached Grosvenor Square, Angela got out of the taxi and looked about her, puzzled. 'I thought we were going to the cinema,' she said. 'Wasn't it good?'

'It was full.'

'I remember,' said Angela, nodding vigorously. 'Five and nines.' Then she sat down again on the pavement.

'Look here,' said Peter to Lady Mary Meadowes. 'You take the taxi back to the cinema. Leave my ticket at the box-office. I'll join you in half an hour. I think I'd better see Angela home and get hold of a doctor.'

'Bumbles,' said Molly. 'I'm coming up too.'

Outside her door Angela suddenly rallied, found her key, opened the flat and walked steadily in. Grainger was still up.

'You need not have stayed in,' said Angela. 'I told you I shouldn't want you.'

'I was worried. You shouldn't have gone out like that,' and then seeing Peter, 'Oh, good evening, my lord.'

Angela turned and saw Peter, as though for the first time. 'Hullo, Peter,' she said. 'Come in.' She fixed Molly with eyes that seemed to focus with difficulty. 'You know,' she said, 'I'm sure I know you quite well, but I can't remember your name.'

'Molly Meadowes,' said Peter. 'We just came to see you home. We must be going along now. Grainger, Mrs Lyne isn't at all well. I think you ought to get her doctor.'

'Molly Meadowes. My dear, I used to stay at Granchester when you were in the nursery. How old that sounds. You're very pretty, Molly, and you're wearing a lovely dress. Come in, both of you.'

Peter frowned at Molly, but she went into the flat.

'Help yourself to something to drink, Peter,' said Angela. She sat down in her armchair by the radio. 'My dear,' she said to Molly, 'I don't think you've seen my flat. I had it done up by David Lennox just before the war. David Lennox. People say unkind things about David Lennox . . . well, you can't blame them . . .' her mind was becoming confused again. She made a resolute attempt to regain control of herself. 'That's a portrait of me by John. Ten years ago; nearly done when I was married. Those are my books . . . my dear, I'm afraid I'm rather distraite this evening. You must forgive me,' and, so saying, she fell into a heavy sleep.

Peter looked about him helplessly. Molly said to Grainger, 'Had we better get her to bed?'

'When she wakes up, I shall be here. I can manage.'

'Sure?'

'Quite sure.'

'Well then, Peter, we'd better get back to our film.'

'Yes,' said Peter. 'I'm awfully sorry for bringing you here.'

'I wouldn't have missed it for anything,' said Molly.

Peter was still puzzled by the whole business.

'Grainger,' he said. 'Had Mrs Lyne been out this evening? To a party or anything?'

'Oh, no, my lord. She's been in all day.'

'Alone?'

'Quite alone, my lord.'

'Extraordinary thing. Well come on, Molly. Good night, Grainger. Take care of Mrs Lyne. I think she ought to see a doctor.'

'I'll take care of her,' said Grainger.

They went down in the lift together, in silence, each full of thought. When they reached the hall Peter said, 'Well, that was rum.'

'Very rum.'

'You know,' said Peter, 'if it had been anyone else but Angela, I should have thought she was tight.'

'Darling, she was plastered.'

'Are you sure?'

'My dear, stinko paralytico.'

'Well, I don't know what to think. It certainly looked like it. But *Angela*... besides her maid said she hadn't been out all the evening. I mean to say people don't get tight alone.'

Suddenly Molly put her arms round Peter's neck and kissed him warmly. 'Bless you,' she said. 'Now we'll go to that cinema.'

It was the first time anyone had ever kissed Peter like that. He was so surprised that in the taxi he made no attempt to follow it up; so surprised that he thought about nothing else all through the film. 'God Save the King' brought him back to reality with a jolt. He was still pensive while he led Molly to supper. It was hysteria, he decided; the girl was naturally upset at the scene they had been through. She's probably frightfully embarrassed about it now; best not to refer to it.

But Molly was not prepared to let the matter drop.

'Oysters,' she said. 'Only a dozen. Nothing else,' and then, though the waiter was still beside her, 'Were you surprised when I kissed you just now?'

'No,' said Peter hastily, 'certainly not. Not at all.'

'Not at all? You mean to say you *expected* me to?'

'No, no. Of course not. You know what I mean.'

'I certainly don't. I think it's very conceited of you not to be surprised. Do you always have this effect on girls, or is it just the uniform?'

'Molly, don't be a beast. If you must know, I *was* surprised.'

'And shocked?'

'No, just surprised.'

'Yes,' said Molly, seeing it was not kind to tease him any more. 'I was surprised, too. I've been wondering about it in the cinema.'

'So have I,' said Peter.

'*That's* how I like you,' said Molly, as though she were a photographer catching a happy expression. She saw the likeness herself and added, 'Hold it.'

'Really, Molly, I don't understand you a bit to-night.'

'Oh but you must, really you must, Peter. I'm sure you were a fascinating little boy.'

'Come to think of it, I believe I was.'

'You mustn't ever try playing the old rip again, Peter. Not with me, at any rate. Now don't pretend you don't understand that. I like you puzzled, Peter, but not *absolutely cretinous*. You know, I nearly despaired of you to-night. You would go on bucking about what a gay dog you'd been. I thought I could never go through with it.'

'Through with what?'

'Marrying you. Mother's terribly keen I should, though I can't think why. I should have thought from her point of view you were about the end. But no, nothing else would do but that I must marry you. So I've tried to be good and I've let you bound away about the good old days till I thought I should have to pour something on your head. Thought I couldn't bear it any more and I'd decided to tell mother it was off. Then we met Mrs Lyne and everything was all right.'

'It seemed awfully awkward to me.'

'Of course it did. You looked like a little boy at his private school when his father has come to the sports in the wrong kind of hat. An adorable little boy.'

'Well,' said Peter, 'I suppose as long as you're satisfied . . . '

'Yes, I think "satisfied" is the word. You'll do. And Sarah and Betty'll be as sick as cats.'

'How did you decide?' asked Margot, when Peter told her of his engagement.

'Well, as a matter of fact, I don't think I did. Molly decided.'

'Yes, that's usually the way. Now I suppose I shall have to do something friendly about that ass Emma Granchester.'

'I really know Lady Metroland very little,' said Lady Granchester. 'But I suppose now I must invite her to luncheon. I'm afraid she's far too smart for us.' And by 'smart' Lady Granchester meant nothing at all complimentary.

But the mothers met and decided on an immediate marriage.

4

THE news of Peter's engagement was not unexpected and, even had it come as a surprise, would have been eclipsed in interest by the story of Angela Lyne's uncharacteristic behaviour at the cinema. Peter and Molly, before parting that night, had resolved to tell no one of the incident; a renunciation from which each made certain implicit reservations. Peter told Margot because he thought she ought to do something about it, Basil because he was still dubious about the true explanation of the mystery and thought that Basil, if anyone could, would throw light on it, and three members of Bratts because he happened to run into them at the bar next morning when his mind was still full of the matter. Molly told her two sisters and Lady Sarah from long habit, because whenever she promised secrecy in any matter she meant, even at the time, to tell these three. These initiates in their turn told their cronies until it was widely known that the temperate, cynical, aloof, impeccably dressed, sharply dignified Mrs Lyne; Mrs Lyne who never 'went out' in a general sense but lived in a rarefied and enviable coterie; Mrs Lyne whose conversation was that of a highly intelligent man, who always cleverly kept out of the gossip columns and picture papers, who for fifteen years had set a high and wholly individual standard of all that Americans meant by 'poise'; this almost proverbial lady had been picked up by Peter in the gutter where she had been thrown struggling by two bouncers from the cinema where she had created a drunken disturbance.

It could scarcely have been more surprising had it been Mrs Stitch herself. It was indeed barely credible and many refused to believe it. Drugs possibly, they conceded, but Drink was out of the question. What Parsnip and Pimpernell were to the intelligentsia, Mrs Lyne and the bottle became to the fashionable world; topic number one.

It was still topic number one three months later at Peter's wedding. Basil persuaded Angela to come to the little party with which Lady Granchester honoured the occasion.

He had gone round to see her when Peter told him the news; not immediately, but within twenty-four hours of hearing it. He found her up and dressed, but indefinably raffish in appearance; her make-up was haphazard and rather garish, like a later Utrillo.

'Angela you look awful.'

'Yes, darling, I feel awful. You're in the army.'

'No, the War Office.'

She began talking intensely and rather wildly about the French. Presently she said, 'I must leave you for a minute,' and went into her bedroom. She came back half a minute later with an abstracted little smile; the inwardly happy smile of a tired old nun – almost. There was a difference.

'Angela,' said Basil, 'if you want a drink you might drink fair with a chap.'

'I don't know what you mean,' she said.

Basil was shocked. There had never been any humbug about Angela before, none where he was concerned anyway.

'Oh, come off it,' he said.

Angela came off it. She began to weep.

'Oh, for Christ's sake,' said Basil.

He went into her bedroom and helped himself to whisky from the bottle by the bed.

'Peter was here the other evening with some girl. I suppose they've told everyone.'

'He told *me.* Why don't you switch to rum? It's much better for you.'

'Is it? I don't think I've ever tasted it. Should I like it?'

'I'll send you some round. When did you start on this bat?'

There was no humbug about Angela now. 'Oh, weeks ago.'

'It's not a bit like you.'

'Isn't it, Basil? Isn't it?'

'You were always bloody to me when I had a bat.'

'Yes, I suppose I was. I'm sorry. But then you see I was in love with you.'

'Was?'

'Oh, I don't know. Fill up the glasses, Basil.'

'That's the girl.'

'"Was" is wrong. I do love you, Basil.'

'Of course you do. Is that how you take it?' he asked, respectfully.

'That's how I take it.'

'Good and strong.'

'Good and strong.'

'But I think we'd be better suited to rum.'

'Doesn't it smell rather?'

'I don't see it matters.'

'Don't want to smell.'

'Whisky smells.'

'Well, I suppose it doesn't matter. It's nice drinking with you, Basil.'

'Of course it's nice. I think it's pretty mean of you to drink without me as you've been doing.'

'I'm not mean.'

'You usen't to be. But you have been lately, haven't you? Drinking by yourself.'

'Yes, that was mean.'

'Now listen, next time you want to go on a bat, let me know. Just ring me up and I'll come round. Then we can drink together.'

'But I want to so often, Basil.'

'Well, I'll come round often. Promise me.'

'I promise.'

'That's the girl.'

The rum was a failure, but in general the new arrangement worked well. Angela drank a good deal less and Basil a good deal more than they had done for the last few weeks and both were happier as a result.

*

Margot tackled Basil on the matter. 'What's the matter with her?' she asked.

'She doesn't like the war.'

'Well, no one does.'

'Don't they? I can't think why not. Anyway, why shouldn't the girl have a drink?'

'You don't think we ought to get her into a home?'

'Good God, no.'

'But she sees nobody.'

'She sees me.'

'Yes, but . . .'

'Honestly, Margot, Angela's fine. A little break like this is what she's been needing all these years. I'll make her come to the wedding if you like and you can see for yourself.'

So Angela came to the wedding. She and Basil did not make the church but they came to the little party at Lady Granchester's house afterwards, and stole the scene. Molly had had her moment of prominence; she had had her double line of troopers and her arch of cavalry sabres; she had had her veil of old lace. In spite of the war it was a pretty wedding. But at her mother's house all eyes were on Mrs Lyne. Even Lady Anchorage and the Duchess of Stayle could not dissemble their interest.

'My dear, *there she is*.'

There she was, incomparably dressed, standing by Basil, talking gravely to Sonia; she wore dark glasses; otherwise there was nothing unusual about her. A footman brought a tray of champagne. 'Is there such a thing as a cup of tea,' she said, 'without cream or sugar?'

Molly and Peter stood at one end of the long drawing-room, Angela at the other. As the guests filed past the bride and bridegroom and came into the straight, you could see them come to the alert at the sight of Angela and draw one another's attention to her. Her own coterie formed round her and she talked like a highly intelligent man. When the last of the guests had shaken hands with them – they were comparatively few – Molly and Peter joined the group at the far end.

'Molly, you are the prettiest girl I've ever seen,' said Angela. 'I'm afraid I was a bore the other night.'

A silly girl would have been embarrassed and said, 'No, not at all.' Molly said, 'Not a *bore*. You were rather odd.'

'Yes,' said Angela. '"Odd" is the word. I'm not always like that, you know.'

'May Peter and I come and see you again? He's only got a week, you know, and then we shall be in London.'

'That's an unusually good girl Peter's picked for himself,' said Angela to Basil when they were alone after the party at her flat. 'You ought to marry someone like that.'

'I could never marry anyone, except, I suppose, you.'

'No, I don't believe you could, Basil.'

When their glasses were filled she said, 'I seem to be getting to the age when I enjoy weddings. I liked that girl this afternoon. D'you know who was here this morning? Cedric.'

'How very odd.'

'It was rather touching really. He came to say good-bye. He's off to-morrow. He couldn't say where, but I guess it's Norway. I never thought of him as a soldier, somehow, but he used to be one till he married me – a very bad one I believe. Poor Cedric, he's had a raw deal.'

'He's not done so badly. He's enjoyed himself messing about with grottoes. And he's had Nigel.'

'He brought Nigel this morning. They gave him a day away from school to say good-bye. You never knew Cedric when I married him. He was most romantic – genuinely. I'd never met anyone like him. Father's friends were all hard-boiled and rich – men like Metroland and Copper. They were the only people I ever saw. And then I met Cedric who was poor and very, very soft-boiled and tall and willowy and very unhappy in a boring smart regiment because he only cared about Russian ballet and baroque architecture. He had the most charming manner and he was always laughing up his sleeve about people like my father and his officers in the regiment. Poor Cedric, it used to be such fun finding things to give him. I bought him an octopus once and we had a case made for its tank, carved with dolphins and covered with silver leaf.'

'It wouldn't have lasted, even if I hadn't come along.'

'No, it wouldn't have lasted. I'm afraid the visit this morning was rather a disappointment to him. He'd planned it all in an attitude of high tragedy, and, my dear, I had such a hangover I had to keep my eyes shut nearly all the time he was here. He's worried about what will happen to the house if he gets killed.'

'Why should he get killed?'

'Why, indeed? Except that he was always such a bad soldier. You know, when the war started I quite made up my mind you were for it.'

'So did my mother. But I'm taking care of that. Which reminds me I ought to go and see Colonel Plum again. He'll be getting restive. I'll go along now.'

'Will he be there?'

'He never leaves. A very conscientious officer.'

Susie was there, too, waiting till the Colonel was free to take her out to dinner. At the sight of the office, some of Basil's elation began to fade away. Basil's job at the War Office looked like going the way of all the others; once secured, it had few attractions for him. Susie was proving a disappointment; in spite of continued remonstrance, she still seemed to prefer Colonel Plum.

'Good evening, handsome,' she said. 'Plummy has been asking for you.'

Basil went through the door marked KEEP OUT.

'Good evening, Colonel.'

'You can call me "sir".'

'None of the best regiments call their commanding officers "sir".'

'You're not in one of the best regiments. You're General Service. What have you been doing all day?'

'You don't think it will improve the tone of the department if I called you "Colonel", sir?'

'I do not. Where have you been and what have you been doing?'

'You think I've been drinking, don't you?'

'I bloody well know you have.'

'But you don't know the reason. You wouldn't understand if I told you. I've been drinking out of chivalry. That doesn't make any sense to you, does it?'

'No.'

'I thought it wouldn't. Coarse grained, sir. If they put on my grave, "He drank out of chivalry", it would simply be the sober truth. But you wouldn't understand. What's more you think I've been idle, don't you?'

'I do.'

'Well, sir, that's where you're wrong. I have been following up a very interesting trail. I hope to have some valuable information very soon.'

'What have you got up to date?'

'You wouldn't sooner wait until I can give you the whole case cut and dried?'

'No.'

'Well, I'm on to a very dangerous woman who calls herself Green. Among her intimates she's known as "Poppet". She pretends to be a painter, but you have only to look at her work to realize it is a cloak for other activities. Her studio is the meeting place for a communist cell. She has an agent in the United States named Parsnip; he has the alias of Pimpernell; he puts it about that he is a poet, two poets in fact, but there again, the work betrays him. Would you like me to quote some Parsnip to you?'

'No.'

'I have reason to believe that Green is the head of an underground organization by which young men of military age are smuggled out of the country. Those are the lines I have been working on. What d'you think of them?'

'Rotten.'

'I was afraid you might say that. It's your own fault. Give me time and I would have had a better story.'

'Now you can do some work. Here's a list of thirty-three addresses of suspected fascists. Check them up.'

'Now?'

'Now.'

'Shan't I keep track of the woman Green?'

'Not in office hours.'

'I can't think what you see in your Plum,' said Basil when he regained the outer office. 'It must simply be snobbery.'

'It's not: it's love. The officer in the pensions office was a full Colonel, so there.'

'I expect you'll be reduced to subalterns, yet. And by the way, lance-corporal, you can call me "sir".'

Susie giggled. 'I believe you're drunk,' she said.

'Drunk with chivalry,' said Basil.

That evening Cedric Lyne left to rejoin his regiment. The forty-eight hours' embarkation leave was over and although he had chosen to start an hour earlier rather than travel by the special train, it was only with difficulty that he found a carriage free from brother officers who had made the same choice. They were going to the North to embark at dawn next day and sail straight into action.

The first-class carriage was quite full, four a side, and the racks were piled high with baggage. Black funnel-shaped shields cast the light on to the passengers' laps; their faces in the surrounding darkness were indistinguishable; a naval pay-master-commander slept peacefully in one corner; two civilians strained their eyes over the evening papers; the other four were soldiers. Cedric sat between two soldiers, stared at the shadowy luggage above the civilians' heads, and ruminated, chewing the last, bitter essence from the events of the last two days.

Because he was thirty-five years of age, and spoke French and was built rather for grace than smartness, they had made Cedric battalion intelligence officer. He kept the war diary, and on wet days was often borrowed by the company commanders to lecture on map reading, security, and the order of battle of a German infantry division. These were Cedric's three lectures. When they were exhausted he was sent on a gas-course and after that on a course of interpretation of air photographs. On exercise he stuck pins in a map and kept a file of field messages.

'There really isn't very much you can do until we get into action,' said his commanding officer. 'You might ring up the photographers in Aldershot about taking that regimental group.'

They put him in charge of the Officers' Mess and made his visits there hideous with complaints.

'We're out of Kümmel again, Cedric.'

'Surely there's some perfectly simple way of keeping the soup hot, Lyne.'

'If officers *will* take the papers to their quarters, the only answer is to order more papers.'

'The Stilton has been allowed to go dry again.'

That had been his life; but Nigel did not know this. For Nigel, at eight years of age, his father was a man-at-arms and a hero. When they were given embarkation leave, Cedric telephoned to Nigel's headmaster and the child met him at their station in the country. Pride in his father and pleasure at an unforeseen holiday made their night at home an enthralling experience for Nigel. The home was given over to empty wards and an idle hospital staff. Cedric and his son stayed in the farm where, before she left, Angela had fitted up a few rooms with furniture from the house. Nigel was full of questions; why Cedric's buttons were differently arranged from the fathers' and brothers' buttons of most of the fellows; what was the difference between a Bren and a Vickers; how much faster were our fighters than the Germans'; whether Hitler had fits, as one fellow said, and, if so, did he froth at the mouth and roll his eyes as the girl at the lodge had once done.

That evening, Cedric took a long farewell of his water garden. It was for the water principally that he and Angela had chosen the place, ten years ago, when they were first engaged. It rose in a clear and copious spring in the hillside above the house and fell in a series of natural cascades to join the considerable stream which flowed more solemnly through the park. He and Angela had eaten a picnic lunch by this spring and looked down on the symmetrical, rectangular building below.

'It'll do,' said Angela. 'I'll offer them fifteen thousand.'

It never embarrassed Cedric to be married to a rich woman. He had not married for money in any gross sense, but he loved the rare and beautiful things which money could buy, and Angela's great fortune made her trebly rare and beautiful in his eyes.

It was surprising that they should have met at all. Cedric had been for years in his regiment, kept there by his father who gave him an allowance, which he could ill spare, on that condition alone. It was that or an office for Cedric and, despite the tedious company, there was just enough pageantry about peace-time soldiering to keep his imagination engaged. Cedric was accomplished; he was a beautiful horseman but hated the rigours of fox-hunting; he was a very fine shot, and because that formed a single tenuous bond with his brother officers and because it was agreeable to do anything pre-eminently well, he accepted invitations to pheasant-shooting in houses where, when they were not at the coverts, he felt lost and lonely. Angela's father had a celebrated shoot in Norfolk; he had also, Cedric was told, a collection of French impressionists. Thither that autumn ten years ago Cedric had gone and had found the pictures too obvious and the birds too tame and the party tedious beyond description, except for Angela, past her debutante days, aloof now and living in a cool and mysterious solitude of her own creation. She had resisted at first every attempt on the defences she had built up against a noisy world and then, quite suddenly, she had accepted Cedric as being like herself a stranger in these parts, as being, unlike herself, full of understanding of another, more splendid, attainable world outside. Angela's father thought Cedric a poor fellow, settled vast sums on them, and let them go their own way.

And this was the way they had gone. Cedric stood by the spring, enshrined, now, in a little temple. The architrave was covered with stalactites, the dome was set with real shells and the clear water bubbled out from the feet of a Triton. Cedric and Angela had bought this temple on their honeymoon at a deserted villa in the hills behind Naples.

Below in the hillside lay the cave which Cedric had bought the summer that Angela had refused to come with him to Salzburg; the summer when she met Basil. The lonely and humiliating years after that summer each had its monument.

'Daddy, what are you waiting for?'

'I'm just looking at the grottoes.'

'But you've seen them thousands of times. They're always the same.'

Always the same; joys for ever; not like men and women with their loves and hates.

'Daddy, there's an aeroplane. Is it a Hurricane?'

'No, Nigel, a Spitfire.'

'How d'you tell the difference?'

Then, on an impulse, he had said, 'Nigel, shall we go to London and see mummy?'

'We might see "The Lion has Wings" too. The fellows say it's awfully decent.'

'All right, Nigel, we'll see both.'

So the two of them went to London by the early morning train. 'Let's surprise her,' said Nigel, but Cedric telephoned first, wryly remembering the story of the pedantic adulterer – 'My dear, it is *I* who am *surprised*; *you* are *astounded*.'

'I am coming round to see Mrs Lyne.'

'She isn't very well this morning.'

'I'm sorry to hear that. Is she able to see people?'

'Yes, I think so, sir. I'll ask . . . yes, madam will be very pleased to see you and Master Nigel.'

They had not met for three years, since they discussed the question of divorce. Cedric understood exactly what Angela had felt about that; it was curious, he reflected, how some people were shy of divorce because of their love of society; they did not want there to be any occasion when their presence might be an embarrassment, they wanted to keep their tickets for the Ascot enclosure. With Angela reluctance came from precisely the opposite motives; she could not brook any intrusion on her privacy; she did not want to answer questions in court or allow the daily paper a single item of information about herself. 'It's not as though you wanted to marry anyone else, Cedric.'

'You don't think the present arrangement makes me look rather foolish?'

'Cedric, what's come over you? You used not to talk like that.'

So he had given way and that year had spanned the stream with a bridge in the Chinese Taste, taken direct from Batty Langley.

In the five minutes of waiting before Grainger took him into Angela's bedroom, he studied David Lennox's grisailles with distaste.

'Are they old, Daddy?'

'No, Nigel, they're not old.'

'They're awfully feeble.'

'They are.' Regency: this was the age of Waterloo and highwaymen and duelling and slavery and revivalist preaching and Nelson having his arm off with no anaesthetic but rum, and Botany Bay – and *this* is what they make of it.

'Well, I prefer the pictures at home, even if they are old. Is that mummy?'

'Yes.'

'Is that old?'

'Older than you, Nigel.'

Cedric turned from the portrait of Angela. What a nuisance John had been about the sittings. It was her father who had insisted on their going to him.

'Is it finished?'

'Yes. It was very hard to make the man finish it, though.'

'It hardly looks finished now, does it Daddy? It's all sploshy.'

Then Grainger opened the door. 'Come in, Cedric,' Angela called from her bed.

Angela was wearing dark glasses. Her make-up things lay on the quilt before her, with which she had been hastily doing her face. Nigel might have asked if it was finished; it was sploshy, like the John portrait.

'I had no idea you were ill,' said Cedric stiffly.

'I'm not really. Nigel, haven't you got a kiss for mummy?'

'Why are you wearing those glasses?'

'My eyes are tired, darling.'

'Tired of what?'

'Cedric,' said Angela petulantly, 'for God's sake don't let him be a bore. Go with Miss Grainger into the next room, darling.'

'Oh, all right,' said Nigel. 'Don't be long, Daddy.'

'You and he seem to be buddies these days.'

'Yes, it's the uniform.'

'Funny your being in the army again.'

'I'm off to-night, abroad.'

'France?'

'I don't think so. I mustn't tell about it. That's why I came to see you.'

'About not talking about not going to France?' said Angela in something of her old teasing way.

Cedric began to talk about the house; he hoped Angela would keep on to it, even if anything happened to him; he thought he saw some glimmerings of taste in the boy; he might grow to appreciate it later. Angela was inattentive and answered absently.

'I'm afraid I'm tiring you.'

'Well, I'm not feeling terribly well to-day. Did you want to see me about anything special?'

'No, I don't think so. Just to say good-bye.'

'Daddy,' came a voice from the next room. 'Aren't you coming?'

'Oh, dear, I wish I could do something about it. I feel there's something I ought to do. It's quite an occasion really, isn't it? I'm not being beastly, Cedric, I really mean it. I think it's sweet of you to come. I only wish I felt up to doing something about it.'

'Daddy, come on. We want to get to Bassett-Lowke's before lunch.'

'Take care of yourself,' said Angela.

'Why?'

'Oh, I don't know. Why will you all ask questions?'

And that had been the end of the visit. At Bassett-Lowke's, Nigel had chosen a model of a Blenheim bomber. 'The fellows *will* be jealous,' he said.

After luncheon they went to see 'The Lion has Wings', and then it was time to put Nigel into the train back to school. 'It's been absolutely ripping, Daddy,' he said.

'Has it really?'

'The rippingest two days I ever spent.'

So after these ripping days Cedric sat in the half-dark, with the pool of light falling on the unread book on his knees, returning to duty.

Basil went to the Café Royal to keep his watch on 'the woman Green'. He found her sitting among her cronies and was greeted with tepid affection.

'So you're in the army now,' she said.

'No, the great uniformed bureaucracy. How are all the Reds?'

'Very well thank you, watching your imperialists making a mess of your war.'

'Been to many communist meetings lately?'

'Why?'

'Just wondering.'

'You sound like a police spy.'

'That's the very last impression I want to make,' and, changing the subject hastily, added, 'Seen Ambrose lately?'

'He's over there now, the lousy fascist.'

Basil looked where she indicated and saw Ambrose at a table by the rail of the opposing gallery, sitting with a little, middle-aged man of nondescript appearance.

'Did you say "fascist"?'

'Didn't you know? He's gone to the Ministry of Information and he's bringing out a fascist paper next month.'

'This is very interesting,' said Basil. 'Tell me some more.'

*

Ambrose sat, upright and poised, with one hand on the stem of his glass and one resting stylishly on the balustrade. There was no particular feature of his clothes which could be mentioned as conspicuous; he wore a dark, smooth suit that fitted perhaps a little closely at waist and wrists, a shirt of plain, cream-coloured silk; a dark, white spotted bow tie; his sleek black hair was not unduly long (he went to the same barber as Alastair and Peter); his pale Semitic face gave no hint of special care and yet it always embarrassed Mr Bentley somewhat to be seen with him in public. Sitting there, gesticulating very slightly as he talked, wagging his head very slightly, raising his voice occasionally in a suddenly stressed uncommon epithet or in a fragment of slang embedded in his precise and literary diction, giggling between words now and then as something which he had intended to say changed shape and became unexpectedly comic in the telling – Ambrose like this caused time to slip back to an earlier age than his own youth or Mr Bentley's, when amid a more splendid décor of red plush and gilt caryatides *fin-de-siècle* young worshippers crowded to the tables of Oscar and Aubrey.

Mr Bentley smoothed his sparse grey hairs and fidgeted with his tie and looked about anxiously for fear he was observed.

The Café Royal, perhaps because of its distant associations with Oscar and Aubrey, was one of the places where Ambrose preened himself, spread his feathers and felt free to take wing. He had left his persecution mania downstairs with his hat and umbrella. He defied the universe.

'The decline of England, my dear Geoffrey,' he said, 'dates from the day we abandoned coal fuel. No, I'm not talking about distressed areas, but about distressed *souls*, my dear. We used to live in a fog, the splendid, luminous, tawny fogs of our early childhood. The golden aura of the Golden Age. Think of it, Geoffrey, there are children now coming to manhood who never saw a London fog. We designed a city which was meant to be seen in a fog. We had a foggy habit of life and a rich, obscure, choking literature. The great catch in the throat of English lyric poetry is just *fog*, my dear, on the vocal cords. And out of the fog we could rule the world; we were a Voice, like the

Voice of Sinai smiling through the clouds. Primitive peoples always choose a God who speaks from a cloud. *Then*, my dear Geoffrey,' said Ambrose, wagging an accusing finger and fixing Mr Bentley with a black accusing eye, as though the poor publisher were personally responsible for the whole thing, '*then*, some busybody invents electricity or oil fuel or whatever it is they use nowadays. The fog lifts, the world sees us as we are, and worse still we see ourselves as we are. It was a carnival ball, my dear, which when the guests unmasked at midnight, was found to be composed entirely of impostors. Such a *rumpus*, my dear.'

Ambrose drained his glass with a swagger, surveyed the café haughtily and saw Basil, who was making his way towards them.

'We are talking of fogs,' said Mr Bentley.

'They're eaten hollow with communism,' said Basil, introducing himself in the part of *agent provocateur*. 'You can't stop a rot that's been going on twenty years by imprisoning a handful of deputies. Half the thinking men in France have begun looking to Germany as their real ally.'

'*Please* Basil, don't start politics. Anyway, we were talking of Fogs, not Frogs.'

'Oh, Fogs.' Basil attempted to tell of a foggy adventure of his own, sailing a yawl round Bear Island, but Ambrose was elated to-night and in no mood for these loose leaves of Conrad drifting in the high wind of his talk. 'We must return to the Present,' he said prophetically.

'Oh dear,' said Mr Bentley. 'Why?'

'Everyone is either looking back or forward. Those with reverence and good taste, like you, my dear Geoffrey, look back to an Augustan age; those with generous hearts and healthy lives and the taste of the devil, like Poppet Green over there, look forward to a Marxian Jerusalem. *We* must accept the Present.'

'You would say, wouldn't you,' said Basil, persevering, 'that Hitler was a figure of the present?'

'I regard him as a page for *Punch*,' said Ambrose. 'To the Chinese scholar the military hero was the lowest of human types, the subject for ribaldry. We must return to Chinese scholarship.'

'It's a terribly difficult language, I believe,' said Mr Bentley.

'I knew a Chink in Valparaiso . . . ' began Basil; but Ambrose was now in full gallop.

'European scholarship has never lost its monastic character,' he said. 'Chinese scholarship deals with taste and wisdom, not with the memorizing of facts. In China the man whom we make a don sat for the Imperial examinations and became a bureaucrat. Their scholars were lonely men of few books and fewer pupils, content with a single concubine, a pine tree and the prospect of a stream. European culture has become conventual; we must make it cenobitic.'

'I knew a hermit in the Ogaden desert once . . . '

'Invasions swept over China; the Empire split up into warring kingdoms. The scholars lived their frugal and idyllic lives undisturbed, occasionally making exquisite private jokes which they wrote on leaves and floated downstream.'

'I read a lot of Chinese poetry once,' said Mr Bentley, 'in the translation, of course. I became fascinated by it. I would read of a sage who, as you say, lived frugally and idyllically. He had a cottage and a garden and a view. Each flower had its proper mood and phase of the climate; he would smell the jasmine after recovering from the toothache and the lotus when drinking tea with a monk. There was a little clearing where the full moon cast no shadow, where his concubine would sit and sing to him when he got drunk. Every aspect of this little garden corresponded to some personal mood of the most tender and refined sort. It was quite intoxicating to read.'

'It is.'

'This sage had no tame dog, but he had a cat and a mother. Every morning he greeted his mother on his knees and every evening, in winter, he put charcoal under her mattress and himself drew the bed-curtains. It sounded the most exquisite existence.'

'It was.'

'And then,' said Mr Bentley, 'I found a copy of the *Daily Mirror* in a railway carriage and I read an article there by Godfrey Winn about his cottage and his flowers and his moods, and for the life of me, Ambrose, I couldn't see the difference between that young gentleman and Yuan Ts'e-tsung.'

It was cruel of Mr Bentley to say this, but it may be argued for him that he had listened to Ambrose for three hours and now that Basil had joined their table he wanted to go home to bed.

The interruption deflated Ambrose and allowed Basil to say, 'These scholars of yours, Ambrose – they didn't care if their empire was invaded?'

'Not a hoot, my dear, not a *tinker's* hoot.'

'And you're starting a paper to encourage this sort of scholarship.'

Basil sat back and ordered a drink, as an advocate in a film will relax, saying in triumph, 'Mr District Attorney, *your* witness.'

There were four hours of darkness to go when Cedric arrived at the port of embarkation. There was a glimmer of light in some of the offices along the quayside, but the quay itself and the ship were in complete darkness; the top-hamper was just discernible as a darker mass against the dark sky. An E.S.O. told Cedric to leave his gear on the quay. The advanced working party were handling that. He left his valise and carried his suitcase up the gangway; at the head an invisible figure directed him to the first-class quarters forward. He found his C.O. in the saloon.

'Hullo, Lyne. You're back already. Lucky. Billy Allgood broke his collar-bone on leave and isn't coming with us. You'd better take charge of the embarkation. There's a hell of a lot to do. Some blasted Highlanders have come to the wrong ship and are all over our troop decks. Had any dinner?'

'I got some oysters in London before starting.'

'Very wise. I tried to get something kept hot. Told them we should all be coming on board hungry, but they're still working peace-time routine here. This is all I could raise.'

He pointed to a large, silvery tray where, disposed on a napkin, lay a dozen lozenges of toast covered with sardines, slivers of cheese and little glazed pieces of tongue. This was the tray that was always brought to the first-class saloon at ten o'clock at night.

'Come back when you've found your cabin.'

Cedric found his cabin, perfectly in order, complete with three towels of different sizes and the photograph of a mustachioed man putting on his life-jacket in the correct manner. He left his suitcase and returned to the C.O.

'Our men will be coming on board in an hour and a half. I don't know what the devil these Highlanders are doing. Find out and clear them off.'

'Very good, Colonel.'

Cedric plunged down again into the darkness and found the E.S.O. They studied the embarkation orders with the aid of a dimmed torch. There was no doubt about it; the Highlanders were in the wrong ship. This was the *Duchess of Cumberland*; they should be in the *Duchess of Clarence*. 'But the *Clarence* isn't here,' said the E.S.O. 'I dare say they were told to go to the *Cumberland* by someone.'

'By whom?'

'Not by me, old man,' said the E.S.O.

Cedric went on board and looked for the C.O. of the Highlanders and found him at length in his cabin asleep in his battledress.

'These are my orders,' said the Highland Colonel, taking a sheaf of typewritten sheets from the pocket on his thigh. They were already tattered and smeared by constant reference. '*Duchess of Cumberland*. Embark 23.00 hrs with full 1097 stores. That's plain enough.'

'But our men come on board in an hour.'

'Can't help you, I'm afraid. These are my orders.'

He was not going to discuss the matter with a subaltern. Cedric fetched his C.O. Colonel to Colonel they talked the thing out and decided to clear the after troop decks. Cedric was sent to wake the Highland duty officer. He found the duty sergeant. Together they went aft to the troop decks.

There were dim lights along the ceiling – electric bulbs recently daubed with blue paint, not yet scratched clear by the troops. Equipment and kit-bags lay about the deck in heaps; there were Bren gun boxes and ammunition and the huge coffin-shaped chests of the anti-tank rifles.

'Oughtn't that to be stored in the armoury?' asked Cedric.

'Not unless you want to get it pinched.'

Amid the heaps of stores half a battalion lay huddled in blankets. Very few of them, on this first night, had slung hammocks. These lay, with the other gear, adding to the piles.

'We'll never get them moved to-night.'

'We've got to try,' said Cedric.

Very slowly the inert mass was got into movement. They began collecting their own gear and swearing monotonously. Working parties began man-handling the stores. They had to go up the ladders on to the main deck, forward through the darkness and down the forward hatches.

Presently a voice from the top of the ladder said, 'Is Lyne down there?'

'Yes.'

'I've been told to bring my company to this troop deck.'

'They'll have to wait.'

'They're coming on board now.'

'Well for God's sake stop them.'

'But isn't this D deck?'

'Yes.'

'Then this is where we are to come to. Who the hell are all these men?'

Cedric went up the ladder and to the head of the gangway. A stream of heavily-laden men of his regiment were toiling up. 'Go back,' ordered Cedric.

'Who the hell's that?' asked a voice from the darkness.

'Lyne. Take your men back to the quay. They can't come on board yet.'

'Oh, but they've got to. D'you realize half of them've had nothing to eat since midday?'

'There's nothing to eat here till breakfast.'

'Oh but, I say, what rot. The R.T.O. at Euston said he'd telegraph through and have a hot meal ready on arrival. Where's the Colonel?'

The line of soldiers on the gangway turned about and began a slow descent. When the last of them was on the quay, invisible in the darkness, their officer came on board.

'You seem to have made a pretty good muck-up,' he said.

The deck was full of the other regiment carrying stores.

'There's a man there smoking,' shouted a ship's officer from above. 'Put that cigarette out.'

Matches began to spurt up on the quay. 'Put those cigarettes out, down there.'

'—y well travelling all the —ing day. No —ing supper. —ed about on the —ing quay. Now a — won't let me have a —ing smoke. I'm —ing —ed with being —ed about by these —ers.'

A dark figure passed Cedric muttering desperately. 'Nominal rolls in triplicate. Nominal rolls in triplicate. Why the devil can't they tell us beforehand they want nominal rolls in triplicate?'

Another dark figure whom Cedric recognized as the E.S.O.

'I say, the men are supposed to strip down their equipment and pack it in green sea bags before embarking.'

'Oh,' said Cedric.

'They don't seem to have done it.'

'Oh.'

'It upsets all the storage arrangements if they don't.'

'Oh.'

An orderly came up. 'Mr Lyne, sir, will you go and see the C.O.?'

Cedric went.

'Look here Lyne, aren't those infernal Scotsmen out of our troop decks yet? I ordered that deck to be clear two hours ago. I thought you were looking after that.'

'I'm sorry, Colonel. They're getting a move on now.'

'I should bloody well hope so. And look here, half our men have had nothing to eat all day. Go up to the purser and see what you can rout out for them. And find out on the bridge exactly what the sailing orders are. When the troops come on board see that everyone knows where everything is. We don't want anything lost. We may be in action before the end of the week. I hear these Highlanders lost a lot of kit on the way up. We don't want them making up deficiencies at our expense.'

'Very good, sir.'

As he went out on deck the ghostly figure brushed past him in the darkness muttering in tones that seemed to echo from another and even worse world. 'Nominal rolls in triplicate. Nominal rolls in triplicate.'

At seven o'clock the Colonel said, 'For God's sake someone take over from Lyne. He seems to have lain down on the job.'

Cedric went to his cabin; he was unspeakably tired; all the events and emotions of the last forty-eight hours were lost in the single longing for sleep; he took off his belt and his shoes and lay on his bunk. Within a quarter of a minute he was unconscious; within five minutes he was woken by the steward placing a tray by his side; it contained tea, an apple, a thin slice of brown bread and butter. That was how the day always began on this ship, whether she was cruising to the midnight sun or West Indies. An hour later another steward passed by striking a musical gong with a little hammer. That was the second stage of the day in this ship. He passed, tinkling prettily, through the first-class quarters, threading his path delicately between valises and kitbags. Unshaven, ill-tempered officers who had not been asleep all night scowled at him as he passed. Nine months ago the ship had been in the Mediterranean and a hundred cultured spinsters had welcomed his music. It was all one to him.

After breakfast the Colonel saw all his officers in the smoking-room. 'We've got to get everything out of the ship,' he said. 'It's got to be loaded tactically. We shan't be sailing until to-night anyway. I've just seen the Captain and he says he isn't fuelled yet. Also we're overloaded and he insists on our putting two hundred men ashore. Also, there's a field hospital coming on board this morning, that we've got to find room for. There is also Field Security Police, Field Force Institute, NAAFI, two Pay Corps officers, four chaplains, a veterinary surgeon, a Press photographer, a naval beach party, some Marine anti-aircraft gunners, an air support liaison unit – whatever that is – and a detachment of Sappers to be accommodated. All ranks are confined to the ship. There will be no communication of any kind with the shore. Duty company will find sentries for the post and telephone boxes on the quay. That's all, gentlemen.'

Everyone said, 'Lyne made nonsense of the embarkation.'

5

WHEN Mr Bentley, in the first flush of patriotic zeal, left publishing and took service with the Ministry of Information, it was agreed between him and the senior partner that his room should be kept for his use and that he should come in whenever he could keep an eye on his interests. Mr Rampole, the senior partner, would see to the routine of the office.

Rampole and Bentley was not a large or a very prosperous firm; it owed its continued existence largely to the fact that both partners had a reasonable income derived from other sources. Mr Bentley was a publisher because ever since he was a boy he had had a liking for books; he thought them a Good Thing; the more of them the merrier. Wider acquaintance had not increased his liking for authors, whom he found as a class avaricious, egotistical, jealous, and ungrateful, but he had always the hope that one day one of these disagreeable people would turn out to be a messiah of genius. And he liked the books themselves; he liked to see in the window of the office the dozen bright covers which were that season's new titles; he liked the sense of vicarious authorship which this spectacle gave him. Not so old Rampole. Mr Bentley often wondered why his senior partner had ever taken to publishing and why, once disillusioned, he persisted in it. Old Rampole deplored the propagation of books. 'It won't do,' he always said whenever Mr Bentley produced a new author, 'no one ever reads first novels.'

Once or twice a year old Rampole himself introduced an author, always with well-justified forecasts of its failure. 'Terrible thing,' he would say. 'Met old So-and-so at the club. Got button-holed. Fellow's just retired from Malay States. Written his reminiscences. We shall have to do them for him.

No getting out of it now. One comfort he won't ever write another book.'

That was one superiority he had over Mr Bentley which he was fond of airing. His authors never came back for more, like Mr Bentley's young friends.

The idea of the *Ivory Tower* was naturally repugnant to old Rampole. 'I've never known a literary review succeed yet,' he said.

He had a certain grudging regard for Ambrose because he was one of the few writers on their list who were incontestably profitable. Other writers always involved an argument, Mr Bentley having an ingenious way of explaining over advances and overhead charges and stock in hand in such a way that he seemed to prove that obvious failures had indeed succeeded. But Ambrose's books sold fifteen thousand copies. He didn't like the fellow, but he had to concede him a certain knack of writing. It shocked him that Ambrose should be so blind to his own interests as to propose such a scheme.

'Has the fellow got money?' he asked Mr Bentley privately.

'Very little, I think.'

'Then what is he thinking of? What's he *after*?'

To Ambrose he said, 'But a literary review, now of all times!'

'Now *is* the time of all times,' said Ambrose. 'Don't you *see*?'

'No, I don't. Costs are up and going higher. Can't get paper. Who'll want to read this magazine anyway? It isn't a woman's paper. It isn't, as I see it, a man's. It isn't even topical. Who's going to advertise in it?'

'I wasn't thinking of having advertisements. I thought of making it something like the old Yellow Book.'

'Well that was a failure,' said old Rampole triumphantly, 'in the end.'

But presently he gave his consent. He always gave his consent in the end to all Mr Bentley's suggestions. That was the secret of their long partnership. He had registered his protest. No one could blame him. It was all Bentley's doing. Often he had opposed Mr Bentley's projects out of habit, on the widest grounds that publication of any kind was undesirable. In the case of the *Ivory Tower* he stood on firm ground and knew it. It gave him positive satisfaction to detect his partner in such indefensible folly. So Mr Bentley's room, which was the most ornamental in the fine old building which they used as their offices, became the editorial room of Ambrose's paper.

There was not, at this stage, much editorial work to be done.

'There's one criticism I foresee,' said Mr Bentley, studying the proof sheets, 'the entire issue seems to be composed by yourself.'

'No one's to guess that,' said Ambrose. 'If you like we'll put some pseudonyms in.' Ambrose had always rather specialized in manifestoes. He had written one at school; he had written a dozen at the University; once, in the late twenties, he and his friends Hat and Malpractice had even issued the invitation to a party in the form of a manifesto. It was one of his many reasons for shunning communism that its manifesto had been written for it, once and for all, by somebody else. Surrounded, as he believed himself to be, by enemies of all kinds, Ambrose found it exhilarating from time to time to trumpet his defiance. The first number of the *Ivory Tower* somewhat belied the serenity and seclusion which it claimed, for Ambrose had a blow for every possible windmill.

The Minstrel Boys or Ivory Tower v. *Manhattan Skyscraper* defined once and for all Ambrose's attitude in the great Parsnip-Pimpernell controversy. *Hermit or Choirmaster* was an expansion of Ambrose's theme at the Café Royal. 'Culture must be cenobitic not conventual.' He struck ferocious unprovoked blows at those who held that literature was of value to the community. Mr J. B. Priestley came in for much personal abuse in these pages. There followed *The Bakelite Tower*, an onslaught on David Lennox and the decorative school of fashionable artists. *Majors and Mandarins* followed, where was defined the proper degree of contempt and abhorrence due to the military, and among the military Ambrose included by name all statesmen of an energetic and war-like disposition.

'It's all very controversial,' said Mr Bentley sadly. 'When you first told me about it, I thought you meant it to be a purely artistic paper.'

'We must show people where we stand,' said Ambrose. 'Art will follow – anyway there's *Monument to a Spartan*.'

'Yes,' said Mr Bentley. 'There's that.'

'It covers fifty pages, my dear. All pure Art.'

He said this with a facetious, shop assistant's intonation as though he was saying, 'All Pure Silk'; he said it as though it were a joke, but in his heart he believed – and he knew Mr Bentley understood him in this sense – he was speaking the simple truth. It *was* all pure art.

He had written it two years ago on his return from Munich after his parting with Hans. It was the story of Hans. Now, after the passage of two years, he could not read it without tears. To publish it was a symbolic action of the laying down of an emotional burden he had carried too long.

Monument to a Spartan described Hans, as Ambrose had loved him, in every mood; Hans immature, the provincial *petit-bourgeois* youth floundering and groping in the gloom of Teutonic adolescence, unsuccessful in his examinations, world-weary, brooding about suicide among the conifers, uncritical of direct authority, unreconciled to the order of the universe; Hans affectionate, sentimental, roughly sensual, guilty; above all, Hans guilty, haunted by the taboos of the forest; Hans credulous, giving his simple and generous acceptance to all the nonsense of Nazi leaders; Hans reverent to those absurd instructors who harangued the youth camps, resentful at the injustices of man to man, at the plots of the Jews and the encirclement of his country, at the blockade and disarmament; Hans loving his comrades, finding in a deep tribal emotion an escape from the guilt of personal love; Hans singing with his Hitler Youth comrades, cutting trees with them, making roads, still loving his old friend, puzzled that he could not fit the old love into the scheme of the new; Hans growing a little older, joining the Brown Shirts, lapped in a kind of be-nighted chivalry, bemused in a twilight where the demagogues and party hacks loomed and glittered like Wagnerian heroes; Hans faithful to his old friend, like a woodcutter's boy in a fairy-tale who sees the whole forest peopled with the great ones of another world and, rubbing his eyes, returns at evening to his hut and his fireside. The Wagnerians shone in Ambrose's story as they did in Hans's eyes. He austerely denied himself any hint of satire. The blustering, cranky, bone-headed party men were all heroes and philosophers. All this Ambrose had recorded with great delicacy and precision at a time when his heart was consumed by the final tragedy. Hans's Storm Troop comrades discover that his friend is a Jew; they have resented this friend before because in their gross minds they knew him to represent something personal and private in a world where only the mob and the hunting-pack had the right to live. So the mob and the hunting-pack fall on Hans's friendship. With a mercy they are far from feeling they save Hans from facing the implications of his discovery. For him, alone, it would have been the great climacteric of his retarded adolescence; the discovery that his own, personal conviction conflicted with the factitious convictions drummed into him by the crooks and humbugs he took for his guides. But the hunting-pack and the mob left Hans no time to devise his own, intense punishment; that at least was spared him in the swift and savage onslaught; that was left to Ambrose returning by train to England.

It was a story which a popular writer would have spun out to 150,000 words; Ambrose missed nothing; it was all there, delicately and precisely, in fifty pages of the *Ivory Tower.*

'Quite frankly, Geoffrey, I regard this as a major work of Art.'

'Yes, Ambrose, I know you do. So do I. I only wish we were publishing it without all the controversial stuff.'

'Not controversial, Geoffrey. We invite acceptance, not argument. We are showing our credentials and *laissez-passer.* That's all.'

'Old Rampole won't like it,' said Mr Bentley.

'We won't let old Rampole see it,' said Ambrose.

*

'I'm on to a very good thing, Colonel.'

'Will you kindly address me as "sir" in this office?'

'You wouldn't prefer to be called "chief"?'

'You'll call me "sir" or get out of that uniform.'

'It's funny,' said Basil. 'I should much sooner be called "chief". In fact that's what Susie does call me. However, sir, may I tell you about my discovery?'

When Basil had told him, Colonel Plum said, 'That's all right as far as it goes. We can't take any action, of course. This fellow Silk is a well-known writer, working in the Ministry of Information.'

'He's a most dangerous type. I know him well. He was living in Munich before the war – never out of the Brown House.'

'That's as may be, but this isn't Spain. We can't go arresting people for what they say in a private conversation in a café. I've no doubt we shall come to that eventually, but at the present stage of our struggle for freedom, it just can't be done.'

'But this paper he's starting.'

'Yes, that's another matter. But Rampole and Bentley are a perfectly respectable little firm. I can't apply for a search warrant until I've got something to go on. We've got pretty wide powers, but we have to be careful how we use them. We'll keep an eye on this paper and if it seems dangerous we'll stop it. Meanwhile, get to work. Here's an anonymous denunciation of a retired admiral in South Kensington. There won't be anything in it. See what the police know about him.'

'Don't we ever investigate night clubs? I'm sure they're bursting with enemy agents.'

Susie said, 'I do. You don't.'

A quiet day at the Ministry of Information. The more energetic neutral correspondents had mostly left the country by now, finding Axis sources a happier hunting-ground for front-page news. The Ministry could get on with its work undisturbed. That afternoon a film was showing in the Ministry theatre; it dealt with otter-hunting and was designed to impress neutral countries with the pastoral beauty of English life. The religious department were all keen filmgoers. Basil found the room empty. On Ambrose's table lay two sets of galley-proofs of the new magazine. Basil pocketed one of them. There was also a passport; Basil took it up with interest. He had never seen an Irish one before. It was made out for a Father Flanagan, S.J., Professor of Dublin University. The photograph showed a cadaverous face of indeterminate age. Father Flanagan was in his leisure from higher education the correspondent of an Irish newspaper. He wanted to visit the Maginot Line during his vacation and after numerous disappointments had found his way to the religious department of the Ministry of Information, where the Roman Catholic director had promised to try and get him a visa. Basil took this too; an additional passport often came in useful. Then he sauntered away.

He took the proofs home and read until dinner, marking a passage here and there as material to his brief. The style throughout was homogeneous but the author's names were multiform. Ambrose rather let himself go on names. 'Huckle-bury Squib', 'Bartholomew Grass', 'Tom Barebones-Abraham'. Only *Monument to a Spartan* bore Ambrose's own name. Later that evening Basil sought Ambrose where he was sure to find him, at the Café Royal.

'I've been reading your magazine,' he said.

'So it *was* you. I thought one of those nasty Jesuits had stolen it. They're always flapping in and out the department like jackdaws. Geoffrey Bentley was in a great stew about it. He doesn't want old Rampole to see a copy until the thing's out.'

'Why should the Jesuits want to show your magazine to old Rampole?'

'They're up to any mischief. What d'you think of it?'

'Well,' said Basil, 'I think you might have made it a bit stronger. You know what you want to do is to shock people a bit. That's the way to put a new magazine across. You can't shock people nowadays with sex, of course; I don't mean that. But suppose you had a little poem in praise of Himmler – something like that?'

'I don't believe that would be a good idea; besides, as far as I know no one has written a poem like that.'

'I dare say I could rake one up for you.'

'No,' said Ambrose. 'What did you think of *Monument to a Spartan*?'

'All the first part is first rate. I suppose they made you put on that ending?'

'Who?'

'The Ministry of Information.'

'They've had nothing to do with it.'

'Haven't they? Well, of course, you know best. I can only say how it reads to an outsider. What I felt was – here is a first-class work of art; something no one but you could have written. And then, suddenly, it degenerates into mere propaganda. Jolly good propaganda, of course; I wish half the stuff your Ministry turns out was as good – but propaganda. An atrocity story – the sort of stuff American journalists turn out by the ream. It glares a bit, you know, Ambrose. Still, of course, we all have to make sacrifices in war time. Don't think I don't respect you for it. But artistically, Ambrose, it's shocking.'

'Is it?' said Ambrose, dismayed. 'Is that how it reads?'

'Leaps to the eye, old boy. Still it ought to give you a leg up in the department.'

'Basil,' said Ambrose solemnly, 'if I thought that was how people would take it, I'd scrap the whole thing.'

'Oh, I shouldn't do that. The first forty-five pages are grand. Why don't you leave it like that, with Hans still full of his illusions, marching into Poland?'

'I might.'

'And you could bring Himmler in, just at the end, in a kind of apotheosis of Nazism.'

'No.'

'Well, Himmler isn't necessary. Just leave Hans in the first exhilaration of victory.'

'I'll think about it.... D'you really mean that intelligent readers would think I was writing propaganda?'

'They couldn't think anything else, old boy, could they?'

A week later by the simple process of going to Rampole and Bentley's office and asking for one, Basil obtained an advance copy of the new magazine. He turned eagerly to the last page and found that *Monument to a Spartan* now ended as he had suggested; he read it again with relish; to anyone ignorant of Ambrose's private history it bore one plain character – the triumphant paean of Hitler Youth; Doctor Ley himself might have been the author. Basil took the magazine with him to the War Office; before approaching Colonel Plum he marked with red chalk the *Monument to a Spartan* and passages in the preceding articles which cast particular ridicule upon the army and the War Cabinet and which urged on the artist the duty of non-resistance to violence. Then he laid it on Colonel Plum's desk.

'I think, sir, you promised to make me a Captain of Marines if I caught a fascist.'

'It was a figurative expression.'

'Meaning what?'

'That you might have done something to excuse your presence in my office. What have you got there?'

'Documentary evidence. A fifth column nest.'

'Well, put it down. I'll have a look at it when I've time.'

It was not Colonel Plum's habit to show enthusiasm before subordinates, but as soon as Basil was gone he began reading the marked passages with close attention. Presently he called for Basil.

'I believe you're on to something here,' he said. 'I'm taking this round to Scotland Yard. Who are these men Squib, Grass and Barebones-Abraham?'

'Don't you think they sound like pseudonyms?'

'Nonsense. When a man chooses an alias he calls himself Smith or Brown.'

'Have it your own way, sir. I shall be interested to see them in the dock.'

'There won't be any dock. We shall get this bunch under a special warrant.'

'Shall I come round to Scotland Yard with you?'

'No.'

'Just for that I won't introduce him to Barebones-Abraham,' said Basil when the Colonel was gone.

'Have we really caught some fifth column at last?' asked Susie.

'I don't know about "we"; *I* have.'

'Will they be shot?'

'Not all of them, I should think.'

'Seems a shame really,' said Susie. 'I expect they're only a bit touched.'

In the pleasure of setting his trap, Basil had not looked forward to its consequences. When Colonel Plum returned to his office two hours later, things seemed to have gone far beyond Basil's control. 'They're pleased as Punch at Scotland Yard,' he said. 'Handing out some very handsome bouquets. The whole thing is buttoned up. We've taken out a special warrant for authors, publishers and printers, but I don't think we need worry the printers much. To-morrow morning the man Silk will be arrested at the Ministry of Information; simultaneously Rampole and Bentley's will be surrounded and entered, all copies of the paper and all correspondence seized. All the office staff will be held pending investigation. What we need now is a description of the men Grass, Squib and Barebones-Abraham. You might get on to that. I'm going round to see the Home Secretary now.'

There was, at first hearing, a lot about this speech which displeased Basil, and more still when he began to turn the thing over in his mind. In the first place Colonel Plum seemed to be getting all the credit and all the fun. It was he himself, Basil felt, who should be going to see the Home Secretary; *he* should have been to Scotland Yard to make arrangements for the morrow's raid; *he* should have had the handsome bouquets of which Colonel Plum had spoken. It was not for this that he had planned the betrayal of an old friend. Colonel Plum was putting on altogether too much dog.

In the second place the sensation of being on the side of the law was novel to Basil and not the least agreeable. Police raids, for Basil, had in the past always meant escaping over the tiles or through the area; it made him ashamed to hear these things spoken of with tolerance and familiarity.

In the third place he was not absolutely happy in his mind about what Ambrose might say. Even though he was to be deprived of the right of public trial, there would presumably be some kind of investigation at which he would be allowed to give an account of himself. Basil's share in editing *Monument to a Spartan* was, he felt, better kept as a good story to tell in the right company at the right time; not to be made the subject of official and semi-legal enquiry.

And in the fourth place Basil had from long association an appreciable softness of disposition towards Ambrose. Other things being equal, he wished him well rather than ill.

These considerations, in that order of importance, worked in Basil's mind.

Ambrose's flat lay in the neighbourhood of the Ministry of Information; it was the top floor of a large Bloomsbury mansion, where the marble stairs changed to deal. Ambrose ascended into what had once been the servants' bedrooms; it was an attic and, so called, satisfied the ascetic promptings which had affected Ambrose in the year of the great slump. There was, however, little else about the flat to suggest hardship. He had the flair of his race for comfort and for enviable possessions. There were expensive continental editions of works on architecture, there were deep armchairs, an object like an ostrich egg sculptured by Brancusi, a gramophone with a prodigious horn and a library of records – these and countless other features made the living-room dear to him. It is true that the bath was served only by a gas-burning apparatus which at the best gave a niggardly trickle of warm water and, at the worst, exploded in a cloud of poisonous vapours, but apparatus of this kind is the hall mark of the higher intellectuals all the world over. Ambrose's bedroom compensated for the dangers and discomforts of the bathroom. In this flat he was served by a motherly old Cockney who teased him at intervals for not marrying.

To this flat Basil came very late that night. He had delayed his arrival on purely artistic grounds. Colonel Plum might deny him the excitements of Scotland Yard and the Home Office, but there should be every circumstance of melodrama here. Basil knocked and rang for some time before he made himself heard. Then Ambrose came to the door in a dressing-gown.

'Oh God,' he said. 'I suppose you're drunk,' for no friend of Basil's who maintained a fixed abode in London could ever consider himself immune from his occasional nocturnal visits.

'Let me in. We haven't a moment to spare.' Basil spoke in a whisper. 'The police will be here at any moment.'

Slightly dazed with sleep, Ambrose admitted him. There are those for whom the word 'police' holds no terror. Ambrose was not of them. All his life he had been an outlaw and the days in Munich were still fresh in his memory when friends disappeared suddenly in the night, leaving no address.

'I've brought you this,' said Basil, 'and this and this.' He gave Ambrose a clerical collar, a black clerical vest ornamented with a double line of jet buttons and an Irish passport. 'You are Father Flanagan returning to Dublin University. Once in Ireland you'll be safe.'

'But surely there's no train at this time.'

'There's one at eight. You mustn't be found here. You can sit in the waiting-room at Euston till it comes in. Have you got a breviary?'

'Of course not.'

'Then read a racing paper. I suppose you've got a dark suit.'

It was significant both of Basil's fine urgency of manner, and of Ambrose's constitutionally guilty disposition, that he was already clothed as a clergyman before he said, 'But what have I done? Why are they after me?'

'Your magazine. It's being suppressed. They're rounding up everyone connected with it.'

Ambrose asked no more. He accepted the fact as a pauper accepts the condition of being perpetually 'moved on'. It was something inalienable from his state; the artist's birthright.

'How did you hear about it?'

'In the War Office.'

'What am I to do about all this?' asked Ambrose helplessly. 'The flat, and the furniture and my books and Mrs Carver.'

'I tell you what. If you like I'll move in and take care of it for you until it's safe to come back.'

'Would you really, Basil?' said Ambrose, touched. 'You're being very kind.'

For some time now Basil had felt himself unfairly handicapped in his pursuit of Susie by the fact of his living with his mother. He had not thought of this solution. It had come providentially, with rapid and exemplary justice all too rare in life; goodness was being rewarded quite beyond his expectations, if not beyond his deserts.

'I'm afraid the geyser is rather a bore,' said Ambrose apologetically.

They were not far from Euston Station. Packing was the work of a quarter of an hour.

'But, Basil, I *must* have *some* clothes.'

'You are an Irish priest. What d'you think the Customs are going to say when they open a trunk full of Charvet ties and crêpe-de-Chine pyjamas?'

Ambrose was allowed one suitcase.

'I'll look after this for you,' said Basil, surveying the oriental profusion of expensive underclothes which filled the many drawers and presses of the bedroom. 'You'll have to walk to the station, you know.'

'Why, for God's sake?'

'Taxi might be traced. Can't take any chances.'

The suitcase had seemed small enough when Basil first selected it as the most priestly of the rather too smart receptacles in Ambrose's box-room; it seemed enormous as they trudged northward through the dark streets of Bloomsbury. At last they reached the classic columns of the railway terminus. It is not a cheerful place at the best of times, striking a chill in the heart of the gayest holiday-maker. Now in war time, before dawn on a cold Spring morning, it seemed the entrance to a sepulchre.

'I'll leave you here,' said Basil. 'Keep out of sight until the train is in. If anyone speaks to you, tell your beads.'

'I haven't any beads.'

'Then contemplate. Go into an ecstasy. But don't open your mouth or you're done.'

'I'll write to you when I get to Ireland.'

'Better not,' said Basil, cheerfully.

He turned away and was immediately lost in the darkness. Ambrose entered the station. A few soldiers slept on benches, surrounded by their kit and equipment. Ambrose found a corner darker, even, than the general gloom. Here, on a packing-case that seemed by its smell to contain fish of a sort, he sat waiting for dawn; black hat perched over his eyes, black overcoat wrapped close about his knees, mournful and black eyes open, staring into the blackness. From the fishy freight below him water oozed slowly on to the pavement making a little pool, as though of tears.

Mr Rampole was not, as many of his club acquaintances supposed, a bachelor, but a widower of long standing. He lived in a small but substantial house at Hampstead and there maintained in servitude a spinster daughter. On this fateful morning his daughter saw him off from the front gate as had been her habit years without number, at precisely 8.45. Mr Rampole paused in the flagged path to comment on the buds which were breaking everywhere in the little garden.

Look well at those buds, old Rampole; you will not see the full leaf.

'I'll be back at six,' he said.

Presumptuous Rampole, who shall tell what the day will bring forth? Not his daughter, who returned, unmoved by the separation, to eat a second slice of toast in the dining-room; not old Rampole, who strode at a good pace towards the Hampstead Underground.

He showed his season ticket to the man at the lift.

'I shall have to get it renewed the day after to-morrow,' he said affably, and tied a knot in the corner of his large white handkerchief to remind him of the fact.

There is no need for that knot, old Rampole; you will never again travel in the Hampstead Underground.

He opened his morning paper as he had done, five days a week, years without number. He turned first to the Deaths, then to the correspondence, then, reluctantly, to the news of the day.

Never again, old Rampole, never again.

The police raid on the Ministry of Information, like so many similar enterprises, fell flat. First the plain clothes men had the utmost difficulty in getting past the gatekeeper.

'Is Mr Silk expecting you?'

'We hope not.'

'Then you can't see him.'

When finally they were identified and allowed to pass, there was a confused episode in the religious department where they found only the Nonconformist minister, whom, too zealously, they proceeded to handcuff. It was explained that Ambrose was unaccountably absent from duty that morning. Two constables were left to await his arrival. All through the day they sat there, casting a gloom over the religious department. The plain clothes men proceeded to Mr Bentley's room where they were received with great frankness and charm.

Mr Bentley answered all their questions in a manner befitting an honest citizen. Yes, he knew Ambrose Silk both as a colleague at the Ministry and, formerly, as one of their authors at Rampole's. No, he had almost nothing to do with publishing these days; he was too busy with all this (an explanatory gesture which embraced the dripping sink, the Nollekens busts and the page of arabesques beside the telephone). Mr Rampole was in entire charge of the publishing firm. Yes, he thought he had heard of some magazine which Silk was starting, the *Ivory Tower*? Was that the name? Very likely. No, he had no copy. Was it already out? Mr Bentley had formed the impression that it was not yet ready for publication. The contributors? Huckle-bury Squib, Bartholomew Grass, Tom Barebones-Abraham? Mr Bentley thought he had heard the names; he might have met them in literary circles in the old days. He had the idea that Barebones-Abraham was rather below normal height, corpulent, bald – yes, Mr Bentley was quite sure he was bald as an egg; he spoke with a stammer and dragged his left leg as he walked. Hucklebury Squib was a very tall young man; easily recognizable for he had lost the lobe of his left ear in extraordinary circumstances when sailing before the mast; he had a front tooth missing and wore gold earrings.

The plain clothes men recorded these details in shorthand. This was the sort of witness they liked, circumstantial, precise, unhesitating.

When it came to Bartholomew Grass, Mr Bentley's invention flagged. He had never seen the man. He rather thought it might be the pseudonym for a woman.

'Thank you, Mr Bentley,' said the chief of the plain clothes men. 'I don't think we need trouble you any more. If we want you I suppose we can always find you here.'

'Always,' said Mr Bentley sweetly. 'I often, whimsically, refer to this little table as my grindstone. I keep my nose to it. We live in arduous times, Inspector.'

A posse of police went to Ambrose's flat, where all they got was a piece of his housekeeper's mind.

'Our man's got away,' they reported when they returned to their superiors.

Colonel Plum, the Inspector of Police, and Basil were summoned late that afternoon to the office of the Director of Internal Security.

'I can't congratulate you,' he said, 'on the way this case has been handled. I'm not blaming you, Inspector, or you, Seal,' and he fixed Colonel Plum with a look of detestation. 'We were clearly on to a very dangerous set of men and you let four out of five slip through your fingers. I've no doubt that at this moment they are sitting in a German submarine, laughing at us.'

'We've got Rampole, sir,' said Colonel Plum. 'I'm inclined to think he's the ringleader.'

'I'm inclined to think he's an old booby.'

'He has behaved in the most hostile and defiant manner throughout. He refuses to give any particulars about any of his accomplices.'

'He threw a telephone directory at one of our men,' said the Inspector, 'and used the following expressions about them: "nincompoops", "jacks-in-office" . . .'

'Yes, yes, I have the report. Rampole is obviously a violent and thoroughly unreasonable type. It won't do him any harm to cool his heels for the rest of the war. But he's not the ringleader. This fellow Barebones-Abraham is the man I want and you haven't been able to find a trace of him.'

'We've got his description.'

'A fat lot of good that is when he's half-way back to Germany. No, the whole thing has been grossly mismanaged. The Home Secretary takes a very poor view of it. *Somebody talked* and I mean to find out who.'

When the interview, painfully protracted, came to an end, the Director told Basil to remain behind.

'Seal,' he said, 'I understand you were the first man to get on to this gang. Have you any idea how they were warned?'

'You put me in a very difficult position, sir.'

'Come, come, my boy, this is no time for petty loyalties when your country's future is at stake.'

'Well, sir, I've felt for some time that there's been too much feminine influence in our department. Have you seen Colonel Plum's secretary?'

'Hokey-pokey, eh?'

'You could call it that, sir.'

'Enemy agent, eh?'

'Oh, no, sir. Have a look at her.'

The Director sent for Susie. When she had gone he said, 'No, not an enemy agent.'

'Certainly not, sir, but a frivolous, talkative girl. Colonel Plum's intimacy. . . . '

'Yes, I quite understand. You did perfectly right to tell me.'

'What did he want, sending for me like that and just staring?' asked Susie.

'I think I've arranged promotion for you.'

'Ooh, you are sweet.'

'I'm just moving into a new flat.'

'Lucky you,' said Susie.

'I wish you'd come and advise me about the decorations. I'm no good at that kind of thing.'

'Oh no?' said Susie in a voice she had learned at the cinema. 'And what would Colonel Plum say?'

'Colonel Plum won't have anything to say. You're rising far above ADDIS.'

'Ooh.'

Next morning Susie received an official intimation that she was to move to the Director's office.

'Lucky you,' said Basil.

She had admired all Ambrose's decorations except the Brancusi sculpture. That had been put away, out of sight, in the box-room.

At Brixton Gaol Mr Rampole enjoyed many privileges that were not accorded to common criminals. There was a table in his cell and a tolerably comfortable chair. He was allowed, at his own expense, some additions to prison fare. He might smoke. *The Times* was delivered to him every morning and for the first time in his life he accumulated a small library. Mr Bentley from time to time brought him papers for which his signature was required. In every way his life was much easier than it would have been in similar circumstances in any country.

But Mr Rampole was not content. There was an obnoxious young man next to him who, when they met at exercise, said 'Heil Mosley,' and at night attempted to tap out messages of encouragement in morse. Moreover Mr Rampole missed his club and his home at Hampstead. In spite of a multitude of indulgences he faced the summer without enthusiasm.

In a soft, green valley where a stream ran through close-cropped, spongy pasture and the grass grew down below the stream's edge and merged there with the water-weeds; where a road ran between grass verges and tumbled walls, and the grass merged into moss which spread upwards and over the tumbled stones of the walls, outwards over the pocked metalling and deep ruts of the road; where the ruins of a police barracks, built to command the road through the valley, burnt in the troubles, had once been white, then black, and now were one green with the grass and the moss and the water-weed; where the smoke of burned turf drifted down from the cabin chimneys and joined the mist that rose from the damp, green earth; where the prints of ass and pig, goose and calf and horse mingled indifferently with those of barefoot children; where the soft, resentful voices rose and fell in the smoky cabins merging with the music of the stream and the treading and shifting and munching of the beasts at pasture; where mist and smoke never lifted and the sun never fell direct, and evening came slowly in infinite gradations of shadow; where the priest came seldom because of the rough road and the long climb home to the head of the valley, and no one except the priest ever came from one month's end to another, there stood an inn which was frequented in by-gone days by fishermen. Here in the summer nights when their sport was over they had sat long over their whiskey and their pipes – professional gentlemen from Dublin and retired military men from England. No one fished the stream now and the few trout that remained were taken by ingenious and illicit means without respect for season or ownership. No one came to stay; sometimes a couple on a walking tour, once or twice a party of motorists, paused for supper, hesitated, discussed the matter and then regretfully pushed on to the next village. Here Ambrose came, perched on an outside-car, from the railway station over the hill six miles distant.

He had discarded his clerical disguise, but there was something about his melancholy air and his precision of speech which made the landlord, who had never had contact before with an intellectual Jew, put him down as a 'spoilt priest'. He had heard about this inn from a garrulous fellow in the packet-boat; it was kept by a distant connexion of this man's wife, and though he had not himself visited the place, he never lost an opportunity of putting in a good word for it.

Here Ambrose settled, in the only bedroom whose windows were unbroken. Here he intended to write a book, to take up again the broken fragments of his artistic life. He spread foolscap paper on the dining-room table and the soft, moist air settled on it and permeated it so that when, on the third day, he sat down to make a start, the ink spread and the lines ran together, leaving what might have been a brush stroke of indigo paint where there should have been a sentence of prose. Ambrose laid down the pen and because the floor sloped where the house had settled, it rolled down the table, and down the floor-boards and under the mahogany sideboard, and lay there among napkin rings and small coins and corks and the sweepings of half a century. And Ambrose wandered out into the mist and the twilight, stepping soundlessly on the soft, green turf.

In London Basil set Susie to work. She wanted to be taken out in the evenings too often and in too expensive a style. He set her to work with needle and silk and embroidery scissors, unpicking the A's from the monograms on Ambrose's crêpe-de-Chine underclothes and substituting in their place a B.

6

LIKE horses in a riding school, line ahead to the leading mark, changing the rein, circling to the leading mark on the opposite wall, changing rein again, line ahead again, orderly and regular and graceful, the aeroplanes manoeuvred in the sharp sunlight. The engines sang in the morning sky, the little black bombs tumbled out, turning over in the air, drifting behind the machines, breaking in silent upheavals of rock and dust which were already subsiding when the sound of the explosions shook the hillside where Cedric Lyne sat with his binoculars, trying to mark their fall.

There was no sign of Spring in this country. Everywhere the land lay frozen and dead, deep snow in the hills, thin ice in the valleys; the buds on the thorn were hard and small and black.

'I think they've found A Company, Colonel,' said Cedric.

Battalion headquarters were in a cave in the side of the hill; a shallow cave made by a single great rock which held up the accumulations of smaller stone which in years had slid down from above and settled round it. The Colonel and the adjutant and Cedric had room to sit here; they had arrived by night and had watched dawn break over the hills. Immediately below them the road led farther inland, climbing the opposing heights in a series of bends and tunnels. At their feet, between them and the opposite escarpment, the land lay frozen and level. The reserve company was concealed there. The headquarter troops formed a small protective perimeter round the cave. Twenty yards away under another rock two signallers lay with a portable wireless set.

'Ack, Beer, Charley, Don... Hullo Lulu, Koko calling; acknowledge my signal; Lulu to Koko – over.'

They had marched forward all the preceding night. When they arrived at the cave Cedric had first been hot and sweaty, then, after they halted in the chill of dawn, cold and sweaty. Now with the sun streaming down on them he was warm and dry and a little sleepy.

The enemy were somewhere beyond the farther hills. They were expected to appear late that afternoon.

'That's what they'll do,' said the Colonel. 'Make their assault in the last hour of daylight so as to avoid a counter-attack. Well, we can hold them for ever on this front. I wish I felt sure of our left flank.'

'The Loamshires are falling back there. They ought to be in position now,' said the adjutant.

'I know. But where are they? They ought to have sent over.'

'All this air activity in front means they'll come this way,' said the adjutant.

'I hope so.'

The high school finished its exercise, took up formation in arrow shape and disappeared droning over the hills. Presently a reconnaissance plane appeared and flew backwards and forwards overhead searching the ground like an old woman after a lost coin.

'Tell those bloody fools to keep their faces down,' said the Colonel.

When the aeroplane had passed he lit his pipe and stood in the mouth of the cave looking anxiously to his left.

'Can you see anything that looks like the Loamshires?'

'Nothing, Colonel.'

'The enemy may have cut in across them yesterday evening. That's what I'm afraid of. Can't you get Brigade?' he said to the signalling corporal.

'No answer from Brigade, sir. We keep trying. Hullo Lulu, Koko calling, acknowledge my signal, acknowledge my signal; Koko to Lulu – over...'

'I've a good mind to push D Company over on that flank.'

'It's outside our boundary.'

'Damn the boundary.'

'We'd be left without a reserve if they come straight down the road.'

'I know, that's what's worrying me.'

An orderly came up with a message. The Colonel read it and passed it to Cedric to file. 'C Company's in position. That's all our forward companies reported. We'll go round and have a look at them.'

Cedric and the Colonel went forward, leaving the adjutant in the cave. They visited the company headquarters and asked a few routine questions. It was a simple defensive scheme, three companies up, one in reserve in the rear. It was suitable ground for defence. Unless the enemy had infantry tanks – and all the reports said he had not – the road could be held as long as ammunition and rations lasted.

'Made a water recce?'

'Yes, Colonel, there's a good spring on the other side of those rocks. We're refilling bottles by relays now.'

'That's right.'

A Company had been bombed, but without casualties, except for a few cuts from splintered rock. They were unshaken by the experience, rapidly digging dummy trenches at a distance from their positions to draw the fire when the aeroplanes returned. The Colonel returned from his rounds in a cheerful mood; the regiment was doing all right. If the flanks held they were sitting pretty.

'We're through to Lulu, sir,' said the signalling corporal.

The Colonel reported to brigade headquarters that he was in position; air activity; no casualties; no sign of enemy troops. 'I've no contact on the left flank . . . yes, I know it's beyond the brigade boundary. I know the Loamshires ought to be there. But *are* they? our . . . Yes, but that flank's completely in the air, if they don't turn up . . .'

It was now midday. Battalion headquarters ate some luncheon – biscuits and chocolate; the adjutant had a flask of whisky. No one was hungry but they drank their bottles empty and sent the orderlies to refill them at the spring B Company had found. When the men came back the Colonel said, 'I'm not happy about the left flank. Lyne, go across and see where those bloody Loamshires are.'

It was two miles along a side track to the mouth of the next pass, where the Loamshires should be in defence. Cedric left his servant behind at battalion headquarters. It was against the rules, but he was weary of the weight of dependent soldiery which throughout the operations encumbered him and depressed his spirits. As he walked alone he was exhilarated with the sense of being one man, one pair of legs, one pair of eyes, one brain, sent on a single intelligible task; one man alone could go freely anywhere on the earth's surface; multiply him, put him in a drove and by each addition of his fellows you subtract something that is of value, make him so much less a man; this was the crazy mathematics of war. A reconnaissance plane came overhead. Cedric moved off the path but did not take cover, did not lie on his face or gaze into the earth and wonder if there was a rear gunner, as he would have done if he had been with headquarters. The great weapons of modern war did not count in single lives; it took a whole section to make a target worth a burst of machine-gun fire; a platoon or a motor lorry to be worth a bomb. No one had anything against the individual; as long as he was alone he was free and safe; there's danger in numbers; divided we stand, united we fall, thought Cedric, striding happily towards the enemy, shaking from his boots all the frustration of corporate life. He did not know it, but he was thinking exactly what Ambrose had thought when he announced that culture must cease to be conventual and become cenobitic.

He came to the place where the Loamshires should have been. There was no sign of them. There was no sign of any life, only rock and ice and beyond, in the hills, snow. The valley ran clear into the hills, parallel with the main road he had left. They may be holding it, higher up, he thought, where it narrows, and he set off up the stony track towards the mountains.

And there he found them; twenty of them under the command of a subaltern. They had mounted their guns to cover the track at its narrowest point and were lying, waiting for what the evening would bring. It was a ragged and weary party.

'I'm sorry I didn't send across to you,' said the subaltern. 'We were all in. I didn't know where you were exactly and I hadn't a man to spare.'

'What happened?'

'It was all rather a nonsense,' said the subaltern, in the classic phraseology of his trade which comprehends all human tragedy. 'They bombed us all day yesterday and we had to go to ground. We made a mile or two between raids but it was sticky going. Then at just before sunset they came clean through us in armoured cars. I managed to get this party away. There may be a few others wandering about, but I rather doubt it. Luckily the Jerries decided to call it a day and settled down for a night's rest. We marched all night and all to-day. We only arrived an hour ago.'

'Can you stop them here?'

'What d'you think?'

'No.'

'No, we can't stop them. We may hold them up half an hour. They may think we're the forward part of a battalion and decide to wait till to-morrow before they attack. It all depends what time they arrive. Is there any chance of your being able to relieve us?'

'Yes. I'll get back right away.'

'We could do with a break,' said the subaltern.

Cedric ran most of the way to the cave. The Colonel heard his story grimly.

'Armoured cars or tanks?'

'Armoured cars.'

'Well, there's a chance. Tell D Company to get on the move,' he said to the adjutant. Then he reported to brigade headquarters on the wireless what he had heard and what he was doing. It was half an hour before D Company was on its way. From the cave they could see them marching along the track where Cedric had walked so exuberantly. As they watched they saw the column a mile away halt, break up and deploy.

'We're too late,' said the Colonel. 'Here come the armoured cars.'

They had overrun the party of Loamshires and were spreading fanwise across the low plain. Cedric counted twenty of them; behind them an endless stream of lorries full of troops. At the first shot the lorries stopped and under cover of the armoured cars the infantry fell in on the ground, broke into open order and began their advance with parade-ground deliberation. With the cars came a squadron of bombers, flying low along the line of the track. Soon the whole battalion area was full of bursting bombs.

The Colonel was giving orders for the immediate withdrawal of the forward companies.

Cedric stood in the cave. It was curious, he thought, that he should have devoted so much of his life to caves.

'Lyne,' said the Colonel. 'Go up to A Company and explain what's happening. If they come in now from the rear the cars may jink round and give the other companies a chance to get out.'

Cedric set out across the little battlefield. All seemed quite unreal to him still.

The bombers were not aiming at any particular target; they were plastering the ground in front of their cars, between battalion headquarters and the mouth of the valley where A Company were dug in. The noise was incessant and shattering. Still it did not seem real to Cedric. It was part of a crazy world where he was an interloper. It was nothing to do with him. A bomb came whistling down, it seemed from directly over his head. He fell on his face and it burst fifty yards away, bruising him with a shower of small stones.

'Thought they'd got him,' said the Colonel. 'He's up again.'

'He's doing all right,' said the adjutant.

The armoured cars were shooting it out with D Company. The infantry spread out in a long line from hillside to hillside and were moving steadily up. They were not firing yet; just tramping along behind the armoured cars, abreast, an arm's length apart. Behind them another wave was forming up. Cedric had to go across this front. The enemy were still out of effective rifle range from him, but spent bullets were singing round him among the rocks.

'He'll never make it,' said the Colonel.

I suppose, thought Cedric, I'm being rather brave. How very peculiar. I'm not the least brave, really; it's simply that the whole thing is so damned silly.

A Company were on the move now. As soon as they heard the firing, without waiting for orders, they were doing what the Colonel intended, edging up the opposing hillside among the boulders, getting into position where they could outflank the outflanking party. It did not matter now whether Cedric reached them. He never did; a bullet got him, killing him instantly while he was a quarter of a mile away.

EPILOGUE
Summer

SUMMER came and with it the swift sequence of historic events which left all the world dismayed and hardly credulous; all, that is to say, except Sir Joseph Mainwaring, whose courtly and ponderous form concealed a peppercorn lightness of soul, a deep unimpressionable frivolity, which left him bobbing serenely on the great waves of history which splintered more solid natures to matchwood. Under the new administration he found himself translated to a sphere of public life where he could do no serious harm to anyone, and he accepted the change as a well-earned promotion. In the dark hours of German victory he always had some light anecdote; he believed and repeated everything he heard; he told how, he had it on the highest authority, the German infantry was composed of youths in their teens, who were intoxicated before the battle with dangerous drugs; 'those who are not mown down by machine guns die within a week,' he said. He told, as vividly as if he had been there and seen it himself, of Dutch skies black with descending nuns, of market women who picked off British officers, sniping over their stalls with sub-machine guns, of waiters who were caught on hotel roofs marking the rooms of generals with crosses as though on a holiday postcard. He believed, long after hope had been abandoned in more responsible quarters, that the French line was intact. 'There is a little bulge,' he explained. 'All we have to do is to pinch it out,' and he illustrated the action with his finger and thumb. He daily maintained that the enemy had outrun his supplies and was being lured on to destruction. Finally when it was plain, even to Sir Joseph, that in the space of a few days England had lost both the entire stores and equipment of her regular army and her only ally; that the enemy were less than twenty-five miles from her shores; that there were only a few battalions of fully armed, fully trained troops in the country; that she was committed to a war in the Mediterranean with a numerically superior enemy; that her cities lay open to air attack from fields closer to home than the extremities of her own islands; that her sea-routes were threatened from a dozen new bases, Sir Joseph said, 'Seen in the proper perspective I regard this as a great and tangible success. Germany set out to destroy our army and failed; we have demonstrated our invincibility to the world. Moreover, with the French off the stage, the last obstacle to our proper understanding with Italy is now removed. I never prophesy, but I am confident that before the year is out they will have made a separate and permanent peace with us. The Germans have wasted their strength. They cannot possibly repair their losses. They have squandered the flower of their army. They have enlarged their boundaries beyond all reason and given themselves an area larger than they can possibly hold down. The war has entered into a new and more glorious phase.'

And in this last statement, perhaps for the first time in his long and loquacious life, Sir Joseph approximated to reality; he had said a mouthful.

A new and more glorious phase: Alastair's battalion found itself overnight converted from a unit in the early stages of training into first-line troops. Their 1098 stores arrived; a vast profusion of ironmongery which, to his pride, included Alastair's mortar. It was a source of pride not free from compensating disadvantages. Now, when the platoon marched, Alastair's pouches were filled with bombs and his back was harnessed to the unnaturally heavy length of steel piping; the riflemen thought they had the laugh of him.

Parachute landings were looked for hourly. The duty company slept in their boots and stood to at dawn and dusk. Men going out of camp carried charged rifles, steel helmets, anti-gas capes. Week-end leave ceased abruptly. Captain Mayfield began to take a censorious interest in the swill tubs; if there was any waste of food, he said, rations would be reduced. The C.O. said, 'There is no such thing nowadays as working hours' and to show what he meant he ordered a series of parades after tea. A training memorandum was issued which had the most formidable effect upon Mr Smallwood; now, when the platoon returned exhausted from field exercises, Mr Smallwood gave them twenty minutes' arms drill before they dismissed; this was the 'little bit extra' for which the memorandum called. The platoon referred to it as '—ing us about'.

Then with great suddenness the battalion got orders to move to an unknown destination. Everyone believed this meant foreign service, and a great breath of exhilaration inflated the camp. Alastair met Sonia outside the guard-room.

'Can't come out to-night. We're moving. I don't know where. I think we're going into action.'

He gave her instructions about where she should go and what she should do while he was away. They now knew that she was to have a child.

There was a special order that no one was to come to the station to see the battalion off; no one in fact was supposed to know they were moving. To make secrecy absolute they entrained by night, disturbing the whole district with the tramp of feet and the roar of lorries going backwards and forwards between camp and station, moving their stores.

Troops in the train manage to achieve an aspect of peculiar raffishness; they leave camp in a state of ceremonial smartness; they parade on the platform as though on the barrack square; they are detailed to their coaches and there a process of transformation and decay sets in; coats are removed, horrible packages of food appear, dense clouds of smoke obscure the windows, in a few minutes the floor is deep in cigarette ends, lumps of bread and meat, waste paper; in repose the bodies assume attitudes of extreme abandon; some look like corpses that have been left too long unburied; others like the survivors of some saturnalian debauch. Alastair stood in the corridor most of the night, feeling that for the first time he had cut away from the old life.

Before dawn it was well known, in that strange jungle process by which news travels in the ranks, that they were not going into action but to 'coastal —ing defence'.

The train travelled, as troop trains do, in a series of impetuous rushes between long delays. At length in the middle of the forenoon they arrived at their destination and marched through a little seaside town of round-fronted stucco early Victorian boarding-houses, an Edwardian bandstand, and a modern, concrete bathing pool, three foot deep, blue at the bottom, designed to keep children from the adventure and romance of the beach. (Here there were no shells or starfish, no jelly-fish to be melted, no smooth pebbles of glass to be found, no bottles that might contain messages from shipwrecked sailors, no waves which, bigger than the rest, suddenly knocked you off your feet. The nurses might sit round this pool in absolute peace of mind.) Two miles out, through a suburb of bungalows and converted railway carriages, there was a camp prepared for them in the park of what, in recent years, had been an unsuccessful holiday club.

That night Alastair summoned Sonia by telephone and she came next day, taking rooms in the hotel. It was a simple and snug hotel and Alastair came there in the evenings when he was off duty. They tried to recapture the atmosphere of the winter and spring, of the days in Surrey when Alastair's life as a soldier had been a novel and eccentric interruption of their domestic routine; but things were changed. The war had entered on a new and more glorious phase. The night in the train when he thought he was going into action stood between Alastair and the old days.

The battalion was charged with the defence of seven miles of inviting coastline, and they entered with relish into the work of destroying local amenities. They lined the sands with barbed wire and demolished the steps leading from esplanade to beach; they dug weapon pits in the corporation's gardens, sandbagged the bow-windows of private houses and with the co-operation of some neighbouring sappers blocked the roads with dragons'-teeth and pill boxes; they stopped and searched all cars passing through this area and harassed the inhabitants with demands to examine their identity cards. Mr Smallwood sat up on the golf course every night for a week, with a loaded revolver, to investigate a light which was said to have been seen flashing there. Captain Mayfield discovered that telegraph posts are numbered with brass-headed nails and believed it to be the work of the fifth column; when mist came rolling in from the sea one evening, the corporal in command of Alastair's section reported an enemy smoke screen, and for miles round word of invasion was passed from post to post.

'I don't believe you're enjoying the army any more,' said Sonia after three weeks of coastal defence.

'It isn't that. I feel I could be doing something more useful.'

'But, darling, you told me your mortar was one of the key points of the defence.'

'So it is,' said Alastair loyally.

'So what?' Then Alastair said, 'Sonia, would you think it bloody of me if I volunteered for special service?'

'Dangerous?'

'I don't suppose so really. But very exciting. They're getting up special parties for raiding. They go across to France and creep up behind Germans and cut their throats in the dark.' He was excited, turning a page in his life, as, more than twenty years ago lying on his stomach before the fire, with a bound volume of *Chums*, he used to turn over to the next instalment of the serial.

'It doesn't seem much of a time to leave a girl,' said Sonia, 'but I can see you want to.'

'They have special knives and tommy-guns and knuckle-dusters; they wear rope-soled shoes.'

'Bless you,' said Sonia.

'I heard about it from Peter Pastmaster. A man in his regiment is raising one. Peter's got a troop in it. He says I can be one of his section commanders; they can fix me up with a commission apparently. They carry rope ladders round their waists and files sewn in the seams of their coats to escape with. D'you mind very much if I accept?'

'No, darling. I couldn't keep you from the rope ladder. Not from the rope ladder I couldn't. I see that.'

Angela had never considered the possibility of Cedric's death. She received the news in an official telegram and for some days would speak to no one, not even to Basil, about the subject. When she mentioned it, she spoke from the middle rather than from the beginning or the end of her progression of thought.

'I knew we needed a death,' she said. 'I never thought it was his.'

Basil said, 'Do you want to marry me?'

'Yes, I think so. Neither of us could ever marry anyone else, you know.'

'That's true.'

'You'd like to be rich, wouldn't you?'

'Will anyone be rich after this war?'

'If anyone is, I shall be. If no one is, I don't suppose it matters so much being poor.'

'I don't know that I want to be rich,' said Basil, after a pause. 'I'm not acquisitive, you know. I only enjoy the funnier side of getting money – not having it.'

'Anyway it's not an important point. The thing is that we aren't separable any more.'

'Let nothing unite us but death. You always thought *I* was going to die, didn't you?'

'Yes.'

'The dog it was that died... Anyway, this is no time to be thinking of marrying. Look at Peter. He's not been married six weeks and there he is joining a gang of desperadoes. What's the sense of marrying with things as they are? I don't see what there is to marriage, if it isn't looking forward to a comfortable old age.'

'The only thing in war time is not to think ahead. It's like walking in the blackout with a shaded torch. You can just see as far as the step you're taking.'

'I shall be a terrible husband.'

'Yes, darling, don't I know it? But you see one can't expect anything to be perfect now. In the old days if there was one thing wrong it spoiled everything; from now on for all our lives, if there's one thing right the day is made.'

'That sounds like poor Ambrose in his Chinese mood.'

Poor Ambrose had moved west. Only the wide, infested Atlantic lay between him and Parsnip. He had taken rooms in a little fishing town and the great waves pounded on the rocks below his windows. The days passed and he did absolutely nothing. The fall of France had no audible echo on that remote shore.

This is the country of Swift, Burke, Sheridan, Wellington, Wilde, T. E. Lawrence, he thought; this is the people who once lent fire to an imperial race, whose genius flashed through two stupendous centuries of culture and success, who are now quietly receding into their own mists, turning their backs on the world of effort and action. Fortunate islanders, thought Ambrose, happy, drab escapists, who have seen the gold lace and the candlelight and left the banquet before dawn revealed stained table linen and a tipsy buffoon!

But he knew it was not for him; the dark, nomadic strain in his blood, the long heritage of wandering and speculation allowed him no rest. Instead of Atlantic breakers he saw the camels swaying their heads resentfully against the lightening sky, as the caravan woke to another day's stage in the pilgrimage.

Old Rampole sat in his comfortable cell and turned his book to catch the last, fading light of evening. He was absorbed and enchanted. At an age when most men are rather concerned to preserve familiar joys than to seek for new, at, to be exact, the age of sixty-two, he had suddenly discovered the delights of light literature.

There was an author on the list of his firm of whom Mr Bentley was slightly ashamed. She wrote under the name of Ruth Mountdragon, a pseudonym which hid the identity of a Mrs Parker. Every year for seventeen years Mrs Parker had written a novel dealing with the domestic adventures of a different family; radically different that is to say in name, exhibiting minor differences of composition and circumstance, but spiritually as indistinguishable as larches; they all had the quality of 'charm'; once it was a colonel's family of three girls in reduced circumstances on a chicken farm, once it was an affluent family on a cruise in the Adriatic, once a newly-married doctor in Hampstead; all the permutations and combinations of upper middle-class life had been methodically exploited for seventeen years; but the charm was constant. Mrs Parker's public was not vast, but it was substantial; it lay, in literary appreciation, midway between the people who liked some books and disliked others, and the people who merely liked reading, inclining rather to the latter group. Mr Rampole knew her name as one of the authors who were not positively deleterious to his pocket, and consequently when his new manner of life and the speculative tendencies which it fostered caused him to take up novel reading he began on her. He was transported into a strange world of wholly delightful, estimable people whom he had rightly supposed not to exist. With each page a deeper contentment settled on the old publisher. He had already read ten books and looked forward eagerly to rereading them when he came to the end of the seventeenth. Mr Bentley was even engaged to bring Mrs Parker to visit him at a future, unspecified date. The prison chaplain was also an admirer of Mrs Parker's. Old Rampole gained great face from disclosing her real name. He half-promised to allow the chaplain to meet her. He was happier than he could remember ever having been.

Peter Pastmaster and the absurdly youthful colonel of the new force were drawing up a list of suitable officers in Bratts Club.

'Most of war seems to consist of hanging about,' he said. 'Let's at least hang about with our own friends.'

'I've a letter from a man who says he's a friend of yours. Basil Seal.'

'Does he want to join?'

'Yes. Is he all right?'

'Perfect,' said Peter. 'A tough nut.'

'Right. I'll put him down with Alastair Trumpington as your other subaltern.'

'No. For God's sake don't do that. But make him liaison officer.'

'You see, I know everything about you,' said Angela.

'There's one thing you don't know,' said Basil. 'If you really want to be a widow again, we'd better marry quick. I don't think I told you. I'm joining a new racket.'

'Basil, what?'

'Very secret.'

'But why?'

'Well, you know, things haven't been quite the same at the War House lately. I don't know why it is, but Colonel Plum doesn't seem to love me as he did. I think he's a bit jealous about the way I pulled off the *Ivory Tower* business. We've never really been matey since. Besides, you know, that racket was all very well in the winter, when there wasn't any real war. It won't do now. There's only one serious occupation for a chap now, that's killing Germans. I have an idea I shall rather enjoy it.'

'Basil's left the War Office,' said Lady Seal.

'Yes,' said Sir Joseph, with sinking heart. Here it was again; the old business. The news from all over the world might be highly encouraging – and, poor booby, he believed it was; we might have a great new secret weapon – and, poor booby, he thought we had; he might himself enjoy a position of great trust and dignity – poor booby, he was going, that afternoon, to address a drawing-room meeting on the subject of hobbies for the A.T.S. – but in spite of all this, Basil was always with him, a grim *memento mori* staring him out of countenance. 'Yes,' he said, 'I suppose he has.'

'He has joined a special corps d'élite that is being organized. They are going to do great things.'

'He has actually joined?'

'Oh, yes.'

'There's nothing I can do to help him?'

'Dear Jo, always so kind. No. Basil has arranged it all himself. I expect that his excellent record at the War Office helped. It isn't every boy who would settle to a life of official drudgery when everyone else was going out for excitement – like Emma's silly girl in the fire brigade. No, he did his duty where he found it. And now he is getting his reward. I am not quite sure what they are going to do, but I know it is very dashing and may well have a decisive effect on the war.'

The grey moment was passed; Sir Joseph, who had not ceased smiling, now smiled with sincere happiness.

'There's a new spirit abroad,' he said. 'I see it on every side.'

And, poor booby, he was bang right.

This book is set in BASKERVILLE. John
Baskerville of Birmingham formed his
ideas of letter-design during his
early career as a writing-master
and engraver of inscriptions.
He retired in middle age,
set up a press of his
own and produced
his first book
in 1757.